THE PORTABLE
Elizabethan Reader

The Viking Portable Library

Each Portable Library volume is made up of
representative works of a favorite modern or
classic author, or is a comprehensive anthology
on a special subject. The format is designed
for compactness and for pleasurable reading.
The books average about 700 pages in length.
Each is intended to fill a need not hitherto met
by any single book. Each is newly edited by an
authority distinguished in his field, who adds
a thoroughgoing introductory essay and other
helpful material. The "Portables" are original
publications in this form. Most of them are
available both in durable cloth and
in stiff paper covers.

THE PORTABLE

Elizabethan

READER

*Edited
& with an Introduction by*
HIRAM HAYDN

NEW YORK · PUBLISHED BY
The Viking Press · 1959

THE PORTABLE ELIZABETHAN READER

Copyright 1946 by The Viking Press, Inc.

Published in December 1946

Published on the same day in the Dominion of Canada
by The Macmillan Company of Canada Limited

Second Printing (B P) June 1955

Third Printing (O P) June 1959

Printed in U. S. A. by The Colonial Press Inc.

For
MARY AND MIKE

Contents

vii

III. AN INQUIRY INTO THE NATURE OF MAN

IV. THE NEW LEARNING

ii. *The Dream of Power*

I. EMPIRE AND THE SHADOW OF MACHIAVELLI

v. The Common Man

vi. The Well of the Past

vii. An Age of Song

Biographical Notes

Ascham, Roger (1515–68). Humanist scholar. For two years he was tutor to Princess Elizabeth. Later he became Latin secretary to Queens Mary and Elizabeth.

Ashley, Robert (1565–1641). Lawyer. He gave up his practice to study and translate continental languages.

Bacon, Francis (1561–1626). Philosopher and Statesman. He was lord chancellor in 1618. His major contribution to philosophy was the inductive method in science, in opposition to the a priori method of Scholasticism.

Breton, Nicholas (1545?–1626?). Pamphleteer in verse and prose. His best work is represented by lyrics in *England's Helicon* and *The Passionate Shepheard* (1604).

Campion, Thomas (1567–1620). Song writer and physician. He wrote treatises on musical theory and wrote masques for the court. Campion's four "Books of Ayres" contained his lyrics, some set to music composed by him.

Chapman, George (1559?–1634). Dramatist and poet. His translations of Homer are classic, the first in English.

Dekker, Thomas (1570?–1641). Playwright of the London common people. His three best plays are *The Shoemaker's Holiday* (1599), *Old Fortunatus* (1600), and *The Honest Whore* (1604).

Dee, John (1527–1608). Astrologer and magician. He was alchemist to the court of Queen Elizabeth.

Digges, Thomas. *See* Introduction to this volume.

Donne, John (1572–1631). Leading preacher and poet. At twenty-four he embarked on the victorious Essex expedition to Cadiz. Later, under the patronage of King James, he became dean of St. Paul's. His prose includes a polemic against the Jesuits and an apology for suicide. His early verse was sensual, realistic, satirical; his later, religious.

Drayton, Michael (1563–1631). His entire career was devoted to poetry. *The Polyolbion* (1613), his greatest work, was a poetic account of the history and topography of England.

Elizabeth (1533–1603). Daughter of Henry VIII and Anne Boleyn, she became queen of a financially shaky realm exhausted by internal religious strife. Her tremendous personal popularity and prudent choice of ministers helped propel England into its renaissance.

Essex, Robert Devereux (1567–1601). The second Earl of Essex, Devereux became a favorite at the court of Elizabeth. He went through a hectic career in and out of court and on the various battlefields where England was involved.

Foxe, John (1516–87). An early Protestant, he left England on Mary Tudor's accession. At Strasbourg he began to publish his *Book of Martyrs*, a history of the persecution of Reformers from Wyclif to 1500.

Florio, John (1553–1625). Famous for his translations of Montaigne, Florio wrote several books on Italian grammar and published an Italian-English dictionary.

Greene, Robert (c.1560–92). Dramatist and pamphleteer. His *Pandosto*, a pastoral story, supplied Shakespeare with plot for *A Winter's Tale*. One of his best plays is *The Honorable History of Friar Bacon and Friar Bungay* (1592).

Greville, Fulke (1554–1628). Poet. A minor writer, he is interesting because his poems and plays deal with almost every battle of ideas of the times. His best known work is the *Life of the Renowned Sir Philip Sidney* (1652).

Hakluyt, Richard (1552?–1616). Geographer. He immersed himself in the history of discovery; then wrote, translated, and published histories of navigation, travel, and discovery. His chief work was *The Principall Navigations, Voiages, and Discoveries of the English Nation* (1598–1600).

Hall, Edward (c.1498–1547). Lawyer and historian. A judge of the sheriff's court in London and M.P. Hall's *Chronicle* was another of Shakespeare's plot sources.

Harvey, Gabriel (1545?–1630). Critic. In defense of his brother, he began a long literary war with Robert Greene and Thomas Nashe. Earlier, while a fellow of Pembroke Hall at Cambridge, he became a close friend of Edmund Spenser.

Holinshed, Raphael (d. c.1580). Historian and chronicler of the British Isles. He was general editor of a project which later became *The Chronicles of England, Scotland, and Ireland* (1578). This work furnished Shakespeare with the plots of *Macbeth, King Lear*, and a part of *Cymbeline*.

Hooker, Richard (1554?–1600). Clergyman of the Church of England, student and lecturer at Oxford. His theory of church and civil government was influential in eighteenth-century England.

Jonson, Ben (1573?–1637). Actor and playwright. A bricklayer as a young man, soldier in Flanders, later an actor. Jonson's versatility was expressed in plays, songs, essays, and critical writings. Leading classicist among the Elizabethans.

Lodge, Thomas (1558–1625). Writer in various media—drama,

poetry, euphuistic prose—he eventually gave up writing to practice medicine.

Lower, Sir William. *See* Introduction to this volume.

Marlowe, Christopher (1564–93). Dramatist and poet. Son of a shoemaker; M.A. from Cambridge. He met a violent death. In his drama he daringly departed from the contemporary cult of imitating the Senecan formula, and unquestionably paved the way for Shakespeare.

Nashe, Thomas (1567–1601). Satirist. Under a pseudonym he wrote anti-Puritan pamphlets. One bitter satire on contemporary society, which attacked Gabriel Harvey, began the feud between them. He is best known for the picaresque *The Unfortunate Traveller* (1594).

Naunton, Sir Robert (1563–1635). Member of Parliament in six successive terms. As secretary of State he expressed strong Protestant opinions and enforced anti-Catholic laws.

Norden, John (1548–1625). Cartographer. He was authorized in 1593 to travel through England and Wales to make maps and charts of those areas. His most interesting work is the *Surveyor's Dialogue* (1608).

North, Thomas (1535?–1601?). Translator. Plutarch's *Lives* was his greatest translation. North's manner and style of writing seriously influenced Elizabethan prose.

Ralegh, Sir Walter (1552?–1618). Navigator. Active as entrepreneur of colonization. A skeptic in religious thought. While imprisoned in the Tower of London he wrote his *History of the World* (1614).

Scot, Reginald (1538–99?). Member of Parliament (1588). *The Discoverie of Witchcraft* was intended to prevent persecution of persons popularly labeled as witches.

Shakespeare, William (1564–1616). Poet and dramatist. Son of a glover of Stratford, he began his playwriting and acting career soon after 1584.

Sidney, Sir Philip (1554–86). Diplomat and soldier. The *Apology for Poetry* was written about 1581. *Astrophel and Stella* (c.1581) was inspired by his love for Penelope Devereux.

Spenser, Edmund (c.1552–99). Poet. His melodious verse was well received in an age responsive to poetry. The uncompleted *Faerie Queene* is his best known work. He had a strong influence on many early seventeenth century poets.

Wotton, Sir Henry (1568–1639). Diplomat and poet. He was ambassador to Venice, where he remained for twenty years from 1624 to his death. He was also provost of Eton.

Wyatt, Sir Thomas (1503?–42). Diplomat. He introduced the sonnet from Italy to England.

Editor's Introduction

Two primary concerns have governed the selection
of the contents of this reader. One has been to represent faithfully both the quality and flavor of Elizabethan
literature, and the temper of the life and thought that
bred that literature. With the scope of this task in mind,
I have omitted many acknowledged classics, preferring
to include less well-known writings that better suggest
the peculiar hopes and fears of the age, its superstitions
and doubts, its faiths and controversies.

My second concern has been to choose material that
may still possess genuine and compelling interest for the
general reader. I have been more interested in selecting
for the non-specialist than for the Elizabethan scholar—
in making the collection stimulating and provocative to
the reader whose interest in the past is mostly in terms
of what meaning the past has for the present, and even
for the future.

We usually think vaguely of the Elizabethan period
as an age of dare-devil adventures, costume drama, and
blood and bombast. This impression is not wholly inaccurate. The pace *was* fast, the personalities spectacular,
the contrasts of Elizabethan life—at least in London—
dramatic. On the one hand existed the color and magnificence of the court, on the other the poverty and
disease and squalor of the city.

But this is still a superficial impression. The paradox

1

was not confined to splendor and misery in London. To anyone who has read more than casually in Elizabethan literature, the deeper paradox is immediately apparent in that literature's combinations of aspiration and despair, piety and brutality, idealism and cynicism, confidence and melancholy, gentility and coarseness.

There are certain periods in human history when events of global and even cosmic significance occur too rapidly for men's thoughts and creeds to catch up to them. We are living in such a time now—a time when scientific progress has taken place so swiftly that we are unprepared to cope with it. The whole structure of our political, social, economic, and especially moral thinking must undergo a drastic revision if we are to readjust ourselves sufficiently to survive. Many of us are inadequate to the adjustment: we had not even been able to evaluate fully and objectively the thought of Darwin and Marx and Freud and Einstein. Then came Hiroshima, and we found ourselves with one foot in the Atomic Age and the other in the eighteenth century.

The Elizabethans experienced a similar dilemma. The end of the sixteenth and the beginning of the seventeenth centuries formed another such time—when the vistas before men expanded too rapidly for all but a handful to grasp their significance. The Elizabethans, too, lived perforce a "bifurcated" existence—with one foot in the Middle Ages and the other in the inchoate Copernican Age. Any just analysis of the paradoxical qualities that we find in their writings must take this fact into consideration—must realize that there was "chaos in God's cabinet." And in the parallel, there may be much for us of the twentieth century to ponder and learn.

Gabriel Harvey, giving his staccato, news-columnist account of the intellectual unrest at Cambridge University in the 1580's, writes to Edmund Spenser: "All inquisitive after News, new Books, new Fashions, new Laws, new Officers, and some after new Elements, and some after new Heavens, and Hells too." It is an apt summary of the intellectual unrest in England at the time—an unrest by no means confined to the academic ivory tower.

The course of events that led to a tremendous upheaval in men's thinking in all sorts of categories—religious, scientific, political, ethical—had developed more slowly in England than on the continent. As in the case of the artistic and esthetic developments of the Renaissance, Italy had led; and the wane of the great flowering of philosophy and art in Italy had coincided largely with the movement's rise in France and Germany, and the advent of the Reformation. As this wave fell off in turn in northern Europe, after the age of Erasmus and Luther and Calvin, Rabelais and Montaigne and the *Pléiade,* it moved on—this time across the channel to England. The final magnificent burgeoning of the Renaissance occurred among the Elizabethans.

By this time, they had inherited the full accumulated weight of more than a century of iconoclasm—in literature, art, religion, philosophy, science, education, and political, economic and historical thinking. The medieval world and the medieval world view were dying,

> And new Philosophy calls all in doubt,
> The Element of fire is quite put out;
> The Sun is lost, and th'earth, and no man's wit
> Can well direct him where to look for it.
> And freely men confess that this world's spent,
> When in the Planets, and the Firmament
> They seek so many new; then see that this
> Is crumbled out again to his Atomies.
> 'Tis all in pieces, all coherence gone;

All just supply, and all Relation:
Prince, Subject, Father, Son, are things forgot,
For every man alone thinks he hath got
To be a Phoenix, and that then can be
None of that kind, of which he is, but he.
This is the world's condition now. . . .

So wrote John Donne, from the commanding vantage-point of 1611, when the Elizabethan Age proper was over, but many of the Elizabethans were seeking, denying, and asserting as vigorously as ever. More than a century of "innovators" had left thoughtful and independent men dizzy and bewildered, the traditionalists utterly confused. England no longer enjoyed that immunity from new and heretical ideas (about heaven and earth alike) that the Huguenot Innocent Gentillet had envied her in his Epistle Dedicatory to his popular *Contra-Machiavel*. Gentillet, describing the evils of the times in France, had written, late in the sixteenth century:

And some there were whom the resemblance of nature or vanity of wit had so deceived, that they derided the everlasting verity of the true God, as if it were but a fable. Rabelais amongst the French, and Agrippa amongst the Germans, were the standard-bearers of that team: which with their scoffing taunts, inveighed not only against the Gospels, but all good arts whatsoever. Those mockers did not as yet openly undermine the groundwork of human society, but only they derided it. But such Cyclopian laughters in the end proved to be only signs and tokens of future evils. For by little and little, that which was taken in the beginning for jests, turned to earnest, and words into deeds. . . .
When our countrymen's minds were sick, and corrupted with these pestilent diseases, and that discipline waxed stale, then came forth the books of Machiavel, a most pernicious writer, which . . . by open means, and as it were a continual assault, utterly destroyed . . . all virtues at once. Insomuch as it took Faith from the princes; authority and majesty from laws; liberty from the people; and peace and

concord from all persons. . . . For what shall I speak of Religion, whereof the Machiavellians had none?

And he concludes,

> But O how happy are ye [Englishmen], both because you have so gracious a Queen, and also for that the infectious Machiavellian doctrine hath not breathed nor penetrated the entrails of most happy England.

Even while he wrote, this rather superficial critic of Machiavelli was inaccurate. "Most happy England" had not only already been invaded by that "most pernicious writer," but also by a host of other innovators—Copernicus, Giordano Bruno, Paracelsus, Agrippa, Cardan, Montaigne, Jean Bodin and Louis LeRoy, to mention only a few. Authority and tradition in all fields of human thought and endeavor had already been challenged.

"The naming of names" varies considerably from writer to writer, but the practice of listing—whether to excoriate or praise—the men who had upset the universal applecart was a favorite practice of the Elizabethans. One of the most interesting and penetrating of these inventories is to be found in John Donne's *Ignatius, His Conclave*, particularly since it was written later than most of these, even post-dating Galileo's discoveries.

Ignatius is explicitly a diatribe against the Jesuit order, and most particularly its founder, Ignatius Loyola. It was written by a Donne whose earlier hesitancy between Catholicism and Anglicanism was over, and who was soon to take Anglican orders. Its polemic nature, however, is not of nearly so much interest to us as the long incidental references to the great innovators, from Columbus down, who had undermined men's traditional thinking and faith. There are few satirical documents that expound so clearly and amusingly the new systems of thought of any time. And the freshness and sly incisiveness of Donne's analyses of the claims of Columbus, Copernicus, Machiavelli, Paracelsus and others, to have done the most to further Satan's unending effort to overthrow God's universal order, make "A Meeting in Hell" a most appropriate introduction to the section I have called "New Horizons."

Of all the new horizons evident, that across the Atlantic was one of the most dramatic and, by this time, the most familiar. In the century since Columbus' first trip, the more fabulous theories about the New World had given way to a greedy conflict for gold and empire; the tales about legendary monsters on land and sea had been replaced by soberer ones about exotic peoples, customs and products. The piece by J. H. included in this collection is a fair sample. Among the drastic dangers of tobacco against which this unknown author warns are the loss of potency and collusion with the devil. Tobacco had clearly become sufficiently familiar to be a proper target for the moralizing reformers of the period.

Although it is still an age of swashbuckling, as contemporary accounts of Drake's voyage around the world make clear, there is a note of dedication in Drayton's ode that is well borne out by the two selections included from Hakluyt's famous collection of *Voyages*. There is a clear parallel between the story of the gallant leadership and indomitable spirit of Sir Humphrey Gilbert, and that of the death of Sir Philip Sidney, recounted in a later section. And this note is sounded again in the story of the search for a northwest passage: a story of the pioneer spirit that pushes on to ever-expanding frontiers, the spirit that dominates the frontispiece to Francis Bacon's *Novum Organum* ("lifted" from the coat of arms of the Spanish royal family), with its picture of a ship sailing beyond the Pillars of Hercules at the end of the known world, and the two words "Plus ultra."

The gallantry of the Queen's "voyagers" is unquestionable; yet this is but one side of the picture. Many of these men went out "to the greater glory of England"— but that greater glory was a euphemism for the ruthless extension of empire, the establishment of colonial supremacy through sea and land power.

In the selection I have chosen from *The Discovery of the Empire of Guiana*, Ralegh is careful to emphasize the humane treatment that his men accord the natives, and to dwell upon the good qualities of these peoples. This tendency, together with his lyric pictures of the land passed on their way up the river, make the passage almost idyllic. Yet the story behind his second expedition to Guiana is sordid enough. Sir Walter had fallen from the Queen's favor and already served a term in the Tower, when her death resulted in the accession of James VI of Scotland. With this shambling gentleman, Ralegh again underwent vicissitudes of fortune and once more wound up in the Tower. This time he was freed to lead the expedition to Guiana. Its goal was twofold: to challenge the authority of the Spaniards in this area, and to secure gold. Success meant restoration to favor; failure meant ruin and death.

Reading the magnificent description that closes the selection, we share the writer's optimism and the freshness of his feeling for *terra incognita*—this vivid and gorgeous new land. Yet the passage ends ominously with the words "and every stone that we stooped to take up, promised either gold or silver by his complexion." Ominously—for the promise remained a promise. On the second expedition, no gold was found; there were disastrous skirmishes with the Spanish, in one of which

Ralegh's son was killed; and Sir Walter returned to England in proud but bitter frustration, eventually to lay his head upon the executioner's block.

It was not, however, the voyagers who suffered most or most often. The exploitation of the natives of the new continents is one of the least savory chapters in the annals of exploration—and the stain was not limited to any one nation or group. It spread and corrupted the ranks of almost all the European invaders. Donne touched satirically upon the situation in his *Ignatius;* of the great litterateurs, Montaigne treated the subject most extensively.

I have found it impossible to keep Montaigne out of this collection of Elizabethan writings. John Florio's translation may not be the most precise and scholarly now available, but it was of immense interest to his contemporaries, whom Montaigne influenced considerably. Moreover, it has two great and pertinent virtues: it is thoroughly Elizabethan in temper, and it is equally faithful to Montaigne himself—to his extraordinary combination of bitter and bland. For this most urbane, aristocratic and apparently desultory of writers and thinkers had in him a capacity for social indignation, bred of a love of justice and a hatred of sham, that made him at times the master of a vitriolic sarcasm.

The synthetic piece I have devised under the title of "Montaigne and the Noble Savage" is composed of two selections, one from the early essay "Of the Cannibals," the other from the later "Of Coaches." In the first of these he is aglow with his enthusiasm for the unspoiled life discovered in the New World. Always something of a primitivist, he rejoices that on the new continents the natural simplicity and beauty of life among these people exceeds the fable of the Golden Age of innocence so often extolled by the poets. This is the piece that inspired Gonzago's famous speech on his "Golden Age" commonwealth in Shakespeare's *Tempest*.

In the second section he has lost none of his enthusiasm: as always, he prefers nature to art. But this essay is no idyll. Like Ronsard in his discussion of the Brazilian colony in his *Discours contre Fortune* ("Docte Villegaignon, tu fais une grand faute") Montaigne is infuriated by the cruelties and butcheries inflicted upon these people in the name of civilization. More, he questions with probing honesty and passion all the scores on which the invaders are so certain of their superiority to these "barbarians." Mercilessly, item by item, he destroys each illusion, and in these two essays reduces the whole story of exploration and colonization to a shambles of pillage. . . .

If the appearance of gold, tobacco, and Indians in London lent solid evidence and even a certain familiarity to strange reports from across the sea, the evidence of the human eye was responsible for as startling and more disquieting reports of conditions in the sky. The sixteenth century "optick Tube" that resulted in the startling news which Galileo proclaimed in his *Siderius Nuncius* proved Hamlet right in his conviction that there were more things in heaven, at least, than Horatio's philosophy had dreamed on. At least from the days of the early followers of Pythagoras, the key-word of dogma has been, "It is He who said it." To the radical empiricist, the ultimate key-word is, "I myself saw (or did) it." And the Elizabethan Age was one of radical empiricism.

At one end of this most exciting period of astronomical exploration (at least until the twentieth century), stands Copernicus, with his great pronouncement of the heliocentric theory of the universe in 1543; at the other, Galileo, with his announcement in 1610 of his observations of the moon, Jupiter and the Milky Way, made through the telescope. The first of these two great figures disturbed men's traditional thinking with his relegation of the earth to a subordinate position in the solar system. The second upset them considerably more with his proof ("I myself saw it") that in the allegedly *eternal* and *immutable* heavens "above" the orb of the moon were evidence of change and many hitherto uncharted stars, and that the moon was not "smooth and luminous," but filled with irregularities that suggested a topography much like that of the earth.

Copernicus and Galileo, the giants, and the lesser but still great figures of Tycho Brahe and Kepler—these are the familiar pioneers. Only lately have we come to know and pay tribute to the part played by Elizabethans, especially by Thomas Digges and Thomas Hariot.

Thomas Digges was unquestionably Copernicus' most important English supporter in the sixteenth century. Others—Robert Recorde, John Dee, and John Field— were conversant with the Copernican theory and gave it serious consideration. But in 1576, Digges added to a new edition of his father's *Prognostication Everlasting* (a standard astrological work) a short piece of his own entitled "A Perfect Description of the Celestial Orbs according to the most ancient doctrine of the Pythagoreans, lately revised by Copernicus and by geometrical demonstrations approved." In this work, Digges, an eminent mathematician, unqualifiedly supports the Copernican theory. The better part of the work actually constitutes the first English translation of those parts of Book I of Copernicus' *De Revolutionibus Orbium Coelestium* containing crucial passages on the heliocentric theory.

But Digges went beyond Copernicus, as well. The

latter had refused to commit himself on the infinity of the universe; Digges explicitly proclaims that infinity, as well as his conviction that the stars, numberless, are scattered throughout infinite space. As he puts it in his diagram—the first known diagram of the universe according to the heliocentric theory to be printed in an English book—"This orb of stars fixed infinitely up extendeth itself in altitude spherically."

In view of the frequent republication of this joint work by the Diggeses, father and son—in 1578, 1583, 1585, 1592, 1596 and 1605—it is clear that the son's tremendously important little treatise had wide circulation in Elizabethan times. It is amazing that we should have lost sight of its importance and remained ignorant of the first edition until recently. Yet it was not until 1934 that the text, with a commentary on its significance, was published in the "Huntington Library Bulletin." This publication was the result of the research of Francis R. Johnson and Sanford V. Larkey, to whom I am indebted for most of the foregoing account.

If Digges was in a genuine sense "the English Copernicus," Hariot was "the English Galileo." Thomas Hariot, mathematician, philosopher, and astronomer, was a friend of Kepler and other distinguished Continental scientific thinkers. As early as 1586, while a member of Ralegh's expedition to Virginia, he had in his possession "a perspective glass whereby was showed many strange sights." In 1607 he made important observations of the comet which later came to be known as "Halley's Comet." By 1609, he was exchanging letters with Kepler on problems of refraction and optics, while working on the principle of a new combination of lenses.

Then, as the letters from his pupil, Sir William Lower, indicate, by 1610 he was using an improved telescope to make important astronomical observations. Whether or not Lower was right in feeling that Hariot, even more than Galileo, was the true pioneer in this work, it seems clear that he proceeded independently. However, being even more interested in mathematics, he never gave to the telescope the central attention that Galileo did. And if, as Lower insists, Hariot allowed others to receive the credit due him, we have no record of any complaint on his part. Like Leonardo, he seems to have been more interested in his discoveries than in the possible fame attendant upon them.[1]

The Lower letters; that of Sir Henry Wotton from Venice; the passage from Ralegh's *History of the World* (Hariot was an intimate of Ralegh's); and the references in Donne's *Ignatius* and "New Philosophy calls all in doubt"—these and many other writings testify to a wide and vital interest in Galileo's findings. But there had already—for more than thirty-five years—been excited comment throughout Europe about strange proceedings in the heavens. The "new star" discovered by Tycho Brahe in 1572, of which Digges also made extensive observations; the second "new star" of 1604, noted and discussed by Kepler and others; the unusually large number of carefully observed comets (especially those of 1577, 1580, and 1585), eclipses, planetary conjunctions, and other astronomical phenomena had produced endless speculation among the learned and consternation among laymen.

Were the Aristotelian-Ptolemaic explanations of the physical universe untrue? Were the "immutable, incorruptible heavens" merely a myth? Or had the age of miracles returned? Or (still more awful thought!)

---

[1] See Marjorie Nicolson, "The 'New Astronomy' and English Literary Imagination," *Studies in Philology*, XXXII, 449-462, for more on Hariot. Miss Nicolson has published widely on the impact of science upon literary imagination.

was the dissolution of the world imminent? Astronomy and astrology were still inseparable in the popular mind, and these strange events gave holiday opportunities to quacks and charlatans of all kinds. Old philosophical theories about the Platonic "great year," esoteric theological figurings about the "Decay of Nature" and the date of Judgment Day, astrological hokum and new astronomical theories based on scientific observation were confused and thrown together to supply a formidable arsenal of prophecy calculated to terrify the ingenuous and unwary.

I have collected a few of these passages under the heading "Portents in the Sky," in an attempt to do justice to varying attitudes. Side by side with fatalistic prophecies and soberer doubts, I have placed the sturdy debunking by Thomas Nashe of the prognostications of Richard Harvey, the younger brother of Gabriel (Nashe's arch-foe). To match and balance the genuine skepticism and concern of Donne (however masked by witty and extravagant imagery), I have included the strong major-key affirmation of Richard Hooker, in the first book of his *Of the Laws of Ecclesiastical Polity*. It is probable that the alarm set forth in some of these passages is not entirely genuine; but the total effect is nonetheless impressive, and nonetheless instructive to those of us who cower in the shadow of the atomic bomb.

Theories and observations combined to make the revolution in the macrocosm spectacular news. In the microcosm, "that little world of man," equally subversive conclusions were abroad, if not so widely and devastatingly advertised. We seldom realize how radical Montaigne's theories about the nature of man seemed to his contemporaries. For centuries, only the most "dangerous" thinkers had challenged the conventional Christian-humanistic concept of man as a primarily rational being, made in the divine image and equipped by nature with reason to guide his life to the goal of virtue and even to assist in his ultimate salvation. This was "the law of nature," as it applied to man—and it was man who was important, not *individual men.*

Yet in the essay "Of Repenting," Montaigne affirms flatly that he is not interested in theoretical generalizations about man, but in studying one particular man—himself. For the first time in the history of literature and thought, an author proposes to follow an individual in all his idiosyncrasies and convolutions—flattering and unpleasant alike. "Others fashion man," he asserts. "I repeat him." He will not swallow the "whole capsule" of man the type, drawn to general laws, but will adopt the empirical approach to the only man he can really know —himself.

This is not the most revolutionary of his essays, but it sets forth the keynote of his pursuit of *"Moi-même."* As he says himself, he speaks the truth—not his bellyful, but as much as he dares. And the older he grows, the more he dares.

Elsewhere, he has drawn as devastating comparisons between man and other animals, as between "civilized" and primitive man. From the famous "Apology for Raymond Sébond" on, his mature thought is devoted to the exposition of his naturalistic philosophy, which sees man as the variable and instinctive child of an infinitely fertile and amoral Nature—who alternately rationalizes his own "universal laws" *after the deed* and accepts the coercion of the laws and customs that he finds around him. These moral imperatives, the "laws of nature," he points out scornfully, are not universal, but "municipal." The only laws of nature he recognizes are those followed by the "uncivilized" peoples of the New World. He is at one with the early Reformation in his conviction that men cannot know and interpret God's design, and he prefers to any acceptance of such trumped-up laws, the chance to investigate all the shadings of personality that he finds in empirical actuality.

Not many of the Elizabethans were bold enough to endorse publicly his conclusions, but they all knew him; most of them referred to him; and many clearly employed his theories in forms that would not endanger their reputations for othodoxy. Despite many speculations, we have little conclusive proof of Shakespeare's debt to him; but worth consideration is the late Ernst Cassirer's statement that without Montaigne's clearly stated exposition of men as complex individuals, it would be difficult to understand how Shakespeare's great complex characters could have emerged from a literature dominated by types.

Gabriel Harvey, writing to Edmund Spenser to reprove him for his old-fashioned and prim notions of morality, does not mention Montaigne, and it is probable that his hedonism and endorsement of "bravery" owe more to Italy—which in the popular mind, connoted Roger Ascham's definition of an Italianate Englishman as a devil incarnate—than to France. But the origin of these ideas is not so important or interesting to us, from our remote observation post, as the fact of their existence. There is no question but that the Elizabethans, with their exuberance and gusto, placed more honest unashamed value on the goods of the flesh than did their fathers of the age of Erasmus and More—all the courtly theories of Platonic love notwithstanding. Such opinions as these of Harvey were boldly expressed by many in a way that would have met with public rebuke, or worse, fifty years before.

A great wave of disillusionment about the ideal values men had long at least officially and formally accepted was taking place. It is apparent in the new attitudes toward the physical constitution of the universe and toward the nature of man himself. It is also apparent in the prevalent attitudes toward education. The work of the Oxford Reformers had done much to remedy and purge the schools and universities of the dregs of degenerate Scholasticism, the piddling remnants of a once great system. Outstanding humanistic teachers like Sir John Cheke, Richard Mulcaster and Roger Ascham had followed in their wake. The preface to *The Schoolmaster* speaks in the humane and enlightened voice that defined the task of the educator as the training of men for virtuous public and private lives—the training of the complete gentleman who found his true end in the ideal of virtuous action.

But already, by the eighties, a tide of reaction had set in again. The cry now was all for a new learning that laid more stress on the empirical, less on the ideal. Gabriel Harvey, who was always sniffing the winds of unrest, describes to Spenser the revolution in progress at Cambridge. The pragmatic political maxims of Machiavelli, the fashionable conduct books that take their models from the court and esteem aristocratic "honor" more than classical morality or traditional Christian virtues, the "relativistic" political and historical studies of Jean Bodin and Louis LeRoy—these and other "heretical" works are described by Harvey with evident enthusiasm.

The current vogue, it is clear, is all for deeds, not theories; for empirical evidence, not hypotheses; for the pragmatic rules of "success," not the absolute laws of idealism; for the new Continental thinkers, not the traditional classical masters. The word "new" recurs again and again. Even discounting somewhat for the volatile excitement of youth, it is apparent that the consciousness of being in the midst of a transitional world is rampant at Cambridge.

If Harvey describes suggestively the uncertain state of flux that characterized this violent reaction from the traditional humanistic studies, we must still wait for Francis Bacon to give both a detailed critique of the old educational order and a fully planned program for a new order. In Book I of *The Advancement of Learning,* Bacon lists the "errors and vanities" to which learning is susceptible. With merciless directness, here as in his *Novum Organum,* he assails the obscurantists, the pedants, the faddists and the servile traditionalists who have always opposed stubbornly the experimenters and original thinkers who sought to establish an organic relation between education and life.

Besides Bacon's analysis, Harvey's excited reportorial account seems superficial. Bacon lists among the "peccant humours," rather than the "formed diseases" of learning, "the extreme affecting of two extremities: the one antiquity, the other novelty. . . ." If Ascham's generation suffered from the former, with its exaggerated devotion to the classical masters, surely Harvey's Cambridge undergraduates erred equally in the direction of novelty.

But the most distinctive note of all in Bacon's inventory of "the diseases and humours of learning" is his anatomy of the errors men had made in their "mistaking or misplacing of the last or furthest end of knowledge." Intellectual curiosity for its own sake; the connoisseur's and dilettante's delight in curious and varied knowledge; the sophist's and aphorist's satisfaction in "victory of wit and contradiction"; the acquisition of knowledge for personal gain, either in terms of reputation, professional advancement, or money—all these he repudiates as "final ends." The last end of knowledge is to develop "a rich storehouse for the glory of the Creator and *the relief of man's estate."* Or, as the father of "Salomon's House" puts it, "The end of our foundation is the knowledge of causes, and secret motions of things; and *the enlarging of the bounds of human empire, to the effecting of all things possible."*

This is the main burden of Bacon's argument, presented systematically in *The Advancement of Learning, Novum Organum,* and the various fragments of the *Great Instauration;* imaginatively in that early piece of "science fiction," the *New Atlantis.* One has only to compare Sir Thomas More's *Utopia* with the latter to comprehend the difference in temper between the earlier humanistic English Renaissance and this last flowering of the Renaissance that sprang up amongst the Elizabethans.

More's values and concerns are all in terms of the establishment of God's "law of nature" among men—all in terms of the development of reason and true virtue in the individual, justice and tolerance in the state. His yardstick is the cardinal virtues of antiquity. But Bacon's vision is one of the harnessing of the physical universe to the end of securing and extending man's intellectual and physical well-being. *His* humanism is not of the classical variety, not immediately concerned with ideal values and the inner man, but rather with the improvement of human living conditions through what we should now call scientific and technological progress. We are still seeking a balance between the two visions— never more desperately than now.

"The enlarging of the bounds of human empire," in this sense, was one Elizabethan dream of power—perhaps the most disinterested and enlightened. Inevitably, in an age of conflict and innovation, of idol-smashing and schism, there were others, more predatory—whether imperialistic or individualistic. Bacon spoke his bit in these respects, too, and all the attempts of doctrinaire twentieth-century scholars to whitewash him into a traditional Christian humanist are ineffectual. Despite his customary politic wariness, he frequently did extol the perspicacity of Machiavelli's, and of Guicciardini's pragmatic political philosophy. Upon occasion, he endorsed power politics. And in the selection I have included here from a speech made in the House of Commons, his genuinely Machiavellian theme of "the best iron in the world" is thoroughly consonant with his scientific philosophy of "a true investigation of the nature of things," rather than the pursuit of pre-conceived ideals or personal ends. His scorn for "reckonings and audits, and *meum* and *teum*" matches his contempt for pedants and narrow-minded, self-seeking professional educators.

The influence of Machiavelli is even more apparent in the essay "Of the True Greatness of Kingdoms." Bacon's attitude toward the importance of military strength and the necessary balance between the aristocracy and the common people is Machiavellian, as is his concluding generalization, which takes for granted the need and desire "to add amplitude and greatness" to one's kingdom. The ultimate goal for both men is the welfare of the given "people," yet in practice the theory is lost in imperialistic power politics and emerges eventually as what amounts to a religion of the state. *Its* health and preservation depend upon growth, which implies expansion; the only alternative, in the cycle of political existence, is decay.

There was another kind of Machiavelism, or pseudo-Machiavelism, popular—or at least notorious—among the Elizabethans. The Gentillet *Contra-Machiavel,* to which I referred earlier, had a great popularity in England, and the emergent picture of Old Nick as the patron saint of all self-seekers who governed their careers only by the ethics of expediency, was widely prevalent. This sort of Machiavelism, applying his advice to the Prince to private careers, merged with the fad of Senecan blood-and-thunder revenge tragedies to produce, chiefly in plays, numerous characters who were a composite of the Lion and the Fox of Machiavellan fame. Shakespeare's Richard III is among the best known.

Bacon's short piece, "Of Boldness," is a soberer and qualified version of Machiavellian "success" counsel. Gabriel Harvey, of all the Elizabethans, made the most thorough cult of *virtù*, or amoral energy. All of his private jottings, finally collected by G. C. Moore Smith under the head of *Marginalia,* disclose his affinity for the Florentine gospel of the winning of worldly success and power through resolution and craftiness. These broken, staccato notes are packed with tributes to Machiavelli and to all men of action who have pushed their way to the top with disregard for traditional moral values—a strange gallery ranging from Caesar to Pietro Aretino. One note in the collection, however, adds ironic pathos to this hymn to achievement. After a characteristic tribute to men of passion and energy, Harvey suddenly whimpers, "But I have done nothing of this sort. Woe to miserable me!" Nor did he ever. The promising, if eccentric and willful young man, eventually passed a long and uneventful provincial life.

The dream of power, among other forms that it assumed, produced an extensive Elizabethan literature of blood and bombast, violence and melodrama. Most of these pieces, particularly those of the theater, are so familiar I have contented myself here with two versions —one "public" and one "private": Marlowe's extravagant but effective picture of Tamburlaine's sack of Babylon, and the Italianate story of the vengeance of Cutwolf, from Thomas Nashe's picaresque novel, *The Unfortunate Traveler.*

An equally well-known, but more exotic form that the dream of power took lay in the unending search for the Philosopher's Stone, and the attendant dreams of commanding the spirit world or encompassing the secret knowledge of alchemy or astrology or the Cabala or other esoteric lore. Behind all these lifetimes devoted to the occult lay one ultimate purpose, one inclusive fantastic dream—the desire and hope of acquiring superhuman power.

The despairing cry, "Yet art thou still but Faustus, and a man," calls up the whole extraordinary sixteenth-century troupe of versatile and talented vagabonds, half-genius and half-charlatan, that wandered the continent, ejected from place after place by popular demand, from fear of their powers and skepticism about their integrity: Paracelsus, he of the awesome collection of names, at once alchemist and genuine physician; Cornelius Agrippa, philosophical mocker and magician; Jerome Cardan, scientist, mathematician, and quack; Giordano Bruno, fanatic and prophetic Copernican philosopher; England's own Dr. John Dee, an eminent mathematician and astronomer, and yet apparently the complete dupe of the spiritualist, Edward Kelley. Even so sound and rational a thinker as Jean Bodin believed literally in the power of witchcraft, and wrote as lengthy a "daemonology" as that of bow-legged King Jamie himself.

There is no need to dwell on *Faustus.* It speaks for itself, with its characteristic Marlovian unevenness—passages of lyric magnificence and mediocre prose side by side; side by side magnificent conceptions and trivial performance. But the first scene is of especial interest in giving historical perspective to Faustus, the insatiable seeker after power and infinite knowledge. As he reviews each field of study, he shows himself unquestionably a child of the new age—rejecting Aristotle's logic for that of Peter Ramus; applying to Justinian's *Institutes* the new scientific and legalistic skeptical arguments; adopting (however ironically) the Calvinistic interpretation of scripture; preferring Paracelsus' medicine to Galen's.

The brief passage from the fantastic book, *A True Relation of Dr. Dee, His Actions with Spirits, &c.*, had perhaps best be left to the ministrations of Freud and Dali. The spirit Gabriel remarks at one point, "Happy is he that hath judgment to understand": reading this piece, we can but echo his sentiments. This scene of Dr. Dee, Edward Kelley, and their intimates, the spirits of Gabriel and Nalvage, has all the symbolism, dissonances, and disconnectedness of a surrealist canvas; it is fascinating, if bewildering.

The other two items in the section "The Lure of Magic" are representative pieces of the period. "White," as distinct from "black" magic, still had many defenders; it had been considered one lawful form of scientific investigation by as revered a figure as Pico della Mirandola. Ralegh's account of the unlawful sort (a chapter from his *History of the World*) affords a clear and classifying definition. It is perhaps of interest to note in passing that his so-called "School of Night," including the "Wizard" Earl of Northumberland, Thomas Hariot, Marlowe, and George Chapman, was accused of illegal occult practices, as well as atheism.

Reginald Scot's *The Discovery of Witchcraft* (1586) was the standard skeptical and rationalistic work on magic of the time. I have balanced several serious "debunking" chapters with samples from his lurid and gusty tales, to give a fair suggestion of the flavor.

Throughout all the sections in this collection, from the prologue on, anti-Catholicism appears again and again. It is inevitable in any collection of representative Elizabethan pieces, for the church that Henry VIII founded and Elizabeth fostered and increased was in the ascendant throughout the period. This was England's first great Anglican age, and although the Puritans, under the leadership of Cartwright, gained in power during the last two decades of the sixteenth century, the time for their full strength had not yet come.

The Anglican church occupied a middle position between that of the Roman Catholic church and that of the early Reformation under the leadership of Luther and Calvin. Independent of Rome, it nevertheless stayed closer to the Mother Church—in its balance between reason and faith, its approval of ecclesiastical hierarchies, and its affiliation with traditional Western institutions and concepts—than to the left wing of the Reformation, with its espousal of the exclusive righteousness of God, the utter corruption of man, its concept of salvation through faith alone, its extreme interpretation of predestination, and its repudiation of man's free will under the governance of reason as relevant to salvation.

These tendencies are apparent in the selection from Richard Hooker's *Of the Laws of Ecclesiastical Polity,* a work officially requested by Archbishop Whitgift as a blast against the Puritan faction led by Cartwright. In this passage, Hooker expounds briefly the theme that he later takes up in detail: the purposive and comprehensive government of the world by God's divine and natural laws. Hooker's work offers substantial evidence of one of the purest and most lucid prose styles in the history of English literature.

Indeed, the whole section is replete with magnificent

prose, from the haunting quality of intenseness and simplicity in John Foxe's account of the death of two early martyrs of the English Reformation to the great rolling organ voice of Donne's sermons. The inclusion of selections from the English *Book of Common Prayer*—in this case the *Book of Christian Prayers* of 1578—needs no explanation or apology. Nor do the portions of the Authorized Bible, save for a reminder that although it was published in the reign of James I, it is most strikingly an Elizabethan product in quality. Echoes of its noble style are evident throughout Elizabethan literature; or perhaps one should say that it is the culmination of the forces peculiar to Elizabethan literature. To refer to only one place where the overtones of its great voice are apparent, I suggest that you turn to the end of Greville's chapter on Sidney's famous scene with the dying soldier on the battlefield: "And when he had pledged this poor soldier, he was presently carried to Arnheim." It is the cadence, the very tone of the New Testament as we know it in the Authorized or King James version; yet it is also utterly characteristic of one Elizabethan accent—limpid, easy, simple, and unforgettable.

The parts of two sermons of Donne's which I have brought together under the title "Corruption and Redemption" form an interesting contrast to the passage from Hooker. Hooker's style is chaste yet warm; classically simple; above all beautifully, rarely clear. Its greatness lies in a cumulative single effect. Donne's, on the contrary, is involved, intricate, heavy with qualifying clauses, studded with striking images that force the reader to stop, full of metaphor and hyperbole and the dramatic contrast and conflict of opposites. Yet, despite these differences and his occasional and uneven brilliances, with him as with Hooker, the total effect is more important than the particular spots; with his long period,

he builds a great sonorous music. It is the familiar difference between Bach and Beethoven, Raphael and
Michelangelo, Velasquez and El Greco, Tolstoy and
Dostoevsky—between the Olympians and the Titans, as
someone has said.

For Donne is still tortured, still insatiably curious, still
a passionate and unfinding seeker, as morbid a dissecter
of death as he has been of love—in his sermons as in his
profane poetry. As often as he repeats, "Because the
Lord was here, our brother is not dead," we remain un-
convinced; he seems to be reassuring himself as much
as us. And in his thundering denunciations of the flesh
we discern the old pull of the flesh.

The combination of Hooker and Donne symbolizes almost all of the English Reformation of the time. In contrast to the moderate and balanced, traditionalist and
enlightened, Anglican church that Hooker officially represents, Donne displays the darker and more excessive,
the prohibitory and hell-and-damnation side of the Reformation. He is not a Puritan, but in many of his sermons he is one with Calvin in his insistence upon man's
utter depravity, one with Luther in his dark daemonic
power, one with both of them in his scorn for the efficacy
of man's natural reason to help in saving his soul. The
roots of his violence may be quite different, but his doctrine of "miserable man" is equally emphatic. . . .

Much of the best Elizabethan literature came from
the court, and from many-sided men who were at once
courtiers, soldiers, statesmen, poets, and men of affairs.
Their versatility was inherent in aristocratic educational
theories of the time; the English equivalent of the Italian
Renaissance ideal of *"L'uomo universale"* was that of the
complete, well-rounded "gentleman"—by which they
meant something much more forceful and effectual than
we do.

"Conduct books" of all kinds had long been popular, including the variety that dealt with the education of the good king or prince—the kind that suffered revolution and reversal at the hands of Machiavelli, with his *Il Principe*. Among the most popular English versions was Sir Thomas Elyot's *The Book Named the Governor*. Around the middle of the sixteenth century, however, a new variety, explicitly concerned with the perfect courtier, began to be imported, chiefly from Italy. Of these, Count Baldassare Castiglione's *Book of the Courtier*, translated by Sir Thomas Hoby, was the great favorite. Sir Philip Sidney, called by Spenser "the President of Chivalry," expressly modeled his life on the ideal set forth by Castiglione.

"The Perfect Courtier," as exemplified by Sidney, is intensely human in his motivations, however pledged to the ideal of honor; and intensely human in his mixture of the almost trivial (for his response on the tennis court is hardly so impressive to us as it seems to have been to Greville) with the heroic, the gentle and patient with the impetuous and obdurate.

I have included in this section the pieces by Dekker and Naunton (the latter written somewhat later) to relieve the rarification of the air. After so exalted an example, it is relaxing to hear from shrewd and common-sense people that some of these great personages were at times sadly lacking in wisdom or generosity, and to learn that gallants of those days were subjected to as merciless a satire as the playboys of ours.

There is no such relief in the second section of "The Creed of the Court," which I have called, in the phrase of Jefferson Butler Fletcher, the great Renaissance scholar, "The Religion of Beauty in Women." Castiglione, under the guidance of Cardinal Bembo, the high priest of "Platonic" love, as it had been reinterpreted in

Renaissance Italy, had set forth in his fourth book an account of the part a good and beautiful lady might play in the courtier's life. As her Platonic lover (*l'amante razionale*), he would ask for no favor beyond an occasional and spiritual kiss, but from her beauty he would receive inspiration to look farther and deeper for true beauty. His soul, mounting the rungs of the Platonic ladder of love and beauty, would come eventually to the perception of true and ultimate spiritual beauty, freed of the flesh, in final union with God.

As described by Castiglione, the progression retains dignity and beauty, if it remains too etherealized for one outspoken gentleman at the court of Urbino, who considers it a strange way to pay tribute to a woman's beauty, and offers the more sensible alternative of "engendering" a child in her. But in actual practice, it came to be what seems most certainly a fashionable pretence for the amusement of courts. From the sponsorship of Isabella d'Este, Vittoria Colonna, and Elizabetta Gonzaga in Italy, the institution was taken up by the court of Marguerite of Navarre and that of Elizabeth, eventually to be reinstated in England by Henrietta Maria. Irreverent scoffers, from Rabelais to the Cavalier poets, had considerable fun with it.

In Elizabethan times, Spenser and Sidney were outstanding singers of its praises. There is much reason to believe that the central concept of *The Faerie Queene* is related to it, and Spenser's introductory letter suggests this. The "Hymn in Honor of Beauty" expressly sets forth one version of the Platonic progression, similar to that developed in Italy by Benivieni in his *Canzona dello Amore celeste et divino*.

Sidney's *Astrophel and Stella* (part of which I have included) is among the most rewarding Elizabethan sonnet sequences celebrating Renaissance Platonic love.

The most rewarding—both because of the quality of the poetry and because of the sincerity and passion that sound through all the elaborate artifice of the conceit involved. The advice that Sidney's muse gives him at the beginning of *Astrophel and Stella*—"Fool, said my muse to me, look in thy heart and write"—seems eventually to have been as effective an imperative to him in loving as in writing. Throughout, the influence of Petrarch, who continually bemoans his lady's refusal to grant him favors, is as strong as that of the Platonic tradition. And of those two famous sonnets that end our selections here—"Thou blind man's mark" and "Leave me, O love"—while the second is expressly Platonic in concept, the first, with its force of frustrated passion's "smoky fire," more than offsets in final effect the elevated serenity of the other.

If churchman to courtier is a considerable journey, courtier to common man is still more considerable. Yet not so considerable as it had once been—witness Hamlet's "The age is grown so picked that the toe of the peasant comes so near the heel of the courtier he galls his kibe."

It is customary to observe that three great modern institutions had their birth in the Renaissance: Protestantism, capitalism, and democracy. There is justification for the generalization, although there were more hints of an emergent democracy than actual manifestations. Democratic implications are concealed in almost all of the new trends we have observed, and one of the surest over-all signs is the way in which these pieces included here under the heading of "The Common Man" reach out tendrils of association to the other sections.

Somewhere amongst his marginalia, Gabriel Harvey wrote in Latin, "The unlettered popularly considered cleverer than the learned." This statement was acutely accurate—and not merely in the sense of one of Harvey's favorite veins: the superiority of the courtier and the man of affairs to the scholar. The age was in twofold revolt against the extreme intellectualism of Scholasticism and the extreme moralism of the humanists who had succeeded the Scholastics. The exaltation of the humble and unlettered is integral to the currents of the early Reformation ("*Surgunt indocti et rapiunt caelum*"); to Montaigne's and his followers' preference for "Nature" over "Art" ("There is a kind of Abecedarie ignorance preceding science: Another doctoral following science: An ignorance which science doth beget, even as it *spoileth* the first"); to the empirical emphasis apparent everywhere in science and education—honor to him who observes or experiences at first hand, and contempt for him who frames his theories "in the narrow cells of the human understanding."

Nowhere was this trend stronger or more important than in the growth of empirical science. In the English universities and at London, as earlier at Padua, the artisans and technicians were coming into their own. Robert Recorde's textbooks on mathematics and astronomy in the vernacular, Digges's Copernican treatise, and the writings of Dee and William Gilbert all demonstrate a consciousness of the contribution these practical scientists were making "without benefit of learning." More, the very fact that these scholars were writing in the vernacular, to effect a joining of systematic mathematics with empirical science, was in itself a powerful proof of and contribution to the movement. During the last half of the sixteenth century, numerous important discoveries and inventions came from men without university educations; the excerpts from Harvey pay tribute to some of them.

The voice of the common man is no less consciously,

but more humorously raised in Thomas Dekker's *The Shoemaker's Holiday* and Thomas Nashe's "I Caught the Bird" (from *The Unfortunate Traveler*). The amusing incident described in the latter, where Jack Wilton proves that "simplicity and plainness shall carry it away," is at once a delightful satire on the "art" of Platonic love and a light-hearted discourse on the theme of "the unlettered popularly considered cleverer. . . ."

Dekker's work holds more serious democratic implications. It is above all a rip-roaring, lusty comedy, one of the best and most readable of Elizabethan times, but it also contains some shrewd thrusts at the speciousness of century-old social codes and classifications. This tale of a shoemaker who becomes Lord Mayor of London (the authentic Simon Eyre, who flourished in the first half of the fifteenth century, is supposed to have been an upholsterer and draper) is dedicated "To all good fellows, professors of the gentle craft, *of what degree soever.*" It is notable that, whenever the gentry and the followers of the "gentle craft" clash—whether in conflicts of wit or open hostility—the shoemakers and their wives and friends come off best.

Ralph's honest and defiant indignation ("Sirrah Hammon, Hammon, dost thou think a shoemaker is so base to be a bawd to his own wife for commodity? Take thy gold, choke with it!" and "The proudest of you that lays hands on her first, I'll lay my crutch 'cross his pate"), and Firk's "Yea, forsooth, no varlet; forsooth, no base; forsooth, I am but mean; no crafty neither, but of the gentle craft" set the tone for the whole play—a tone to which the King adds his benediction in the final scene, when he rebukes the Earl of Lincoln for his allegations about "base blood." And we finish the play with the oft-repeated phrases of Simon Eyre, the madcap shoemaker-mayor, ringing in our ears: "Prince am I none, yet am I nobly born, as being the sole son of a shoemaker."

The broadside ballads take their place naturally in this section as the poetry of the people. These ballads were sold by ballad singers on the street-corner. They were printed on a single sheet and ornamented with woodcuts; they often found their way to the walls of homes and taverns as decorations. They are described by John Earle in his *Microcosmography* as the work of "pot-poets," that "go out in single sheets, and are chanted from market to market to a vile tune and a worse throat, whilst the poor country wench melts like her butter to hear them." Among the best known of the professional ballad writers were William Elderton, to whose red nose Nashe refers in his blast against Richard Harvey's astrological predictions, and Thomas Deloney, who also wrote prose romances about craftsmen. . . .

The greater part of this Reader has been devoted to "new horizons" of all sorts, although only the first section has been so titled. I do not believe that such an emphasis is distorted; the selections themselves justify my contention that the Elizabethan period was an age of transition between one world and the other, much as our own is. But the earlier Renaissance had been preeminently marked by a great revival of classical learning and a tremendous reverence for antiquity. That favorite figure of sixteenth- and seventeenth-century writers, Janus of the two faces, is particularly pertinent to the character of the age. The Renaissance begins with its face turned to the great stretch of the past; it ends with its face turned toward the illimitable vistas of the future.

In England, the Erasmus-Oxford movement of the early sixteenth century had stressed the noble documents of classical letters and learning, and their appli-

cability to the present. In Elizabethan times, a strong
reaction had set in. Yet the interest continued, if diminished and somewhat altered. There were the great translations—North's Plutarch and Chapman's Homer. There
were the sturdy historians of England—notably Holinshed and Halle, whose *Chronicles* were an endless
source of material for Shakespeare and a contributing
force to that wave of nationalistic and patriotic feeling
that marked Elizabeth's reign.

Scattered throughout the Reader, according to subject matter, are excerpts of Sir Walter Ralegh's somber
but sonorous prose. His greatest undertaking, a labor of
his Tower years, was his unfinished but monumental
History of the World. The selection from his preface to
this work forms a fitting introduction to the section
called "The Well of the Past." His meditations on history
convey effectively a sense of that vast expanse of space
and time already lost, already "behind." And the bitter
irony of the final paragraphs closes with equal effec-
tiveness the gap between that past and the present. The
injunction about vanity from *Ecclesiastes* hovers sar-
donically over these pages, as it does—together with the
carpe diem theme—over the turbulent, gusty and bewildering days of the Elizabethan Age. . . .

The book closes with a section of lyric poetry. There
is no need to dwell on this section in the introduction,
for there has never before or since been so glorious an
outpouring of song in all the rest of the ages of man.
Anyone who reads poetry, reads the Elizabethans. The
problem has not been whom to include, but whom to
exclude. I have been guided by two or three major
principles: to give the full flavor of a few poets, rather
than a nibble at many; to choose—when such a choice
was necessary among poets of equal, or almost equal,
merit—interesting historical figures rather than dull or

obscure ones; to do as much justice as possible, within the space allotted, to different *kinds* of poets.

But in the last analysis, such a selection must be largely guided by personal and subjective preferences. I have begun the section with a part of Sidney's "Apology for Poetry" because I felt that at least a sample of the many Elizabethan critical essays should be included, and this seems to me the best. I have given space to Sir Thomas Wyatt and not to the Earl of Surrey because, while both pre-date Elizabeth's succession to the throne and the full "age of song" (They dominate, however, *Tottel's Miscellany* of 1557, which may be considered to inaugurate the literary Elizabethan Age), Wyatt—in his honest passion, his simple lyricism and his verbal felicity—seems to me representative of the happiest Elizabethan singers, while the colder, more resplendent Surrey foreshadows a less appealing side of the later lyricists. I have included Elizabeth—the only woman in the whole collection—and Essex for obvious sentimental reasons.

For the rest, we find Ralegh, Spenser, Breton, Greene, Lodge, Drayton, Campion, Jonson, and Donne. Sidney, Marlowe, Chapman, Greville, Dekker and the ballad-makers appear elsewhere in the book. Along with Surrey, Sackville, Lyly, Gascoigne, Oxford, Dyer, Watson, Daniel, the two Davies, Harington, Marston, Heywood, Beaumont, Fletcher, and others are missing altogether. It was inevitable. Where there is such prodigal richness, there must be some waste.

The casualties in other kinds of literature are as great. None of the body of Spenser's *Faerie Queene;* Sidney's *Arcadia;* Jonson's *Volpone;* Marlowe's *Edward IV* and *Hero and Leander;* the popular moral tales in verse of *The Mirror of Magistrates;* the plays of Kyd, Peele, Marston, Chapman; the prose romances of Barnaby

Rich, Greene, Lodge—one could go on and on. Elizabeth's reign was from 1558 to 1603. I have taken as my terminal points the publication of *Tottel's Miscellany* in 1557 and the death of Francis Bacon in 1626—a stretch of almost seventy years, seventy of the most eventful years in human life and literature. And I have been guided, as I said at the outset, by a determination to select representative material and material possessing readability and interest for the twentieth century.

The one greatest omission is no omission at all. Over the whole book, over all its parts, looms the gigantic shadow of Will Shakespeare. Literally, he is represented by one tiny selection in the group called "Portents in the Sky." Actually, he is represented everywhere. This is his world, and the book might as justly be called *A Shakespearean Reader*. Star-gazers, children of the Golden Age, pedants and scientists, "Machiavellian" tyrants and climbers, witches and magicians, Puritans, courtiers, exponents and ridiculers of Platonic love, craftsmen and artisans, the great figures of England's and the world's past—all these and a host of others people his plays as they do these pages. The Viking Portable Library already contains a *Portable Shakespeare:* the two volumes are complementary as few can be.

Read well, and you will find in these pages some of the causes of Hamlet's brooding melancholy, as well as the model for the courtier-scholar-soldier Ophelia describes; snatches of the London in which Falstaff reveled; the dark and mysterious world in which Macbeth met the witches; the sunnier but no less mysterious one that Prospero governed; Gonzago's "commonwealth;" Hotspur's fiery and exclusive devotion to honor; the Duke's speech in *Measure for Measure* about the current craze for novelty; Edmund's naturalistic skepticism; Iago's malevolent scheming; the codes of honor and love satirically treated in *Troilus and Cressida;* the Machiavellian policy of Claudius and the cruder Machiavellian career of Richard III; the court of *Love's Labour's Lost,* the pastoral Arden of *As You Like It,* and the seacoast of Bohemia in *A Winter's Tale;* the great antique worlds in which Antony and Cleopatra, Coriolanus and Brutus and Caesar lived and strove and died; and that storm-shaken and disintegrating world of Lear's.

This book, in short, is that theater of life to which Shakespeare refers so often—in Jacques' famous "All the world's a stage"; in Prospero's equally famous "These our actors"; in Macbeth's "Life's but a walking shadow, a poor player"; and in Isabella's "Man, proud man, drest in a little brief authority." It is the rich and varied world in which Will Shakespeare lived and died—that world which he half recorded, half re-created in his magnificent plays.

"Others abide our question; thou art free." Here are some of those others, brought before you again, to receive your verdict after three and a half centuries.

HIRAM HAYDN

EDITOR'S NOTE

My thanks are due especially to Miss Mary Louise Hammer, for her extensive help both in preparing the final manuscript and proofreading those parts which required a modernizing of the spelling. I also wish to acknowledge the assistance of Miss Irene Orgel for her part in modernizing the spelling and typing the revision, and that of Mrs. Willard Freeman for her stenographic help.

For several suggestions for additions to the Reader, I

am grateful to Professors Oscar James Campbell and Marc Friedlaender. I owe a still greater debt to Mr. Campbell for the privilege of having first encountered many of these Elizabethans under his guidance—would there were more teachers like him.

To Professor Marjorie Hope Nicolson, my thanks for help on the section "The Upheaval in the Heavens"—to which she suggested the addition of Sir Henry Wotton's letter to the Earl of Salisbury.

A word of explanation concerning the procedure I have followed with regard to spelling, punctuation, etc., may be in order. With few exceptions (one is the word "shew," characteristic and yet perfectly clear), the spelling has been modernized. The punctuation has been altered to modern practice, for the sake of clarification, except where it seemed so integral a part of the style (as in Donne's *Sermons* and Harvey's writings) that it should be left intact. I have, however, for the most part retained the heavy Elizabethan use of the comma. I have also followed their practice in capitalization, with the feeling that perhaps some of the quaintness and flavor lost in the modernization of the spelling might thus be preserved, without disturbing the twentieth-century reader.

H. H.

PART ONE
New Horizons

John Donne

A MEETING IN HELL

I was in Ecstasy, and

> My little wandering sportful Soul,
> Guest, and Companion of my body

had liberty to wander through all places, and to survey and reckon all the rooms, and all the volumes of the heavens, and to comprehend the situation, the dimensions, the nature, the people, and the policy, both of the swimming Islands, the Planets, and of all those which are fixed in the firmament. Of which, I think it an honester part as yet to be silent, than to do Galileo wrong by speaking of it, who of late hath summoned the other worlds, the Stars to come nearer to him, and give him an account of themselves. Or to Kepler, who (as himself testifies of himself) ever since Tycho Brahe's death hath received it into his care, that no new thing should be done in heaven without his knowledge. For by the law, Prevention must take place; and therefore what they have found and discovered first, I am content they speak and utter first. Yet this they may vouchsafe to take from me, that they shall hardly find Enoch or Elias anywhere in their circuit. When I had surveyed all the Heavens, then as

> The Lark by busy and laborious ways,
> Having climbed up the ethereal hill, doth raise
> His Hymns to Phoebus' Harp, And striking then
> His sails, his wings, doth fall down back again
> So suddenly, that one may safely say
> A stone came lazily, that came that way.

In the twinkling of an eye, I saw all the rooms in Hell open to my sight. And by the benefit of certain spectacles, I know not of what making, but, I think, of the same, by which Gregory the Great, and Bede did discern so distinctly the souls of their friends, when they were discharged from their bodies, and sometimes the souls of such men as they knew not by sight, and of some that were never in the world, and yet they could distinguish them flying into Heaven, or conversing with living men, I saw all the channels in the bowels of the Earth; and all the inhabitants of all nations, and of all ages were suddenly made familiar to me. I think truly, Robert Aquinas when he took Christ's long Oration, as he hung upon the Cross, did use some such instrument as this, but applied to the ear: And so I think did he, which dedicated to Adrian VI, that Sermon which Christ made in praise of his father Joseph: for else how did they hear that, which none but they ever heard?

As for the Suburbs of Hell (I mean both Limbo and Purgatory) I must confess I passed them over so negligently, that I saw them not: and I was hungrily carried, to find new places, never discovered before. For Purgatory did not seem worthy to me of much diligence, because it may seem already to have been believed by some persons, in some corners of the Roman Church, for about fifty years; that is, ever since the Council of Trent had a mind to fulfill the prophecies of Homer,

Virgil, and the other Patriarchs of the Papists; and being not satisfied with making one Transsubstantiation, purposed to bring in another: which is to change fables into Articles of faith.

Proceeding therefore to more inward places, I saw a secret place, where there were not many, beside Lucifer himself; to which, only they had title, which had so attempted any innovation in this life, that they gave an affront to all antiquity, and induced doubts, and anxieties, and scruples, and after, a liberty of believing what they would; at length established opinions, directly contrary to all established before. . . .

Now to this place, not only such endeavor to come, as have innovated in matters, directly concerning the soul, but they also which have done so, either in the Arts, or in conversation, or in anything that exerciseth the faculties of the soul, and may so provoke to quarrelsome and brawling controversies: *For so the truth be lost, it is no matter how.* But the gates are seldom opened, nor scarce oftener than once in an Age.

But my destiny favored me so much, that I was present then, and saw all the pretenders, and all that affected an entrance, and Lucifer himself, who then came out into the outward chamber, to hear them plead their own Causes. As soon as the door creaked, I spied a certain Mathematician, which till then had been busied to find, to deride, to detrude Ptolemy; and now with an erect countenance, and settled pace, came to the gates, and with hands and feet (scarce respecting Lucifer himself) beat the doors, and cried, "Are these shut against me, to whom all the Heavens were ever open, who was a Soul to the Earth, and gave it motion?"

By this I knew it was Copernicus. For though I had never heard ill of his life, and therefore might wonder to find him there; yet when I remembered, that the

Papists have extended the name, and the punishment of Heresy, almost to everything, and that as yet I used Gregory's and Bede's spectacles, by which one saw Origen, who deserved so well of the Christian Church, burning in Hell, I doubted no longer, but assured myself that it was Copernicus which I saw.

To whom Lucifer said, "Who are you? For though even by this boldness you seem worthy to enter, and have attempted a new faction even in Hell, yet you must first satisfy those, which stand about you, and which expect the same fortune as you do."

"Except, O Lucifer," answered Copernicus, "I thought thee of the race of the star Lucifer, with which I am so well acquainted, I should not vouchsafe thee this discourse. I am he, which pitying thee who wert thrust into the Center of the world, raised both thee, and thy prison, the Earth, up into the Heavens; so as by my means God doth not enjoy his revenge upon thee. The Sun, which was an officious spy, and a betrayer of faults, and so thine enemy, I have appointed to go into the lowest part of the world. Shall these gates be open to such as have innovated in small matters? And shall they be shut against me, who have turned the whole frame of the world, and am thereby almost a new Creator?"

More than this he spoke not. Lucifer stuck in a meditation. For what should he do? It seemed unjust to deny entry to him which had deserved so well, and dangerous to grant it, to one of so great ambitions, and undertakings. Nor did he think that himself had attempted greater matters before his fall. Something he had which he might have conveniently opposed, but he was loath to utter it, lest he should confess his fear.

But Ignatius Loyola which was got near his chair, a subtle fellow, and so indued with the Devil, that he was able to tempt, and not only that, but (as they say) even to possess the Devil, apprehended this perplexity in Lucifer. And making himself sure of his own entrance, and knowing well, that many thousands of his family aspired to that place, he opposed himself against all others. He was content they should be damned, but not that they should govern. And though when he died he was utterly ignorant in all great learning, and knew not so much as Ptolemey's or Copernicus' name, but might have been persuaded, that the words Almagest, Zenith, and Nadir, were Saints' names, and fit to be put into the Litany, and *Ora pro nobis* joined to them; yet after he had spent some time in Hell, he had learnt somewhat of his Jesuits, which daily came thither. And whilst he stayed at the threshold of Hell; that is, from the time when he delivered himself over to the Pope's will, he took a little taste of learning. Thus furnished, thus he undertakes Copernicus.

"Do you think to win our Lucifer to your part, by allowing him the honor of being of the race of that star? Who was not only made before all the stars, but being glutted with the glory of shining there, transferred his dwelling and Colonies unto this Monarchy, and thereby gave our Order a noble example, to spy, to invade, and to possess foreign kingdoms. Can our Lucifer, or his followers have any honor from that star Lucifer, which is but Venus? Whose face how much we scorn, appears by this, that, for the most part we use her adversely and preposterously. Rather let our Lucifer glory in Lucifer the Calaritan Bishop; not therefore because he is placed amongst Heretics, only for affirming the propagation of the soul; but especially for this, that he was the first that opposed the dignity of Princes, and imprinted the names of Antichrist, Judas, and other stigmatic marks upon the Emperor.

"But for you, what new thing have you invented, by

which our Lucifer gets anything? What cares he whether the earth travel, or stand still? Hath your raising up of the earth into heaven, brought men to that confidence, that they build new towers or threaten God again? Or do they out of this motion of the earth conclude, that there is no Hell, or deny the punishment of sin? Do not men believe? Do they not live just as they did before?

"Besides, this detracts from the dignity of your learning, and derogates from your right and title of coming to this place, that those opinions of yours may very well be true. If therefore any man have honor or title to this place in this matter, it belongs wholly to our Clavius, who opposed himself opportunely against you, and the truth, which at that time was creeping into every man's mind. He only can be called the Author of all contentions, and school-combats in this cause; and no greater profit can be hoped for herein, but that for such brabbles, more necessary matters be neglected. And yet not only for this is our Clavius to be honored, but for the great pains also which he took in the Gregorian Calendar, by which both the peace of the Church, and Civil businesses have been egregiously troubled: nor hath Heaven itself escaped his violence, but hath ever since obeyed his appointments: so that St. Stephen, John the Baptist, and all the rest, which have been commanded to work miracles at certain appointed days, where their Relics are preserved, do not now attend till the day come, as they were accustomed, but are awaked ten days sooner, and constrained by him to come down from heaven to do that business.

"But your inventions can scarce be called yours, since long before you, Heraclitus, Ecphantus, and Aristarchus thrust them into the world: who notwithstanding content themselves with lower rooms amongst the other Philosophers, and aspire not to this place, reserved only for Antichristian Heroes: neither do you agree so well amongst yourselves, as that you can be said to have made a Sect, since, as you have perverted and changed the order and Scheme of others: so Tycho Brahe hath done by yours, and others by his. Let therefore this little Mathematician (dread Emperor) withdraw himself to his own company. And if hereafter the fathers of our Order can draw a Cathedral Decree from the Pope, by which it may be defined as a matter of faith: That the earth doth not move; and an Anathema inflicted upon all which hold the contrary: then perchance both the Pope which shall decree that, and Copernicus his followers (if they be Papists) may have the dignity of this place."

Lucifer signified his assent; and Copernicus, without muttering a word, was as quiet, as he thinks the sun.

Then he which stood next him, entered into his place. To whom Lucifer said: "And who are you?"

He answered, "Philippus Aureolus Theophrastus Paracelsus Bombast of Hohenheim." At this Lucifer trembled, as if it were a new Exorcism, and he thought it might well be the first verse of St. John, which is always employed in Exorcisms, and might now be taken out of the Welsh, or Irish Bibles. But when he understood that it was but the web of his name, he recollected himself, and raising himself upright, asked what he had to say to the great Emperor Satan, Lucifer, Beelzebub, Leviathan, Abaddon.

Paracelsus replied, "It were an injury to thee, O glorious Emperor, if I should deliver before thee, what I have done, as though all those things had not proceeded from thee, which seemed to have been done by me, thy organ and conduit: yet since I shall rather be thy trumpet herein, than mine own, some things may be uttered by me. Besides therefore that I brought all Methodical

Physicians, and the art itself into so much contempt, that that kind of physic is almost lost; this also was ever my principal purpose, that no certain new Art, nor fixed rules might be established, but that all remedies might be dangerously drawn from my uncertain, ragged, and imperfect experiments, in trial whereof, how many men have been made carcases? And falling upon those times which did abound with paradoxical, and unusual diseases, of all which, the pox, which then began to rage, was almost the center and sink; I ever professed an assured and an easy cure thereof, lest I should deter any from their licentiousness. And whereas almost all poisons are so disposed and conditioned by nature, that they offend some of the senses, and so are easily discerned and avoided, I brought it to pass, that that treacherous quality of theirs might be removed, and so they might safely be given without suspicion, and yet perform their office as strongly. All this I must confess, I wrought by thy minerals and by thy fires, but yet I cannot despair of my reward, because I was thy first Minister and instrument, in these innovations."

By this time Ignatius had observed a tempest risen in Lucifer's countenance: for he was just of the same temper as Lucifer, and therefore suffered with him in everything, and felt all his alterations. That therefore he might deliver him from Paracelsus, he said, "You must not think sir, that you may here draw out an oration to the proportion of your name. It must be confessed, that you attempted great matters, and well becoming a great officer of Lucifer, when you undertook not only to make a man, in your Alembics, but also to preserve him immortal. And it cannot be doubted, but that out of your Commentaries upon the Scriptures, in which you were utterly ignorant, many men have taken occasion of erring, and thereby this kingdom much indebted to you.

"But must you therefore have access to this secret place? What have you compassed, even in Physic itself, of which we Jesuits are ignorant? For though our Ribadenegra have reckoned none of our Order, which hath written in Physic, yet how able and sufficient we are in that faculty, I will be tried by that Pope, who hath given a privilege to Jesuits to practice Physic, and to be present at Death-beds, which is denied to other Orders. For why should he deny us their bodies whose souls he delivers to us? And since he hath transferred upon us the power to practice Physic, he may justly be thought to have transferred upon us the Art itself, by the same Omnipotent Bull; since he which grants the end, is by our Rules of law presumed to have granted all means necessary to that end.

"Let me (dread Emperor) have leave to speak truth before thee; these men abuse and profane too much thy metals, which are the bowels, and treasure of thy kingdom. For what doth Physic profit thee? Physic is a soft, and womanish thing. For since no medicine doth naturally draw blood, that science is not fit nor worthy of our study.

"Besides why should those things, which belong to you, be employed to preserve from diseases, or to procure long life? Were it not fitter, that your brother, and colleague, the Bishop of Rome, which governs upon the face of your earth, and gives daily increase to your kingdom, should receive from you these helps and subsidies? To him belongs all the Gold, to him all the precious stones, concealed in your entrails, whereby he might bait and ensnare the Princes of the earth, through their Lord, and counsellors means to his obedience, and to receive his commandments, especially in these times, when almost everywhere his ancient rights and tributes are denied unto him. To him belongs your Iron, and the

ignobler metals, to make engines. To him belong your
Minerals apt for poison. To him, the Saltpeter, and all
the Elements of Gun-powder, by which he may demolish and overthrow Kings and Kingdoms, and Courts,
and seats of Justice.

"Neither doth Paracelsus truly deserve the name of
Innovator, whose doctrine, Severinus and his other followers do refer to the most ancient times. Think therefore yourself well satisfied, if you be admitted to govern
in chief that Legion of homicide-Physicians, and of
Princes which shall be made away by poison in the
midst of their sins, and of women tempting by paintings
and face-physic. Of all which sorts great numbers will
daily come hither out of your Academy."

Content with this sentence, Paracelsus departed; and
Machiavelli succeeded, who having observed Ignatius
his forwardness, and sauciness, and how, uncalled, he
had thrust himself into the office of king's Attorney,
thought this stupid patience of Copernicus, and Paracelsus (men which tasted too much of their Germany) unfit for a Florentine: and therefore had provided some
venomous darts, out of his Italian Arsenal, to cast against
this worn soldier of Pampelune, this French-Spanish
mongrel, Ignatius.

But when he thought better upon it, and observed that
Lucifer ever approved whatsoever Ignatius said, he suddenly changed his purpose; and putting on another resolution, he determined to direct his speech to Ignatius,
as to the principal person next to Lucifer, as well by this
means to sweeten and mollify him, as to make Lucifer
suspect, that by these honors and specious titles offered
to Ignatius, and entertained by him, his own dignity
might be eclipsed, or clouded; and that Ignatius by winning to his side politic men, exercised in civil businesses,

might attempt some innovation in that kingdom. Thus therefore he began to speak.

"Dread Emperor, and you, his watchful and diligent Genius, Father Ignatius, Archchancellor of this Court, and highest Priest of this highest Synagogue (except the primacy of the Roman Church reach also unto this place) let me before I descend to myself, a little consider, speak, and admire your stupendous wisdom, and the government of this state. You may vouchsafe to remember (great Emperor) how long after the Nazarene's death, you were forced to live a solitary, a barren, and an Eremitical life: till at last (as it was ever your fashion to imitate heaven) out of your abundant love, you begot this dearly beloved son of yours, Ignatius, which stands at your right hand. And from both of you proceeds a spirit, whom you have sent into the world, who triumphing both with Mitre and Crown, governs your Militant Church there. As for those sons of Ignatius who either he left alive, or were born after his death, and your spirit, the Bishop of Rome; how justly and properly may they be called Equivocal men? And not only Equivocal in that sense, in which the Pope's Legates, at your Nicene Council were called Equivocal, because they did agree in all their opinions, and in all their words: but especially because they have brought into the world a new art of Equivocation. O wonderful, and incredible Hypercritics, who, not out of marble fragments, but out of the secretest Records of Hell itself: that is out of the minds of Lucifer, the Pope, and Ignatius (persons truly equivocal), have raised to life again the language of the Tower of Babel, so long concealed, and brought us again from understanding one another.

"For my part (O noble pair of Emperors) that I may freely confess the truth, all which I have done, wheresoever there shall be mention made of the Jesuits, can be reputed but childish; for this honor I hope will not be denied me, that I brought in an Alphabet, and provided certain Elements, and was some kind of schoolmaster in preparing them a way to higher undertakings; yet it grieves me, and makes me ashamed, that I should be ranked with this idle and Chimerical Copernicus, or this cadaverous vulture, Paracelsus. I scorn that those gates, into which men could conceive any hope of entrance, should not voluntarily fly open to me. Yet I can better endure the rashness and fellowship of Paracelsus, than the other: because he having been conveniently practiced in the butcheries, and mangling of men, he had the reason to hope for favor of the Jesuits.

"For I myself went always that way of blood, and therefore I did ever prefer the sacrifices of the Gentiles, and of the Jews, which were performed with effusion of blood (whereby not only the people, but the Priests also were animated to bold enterprises) before the soft and wanton sacrifices of Christians. If I might have had my choice, I should rather have wished, that the Roman Church had taken the Bread, than the Wine, from the people, since in the wine there is some color, to imagine and represent blood. Neither did you (most Reverend Bishop of this Diocese, Ignatius) abhor from this way of blood. For having consecrated your first age to the wars, and grown somewhat unable to follow that course, by reason of a wound; you did presently begin to think seriously of a spiritual war, against the Church, and found means to open ways, even into Kings' chambers, for your executioners. Which dignity, you did not reserve only to your own Order, but (though I must confess, that the foundation, and the nourishment of this Doctrine remains with you, and is peculiar to you, out of your infinite liberality) you have vouchsafed sometime, to use the hands of other men in these employments. And therefore as well as they, who have so often in vain attempted it in England, as they which have brought their great purposes to effect in France, are indebted only to you for their courage and resolution.

"But yet although the entrance into this place may be decreed to none, but the Innovators, and only such of them as have dealt in Christian business; and of them also, to those only which have had the fortune to do much harm, I cannot see but that next to the Jesuits, I must be invited to enter, since I did not only teach those ways, by which, through perfidiousness and dissembling of Religion, a man might possess, and usurp upon the liberty of free Commonwealths; but also did arm and furnish the people with my instructions, how when they were under this oppression, they might safeliest conspire, and remove a tyrant, or revenge themselves of their Prince, and redeem their former losses; so that from both sides, both from Prince and People, I brought an abundant harvest, and a noble increase to this kingdom."

By this time I perceived Lucifer to be much moved with this Oration, and to incline much towards Machiavelli. For he did acknowledge him to be a kind of Patriarch, of those whom they call Laymen. And he had long observed, that the Clergy of Rome tumbled down to Hell daily, easily, voluntarily, and by troupes, because they were accustomed to sin against their conscience, and knowledge; but that the Laity sinning out of a slothfulness, and negligence of finding the truth, did rather offend by ignorance, and omission. And therefore he thought himself bound to reward Machiavelli, which had awakened this drowsy and implicit Laity to greater, and more bloody undertakings. Besides this, since Ignatius could not be denied the place, whose ambitions and

turbulencies Lucifer understood very well, he thought
Machiavelli a fit and necessary instrument to oppose
against him; that so the scales being kept even by their
factions, he might govern in peace, and two poisons
mingled might do no harm.

But he could not hide this intention from Ignatius,
more subtle than the Devil, and the verier Lucifer of the
two. Therefore Ignatius rushed out, threw himself down
at Lucifer's feet, and grovelling on the ground adored
him. . . .

[Ignatius launches a long assault on Machiavelli's pre-
tensions and unworthiness. Lucifer finally reluctantly
dismisses the Florentine.]

Truly I thought this Oration of Ignatius very long:
and I began to think of my body which I had so long
abandoned, lest it should putrify, or grow moldy, or be
buried; yet I was loath to leave the stage, till I saw the
play ended. And I was in hope, that if any such thing
should befall my body, the Jesuits, who work Miracles
so familiarly, and whose reputation I was so careful of
in this matter, would take compassion upon me, and
restore me again. But as I had sometimes observed,

> Feathers or straws swim on the water's face
> Brought to the bridge, where through a narrow place
> The water passes, thrown back, and delayed;
> And having danced a while, and nimbly played
> Upon the watery circles, then have been
> By the streams liquid snares, and jaws sucked in
> And sunk into the womb of that swollen bourne,
> Leave the beholder desperate of return.

So I saw Machiavelli often put forward, and often
thrust back, and at last vanish. And looking earnestly
upon Lucifer's countenance, I perceived him to be
affected towards Ignatius, as Princes, who though they
envy and grudge, that their great Officers should have

such immoderate means to get wealth; yet they dare not complain of it, lest thereby they should make them odious and contemptible to the people; so that Lucifer now suffered a new Hell: that is, the danger of a Popular Devil, vainglorious, and inclined to innovations there. Therefore he determined to withdraw himself into his inward chamber, and to admit none but Ignatius: for he could not exclude him, who had deserved so well; neither did he think it safe to stay without, and give him more occasions to amplify his own worth, and undervalue all them there in public, and before so many vulgar Devils.

But as he rose, a whole army of souls besieged him. And all which had invented any new thing, even in the smallest matters, thronged about him, and importuned an admission. Even those which had but invented new attire for women, and those whom Pancirollo hath recorded in his *Commentaries* for invention of Porcelain dishes, of Spectacles, of Quintans, of stirrups, and of Caviari, thrust themselves into the troupe. And of those, which pretended that they had squared the circle, the number was infinite. But Ignatius scattered all this cloud quickly, by commanding, by chiding, by deriding, and by force and violence.

Amongst the rest, I was sorry to see him use Pietro Aretino so ill as he did. For though Ignatius told him true when he boasted of his licentious pictures, that because he was not much learned, he had left out many things of that kind, with which the ancient histories and poems abound; and that therefore Aretino had not only not added any new invention, but had also taken away all courage and spurs from youth, which would rashly trust, and rely upon his diligence, and seek no further, and so lose that infinte and precious treasure of Antiquity. . . .

But for all this, since Aretino was one who, by a long custom of libelous and contumelious speaking against Princes, had got such a habit, that at last he came to diminish and disesteem God himself, I wonder truly, that this Arch-Jesuit, though he would not admit him to any eminent place in his Triumphant Church, should deny him an office of lower estimation. For truly to my thinking, he might have been fit, either to serve Ignatius, as master of his pleasures, or Lucifer as his Crier. For whatsoever Lucifer durst think, this man durst speak. But Ignatius, who thought himself sufficient for all uses, thrust him away, and when he offered upward, offered his staff at him.

Nor did he use Christopher Columbus with any better respect; who having found all ways in the earth, and sea open to him, did not fear any difficulty in Hell, but when he offered to enter, Ignatius stayed him, and said: "You must remember, sir, that if this kingdom have got anything by the discovery of the West Indies, all that must be attributed to our Order. For if the opinion of the Dominicans had prevailed, *That the inhabitants should be reduced, only by preaching and without violence,* certainly their two-hundred thousand of men would scarce in so many ages have been brought to one-hundred and fifty, which by our means was so soon performed. And if the law, made by Ferdinand, only against Cannibals: *That all which would not be Christians should be bondslaves,* had not been extended into other Provinces, we should have lacked men, to dig us out that benefit, which their countries afford.

"Except we when we took away their old Idolatry, had recompensed them with a new one of ours; except we had obtruded to those ignorant and barbarous people sometimes natural things, sometimes artificial, and counterfeit, instead of Miracles; and except we had been always ready to convey, and to apply this medicine made of this precious American dung, unto the Princes of Europe, and their Lords, and Counsellors, the profit by the only discovery of these places (which must of necessity be referred to fortune) would have been very little; yet I praise your perseverance, and your patience; which since that seems to be your principal virtue, you shall have good occasion to exercise here, when you remain in a lower and remoter place, than you think belongs to your merits. . . ."

[Through Ignatius' further wiles, all the rest of the candidates are dismissed.]

Therefore Lucifer . . . despairing of bringing in another, began earnestly to think, how he might leave Ignatius out. This therefore he said to him: "I am sorry my Ignatius, that I can neither find in others, deserts worthy of this place, nor any room in this place worthy of your deserts. If I might die, I see there would be no long strife for a successor. For if you have not yet done that act which I did at first in Heaven, and thereby got this Empire, this may excuse you, that no man hath been able to tell you what it was. For if any of the Ancients say true, when they call it Pride, or Licentiousness, or Lying: or if it be in any of the Casuists which profess the Art of sinning, you cannot be accused of having omitted it.

"But since I may neither forsake this kingdom, nor divide it, this only remedy is left: I will write to the Bishop of Rome: he shall call Galileo the Florentine to him; who by this time hath thoroughly instructed himself of all the hills, woods, and Cities in the new world, the Moon. And since he effected so much with his first Glasses, that he saw the Moon, in so near a distance that he gave himself satisfaction of all, and the least parts in her, when now being grown to more perfection in his Art, he shall have made new Glasses, and they received a hallowing from the Pope, he may draw the Moon, like a boat floating upon the water, as near the earth as he will.

"And thither (because they ever claim that those employments of discovery belong to them) shall all the Jesuits be transferred, and easily unite and reconcile the Lunatic Church to the Roman Church; without doubt, after the Jesuits have been there a little while, there will soon grow naturally a Hell in that world also: over which, you, Ignatius, shall have dominion, and establish your kingdom and dwelling there. And with the same ease as you pass from the earth to the Moon, you may pass from the Moon to the other stars, which are also thought to be worlds, and so you may beget and propagate many Hells, and enlarge your Empire, and come nearer unto that high seat which I left at first. . . ."

[Ignatius refuses this compromise measure, and insists upon the coveted seat. Lucifer finally yields.]

Upon this I came back again, to spy (if the gates were still open) with what affection Ignatius, and they who were in ancient possession of that place, behaved themselves towards one another. And I found him yet in the porch, and there beginning a new contention: for having presently cast his eyes to the principal place, next to Lucifer's own Throne, and finding it possessed, he stopped Lucifer, and asked him, who it was that sat there.

It was answered, that it was Pope Boniface; to whom, as to a principal Innovator, for having first challenged the name of Universal Bishop, that honor was afforded.

"Is he an Innovator?" thundered Ignatius. "Shall I suffer this, when all my Disciples have labored all this while to prove to the world, that all the Popes before his time did use that name? And that Gregory did not reprehend the Patriarch John for taking to himself an Antichristian name, but for usurping a name which was due to none but the Pope. And could it be fit for you, Lucifer (who in this were either unmindful of the Roman Church, or else too weak and incapable of her secrets and mysteries), to give way to any sentence in Hell, which (though it were according to truth) yet differed from the Jesuit's Oracles?"

With this Ignatius flies upwards, and rushes upon Boniface, and throws him out of his Seat. And Lucifer went up with him as fast, and gave him assistance, lest, if he should forsake him, his own seat might be endangered.

[FROM *Ignatius, His Conclave*]

Michael Drayton

TO THE VIRGINIAN VOYAGE

You brave heroic minds
Worthy your country's name,
  That honour still pursue,
  Go, and subdue,
Whilst loit'ring hinds
Lurk here at home, with shame.

Britons, you stay too long;
Quickly aboard bestow you,
  And with a merry gale
  Swell your stretched sail,
With vows as strong
As the winds that blow you.

Your course securely steer,
West and by south forth keep,
  Rocks, lee-shores, nor shoals,
  When Æolus scowls,
You need not fear,
So absolute the deep.

And cheerfully at sea,
Success you still entice,
   To get the pearl and gold,
   And ours to hold,
Virginia,
Earth's only paradise,

Where nature hath in store
Fowl, venison, and fish,
   And the fruitful'st soil
   Without your toil
Three harvests more,
All greater than your wish.

And the ambitious vine
Crowns with his purple mass,
   The cedar reaching high
   To kiss the sky,
The cypress, pine,
And useful sassafras.

To whose the golden age
Still nature's laws doth give,
   No other cares that tend,
   But them to defend
From winter's age,
That long there doth not live.

Whenas the luscious smell
Of that delicious land,
   Above the seas that flows,
   The clear wind throws,
Your hearts to swell
Approaching the dear strand,

In kenning of the shore,
Thanks to God first given,
   O you, the happi'st men,
   Be frolic then,
Let cannons roar,
Frighting the wide heaven.

And in regions far
Such heroes bring ye forth
   As those from whom we came,
   And plant our name
Under that star
Not known unto our north.

And as there plenty grows
Of laurel everywhere,
   Apollo's sacred tree,
   You it may see
A poet's brows
To crown, that may sing there.

Thy voyages attend,
Industrious Hakluyt,
   Whose reading shall enflame
   Men to seek fame,
And much commend
To after times thy wit.

Richard Hakluyt

THE DEATH OF
SIR HUMPHREY GILBERT

THE WIND was large for England at our return, but
very high, and the sea rough, insomuch as the frigate, wherein the General went, was almost swallowed
up.

Monday in the afternoon we passed in sight of Cape
Race, having made as much way in little more than two
days and nights back again, as before we had done in
eight days from Cape Race unto the place where our
ship perished. Which hindrance thitherward, and speed
back again, is to be imputed unto the swift current, as
well as to the winds, which we had more large in our return. This Monday the General came aboard the *Hind,*
to have the surgeon of the *Hind* to dress his foot, which
he hurt by treading upon a nail: at which time we comforted each other with hope of hard success to be all
past, and of the good to come. So agreeing to carry out
lights always by night, that we might keep together, he
departed into his frigate, being by no means to be entreated to tarry in the *Hind,* which had been more for
his security. Immediately after followed a sharp storm,
which we overpassed for that time, praised be God.

The weather fair, the General came aboard the *Hind*
again, to make merry together with the captain, master,
and company, which was the last meeting, and continued there from morning until night. During which

time there passed sundry discourses touching affairs past and to come, lamenting greatly the loss of his great ship, more of the men, but most of all his books and notes, and what else I know not, for which he was out of measure grieved, the same doubtless being some matter of more importance than his books, which I could not draw from him: yet by circumstance I gathered the same to be the ore which Daniel the Saxon had brought unto him in the Newfoundland. Whatsoever it was, the remembrance touched him so deep as, not able to contain himself, he beat his boy in great rage, even at the same time, so long after the miscarrying of the great ship, because upon a fair day, when we were becalmed upon the coast of the Newfoundland near unto Cape Race, he sent his boy aboard the *Admiral* to fetch certain things: amongst which, this being chief, was yet forgotten and left behind. After which time he could never conveniently send again aboard the great ship, much less he doubted her ruin so near at hand.

Herein my opinion was better confirmed diversely, and by sundry conjectures, which maketh me have the greater hope of this rich mine. For whereas the General had never before good conceit of these north parts of the world, now his mind was wholly fixed upon the Newfoundland. And as before he refused not to grant assignments liberally to them that required the same into these north parts, now he became contrarily affected, refusing to make any so large grants, especially of St. John's, which certain English merchants made suit for, offering to employ their money and travail upon the same yet neither by their own suit, nor of others of his own company, whom he seemed willing to pleasure, it could be obtained. Also laying down his determination in the spring following for disposing of his voyage then to be re-attempted: he assigned the captain and master of the *Golden Hind* unto the south discovery, and reserved unto himself the north, affirming that this voyage had won his heart from the south, and that he was now become a northern man altogether.

Last, being demanded what means he had, at his arrival in England, to compass the charges of so great preparation as he intended to make the next spring, having determined upon two fleets, one for the south, another for the north; "Leave that to me," he replied. "I will ask a penny of no man. I will bring good tidings unto her Majesty, who will be so gracious to lend me £10,000." He willed us therefore to be of good cheer; for he did thank God, he said, with all his heart for that he had seen, the same being enough for us all, and that we needed not to seek any further. And these last words he would often repeat, with demonstration of great fervency of mind, being himself very confident and settled in belief of inestimable good by this voyage; which the greater number of his followers nevertheless mistrusted altogether, not being made partakers of those secrets, which the General kept unto himself. Yet all of them that are living may be witnesses of his words and protestations, which sparingly I have delivered.

Leaving the issue of this good hope unto God, who knoweth the truth only, and can at His good pleasure bring the same to light, I will hasten to the end of this tragedy, which must be knit up in the person of our General. And as it was God's ordinance upon him, even so the vehement persuasion and entreaty of his friends could nothing avail to divert him of a wilful resolution of going through in his frigate; which was overcharged upon the decks with fights, nettings, and small artillery, too cumbersome for so small a boat that was to pass through the ocean sea at that season of the year, when by course we might expect much storm of foul weather. Whereof, indeed, we had enough.

But when he was entreated by the captain, master, and other his well-willers of the *Hind* not to venture in the frigate, this was his answer: "I will not forsake my little company going homeward, with whom I have passed so many storms and perils."

And in very truth he was urged to be so over hard by hard reports given of him that he was afraid of the sea; albeit this was rather rashness than advised resolution, to prefer the wind of a vain report to the weight of his own life. Seeing he would not bend to reason, he had provision out of the *Hind*, such as was wanting aboard his frigate. And so we committed him to God's protection, and set him aboard his pinnace, we being more than 300 leagues onward of our way home.

By that time we had brought the Islands of Azores south of us; yet we then keeping much to the north, until we had got into the height and elevation of England, we met with very foul weather and terrible seas, breaking short and high, pyramid-wise. The reason whereof seemed to proceed either of hilly grounds high and low within the sea, as we see hills and vales upon the land, upon which the seas do mount and fall, or else the cause proceedeth of diversity of winds, shifting often in sundry points, all which having power to move the great ocean, which again is not presently settled, so many seas do encounter together, as there had been diversity of winds. Howsoever it cometh to pass, men which all their lifetime had occupied the sea never saw more outrageous seas. We had also upon our mainyard an apparition of a little fire by night, which seamen do call Castor and Pollux. But we had only one, which they take an evil sign of more tempest; the same is usual in storms.

Monday, the 9 of September, in the afternoon, the frigate was near cast away, oppressed by waves, yet at that time recovered; and giving forth signs of joy, the General, sitting abaft with a book in his hand, cried out to us in the *Hind*, so oft as we did approach within hearing, "We are as near to heaven by sea as by land!" Reiterating the same speech, well beseeming a soldier, resolute in Jesus Christ, as I can testify he was.

The same Monday night, about twelve of the clock, or not long after, the frigate being ahead of us in the *Golden Hind*, suddenly her lights were out, whereof as it were in a moment we lost the sight, and withal our watch cried "The General was cast away," which was too true. For in that moment the frigate was devoured and swallowed up of the sea. Yet still we looked out all that night, and ever after until we arrived upon the coast of England; omitting no small sail at sea, unto which we gave not the tokens between us agreed upon to have perfect knowledge of each other, if we should at any time be separated.

[FROM *Principal Voyages of the English Nation*]

SEARCH FOR
THE NORTHWEST PASSAGE

THE SEVENTH of July being very desirous to search the habitation of this country, I went myself with our new pinnace into the body of the land, thinking it to be a firm continent, and passing up a very large river, a great flaw of wind took me, whereby we were constrained to seek succour for that night, which being had,

I landed with the most part of my company, and went to the top of a high mountain, hoping from thence to see into the country: but the mountains were so many and so mighty as that my purpose prevailed not: whereupon I again returned to my pinnace, and willing divers of my company to gather mussels for my supper, whereof in this place there was great store, myself having espied a very strange sight, especially to me that never before saw the like, which was a mighty whirlwind taking up the water in very great quantity, furiously mounting it into the air, which whirlwind was not for a puff or blast, but continual, for the space of three hours, with very little intermission, which since it was in the course that I should pass, we were constrained that night to take up our lodging under the rocks.

The next morning the storm being broken up, we went forward in our attempt, and sailed into a mighty great river directly into the body of the land, and in brief, found it to be no firm land, but huge, waste, and desert isles with mighty sounds, and inlets passing between sea and sea. Whereupon we returned towards our ships, and landing to stop a flood, we found the burial of these miscreants; we found of their fish in bags, plaices, and caplin dried, of which we took only one bag and departed.

The ninth of this month we came to our ships, where we found the people desirous in their fashion of friendship and barter: our mariners complained heavily against the people, and said that my lenity and friendly using of them gave them stomach to mischief: "for they have stolen an anchor from us, they have cut our cable very dangerously, they have cut our boats from our stern, and now since your departure, with slings they spare us not with stones of half a pound weight: and will you still endure these injuries? It is a shame to bear

them." I desired them to be content and said, I doubted
not but all should be well. The tenth of this month I
went to the shore, the people following me in their
canoes: I tolled them on shore, and used them with
much courtesy, and then departed aboard, they following me and my company. I gave some of them bracelets,
and caused seven or eight of them to come aboard,
which they did willingly, and some of them went into
the top of the ship: and thus courteously using them, I
let them depart: the sun was no sooner down, but they
began to practise their devilish nature, and with slings
threw stones very fiercely into the *Moonlight,* and struck
one of her men then boatswain, that he overthrew
withal: whereat being moved, I changed my courtesy,
and grew to hatred; myself in my own boat well manned
with shot, and the bark's boat likewise pursued them,
and gave them divers shot, but to small purpose, by
reason of their swift rowing: so small content we returned.

The eleventh of this month there came five of them to
make a new truce: the master of the Admiral came to
me to shew me of their coming, and desired to have
them taken and kept as prisoners until we had his anchor
again: but when he saw that the chief ringleader and
master of mischief was one of the five, he then was
vehement to execute his purpose, so it was determined
to take him: he came crying Ylyaoute, and striking his
breast offered a pair of gloves to sell, the master offered
him a knife for them: so two of them came to us, the
one was not touched, but the other was soon captive among us: then we pointed to him and his fellows
for our anchor, which being had, we made signs that he
should be set at liberty within one hour after he came
aboard; the wind came fair, whereupon we weighed and
set sail, and so brought the fellow with us: one of his

fellows still following our ship close aboard, talked with him and made a kind of lamentation, we still using him well with Ylyaoute, which was the common course of courtesy. At length this fellow aboard us spake four or five words unto the other and clapped his two hands upon his face, whereupon the other doing the like, departed as we suppose with heavy cheer. We judged the covering of his face with his hands and bowing of his body down, signified his death. At length he became a pleasant companion among us. I gave him a suit of frieze after the English fashion, because I saw he could not endure the cold, of which he was very joyful, he trimmed up his darts, and all his fishing tools, and would make oakum, and set his hand to a rope's end upon occasion. He lived with the dry caplin that I took when I was searching in the pinnace, and did eat dry Newland fish.

All this while, God be thanked, our people were in very good health, only one young man excepted, who died at sea the fourteenth of this month, and the fifteenth, according to the order of the sea, with praise given to God by service, was cast overboard.

The seventeenth of this month being in the latitude of 63 degrees 8 minutes, we fell upon a most mighty and strange quantity of ice in one entire mass, so big as that we knew not the limits thereof, and being withal so very high in form of a land, with bays and capes and like high cliff land, as that we supposed it to be land, and therefore sent our pinnace off to discover it: but at her return we were certainly informed that it was only ice, which bred great admiration to us all considering the huge quantity thereof, incredible to be reported in truth as it was, and therefore I omit to speak any further thereof. This only I think, that the like before was never seen: and in this place we had very stickle and strong currents.

We coasted this mighty mass of ice until the thirtieth of July, finding it a mighty bar to our purpose: the air in this time was so contagious and the sea so pestered with ice, as that all hope was banished of proceeding: for the twenty-fourth of July all our shrouds, ropes and sails were so frozen, and compassed with ice, only by a gross fog, as seemed to me more than strange, since the last year I found this sea free and navigable, without impediments.

Our men through this extremity began to grow sick and feeble, and withal hopeless of good success: whereupon very orderly, with good discretion they entreated me to regard the state of this business, and withal advised me that in conscience I ought to regard the safety of mine own life with the preservation of theirs, and that I should not through my overboldness leave their widows and fatherless children to give me bitter curses. This matter in conscience did greatly move me to regard their estates: yet considering the excellency of the business if it might be attained, the great hope of certainty by the last year's discovery, and that there was yet a third way not put in practice, I thought it would grow to my great disgrace, if this action by my negligence should grow into discredit: whereupon seeking help from God, the fountain of all mercies, it pleased his divine majesty to move my heart to prosecute that which I hope shall be to his glory, and to the contentation of every Christian mind. Whereupon falling into consideration that the *Mermaid,* albeit a very strong and sufficient ship, yet by reason of her burthen was not so convenient and nimble as a smaller bark, especially in such desperate hazards: further having in account her great charge to the adventurers being at 100 livres the month, and that in doubtful service: all the premises considered with divers other things, I determined to furnish the *Moonlight* with revictualling and sufficient men, and to proceed in this action as God should direct me. Whereupon I altered our course from the ice, and bare east-south-east to recover the next shore where this thing might be performed: so with favourable wind it pleased God that the first of August we discovered the land in latitude 66 degrees 33 minutes and in longitude from the meridian of London 70 degrees void of trouble without snow or ice.

The second of August we harboured ourselves in a very excellent good road, where with all speed we graved the *Moonlight,* and revictualled her: we searched this country with our pinnace while the bark was trimming, which William Eston did: he found all this land to be only islands, with a sea on the east, a sea on the west, and a sea on the north. In this place we found it very hot, and we were very much troubled with a fly which is called mosquito, for they did sting grievously. The people of this place at our first coming in caught a seal, and with bladders fast tied to him sent him unto us with the flood, so as he came right with our ships, which we took as a friendly present from them.

The fifth of August I went with the two masters and others to the top of a hill, and by the way William Eston espied three canoes lying under a rock, and went unto them: there were in them skins, darts, with divers superstitious toys, whereof we diminished nothing, but left upon every boat a silk point, a bullet of lead, and a pin. The next day being the sixth of August, the people came unto us without fear, and did barter with us for skins, as the other people did: they differ not from the other, neither in their canoes nor apparel, yet is their pronunciation more plain than the others, and nothing hollow in the throat. Our savage aboard us kept himself close, and made show that he would fain have another companion. Thus being provided, I departed from this land the twelfth of August at six of the clock in the morning, where I left the *Mermaid* at an anchor: the fourteenth sailing west about fifty leagues, we discovered land, being in latitude 66 degrees 19 minutes: this land is seventy leagues from the other from whence we came. This fourteenth day from nine a-clock at night till three a-clock in the morning, we anchored by an island of ice, twelve leagues off the shore, being moored to the ice.

The fifteenth day at three a-clock in the morning we departed from this land to the south, and the eighteenth of August we discovered land north-west from us in the morning, being a very fair promontory, in latitude 65 degrees, having no land on the south. Here we had great hope of a through passage.

This day at three a-clock in the afternoon we again discovered land south-west and by south from us, where at night we were becalmed. The nineteenth of this month at noon, by observation, we were in 64 degrees 20 minutes. From the eighteenth day at noon unto the nineteenth at noon, by precise ordinary care, we had sailed fifteen leagues south and by west, yet by art and more exact observation, we found our course to be south-west, so that we plainly perceived a great current striking to the west.

This land is nothing in sight but isles, which increaseth our hope. This nineteenth of August at six a-clock in the afternoon, it began to snow, and so continued all night with foul weather, and much wind, so that we were constrained to lie at hull all night five leagues off the shore: in the morning, being the twentieth of August, the fog and storm breaking up, we bare in with the land, and at nine a-clock in the morning we anchored in a very fair and safe road and locked for all weathers. At ten of the clock I went on shore to the top of a very high hill, where I perceived that this land was islands: at four of the clock in the afternoon we weighed anchor, having a fair north-north-east wind, with very fair weather; at six of the clock we were clear without the land, and so shaped our course to the south, to discover the coast, whereby the passage may be through God's mercy found.

We coasted this land till the eight-and-twentieth of August, finding it still to continue towards the south, from the latitude of 67 to 57 degrees: we found marvellous great store of birds, gulls and mews, incredible to be reported, whereupon being calm weather, we lay one glass upon the lee, to prove for fish, in which space we caught 100 of cod, although we were but badly provided for fishing, not being our purpose. This eight-and-twentieth having great distrust of the weather, we arrived in a very fair harbour in the latitude of 56 degrees, and sailed ten leagues into the same, being two leagues broad, with very fair woods on both sides: in this place we continued until the first of September, in which time we had two very great storms. I landed, and went six miles by guess into the country, and found that the woods were fir, pineapple, alder, yew, withy, and birch: here we saw a black bear: this place yieldeth great store of birds, as pheasant, partridge, Barbary hens or the like, wild geese, ducks, blackbirds, jays, thrushes, with other kinds of small birds. Of the partridge and pheasant we killed great store with bow and arrows: in this place at the harbour mouth we found great store of cod.

The first of September at ten a-clock we set sail, and coasted the shore with very fair weather. The third day being calm, at noon we struck sail, and let fall a cadge anchor, to prove whether we could take any fish, being in latitude 54 degrees 30 minutes, in which place we found great abundance of cod, so that the hook was no sooner overboard, but presently a fish was taken. It was the largest and the best-fed fish that ever I saw, and divers fishermen that were with me said that they never saw a more sauvle or better skull of fish in their lives: yet had they seen great abundance.

The fourth of September at five a-clock in the afternoon we anchored in a very good road among great store of isles, the country low land, pleasant and very full of fair woods. To the north of this place eight leagues, we had a perfect hope of the passage, finding a mighty great sea passing between two lands west. The south land to our judgement being nothing but isles, we greatly desired to go into this sea, but the wind was directly against us. We anchored in four fathom fine sand. In this place is fowl and fish mighty store.

The sixth of September having a fair north-north-west wind, having trimmed our bark we purposed to depart, and sent five of our sailors, young men, ashore to an island, to fetch certain fish which we purposed to weather, and therefore left it all night covered upon the isle: the brutish people of this country lay secretly lurking in the wood, and upon the sudden assaulted our men: which when we perceived, we presently let slip our cables upon the hawse, and under our foresail bore into the shore, and with all expedition discharged a double musket upon them twice, at the noise whereof they fled: notwithstanding to our very great grief, two of our men were slain with their arrows, and two grievously wounded, of whom at this present we stand in very great doubt, only one escaped by swimming, with an arrow shot through his arm. These wicked miscreants never offered parley or speech, but presently executed their cursed fury.

This present evening it pleased God further to increase our sorrows with a mighty tempestuous storm, the wind being north-north-east, which lasted unto the tenth of this month very extreme. We unrigged our ship, and purposed to cut down our masts, the cable of our sheet-anchor broke, so that we only expected to be driven on shore among these cannibals for their prey. Yet in this deep distress the mighty mercy of God, when hope was past, gave us succour, and sent us a fair lee, so as we recovered our anchor again, and new moored our ship: where we saw that God manifestly delivered us: for the strains of one of our cables were broken, and we only rode by an old junk. Thus being freshly moored a new storm arose, the wind being west-north-west, very forcible, which lasted unto the tenth day at night.

The eleventh day with a fair west-north-west wind we departed with trust in God's mercy, shaping our course for England, and arrived in the west country in the beginning of October.

[FROM *Principal Voyages of the English Nation*]

Sir Walter Ralegh

THE DISCOVERY OF GUIANA

ON BOTH sides of this river, we passed the most beautiful country that ever mine eyes beheld: and whereas all that we had seen before was nothing but woods, prickles, bushes, and thorns, here we beheld plains of twenty miles in length, the grass short and green, and in divers parts groves of trees by themselves, as if they had been by all the art and labour in the world so made of purpose: and still as we rowed, the deer came down feeding by the water's side, as if they had been used to a keeper's call. Upon this river there were great store of fowl, and of many sorts: we saw in it divers sorts of strange fishes and of marvellous bigness, but for Lagartos it exceeded, for there were thousands of those ugly serpents, and the people call it for the abundance of them the river of Lagartos in their language. I had a Negro, a very proper young fellow, that leaping out of the galley to swim in the mouth of this river was in all our sights taken and devoured with one of those Lagartos.

In the meanwhile our companies in the galley thought we had been all lost (for we promised to return before night) and sent the *Lion's Whelps* ship's boat with Captain Whiddon to follow us up the river, but the next day after we had rowed up and down some four score miles we returned, and went on our way up the great river, and when we were even at the last cast for want of victuals, Captain Gifford being before the galley and the rest of the boats, seeking out some place to land upon the banks to make fire, espied four canoes coming down the river and with no small joy caused his men to try the uttermost of their strengths, and after awhile two of the four gave over and ran themselves ashore, every man betaking himself to the fastness of the woods, the two other lesser got away, while he landed to lay hold on these, and so turned into some by-creek, we knew not whither: those canoes that were taken were loaden with bread, and were bound for Marguerita in the West Indies, which those Indians (called Arwacas) purposed to carry thither for exchange. But in the lesser there were three Spaniards, who, having heard of the defeat of their governor in Trinidado, and that we purposed to enter Guiana, came away in those canoes: one of them was a cavaliero, as the captain of the Arwacas after told us, another a soldier, and the third a refiner.

In the meantime nothing on the earth could have been more welcome to us next unto gold than the great store of very excellent bread which we found in these canoes, for now our men cried, "Let us go on, we care not how far." After that Captain Gifford had brought the two canoes to the galley, I took my barge and went to the bank's side with a dozen shot, where the canoes first ran themselves ashore, and landed there, sending out Captain Gifford and Captain Thyn on one hand, and Captain Calfield on the other, to follow those that were fled into the woods, and as I was creeping through the bushes, I saw an Indian basket hidden, which was the refiner's basket, for I found in it his quicksilver, salt-petre, and divers things for the trial of metals, and also the dust of such ore as he had refined, but in those canoes which escaped there was a good quantity of ore and gold.

I then landed more men and offered five hundred pound to what soldier soever could take one of those three Spaniards that we thought were landed. But our labours were in vain in that behalf, for they put themselves into one of the small canoes: and so while the greater canoes were in taking they escaped: but seeking after the Spaniards we found the Arwacas hidden in the woods which were pilots for the Spaniards, and rowed their canoes: of which I kept the chiefest for a pilot and carried him with me to Guiana, by whom I understood where and in what countries the Spaniards had laboured for gold, though I made not the same known to all: for when the springs began to break and the rivers to raise themselves so suddenly as by no means we could abide the digging of any mine, especially for that the richest are defended with rocks of hard stone which we call the White Spar, and that it required both time, men, and instruments fit for such a work, I thought it best not to hover thereabouts, lest if the same had been perceived by the company, there would have been by this time many barks and ships set out, and perchance other nations would also have gotten of ours for pilots, so as both ourselves might have been prevented, and all our care taken for good usage of the people been utterly lost by those that only respect present profit, and such violence or insolence offered, as the nations which are borderers would have changed their desire of our love and defence into hatred and violence. And for any longer stay to have brought a more quantity (which I hear hath been often objected) whosoever had seen or proved the fury of that river after it began to arise, and had been a month and odd days as we were from hearing aught from our ships, leaving them meanly manned, above four hundred miles off, would perchance have turned somewhat sooner than we did, if all the mountains had been gold or rich stones. And to say the truth all the branches and small rivers which fell into Orenoque were raised with such speed, as if we waded them over the shoes in the morning outward we were covered to the shoulders homeward the very same day: and to stay to dig out gold with our nails had been *Opus laboris* but not *Ingenii:* such a quantity as would have served our turns we could not have had, but a discovery of the mines to our infinite disadvantage we had made, and that could have been the best profit of further search or stay; for those mines are not easily broken nor opened in haste, and I could have returned a good quantity of gold ready cast if I had not shot at another mark than present profit.

This Arwacan pilot, with the rest, feared that we would have eaten them, or otherwise have put them to some cruel death, for the Spaniards to the end that none of the people in the passage towards Guiana or in Guiana itself might come to speech with us persuaded all the nations that we were men-eaters and cannibals: but when the poor men and women had seen us and that we gave them meat and to every one some thing or other which was rare and strange to them, they began to conceive the deceit and purpose of the Spaniards, who indeed (as they confessed) took from them both their wives and daughters daily, and used them for the satisfying of their own lusts, especially such as they took in this manner by strength. But I protest before the majesty of the living God, that I neither know nor believe that any of our company one or other, by violence or otherwise, ever knew any of their women, and yet we saw many hundreds, and had many in our power, and of those very young, and excellently favoured which came among us without deceit, stark naked.

Nothing got us more love among them than this usage, for I suffered not any man to take from any of the nations so much as a pina or a potato root without giving them contentment, nor any man so much as to offer to touch any of their wives or daughters: which course, so contrary to the Spaniards (who tyrannize over them in all things) drew them to admire her Majesty, whose commandment I told them it was, and also wonderfully to honour our nation. But I confess it was a very impatient work to keep the meaner sort from spoil and stealing when we came to their houses, which because in all I could not prevent, I caused my Indian interpreter at every place when we departed to know of the loss or wrong done, and if aught were stolen or taken by violence, either the same was restored and the party punished in their sight, or else it was paid for to their uttermost demand. They also much wondered at us after they heard that we had slain the Spaniards at Trinidado, for they were before resolved that no nation of Christians durst abide their presence, and they wondered more when I had made them know of the great overthrow that her Majesty's army and fleet had given them of late years in their own countries.

After we had taken in this supply of bread with divers baskets of roots which were excellent meat, I gave one of the canoes to the Arwacas which belonged to the Spaniards that were escaped, and when I had dismissed all but the captain (who by the Spaniards was christened Martin) I sent back in the same cause the old Ciawan and Ferdinando my first pilot, and gave them both such things as they desired with sufficient victual to carry them back, and by them wrote a letter to the ships which they promised to deliver, and performed it, and then I went on with my new hired pilot Martin the Arwacan: but the next or second day after, we came aground again with our galley, and were like to cast her away, with all our victual and provision, and so lay on the sand one whole night and were far more in despair at this time to free her than before, because we had no tide of flood to help us, and therefore feared that all our hopes would have ended in mishaps: but we fastened an anchor upon the land and with main strength drew her off.

And so the fifteenth day we discovered afar off the mountains of Guiana to our great joy, and towards the evening had a slent of a northerly wind that blew very strong, which brought us in sight of the great river of Orenoque, out of which this river descended wherein we were: we descried afar off three other canoes as far as we could discern them, after whom we hastened with our barge and wherries, but two of them passed out of sight, and the third entered up the great river on the right hand to the westward, and there stayed out of sight, thinking that we meant to take the way eastward towards the province of Carapana, for that way the Spaniards keep, not daring to go upwards to Guiana, the people in those parts being all their enemies, and those in the canoes thought us to have been those Spaniards that were fled from Trinidado, and had escaped killing: and when we came so far down as the opening of that branch into which they slipped, being near them with our barge and wherries, we made after them, and ere they could land, came within call, and by our interpreter told them what we were, wherewith they came back willingly aboard us: and of such fish and Tortugas eggs as they had gathered, they gave us, and promised in the morning to bring the lord of that part with them, and to do us all other services they could.

That night we came to an anchor at the parting of three goodly rivers (the one was the river of Amana by which we came from the north and ran athwart towards the south, the other two were of Orenoque which crossed from the west and ran to the sea towards the east) and landed upon a fair sand, where we found thousands of Tortugas eggs, which are very wholesome meat and greatly restoring, so as our men were now well filled and highly contented both with the fare, and nearness of the land of Guiana which appeared in sight. In the morning there came down according to promise the lord of that border called Toparimaca, with some thirty or forty followers and brought us divers sorts of fruits, and of his wine, bread, fish, and flesh, whom we also feasted as we could, at least he drank good Spanish wine (whereof we had a small quantity in bottles) which above all things they love. I conferred with this Toparimaca of the next way to Guiana, who conducted our galley and boats to his own port, and carried us from thence some mile and a half to his town, where some of our captains caroused of his wine till they were reasonable pleasant, for it is very strong with pepper, and the juice of divers herbs, and fruits digested and purged;

they keep it in great earthen pots of ten or twelve gallons very clean and sweet, and are themselves at their meetings and feasts the greatest carousers and drunkards of the world.

When we came to his town we found two cassiques, whereof one of them was a stranger that had been up the river in trade, and his boats, people, and wife encamped at the port where we anchored, and the other was of that country a follower of Toparimaca: they lay each of them in a cotton hamaca, which we call Brazil beds, and two women attending them with six cups and a little ladle to fill them, out of an earthen pitcher of wine, and so they drank each of them three of those cups at a time, one to the other, and in this sort they drink drunk at their feasts and meetings.

That cassique that was a stranger had his wife staying at the port where we anchored, and in all my life I have seldom seen a better-favoured woman. She was of good stature, with black eyes, fat of body, of an excellent countenance, her hair almost as long as herself, tied up again in pretty knots, and it seemed she stood not in that awe of her husband as the rest, for she spake and discoursed, and drank among the gentlemen and captains, and was very pleasant, knowing her own comeliness and taking great pride therein. I have seen a lady in England so like her, as but for the difference of colour I would have sworn might have been the same. . . .

When we ran to the tops of the first hills of the plains adjoining to the river, we beheld that wonderful breach of waters, which ran down Caroli: and might from that mountain see the river how it ran in three parts, above twenty miles off, and there appeared some ten or twelve overfalls in sight, every one as high over the other as a church-tower, which fell with that fury that the rebound of waters made it seem as if it had been all covered over with a great shower of rain: and in some places we took it at the first for a smoke that had risen over some great town. For mine own part, I was well persuaded from thence to have returned, being a very ill footman, but the rest were all so desirous to go near the said strange thunder of waters, as they drew me on by little and little, till we came into the next valley, where we might better discern the same. I never saw a more beautiful country, nor more lively prospects, hills so raised here and there over the valleys, the river winding into divers branches, the plains adjoining without bush or stubble, all fair green grass, the ground of hard sand easy to march on, either for horse or foot, the deer crossing in every path, the birds towards the evening singing on every tree with a thousand several tunes, cranes and herons of white, crimson, and carnation perching on the river's side, the air fresh with a gentle easterly wind, and every stone that we stooped to take up, promised either gold or silver by his complexion.

[FROM *Discovery of the Empire of Guiana*]

J. H.

WORK FOR CHIMNEY SWEEPS: A WARNING AGAINST TOBACCO

THE FOURTH REASON

THE FOURTH argument against this newcome simple, was that it drieth up and withereth our unctuous and radical moisture in us, and thereby seemeth an utter enemy to the continuance and propagation of mankind.

This may be proved in this sort. That thing which depriveth the body of nourishment and food, doth also wither and dry up our natural and radical moisture (because this hath his refreshing and sustenance from the purest part of the blood engendered of our nourishments). But Tobacco was shewed before to deprive us of our nourishment, in that it spendeth and evacuateth out of us by spitting and sweats and otherwise much of that matter that in time would prove in us good blood and good food for our bodies. And therefore Tobacco must needs be said to be a great decayer and witherer of our radical moisture before specified.

Moreover Tobacco by means of his great heat and immeasureable dryness, dissipateth natural heat and kind warmth in our bodies, and thereby is cause of defect of good concoction and perfect digestion in us. The humours therefore in us by this means made crude and raw, can be no fit aliment or nutriment for the unctuous and substantial humidity wherein with moderate and kindly heat the Philosopher esteemed the life of man to consist.

And last of all, whereas the sperm and seed of man, is supposed (by the Physicians and natural Philosophers also) to be framed of the purest and finest part of his blood by the action and virtue of kindly warmth working therein; the blood being now undigested and crude, and the natural heat perverted and corrupted by the immoderate use of this hellish smoke, reeking forth of Pluto's forge, what sperm or seed shall we expect to come from them that daily use or rather shamefully abuse this so apparent an enemy to the propagation thereof, as well if you respect the material cause of seed consisting in the perfectest and most concocted parts of the blood as his efficiency (resting in the moderation of natural heat) both greatly altered and decayed by the use of Tobacco.

Hereby it must needs in consequence follow, that the continuation and propagation of mankind (consisting principally in his perfect and uncorrupt seed) is in those men much abridged.

And for certain proof that Tobacco drieth up the sperm and seed of man, I hear by faithful relation of such as have much used it; that whereas before the use thereof, they had been long molested with a flux of seed, commonly called with us the running of the reins and of the Physician Gomorrhaea (proceeding in them by reason of great quantity and abundance of that matter seeking vent forth of the body), they were in short space eased of this effect by the only use of this medicine. For no doubt, this fiery fume, dried up the superfluity of that matter, which by reason of her thin and great quantity easily dropped from them. But if they persist over long in the practice thereof, no doubt more of that spermatical humidity will be dried up in them, than will be convenient for their health, or for the increase of their like; whereby the propagation and continuation of mankind in this world must need be abridged. . . .

THE SEVENTH REASON

The seventh reason against Tobacco was, that this herb seemed to be first found out and invented by the Devil, and first used and practiced by the Devil's priests, and therefore not to be used of us Christians.

That the Devil was the first author hereof, Monardus in his Treatise of Tobacco doth sufficiently witness, saying: The Indian Priests (who no doubt were instruments of the devil whom they serve) do ever before they answer to questions propounded to them by their Princes, drink of this Tobacco fume, with the vigor and strength whereof, they fall suddenly to the ground, as dead men, remaining so, according to the quantity of the smoke that they had taken. And when the herb had done his work, they revive and wake, giving answers according to the visions and illusions which they saw whilst they were wrapt in that order.

And they interpreted their demands as to them seemed best, or as the Devil had counselled them, giving continual doubtful answers, in such sort, that howsoever they fell out, they might turn it to their purpose, like unto the Oracle of Apollo, who might be understood, that either he might overthrow the Romans, or that the Romans might overcome him.

But yet in more plain words, the same Monardus a little after declareth the Devil to be the author of Tobacco, and of the knowledge thereof, saying: And as the Devil is a deceiver, and hath the knowledge of the virtue of herbs; so he did shew them the virtue of this herb, by means whereof they might see the imaginations and Visions that he representeth unto them, and by that means doth deceive them.

Wherefore in mine opinion this practice is the more to be eschewed of us Christains, who follow and profess Christ as the only verity and truth, and detest and abhor the Devil, as a liar and deceiver of mankind.

[FROM *A Warning for Tobacconists*]

John Florio

MONTAIGNE AND
THE NOBLE SAVAGE

I HAVE had long time dwelling with me a man, who for the space of ten or twelve years had dwelt in that other world, which in our age was lately discovered in those parts where Villegaignon first landed, and surnamed Antarctic France. This discovery of so infinite and vast a country, seemeth worthy great consideration. I wot not whether I can warrant myself, that some other be not discovered hereafter, since so many worthy men, and better learned than we are, have so many ages been deceived in this. I fear me our eyes be greater than our bellies, and that we have more curiosity than capacity. We embrace all, but we fasten nothing but wind. . . .

This servant I had, was a simple and rough-hewn fellow: a condition fit to yield a true testimony. For, subtle people may indeed mark more curiously, and observe things more exactly, but they amplify and gloss them: and the better to persuade, and make their interpretations of more validity, they cannot choose but somewhat alter the story. They never represent things truly, but fashion and mask them according to the visage they saw them in; and to purchase credit to their judgement, and draw you on to believe them, they commonly adorn, enlarge, yea, and Hyperbolize the matter. Wherein is required either a most sincere Reporter, or a man so simple that he may have no invention to build upon, and to give a true likelihood unto false devices, and be not wedded to his own will. Such a one was my man; who besides his own report, hath many times shewed me divers Mariners, and Merchants, whom he had known in that voyage.

So am I pleased with his information, that I never inquire what Cosmographers say of it. We had need of Topographers to make us particular narrations of the places they have been in. For some of them, if they have the advantage of us, that they have seen Palestine, will challenge a privilege, to tell us news of all the world besides. I would have every man write what he knows, and no more: not only in that, but in all other subjects. For one may have particular knowledge of the nature of one river, and experience of the quality of one fountain, that in other things knows no more than another man: who nevertheless to publish this little scantling, will undertake to write of all the Physics. From which vice proceed divers great inconveniences.

Now (to return to my purpose) I find (as far as I have been informed) there is nothing in that nation, that is either barbarous or savage, unless men call that barbarism which is not common to them. As indeed, we have no other aim of truth and reason, than the example and Idea of the opinions and customs of the country we live in. There is ever perfect religion, perfect policy, perfect and complete use of all things. They are even savage, as we call those fruits wild, which nature of herself, and of her ordinary progress hath produced: whereas indeed they are those which ourselves have altered by our artificial devices, and diverted from their common order, we should rather term savage. In those are the true and most profitable virtues, and natural properties most lively and vigorous, which in these we have bastardized, applying them to the pleasure of our corrupted taste. And if notwithstanding, in divers fruits of those countries that were never tilled, we shall find, that in respect of ours they are most excellent, and as delicate unto our taste; there is no reason, art should gain the point of honour of our great and puissant mother Nature. We have so much by our inventions surcharged the beauties and riches of her works, that we have altogether overchoked her: yet where ever her purity shineth, she makes our vain and frivolous enterprises wonderfully ashamed.

> *Et veniunt hederae sponte sua melius,*
> *Surgit et in solis formosior arbutus antris,*
> *Et volucres nulla dulcius arte canunt.*
> —*Propertius i. El. ii. 10.*

> Ivies spring better of their own accord,
> Unhaunted plots much fairer trees afford.
> Birds by no art much sweeter notes record.

All our endeavor or wit, cannot so much as reach to represent the nest of the least birdlet, its contexture, beauty, profit and use, no more the web of a silly spider. "All things," saith Plato, "are produced, either by nature, by fortune, or by art. The greatest and fairest by one or other of the two first, the least and imperfect by the last." Those nations seem therefore so barbarous unto me, because they have received very little fashion from human wit, and are yet near their original naturality. The laws of nature do yet command them, which are but little bastardized by ours. And that with such purity, as I am sometimes grieved the knowledge of it came no sooner to light, at what time there were men, that better than we could have judged of it. I am sorry Lycurgus and Plato had it not: for meseemeth that what in those nations we see by experience, doth not only exceed all the pictures wherewith licentious Poesy hath proudly embellished the golden age, and all her quaint inventions to feign a happy condition of man, but also the conception and desire of Philosophy. They could not imagine a genuity so pure and simple, as we see it by experience; nor ever believe our society might be maintained with so little art and human combination.

It is a nation, would I answer Plato, that hath no kind of traffic, no knowledge of Letters, no intelligence of numbers, no name of magistrate, nor of politic superiority; no use of service, of riches or of poverty; no contracts, no successions, no partitions, no occupation but idle; no respect of kindred, but common, no apparel but natural, no manuring of lands, no use of wine, corn, or metal. The very words that import lying, falsehood, treason, dissimulations, covetousness, envy, detraction, and pardon, were never heard of amongst them. How dissonant would he find his imaginary commonwealth from this perfection!

Hos natura modos primum dedit.

Nature at first uprise,
These manners did devise.

Furthermore, they live in a country of so exceeding pleasant and temperate situation, that as my testimonies have told me, it is very rare to see a sick body amongst them; and they have further assured me, they never saw any man there, either shaking with the palsy, toothless, with eyes dropping, or crooked and stooping through age. They are seated along the seacoast, encompassed toward the land with huge and steepy mountains, having between both, a hundred leagues or thereabout of open and champaigne ground. They have great abundance of fish and flesh, that have no resemblance at all with ours, and eat them without any sauces, or skill of Cookery, but plain boiled or broiled. The first man that brought a horse thither, although he had in many other voyages conversed with them, bred so great a horror in the land, that before they could take notice of him, they slew him with arrows.

Their buildings are very long, and able to contain two or three hundred souls, covered with barks of great trees, fastened in the ground at one end, interlaced and joined close together by the tops, after the manner of some of our Granges; the covering whereof hangs down to the ground, and steadeth them as a flank. They have a kind of wood so hard, that riving and cleaving the same, they make blades, swords, and gridirons to broil their meat with. Their beds are of a kind of cotton cloth, fastened to the house roof, as our ship cabins: every one hath his several couch; for the women lie from their husbands. They rise with the Sun, and feed for all day, as soon as they are up: and make no more meals after that. They drink not at meat, as Suidas reporteth of some other people of the East, which drank after meals, but drink many times a day, and are much given to pledge carouses. Their drink is made of a certain root, and of the color of our Claret wines, which lasteth but two or three days; they drink it warm: It hath somewhat a sharp taste, wholesome for the stomach, nothing heady, but laxative for such as are not used unto it, yet very pleasing to such as are accustomed unto it. Instead of bread, they use a certain white composition, like unto Corianders confected. I have eaten some, the taste whereof is somewhat sweet and wallowish.

They spend the whole day in dancing. Their young men go hunting after wild beasts with bows and arrows. Their women busy themselves therewhilst with warming of their drink, which is their chiefest office. Some of their old men, in the morning before they go to eating, preach in common to all the household, walking from one end of the house to the other, repeating one selfsame sentence many times, till he have ended his turn (for their buildings are a hundred paces in length). He commends but two things unto his auditory: First, valour against their enemies, then lovingness unto their wives. . . .

We may then well call them barbarous, in regard of reason's rules, but not in respect of us that exceed them in all kind of barbarism. Their wars are noble and generous, and have as much excuse and beauty, as this human infirmity may admit: they aim at nought so much, and have no other foundation amongst them, but the mere jealousy of virtue. They contend not for the gaining of new lands; for to this day they yet enjoy that natural uberty and fruitfulness, which without labouring toil, doth in such plenteous abundance furnish them with all necessary things, that they need not enlarge their limits. They are yet in that happy estate, as they desire no more, than what their natural necessities direct them: whatsoever is beyond it, is to them superfluous.

Those that are much about one age, do generally intercall one another brethren, and such as are younger, they call children, and the aged are esteemed as fathers to all the rest. These leave this full possession of goods in common, and without division to their heirs, without other claim or title, but that which nature doth plainly impart unto all creatures, even as she brings them into the world.

If their neighbours chance to come over the mountains to assail or invade them, and that they get the victory over them, the Victors' conquest is glory, and the advantage to be and remain superior in valour and virtue: else have they nothing to do with the goods and spoils of the vanquished, and so return into their country, where they neither want any necessary thing, nor

lack this great portion, to know how to enjoy their condition happily, and are contented with what nature af-
fordeth them. . . .

Surely, in respect of us these are very savage men: for
either they must be so in good sooth, or we must be so
indeed: There is a wondrous distance between their
form and ours. Their men have many wives, and by how
much more they are reputed valiant, so much the
greater is their number. The manner and beauty in their
marriages is wondrous strange and remarkable: For, the
same jealousy our wives have to keep us from the love
and affection of other women, the same have theirs to
procure it. Being more careful for their husbands'
honour and content, than of anything else: They endeavour and apply all their industry, to have as many
rivals as possibly they can, forasmuch as it is a testimony
of their husbands' virtue. Our women would count it a
wonder, but it is not so: It is virtue properly Matri-
monial; but of the highest kind. And in the Bible, Leah,
Rachel, Sara, and Jacob's wives, brought their fairest
maiden servants unto their husbands' beds. . . .

Three of that nation, ignorant how dear the knowledge of our corruptions will one day cost their repose,
security, and happiness, and how their ruin shall proceed from this commerce, which I imagine is already
well advanced (miserable as they are to have suffered
themselves to be so cozened by a desire of new-fangled
novelties, and to have quit the calmness of their climate,
to come and see ours) were at Rouen in the time of our
late King Charles the Ninth, who talked with them a
great while. They were shewed our fashions, our pomp,
and the form of a fair City; afterward some demanded
their advice, and would needs know of them what things
of note and admirable they had observed amongst us.

They answered three things, the last of which I have

forgotten, and am very sorry for it; the other two I yet remember. They said: "First, they found it very strange, that so many tall men with long beards, strong and well-armed, as it were about the King's person (it is very likely they meant the Switzers of his guard) would submit themselves to obey a beardless child, and that we did not rather choose one amongst them to command the rest. Secondly (they have a manner of phrase whereby they call men but a moiety one of another), they had perceived, there were men amongst us full gorged with all sorts of commodities, and others which hunger-starved, and bare with need and poverty, begged at their gates: and found it strange, these moieties so needy could endure such an injustice, and that they took not the others by the throat, or set fire on their houses.

I talked a good while with one of them, but I had so bad an interpreter, and who did so ill apprehend my meaning, and who through his foolishness was so troubled to conceive my imaginations, that I could draw no great matter from him. Touching that point, wherein I demanded of him, what good he received by the superiority he had amongst his countrymen (for he was a Captain and our Mariners called him King) he told me, it was to march foremost in any charge of war. Further, I asked him, how many men did follow him. He shewed me a distance of place, to signify they were as many as might be contained in so much ground, which I guessed to be about four or five thousand men. Moreover I demanded, if when wars were ended, all his authority expired; he answered, that he had only this left him, which was, that when he went on progress, and visited the villages depending of him, the inhabitants prepared paths and highways athwart the hedges of their woods, for him to pass through at ease.

All that is not very ill; but what of that? They wear no kind of breeches nor hosen.

[FROM *Of the Cannibals*]

Our world hath of late discovered another (and who can warrant us whether it be the last of his brethren, since both the Demons, the Sibyls, and all we have hitherto been ignorant of this?) no less-large, fully-peopled, all-things-yielding, and mighty in strength, than ours: nevertheless so new and infantine, that he is yet to learn his ABC. It is not yet full fifty years that he knew neither letters, nor weight, nor measures, nor apparel, nor corn, nor vines. But was all naked, simply-pure, in Nature's lap, and lived but with such means and food as his mother-nurse afforded him.

If we conclude aright of our end, and the foresaid Poet of the infancy of this age, this late-world shall but come to light, when ours shall fall into darkness. The whole Universe shall fall into a palsy or convulsion of sinews: one member shall be maimed or shrunken, another nimble and in good plight. I fear, that by our contagion, we shall directly have furthered his declination, and hastened his ruin; and that we shall too dearly have sold him our opinions, our new-fangles and our Arts. It was an unpolluted, harmless infant world; yet have we not whipped and submitted the same unto our discipline, or schooled him by the advantage of our valour or natural forces, nor have we instructed him by our justice and integrity; nor subdued by our magnanimity. Most of their answers, and a number of the negotiations we have had with them witness that they were nothing short of us, nor beholding to us for any excellency of natural wit or perspicuity, concerning pertinency.

The wonderful, or as I may call it, amazement-breed-

ing magnificence of the never-like seen Cities of Cuzco
and Mexico, and amongst infinite such like things, the
admirable Garden of that King, where all the Trees, the
fruits, the Herbs and Plants, according to the order and
greatness they have in a Garden, were most artificially
framed in gold: as also in his Cabinet, all the living
creatures that his Country or his Seas produced, were
cast in gold; and the exquisite beauty of their works, in
precious Stones, in Feathers, in Cotton and in Painting:
shew that they yielded as little unto us in cunning and
industry. But concerning unfeigned devotion, awful observance of laws, unspotted integrity, bounteous liberality, due loyalty and free liberty, it hath greatly availed
us, that we had not so much as they: By which advantage, they have lost, cast away, sold, undone, and
betrayed themselves.

Touching hardiness and undaunted courage, and as
for matchless constancy, unmoved assuredness, undis-
mayed resolution against pain, smarting, famine and
death itself; I will not fear to oppose the examples which
I may easily find amongst them, to the most famous
ancient examples, we may with all our industry discover
in all the Annals and memories of our known old World.
For, as for those which have subdued them, let them lay
aside the wiles, the policies and stratagems, which they
have employed to cozen, to coney-catch, and to circumvent them; and the just astonishment which those nations might justly conceive, by seeing so unexpected an
arrival of bearded men; divers in language, in habit, in
religion, in behaviour, in form, in countenance; and from
a part of the world so distant, and where they never
heard any habitation was: mounted upon great and unknown monsters; against those, who had never so much
as seen any horse, and less any beast whatsoever apt to
bear, or taught to carry either man or burden; covered

with a shining and hard skin, and armed with slicing-keen weapons and glittering armour: against them, who for the wonder of the glistering of a looking-glass or of a plain knife, would have changed or given inestimable riches in Gold, Precious Stones, and Pearls; and who had neither the skill nor the matter wherewith at any leisure, they could have pierced our steel; to which you may add the flashing-fire and thundering roar of shot and Harquebuses; able to quell and daunt even Caesar himself, had he been so suddenly surprized and as little experienced as they were: and thus to come unto, and assault silly-naked people, saving where the invention of weaving of Cotton cloth was known and used: for the most altogether unarmed, except some bows, stones, staves and wooden bucklers: unsuspecting poor people, surprized under colour of amity and well-meaning faith overtaken by the curiosity to see strange and unknown things: I say, take this disparity from the conquerors, and you deprive them of all the occasions and cause of so many unexpected victories.

When I consider that stern-untamed obstinacy, and undaunted vehemence, wherewith so many thousands of men, of women and children, do so infinite times present themselves unto inevitable dangers, for the defence of their Gods and liberty: this generous obstinacy to endure all extremities, all difficulties and death, more easily and willingly, than basely to yield unto their domination, of whom they have so abominably been abused: some of them choosing rather to starve with hunger and fasting, being taken, than to accept food at their enemy's hands, so basely victorious: I perceive, that whosoever had undertaken them man to man, without odds of arms, of experience or of number, should have had as dangerous a war, or perhaps more, as any we see amongst us.

Why did not so glorious a conquest happen under Alexander, or during the time of the ancient Greeks and Romans? Or why befell not so great a change and alteration of Empires and people, under such hands as would gently have polished, reformed and civilized, what in them they deemed to be barbarous and rude: or would have nourished and fostered those good seeds, which nature had there brought forth: adding not only to the manuring of their grounds and ornaments of their cities, such arts as we had; and that no further then had been necessary for them, but therewithall joining unto the original virtues of the country, those of the ancient Grecians and Romans? What [reparation] and what reformation would all that far-spreading world have found, if the examples, demeanours and policies, wherewith we first presented them, had called and allured those uncorrupted nations, to the admiration and imitation of virtue, and had established between them and us a brotherly society and mutual correspondency? How easy a matter had it been, profitably to reform, and christianly to instruct, minds yet so pure and new, so willing to be taught, being for the most part endowed with so docile, so apt and so yielding natural beginnings? Whereas contrarywise, we have made use of their ignorance and inexperience, [to] draw them more easily unto treason, fraud, luxury, avarice and all manner of inhumanity and cruelty, by the example of our life and pattern of our customs. Who ever raised the service of merchandise and benefit of traffic to so high a rate? So many goodly cities ransacked and razed; so many nations destroyed and made desolate; so infinite millions of harmless people of all sexes, states and ages, massacred, ravaged and put to the sword; and the richest, the fairest and the best part of the world topsy-turvied, ruined and defaced for the traffic of Pearls and Pepper:

Oh mechanical victories, oh base conquest! Never did greedy revenge, public wrongs or general enmities, so moodily enrage, and so passionately incense men against men, unto so horrible hostilities, bloody dissipation, and miserable calamities.

Certain Spaniards coasting along the Sea in search of mines, fortuned to land in a very fertile, pleasant and well-peopled country: unto the inhabitants whereof they declared their intent, and shewed their accustomed persuasions; saying: That they were quiet and well-meaning men, coming from far countries, being sent from the King of Castile, the greatest King of the habitable earth, unto whom the Pope, representing God on earth, had given the principality of all the Indies. That if they would become tributaries to him, they should be most kindly used and courteously entreated: They required of them victuals for their nourishment; and some gold for the behoof of certain Physical experiments. Moreover, they declared unto them, the believing in one only God, and the truth of our religion, which they persuaded them to embrace, adding thereto some threats.

Whose answer was this: That happily they might be quiet and well-meaning, but their countenance shewed them to be otherwise: As concerning their King, since he seemed to beg, he shewed to be poor and needy: And for the Pope, who had made that distribution, he expressed himself a man loving dissension, in going about to give unto a third man, a thing which was not his own: so to make it questionable and litigious amongst the ancient possessors of it. As for victuals, they should have part of their store: And for gold, they had but little, and that it was a thing they made very small account of, as merely unprofitable for the service of their life, whereas all their care was but how to pass it happily and pleasantly: and therefore, what quantity soever they should find, that only excepted which was employed about the service of their Gods, they might boldly take it. As touching one only God, the discourse of him had very well pleased them: but they would by no means change their religion, under which they for so long time lived so happily: and that they were not accustomed to take any counsel, but of their friends and acquaintance. As concerning their menaces, it was a sign of want of judgment, to threaten those, whose nature, condition, power and means was to them unknown. And therefore they should with all speed hasten to avoid their dominions (forsomuch as they were not wont to admit or take in good part the kindnesses and remonstrances of armed people, namely of strangers); otherwise they would deal with them as they had done with such others, shewing them the heads of certain men sticking upon stakes about their City, which had lately been executed. *Lo, here an example of the stammering of this infancy.*

But so it is, neither in this, nor in infinite other places, where the Spaniards found not the merchandise they sought for, neither made stay or attempted any violence, whatsoever other commodity the place yielded: witness my Cannibals. Of two the most mighty and glorious Monarchs of that world, and peradventure of all our Western parts, Kings over so many Kings: the last they deposed and overcame: he of Peru, having by them been taken in a battle, and set at so excessive a ransom, that it exceedeth all belief, and that truly paid: and by his conversation having given them apparent signs of a free, liberal, undaunted and constant courage, and declared to be of a pure, noble, and well-composed understanding; a humour possessed the conquerors, after they had most insolently exacted from him a Million, three hundred five and twenty thousand, and five hundred weights of gold; besides the silver and other precious things, which amounted to no less a sum (so that their horses were all shod of massive gold) to discover (what disloyalty or treachery soever it might cost them) what the remainder of this King's treasure might be, and without controlment enjoy whatever he might have hidden or concealed from them.

Which to compass, they forged a false accusation and proof against him; That he practiced to raise his provinces, and intended to induce his subjects to some insurrection, so to procure his liberty. Whereupon, by the very judgment of those who had complotted this forgery and treason against him, he was condemned to be publicly hanged and strangled: having first made him to redeem the torment of being burned alive, by the baptism which at the instant of his execution, in charity they bestowed upon him. A horrible and the like never heard of accident: which nevertheless he undismayedly endured with an unmoved manner, and truly royal gravity, without ever contradicting himself either in countenance or speech. And then, somewhat to mitigate and circumvent those silly unsuspecting people, amazed and astonished at so strange a spectacle, they counterfeited a great mourning and lamentation for his death, and appointed his funerals to be solemnly and sumptuously celebrated.

The other King of Mexico, having a long time manfully defended his besieged City, and in the tedious siege, shewed whatever pinching sufferance, and resolute perseverance can effect, if ever any courageous Prince or warlike people shewed the same; and his disastrous success having delivered him alive into his enemy's hands, upon conditions to be used as beseemed a King: who during the time of his imprisonment, did never make the least shew of anything unworthy that glorious title. After which victory, the Spaniards not

finding that quantity of gold they had promised themselves, when they had ransacked and ranged all corners,
they by means of the cruellest tortures and horriblest
torments they could possibly devise, began to wrest and
draw some more from such prisoners as they had in keeping. But unable to profit anything that way, finding
stronger hearts than their torments, they in the end fell
to such moody outrages, that contrary to all law of nations, and against their solemn vows and promises, they
condemned the King himself and one of the chiefest
Princes of his Court, to the Rack, one in presence of
another.

The Prince, environed round with hot burning coals,
being overcome with the exceeding torment, at last in
most piteous sort turning his dreary eyes toward his
Master, as if he asked mercy of him for that he could
endure no longer, the king, fixing rigorously and fiercely
his looks upon him, seeming to upbraid him with his
remissness and pusilanimity, with a stern and settled
voice uttered these few words unto him, "What? Sup-
posest thou I am in a cold bath? Am I at more ease than
thou art?"

Whereat the silly wretch immediately fainted under
the torture, and yielded up the ghost. The king, half
roasted, was carried away: not so much for pity (for
what ruth could ever enter so barbarous minds, who
upon the surmised information of some odd piece or
vessel of gold, they intended to get, would broil a man
before their eyes, and not a man only, but a king, so
great in fortune and so renowned in desert?) but forasmuch as his unmatched constancy did more and more
make their inhuman cruelty ashamed. They afterward
hanged him, because he had courageously attempted
by arms to deliver himself out of so long captivity and
miserable subjection; where he ended his wretched life,

worthy an high-minded and never daunted Prince. At another time, in one same fire, they caused to be burned all alive four hundred common men, and threescore principal Lords of a Province, whom by the fortune of war they had taken prisoners.

These narrations we have out of their own books: for they do not only avouch, but vauntingly publish them. May it be, they do it for a testimony of their justice or zeal toward their religion? Verily they are ways over-different and enemies to so sacred an end. Had they proposed unto themselves to enlarge and propagate our religion, they would have considered, that it is not amplified by possession of lands, but of men: and would have been satisfied with such slaughters, as the necessity of war bringeth, without indifferently adding thereunto so bloody a butchery, as upon savage beasts; and so universal as fire or sword could ever attain unto; having purposely preserved no more than so many miserable bond-slaves, as they deemed might suffice for the digging, working and service of their mines, so that divers of their chieftains have been executed to death, even in the places they had conquered, by the appointment of the Kings of Castile, justly offended at the seldom seen horror of their barbarous demeanours, and well nigh all disesteemed, contemned and hated. God hath meritoriously permitted, that many of their great pillages, and ill-gotten goods, have either been swallowed up by the revenging Seas in transporting them, or consumed by the intestine wars and civil broils, wherewith themselves have devoured one another; and the greatest part of them have been overwhelmed and buried in the bowels of the earth, in the very places they found them, without any fruit of their victory.

Touching the objection which some make, that the receipt, namely in the hands of so thrifty, wary and wise a Prince, doth so little answer the fore-conceived hope, which was given unto his predecessors, and the said former abundance of riches, they met withal at the first discovery of this new-found world (for although they bring home great quantity of gold and silver, we perceive the same to be nothing, in respect of what might be expected thence), it may be answered, that the use of money was there altogether unknown; and consequently that all their gold was gathered together, serving to no other purpose, than for shew, state and ornament, as a movable reserved from father to son by many puissant Kings, who exhausted all their mines, to collect so huge a heap of vessels or statues for the ornament of their Temples, and embellishing of their Palaces: whereas all our gold is employed in commerce and traffic between man and man. We mince and alter it into a thousand forms: we spend, we scatter and disperse the same to several uses.

Suppose our Kings should thus gather and heap up all the gold they might for many ages hoard up together, and keep it close and untouched. Those of the kingdom of Mexico were somewhat more civilized, and better artists, than other nations of that world. And as we do, so judged they, that this Universe was near his end: and took the desolation we brought amongst them as an infallible sign of it. They believed the state of the world, to be divided into five ages, as in the life of five succeeding Suns, whereof four had already ended their course or time; and the same which now shined upon them, was the fifth and last. The first perished together with all other creatures by an universal inundation of waters. The second by the fall of the heavens upon us which stifled and overwhelmed every living thing: in which age they affirm the Giants to have been, and shewed the Spaniards certain bones of them, according to whose proportion the stature of men came to be of the height of twenty handfuls. The third was consumed by a violent fire, which burned and destroyed all. The fourth by a whirling emotion of the air and winds, which with the violent fury of itself removed and over-threw divers high mountains: saying, that men died not of it, but were transformed into Monkeys. (Oh what impressions doth not the weakness of man's belief admit?)

After the consummation of this fourth Sun, the world continued five and twenty years in perpetual darkness: in the fifteenth of which one man and one woman were created, who renewed the race of mankind. Ten years after, upon a certain day, the Sun appeared as newly created: from which day beginneth ever since the calculation of their years. On the third day of whose creation, died their ancient Gods; their new ones have day by day been born since. In what manner this last Sun shall perish, my author could not learn of them. But their number of this fourth change, doth jump and meet with that great conjunction of the Stars, which eight hundred and odd years since, according to the Astrologians' supposition, produced divers great alterations and strange novelties in the world.

Concerning the proud pomp and glorious magnificence, by occasion of which I am fallen into this discourse, nor Greece, nor Rome, nor Egypt, can (be it in profit, or difficulty or nobility) equal or compare sundry and divers of their works. The causeway or highway which is yet to be seen in Peru, erected by the Kings of that country, stretching from the city of Quito, unto that of Cuzco (containing three hundred leagues in length) straight, even, and fine, and twenty paces in breadth curiously paved, raised on both sides with goodly, high masonry walls, all along which, on the inner side there are two continual running streams, pleasantly beset with beauteous trees, which they call Moly. In framing of which, where they meet any mountains or rocks, they have cut, razed and levelled them, and filled all hollow places with lime and stone. At the end of every day's journey, as stations, there are built stately great palaces, plenteously stored with all manner of good victuals, apparel and arms, as well for daily wayfaring men, as for such armies that might happen to pass that way. In the estimation of which work I have especially considered the difficulty, which in that place is particularly to be remembered. For they built with no stones that were less than ten foot square: They had no other means to carry or transport them, than by mere strength of arms to draw and drag the carriage they needed: they had not so much as the art to make scaffolds; nor knew other device, than to raise so much earth or rubbish, against their building, according as the work riseth, and afterward to take it away again.

But return we to our coaches. Instead of them, and of all other carrying beasts, they caused themselves to be carried by men, and upon their shoulders. This last King of Peru, the same day he was taken, was thus carried upon rafters or beams of massive Gold, sitting in a fair chair of state, likewise all of gold, in the middle of his battle. Look how many of his porters as were slain, to make him fall (for all their endeavour was to take him alive) so many others took and underwent presently the place of the dead: so that they could never be brought down or made to fall, what slaughter soever was made of those kind of people, until such time as a horseman furiously ran to take him by some part of his body, and so pulled him to the ground.

[FROM *Of Coaches*]

II. The Upheaval in the Heavens

Thomas Digges

IN SUPPORT OF COPERNICUS

TO THE READER

Having of late, gentle Reader, corrected and reformed sundry faults that by negligence in printing
have crept into my father's *General Prognostication:*
Among other things I found a description or Model of
the world and situation of Spheres Celestial and Elementary according to the doctrine of Ptolemy, whereunto all Universities (led thereto chiefly by the authority
of Aristotle) since then have consented. But in this our
age one rare wit (seeing the continual errors that from
time to time more & more have been discovered, besides
the infinite absurdities in their Theorickes, which they
have been forced to admit that would not confess any
mobility in the ball of the earth) hath by long study,
painful practise, and rare invention delivered a new
Theorick or model of the world, shewing that the Earth
resteth not in the Center of the whole world, but only in
the Center of this our mortal world or Globe of Ele-

ments, which environed and enclosed in the Moon's Orb, and together with the whole Globe of mortality is carried yearly round about the Sun, which like a king in the middest of all reigneth and giveth the laws of motion to the rest, spherically dispersing his glorious beams of light through all this sacred Celestial Temple. And the Earth itself to be one of the Planets, having his peculiar & straying courses turning every twenty-four hours round upon his own Center, whereby the Sun and great Globe of fixed stars seem to sway about and turn, albeit indeed they remain fixed.

So many ways is the sense of mortal men abused, but reason and deep discourse of wit having opened these things to Copernicus, & the same being with demonstrations Mathematical most apparently by him to the world delivered, I thought it convenient together with the old Theorick also to publish this, to the end such noble English minds (as delight to reach above the baser sort of men) might not be altogether defrauded of so noble a part of Philosophy. And to the end it might manifestly appear that Copernicus meant not, as some have fondly excused him, to deliver these grounds of the Earth's mobility only as Mathematical principles, feigned & not as Philosophical truly averred. I have also from him delivered both the Philosophical reasons by Aristotle and others produced to maintain the Earth's stability, and also their solutions and insufficiency, wherein I cannot a little commend the modesty of that grave Philosopher Aristotle, who seeing (no doubt) the insufficiency of his own reasons in seeking to confute the Earth's motion, useth these words: *De his explicatum est ea qua potuimus facultate*. Howbeit, his disciples have not with like sobriety maintained the same.

Thus much for my own part in this case I will only say: There is no doubt but of a true ground truer effects may be produced than of principles that are false, and of true principles falsehood or absurdity cannot be inferred. If therefore the Earth be situated immovable in the Center of the world, why find we not Theorickes upon that ground to produce effects as true and certain as these of Copernicus? why cast we not away those *circulos aequantes* and motions irregular, seeing our own Philosopher, Aristotle himself, the light of our Universities, hath taught us: *Simplicis corporis simplicem oportet esse motum*. But if contrary it be found, impossible (the Earth's stability being granted) but that we must necessarily fall into these absurdities, and cannot by any mean avoid them. Why shall we so much dote in the appearance of our senses, which many ways may be abused, and not suffer ourselves to be directed by the rule of Reason, which the great God hath given us a Lamp to lighten the darkness of our understanding and the perfect guide to lead us to the golden branch of Verity amid the forest of errors.

Behold a noble Question to be of the Philosophers and Mathematicians of our Universities argued not with childish Invectives, but with grave reasons Philosophical and irreprovable Demonstrations Mathematical. And let us not in matters of reason be led away with authority and opinions of men. . . .

The Globe of Elements enclosed in the Orb of the Moon I call the Globe of Mortality because it is the peculiar Empire of death. For above the Moon they fear not his force. . . . In the midst of this Globe of Mortality hangeth this dark star or ball of earth and water, balanced and sustained in the midst of the thin air only with that propriety which the wonderful workman hath given at the Creation to the Center of this Globe with his magnetical force vehemently to draw and hale unto itself all such other Elemental things as retain the like nature. This ball every twenty-four hours by natural, uniform and wonderful sly & smooth motion rolleth round, making with his Period our natural day, whereby it seems to us that the huge infinite immovable Globe should sway and turn about.

The Moon's Orb that environeth and containeth this dark star and the other mortal, changeable, corruptible Elements & Elementary things is also turned round every 29 days, 31 minutes, 50 seconds, 8 thirds, 9 fourths, and 20 fifths, and this Period may most aptly be called the Month. The rest of the Planets' motions appear by the Picture and shall more largely be hereafter spoken of.

Herein, good Reader, I have waded farther than the vulgar sort of Demonstrative & Practice, & God sparing life, I mean though not as a Judge to decide, yet at the Mathematical bar in this case to plead in such sort, as it shall manifestly appear to the World whether it be possible upon the Earth's stability to deliver any true or probable Theorick, & then refer the pronouncing of sentence to the grave Senate of indifferent discreet Mathematical Readers.

Farewell, and respect my travail as thou shalt see them tend to the advancement of truth and discovering the Monstrous loathsome shape of error.

A PERFECT DESCRIPTION OF THE CELES-
TIAL ORBS ACCORDING TO THE MOST
ANCIENT DOCTRINE OF THE PYTHAGO-
REANS, LATELY REVIVED BY COPERNI-
CUS AND BY GEOMETRICAL DEMON-
STRATIONS APPROVED

Although in this most excellent and difficult part of Philosophy in all times have been sundry opinions touching the situation and moving of the bodies Celestial, yet in certain principles all Philosophers of any account, of all ages have agreed and consented. First, that the Orb of the fixed stars is of all other the most high, the farthest distant, and comprehendeth all the other spheres of wandering stars. And of these straying bodies called Planets, the old philosophers thought it a good ground in reason that the nearest to the center should most swiftly move, because the circle was least and thereby the sooner overpassed, and the farther distant the more slowly. Therefore as the Moon, being swiftest in course, is found also by measure nearest, so have all agreed that the Orb of Saturn, being in moving the slowest of all the Planets, is also the highest: Jupiter the next, and then Mars, but of Venus & Mercury there hath been great controversy, because they stray not every way from the Sun as the rest do. And therefore some have placed them above the Sun, as Plato in his *Timæus:* others beneath, as Ptolemy and the greater part of them that followed him. Alpetragius maketh Venus above the Sun and Mercury beneath, and sundry reasons have been of all sides alleged in defense of their opinions.

They that follow Plato (supposing that all stars should have obscure & dark bodies shining with borrowed light like the Moon) have alleged that if those Planets were lower than the Sun, then should they sometimes obscure some part of the body of the Sun, and also shine not with a light circular, but segmentary, and that variable as in the Moon: Which when they see by experience at no time to happen, they conclude with Plato. On the contrary part such as will maintain them beneath, frame a likelihood by reason of the large space between the Orbs of Sun and Moon. For the greatest distance of the Moon is but .64.½ semi-diameters of the Earth, & to the nearest of the Sun are .1160.—so that there remaineth between the Moon and the Sun .1095. semi-diameters of the earth. And therefore that so huge a space should not remain empty, there they situate the Orbs of Mercury and Venus. And by the distance of their *Absides* whereby they search the thickness of their Orbs they find that they of all the rest best answer that situation, so as the lowest of Mercury's Orb may reach down almost to the highest of the Moon's, & the top of Mercury to the inferior part of Venus' sphere, which with his *Abis* should reach almost to the Sun. For between the *Absides* of Mercury by their Theoricks they supputate .177. semi-diameters of the earth and then the crassitude of Venus' Orb being .910. semi-diameters, doeth very nearly supply and fill the residue. They therefore will not confess that these Planets have any obscurity in their bodies like the Moon, but that either with their own proper light or else being thoroughly pierced with solar beams, they shine and show Circular. And having a straying course of latitude they seldom pass between the Sun and us, or if they should, their bodies being so small, could scarcely hide the hundreth part of the Sun, and so small a spot in so noble a light could hardly be discerned. And yet Averroes in his Paraphrasis on Ptolemy affirmeth that he saw a little spot in the Sun at such time as by Calculation he had forecast a corporal Conjunction.

But how weak this their reason is, it may soon appear if we consider how from the Earth to the lowest of the Moon's Orb there is .38. semi-diameters of the earth, or by the truer computation according to Copernicus .52.— and yet in all that so huge a space we know nothing but the air or fiery Orb if any such be. Again the Diameter of the circle whereby Venus should be carried nearly .45. grades distant from the Sun, must needs be six times greater at the least than the distance of that circle's lowest part from the Earth, then if that whole circle comprehended within the Orb of Venus should be turned about the Earth (as needs it must). If we will not attribute to the Earth any motion we may easily consider what rule in the heavens so vast & huge an Epicycle, containing a space so many times greater than the Earth, air & Orbs of the Moon and Mercury also, will make, especially being turned round about the earth.

Again, that reason of Ptolemy that the Sun must needs be placed in the midst of those Planets that wander from him at liberty and those that are as it were combined to him, is proved senseless by the motion of the Moon, whom we see no less to stray from the Sun than any of those other three superior Planets. But if they will needs have these two Planets' Orbs within an Orb of the Sun, what reason can they give why they should not depart from the Sun at large, as the other Planets do, considering the increase of swiftness in their motion must accompany the inferior situation, or else the whole order of Theoricks should be disturbed. It is therefore evident that either there must be some other Centre, whereunto the order of these Orbs should be referred, or else no reason in their order nor cause apparent why we should rather to Saturn than to Jupiter or any of the rest attribute the higher or remoter Orb. And therefore seemeth it worthy of consideration that Martianus Capella wrote in his *Encyclopedia* and certain other Latins held, affirming that Venus and Mercury do run about the Sun in their spheres peculiar, & therefore could not stray farther from the Sun than the capacity of their Orbs would give them leave, because they encompass not the Earth as the others do, but have their *Absides* after another manner conversed, what other thing would they hereby signify but that the Orbs of these Planets should environ the Sun as their Center. So may the sphere of Mercury, being not of half the amplitude of Venus' Orb, be well situated within the same.

And if in like sort, we situate the Orbs of Saturn, Jupiter, and Mars, referring them as it were to the same Center, so as their capacity be such as they contain and circulate also the Earth, happily we shall not err, as by evident Demonstrations in the residue of Copernicus' *Revolutions* is demonstrated. For it is apparent that these Planets near the Sun are always least, and farthest distant and opposite are much greater in sight & nearer to us, whereby it cannot be but the centre of them is rather to the Sun than to the Earth to be referred: as in the Orbs of Venus and Mercury also. But if all these to the Sun as a centre in this manner be referred, then must there needs between the convex Orb of Venus and the concave of Mars an huge space be left, wherein the Earth & Elementary frame enclosed with the Lunar Orb of duty must be situated. For from the Earth the Moon may not be far removed, being without controversy of all other nearest in place and nature to it: especially considering between the same Orbs of Venus and Mars there is room sufficient.

Therefore need we not be ashamed to confess this whole globe of Elements enclosed with the Moon's sphere, together with the Earth as the Centre of the same, to be by this great Orb, together with the other Planets about the Sun, turned, making by his revolution our year. And whatsoever seems to us to proceed by the moving of the Sun, the same to proceed indeed by the revolution of the Earth, the Sun still remaining fixed & immovable in the middest. And the distance of the Earth from the Sun to be such, as being compared with the other Planets, maketh evident alterations and diversity of Aspects; but if it be referred to the Orb of stars fixed, then hath it no proportion sensible, but as a point or a Center to a circumference—which I hold far more reasonable to be granted, than to fall into such an infinite multitude of absurd imaginations, as they were feign to admit that will needs wilfully maintain the Earth's stability in the Centre of the world. But rather herein to direct ourselves by that wisdom we see in all God's natural works, where we may behold one thing rather endued with many virtues and effects, than any superfluous or unnecessary part admitted.

And all these things, although they seem hard, strange, & incredible, yet to any reasonable man that hath his understanding ripened with Mathematical demonstration, Copernicus in his *Revolutions,* according to his promise, hath made them more evident and clear than the Sunbeams. These grounds therefore admitted, which no man reasonably can impugn, that the greater orb requireth the longer time to run his Period: The orderly and most beautiful frame of the Heavens doth ensue.

The first and highest of all is the immovable sphere of fixed stars, containing itself and all the Rest, and therefore fixed: as the place universal of Rest, whereunto the motions and positions of all inferior spheres are to be compared. For albeit sundry Astrologians finding alteration in the declination and Longitude of stars, have thought that the same also should have his motion peculiar: Yet Copernicus, by the motions of the Earth, solveth all, and utterly cutteth off the ninth and tenth spheres, which, contrary to all sense, the maintainers of the earth's stability have been compelled to imagine.

The first of the movable Orbs is that of Saturn, which, being of all other next unto that infinite Orb immovable, garnished with lights innumerable, is also in his course most slow, & once only in thirty years passeth his Period. The second is Jupiter, who in twelve years performeth his circuit. Mars in two years runneth his circular race. Then followeth the great Orb wherein the globe of mortality, enclosed in the Moon's Orb as an Epicycle and holding the Earth as a Centre by his own weight resting always permanent, in the middest of the air is carried round once in a year.

In the fifth place is Venus, making her revolution in nine months. In the sixth is Mercury, who passeth his circuit in eighty days.

In the middest of all is the Sun. For in so stately a temple as this, who would desire to set his lamp in any other better or more convenient place than this, from whence uniformly it might distribute light to all. For not unfitly it is of some called the lamp or light of the world, of others the mind, of others the Ruler of the world.

Ad cuius numeros & dii moveantur & orbes accipiant leges praescriptaque faedera servent

Trismegistus calleth him the visible god. Thus doth the Sun, like a king sitting on his throne, govern his courts of inferior powers: Neither is the Earth defrauded of the service of the Moon, but as Aristotle saith of all other, the Moon with the Earth hath nearest alliance, so here are they matched accordingly.

In this form of Frame may we behold such a wonderful Symmetry of notions and situations, as in no other can be proponed: The times whereby we the Inhabitants of the Earth are directed, are constituted by the revolutions of the Earth; the circulation of her Centre causeth the year; the conversion of her circumference maketh the natural day; and the revolution of the Moon produceth the month. By the only view of this Theorick, the cause and reason is apparent why in Jupiter the progressions and Retrogradations are greater than in Saturn, and less than in Mars; why also in Venus they are more than in Mercury. And why such changes from Direct to Retrograde, Stationary, etc., happeneth notwithstanding more rifely in Saturn than in Jupiter, & yet more rarely in Mars; why in Venus not so commonly as in Mercury. Also why Saturn, Jupiter and Mars are nearer the earth in their Acronical than in their Cosmical or Heliacal rising. Especially Mars, who rising at the Sunset, sheweth in his ruddy fiery colour equal in quantity with Jupiter, and contrariwise, setting little after the Sun, is scarcely to be discerned from a Star of the second light.

All which alterations apparently follow upon the Earth's motion. And that none of these do happen in the fixed stars, it plainly argueth their huge distance and immeasurable Altitude, in respect whereof this great Orb wherein the Earth is carried is but a point, and utterly without sensible proportion, being compared to that heaven. For as it is in perspective demonstrated: Every quantity hath a certain proportionable distance whereunto it may be discerned, and beyond the same it may not be seen. This distance therefore of that immovable heaven is so exceeding great, that the whole *Orbis Magnus* vanisheth away, if it be conferred to that heaven.

Herein can we never sufficiently admire this wonderful & incomprehensible huge frame of God's work proponed to our senses. Seeing first this ball of the Earth wherein we move, to the common sort seemeth great, and yet in respect of the Moon's Orb is very small, but compared with *Orbis Magnus* wherein it is carried, it scarcely retaineth any sensible proportion—so marvelously is that Orb of Annual motion greater than this little dark star wherein we live. But that *Orbis Magnus*, being, as is before declared, but as a point in respect of the immensity of that immovable heaven, we may easily consider what little portion of God's frame our Elementary corruptible world is, but never sufficiently be able to admire the immensity of the Rest. Especially of that fixed Orb, *garnished with lights innumerable and reaching up in Spherical Altitude without end.*

Of which lights Celestial, it is to be thought that we only behold such as are in the inferior parts of the same Orb, and as they are higher, so seem they of less and lesser quantity, even till our sight, being not able farther to reach or conceive, the greatest part rest, by reason of their wonderful distance, invisible unto us. And this may well be thought of us to be the glorious court of the great God, whose unsearchable works invisible we may partly by these, his visible, conjecture, to whose infinite power and majesty *such an infinite place* surmounting all other, both in quantity and quality, only is convenient. But because the world hath so long a time been carried with an opinion of the Earth's stability, as the contrary cannot but be now very impersuasible, I have thought good out of Copernicus also to give a taste of the reasons philosophical alleged for the Earth's stability, and their solutions, that such as are not able with Geometrical eyes to behold the secret perfection of Copernicus' Theorick, may yet by these familiar, natural reasons be induced to search farther, and not rashly to condemn for fantastical, so ancient doctrine revived, and by Copernicus so demonstratively approved.

WHAT REASONS MOVED ARISTOTLE AND
OTHERS THAT FOLLOWED HIM TO
THINK THE EARTH TO REST IMMOV-
ABLE AS A CENTRE TO THE WHOLE
WORLD

The most effectual reasons that they produce to prove the Earth's stability in the middle or lowest part of the world, is that of Gravity and Levity. For of all other the Element of the Earth, say they, is most heavy, and all ponderous things are carried unto it, striving as it were to sway even down to the inmost part thereof. For the Earth, being round, into the which all weighty things on every side fall, making right angles on the superficies, must needs—if they were not stayed on the superficies —pass to the Center, seeing every right line that falleth perpendicularly upon the Horizon in that place where it toucheth the Earth must needs pass by the Centre. And those things that are carried toward that Medium, it is likely that there also they would rest. So much therefore, the rather shall the Earth rest in the middle, and (receiving all things into itself that fall) by his own weight shall be most immovable.

Again they seek to prove it by reason of motion and his nature, for of one and the same a simple body, the motion must also be simple, saith Aristotle. Of simple motions there are two kinds, right and circular. Right are either up or down: so that every simple motion is either downward toward the Center, or upward from the Center, or circular about the Centre. Now unto the Earth and water, in respect of their weight, the motion downward is convenient to seek the Center. To air and fire, in regard of their lightness, upward and from the Center. So is it meet to these elements to attribute the right or straight motion, and to the heavens only it is proper circularly about this mean or Center to be turned round. Thus much Aristotle.

If therefore, saith Ptolemy of Alexandria, the Earth should turn but only by the daily motion, things quite contrary to these should happen. For his motion should be most swift and violent that in twenty-four hours should let pass the whole circuit of the Earth, and those things which by sudden turning are stirred, are altogether unmeet to collect, but rather to disperse things united, unless they should by some firm fastening be kept together. And long ere this, the Earth, being dissolved in pieces, should have been scattered through the heavens—which were a mockery to think of, and much more beasts and all other weights that are loose could not remain unshaken. And also things falling should not light on the place's perpendicular under them; neither should they fall directly thereto, the same being violently in the mean carried away. Clouds also, and other things hanging in the air, should always seem to us to be carried toward the West.

THE SOLUTION OF THESE REASONS, WITH THEIR INSUFFICIENCY

These are the causes and such other wherewith they approve the Earth to rest in the middle of the world, and that out of all question. But he that will maintain the Earth's mobility may say that this motion is not violent but natural. And these things which are naturally moved have effects contrary to such as are violently carried. For such motions wherein force and violence is used, must needs be dissolved and cannot be of long continuance; but those which by nature are caused, remain still in their perfect estate and are conserved and kept in their most excellent constitution. Without cause, therefore, did Ptolemy fear lest the Earth and all earthly things should be torn in pieces by this revolution of the Earth caused by the working of nature, whose operations are far different from those of Art, or such as human intelligence may reach unto.

But why should he not much more think and misdoubt the same of the world, whose motion must of necessity be so much more swift and vehement than this of the Earth, as the Heaven is greater than the Earth? Is therefore the Heaven made so huge in quantity that it might with unspeakable vehemency of motion be severed from the Centre, lest, happily resting, it should fall, as some Philosophers have affirmed? Surely if this reason should take place, the Magnitude of the Heaven should infinitely extend. For the more this motion should violently be carried higher, the greater should the swiftness be, by reason of the increasing of the circumference, which must of necessity in twenty-four hours be passed over, and in like manner by increase of the motion, the Magnitude must also necessarily be augmented. Thus should the swiftness increase the Magnitude, and the Magnitude the swiftness, infinitely.

But according to that ground of nature, whatsoever is infinite can never be passed over. The Heaven therefore of necessity must stand and rest fixed. But, say they, without the Heaven there is no body, no place, no emptiness—no, not anything at all whither heaven should or could farther extend. But this surely is very strange, that nothing should have such efficient power to restrain something, the same having a very essence and being. Yet if we would thus confess that the Heaven were indeed infinite upward, and only finite downward in respect of his spherical concavity, Much more perhaps might that saying be verified, that without the Heaven

is nothing, seeing everything in respect of the infinite-
ness thereof had place sufficient within the same. But
then must it of necessity remain immovable. For the
chiefest reason that hath moved some to think the
Heaven limited was Motion, which they thought without controversy to be indeed in it.

But whether the world have his bounds or be indeed
infinite and without bounds, let us leave that to be discussed of Philosophers. Sure we are that the Earth is not
infinite, but hath a circumference limited, seeing therefore all Philosophers consent that limited bodies may
have Motion, and infinite cannot have any. Why do we
yet stagger to confess motion in the Earth, being most
agreeable to his form and nature, whose bounds also
and circumference we know, rather than to imagine
that the whole world should sway and turn, whose end
we know not, nor possibly can of any mortal man be
known. And therefore the true Motion indeed to be in
the Earth, and the appearance only in the Heaven: And
that these appearances are no otherwise than if the Vir-
gilian *Aeneas* should say:

Provehimur portu, terraeque urbesque recedunt.

For a ship carried in a smooth Sea with such tranquillity doth pass away, that all things on the shores and
the Seas to the sailors seem to move, and themselves
only quietly to rest, with all such things as are aboard
them; so surely may it be in the Earth, whose Motion
being natural and not forcible, of all other is most uniform and unperceivable, whereby to us that sail therein
the whole world may seem to roll about. But what shall
we then say of Clouds and other things hanging or resting in the air or tending upward, but that not only the
Earth and Sea, making one globe, but also no small part
of the air is likewise circularly carried, and in like sort

all such things as are derived from them or have any manner of alliance with them. Either for that the lower Region of the air, being mixed with Earthly and watery vapours, follow the same nature of the Earth. Either that it be gained and gotten from the Earth by reason of Vicinity or Contiguity.

Which if any man marvel at, let him consider how the old Philosophers did yield the same reason for the revolution of the highest Region of the air, wherein we may sometimes behold Comets carried circularly no otherwise than the bodies Celestial seem to be, and yet hath that Region of the air less convenience with the Orbs Celestial, than this lower part with the Earth. But we affirm that part of the air in respect of his great distance to be destitute of this Motion Terrestrial, and that this part of the air that is next to the Earth doth appear most still and quiet by reason of his uniform natural accompanying of the Earth, and likewise things that hang therein, unless by winds or other violent accident they be tossed to and fro. For the wind in the air, is nothing else but as the wave in the Sea: And of things ascending and descending in respect of the world, we must confess them to have mixed motion of right & circular, albeit it seem to us right & straight: No otherwise than if in a ship under sail, a man should softly let a plummet down from the top along by the mast even to the deck. This plummet passing always by the straight mast, seemeth also to fall in a right line, but being by discourse of reason weighed, his Motion is found mixed of right and circular. For such things as naturally fall downward, being of earthly nature, there is no doubt but as parts they retain the nature of the whole.

No otherwise is it of these things that by fiery force are carried upward. For the earthly fire is chiefly nourished with earthly matter, and flame is defined to be nought else but a burning fume or smoke, and the property of fire is to extend the subject whereunto it entereth —the which it doth with so great violence as by no means or engines it can be constrained, but that with breach of bands it will perform his nature. This motion extensive is from the Centre to the circumference, so that if any earthly part be fired, it is carried violently upward. Therefore, whereas they say that of simple bodies the motion is altogether simple, of the circular it is chiefly verified, so long as the simple body remaineth in his natural place and perfect unity of composition. For in the same place there can be no other motion but circular, which remaining wholly in itself is most like to rest and immobility. But right or straight motion only happen to those things that stray and wander, or by any means are thrust out of their natural place. But nothing can be more Repugnant to the form and Ordinance of the world, than that things naturally should be out of their natural place. This kind of motion therefore that is by right line is only accident to those things that are not in their right state or perfection natural, while parts are disjoined from their whole body, and covet to return to the unity thereof again.

Neither do these things which are carried upward or downward besides this circular moving make any simple, uniform, or equal motion, for with their levity or ponderosity of their body, they cannot be tempered, but always as they fall (beginning slowly) they increase their motion, and the farther the more swiftly; whereas contrariwise this our earthly fire (for other we cannot see) we may behold, as it is carried upward, to vanish and decay—as it were, confessing the cause of violence to proceed only from his matter Terrestrial. The circular motion always continueth uniform and equal, by reason of his cause, which is indeficient and always continuing.

But the other hasteneth to end and to attain that place where they leave linger to be heavy or light, and having attained that place, their motion ceaseth. Seeing therefore this circular motion is proper to the whole, as straight is only unto parts, we may say that circular doth rest with straight as *animal cum aegro*. And whereas Aristotle hath distributed *simplicem motum* into these three kinds: *a medio, ad medium,* and *circa medium,* it must be only in reason and imagination, as we likewise sever in consideration Geometrical a point, a line, and a superficies, whereas indeed neither can stand without other, nor any of them without a body.

Hereto we may adjoin that the condition of immobility is more noble and divine than that of change, alteration, or instability, & therefore more agreeable to Heaven than to this Earth, where all things are subject to continual mutability. And seeing by evident proof of Geometrical mensuration, we find that the Planets are sometimes nearer to us and sometimes more remote, and that therefore even the maintainers of the Earth's stability are enforced to confess that the Earth is not their Orb's Centre, this motion *circa medium* must in more general sort be taken, and that it may be understood that every Orb hath his peculiar *medium* and Centre, in regard whereof this simple and uniform motion is to be considered. Seeing therefore that these Orbs have several Centres, it may be doubted whether the Centre of this earthly Gravity be also the Centre of the world. For Gravity is nothing else but a certain proclivity or natural coveting of parts to be coupled with the whole, which by divine providence of the Creator of all is given & impressed into the parts, that they should restore themselves into their unity and integrity concurring in spherical form, which kind of propriety or affection it is likely also that the Moon and other glorious bodies want not to knit & combine their parts together, and to maintain them in their round shape, which bodies notwithstanding are by sundry motions, sundry ways conveyed.

Thus as it is apparent by these natural reasons that the mobility of the Earth is more probable and likely than the stability. So if it be Mathematically considered, and with Geometrical Mensurations every part of every Theorick examined: the discreet Student shall find that Copernicus not without great reason did propone this ground of the Earth's Mobility.

[FROM *A Perfect Description of the Celestial Orbs*]

PORTENTS IN THE SKY

Robert Ashley

IN THE SHADOW OF THE GREAT YEAR

THERE ARE certain periods appointed for the world, which while they endure, all things do come to their vigour; and which being ended, they do all perish: but all of them end their course within the revolution of the Great Year. And . . . when the one cometh to end, and the other is ready to begin, there are many strange signs seen both in earth and in heaven. Wherefore many are of opinion that some great alteration doth approach, considering the signs which within these few years have appeared in heaven, in the stars, in the elements, and in all nature. . . . [Some authorities believe] that there have already been seven Great Years in the space of five thousand, five hundred and thirty years . . . and that the eighth shall be in the year of Christ 1604.

[FROM *Of the Interchangeable Course or Variety of Things in the Whole World*, by Louis LeRoy, translated by Robert Ashley, 1594.]

John Norden

THE APPROACHING END

I

The greatest changes and most rare events,
In States, in Kingdoms, and in greatest sects,
Are said to issue of the Spheres' dissents
The eight and ninth, not by their joint aspects,
    Their awkward movings breed rarest effects,
        Not by their Nature's inclination,
        But by their motive Trepidation.

II

Besides conjunction of Triplicities,
Of Saturn, Jupiter, and Mars aspecting,
Are held most powerful Principalities,
Greatest Alterations effecting,
    Their triplicities duely respecting:
        Fiery, or airy, watery, or earthly,
        The event corresponds the triplicity.

III

Of such, some count seven since the world began
(Five thousand, five hundred, sixty two years),
The Eighth shall be when four years more are come,
By testy of the best Astrologers,
    Presaged thus, it may well summon tears,
        That he that rules may moderate his ire,
        Lest World consume with fearful gusts of fire.

IV

Seneca reports Belus to foresee
The universal deluge ere it came:
And when the conflagration should be,
To burn the mass, as water drowned the same,
   When of the Stars such Opposition came,
      As one right line might pierce their Circles all
      In Cancer sign: this last effect should fall.

V

The antique Poets in their Poems telled
Under their fondest Fables, Mysteries:
By Phaeton, how heaven's Powers rebelled
In Fire's force, and by the histories
   Of Pyrrha and Deucalian there lies,
      The like of water's impetuity,
      In part concurring with divinity—

VI

Which hath revealed the World's destruction
By water past, her future fall by Fire:
But holds the cause, Sin, not conjunction
Of Fire or Water's self-revenging ire:
   The Powers divine commove them to conspire
      To make the earth and earthly Bodies nought,
      That do defile, what he so pure hath wrought.

VII

The Priests of Egypt gazing on the stars,
Are said to see the World's sad ruins past,
That had betide by Fire and Water's jars:
And how the World inconstant and unchaste,

Assailed by these, cannot alike stand fast.
　　Earthquakes and Wars, Famine, Hate, and Pest,
　　Bring perils to the Earth, and Man's unrest.

VIII

We at the present see Time's changing state,
And Nature's fearful alterations,
As if Time now did preach the Heavens' debate,
And Stars to band in dismal factions.
　　Strange Signs are seen, divine probations,
　　　　That some Effect will follow of Admire,
　　　　Too late, when come, to say it will retire.

IX

The Sun and Moon eclipsed ne'er so much,
Comets and strange Impressions in the Air:
The Tides and swelling Floods were never such:
The Earth doth tremble, Nature doth impair,
　　Hideous Monsters now possess the Chair,
　　　　Where erst dame Nature's true begotten seed
　　　　Sat truly graced in her proper weed.

X

Such changes never have been seen of yore,
In Countries and in Kingdoms, as of late,
Manners, and Laws, and Religion's lore,
Never were prized at so mean a rate:
　　Such are the changes of this Earth's estate,
　　　　It may be said, Time's wings begin to fry,
　　　　Now couching low, that erst did soar so high.

XI

Yea, now is proved the progress of the Sun
To differ far from pristine gradience:

The Solstices and Equinoxes run,
As in pretended disobedience.
   The Sun observed by Art's Diligence,
      Is found in fourteen hundred years to fall,
      Near twelve Degrees towards the Center ball.

XII

The Zodiac and all her parts and signs,
Alter the course, that first they were assigned,
And all the orb of Heaven so combines,
As she unto her Period inclined.
   Time past, far greater than that is behind,
      Doth prove the Heavens in their greatest Pride,
      Subject to changes and to wave aside.

XIII

Some eke affirm the earthly Sphere to err:
First set the Center of the concave Spheres
Now start aside (supposed not to stir).
If so, the Power that Earth and Heaven Steers
   By it foreshows the purpose that he bears,
      That all the Creatures that he made so fast,
      Shall by degrees alter, wear and wast.

                [FROM *Vicissitudo Rerum*]

Fulke Greville

NATURE, THE QUEEN OF CHANGE

All which best root, and spring in new foundations
Of States or Kingdoms; and again in age,
Or height of pride and power, feel declination;
Mortality is Change's proper stage:

    States have degrees, as human bodies have,
    Spring, Summer, Autumn, Winter, and the grave.

But further now the Eternal Wisdom shows,
That though God do preserve thus for a time,
This Equilibrium, wherein Nature goes,
By passing humours, not to overclimb,
    Yet he both by the cure, and the disease,
    Proves Dissolution all at length must seize.

For surely, if it had been God's intent
To give Man here eternally possession,
Earth had been free from all misgovernment,
War, Malice, could not then have had progression,
    Man (as at first) had been man's nursing brother,
    And not, as since, one Wolf to another.

For only this Antipathy of mind
Hath ever been the bellows of Sedition;
Where each man kindling one, inflames Mankind,
Till on the public they inflict perdition,
    And as Man unto Man, so State to State
    Inspired is, with the venom of this hate.

And what does all these mutinies include,
But dissolution first of Government?
Then a dispeopling of the earth by feud,
As if our Maker to destroy us meant?
    For states are made of Men, and Men of dust,
    The moulds are frail, disease consume them must.

Now as the Wars prove man's mortality;
So do the oppositions here below,
Of Elements, the contrariety,

Of constellations, which above do shew,
Of qualities in flesh, will in the spirits;
Principles of discord, not of concord made,
All prove God meant not Man should here inherit
A time-made World, which with time should not fade;
    But as Noah's flood once drowned woods, hills, &
        plain,
    So should the fire of Christ waste all again.

[FROM *A Treatise of Wars*]

John Donne

NEW PHILOSOPHY CALLS ALL IN DOUBT

So did the world from the first hour decay,
That evening was beginning of the day,
And now the Springs and Summers which we see,
Like sons of women after fifty be.
And new Philosophy calls all in doubt,
The Element of fire is quite put out;
The Sun is lost, and th' earth, and no man's wit
Can well direct him where to look for it.
And freely men confess that this world's spent,
When in the Planets, and the Firmament
They seek so many new; then see that this
Is crumbled out again to his Atomies.
'Tis all in pieces, all coherence gone;
All just supply, and all Relation:
Prince, Subject, Father, Son, are things forgot,
For every man alone thinks he hath got
To be a Phœnix, and that then can be
None of that kind, of which he is, but he.
This is the world's condition now. . . . .

We think the heavens enjoy their Spherical,
Their round proportion embracing all.
But yet their various and perplexed course,
Observ'd in divers ages, doth enforce
Men to find out so many eccentric parts,
Such divers down-right lines, such overthwarts,
As disproportion that pure form: it tears
The Firmament in eight and forty shares,
And in these Constellations then arise
New stars, and old do vanish from our eyes:
As though heav'n suffered earthquakes, peace or war,
When new Towers rise, and old demolish'd are.
They have impal'd within a Zodiac
The free-born Sun, and keep twelve Signs awake
To watch his steps; the Goat and Crab control,
And fright him back, who else to either Pole
(Did not these Tropics fetter him) might run:
For his course is not round; nor can the Sun
Perfect a Circle, or maintain his way
One inch direct; but where he rose to-day
He comes no more, but with a cozening line,
Steals by that point, and so is Serpentine:
And seeming weary with his reeling thus,
He means to sleep, being now fall'n nearer us.
So, of the Stars, which boast that they do run
In Circle still, none ends where he begun.
All their proportion 's lame, it sinks, it swells.
For of Meridians, and Parallels,
Man hath weav'd out a net, and this net thrown
Upon the Heavens, and now they are his own.
Loth to go up the hill, or labour thus
To go to heaven, we make heaven come to us.
We spur, we rein the stars, and in their race
They 're diversely content t' obey our pace.

[FROM *An Anatomy of the World: The First Anniversary*]

William Shakespeare

THESE LATE ECLIPSES

GLOUCESTER. These late eclipses in the sun and moon portend no good to us. Though the wisdom of nature can reason it thus and thus, yet nature finds itself scourged by the sequent effects. Love cools, friendship falls off, brothers divide. In cities, mutinies; in countries, discord; in palaces, treason; and the bond cracked between son and father. This villain of mine comes under the prediction; there 's son against father: the King falls from bias of nature; there 's father against child. We have seen the best of our time. Machinations, hollowness, treachery, and all ruinous disorders, follow us disquietly to our graves. . . .   [*Exit.*

EDMUND. This is the excellent foppery of the world, that, when we are sick in fortune—often the surfeit of our own behaviour—we make guilty of our disasters the sun, the moon, and the stars; as if we were villains by necessity; fools by heavenly compulsion; knaves, thieves, and treachers by spherical predominance; drunkards, liars, and adulterers by an enforced obedience of planetary influence; and all that we are evil in, by a divine thrusting on. An admirable evasion of whoremaster man, to lay his goatish disposition to the charge of a star! My father compounded with my mother under the dragon's tail, and my nativity was under Ursa Major; so that it follows I am rough and lecherous. 'Sfoot! I should have been that I am, had the maidenliest star in the firmament twinkled on my bastardizing. Edgar—

Enter EDGAR.

and pat he comes, like the catastrophe of the old comedy. My cue is villainous melancholy, with a sigh like Tom o' Bedlam. O, these eclipses do portend these divisions! Fa, sol, la, mi.

[FROM *King Lear*, I, ii]

Thomas Nashe

THE STARS' DISTEMPERATURES DISPROVED

I

ANOTHER sort of men there are, who though not addicted to such counterfeit curiosity, yet are they infected with a farther improbability; challenging knowledge unto themselves of deeper mysteries, when, as with Thales Milesius, they see not what is under their feet; searching more curiously into the secrets of nature, when as in respect of deeper knowledge, they seem mere naturals; coveting with the Phoenix to approach so nigh to the sun, that they are scorched with his beams, and confounded with his brightness. Who made them so privy to the secrets of the Almighty, that they should foretell the tokens of his wrath, or terminate the time of his vengeance? But lightly some news attends the end of every Term; some Monsters are booked, though not bred against vacation times, which are straightway diversely dispersed into every quarter, so that at length they become the Alehouse talk of every Carter. Yea, the Country Plowman feareth a Calabrian flood in the midst of a furrow, and the silly Shepherd committing his wandering sheep to the custody of his wappe, in his field naps dreameth of flying Dragons, which for fear lest he should see to the loss of his sight, he falleth asleep; no

star he seeth in the night but seemeth a Comet; he
lighteth no sooner on a quagmire, but he thinketh this
is the foretold Earthquake, whereof his boy hath the
Ballad.

Thus are the ignorant deluded, the simple misused,
and the sacred Science of Astronomy discredited.

[FROM *The Anatomy of Absurdity*]

II

Gentlemen, I am sure you have heard of a ridiculous
Ass that many years since sold lies by the great, and
wrote an absurd *Astrological Discourse* of the terrible
Conjunction of Saturn and Jupiter, wherein (as if he had
lately cast the Heaven's water, or been at the anato-
mizing of the Sky's entrails in Surgeon's hall) he prophe-
cieth of such strange wonders to ensue from stars'
distemperature and the unusual adultery of Planets, as
none but he that is Bawd to those celestial bodies could
ever descry. What expectation there was of it both in
town and country, the amazement of those times may
testify: and the rather because he pawned his credit
upon it, in these express terms: "If these things fall not
out in every point as I have wrote, let me forever hereafter lose the credit of my Astronomy."

Well, so it happened that he happened not to be a
man of his word; his Astronomy broke his day with his
creditors, and Saturn and Jupiter proved honester men
than all the World took them for. Whereupon the poor
Prognosticator was ready to run himself through with
his Jacob's Staff, and cast himself headlong from the top
of a Globe (as a mountain) and break his neck. The
whole University hissed at him; Tarlton at the Theatre
made jests of him; and Elderton consumed his ale-
crammed nose to nothing, in bearbaiting him with whole
bundles of ballads. Would you, in likely reason, guess it

were possible for any shame-swollen toad to have the spit-proof face to outlive this disgrace? It is, dear brethren, *Vivit, imo vivit;* and, which is more, he is a Vicar.

[FROM *Pierce Penniless, His Supplication to the Devil*]

III

I found the *Astrological Discourse* the other night in the Chronicle. Gabriel Harvey will outface us, it is a work of such deep art and judgment, when it is expressly passed under record for a cozening prognostication. The words are these, though somewhat abbreviated; for he makes a long circumlocution of it.

In the year 1583, by means of an *Astrological Discourse* upon the great and notable conjunction of Saturn and Jupiter, the common sort of people were almost driven out of their wits, and knew not what to do: but when no such thing happened, they fell to their former security, and condemned the discourser of extreme madness and folly.

Ipsissima sunt Aristotelis verba, they are the very words of John Tell-truth, in the 1357 folio of the last edition of the great Chronicle of England.

[FROM *Four Letters Confuted*]

Richard Hooker

THE REIGN OF LAW

WHEREFORE to come to the law of nature: albeit thereby we sometimes mean that manner of working which God hath set for each created thing to keep; yet forasmuch as those things are termed most properly natural agents, which keep the law of their kind unwittingly, as the heavens and elements of the world, which can do no otherwise than they do; and forasmuch as we give unto intellectual natures the name of Voluntary agents, that so we may distinguish them from the other; expedient it will be, that we sever the law of nature observed by the one from that which the other is tied unto. Touching the former, their strict keeping of one tenure, statute, and law, is spoken of by all, but hath in it more than men have as yet attained to know, or perhaps ever shall attain, seeing the travail of wading herein is given of God to the sons of men, that perceiving how much the least thing in the world hath in it more than the wisest are able to reach unto, they may by this means learn humility.

Moses, in describing the work of creation, attributeth speech unto God: "God said, Let there be light: let there be a firmament: let the waters under the heaven be gathered together into one place: let the earth bring forth: let there be lights in the firmament of heaven." Was this only the intent of Moses, to signify the infinite greatness of God's power by the easiness of His accomplishing such effects, without travail pain, or labour? Surely it seemeth that Moses had herein besides this a further purpose, namely, first to teach that God did not work as a necessary but a voluntary agent, intending beforehand and decreeing with himself that which did outwardly proceed from Him: secondly, to shew that God did then institute a law natural to be observed by creatures, and therefore according to the manner of laws, the institution thereof is described, as being established by solemn injunction. His commanding those things to be which are, and to be in such sort as they are, to keep that tenure and course which they do, importeth the establishment of nature's law.

This world's first creation, and the preservation since of things created, what is it but only so far forth a manifestation by execution, what the eternal law of God is concerning things natural? And as it cometh to pass in a kingdom rightly ordered, that after a law is once published, it presently takes effect far and wide, all states framing themselves thereunto; even so let us think it fareth in the natural course of the world: since the time that God did first proclaim the edicts of His law upon it, heaven and earth have hearkened unto His voice, and their labour hath been to do His will: He "made a law for the rain;" He gave His "decree unto the sea, that the waters should not pass His commandment."

Now if nature should intermit her course, and leave altogether though it were but for a while the observation of her own laws; if those principal and mother elements of the world, whereof all things in this lower world are made, should lose the qualities which now they have; if the frame of that heavenly arch erected over our heads should loosen and dissolve itself; if celestial spheres should forget their wonted motions, and by irregular volubility turn themselves any way as it might happen; if the prince of the lights of heaven, which now as a giant doth run his unwearied course, should as it were through a languishing faintness begin to stand and to rest himself; if the moon should wander from her beaten way, the times and seasons of the year blend themselves by disordered and confused mixture, the winds breathe out their last gasp, the clouds yield no rain, the earth be defeated of heavenly influence, the fruits of the earth pine away as children at the withered breasts of their mother no longer able to yield them relief: what would become of man himself, whom these things now do all serve? See we not plainly that obedience of creatures unto the law of nature is the stay of the whole world?

Notwithstanding with nature it cometh sometimes to pass as with art. Let Phidias have rude and obstinate stuff to carve, though his art do that it should, his work will lack that beauty which otherwise in fitter matter it might have had. He that striketh an instrument with skill may cause notwithstanding a very unpleasant sound, if the string whereon he striketh chance to be uncapable of harmony. In the matter whereof things natural consist, that of Theophrastus taketh place, Πολὺ τὸ οὐχ ὑπακοῦον οὐδὲ δεχόμενον τὸ εὖ. "Much of it is oftentimes such as will by no means yield to receive that impression which were best and most perfect." Which defect in the matter of things natural, they who gave themselves unto the contemplation of nature amongst the heathen observed often: but the true original cause thereof, divine malediction, laid for the sin of man upon these creatures which God had made for the use of man, this being an article of that saving truth which God hath revealed unto his Church, was above the reach of their merely natural capacity and understanding. But howsoever these swervings are now and then incident into the course of nature, nevertheless so constantly the laws of nature are by natural agents observed, that no man denieth but those things which nature worketh are wrought, either always or for the most part, after one and the same manner.

ON LOOKING THROUGH A TELE-SCOPE: GALILEO AND HARIOT

Sir William Lower

THE MAN IN THE MOON

(To Thomas Hariot)

I HAVE received the perspective Cylinder that you promised me and am sorry that my man gave you not more warning, that I might have had also the two or three more that you mentioned to choose for me. Henceforward he shall have order to attend you better and to defray the charge of this and others, that he forgot to pay the workman. According as you wished I have observed the Moon in all his changes. In the new I discover manifestly the earth shine, a little before the Dichotomy, that spot which represents unto me the Man in the Moon (but without a head) is first to be seen. A little after near the brim of the gibbous parts towards the upper corner appear luminous parts like stars much brighter than the rest and the whole brim along, looks like unto the Description of Coasts in the Dutch book of voyages. In the full she appears like a tart that my cook made me the last Week, here a vein of bright stuff, and there of dark, and so confusedly all over. I must confess I can see none of this without my cylinder. Yet an ingenious young man that accompanies me here often, and loves you, and these studies much, sees many of these things even without the help of the instrument, but with it sees them most plainly. I mean the young Mr. Protheroe.

Kepler I read diligently, but therein I find what it is to be so far from you. For as himself, he hath almost put me out of my wits. His *Aequanes*, bisections of eccentricities, librations in the diameters of Epicycles, revolutions in Ellipses, have so thoroughly seized upon my imagination as I do not only ever dream of them, but oftentimes awake lose myself, and power of thinking with too much wanting to it. Not of his causes, for I cannot fancy those magnetical natures. But about his theory which methinks (although I cannot yet overmaster many of his particulars) he establisheth soundly and as you say overthrow the circular Astronomy.

Do you not here startle, to see every day some of your inventions taken from you; for I remember long since you told me as much, that the motions of the planets were not perfect circles. So you taught me the curious way to observe weight in Water, and within a while after Ghetaldi comes out with it in print. A little before Vieta [anticipated] you of the garland of the great Invention of Algebra. All these were your dues and many others that I could mention; and yet too great reservedness had robbed you of these glories. But although the inventions be great, the first and last I mean, yet when I survey your storehouse, I see they are the smallest things and such as in comparison of many others are of small or no value. Only let this remember you, that it is possible by too much procrastination to be prevented in the honor of some of your rarest inventions and speculations. Let your Country and friends enjoy the comforts they would have in the true and great honor you would purchase yourself by publishing some of your choice works, but you know best what you have to do. Only I, because I wish you all good, with this, and sometimes the more longingly, because in one of your letters you gave me some kind of hope thereof.

But again to Kepler. I have read him twice over cursorily. I read him now with Calculation. Sometimes I find a difference of minutes, sometimes false prints, and sometimes an utter confusion in his accounts. These difficulties are so many, and often as here again I want your conference, for I know an hour with you, would advance my studies more than a year here. To give you a taste of some of these difficulties that you may judge of my capacity, I will send you only this one. For this theory I am much in love with these particulars:

1. His permutation of the medial to the apparent motions, for it is more rational that all dimensions as of Eccentricities, apogacies, etc. . . . should depend rather of the habitude to the sun, than to the imaginary circle of orbis annuus.

2. His elliptical *iter planetarum,* for methinks it shews a Way to the solving of the unknown walks of comets. For as his Ellipsis in the Earth's motion is more a circle and in Mars is more long and in some of the other planets may be longer again, so in those comets that are appeared fixed the ellipsis may be nearly a right line.

3. His fancy of *ecliptica media* or his *via regia* of the sun, unto which the walk of all the other planets is oblique, more or less; even the *ecliptica vera* under which the earth walks his year's journey; by which he solves handsomely the mutation of the stars' latitudes.

Indeed I am much delighted with his book, but he is so tough in many places as I cannot bite him. I pray write me some instructions in your next, how I may deal with him to overmaster him for I am ready to take pains, *te modo jura dantem indigeo, dictatorem exposco.*

But in his book I am much out of love with these

particulars. 1. First his many and intolerable atechnies, whence derive those many and uncertain assays of calculation. 2. His finding fault with Vieta for mending the like things in Ptolemy, Copernicus. . . . But see the justice: Vieta speaks slightly of Copernicus, a greater than Atlas. Kepler speaks as slightly of Vieta, a greater than Apollonius whom Kepler everywhere admires. For whosoever can do the things that Kepler cannot do, shall be to him great Apollonius.

But enough of Kepler. Let me once again entreat your counsel how to read him with best profit, for I am wholly possessed with Astronomical speculations and desires. For your declaration of Vieta's appendicle it is so full and plain, as you have abundantly satisfied my desire, for which I yield you the thanks I ought. Only in a word tell me whether by it he can solve Copernicus, the fifth chapter of his fifth book.

The last of Vieta's problems you leave to speak of because (you say) I had a better of you, which was more universal and more easily demonstrated, and findeth the point, as well out of the plane of the triangle given, as in the plane. I pray here help my memory or understanding for although I have bethought myself *usque ad insaniam,* I cannot remember or conceive what proposition you mean. If I have had such a one of you, tell me what one it is and by what tokens I may know it; if I have not had, then let me now have it, for you know how much I love your things and of all ways of teaching for richness and fullness, for stuff and form, yours unto me are incomparably most satisfactory. If your leisure give you leave impart also unto me somewhat else of your riches in this argument.

Let me entreat you to advise and direct this bearer Mr. Vaughan when and how to provide himself of a fit sphere; that by the contemplation of that our imaginations here may be relieved in many speculations that perplex our understandings with diagrams in plano. He hath money to provide do you but tell him where they are to be had and what manner of sphere (I mean with what and how many circles) will be most useful for us to these studies.

After all this I must needs tell you my sorrows. God that gave him, hath taken from me my only son, by continual and strange fits of Epilepsy or Apoplexy, when in appearance, as he was most pleasant and goodly, he was most healthy, but amongst other things, I have learned of you to settle and submit my desires to the will of God; only my wife with more grief bears this affliction, yet now again she begins to be comforted.

Let me hear from you and according to your leisure and friendship have directions in the course of studies I am in. Above all things take care of your health, keep correspondence with Kepler and whereinsoever you can have use of me, require it with all liberty. So I rest ever,

Your assured and true friend to be used in

all things that you please.

WILLIAM LOWER

Tra'vent on Mount Martin

Let me not make myself more able than there is cause. I cannot order the calculation by the construction you sent me of Vieta's third problem, to find the distances of C & D & B from the Apogen or the proportion of ia. to ac. the eccentricity. I took Copernicus, third observations in the sixth chap. of his fifth book. Therefore help here once again.

Addressed: To his especial good friend

Mr. Thomas Hariot at Sion near London.

Sir Henry Wotton

THE MATHEMATICAL PROFESSOR AT PADUA

(To the Earl of Salisbury)

March 13, 1610

Now touching the occurrences of the present, I send herewith unto his Majesty the strangest piece of news (as I may justly call it) that he hath ever yet received from any part of the world; which is the annexed book (come abroad this very day) of the Mathematical Professor at Padua, who by the help of an optical instrument (which both enlargeth and approximateth the object), invented first in Flanders, and bettered by himself, hath discovered four new planets rolling about the sphere of Jupiter, besides many other unknown fixed stars; likewise, the true cause of the *Via Lactae*, so long searched; and lastly, that the moon is not spherical, but endued with many prominences, and, which is of all the strangest, illuminated with the solar light by reflection from the body of the earth, as he seemeth to say. So as upon the whole subject he hath first overthrown all former astronomy—for we must have a new sphere to save the appearances—and next all astrology. For the virtue of these new planets must needs vary the judicial part, and why may there not yet be more? These things I have been bold thus to discourse unto your Lordship, whereof here all corners are full. And the author runneth a fortune to be either exceeding famous or exceeding ridiculous. By the next ship your Lordship shall receive from me one of the above-named instruments, as it is bettered by this man.

Sir William Lower

THE PERSPECTIVE CYLINDER

(To Thomas Hariot)

June 21, 1610

I GAVE your letter a double welcome, both because it came from you and contained news of that strange nature; although that which I craved, you have reserved till another time. Methinks my diligent Galileo hath done more in his three-fold discovery than Magellan in opening the straits to the South Sea or the Dutchmen that were eaten by bears in Nova Zembla. I am sure with more ease and safety to himself and more pleasure to me. I am so affected with this news as I wish summer were past that I might observe these phenomena also.

In the moon I had formerly observed a strange spottedness all over, but had no conceit that any part thereof might be shadows; since I have observed three degrees in the dark parts, of which the lighter sort hath some resemblance of shadiness—but that they grow shorter or longer I cannot yet perceive. There are three stars in Orion below the three in his girdle so near together as they appeared unto me always like a long star, insomuch as about four years since I was a writing you news out of Cornwall of a view, a strange phenomenon. But asking some that had better eyes than myself, they told me, they were three stars lying close together in a right line. These stars with my cylinder this last winter I often observed, and it was long ere I believed that I saw them, they appearing through the Cylinder so far and distinctly asunder that without I cannot yet dissever.

The discovery of these made me then observe the seven stars also in ♉, which before I always rather believed to be, seven, then ever could number them. Through my Cylinder I saw these also plainly and far asunder, and more then seven too. But because I was prejudged with that number, I believed not mine eyes nor was careful to observe how many; the next winter now that you have opened mine eyes you shall hear much from me of this argument. Of the third and greatest (that I confess pleased me most) I have least to say, saving that just at the instant that I received your letters we Traventine Philosophers were considering of Kepler's reasons by which he endeavors to overthrow Nolanus' and Gilbert's opinions concerning the immensity of the Sphere of the stars and that opinion particularly of Nolanus, by which he affirmed that the eye being placed in any part of the Universe the appearance would be still all one as unto us here.

When I was saying that although Kepler had said something to most that might be urged for that opinion of Nolanus, yet of one principal thing he had not thought; for although it may be true that to the eye placed in any star of ⊗, the stars in Capricorn will vanish, yet he hath not therefore so soundly concluded (as he thinks) that therefore towards the part of the world there will be a voidness or thin scattering of little stars whereas else round about there will appear huge stars close thrust together: for said I (having heard you say often as much) what is in that huge space between the stars and Saturn, there remain ever fixed infinite numbers which may supply the appearance to the eye that shall be placed in ⊗, which by reason of their lesser magnitudes do fly our sight what is about ♄. ♃. ♂. etc., there move other planets also which appear not.

Just as I was saying this, comes your letter, which, when I had read:

"Lo," quoth I, "what I spoke probably experience hath made good!"

We both with wonder and delight fell to considering your letter. We are here so on fire with these things that I must renew my request and your promise to send me of all sorts of these Cylinders. My man shall deliver you money for any charge requisite, and content your man for his pains and skill. Send me so many as you think needful unto these observations, and in requital, I will send you store of observations. Send me also one of Galileo's books, if any yet be come over and you can get them. Concerning my doubt in Kepler, you see what it is to be so far from you. What troubled me a month you satisfied in a minute.

I have supplied very fitly my want of a sphere, in the dissolution of a hogshead, for the hopes thereof have framed me a very fine one. I pray also at your leisure answer the other points of my last letter concerning Vieta, Kepler and yourself. I have nothing to present you in counter, but gratitude with a will in act to be useful unto you and a power *inproxima potentia;* which I will not leave also till I have brought *ad actum.* If you in the mean time can further it, tell wherein I may do you service, and see how wholly you shall dispose of me.

Your most assured and loving friend

Tra'venti, the longest day of 1610.

WILLIAM LOWER

Addressed: To his especial good friend
    Mr. Thomas Hariot
    at Sion nere London.

Sir Walter Ralegh

VENUS AND THE "WORTHY ASTROLOGER"

AND SURELY it is not improbable, that the flood of Ogyges, being so great as histories have reported it, was accompanied with much alteration of the air sensibly discerned in those parts, and some unusual face of the skies. Varro, in his books *De Gente Populi Romani,* (as he is cited by St. Augustine) reporteth out of Castor, that so great a miracle happened in the star of Venus, as never was seen before nor in after-times: for the colour, the greatness, the figure, and the course of it were changed. This fell out, as Adrastus Cyzicenus, and Dion Neapolites, famous mathematicians, affirmed, in the time of Ogyges.

Now concerning the course of that or any planet, I do not remember that I have anywhere read of so good astrologers flourishing among the Greeks or elsewhere, in those days, as were likely to make any calculation of the revolutions of the planets so exact that it should need no reformation. Of the colour and magnitude, I see no reason why the difference found in the star of Venus should be held miraculous; considering that lesser mists and fogs than those which covered Greece with so long darkness, do familiarly present our senses with as great alterations in the sun and moon. That the figure should vary, questionless it was very strange; yet I cannot hold it any prodigy; for it stands well with good reason, that the side of Venus which the sun beholds, being enlightened by him, the opposite half should remain shadowed; whereby that planet would, unto our eyes, descrying only that part whereon the light falleth, appear to be horned, as the moon doth seem; if distance, as in other things, did not hinder the apprehension of our senses.

Galilæus, a worthy astrologer now living, who, by the help of perspective glasses, hath found in the stars many things unknown to the ancients, affirmeth so much to have been discovered in Venus by his late observations. Whether some watery dispostion of the air might present as much to them that lived with Ogyges, as Galilæus hath seen through his instrument, I cannot tell; sure I am, that the discovery of a truth formerly unknown, doth rather convince man of ignorance, than nature of error. One thing herein is worthy to be noted, that this great but particular flood of Ogyges was (as appeareth by this of St. Augustine) accompanied with such unusual (and therefore the more dreadful, though natural) signs testifying the concurrence of causes with effects in that inundation; whereas the flood of Noah, which was general, and altogether miraculous, may seem to have had no other token, or foreshewing, than the long preaching of Noah himself, which was not regarded; for they were eating and drinking, when the flood came suddenly, and took them all away.

[FROM *History of the World*]

III. An Inquiry into the Nature of Man

John Florio

MONTAIGNE ON REPENTANCE

OTHERS fashion man; I repeat him, and represent a particular one, but ill made, and when, were I to form a new, he should be far other than he is; but he is now made. And though the lines of my picture change and vary, yet lose they not themselves. The world runs all on wheels. All things therein move without intermission; yea, the earth, the rocks of Caucasus, and the Pyramids of Egypt, both with the public and their own motion. *Constancy itself is nothing but a languishing and wavering dance.* I cannot settle my object; it goeth so unquietly and staggering, with a natural drunkenness. I take it in this plight, as it is at the instant I amuse myself about it. I describe not the essence, but the passage; not a passage from age to age—or as the people reckon—from seven years to seven; but from day to day, from minute to minute. My history must be fitted to the present. I may soon change, not only fortune, but intention. It is a counter-rule of divers and variable accidents, and irresolute imaginations, and sometimes con-

151

trary: whether it be that myself am other, or that I apprehend subjects by other circumstances and considerations. Howsoever, I may perhaps gainsay myself, but truth (as Demades said) I never gainsay: Were my mind settled, I would not essay, but resolve myself. It is still an apprentice and a probationer. I propose a mean life, and without luster: 'Tis all one. *They* fasten all moral Philosophy as well to a popular and private life, as to one of richer stuff. *Every man beareth the whole stamp of human condition,* [they say]: authors communicate themselves unto the world by some special and strange mark; I the first, by my general disposition; as *Michael de Montaigne;* not as a Grammarian, or a Poet, or a Lawyer.

If the world complain, I speak too much of myself, I complain, it thinks no more of itself. But is it reason, that being so private in use, I should pretend to make myself public in knowledge? Or is it reason, I should produce into the world, where fashion and art have such sway and command, the raw and simple effects of nature; and of a nature as yet exceeding weak? To write books without learning, is it not to make a wall without stone or such like thing? Conceits of music are directed by art; mine by hap. Yet have I this according to learning, that never man handled subject, he understood or knew, better than I do this I have undertaken; being therein the cunningest man alive.

Secondly, that never man waded further into his matter, nor more distinctly sifted the parts and dependencies of it, nor arrived more exactly and fully to the end he proposed unto himself. To finish the same, I have need of naught but faithfulness: which is therein as sincere and pure as may be found. I speak truth, not my belly-full, but as much as I dare: and I dare the more, the more I grow into years: for it seemeth, custom alloweth old age more liberty to babble, and indiscretion to talk of itself. It cannot herein be, as in trades: where the Craftsman and his work do often differ. Being a man of so sound and honest conversation, writ he so foolishly? Are such learned writings come from a man of so weak a conversation? who hath but an ordinary conceit, and writeth excellently, one may say his capacity is borrowed, not of himself. A skillful man is not skillful in all things: but a sufficient man, is sufficient everywhere, even unto ignorance.

Here my book and myself march together, and keep one pace. Elsewhere one may commend or condemn the work, without the workman; here not: who toucheth one toucheth the other. He who shall judge of it without knowing him, shall wrong himself more than me; he that knows it, hath wholly satisfied me. Happy beyond my merit, if I get this only portion of public approbation, as I may cause men of understanding to think, I had been able to make use and benefit of learning, had I been endowed with any: and deserved better help of memory. Excuse we here what I often say, that I seldom repent myself, and that my conscience is contented with itself; not of an Angel's or a horse's conscience, but as of a man's conscience. Adding ever this clause, not of ceremony, but of true and essential submission: that *I speak inquiring and doubting, merely and simply referring myself, from resolution, unto common and lawful opinions.* I teach not; I report. No vice is absolutely vice, which offendeth not, and a sound judgment accuseth not. For, the deformity and incommodity thereof is so palpable, as peradventure they have reason, who say, it is chiefly produced by sottishness and brought forth by ignorance; so hard is it, to imagine one should know it without hating it. *Malice sucks up the greatest part of her own venom, and therewith poisoneth herself. Vice, leaveth, as an ulcer in the flesh, a repentance in the soul, which still scratcheth and bloodieth itself.* For reason effaceth other griefs and sorrows, but engendereth those of repentance: the more irksome, because inward: As the cold and heat of agues is more offensive than that which comes outward.

I account vices (but each according to their measure) not only those which reason disallows, and nature condemns, but such as man's opinion hath forged as false and erroneous, if laws and customs authorize the same. In like manner there is no goodness but gladdeth an honest disposition. There is truly I wot not what kind of congratulation, of well doing, which rejoiceth in ourselves, and a generous jollity, that accompanieth a good conscience. A mind courageously vicious, may happily furnish itself with security, but she cannot be fraught, with this self-delight and satisfaction. It is no small pleasure, for one to feel himself preserved from the contagion of an age, so infected as ours, and to say to himself; could a man enter and see even into my soul, yet should he not find me guilty, either of the affliction or ruin of anybody, nor culpable of envy or revenge, nor of public offense against the laws, nor tainted with innovation, trouble or sedition; nor spotted with falsifying of my word: and although the liberty of times allowed and taught it every man, yet could I never be induced to touch the goods or dive into the purse of any French man, and have always lived upon mine own, as well in time of war, as peace: nor did I ever make use of any poor man's labor, without reward.

These testimonies of an unspotted conscience are very pleasing, which natural joy is a great benefit unto us: and the only payment never faileth us. To ground the recompense of virtuous actions upon the approbation of others, is to undertake a most uncertain or troubled foundation, namely in an age so corrupt and times so ignorant, as this is: the vulgar people's good opinion is injurious. Whom trust you in seeing what is commendable? God keep me from being an honest man, according to the description I daily see made of honour, each one by himself. *Quae fuerant vitia, mores sunt: What erst were vices are now grown fashions.*

Some of my friends, have sometimes attempted to school me roundly, and sift me plainly, either of their own motion, or invited by me, as to an office, which to a well-composed mind, both in profit and lovingness, exceedeth all the duties of sincere amity. Such have I ever entertained with open arms of courtesy, and kind acknowledgment. But now, to speak from my conscience, I often found so much false measure in their reproaches and praises, that I had not greatly erred if I had rather erred, than done well after their fashion. Such as we especially, who live a private life not exposed to any gaze but our own, ought in our hearts establish a touchstone, and there to touch our deeds and try our actions; and accordingly, now cherish and now chastise ourselves.

I have my own laws and tribunal, to judge of me, whither I address myself more than anywhere else. I restrain my actions according to other, but extend them according to myself. None but yourself knows rightly whether you be demiss and cruel, or loyal and devout. Others see you not, but guess you by uncertain conjectures. They see not so much your nature as your art. Adhere not then to their opinion, but hold unto your own. *Tuo tibi judicio est utendum. Virtutis et viciorum grave ipsius conscientiae pondus est: qua sublata jacent omnia. You must use your own judgment. The weight of the very conscience of vice and virtues is heavy: take that away, and all is down.*

But whereas it is said, that repentance nearly followeth sin, seemeth not to imply sin placed in his rich array, which lodgeth in us as in his proper mansion. One may disavow and disclaim vices, that surprise us, and whereto our passions transport us: but those, which by long habit are rooted in a strong, and anchored in a powerful will, are not subject to contradiction. *Repentance is but a denying of our will, and an opposition of our fantasies,* which diverts us here and there. It makes some disavow his former virtue and continence.

> *Quae mens est hodie, cur eadem non puero fuit,*
> *Vel cur his animis incolumes non redeunt genae?*

> Why was not in a youth same mind as now?
> Or why bears not this mind a youthful brow?

That is an exquisite life, which even in his own private keepeth itself in awe and order. Everyone may play the juggler, and represent an honest man upon the stage; but within, and in bosom, where all things are lawful, where all is concealed; to keep a due rule or formal decorum, that's the point. The next degree, is to be so in one's own home, and in his ordinary actions, whereof we are to give account to nobody: wherein is no study, nor art. And therefore Bias describing the perfect state of a family, whereof (saith he) the master, be such inwardly by himself, as he is outwardly, for fear of the laws, and respect of men's speeches. And it was a worthy saying of Julius Drusus, to those workmen, which for three thousand crowns, offered so to reform his house, that his neighbors should no more overlook into it: I will give you six thousand (said he) and contrive it so, that on all sides every man may look into it. The custom of Agesilaus is remembered with honour, who in his travail was wont to take up his lodging in churches, that the people, and Gods themselves might pry into his private actions. Some have been admirable to the world, in whom nor his wife, nor his servants ever noted anything remarkable. *Few men have been admired of their familiars. No man hath been a Prophet, not only in his house, but in his own country*, saith the experience of histories. Even so in things of naught. And in this base example, is the image of greatness discerned. In my climate of Gascony they deem it a jest to see me in print. The further the knowledge which is taken of me is from my home, of so much more worth am I. In Guienne I pay Printers; in other places they pay me. Upon this accident they ground, who living and present keep close-lurking, to purchase credit when they shall be dead and absent. I had rather have less. And I cast not myself into the world, but for the portion I draw from it. That done, I quit it.

The people attend on such a man with wonderment, from a public act, unto his own doors: together with his robes he leaves of his part; falling so much the lower, by how much higher he was mounted. View him within: there all is turbulent, disordered and vile. And were order and formality found in him, a lively, impartial, and well-sorted judgment is required, to perceive and fully to discern him in these base and private actions. Considering that order is but a dumpish and drowsy virtue: to gain a Battle, perform an Ambassage, and govern a people, are noble and worthy actions; to chide, laugh, sell, pay, love, hate, and mildly and justly to converse both with his own and with himself; not to relent, and not gainsay himself, are things more rare, more difficult and less remarkable.

Retired lives sustain that way, whatever some say, offices as much more crabbed, and extended, than other lives do. And private men (saith Aristotle) serve virtue more hardly, and more highly attend her, than those

which are magistrates or placed in authority. We prepare ourselves unto eminent occasions, more for glory
than for conscience. *The nearest way to come unto
glory, were to do that for conscience, which we do for
glory.* And me seemeth the virtue of Alexander representeth much less vigor in her large Theater, than that
of Socrates, in his base and obscure excercitation. I
easily conceive Socrates, in the room of Alexander; Alexander in that of Socrates I cannot. If any ask the one,
what he can do, he will answer, *"Conquer the world"*;
let the same question be demanded of the other, he will
say, *"Lead my life conformably to its natural condition"*; A science much more generous, more important,
and more lawful.

*The worth of the mind consisteth not in going high,
but in marching orderly.* Her greatness is not exercised
in greatness; in mediocrity it is. As those, which judge
and touch us inwardly, make no great account of the
brightness of our public actions: and see they are but
streaks and points of clear Water, surging from a bottom, otherwise slimy and full of mud: So those who
judge us by this gay outward appearance, conclude the
same of our inward constitution, and cannot couple
popular faculties as theirs are, unto these other faculties,
which amaze them so far from their level. So do we attribute savage shapes and ugly forms unto devils. As
who doth not ascribe high-raised eyebrows, open nostrils,
stern frightful visage, and a huge body unto Tamburlaine, as is the form or shape of the imagination we have
fore-conceived by the bruit of his name? Had any heretofore shewed me Erasmus, I could hardly have been induced to think, but whatsoever he had said to his boy or
hosts, had been Adages and Apothegms. We imagine
much more fitly an Artificer upon his closet stool or on
his wife, than a great judge, reverend for his carriage

and regardful for his sufficiency; we think, that from those high thrones they should not abase themselves so low, as to live. As vicious minds are often incited to do well by some strange impulsion, so are virtuous spirits moved to do ill. They must then be judged by their settled estate, when they are near themselves, and as we say, at home, if at any time they be so; or when they are nearest unto rest, and in their natural seat. *Natural inclinations are by institution helped and strengthened, but they neither change nor exceed.* A thousand natures in my time, have, athwart a contrary discipline, escaped toward virtue or toward vice.

> *Sic ubi desuetae silvis in carcere clausae,*
> *Mansuevere ferae, et vultus posuere minaces,*
> *Atque hominem didicere pati, si torrida parvus*
> *Venit in ora cruor, redeunt rabiesque furorque,*
> *Admonitaeque tument gustato sanguine fauces,*
> *Fervet, et a trepido vix abstinet irae magistro.*

> So when wild beasts, disused from the wood,
> Fierce looks laid-down, grow tame, closed in a cage
> Taught to bear man, if then a little blood
> Touch their hot lips, fury returns and rage;
> Their jaws by taste admonished swell with veins,
> Rage boils, and from faint keeper scarce abstains.

These original qualities are not grubbed out; they are but covered, and hidden. The Latin tongue is to me in a manner natural; I understand it better than French; but it is now forty years, I have not made use of it to speak, nor much to write: yet in some extreme emotions and sudden passions, wherein I have twice or thrice fallen, since my years of discretion; and namely once, when my Father, being in perfect health, fell all along upon me in a swoon, I have ever, even from my very heart, uttered my first words in Latin: Nature rushing and by force expressing itself, against so long a custom; the like example is alleged of divers others. *Those which in my time, have attempted to correct the fashions of the world by new opinions, reform the vices of appearance; those of essence they leave untouched if they increase them not.*

And their increase is much to be feared. We willingly protract all other well-doing upon these external reformations, of less cost, and of greater merit; whereby we satisfy good cheap, other natural, consubstantial, and intestine vices. Look a little into the course of our experience. There is no man (if he listen to himself) that doth not discover in himself a peculiar form of his, a swaying form, which wrestleth against the institution, and against the tempests of passions which are contrary unto him. As for me, I feel not myself much agitated by a shock; I commonly find myself in mine own place, as are sluggish and lumpish bodies. If I am not close and near unto myself, I am never far off: my debauches or excesses transport me not much. There is nothing extreme and strange, yet have I sound fits and vigorous lusts. The true condemnation, and which toucheth the common fashion of our men, is, that their very retreat is full of corruption and filth; the idea of their amendment blurred and deformed; their repentance crazed and faulty, very near as much as their sin. Some, either because they are so fast and naturally joined unto vice, or through long custom, have lost all sense of its ugliness. To others (of whose rank I am) vice is burdensome, but they counter-balance it with pleasure, or other occasions: and suffer it, and at a certain rate lend themselves unto it, though basely and viciously. Yet might happily so remote a disproportion of measure be imagined, where with justice, the pleasure might excuse the offence, as we say of profit. Not only being accidental, and out of sin, as in thefts, but even in the very exercise of it, as in the acquaintance or copulation

with women; where the provocation is so violent, and as
they say, sometimes unresistable.

In a town of a kinsman of mine, the other day, being
in Armignac, I saw a country man, commonly surnamed
the Thief: who himself reported his life to have been
thus. Being born a beggar, and perceiving, that to get
his bread by the sweat of his brow and labor of his
hands, would never sufficiently arm him against penury,
he resolved to become a Thief; and that trade had employed all his youth safely, by means of his bodily
strength: for he ever made up Harvest and Vintage in
other men's grounds; but so far off, and in so great
heaps, that it was beyond imagination, one man should
in one night carry away so much upon his shoulders: and
was so careful to equal the prey, and disperse the mischief he did, that the spoil was of less import to every
particular man.

He is now in old years indifferently rich; for a man
of his condition (Godamercy his trade), which he is not
ashamed to confess openly. And to reconcile himself
with God, he affirmeth, to be daily ready, with his
gettings, and other good turns, to satisfy the posterity of
those he hath heretofore wronged or robbed; which if
himself be not of ability to perform (for he cannot do all
at once) he will charge his heirs withal, according to the
knowledge he hath, of the wrongs by him done to every
man. By this description, be it true or false, he respect-
eth theft, as a dishonest and unlawful action, and hateth
the same: yet less than pinching want: He repents but
simply; for in regard it was so counterbalanced and recompensed, he repenteth not. That is not that habit
which incorporates us unto vice, and confirmeth our
understanding in it; nor is it that boisterous wind, which
by violent blasts dazzeleth and troubleth our minds, and
at that time confounds, and overwhelms both us, our

judgment, and all into the power of vice. What I do, is ordinarily full and complete, and I march (as we say) all in one pace: I have not many motions, that hie themselves and slink away from my reason, or which very near are not guided by the consent of all my parts, without division, or intestine sedition: my judgment hath the whole blame, or commendation; and the blame it hath once, it hath ever: for, almost from its birth, it hath been one of the same inclination, course and force. And in matters of general opinions, even from my infancy, I ranged myself to the point I was to hold. Some sins there are outrageous, violent and sudden; leave we them.

But those other sins, so often reassumed, determined and advised upon, whether they be of complexion, or of profession and calling, I cannot conceive how they should so long be settled in one same courage, unless the reason and conscience of the sinner were thereunto inwardly privy and constantly willing. And how to imagine or fashion the repentance thereof, which he vaunteth, doth sometimes visit him, seemeth somewhat hard unto me. I am not of Pythagoras' Sect, that men take a new soul, when to receive Oracles, they approach the images of Gods, unless he would say with all, that it must be a strange one, new, and lent him for the time: our own, giving so little sign of purification, and cleanness worthy of that office. They do altogether against the Stoical precepts, which appoint us to correct the imperfections and vices we find in ourselves, but withal forbid us to disturb the quiet of our mind. They make us believe, they feel great remorse, and are inwardly much displeased with sin; but of amendment, correction or intermission, they shew us none. *Surely there can be no perfect health, where the disease is not perfectly removed.* Were repentance put in the scale of the balance, it would weigh down sin. *I find no humour so easy to be counterfeited as Devotion:* If one conform not his life and conditions to it, her essence is abstruse and concealed, her appearance gentle and stately.

For my part, I may in general wish to be other than I am; I may condemn and dislike my universal form; I may beseech God to grant me an undefiled reformation, and excuse my natural weakness; but meseemeth I ought not to term this repentance no more than the displeasure of being neither Angel nor Cato. My actions are squared to what I am and to my condition. I cannot do better: and *repentance doth not properly concern what is not in our power; sorrow doth.* I may imagine infinite dispositions of a higher pitch, and better governed than mine, yet do I nothing better my faculties; no more than mine arm becommeth stronger, or my wit more excellent, by conceiving some others to be so. If to suppose and wish a more nobler working than ours, might produce the repentance of our own, we should then repent us of our most innocent actions: for so much as we judge that in a more excellent nature, they had been directed with greater perfection and dignity; and ourselves would do the like.

When I consult with my age of my youth's proceedings, I find that commonly (according to my opinion) I managed them in order. This is all my resistance is able to perform. I flatter not myself: in like circumstances, I should ever be the same. It is not a spot, but a whole dye that stains me. I acknowledge no repentance [that] is superficial, mean and ceremonious. It must touch me on all sides, before I can term it repentance. It must pinch my entrails, and afflict them as deeply and thoroughly, as God himself beholds me. When in negotiating, many good fortunes have slipped me for want of good discretion, yet did my projects make good choice, according to the occurrences presented unto them. Their manner is ever to take the easier and surer side. I find that in my former deliberations, I proceeded, after my rules, discreetly for the subject's state propounded to me; and in like occasions, would proceed alike a hundred years hence. I respect not what now it is, but what it was, when I consulted of it.

The consequence of all designs consists in the seasons; occasions pass, and matters change incessantly. I have in my time run into some gross, absurd, and important errors; not for want of good advice, but of good hap. There are secret and undivinable parts in the objects men do handle; especially in the nature of men and mute conditions, without shew, and sometimes unknown of the very possessors, produced and stirred up by sudden occasions. If my wit could neither find nor presage them, I am not offended with it; the function thereof is contained within its own limits. If the success [beat] me, and favour the side I refused; there is no remedy; I fall not out with myself: I accuse my fortune, not my endeavour: that's not called repentance. Phocion had given the Athenians some counsel, which was not followed: the matter, against his opinion, succeeding happily. "How now, Phocion," quoth one. "Art thou pleased the matter hath thrived so well?"

"Yea," said he, "and I am glad of it, yet repent not the advice I gave."

When any of my friends come to me for counsel, I bestow it frankly and clearly, not (as well-high all the world doth) wavering at the hazard of the matter, whereby the contrary of my meaning may happen: that so they may justly find fault with my advice: for which I care not greatly. For they shall do me wrong, and it became not me to refuse them that duty. I have nobody to blame for my faults or misfortunes, but myself. For in effect I seldom use the advice of others unless it be for compliment's sake, and where I have need of instruction or knowledge of the fact. Marry, in things wherein naught but judgment is to be employed; strange reasons may serve to sustain, but not to divert me. I lend a favourable and courteous ear unto them all. But (to my remembrance) I never believed any but mine own. With me they are but Flies and Moths, which distract my will. I little regard mine own opinions, other men's I esteem as little: Fortune pays me accordingly. If I take no counsel I give as little. I am not much sought after for it, and less credited when I give it: neither know I any enterprise, either private or public, that my advice hath directed and brought to conclusion. Even those whom fortune had someway tied thereunto, have more willingly admitted the direction of others' conceits, than mine. As one that am as jealous of the rights of my quiet, as of those of my authority; I would rather have it thus.

Where leaving me, they jump with my profession, which is, wholly to settle and contain me in myself. It is a pleasure unto me, to be disinterested of other men's affairs, and disengaged from their contentions. When suits or businesses be overpassed, howsoever it be, I grieve little at them. For, the imagination that they must necessarily happen so, puts me out of pain. Behold them in the course of the Universe, and enchained in Stoical causes. Your fantasy cannot by wish or imagination, remove one point of them, but the whole order of things must reverse both what is past, and what is to come. Moreover, I hate that accidental repentance which old age brings with it.

He that in ancient times said, he was beholden to years, because they had rid him of voluptuousness, was not of mine opinion. I shall never give impuissance thanks, for any good it can do me. *Nec tam aversa unquam videbitur ab opere suo providentia, ut debilitas inter optima inventa sit.* "Nor shall foresight ever be seen so averse from her own work, that weakness be found to be one of the best things." Our appetites are rare in old age: the blow overpassed, a deep satiety seizeth upon us: *Therein I see no conscience.* Fretting care and weakness, imprint in us an effeminate and drowzy virtue.

We must not suffer ourselves so fully to be carried into natural alterations, as to corrupt or adulterate our judgment by them. Youth and pleasure have not heretofore prevailed so much over me, but I could ever (even in the midst of sensualities) discern the ugly face of sin: nor can the distaste which years bring on me, at this instant, keep me from discerning that of voluptuousness in vice. Now I am no longer in it, I judge of it as if I were still there. I, who lively and attentively examine my reason, find it to be the same that possessed me in my most dissolute and licentious age; unless perhaps, they being enfeebled and impaired by years, do make some difference: And find, that what delight it refuseth to afford me in regard of my bodily health, it would no more deny me, than in times past, for the health of my soul. To see it out of combat, I hold it not the more courageous. My temptations are so mortified and crazed, as they are not worthy of its oppositions; holding but my hand before me, I becalm them. Should one present that former concupiscence unto it, I fear it would be of less power to sustain it than heretofore it hath been. I see in it, by itself, no increase of judgment, nor access of brightness, what it now judgeth, it did then. Wherefore if there be any amendment, 'tis but diseased. *Oh miserable kind of remedy, to be beholden unto sickness for our health.*

It is not for our mishap, but for the good success of our judgment to perform this office. Crosses and afflictions, make me do nothing but curse them. They are for people, that cannot be awaked but by the whip: the course of my reason is the nimbler in prosperity; it is much more distracted and busied in the digesting of mischiefs, than of delights. I see much clearer in fair weather. Health forewarneth me, as with more pleasure, so to better purpose than sickness. I approached the nearest I could unto amendment and regularity, when I should have enjoyed the same; I should be ashamed and vexed, that the misery and mishap of my old age could exceed the health, attention and vigor of my youth: and that I should be esteemed, not for what I have been, but for what I am left to be. The happy life (in my opinion) not (as said Antisthenes) the happy death, is it that makes man's happiness in this world.

I have not preposterously busied myself to tie the tail of a Philosopher, unto the head and body of a varlet: nor that this paltry end, should disavow and belie the fairest, soundest, and longest part of my life. I will present myself, and make a general muster of my whole, everywhere uniformly. Were I to live again, it should be as I have already lived. I neither deplore what is past, nor dread what is to come: and if I be not deceived, the inward parts have nearly resembled the outward. It is one of the chiefest points wherein I am beholden to fortune, that in the course of my body's estate, each thing hath been carried in season. I have seen the leaves, the blossoms, and the fruit; and now see the drooping and withering of it. Happily, because naturally. I bear my present miseries the more gently, because they are in season, and with greater favour make me remember the long happiness of my former life. In like manner, my discretion may well be of like proportion in the one and the other time: but sure it was of much more performance, and had a better grace, being fresh, jolly and full of spirit, than now that it is worn, decrepit and toilsome.

I therefore renounce these casual and dolorous reformations. *God must touch our hearts; our conscience must amend of itself,* and not by reinforcement of our reason, nor by the enfeebling of our appetites. Voluptuousness in itself is neither pale nor discoloured, to be discerned by bleary and troubled eyes. We should affect temperance and chastity for itself, and for God's cause, who hath ordained them unto us: that which Catarrhs bestow upon us, and which I am beholden to my colic [for, is] neither temperance nor chastity. A man cannot boast of condemning or combating sensuality, if he see her not, or know not her grace, her force and most attractive beauties. I know them both, and therefore may speak it.

But methinks our souls in age are subject unto more importunate diseases and imperfections, than they are in youth. I said so being young, when my beardless chin was upbraided me; and I say it again, now that my gray beard gives me authority. We entitle wisdom, the forwardness of our humours, and the distaste of present things; but in truth we abandon not vices, so much as we change them; and in my opinion for the worse. Besides a silly and ruinous pride, cumbersome tattle, wayward and unsociable humours, superstition and a ridiculous carking for wealth, when the use of it is well-nigh lost, I find the more envy, injustice and lewdness in it. It sets more wrinkles in our minds, than on our foreheads: nor are there any spirits, or very rare ones, which in growing old taste now sourly and mustily.

Man marcheth entirely towards his increase and decrease. View but the wisdom of Socrates, and divers circumstances of his condemnation, I daresay he something lent himself unto it by prevarication of purpose; being so near, and at the age of seventy, to endure the benumbing of his spirit's richest pace, and the dimming of his accustomed brightness. What Metamorphoses have I seen it daily make in divers of mine acquaintances? It is a powerful malady, which naturally and imperceptibly glideth unto us: There is required great provision of study, heed and precaution, to avoid the imperfections wherewith it chargeth us; or at least to weaken their further progress. I find that notwithstanding all my entrenchings, by little and little it getteth ground upon me: I hold out as long as I can, but know not whither at length it will bring me. Hap what hap will, I am pleased the world know from what height I tumbled.

[FROM *Of Repenting*]

Gabriel Harvey

NEW FASHIONS IN MORALS

SIR, YOUR new complaint of the new world is nigh as old as Adam and Eve, and full as stale as the stalest fashion that hath been in fashion since Noah's flood. You cry out of a false and treacherous world, and therein are passing eloquent and pathetical in a degree above the highest. Now I beseech you, Sir, did not Abel live in a false and treacherous world, that was so villainously and cruelly murdered of his own very brother? Nay, did not old Grandsire himself live in a false and treacherous world, that was so subtly and fraudulently put beside so incomparably rich and goodly possession as Paradise was?

The stories to this effect—Tower of Babel, Sodom— are notoriously known; there be infinite thousands of examples to prove that the first men in the world were as well our masters in villainy as either predecessors in time or fathers in consanguinity. Let us not be so injurious to remainder antiquity as to deprive the farthest off, of his due commendation, neither must we be so partially affectionate towards any as, against our own consciences, to conceal these notorious and infamous treacheries. Undoubtedly the very world itself millions of years before the Creation was predestinate to be a schoolhouse and shop of all villainies, and even then I suppose the ill-favored sprites and devils that now so trouble and infect the world were a-devising and premeditating those infinite several kinds and varieties of wickedness, that immediately after the Creation and ever since they have so basely blown abroad and so cunningly planted in every quarter and corner of the world. . . .

You suppose the first age was the Golden Age. It is nothing so. Bodin defendeth the Golden Age to flourish now, and our first grandfathers to have rubbed through in the Iron and Brazen Age at the beginning, when all things were rude and unperfect in comparison with the exquisite fineness and delicacy that we have grown to in these days.

You suppose it a foolish mad world, wherein all things are over-ruled by fancy. What greater error? All things else are but trouble of mind and vexation of spirit. Until a man's fancy be satisfied, he wanteth his most sovereign contentment, and cannot be at quiet in himself. You suppose most of these bodily and sensual pleasures are to be abandoned as unlawful, and the inward contemplative delights of the mind more zealously to be embraced as most commendable.

Good Lord, you a gentleman, a courtier, a youth, and go about to revive so old and stale a bookish opinion, dead and buried many hundred years before you or I

knew whether there were any world or no! You are sure
the sensible and tickling pleasures of the tasting, feeling,
smelling, seeing, and hearing are very recreative and
delectable indeed. Your other delights, proceeding of
some strange melancholy conceits and speculative imaginations discoursed at large in your fancy and brain,
are but imaginary and fantastical delights, and, but for
names' sake, might as well and more truly be called the
extremest labors and miserablest torments under the sun.

You suppose us students happy, and think the air
preferred that breatheth on these same great learned
philosophers and profound clerks. Would to God you
were one of these men but a seven-night. I doubt not
but you would swear ere Sunday next, that there were
not the like woeful and miserable creatures to be found
within the compass of the whole world again. None so
injurious to themselves, so tyrannous to their servants,
so niggardly to their kinsfolks, so rigorous to their acquaintance, so unprofitable to all, so untoward for the
commonwealth, and so unfit for the world, mere book-
worms and very idols, the most intolerable creatures to
come in any good sociable company that ever God created. Look them in the face: you will straightways affirm they are the driest, leanest, ill-favoredest, abjectest,
base-mindedest carrions and wretches that ever you set
your eye on.

To be short, and to cut off a number of such by-
supposes, your greatest and most erroneous suppose is
that Reason should be mistress and Appetite attend on
her ladyship's person as a poor servant and handmaiden
of hers. Now that had been a probable defense and
plausible speech a thousand years since. There is a variable course and revolution of all things. Summer getteth
the upper hand of winter, and winter again of summer.
Nature herself is changeable, and most of all delighted

with vanity; and art, after a sort her ape, conformeth herself to the like mutability. The moon waxeth and waneth; the sea ebbeth and floweth; and as flowers, so ceremonies, laws, fashions, customs, trades of living, sciences, devices, and all things else in a manner flourish their time and then fade to nothing. . . .

So it standeth with men's opinions and judgments in matters of doctrine and religion. On forty years the knowledge in the tongues and eloquence carrieth the credit and flaunteth it out in her satin doublet and velvet hose. Then expireth the date of her bravery, and every man having enough of her, philosophy and knowledge in divers natural moral matters, must give her the Camisade and bear the sway another while. Every man seeth what she can do. At last cometh bravery and jointeth them both.

[FROM *Letter Book: To Edmund Spenser*]

IV. The New Learning

Roger Ascham

THE SCHOOLMASTER

W HEN THE great Plague was at London, the Year
1563, the Queen's Majesty, Queen Elizabeth, lay
at her Castle of Windsor: Where, upon the tenth day of
December, it fortuned, that in Sir William Cecil's chamber, her Highness's principal Secretary, there dined together these Personages: Mr. Secretary himself; Sir
William Petre; Sir John Mason; Dr. Wotton; Sir Richard
Sackville, Treasurer of the Exchequer; Sir Walter Mildmay, Chancellor of the Exchequer; Mr. Haddon, Master
of Requests; Mr. John Astely, Master of the Jewel
House; Mr. Bernard Hampton; Mr. Nicasius; and I. Of
which number, the most part were of Her Majesty's
most honorable Privy Council, and the rest serving her
in very good place. I was glad then, and do rejoice yet
to remember, that my chance was so happy to be there
that day, in the Company of so many wise and good
Men together, as hardly then could have been picked
out again out of all England beside.

Mr. Secretary hath this accustomed manner: though
his head be never so full of most weighty Affairs of the

173

Realm, yet at dinner time he doth seem to lay them always aside; and findeth ever fit Occasion to talk pleasantly of other matters, but most gladly of some matter of Learning, wherein he will courteously hear the Mind of the meanest at his Table.

Not long after our sitting down, "I have strange News brought me," saith Mr. Secretary, "this morning, that divers Scholars of Eton be run away from the School for fear of beating." Whereupon Mr. Secretary took Occasion to wish, that some more Discretion were in many Schoolmasters, in using Correction, than commonly there is; who many times punish rather the weakness of Nature, than the Fault of the Scholar; whereby many Scholars, that might else prove well, be driven to hate Learning before they know what Learning meaneth; and so are made willing to forsake their Book, and be glad to be put to any other kind of Living.

Mr. Petre, as one somewhat severe of Nature, said plainly that the Rod only was the Sword, that must keep the School in Obedience, and the Scholar in good Order. Mr. Wotton, a Man mild of nature, with soft voice and few words, inclined to Mr. Secretary's Judgement, and said, "In mine Opinion the Schoolhouse should be in deed, as it is called by name, the House of play and pleasure, and not of Fear and Bondage; and as I do remember, so saith Socrates in one place of Plato. And therefore if a Rod carry the fear of a Sword, it is no marvel, if those that be fearful of Nature, choose rather to forsake the Play, than to stand always within the fear of a Sword in a fond man's handling."

Mr. Mason, after his manner, was very merry with both parties, pleasantly playing both with the shrewd Touches of many curst Boys, and with the small Discretion of many lewd Schoolmasters. Mr. Haddon was fully of Mr. Petre's Opinion, and said that the best Schoolmaster of our time was the greatest Beater and named the Person.

"Though," quoth I, "it was his good Fortune, to send from his School unto the University one of the best Scholars indeed of all our time; yet wise Men do think, that that came so to pass, rather by the great Towardness of the Scholar, than by the great Beating of the Master: and whether this be true or no, you yourself are best witness." I said somewhat farther in the matter, how, and why, young Children were sooner allured by Love, than driven by Beating, to attain good Learning: wherein I was the bolder to say my mind, because Mr. Secretary courteously provoked me thereunto; or else in such a Company, and namely in his Presence, my wont is, to be more willing to use mine Ears, than to occupy my Tongue.

Sir Walter Mildmay, Mr. Astely, and the rest, said very little: only Sir Richard Sackville said nothing at all. After dinner, I went up to read with the Queen's Majesty. We read then together in the Greek tongue, as I well remember, that noble Oration of Demosthenes against Æschines, for his false dealing in his Embassage to King Philip of Macedon. Sir Richard Sackville came up soon after, and finding me in her Majesty's privy Chamber, he took me by the hand, and carrying me to a Window, said:

"Mr. Ascham, I would not for a good deal of Money have been this day absent from dinner. Where, though I said nothing, yet I gave as good Ear, and do consider as well the Talk that passed, as any one did there. Mr. Secretary said very wisely, and most truly, that many young Wits be driven to hate Learning, before they know what Learning is. I can be good witness to this myself; for a fond Schoolmaster, before I was fully fourteen years old, drave me so with fear of Beating from all Love of Learning, as now, when I know what difference it is, to have Learning, and to have little, or none at all, I feel it my greatest Grief, and find it my greatest Hurt, that ever came to me, that it was my so ill chance, to light upon so lewd a Schoolmaster.

"But seeing it is but vain to lament things past, and also Wisdom to look to things to come, surely, God willing, if God lend me Life, I will make this my mishap some Occasion of good hap to little Robert Sackville, my son's son. For whose bringing up, I would gladly, if it so please you, use specially your good Advice. I hear say you have a son much of his age; we will deal thus together: point you out a Schoolmaster, who by your Order shall teach my Son and yours, and for all the rest, I will provide, yea though they three do cost me a couple of hundred pounds by year; and beside, you shall find me as fast a Friend to you and yours, as perchance any you have." Which Promise the worthy Gentleman surely kept with me until his dying day.

We had then farther Talk together of bringing up of Children; of the Nature of quick and hard Wits; of the right choice of a good Wit; of Fear, and Love in teaching Children. We passed from Children and came to young Men, namely, Gentleman: We talked of their too much Liberty, to live as they lust; of their letting loose too soon overmuch Experience of ill, contrary to the good order of many good old Commonwealths of the Persians and Greeks; of Wit gathered, and good Fortune gotten by some, only by Experience without Learning. And, lastly, he required of me very earnestly to shew what I thought of the common going of Englishmen into Italy.

"But," saith he, "because this place, and this time will not suffer so long Talk, as these good matters require, therefore I pray you, at my Request, and at your Leisure, put in some Order of writing, the chief points of this our Talk, concerning the right Order of teaching, and Honesty of living, for the good bringing up of Children and young Men. And surely, beside contenting me, you shall both please and profit very many others."

I made some Excuse by lack of Ability, and weakness of Body.

"Well," saith he, "I am not now to learn what you can do: our dear Friend, good Mr. Goodricke, whose Judgement I could well believe, did once for all satisfy me fully therein. Again, I heard you say not long ago, that you may thank Sir John Cheke for all the Learning you have; and I know very well myself, that you did teach the Queen. And therefore, seeing God did so bless you, to make you the Scholar of the best Master, and also the Schoolmaster of the best Scholar, that ever were in our time; surely, you should please God, benefit your Country, and honest your own Name; if you would take the Pains to impart to others, what you learned of such a Master, and how you taught such a Scholar. And in uttering the Stuff ye received of the one, in declaring the Order ye took with the other, ye shall never lack Matter, nor Manner, what to write, nor how to write, in this kind of Argument."

I, beginning some farther Excuse, suddenly was called to come to the Queen. The night following, I slept little; my head was so full of this our former Talk, and I so mindful somewhat to satisfy the honest Request of so dear a Friend. I thought to prepare some little Treatise for a New Year's Gift that Christmas; but, as it chanceth to busy Builders, so, in building this my poor Schoolhouse (the rather because the Form of it is somewhat new, and differing from others), the Work rose daily higher and wider, than I thought it would at the Beginning.

And though it appear now, and be in very deed, but a small Cottage, poor for the Stuff, and rude for the Workmanship; yet in going forward I found the Site so good, as I was loath to give it over; but the Making so costly, outreaching my Ability, as many times I wished that some one of those three, my dear Friends, with full Purses, Sir Thomas Smith, Mr. Haddon, or Mr. Watson had had the doing of it. Yet, nevertheless I myself spending gladly that little, that I gat at home by good Sir John Cheke, and that that I borrowed abroad of my friend Sturmius, beside somewhat that was left me in Reversion by my old Masters, Plato, Aristotle, and Cicero; I have at last patched it up, as I could, and as you see. If the Matter be mean, and meanly handled, I pray you bear both with me, and it; for never Work went up in worse Weather, with more Lets, and Stops, than this poor Schoolhouse of mine. Westminster Hall can bear some witness, beside much weakness of body, but more trouble of mind, by some such sores, as grieve me to touch them myself; and therefore I purpose not to open them to others.

And in the midst of outward Injuries, and inward Cares, to increase them withal, good Sir Richard Sackville dieth, that worthy Gentleman, "that earnest Favorer and furtherer of God's true Religion; that faithful Servitor to his Prince and Country; a Lover of Learning, and all learned Men; wise in all doings; courteous to all persons, shewing Spite to none, doing Good to many; and as I well found, to me so fast a Friend, as I never lost the like before." When he was gone, my heart was dead; there was not one, that wore a black Gown for him, who carried a heavier Heart for him, than I. When he was gone, I cast this Book away; I could not look upon it, but with weeping eyes, in remembering him, who was the only setter on, to do it; and would have been not only a glad Commender of it, but also a sure and certain Comfort to me, and mine for it.

Almost two years together, this Book lay scattered and neglected, and had been quite given over of me, if the Goodness of one had not given me some Life and Spirit again. God the mover of goodness, prosper always him and his, as he hath many times comforted me and mine; and, I trust to God, shall comfort more and more. Of whom most justly I may say, and very oft, and always gladly I am wont to say, that sweet verse of Sophocles, spoken by Œdipus to worthy Theseus:

Ἔχω γὰρ ἃ ἔχω διὰ σὲ, κ'οὐκ ἄλλον βροτῶν.

This Hope hath helped me to end this Book; which if he allow, I shall think my Labors well employed, and shall not much esteem the misliking of any others. And I trust he shall think the better of it, because he shall find the best part thereof to come out of his School, whom he of all Men loved and liked best.

Yet some Men, friendly enough of Nature, but of small Judgement in Learning, do think I take too much pains, and spend too much time, in setting forth these children's Affairs. But those good Men were never brought up in Socrates's School, who saith plainly, "No man goeth about a more godly Purpose, than he that is mindful of the good bringing up both of his own and other men's Children."

Therefore, I trust, good and wise men will think well of this my doing. And of other, that think otherwise, I will think myself, they are but men, to be pardoned for their Folly, and pitied for their Ignorance.

In writing this Book, I have had earnest Respect to three special points, truth of Religion, Honesty in living, right Order in Learning. In which three ways, I pray God, my poor Children may diligently walk: for whose sake, as Nature moved, and Reason required, and Necessity also somewhat compelled, I was the willinger to take these Pains.

For, seeing at my death I am not like to leave them any great Store of living, therefore in my life time, I thought good to bequeath unto them, in this little Book, as in my Will and Testament, the right way to good Learning: which if they follow, with the fear of God, they shall very well come to Sufficiency of living.

I wish also, with all my heart, that young Mr. Robert Sackville, may take that Fruit of this labor, that his worthy Grandfather purposed he should have done. And if any other do take either profit or pleasure hereby, they have cause to thank Mr. Robert Sackville, for whom specially this my *Schoolmaster* was provided.

And one thing I would have the Reader consider in reading this Book, that because no Schoolmaster hath charge of any Child, before he enter into his School; therefore I, leaving all former Care of their good bringing up to wise and good Parents, as a matter not belonging to the Schoolmaster, I do appoint this my *Schoolmaster* then and there to begin, where his Office and Charge beginneth. Which charge lasteth not long, but until the Scholar be made able to go to the University, to proceed in Logic, Rhetoric, and other kind of Learning.

Yet if my Schoolmaster, for love he beareth to his Scholar, shall teach him somewhat for his furtherance, and better Judgement in learning, that may serve him seven years after in the University, he doth his Scholar no more wrong, nor deserveth no worse name thereby, than he doth in London—who, selling Silk or Cloth unto his Friend, doth give him better Measure then either his promise or bargain was.

[FROM The preface to *The Schoolmaster*, Farewell in Christ]

Gabriel Harvey

REVOLUTION AT CAMBRIDGE

B UT I beseech you, what News all this while at Cambridge? That was wont to be ever one great Question. What? *Det mihi Mater ipsa bonam veniam, eius
ut aliqua mihi liceat Secreta, uni cuidam de eodem
gremio obsequentissimo filio, revelare: et sic paucis
habeto. Nam alias fortasse pluribus: nunc non placet,
non vacat, molestum esset.* Tully and Demosthenes
nothing so much studied, as they were wont: Livy, and
Salust possibly rather more, than less: Lucian never so
much: Aristotle much named, but little read: Xenophon
and Plato, reckoned amongst Discoursers, and conceited
Superficial fellows: much verbal and sophistical jan-
gling: little subtle and effectual disputing; noble and
royal Eloquence, the best and persuasiblest Eloquence:
no such Orators again, as red-headed Angels: an exceeding great difference between the countenances, and
ports of those, that are brave and gallant, and of those,
that are basely, or meanly apparelled: between the
learned and unlearned, Tully, and Tom Tooly, in effect
none at all.

Machiavelli a great man: Castiglione of no small reputation: Petrarch, and Boccaccio in every man's mouth:
Galateo and Guazzo never so happy: over many acquainted with Unico Aretino: the French and Italian
when so highly regarded of Scholars? the Latin and
Greek, when so lightly? the Queen Mother at the beginning, or end of every conference: many bargains of

Monsieur: Shymeirs a noble gallant fellow: all inquisitive after News, new Books, new Fashions, new Laws, new Officers, and some after new Elements, and some after new Heavens and Hells too. Turkish affairs familiarly known: castles buried in the Air: much ado, and little help: Jack would fain be a Gentleman: in no age so little so much made of, everyone highly in his own favor, thinking no man's penny, so good silver as his own: Something made of Nothing, in spite of Nature: Numbers made of Ciphers, in spite of Art: Geometrical Proportion seldom, or never used, Arithmetical over much abused: Oxen and Asses (notwithstanding the absurdity it seemed to Plautus) draw both together in one and the same Yoke: *conclusio fere sequitur deteriorem partem.*

The Gospel taught, not learned: Charity key cold: nothing good, but by Imputation: the Ceremonial Law, in word abrogated: the Judicial in effect disannulled: the Moral indeed abandoned: the Light, the Light in every man's Lips, but mark me their eyes, and tell me, if they look not liker Owlets, or Bats, than Eagles: as of old Books, so of ancient Virtue, Honesty, Fidelity, Equity, new Abridgements: every day fresh span new Opinions: Heresy in Divinity, in Philosophy, in Humanity, in Manners, grounded much upon hearsay: Doctors contemned: the Text known of most, understood of few: magnified of all, practiced of none: the Devil not so hated, as the Pope: many Invectives, small amendment: Skill they say controlled of Will: and Goodness mastered of Goods: but Agent, and Patient much alike, neither Barrel greatly better Herring.

No more ado about Caps and Surplices: Master Cartwright nigh forgotten: the man you wot of, conformable, with his square Cap on his round head: and Non-resident at pleasure: and yet Non-residents never better baited, but not one the fewer, either I believe in Act, or

I believe in Purpose. A number of our preachers fib to French Soldiers, at the first, more than Men, in the end less than Women. Some of our pregnantest and soonest ripe Wits, of Hermogenes' metal for all the world: Old men and Counsellors amongst Children: Children amongst Counsellors, and old men: Not a few double sacred Tani, and Changeable chameleons: over many Claw-backs and Pick-thanks: Reeds shaken of every Wind: Jacks of both sides: Aspen leaves: painted Sheaths, and Sepulchres: Asses in Lions' skins. . . .

Concerning the chiefest general point of your Mastership's letter, yourself are not ignorant that scholars in our age are rather now Aristippi than Diogenes: and rather active than contemplative philosophers: coveting above all things under heaven to appear somewhat more than scholars if themselves wist how; and of all things in the world most detesting that spiteful malicious proverb, of greatest Clerks, and not wisest men. The date whereof they defend was expired when Duns Scotus and Thomas Aquinas with the whole rabblement of Schoolmen were abandoned our schools and expelled the University.

And now of late forsooth to help countenance out the matter they have gotten Philbertes Philosopher of the Court, the Italian Archbishop's brave Galatro, Castiglione's fine *Cortegiano*, Bengalasso's Civil Instructions to his Nephew Seignor Princisca Ganzar: Guazzo's new Discourses of courteous behavior, Jovio's and Rasseli's *Emblems* in Italian, Paradine's in French, Plutarch in French, Frontine's *Stratagems*, Polyene's *Stratagems*, Polonica, Apodemica, Guigiandine, Philip de Comines, and I know not how many outlandish braveries besides of the same stamp.

Shall I hazard a little farther: and make you privy to all our privities indeed. Thou knowest *non omnibus dor-*

mio et tibi habeo non huic. Aristotle's *Organon* is nigh-hand as little read as Duns's *Quodlibet.* His economics and politics everyone oweth by rote. You can not step into a scholar's study but (ten to one) you shall lightly find open either Bodin's *De Republica* or LeRoy's *Exposition* upon Aristotle's *Politics* or some other like French or Italian Politic Discourses.

And I warrant you some good fellows amongst us begin now to be prettily well acquainted with a certain parlous book called, as I remember me, *Il Principe* di Niccolo Machiavelli, and I can peradventure name you an odd crew or two that are as cunning in his *Discorsi sopra la prima Deca di Livio,* in his *Historia Fiorentina,* and in his Dialogues *della Arte della Guerra* too, and in certain gallant Turkish Discourses too, as University men were wont to be in their *parva Logicalia* and *Magna Moralia* and *Physicalia* of both sorts; *verbum intelligenti sat;* you may easily conjecture the rest yourself; especially being one that can as soon as another spy light at a little hole.

But, howsoever, most of us have expired the setting down, or rather setting up of this conclusion touching the expiring of the foresaid date as a most necessary University principle and main foundation of all our credit abroad; methinks still for some special commonwealth affairs and many particular matters of counsel and policy, besides daily fresh news and a thousand both ordinary and extraordinary occurrences and accidents in the world, we are yet (notwithstanding all and singular the premises) to take instructions and advertisements at your lawyers' and courtiers' hands, that are continually better trained and more lively experienced therein, than we University men are or possibly can be, or else peradventure when we shall stand most in our own conceits we may haply deceive and disgrace ourselves most, and in some by-matters when we least think of it, commit greater errors, and more foully overshoot ourselves than we be yet aware of or can conjecturally imagine.

[FROM *Letter Book: To Edmund Spenser*]

Francis Bacon

THE DISEASES AND HUMOURS OF LEARNING

Now I proceed to those errors and vanities which have intervened amongst the studies themselves of the learned, which is that which is principal and proper to the present argument; wherein my purpose is not to make a justification of the errors, but by a censure and separation of the errors to make a justification of that which is good and sound, and to deliver that from the aspersion of the other. For we see that it is the manner of men to scandalize and deprave that which retaineth the state and virtue, by taking advantage upon that which is corrupt and degenerate: as the heathens in the primitive church used to blemish and taint the Christians with the faults and corruptions of heretics. But nevertheless I have no meaning at this time to make any exact animadversion of the errors and impediments in matters of learning, which are more secret and remote from vulgar opinion, but only to speak unto such as do fall under or near unto a popular observation.

There be therefore chiefly three vanities in studies, whereby learning hath been most traduced. For those things we do esteem vain, which are either false or frivolous, those which either have no truth or no use: and those persons we esteem vain, which are either credulous or curious; and curiosity is either in matter or words: so that in reason as well as in experience there fall out to be these three distempers (as I may term them) of learning: the first, fantastical learning; the second, contentious learning; and the last, delicate learning; vain imaginations, vain altercations, and vain affectations; and with the last I will begin. Martin Luther, conducted (no doubt) by an higher Providence, but in discourse of reason, finding what a province he had undertaken against the bishop of Rome and the degenerate traditions of the church, and finding his own solitude, being no ways aided by the opinions of his own time, was enforced to awake all antiquity, and to call former times to his succours to make a party against the present time: so that the ancient authors, both in divinity and in humanity, which had long time slept in libraries, began generally to be read and revolved. This by consequence did draw on a necessity of a more exquisite travail in the languages original, wherein those authors did write, for the better understanding of those authors, and the better advantage of pressing and applying their words. And thereof grew again a delight in their manner of style and phrase, and an admiration of that kind of writing; which was much furthered and precipitated by the enmity and opposition that the propounders of those primitive but seeming new opinions had against the Schoolmen; who were generally of the contrary part, and whose writings were altogether in a different style and form; taking liberty to coin and frame new terms of art to express their own sense, and to avoid circuit of speech, without regard to the pureness, pleasantness, and (as I may call it) lawfulness of the phrase or word. And again, because the great labour then was with the people (of whom the Pharisees were wont to say, "*Ex-ecrabilis ista turba, quae non novit legem*"), for the winning and persuading of them, there grew of necessity in chief price and request eloquence and variety of discourse, as the fittest and forciblest access into the capacity of the vulgar sort: so that these four causes concurring, the admiration of ancient authors, the hate of the Schoolmen, the exact study of languages, and the efficacy of preaching, did bring in an affectionate study of eloquence and copie of speech, which then began to flourish.

This grew speedily to an excess; for men began to hunt more after words than matter; more after the choiceness of the phrase, and the round and clean composition of the sentence, and the sweet falling of the clauses, and the varying and illustration of their works with tropes and figures, than after the weight of matter, worth of subject, soundness of argument, life of invention, or depth of judgement. Then grew the flowing and watery vein of Osorius, the Portugal bishop, to be in price. Then did Sturmius spend such infinite and curious pains upon Cicero the Orator, and Hermogenes the Rhetorician, besides his own books of Periods and Imitation, and the like. Then did Car of Cambridge and Ascham with their lectures and writings almost deify Cicero and Demosthenes, and allure all young men that were studious unto that delicate and polished kind of learning. Then did Erasmus take occasion to make the scoffing echo, "*Decem annos consumpsi in legendo Cicerone*"; and the echo answered in Greek *One, Asine.* Then grew the learning of the Schoolmen to be utterly despised as barbarous. In sum, the whole inclination and bent of those times was rather towards copie than weight.

Here therefore is the first distemper of learning, when

men study words and not matter; whereof, though I have represented an example of late times, yet it hath been and will be *secundum majus et minus* in all time. And how is it possible but this should have an operation to discredit learning, even with vulgar capacities, when they see learned men's works like the first letter of a patent, or limned book; which though it hath large flourishes, yet it is but a letter? It seems to me that Pygmalion's frenzy is a good emblem or portraiture of this vanity: for words are but the images of matter; and except they have life of reason and invention, to fall in love with them is all one as to fall in love with a picture.

But yet notwithstanding it is a thing not hastily to be condemned, to clothe and adorn the obscurity even of philosophy itself with sensible and plausible elocution. For hereof we have great examples in Xenophon, Cicero, Seneca, Plutarch, and of Plato also in some degree; and hereof likewise there is great use: for surely, to the severe inquisition of truth and the deep progress into philosophy, it is some hindrance; because it is too early satisfactory to the mind of man, and quencheth the desire of further search, before we come to a just period. But then if a man be to have any use of such knowledge in civil occasions, of conference, counsel, persuasion, discourse, or the like, then shall he find it prepared to his hands in those authors which write in that manner. But the excess of this is so justly contemptible, that as Hercules, when he saw the image of Adonis, Venus' minion, in a temple, said in disdain, *"Nil sacri es"*; so there is none of Hercules' followers in learning, that is, the more severe and laborious sort of inquirers into truth, but will despise those delicacies and affectations, as indeed capable of no divineness. And thus much of the first disease or distemper of learning.

The second which followeth is in nature worse than

the former: for as substance of matter is better than beauty of words, so contrariwise vain matter is worse than vain words: wherein it seemeth the reprehension of St. Paul was not only proper for those times, but prophetical for the times following; and not only respective to divinity, but extensive to all knowledge: *"Devita profanas vocum novitates, et oppositiones falsi nominis scientiae."* For he assigneth two marks and badges of suspected and falsified science: the one, the novelty and strangeness of terms; the other, the strictness of positions, which of necessity doth induce oppositions, and so questions and altercations. Surely, like as many substances in nature which are solid do putrify and corrupt into worms; so it is the property of good and sound knowledge to putrify and dissolve into a number of subtle, idle, unwholesome, and (as I may term them) vermiculate questions, which have indeed a kind of quickness and life of spirit, but no soundness of matter or goodness of quality. This kind of degenerate learning did chiefly reign amongst the Schoolmen: who having sharp and strong wits, and abundance of leisure, and small variety of reading, but their wits being shut up in the cells of a few authors (chiefly Aristotle their dictator) as their persons were shut up in the cells of monasteries and colleges, and knowing little history, either of nature or time, did out of no great quantity of matter and infinite agitation of wit spin out unto us those laborious webs of learning which are extant in their books. For the wit and mind of man, if it work upon matter, which is the contemplation of the creatures of God, worketh according to the stuff and is limited thereby; but if it work upon itself, as the spider worketh his web, then it is endless, and brings forth indeed cobwebs of learning, admirable for the fineness of thread and work, but of no substance or profit.

This same unprofitable subtility or curiosity is of two sorts; either in the subject itself that they handle, when it is a fruitless speculation or controversy (whereof there are no small number both in divinity and philosophy), or in the manner or method of handling of a knowledge, which amongst them was this: upon every particular position or assertion to frame objections, and to those objections, solutions; which solutions were for the most part not confutations, but distinctions: whereas indeed the strength of all sciences, is as the strength of the old man's faggot, in the bond. For the harmony of a science, supporting each part the other, is and ought to be the true and brief confutation and suppression of all the smaller sort of objections. But, on the other side, if you take out every axiom, as the sticks of the faggot, one by one, you may quarrel with them and bend them and break them at your pleasure: so that as was said of Seneca, *"Verborum minutiis rerum frangit pondera,"* so a man may truly say of the Schoolmen, *"Quaestionum minutiis scientiarum frangunt soliditatem."* For were it not better for a man in a fair room to set up one great light, or branching candlestick of lights, than to go about with a small watch candle into every corner? And such is their method, that rests not so much upon evidence of truth proved by arguments, authorities, similitudes, examples, as upon particular confutations and solutions of every scruple, cavillation, and objection; breeding for the most part one question as fast as it solveth another; even as in the former resemblance, when you carry the light into one corner, you darken the rest; so that the fable and fiction of Scylla seemeth to be a lively image of this kind of philosophy or knowledge; which was transformed into a comely virgin for the upper parts; but then *"Candida succinctam latrantibus inquina monstris":* so the generalities of the Schoolmen are for a while

good and proportionable; but then when you descend
into their distinctions and decisions, instead of a fruitful
womb for the use and benefit of man's life, they end in
monstrous altercations and barking questions. So as it is
not possible but this quality of knowledge must fall under popular contempt, the people being apt to contemn
truth upon occasion of controversies and altercations,
and to think they are all out of their way which never
meet. And when they see such digladiation about sub-
tilties, and matter of no use or moment, they easily fall
upon that judgement of Dionysius of Syracusa, "*Verba
ista sunt senum otiosorum.*"

Notwithstanding, certain it is that if those Schoolmen
to their great thirst of truth and unwearied travail of wit
had joined variety and universality of reading and contemplation, they had proved excellent lights, to the great
advancement of all learning and knowledge; but as they
are, they are great undertakers indeed, and fierce with
dark keeping. But as in the inquiry of the divine truth,
their pride inclined to leave the oracle of God's word,
and to vanish in the mixture of their own inventions; so
in the inquisition of nature, they ever left the oracle of
God's works, and adored the deceiving and deformed
images which the unequal mirror of their own minds, or
a few received authors or principles, did represent unto
them. And thus much for the second disease of learning.

For the third vice or disease of learning, which concerneth deceit or untruth, it is of all the rest the foulest;
as that which doth destroy the essential form of knowledge, which is nothing but a representation of truth:
for the truth of being and the truth of knowing are one,
differing no more than the direct beam and the beam
reflected. This vice therefore brancheth itself into two
sorts: delight in deceiving and aptness to be deceived,
imposture and credulity; which, although they appea

to be of a diverse nature, the one seeming to proceed of cunning and the other of simplicity, yet certainly they do for the most part concur: for, as the verse noteth,

Percontatorem fugito, nam garrulus idem est,

an inquisitive man is a prattler; so upon the like reason a credulous man is a deceiver: as we see it in fame, that he that will easily believe rumours, will as easily augment rumours and add somewhat to them of his own; which Tacitus wisely noteth, when he saith, *"Fingunt simul creduntque"*: so great an affinity hath fiction and belief.

This facility of credit and accepting or admitting things weakly authorized or warranted, is of two kinds according to the subject: for it is either a belief of history, or, as the lawyers speak, matter of fact; or else of matter of art and opinion. As to the former, we see the experience and inconvenience of this error in ecclesiastical history; which hath too easily received and registered reports and narrations of miracles wrought by martyrs, hermits, or monks of the desert, and other holy men, and their relics, shrines, chapels, and images: which though they had a passage for a time by the ignorance of the people, the superstitious simplicity of some, and the politic toleration of others, holding them but as divine poesies; yet after a period of time, when the mist began to clear up, they grew to be esteemed but as old wives' fables, impostures of the clergy, illusions of spirits, and badges of Antichrist, to the great scandal and detriment of religion.

So in natural history, we see there hath not been that choice and judgement used as ought to have been; as may appear in the writings of Plinius, Cardanus, Albertus, and divers of the Arabians, being fraught with much fabulous matter, a great part not only untried, but

notoriously untrue, to the great derogation of the credit
of natural philosophy with the grave and sober kind of
wits: wherein the wisdom and integrity of Aristotle is
worthy to be observed; that, having made so diligent
and exquisite a history of living creatures, hath mingled
it sparingly with any vain or feigned matter: and yet on
the other side hath cast all prodigious narrations, which
he thought worthy the recording, into one book: excellently discerning that matter of manifest truth, such
whereupon observation and rule was to be built, was not
to be mingled or weakened with matter of doubtful
credit; and yet again, that rarities and reports that seem
uncredible are not to be suppressed or denied to the
memory of men.

And as for the facility of credit which is yielded to
arts and opinions, it is likewise of two kinds; either when
too much belief is attributed to the arts themselves, or
to certain authors in any art. The sciences themselves,
which have had better intelligence and confederacy with
the imagination of man than with his reason, are three
in number; astrology, natural magic, and alchemy: of
which sciences, nevertheless, the ends or pretences are
noble. For astrology pretendeth to discover that correspondence or concatenation which is between the superior globe and the inferior: natural magic pretendeth
to call and reduce natural philosophy from variety of
speculations to the magnitude of works: and alchemy
pretendeth to make separation of all the unlike parts of
bodies which in mixtures of nature are incorporate. But
the derivations and prosecutions to these ends, both in
the theories and in the practices, are full of error and
vanity; which the great professors themselves have
sought to veil over and conceal by enigmatical writings,
and referring themselves to auricular traditions and such
other devices, to save the credit of impostures. And yet

surely to alchemy this right is due, that it may be compared to the husbandman whereof Aesop makes the fable; that, when he died, told his sons that he had left unto them gold buried underground in his vineyard; and they digged over all the ground, and gold they found none; but by reason of their stirring and digging the mould about the roots of their vines, they had a great vintage the year following: so assuredly the search and stir to make gold hath brought to light a great number of good and fruitful inventions and experiments, as well for the disclosing of nature as for the use of man's life.

And as for the overmuch credit that hath been given unto authors in sciences, in making them dictators, that their words should stand, and not consuls to give advice; the damage is infinite that sciences have received thereby, as the principal cause that hath kept them low at a stay without growth or advancement. For hence it hath comen, that in arts mechanical the first deviser comes shortest, and time addeth and perfecteth; but in sciences the first author goeth furthest, and time leeseth and corrupteth. So we see, artillery, sailing, printing, and the like, were grossly managed at the first, and by time accommodated and refined: but contrariwise, the philosophies and sciences of Aristotle, Plato, Democritus, Hippocrates, Euclides, Archimedes, of most vigour at the first and by time degenerate and imbased; whereof the reason is no other, but that in the former many wits and industries have contributed in one; and in the latter many wits and industries have been spent about the wit of some one, whom many times they have rather depraved than illustrated. For as water will not ascend higher than the level of the first springhead from whence it descendeth, so knowledge derived from Aristotle, and exempted from liberty of examination, will not rise again higher than the knowledge of Aristotle. And therefore

although the position be good, *"Oportet discentem cre-
dere,"* yet it must be coupled with this, *"Oportet edoctum
judicare";* for disciples do owe unto masters only a temporary belief and a suspension of their own judgement
till they be fully instructed, and not an absolute resignation or perpetual captivity: and therefore, to conclude
this point, I will say no more, but so let great authors
have their due, as time, which is the author of authors,
be not deprived of his due, which is, further and further
to discover truth. Thus have I gone over these three
diseases of learning; besides the which there are some
other rather peccant humours than formed diseases,
which nevertheless are not so secret and intrinsic but
that they fall under a popular observation and traducement, and therefore are not to be passed over.

The first of these is the extreme affecting of two extremities: the one antiquity, the other novelty; wherein
it seemeth the children of time do take after the nature
and malice of the father. For as he devoureth his children, so one of them seeketh to devour and suppress the
other; while antiquity envieth there should be new additions, and novelty cannot be content to add but it must
deface: surely the advice of the prophet is the true direction in this matter, *"State super vias antiquas, et videte
quaenam sit via recta et bona et ambulate in ea."* Antiquity deserveth that reverence, that men should make
a stand thereupon and discover what is the best way;
but when the discovery is well taken, then to make progression. And to speak truly, *"Antiquitas saeculi juven-
tus mundi."* These times are the ancient times, when the
world is ancient, and not those which we account ancient *ordine retrogrado,* by a computation backward
from ourselves.

Another error induced by the former is a distrust that
anything should be now to be found out, which the

world should have missed and passed over so long time; as if the same objection were to be made to time, that Lucian maketh to Jupiter and other the heathen gods; of which he wondereth that they begot so many children in old time, and begot none in his time; and asketh whether they were become septuagenary, or whether the law *Papia*, made against old men's marriages, had restrained them. So it seemeth men doubt lest time is become past children and generation; wherein contrariwise we see commonly the levity and unconstancy of men's judgements, which till a matter be done, wonder that it can be done; and as soon as it is done, wonder again that it was no sooner done: as we see in the expedition of Alexander into Asia, which at first was prejudged as a vast and impossible enterprise; and yet afterwards it pleaseth Livy to make no more of it than this, *"Nil aliud quam bene ausus vana contemnere."* And the same happened to Columbus in the western navigation. But in intellectual matters it is much more common; as may be seen in most of the propositions of Euclid; which till they be demonstrate, they seem strange to our assent; but being demonstrate, our mind accepteth of them by a kind of relation (as the lawyers speak) as if we had known them before.

Another error, that hath also some affinity with the former, is a conceit that of former opinions or sects after variety and examination the best hath still prevailed and suppressed the rest; so as if a man should begin the labour of a new search, he were but like to light upon somewhat formerly rejected, and by rejection brought into oblivion: as if the multitude, or the wisest for the multitude's sake, were not ready to give passage rather to that which is popular and superficial, than to that which is substantial and profound; for the truth is, that time seemeth to be of the nature of a river or

stream, which carrieth down to us that which is light
and blown up, and sinketh and drowneth that which is
weighty and solid.

Another error, of a diverse nature from all the former,
is the over-early and peremptory reduction of knowledge into arts and methods; from which time commonly
sciences receive small or no augmentation. But as young
men, when they knit and shape perfectly, do seldom
grow to a further stature; so knowledge, while it is in
aphorisms and observations, it is in growth but when it
once is comprehended in exact methods, it may perchance be further polished and illustrate and accommodated for use and practice; but it increaseth no more
in bulk and substance.

Another error which doth succeed that which we last
mentioned, is, that after the distribution of particular
arts and sciences, men have abandoned universality, or
philosophia prima: which cannot but cease and stop all
progression. For no perfect discovery can be made upon
a flat or a level: neither is it possible to discover the
more remote and deeper parts of any science, if you
stand but upon the level of the same science, and ascend not to a higher science.

Another error hath proceeded from too great a reverence, and a kind of adoration of the mind and understanding of man; by means whereof, men have with-
drawn themselves too much from the contemplation of
nature, and the observations of experience, and have
tumbled up and down in their own reason and conceits.
Upon these intellectualists, which are notwithstanding
commonly taken for the most sublime and divine philosophers, Heraclitus gave a just censure, saying, "Men
sought truth in their own little worlds, and not in the
great and common world"; for they disdain to spell, and
so by degrees to read in the volume of God's works: and

contrariwise by continual meditation and agitation of wit do urge and as it were invocate their own spirits to divine and give oracles unto them, whereby they are deservedly deluded.

Another error that hath some connexion with this latter is, that men have used to infect their meditations, opinions, and doctrines, with some conceits which they have most admired, or some sciences which they have most applied; and given all things else a tincture according to them, utterly untrue and unproper. So hath Plato intermingled his philosophy with theology, and Aristotle with logic; and the second school of Plato, Proclus and the rest, with the mathematics. For these were the arts which had a kind of primogeniture with them severally. So have the alchemists made a philosophy out of a few experiments of the furnace; and Gilbertus our countryman hath made a philosophy out of the observations of a loadstone. So Cicero, when, reciting the several opinions of the nature of the soul, he found a musician that held the soul was but a harmony, saith pleasantly, "*Hic ab arte sua non recessit*," &c. But of these conceits Aristotle speaketh seriously and wisely when he saith, "*Qui respiciunt ad pauca de facili pronunciant.*"

Another error is an impatience of doubt, and haste to assertion without due and mature suspension of judgement. For the two ways of contemplation are not unlike the two ways of action commonly spoken of by the ancients: the one plain and smooth in the beginning, and in the end impassable; the other rough and troublesome in the entrance, but after a while fair and even: so it is in contemplation; if a man will begin with certainties, he shall end in doubts; but if he will be content to begin with doubts, he shall end in certainties.

Another error is in the manner of the tradition and delivery of knowledge, which is for the most part magis-

tral and peremptory, and not ingenuous and faithful;
in a sort as may be soonest believed, and not easiliest examined. It is true that in compendious treatises for practice that form is not to be disallowed: but in the true
handling of knowledge, men ought not to fall either on
the one side into the vein of Velleius the Epicurean, *"Nil
tam metuens, quam ne dubitare aliqua de re videretur"*;
nor on the other side into Socrates his ironical doubting
of all things; but to propound things sincerely with more
or less asseveration, as they stand in a man's own judgement proved more or less.

Other errors there are in the scope that men propound to themselves, whereunto they bend their en-
deavours; for whereas the more constant and devote
kind of professors of any science ought to propound to
themselves to make some additions to their science, they
convert their labours to aspire to certain second prizes:
as to be a profound interpreter or commenter, to be a
sharp champion or defender, to be a methodical com-
pounder or abridger, and so the patrimony of knowledge
cometh to be sometimes improved, but seldom augmented.

But the greatest error of all the rest is the mistaking
or misplacing of the last or furthest end of knowledge.
For men have entered into a desire of learning and
knowledge, sometimes upon a natural curiosity and inquisitive appetite; sometimes to entertain their minds
with variety and delight; sometimes for ornament and
reputation; and sometimes to enable them to victory of
wit and contradiction; and most times for lucre and profession; and seldom sincerely to give a true account of
their gift of reason, to the benefit and use of men: as if
there were sought in knowledge a couch whereupon to
rest a searching and restless spirit; or a terrace for a
wandering and variable mind to walk up and down with

a fair prospect; or a tower of state for a proud mind to raise itself upon; or a fort or commanding ground for strife and contention; or a shop for profit or sale; and not a rich storehouse for the glory of the Creator and the relief of man's estate. But this is that which will indeed dignify and exalt knowledge, if contemplation and action may be more nearly and straitly conjoined and united together than they have been; a conjunction like unto that of the two highest planets, Saturn, the planet of rest and contemplation, and Jupiter, the planet of civil society and action. Howbeit, I do not mean, when I speak of use and action, that end before-mentioned of the applying of knowledge to lucre and profession; for I am not ignorant how much that diverteth and interrupteth the prosecution and advancement of knowledge, like unto the golden ball thrown before Atalanta, which while she goeth aside and stoopeth to take up, the race is hindered,

Declinat cursus, aurumque volubile tollit.

Neither is my meaning, as was spoken of Socrates, to call philosophy down from heaven to converse upon the earth; that is, to leave natural philosophy aside, and to apply knowledge only to manners and policy. But as both heaven and earth do conspire and contribute to the use and benefit of man; so the end ought to be, from both philosophies to separate and reject vain speculations, and whatsoever is empty and void, and to preserve and augment whatsoever is solid and fruitful: that knowledge may not be as a courtesan, for pleasure and vanity only, or as a bond-woman, to acquire and gain to her master's use; but as a spouse, for generation, fruit, and comfort.

Thus have I described and opened, as by a kind of dissection, those peccant humours (the principal of them) which have not only given impediment to the proficience of learning, but have given also occasion to the traducement thereof: wherein if I have been too plain, it must be remembered, "*fidelia vulnera amantis, sed dolosa oscula malignantis.*" This I think I have gained, that I ought to be the better believed in that which I shall say pertaining to commendation; because I have proceeded so freely in that which concerneth censure. And yet I have no purpose to enter into a laudative of learning, or to make a hymn to the Muses (though I am of opinion that it is long since their rites were duly celebrated), but my intent is, without varnish or amplification justly to weigh the dignity of knowledge in the balance with other things, and to take the true value thereof by testimonies and arguments divine and human.

[FROM *The Advancement of Learning, Book I*]

SALOMON'S HOUSE

THERE reigned in this island, about 1,900 years ago, a king, whose memory of all others we most adore; not superstitiously, but as a divine instrument, though a mortal man: his name was Solamona; and we esteem him as the lawgiver of our nation. This king had a large heart, inscrutable for good, and was wholly bent to make his kingdom and people happy. He therefore taking into consideration how sufficient and substantive this land was, to maintain itself without any aid at all of the foreigner; being 5,600 miles in circuit, and of rare fertility of soil, in the greatest part thereof; and finding also the shipping of this country mought be plentifully set on work, both by fishing and by transportations from port to port, and likewise by sailing unto some small islands that are not far from us, and are under the crown and laws of this State; and recalling into his memory the happy and flourishing estate wherein this land then was, so as it might be a thousand ways altered to the worse, but scarce any one way to the better; though nothing wanted to his noble and heroical intentions, but only (as far as human foresight mought reach) to give perpetuity to that which was in his time so happily established. Therefore amongst his other fundamental laws of this kingdom he did ordain the interdicts and prohibitions which we have touching entrance of strangers; which at that time (though it was after the calamity of America) was frequent: doubting novelties and commixture of manners. It is true, the like law against the admission of strangers without licence is an ancient law in the kingdom of China, and yet continued in use. But there it is a poor thing; and hath made them a curious, ignorant, fearful, foolish nation. But our lawgiver made his law of another temper. For first, he hath preserved all points of humanity, in taking order and making provision for the relief of strangers distressed; whereof you have tasted."

At which speech (as reason was) we all rose up, and bowed ourselves. He went on:

"That king also still desiring to join humanity and policy together; and thinking it against humanity, to detain strangers here against their wills; and against policy, that they should return, and discover their knowledge of this estate, he took this course: he did ordain, that of the strangers that should be permitted to land, as many (at all times) might depart as would; but as many as would stay, should have very good conditions, and means to live from the State. Wherein he saw so far, that now in so many ages since the prohibition, we have memory not of one ship that ever re-

turned, and but of thirteen persons only, at several
times, that chose to return in our bottoms. What those
few that returned may have reported abroad I know not.
But you must think, whatsoever they have said, could
be taken where they came but for a dream. Now for our
traveling from hence into parts abroad, our lawgiver
thought fit altogether to restrain it. So is it not in China.
For the Chinese sail where they will, or can; which
showeth, that their law of keeping out strangers is a
law of pusillanimity and fear. But this restraint of ours
hath one only exception, which is admirable; preserving
the good which cometh by communicating with strangers, and avoiding the hurt: and I will now open it to
you. And here I shall seem a little to digress, but you
will by and by find it pertinent.

"Ye shall understand, my dear friends, that amongst
the excellent acts of that king, one above all hath the
pre-eminence. It was the erection and institution of an
order, or society, which we call Salomon's House; the
noblest foundation, as we think, that ever was upon the
earth, and the lantern of this kingdom. It is dedicated to
the study of the works and creatures of God. Some think
it beareth the founder's name a little corrupted, as if it
should be Solamona's House. But the records write it as
it is spoken. So as I take it to be denominate of the king
of the Hebrews, which is famous with you, and no
stranger to us; for we have some parts of his works
which with you are lost; namely, that Natural History
which he wrote of all plants, from the cedar of Libanus
to the moss that groweth out of the wall; and of all
things that have life and motion. This maketh me think
that our king finding himself to symbolize, in many
things, with that king of the Hebrews (which lived
many years before him) honoured him with the title of
this foundation. And I am the rather induced to be of

this opinion, for that I find in ancient records, this order or society is sometimes called Salomon's House, and sometimes the College of the Six Days' Works; whereby I am satisfied that our excellent king had learned from the Hebrews that God had created the world, and all that therein is, within six days: and therefore he instituting that house, for the finding out of the true nature of all things (whereby God might have the more glory in the workmanship of them, and men the more fruit in the use of them), did give it also that second name.

"But now to come to our present purpose. When the king had forbidden to all his people navigation into any part that was not under his crown, he made nevertheless this ordinance: that every twelve years there should be set forth out of this kingdom two ships, appointed to several voyages; that in either of these ships there should be a mission of three of the fellows or brethren of Salomon's House, whose errand was only to give us knowledge of the affairs and state of those countries to which they were designed; and especially of the sciences, arts, manufactures, and inventions of all the world; and withal to bring unto us books, instruments, and patterns in every kind: that the ships, after they had landed the brethren, should return; and that the brethren should stay abroad till the new mission. These ships are not otherwise fraught than with store of victuals, and good quantity of treasure to remain with the brethren, for the buying of such things, and rewarding of such persons, as they should think fit. Now for me to tell you how the vulgar sort of mariners are contained from being discovered at land, and how they that must be put on shore for any time, colour themselves under the names of other nations, and to what places these voyages have been designed, and what places of rendezvous are appointed for the new missions, and the like circumstances of the practice, I may not do it, neither is it much to your desire. But thus you see we maintain a trade, not for gold, silver, or jewels, nor for silks, nor for spices, nor any other commodity of matter; but only for God's first creature, which was light: to have light, I say, of the growth of all parts of the world."

And when he had said this, he was silent, and so were we all; for indeed we were all astonished to hear so strange things so probably told. And he perceiving that we were willing to say somewhat, but had it not ready, in great courtesy took us off, and descended to ask us questions of our voyage and fortunes, and in the end concluded that we might do well to think with ourselves, what time of stay we would demand of the State, and bade us not to scant ourselves; for he would procure such time as we desired. Whereupon we all rose up and presented ourselves to kiss the skirt of his tippet, but he would not suffer us, and so took his leave. . . .

Three days after the Jew came to me again, and said, "Ye are happy men; for the father of Salomon's House taketh knowledge of your being here, and commanded me to tell you, that he will admit all your company to his presence, and have private conference with one of you, that ye shall choose; and for this hath appointed the next day after tomorrow. And because he meaneth to give you his blessing, he hath appointed it in the forenoon."

We came at our day and hour, and I was chosen by my fellows for the private access. We found him in a fair chamber, richly hanged, and carpeted under foot, without any degrees to the state. He was set upon a low throne richly adorned and a rich cloth of state over his head, of blue satin embroidered. He was alone, save that he had two pages of honour, on either hand one, finely attired in white. His under garments were the like that we saw him wear in the chariot; but instead of his gown, he had on him a mantle with a cape, of the same fine black, fastened about him. When we came in, as we were taught, we bowed low at our first entrance; and when we were come near his chair, he stood up, holding forth his hand ungloved, and in posture of blessing; and we every one of us stooped down, and kissed the hem of his tippet. That done, the rest departed, and I remained. Then he warned the pages forth of the room, and caused me to sit down beside him, and spake to me thus in the Spanish tongue:

"God bless thee, my son; I will give thee the greatest jewel I have. For I will impart unto thee, for the love of God and men, a relation of the true state of Salomon's House. Son, to make you know the true state of Salomon's House, I will keep this order. First, I will set forth unto you the end of our foundation. Secondly, the preparations and instruments we have for our works. Thirdly, the several employments and functions whereto our fellows are assigned. And fourthly, the ordinances and rites which we observe.

"The end of our foundation is the knowledge of causes, and secret motions of things; and the enlarging of the bounds of human empire, to the effecting of all things possible.

"The preparations and instruments are these. We have large and deep caves of several depths: the deepest are sunk six hundred fathoms; and some of them are digged and made under great hills and mountains; so that if you reckon together the depth of the hill, and the depth of the cave, they are, some of them, above three miles deep. For we find that the depth of a hill, and the depth of a cave from the flat, is the same thing; both remote alike from the sun and heaven's beams, and from the open air. These caves we call the lower region, and we use them for all coagulations, indurations, refrigerations, and conservations of bodies. We use them likewise for the imitation of natural mines, and the producing also of new artificial metals, by compositions and materials which we use, and lay there for many years. We use them also sometimes (which may seem strange) for curing of some diseases, and for prolongation of life, in some hermits that choose to live there, well accommodated of all things necessary, and indeed live very long; by whom also we learn many things.

"We have burials in several earths, where we put divers cements, as the Chinese do their porcelain. But we have them in greater variety, and some of them more fine. We also have great variety of composts and soils, for the making of the earth fruitful.

"We have high towers, the highest about half a mile in height, and some of them likewise set upon high mountains, so that the vantage of the hill, with the tower, is in the highest of them three miles at least. And these places we call the upper region, accounting the air between the high places and the low as a middle region. We use these towers, according to their several heights and situations, for insulation, refrigeration, conservation, and for the view of divers meteors—as winds, rain, snow, hail; and some of the fiery meteors also. And upon them, in some places, are dwellings of hermits, whom we visit sometimes, and instruct what to observe.

"We have great lakes, both salt and fresh, whereof we have use for the fish and fowl. We use them also for burials of some natural bodies, for we find a difference in things buried in earth, or in air below the earth, and things buried in water. We have also pools, of which some do strain fresh water out of salt, and others by art do turn fresh water into salt. We have also some rocks in the midst of the sea, and some bays upon the shore for some works, wherein is required the air and vapour of the sea. We have likewise violent streams and cataracts, which serve us for many motions; and likewise engines for multiplying and enforcing of winds to set also on divers motions.

"We have also a number of artificial wells and fountains, made in imitation of the natural sources and baths, as tincted upon vitriol, sulphur, steel, brass, lead, nitre, and other minerals; and again, we have little wells for infusions of many things, where the waters take the virtue quicker and better than in vessels or basins. And amongst them we have a water, which we call Water of Paradise, being by that we do to it made very sovereign for health and prolongation of life.

"We have also great and spacious houses, where we imitate and demonstrate meteors—as snow, hail, rain, some artificial rains of bodies, and not of water, thunders, lightnings; also generations of bodies in air—as frogs, flies, and divers others.

"We have also certain chambers, which we call chambers of health, where we qualify the air as we think good and proper for the cure of divers diseases, and preservation of health.

"We have also fair and large baths, of several mixtures, for the cure of diseases, and the restoring of man's body from arefaction; and others for the confirming of it in strength of sinews, vital parts, and the very juice and substance of the body.

"We have also large and various orchards and gardens, wherein we do not so much respect beauty as variety of ground and soil, proper for divers trees and herbs, and some very spacious, where trees and berries are set, whereof we make divers kinds of drinks, besides the vineyards. In these we practise likewise all conclusions of grafting and inoculating, as well of wild-trees as fruit-trees, which produceth many effects. And we make by art, in the same orchards and gardens, trees and flowers, to come earlier or later than their seasons, and to come up and bear more speedily than by their natural course they do. We make them also by art greater much than their nature; and their fruit greater and sweeter, and of differing taste, smell, colour, and figure, from their nature. And many of them we so order as they become of medicinal use.

"We have also means to make divers plants rise by mixtures of earths without seeds, and likewise to make divers new plants, differing from the vulgar, and to make one tree or plant turn into another.

"We have also parks, and enclosures of all sorts, of beasts and birds; which we use not only for view or rareness, but likewise for dissections and trials, that thereby we may take light what may be wrought upon the body of man. Wherein we find many strange effects: as continuing life in them, though divers parts, which you account vital, be perished and taken forth; resuscitating of some that seem dead in appearance, and the like. We try also all poisons, and other medicines upon them, as well of chirurgery as physic. By art likewise we make them greater or taller than their kind is, and contrariwise dwarf them and stay their growth; we make them more fruitful and bearing than their kind is, and contrariwise barren and not generative. Also we make them differ in colour, shape, activity, many ways. We find means to make commixtures and copulations of divers kinds, which have produced many new kinds, and them not barren, as the general opinion is. We make a number of kinds, of serpents, worms, flies, fishes, of putrefaction, whereof some are advanced (in effect) to be perfect creatures, like beasts or birds, and have sexes, and do propagate. Neither do we this by chance, but we know beforehand of what matter and commixture, what kind of those creatures will arise.

"We have also particular pools where we make trials upon fishes, as we have said before of beasts and birds.

"We have also places for breed and generation of those kinds of worms and flies which are of special use; such as are with you your silkworms and bees.

"I will not hold you long with recounting of our brew-houses, bake-houses, and kitchens, where are made divers drinks, breads, and meats, rare and of special effects. Wines we have of grapes, and drinks of other juice, of fruits, of grains, and of roots, and of mixtures with honey, sugar, manna, and fruits dried and decocted; also of the tears or woundings of trees, and of the pulp of canes. And these drinks are of several ages, some to the age or last of forty years. We have drinks also brewed with several herbs, and roots and spices; yea, with several fleshes and white-meats; whereof some of the drinks are such as they are in effect meat and drink both, so that divers, especially in age, do desire to live with them with little or no meat or bread. And above all we strive to have drinks of extreme thin parts, to insinuate into the body, and yet without all biting, sharpness, or fretting; insomuch as some of them, put upon the back of your hand, will with a little stay pass through to the palm, and taste yet mild to the mouth. We have also waters, which we ripen in that fashion, as they become nourishing, so that they are indeed excellent drinks, and many will use no other. Bread we have of several grains, roots, and kernels; yea, and some of flesh, and fish, dried; with divers kinds of leavenings and seasonings; so that some do extremely move appetites, some do nourish so, as divers do live of them, without any other meat, who live very long. So for meats, we have some of them so beaten, and made tender, and mortified, yet without all corrupting, as a weak heat of the stomach will turn them into good chilus, as well as a strong heat would meat otherwise prepared. We have some meats also, and breads, and drinks, which taken by men, enable them to fast long after; and some other, that used make the very flesh of men's bodies sensibly more hard and tough, and their strength far greater than otherwise it would be.

"We have dispensatories or shops of medicines; wherein you may easily think, if we have such variety of plants, and living creatures, more than you have in Europe (for we know what you have), the simples, drugs and ingredients of medicines, must likewise be in so much the greater variety. We have them likewise of divers ages, and long fermentations. And for their preparations, we have not only all manner of exquisite distillations and separations, and especially by gentle heats, and percolations through divers strainers, yea, and substances; but also exact forms of composition, whereby they incorporate almost as they were natural simples.

"We have also divers mechanical arts, which you have not; and stuffs made by them, as papers, linen, silks, tissues, dainty works of feathers of wonderful lustre, excellent dyes, and many others: and shops likewise, as well for such as are not brought into vulgar use amongst us, as for those that are. For you must know, that of the things before recited, many of them are grown into use throughout the kingdom, but yet, if they did flow from our invention, we have of them also for patterns and principles.

"We have also furnaces of great diversities, and that keep great diversity of heats: fierce and quick, strong and constant, soft and mild; blown, quiet, dry, moist, and the like. But above all we have heats, in imitation of the sun's and heavenly bodies' heats, that pass divers inequalities, and (as it were) orbs, progresses, and returns, whereby we produce admirable effects. Besides, we have heats of dungs, and of bellies and maws of living creatures and of their bloods and bodies, and of hays and herbs laid up moist, of lime unquenched, and such like. Instruments also which generate heat only by motion. And farther, places for strong insulations; and again, places under the earth, which by nature or art yield heat. These divers heats we use as the nature of the operation which we intend requireth.

"We have also perspective houses, where we make demonstrations of all lights and radiations, and of all colours; and out of things uncoloured and transparent, we can represent unto you all several colours, not in rainbows (as it is in gems and prisms), but of themselves single. We represent also all multiplications of light, which we carry to great distance, and make so sharp, as to discern small points and lines. Also all colourations of light; all delusions and deceits of the sight, in figures, magnitudes, motions, colours; all demonstrations of shadows. We find also divers means yet unknown to you, of producing of light, originally from divers bodies. We procure means of seeing objects afar off, as in the heaven and remote places; and represent things near as afar off, and things afar off as near; making feigned distances. We have also helps for the sight, far above spectacles and glasses in use. We have also glasses and means to see small and minute bodies, perfectly and distinctly; as the shapes and colours of small flies and worms, grains, and flaws in gems which cannot otherwise be seen, observations in urine and blood not otherwise to be seen. We make artificial rainbows, halos, and circles about light. We represent also all manner of reflections, refractions, and multiplications of visual beams of objects.

"We have also precious stones of all kinds, many of them of great beauty and to you unknown; crystals likewise, and glasses of divers kinds; and amongst them some of metals vitrificated, and other materials, besides those of which you make glass. Also a number of fossils and imperfect minerals, which you have not. Likewise loadstones of prodigious virtue: and other rare stones, both natural and artificial.

"We have also sound-houses, where we practise and demonstrate all sounds and their generation. We have harmonies which you have not, of quarter-sounds and lesser slides of sounds. Divers instruments of music likewise to you unknown, some sweeter than any you have; together with bells and rings that are dainty and sweet. We represent small sounds as great and deep; likewise great sounds, extenuate and sharp; we make divers tremblings and warblings of sounds, which in their original are entire. We represent and imitate all articulate sounds and letters, and the voices and notes of beasts and birds. We have certain helps, which set to the ear do further the hearing greatly. We have also divers strange and artificial echoes, reflecting the voice many times, and as it were tossing it; and some that give back the voice louder than it came, some shriller and some deeper; yea, some rendering the voice, differing in the letters or articulate sound from that they receive. We have also means to convey sounds in trunks and pipes, in strange lines and distances.

"We have also perfume-houses, wherewith we join also practices of taste. We multiply smells, which may seem strange: we imitate smells, making all smells to breathe out of other mixtures than those that give them. We make divers imitations of taste likewise, so that they will deceive any man's taste. And in this house we contain also a confiture-house, where we make all sweetmeats, dry and moist, and divers pleasant wines, milks, broths, and salads, far in greater variety than you have.

"We have also engine-houses, where are prepared engines and instruments for all sorts of motions. There we imitate and practise to make swifter motions than any you have, either out of your muskets or any engine that you have; and to make them and multiply them more easily and with small force, by wheels and other means, and to make them stronger and more violent than yours are, exceeding your greatest cannons and basilisks. We represent also ordnance and instruments of war and engines of all kinds; and likewise new mixtures and compositions of gunpowder, wild-fires burning in water and unquenchable, also fire-works of all variety, both for pleasure and use. We imitate also flights of birds; we have some degrees of flying in the air. We have ships and boats for going under water and brooking of seas, also swimming-girdles and supporters. We have divers curious clocks, and other like motions of return, and some perpetual motions. We imitate also motions of living creatures by images of men, beasts, birds, fishes, and serpents; we have also a great number of other various motions, strange for equality, fineness, and subtilty.

"We have also a mathematical-house, where are represented all instruments, as well of geometry as astronomy, exquisitely made.

"We have also houses of deceits of the senses, where we represent all manner of feats of juggling, false apparitions, impostures and illusions, and their fallacies. And surely you will easily believe that we, that have so many things truly natural which induce admiration, could in a world of particulars deceive the senses if we would disguise those things, and labour to make them seem more miraculous. But we do hate all impostures and lies, insomuch as we have severely forbidden it to all our fellows, under pain of ignominy and fines, that they do not show any natural work or thing adorned or swelling, but only pure as it is, and without all affectation of strangeness.

"These are, my son, the riches of Salomon's House.

"For the several employments and offices of our fellows, we have twelve that sail into foreign countries under the names of other nations (for our own we conceal), who bring us the books and abstracts, and patterns of experiments of all other parts. These we call Merchants of Light.

"We have three that collect the experiments which are in all books. These we call Depredators.

"We have three that collect the experiments of all mechanical arts, and also of liberal sciences, and also of practises which are not brought into arts. These we call Mystery-men.

"We have three that try new experiments, such as themselves think good. These we call Pioneers or Miners.

"We have three that draw the experiments of the former four into titles and tables, to give the better light for the drawing of observations and axioms out of them. These we call Compilers.

"We have three that bend themselves, looking into the experiments of their fellows, and cast about how to draw out of them things of use and practice for man's life and knowledge, as well for works as for plain demonstration of causes, means of natural divinations, and the easy and clear discovery of the virtues and parts of bodies. These we call dowry-men or Benefactors.

"Then after divers meetings and consults of our whole number, to consider of the former labours and collections, we have three that take care out of them to direct new experiments, of a higher light, more penetrating into Nature than the former. These we call Lamps.

"We have three others that do execute the experiments so directed, and report them. These we call Inoculators.

"Lastly, we have three that raise the former discoveries by experiments into greater observations, axioms, and aphorisms. These we call Interpreters of Nature.

"We have also, as you must think, novices and apprentices, that the succession of the former employed men do not fail; besides a great number of servants and attendants, men and women. And this we do also: we have consultations, which of the inventions and experiences which we have discovered shall be published, and which not: and take all an oath of secrecy for the concealing of those which we think fit to keep secret: though some of those we do reveal sometimes to the State, and some not.

"For our ordinances and rites, we have two very long and fair galleries: in one of these we place patterns and samples of all manner of the more rare and excellent inventions: in the other we place the statues of all principal inventors. There we have the statue of your Columbus, that discovered the West Indies: also the inventor of ships: your Monk that was the inventor of ordnance and of gunpowder: the inventor of music: the inventor of letters: the inventor of printing: the inventor of observations of astronomy: the inventor of works in metal: the inventor of glass: the inventor of silk of the worm: the inventor of wine: the inventor of corn and bread: the inventor of sugars: and all these by more certain tradition than you have. Then we have divers inventors of our own, of excellent works, which since you have not seen, it were too long to make descriptions of them; and besides, in the right understanding of those descriptions you might easily err. For upon every invention of value we erect a statue to the inventor, and give him a liberal and honourable reward. These statues are some of brass, some of marble and touchstone, some of cedar and other special woods gilt and adorned; some of iron, some of silver, some of gold.

"We have certain hymns and services, which we say daily, of laud and thanks to God for His marvellous works. And forms of prayer, imploring His aid and blessing for the illumination of our labours, and the turning of them into good and holy uses.

"Lastly, we have circuits or visits, of divers principal cities of the kingdom; where, as it cometh to pass, we do publish such new profitable inventions as we think good. And we do also declare natural divinations of diseases, plagues, swarms of hurtful creatures, scarcity, tempests, earthquakes, great inundations, comets, temperature of the year, and divers other things; and we give counsel thereupon, what the people shall do for the prevention and remedy of them."

And when he had said this he stood up; and I, as I had been taught, knelt down; and he laid his right hand upon my head, and said, "God bless thee, my son, and God bless this relation which I have made. I give thee leave to publish it, for the good of other nations; for we here are in God's bosom, a land unknown."

[FROM *New Atlantis*]

PART TWO

The Dream of Power

I. Empire and the Shadow of Machiavelli

Francis Bacon

THE BEST IRON IN THE WORLD

For greatness (Mr. Speaker) I think a man may speak it soberly and without bravery, that this kingdom of England, having Scotland united, Ireland reduced, the sea provinces of the Low Countries contracted, and shipping maintained, is one of the greatest monarchies, in forces truly esteemed, that hath been in the world. For certainly the kingdoms here on earth have a resemblance with the kingdom of heaven, which our Saviour compareth not to any great kernel or nut, but to a very small grain, yet such a one as is apt to grow and spread. And such do I take to be the constitution of this kingdom, if indeed we shall refer our counsels to greatness and power, and not quench them too much with consideration of utility and wealth.

For (Mr. Speaker) was it not, think you, a true answer that Solon of Greece made to the rich King Croesus of Lydia, when he showed unto him a great quantity of gold that he had gathered together, in ostentation of his greatness and might. But Solon said to him, contrary to his expectation, "Why, sir, if another come that hath better iron than you, he will be lord of all your gold."

Neither is the authority of Machiavel to be despised, who scorneth the proverb of estate taken first from a speech of Mucianus, that "Moneys are the sinews of wars"; and saith there are no true sinews of war but the very sinews of the arms of valiant men.

Nay more (Mr. Speaker), whosoever shall look into the seminary and beginnings of the monarchies of the world, he shall find them founded in poverty. Persia, a country barren and poor, in respect of the Medes whom they subdued. Macedon, a kingdom ignoble and mercenary, until the time of Philip the son of Amyntas. Rome had poor and pastoral beginnings. The Turks, a band of Sarmatian Scythes, that in a vagabond manner made impression upon that part of Asia which is yet called Turcomania; out of which, after much variety of fortune, sprang the Ottoman family, now the terror of the world. So we know the Goths, Vandals, Alans, Huns, Lombards, Normans, and the rest of the northern people, in one age of the world made their descent or expedition upon the Roman empire, and came not as rovers to carry away prey and be gone again, but planted themselves in a number of fruitful and rich provinces, where not only their generations, but their names remain till this day; witness Lombardy, Catalonia, a name compounded of Goth and Alane, Andaluzio, a name corrupted from Vandelicia, Hungary, Normandy, and others.

Nay, the fortune of the Swisses of late years, which are bred in a barren and mountainous country, is not to be forgotten, who first ruined the Duke of Burgundy, the same who had almost ruined the kingdom of France; what time; after the battle of Grançon, the rich jewel of Burgundy, prized at many thousands, was sold for a few

pence by a common Swiss, that knew no more what a
jewel meant than did Aesop's cock. And again the same
nation, in revenge of a scorn, was the ruin of the French
king's affairs in Italy, Lewis XII. For that king, when he
was pressed somewhat rudely by an agent of the Swisses
to raise their pensions, brake into words of choler:
"What," said he, "will these villains of the mountains put
a tax upon me?" Which words lost him his duchy of
Milan, and chased him out of Italy.

All which examples (Mr. Speaker) do well prove
Solon's opinion of the authority and mastery that iron
hath over gold. And therefore if I should speak unto you
mine own heart, methinks we should a little disdain that
the nation of Spain, which howsoever of late it hath
grown to rule, yet of ancient times served many ages,
first under Carthage, then under Rome, after under
Saracens, Goths, and others, should of late years take
unto themselves that spirit as to dream of a monarchy in
the West, according to that device, *Video solem orien-
tem in occidente,* only because they have ravished from
some wild and unarmed people mines and store of gold;
and on the other side, that this island of Brittany, seated
and manned as it is, and that hath (I make no question)
the best iron in the world, that is the best soldiers of the
world, should think of nothing but reckonings and
audits, and *meum* and *tuum,* and I cannot tell what.

[*Speech in House of Commons,* Feb. 17, 1606-1607]

OF THE TRUE GREATNESS
OF KINGDOMS

THE SPEECH of Themistocles, the Athenian, which
was haughty and arrogant in taking so much to
himself, had been a grave and wise observation and
censure, applied at large to others. Desired at a feast to

touch a lute, he said, "He could not fiddle, but yet he could make a small town a great city." These words (holpen a little with a metaphor) may express two different abilities in those that deal in business of estate; for if a true survey be taken of counsellors and statesmen, there may be found (though rarely) those which can make a small state great, and yet cannot fiddle: as, on the other side, there will be found a great many that can fiddle very cunningly, but yet are so far from being able to make a small state great, as their gift lieth the other way; to bring a great and flourishing estate to ruin and decay. And certainly, those degenerate arts and shifts whereby many counsellors and governors gain both favour with their masters and estimation with the vulgar, deserve no better name than fiddling; being things rather pleasing for the time, and graceful to themselves only, than tending to the weal and advancement of the state which they serve. There are also (no doubt) counsellors and governors which may be held sufficient (*negotiis pares*), able to manage affairs, and to keep them from precipices and manifest inconveniences; which nevertheless are far from the ability to raise and amplify an estate in power, means, and fortune. But be the workmen what they may be, let us speak of the work; that is, the true greatness of kingdoms and estates, and the means thereof—an argument fit for great and mighty princes to have in their hand; to the end that neither by over-measuring their forces they lose themselves in vain enterprises: nor, on the other side, by undervaluing them they descend to fearful and pusillanimous counsels.

The greatness of an estate in bulk and territory doth fall under measure; and the greatness of finances and revenue doth fall under computation. The population may appear by musters; and the number and greatness of cities and towns by cards and maps; but yet there is not anything amongst civil affairs more subject to error than the right valuation and true judgement concerning the power and forces of an estate. The kingdom of heaven is compared, not to any great kernel or nut, but to a grain of mustard-seed; which is one of the least grains, but hath in it a property and spirit hastily to get up and spread. So are there states great in territory, and yet not apt to enlarge or command; and some that have but a small dimension of stem, and yet apt to be the foundations of great monarchies.

Walled towns, stored arsenals and armouries, goodly races of horse, chariots of war, elephants, ordnance, artillery, and the like; all this is but a sheep in a lion's skin, except the breed and disposition of the people be stout and warlike. Nay, number itself in armies importeth not much where the people is of weak courage; for (as Virgil saith), "It never troubles a wolf how many the sheep be." The army of the Persians in the plains of Arbela was such a vast sea of people as it did somewhat astonish the commanders in Alexander's army, who came to him therefore and wished him to set upon them by night; but he answered, "He would not pilfer the victory"; and the defeat was easy. When Tigranes, the Armenian, being encamped upon a hill with four hundred thousand men, discovered the army of the Romans, being not above fourteen thousand, marching towards him, he made himself merry with it, and said, "Yonder men are too many for an ambassage, and too few for a fight"; but before the sun set, he found them enow to give him the chase with infinite slaughter. Many are the examples of the great odds between number and courage: so that a man may truly make a judgement that the principal point of greatness in any state is to have a race of military men. Neither is money the sinews of war (as it is trivially said), where the sinews of men's arms in base and effeminate people are failing: for Solon said well to Croesus (when in ostentation he showed him his gold), "Sir, if any other come that hath better iron than you, he will be master of all this gold." Therefore, let any prince or state think soberly of his forces, except his militia of natives be of good and valiant soldiers; and let princes, on the other side, that have subjects of martial disposition, know their own strength, unless they be otherwise wanting unto themselves. As for mercenary forces (which is the help in this case), all examples show that, whatsoever estate or prince doth rest upon them, *he may spread his feathers for a time, but he will mew them soon after.*

The blessing of Judah and Issachar will never meet; *that the same people or nation should be both the lion's whelp and the ass between burdens;* neither will it be that a people overlaid with taxes should ever become valiant and martial. It is true that taxes, levied by consent of the estate, do abate men's courage less; as it hath been seen notably in the excises of the Low Countries; and, in some degree, in the subsidies of England; for you must note that we speak now of the heart and not of the purse; so that although the same tribute and tax laid by consent or by imposing be all one to the purse, yet it works diversely upon the courage. So that you may conclude *that no people overcharged with tribute is fit for empire.*

Let states that aim at greatness take heed how their nobility and gentlemen do multiply too fast; for that maketh the common subject grow to be a peasant and base swain, driven out of heart, and in effect but the gentleman's labourer. Even as you may see in coppice woods; *if you leave your staddles too thick, you shall never have clean underwood, but shrubs and bushes.* So in countries, if the gentlemen be too many the commons will be base: and you will bring it to that that not the hundred poll will be fit for an helmet: especially as to the infantry, which is the nerve of an army; and so there will be great population and little strength. This which I speak of hath been nowhere better seen than by comparing of England and France; whereof England, though far less in territory and population, hath been (nevertheless) an overmatch; in regard the middle people of England make good soldiers, which the peasants of France do not. And herein the device of King Henry VII (whereof I have spoken largely in the history of his life) was profound and admirable, in making farms and houses of husbandry of a standard, that is, maintained with such a proportion of land unto them as may breed a subject to live in convenient plenty, and no servile condition; and to keep the plough in the hands of the owners, and not mere hirelings; and thus indeed you shall attain to Virgil's character, which he gives to ancient Italy:

Terra potens armis atque ubere glebae.

Neither is that state (which, for anything I know, is almost peculiar to England, and hardly to be found anywhere else, except it be perhaps in Poland) to be passed over; I mean the state of free servants and attendants upon noblemen and gentlemen, which are no ways inferior unto the yeomanry for arms; and therefore, out of all question, the splendour and magnificence and great retinues and hospitality of noblemen and gentlemen received into custom doth much conduce unto martial greatness; whereas, contrariwise, the close and reserved living of noblemen and gentlemen causeth a penury of military forces.

By all means it is to be procured that the trunk of

Nebuchadnezzar's tree of monarchy be great enough to bear the branches and the boughs; that is, that the natural subjects of the crown or state bear a sufficient proportion to the stranger subjects that they govern. Therefore all states that are liberal of naturalization towards strangers are fit for empire; for to think that a handful of people can, with the greatest courage and policy in the world, embrace too large extent of dominion, it may hold for a time but it will fail suddenly. The Spartans were a nice people in point of naturalization; whereby, while they kept their compass, they stood firm; but when they did spread, and their boughs were becomen too great for their stem, they became a windfall upon the sudden. Never any state was in this point so open to receive strangers into their body as were the Romans; therefore it sorted with them accordingly, for they grew to the greatest monarchy. Their manner was to grant naturalization (which they called *jus civitatis*) and to grant it in the highest degree, that is, not only *jus commercii, jus connubii, jus haereditatis;* but also, *jus suffragii,* and *jus honorum;* and this not to singular persons alone, but likewise to whole families; yea, to cities and sometimes to nations. Add to this their custom of plantation of colonies, whereby the Roman plant was removed into the soil of other nations; and, putting both constitutions together, you will say that it was not the Romans that spread upon the world, but it was the world that spread upon the Romans; and that was the sure way of greatness. I have marvelled sometimes at Spain, how they clasp and contain so large dominions with so few natural Spaniards; but sure the whole compass of Spain is a very great body of a tree, far above Rome and Sparta at the first; and besides, though they have not had that usage to naturalize liberally, yet they have that which is next to it; that is, *to employ almost*

*indifferently all nations in their militia of ordinary sol-
diers;* yea, and sometimes in their highest commands;
nay, it seemeth at this instant they are sensible of this
want of natives; as by the *pragmatical sanction,* now
published, appeareth.

It is certain that sedentary and within-door arts and
delicate manufactures (that require rather the finger
than the arm) have in their nature a contrariety to a
military disposition; and generally all warlike people
are a little idle, and love danger better than travail;
neither must they be too much broken of it if they shall
be preserved in vigour. Therefore it was great advantage
in the ancient states of Sparta, Athens, Rome, and others,
that they had the use of slaves, which commonly did rid
those manufactures; but that is abolished in greatest
part by the Christian law. That which cometh nearest
to it is to leave those arts chiefly to strangers (which for
that purpose are the more easily to be received), and to
contain the principal bulk of the vulgar natives within
those three kinds, tillers of the ground, free servants,
and handicraftsmen of strong and manly arts, as smiths,
masons, carpenters, &c., not reckoning professed soldiers.

But, above all, for empire and greatness it importeth
most that a nation do profess arms as their principal
honour, study, and occupation; for the things which we
formerly have spoken of are but habilitations towards
arms; and what is habilitation without intention and act?
Romulus, after his death (as they report or feign), sent
a present to the Romans, that above all they should intend arms, and then they should prove the greatest empire of the world. The fabric of the state of Sparta was
wholly (though not wisely) framed and composed to
that scope and end; the Persians and Macedonians had
it for a flash; the Gauls, Germans, Goths, Saxons, Normans, and others, had it for a time; the Turks have it at

this day, though in great declination. Of Christian Europe, they that have it are in effect only the Spaniards. But it is so plain *that every man profiteth in that he most intendeth,* that it needeth not to be stood upon: it is enough to point at it; that no nation which doth not directly profess arms may look to have greatness fall into their mouths; and on the other side, it is a most certain oracle of time, that those states that continue long in that profession (as the Romans and Turks principally have done) do wonders; and those that have professed arms but for an age have, notwithstanding, commonly attained that greatness in that age which maintained them long after, when their profession and exercise of arms had grown to decay.

Incident to this point is for a state to have those laws or customs which may reach forth unto them just occasions (as may be pretended) of war; for there is that justice imprinted in the nature of men, that they enter not upon wars (whereof so many calamities do ensue), but upon some at the least specious grounds and quarrels. The Turk hath at hand, for cause of war, the propagation of his law or sect, a quarrel that he may always command. The Romans, though they esteemed the extending the limits of their empire to be great honour to their generals when it was done, yet they never rested upon that alone to begin a war. First therefore let nations that pretend to greatness have this, that they be sensible of wrongs, either upon borderers, merchants, or politic ministers; and that they sit not too long upon a provocation: secondly, let them be prest and ready to give aids and succours to their confederates; as it ever was with the Romans; insomuch as if the confederate had leagues defensive with divers other states, and upon invasion offered did implore their aids severally, yet the Romans would ever be the foremost, and leave it to none other to have the honour. As for the wars which were anciently made on the behalf of a kind of party or tacit conformity of estate, I do not see how they may be well justified: as when the Romans made a war for the liberty of Graecia: or when the Lacedaemonians and Athenians made wars to set up or pull down democracies and oligarchies: or when wars were made by foreigners under the pretence of justice or protection, to deliver the subjects of others from tyranny and oppression; and the like. Let it suffice, that no estate expect to be great that is not awake upon any just occasion of arming.

No body can be healthful without exercise, neither natural body nor politic; and certainly to a kingdom or estate a just and honourable war is the true exercise. A civil war indeed, is like the heat of a fever; but a foreign war is like the heat of exercise, and serveth to keep the body in health; for in a slothful peace both courages will effeminate and manners corrupt. But howsoever it be for happiness, without all questions for greatness, it maketh to be still for the most part in arms; and the strength of a veteran army (though it be a chargeable business), always on foot, is that which commonly giveth the law, or at least the reputation amongst all neighbour states, as may well be seen in Spain, which hath had, in one part or other, a veteran army almost continually now by the space of six-score years.

To be master of the sea is an abridgement of a monarchy. Cicero, writing to Atticus of Pompey his preparation against Caesar, saith, *"Consilium Pompeii plane Themistocleum est; putat enim qui mari potitur eum rerum potiri";* and without doubt Pompey had tired out Caesar if upon vain confidence he had not left that way. We see the great effects of battles by sea: the battle of Actium decided the empire of the world; the battle of Lepanto arrested the greatness of the Turk. There be many examples where sea-fights have been final to the war: but this is when princes or states have set up their rest upon the battles. But thus much is certain; that he that commands the sea is at great liberty, and may take as much and as little of the war as he will; whereas those that be strongest by land are many times nevertheless in great straits. Surely at this day with us of Europe the vantage of strength at sea (which is one of the principal dowries of this kingdom of Great Britain) is great; both because most of the kingdoms of Europe are not merely inland, but girt with the sea most part of their compass; and because the wealth of both Indies seems in great part but an accessory to the command of the seas.

The wars of latter ages seem to be made in the dark, in respect of the glory and honour which reflected upon men from the wars in ancient time. There be now, for martial encouragement, some degrees and orders of chivalry, which nevertheless are conferred promiscuously upon soldiers and no soldiers; and some remembrance perhaps upon the scutcheon, and some hospitals for maimed soldiers, and such-like things; but in ancient times, the trophies erected upon the place of the victory; the funeral laudatives and monuments for those that died in the wars; the crowns and garlands personal; the style of emperor which the great kings of the world after borrowed; the triumphs of the generals upon their return; the great donatives and largesses upon the disbanding of the armies, were things able to inflame all men's courages. But above all, that of the triumph amongst the Romans was not pageants or gaudery, but one of the wisest and noblest institutions that ever was; for it contained three things: honour to the general, riches to the treasury out of the spoils, and donatives to the army. But that honour perhaps were not fit for monarchies, except it be in the person of the monarch

himself or his sons; as it came to pass in the times of the
Roman emperors, who did impropriate the actual triumphs to themselves and their sons for such wars as they
did achieve in person, and left only for wars achieved by
subjects some triumphal garments and ensigns to the
general.

To conclude: no man can *by care taking* (as the
Scripture saith) *add a cubit to his stature* in this little
model of a man's body; but in the great frame of kingdoms and commonwealths it is in the power of princes
or estates to add amplitude and greatness to their kingdoms; for by introducing such ordinances, constitutions,
and customs, as we have now touched, they may sow
greatness to their posterity and succession: but these
things are commonly not observed, but left to take their
chance.

[FROM *Essays*]

OF BOLDNESS

IT IS a trivial grammar-school text, but yet worthy a
wise man's consideration: question was asked of
Demosthenes, what was the chief part of an orator? he
answered, Action: what next? Action: what next again?
Action. He said it that knew it best, and had by nature
himself no advantage in that he commended. A strange
thing, that that part of an orator which is but superficial, and rather the virtue of a player, should be placed
so high above those other noble parts of invention,
elocution, and the rest; nay almost alone, as if it were
all in all. But the reason is plain. There is in human
nature generally more of the fool than of the wise; and
therefore those faculties by which the foolish part of
men's minds is taken are most potent. Wonderful like is

the case of boldness in civil business; what first? Boldness; what second and third? Boldness: and yet boldness is a child of ignorance and baseness, far inferior to other parts: but, nevertheless, it doth fascinate and bind hand and foot those that are either shallow in judgement or weak in courage, which are the greatest part; yea, and prevaileth with wise men at weak times. Therefore we see it hath done wonders in popular states, but with senates and princes less; and more ever upon the first entrance of bold persons into action than soon after; for boldness is an ill keeper of promise. Surely as there are mountebanks for the natural body, so are there mountebanks for the politic body; men that undertake great cures, and perhaps have been lucky in two or three experiments, but want the grounds of science, and therefore cannot hold out. Nay, you shall see a bold fellow many times do Mahomet's miracle. Mahomet made the people believe that he would call a hill to him, and from the top of it offer up his prayers for the observers of his law. The people assembled: Mahomet called the hill to come to him again and again; and when the hill stood still, he was never a whit abashed, but said, "If the hill will not come to Mahomet, Mahomet will go to the hill." So these men, when they have promised great matters and failed most shamefully, yet (if they have the perfection of boldness) they will but slight it over, and make a turn, and no more ado. Certainly to men of great judgement, bold persons are a sport to behold; nay, and to the vulgar also boldness hath somewhat of the ridiculous; for if absurdity be the subject of laughter, doubt you not but great boldness is seldom without some absurdity. Especially it is a sport to see when a bold fellow is out of countenance, for that puts his face into a most shrunken and wooden posture, as needs it must; for in bashfulness the spirits do a little go and come; but with bold

men, upon like occasion, they stand at a stay; like a stale
at chess, where it is no mate, but yet the game cannot
stir. But this last were fitter for a satire than for a serious
observation. This is well to be weighed, that boldness is
ever blind; for it seeth not dangers and inconveniences:
therefore it is ill in counsel, good in execution; so that
the right use of bold persons is, that they never command in chief, but be seconds and under the direction
of others; for counsel it is good to see dangers, and
in execution not to see them except they be very great.

[FROM Essays]

Gabriel Harvey

THE CULT OF VIRTÙ

1. A right fellow to practice in the
world: one, that knoweth fashions: and
prettily spiced with the powder of experience and meetly well-tempered with the
powder of experience.

*Knowledge
of the world:
Machiavelli
and Aretino.*

Machiavelli and Aretino knew fashions,
and were acquainted with the cunning of
the world.

Machiavelli and Aretino were not to
learn how to play their parts, but were
prettily beaten to the doings of the world.

Machiavelli and Aretino knew the lessons by heart and were not to seek how to
use the wicked world, the flesh, and the
Devil. They had learned cunning enough:
and had seen fashions enough: and could

and would use both, with advantage enough. Two courtisan politicians.

2. Scholars, and common youths, even amongst the lustiest, and bravest courtiers; are yet to learn the lesson in the world.

Vita, militia: vel Togata, vel Armata.

First cast to shoot right: then be sure to shoot home.

Life is warfare: act accordingly.

Let not short shooting lose your game. Aim straight, draw home. *Risoluto per tutto.*

3. Curious in deliberatory, and Judicial Decisions: furious in active expeditions, and executions.

Orderly and Methodical proceeding.

What would Speculator, or Machiavelli advise in this Case?

What would Caesar do, or suffer in this case?

The cunning of the Fox: Machiavelli and Ulysses. The courage of the Lion: Caesar.

How would Ulysses discourse, or, dispatch this matter?

How would the wisest Head; the finest Tongue; the valiantest and activest Heart, behave and bestir himself in this Case?

What course of proceeding, or conveyance, would the cunningest, and deepest wit in the world, take?

4. He is not wise, that is not wise for himself.

Live for yourself.

Wealth and honor . . . Prompt action . . . Boldness, eloquence, and winning manners lead to success . . . The power

of gold . . . Self-confidence . . . Be serpent and dove, lamb and wolf (The Lion
and the Fox) . . . Lose not time.

5. *Quicquid est in Deo, est Deus;*   Virtù.
   Quicquid est in Viro, sit   2
   Virtus, et vis.
   Quicquid cogitat, Vigor:
   Quicquid loquitur, Emphasis:
   Quicquid agit, Dynamis:
   Quicquid patitur, Alacritas.

6. The only brave way to learn all   *Scholars,*
things with no study, and much pleasure.   *and livers*
   Robin Goodfellow's Table Philosophy,   *of Life.*
good sociable Lessons.

7. Fire will out; and feats will shew his
cunning. . . .
          Mihi solus Caesar plusquam
          Omnes Libri.
Idle Heads are always in your *trans-*
cendentibus and *in nubibus:* politic Wits,
evermore *in concreto activo* . . . *omnis*
theoria puerilis, sine virili praxi.

8. *Regula Regularum.* To seek and enforce all possible advantage.

9. *Inutiles Cardani subtilitates negli-*
gendae: Sola pragmatica, et Cosmopolitica
curanda: that carry meat in the mouth; and
are daily in *esse. Quae alunt familiam et*
parasitos: quae semper aedificant.

In verbis Emphati-
   cus:
In factis energeticus:
In utrisque Indus-
   trius,
Rerum potitur.
	L'emfatico ben
	   parlà:
	L'inquisitivo ben sà:
	L'energetico ben fà:
	L'industrio ben hà.
		The path to
		Success.

10. No shield invincible, but the Heart of Confidence and the Hand of Industry. Industry, witty, and judicious Labor; extensively improved and amounting to the highest degree of valor, as well indefatigable, as violent.

A Heart of Confidence, a Hand of Industry.

Industry, is the fifth Element: and Confidence, the life and vigor of all five.

11. Give me possession: and take you possibility.

Matters in *esse* and persons in possession, bear all the sway.

12. The most pregnant Rule, and Sovereign Maxim, of my whole Virtue, and Fortune: no body, without Exercise: no mind, without cheerfulness: no Fortune, without Audacity: no Treasure, like a nimble and durable Body: with a lively and ever-cheery mind: and an invincible confidence in all entertainments, and actions. Your daily charge, to exercise, to laugh: to proceed boldly. And then Eloquence, and Industry, will achieve all: the two heroical singularities of Angelus Furius; still excelling all, *Peritia, Assuetudine, Zelo.*

The Rule of Rules.

13. In any excellent action: *più oltra*,   Più oltra.
the bravest, and Imperialest posy in the
world. You do well: do still better, and better: *più oltra*. Another doth, or speaketh,
excellently well: Do you, and speak you
better: *più oltra*.

An Iron Body: A Silver mind: A Golden
Fortune: A heavenly felicity upon Earth.
But ever excel more, and more: *più oltra*.

Aretino's glory, to be himself: to speak,   *Aretino.*
and write like himself: to imitate none but
himself, and ever to maintain his own singularity.

Angeli Autores, Orpheus et Proaeresius: *The most*
Furii, Fortius, Aretinus, Lutherus, etiam   *worthy and*
Agrippa in mathematicis, Machiavellus in   *excellent*
politicis.   *authors.*

Art, little worth, unless it be transformed
into Nature.

A Lusty Body: and a Brave Mind: ye
mighty doers in the world. Heroical valor,
nothing else.

Experience, is A man, and A perfect   *Experience*
Creature: Theory, is but A Child, or A   *a Man,*
monster: *ex ultima Tabula physicae Ra-*   *and theory*
meae, in Platonica fabula Aristaei, et Protei.   *a Child.*

14. Gallant Audacity, is never out of
countenance: But hath ever A Tongue, and
A Hand at will.

Begin with resolution: and follow it thoroughly for life.

Reason and Industry, cunningly, and ef-
fectually employed, will prevail.

The most easy, and flowing composition,
ever best: with gallant words.

No such Touchstone, to prove A Man, as his own Tongue.

He that would be thought A Man, or seem anything worth; must be A Great Doer, or A Great Speaker: He is A Cipher, and but a peakgoose, that is neither of both: He is the Right man, that is Both: He that cannot be Both, let him be One at least, if he mean to be accounted anybody: or farewell all hope of value.

Be a great Doer, or a great Speaker.

		The way to Advancement.
15. Three causes of Advancement.	1. Art.	
	2. Industry without art.	
	Experiments of all fortunes.	
	Great marriages.	
	Some egregious Act.	
	3. Service in war, in peace.	

16. The Marii and the Sforzas, great men, of great power, more endowed with a fiery spirit than with mental power: M. Furius Camillus, L. Papirius Cursor, C. Caecilius Metellus Celer, Richard I coeur de Lion. The great multitude applauds these passionate men, and counts them alone Men. They are thought fiery and powerful. . . .

Fiery natures.

But I have done nothing of this sort. Woe to miserable me, until I also do something striking and worthy of admiration—in a fashion both effective and expressive. Would that there were no one in the world more famous than I!

Vae misero mihi!

[FROM *Marginalia*]

Christopher Marlowe

THE SACKING OF BABYLON

TAMBURLAINE: Now crouch, ye kings of greatest
    Asia,
And tremble when ye hear this Scourge will come
That whips down cities and controlleth crowns,
Adding their wealth and treasure to my store.
The Euxine sea, north to Natolia;
The Terrene, west; the Caspian, north northeast;
And on the south, Sinus Arabicus;
Shall all be laden with the martial spoils
We will convey with us to Persia.
Then shall my native city Samarcanda,
And crystal waves of fresh Jaertis' stream,
The pride and beauty of her princely seat,
Be famous through the furthest continents;
For there my palace royal shall be placed,
Whose shining turrets shall dismay the heavens,
And cast the fame of Ilion's tower to hell:
Thorough the streets, with troops of conquered kings,
I'll ride in golden armour like the sun;
And in my helm a triple plume shall spring,

Spangled with diamonds, dancing in the air,
To note me emperor of the three-fold world,
Like to an almond tree y-mounted high
Upon the lofty and celestial mount
Of ever-green Selinus, quaintly decked
With blooms more white than Erycina's brows,
Whose tender blossoms tremble every one
At every little breath that thorough heaven is blown.
Then in my coach, like Saturn's royal son
Mounted his shining chariot gilt with fire,
And drawn with princely eagles through the path
Paved with bright crystal and enchased with stars,
When all the gods stand gazing at his pomp,
So will I ride through Samarcanda streets,
Until my soul, dissevered from this flesh,
Shall mount the milk-white way and meet him there.
To Babylon, my lords, to Babylon!   [*Exeunt.*

Enter the GOVERNOR OF BABYLON, MAXIMUS, *and others, upon the walls.*

GOV. What saith Maximus?

MAX. My lord, the breach the enemy hath made
Gives such assurance of our overthrow,
That little hope is left to save our lives,
Or hold our city from the conqueror's hands.
Then hang out flags, my lord, of humble truce,
And satisfy the people's general prayers,
That Tamburlaine's intolerable wrath
May be suppressed by our submission.

GOV. Villain, respectest thou more thy slavish life
Than honour of thy country or thy name?
Is not my life and state as dear to me,
The city and my native country's weal,
As any thing of price with thy conceit?
Have we not hope, for all our battered walls,
To live secure and keep his forces out,

When this our famous lake of Limnasphaltis
Makes walls afresh with every thing that falls
Into the liquid substance of his stream,
More strong than are the gates of death or hell?
What faintness should dismay our courages,
When we are thus defenced against our foe,
And have no terror but his threatening looks?

   Enter, above, a CITIZEN, *who kneels to the* GOVERNOR.

  CIT. My lord, if ever you did deed of ruth,
And now will work a refuge to our lives,
Offer submission, hang up flags of truce,
That Tamburlaine may pity our distress,
And use us like a loving conqueror.
Though this be held his last day's dreadful siege,
Wherein he spareth neither man nor child,
Yet are there Christians of Georgia here,
Whose state he ever pitied and relieved,
Will get his pardon, if your grace would send.

  GOV. How is my soul environed!
And this eternized city Babylon
Filled with a pack of faintheart fugitives
That thus entreat their shame and servitude!

   Enter, above, a SECOND CITIZEN.

  SEC. CIT. My lord, if ever you will win our hearts,
Yield up the town, save our wives and children;
For I will cast myself from off these walls,
Or die some death of quickest violence,
Before I bide the wrath of Tamburlaine.

  GOV. Villains, cowards, traitors to our state!
Fall to the earth, and pierce the pit of hell,
That legions of tormenting spirits may vex
Your slavish bosoms with continual pains.
I care not, nor the town will never yield
As long as any life is in my breast.

   Enter THERIDAMAS *and* TECHELLES, *with* SOLDIERS.

THER. Thou desperate governor of Babylon,
To save thy life, and us a little labour,
Yield speedily the city to our hands,
Or else be sure thou shalt be forced with pains
More exquisite than ever traitor felt.

GOV. Tyrant, I turn the traitor in thy throat,
And will defend it in despite of thee.
Call up the soldiers to defend these walls.

TECH. Yield, foolish governor; we offer more
Than ever yet we did to such proud slaves
As durst resist us till our third day's siege.
Thou seest us prest to give the last assault,
And that shall bide no more regard of parley.

GOV. Assault and spare not; we will never yield.

                      [*Alarms: and they scale the walls.*
Enter TAMBURLAINE, *drawn in his chariot by the*
Kings of TREBIZON *and* SORIA; AMYRAS, CELEBINUS,
USUMCASANE; ORCANES, *King of Natolia, and the King*
of JERUSALEM, *led by* SOLDIERS; *and others.*

TAMB. The stately buildings of fair Babylon,
Whose lofty pillars, higher than the clouds,
Were wont to guide the seaman in the deep,
Being carried thither by the cannon's force,
Now fill the mouth of Limnasphaltis' lake,
And make a bridge unto the battered walls.
Where Belus, Ninus, and great Alexander
Have rode in triumph, triumphs Tamburlaine,
Whose chariot-wheels have burst the Assyrians' bones,
Drawn with these kings on heaps of carcasses.
Now in the place, where fair Semiramis,
Courted by kings and peers of Asia,
Hath trod the measures, do my soldiers march;
And in the streets, where brave Assyrian dames
Have rid in pomp like rich Saturnia,

With furious words and frowning visages
My horsemen brandish their unruly blades.

Re-enter THERIDAMAS *and* TECHELLES, *bringing in the*
GOVERNOR OF BABYLON

Who have ye there, my lords?

THER. The sturdy governor of Babylon,
That made us all the labour for the town,
And used such slender reckoning of your majesty.

TAMB. Go, bind the villain; he shall hang in chains
Upon the ruins of this conquered town.
Sirrah, the view of our vermilion tents,
Which threatened more than if the region
Next underneath the element of fire
Were full of comets and of blazing stars,
Whose flaming trains should reach down to the earth,
Could not affright you; no, nor I myself,
The wrathful messenger of mighty Jove,
That with his sword hath quailed all earthly kings,
Could not persuade you to submission,
But still the ports were shut: villain, I say,
Should I but touch the rusty gates of hell,
The triple headed Cerberus would howl,
And wake black Jove to crouch and kneel to me;
But I have sent volleys of shot to you.
Yet could not enter till the breach was made.

GOV. Nor, if my body could have stopped the breach,
Shouldst thou have entered, cruel Tamburlaine.
'Tis not thy bloody tents can make me yield,
Nor yet thyself, the anger of the Highest;
For though thy cannon shook the city walls,
My heart did never quake, or courage faint.

TAMB. Well, now I'll make it quake. Go draw him up,
Hang him in chains upon the city walls,
And let my soldiers shoot the slave to death.

GOV. Vile monster, born of some infernal hag,
And sent from hell to tyrannize on earth,
Do all thy worst; nor death nor Tamburlaine,
Torture or pain, can daunt my dreadless mind.

TAMB. Up with him, then! his body shall be scarred.

GOV. But, Tamburlaine, in Limnasphaltis' lake
There lies more gold than Babylon is worth,
Which, when the city was besieged, I hid:
Save but my life, and I will give it thee.

TAMB. Then, for all your valour, you would save your
life?
Whereabout lies it?

GOV. Under a hollow bank, right opposite
Against the western gate of Babylon.

TAMB. Go thither, some of you, and take his gold:
The rest forward with execution.
Away with him hence, let him speak no more.
I think I make your courage something quail.
When this is done, we'll march from Babylon,
And make our greatest haste to Persia.
These jades are broken winded and half-tired;
Unharness them, and let me have fresh horse.
So. Now their best is done to honour me.
Take them and hang them both up presently.

KING OF TREB. Vile tyrant! barbarous bloody Tamburlaine!

TAMB. Take them away, Theridamas; see them des-
patched.

THER. I will, my lord.

[*Exit with the Kings of* TREBIZON *and* SORIA.

TAMB. Come, Asian viceroys; to your tasks awhile,
And take such fortune as your fellows felt.

ORC. First let thy Scythian horse tear both our limbs,
Rather than we should draw thy chariot,

And like base slaves abject our princely minds
To vile and ignominious servitude.

    KING OF JER. Rather lend me thy weapon, Tamburlaine,

That I may sheathe it in this breast of mine.
A thousand deaths could not torment our hearts
More than the thought of this doth vex our souls.

    AMY. They will talk still, my lord, if you do not bridle them.

    TAMB. Bridle them, and let me to my coach.

    [*Attendants bridle* ORCANES, *King of Natolia, and the King of* JERUSALEM, *and harness them to the chariot. The* GOVERNOR OF BABYLON *appears hanging in chains on the walls. Re-enter* THERIDAMAS.

    AMY. See now, my lord, how brave the captain hangs.

    TAMB. 'Tis brave indeed, my boy. Well done!
Shoot first, my lord, and then the rest shall follow.

    THER. Then have at him, to begin withal.

                  [THERIDAMAS *shoots at the* GOVERNOR.

    GOV. Yet save my life, and let this wound appease
The mortal fury of great Tamburlaine!

    TAMB. No, though Asphaltis' lake were liquid gold,
And offered me as ransom for thy life,
Yet shouldst thou die. Shoot at him all at once.

                        [*They shoot.*

So, now he hangs like Bagdet's governor,
Having as many bullets in his flesh
As there be breaches in her battered wall.
Go now, and bind the burghers hand and foot,
And cast them headlong in the city's lake.
Tartars and Persians shall inhabit there;
And to command the city, I will build
A citadel, that all Africa,
Which hath been subject to the Persian king,

Shall pay me tribute for in Babylon.

    TECH. What shall be done with their wives and chil-
       dren, my lord?

    TAMB. Techelles, drown them all, man, woman, and
       child;

Leave not a Babylonian in the town.

    TECH. I will about it straight. Come, soldiers.

                          [Exit with SOLDIERS.

    TAMB. Now, Casane, where's the Turkish Alcoran,

And all the heaps of superstitious books

Found in the temples of that Mahomet

Whom I have thought a god? They shall be burnt.

    USUM. Here they are, my lord.

    TAMB. Well said. Let there be a fire presently.

                              [They light a fire.

In vain, I see, men worship Mahomet.

My sword hath sent millions of Turks to hell,

Slew all his priests, his kinsmen, and his friends,

And yet I live untouched by Mahomet.

There is a God, full of revenging wrath,

From whom the thunder and the lightning breaks,

Whose Scourge I am, and him will I obey.

So, Casane, fling them in the fire.

                           [They burn the books.

Now Mahomet, if thou have any power,

Come down thyself and work a miracle:

Thou art not worthy to be worshipped

That suffers flames of fire to burn the writ

Wherein the sum of thy religion rests.

Why sendest thou not a furious whirlwind down,

To blow thy Alcoran up to thy throne,

Where men report thou sittest by God himself,

Or vengeance on the head of Tamburlaine

That shakes his sword against thy majesty,

And spurns the abstracts of thy foolish laws?

Well, soldiers, Mahomet remains in hell;
He cannot hear the voice of Tamburlaine.
Seek out another godhead to adore,
The God that sits in heaven, if any god;
For he is God alone, and none but he.

    Re-enter TECHELLES.

    TECH. I have fulfilled your highness' will, my lord:
Thousands of men, drowned in Asphaltis' lake,
Have made the water swell above the banks,
And fishes fed by human carcasses,
Amazed, swim up and down upon the waves,
As when they swallow assafoetida,
Which makes them fleet aloft and gasp for air.

    TAMB. Well then, my friendly lords, what now remains,
But that we leave sufficient garrison
And presently depart to Persia,
To triumph after all our victories?

    THER. Aye, good my lord, let us in haste to Persia;
And let this captain be removed the walls
To some high hill about the city here.

    TAMB. Let it be so; about it, soldiers.
But stay; I feel myself distempered suddenly.

    TECH. What is it dares distemper Tamburlaine?

    TAMB. Something, Techelles; but I know not what.
But forth, ye vassals. Whatsoe'er it be,
Sickness or death can never conquer me.   [*Exeunt.*

    [FROM *The Bloody Conquests of Mighty Tamburlaine*, Part II,
iv, 3; v, 1]

Thomas Nashe

THE VENGEANCE OF CUTWOLF

PREPARE your ears and your tears, for never till this thrust I any tragical matter upon you. Strange and wonderful are God's judgments; here shine they in their glory. Chaste Heraclide, thy blood is laid up in heaven's treasury; not one drop of it was lost but lent out to usury: water poured forth sinks down quietly into the earth, but blood spilt on the ground sprinkles up to the firmament. Murder is wide-mouthed, and will not let God rest till he grant revenge. Not only the blood of the slaughtered innocent, but the soul ascendeth to his throne, and there cries out and exclaims for justice and recompense. Guiltless souls that live every hour subject to violence, and with your despairing fears do much impair God's providence: fasten your eyes on this spectacle that will add to your faith. Refer all your oppressions, afflictions, and injuries to the even-balanced eye of the Almighty; he it is that when your patience sleepeth, will be most exceeding mindful of you.

This is but a gloss upon the text; thus Cutwolf begins his insulting oration:

Men and people that have made holy day to behold my pained flesh toil on the wheel, expect not of me a whining penitent slave, that shall do nothing but cry and say his prayers and so be crushed in pieces. My body is little, but my mind is as great as a giant's: the soul which is in me, is the very soul of Julius Caesar by reversion; my name is Cutwolf, neither better nor worse

by occupation, but a poor Cobbler of Verona. Cobblers
are men, and kings are no more. The occasion of my
coming hither at this present, is to have a few of my
bones broken (as we are all born to die) for being the
death of the Emperor of homicides, Esdras of Granada.

About two years since in the streets of Rome he slew
the only and eldest brother I had named Bartoll, in quar-
relling about a courtesan. The news brought to me as I
was sitting in my shop under a stall knocking in of tacks.
I think I raised up my bristles, sold pritch-awl, sponge,
blacking tub, and punching iron, bought me rapier and
pistol, and to go I went. Twenty months together I pursued him, from Rome to Naples, from Naples to Caiete,
passing over the river, from Caiete to Siena, from Siena
to Florence, from Florence to Parma, from Parma to
Pavia, from Pavia to Syon, from Syon to Geneva, from
Geneva back again towards Rome: where in the way it
was my chance to meet him in the nick here at Bologna,
as I will tell you how.

I saw a great fray in the streets as I passed along, and
many swords walking, whereupon drawing nearer, and
inquiring who they were, answer was returned me it
was that notable Bandetto Esdras of Granada. O so I
was tickled in the spleen with that word; my heart
hopped and danced, my elbows itched, my fingers
frisked; I knew not what should become of my feet, nor
knew what I did for joy. The fray parted. I thought it not
convenient to single him out (being a sturdy knave) in
the street, but to stay till I had got him at more advantage. To his lodging I dogged him, lay at the door all
night where he entered, for fear he should give me the
slip any way. Betimes in the morning I rung the bell
and craved to speak with him. Now to his chamber
door I was brought, where knocking, he rose in his shirt
and let me in. And when I was entered, he bade me lock

the door and declare my errand, and so he slipped to bed again.

"Marry, this," quoth I, "is my errand. Thy name is Esdras of Granada, is it not? Most treacherously thou slewest my brother Bartoll about two years ago in the streets of Rome: his death am I come to revenge. In quest of thee ever since above three thousand miles have I travelled. I have begged to maintain me the better part of the way, only because I would intermit no time from my pursuit in going back for money. Now have I got thee naked in my power, die thou shalt, though my mother and my grandmother, dying, did entreat for thee. I have promised the devil thy soul within this hour. Break my word I will not; in thy breast I intend to bury a bullet. Stir not, quinch not, make no noise: for if thou dost it will be worse for thee."

Quoth Esdras, "Whatever thou best at whose mercy I lie spare me, and I will give thee as much gold as thou wilt ask. Put me to any pains, my life reserved, and I willingly will sustain them: cut off my arms and legs, and leave me as a leper to some loathsome hospital, where I may but live a year to pray and repent me. For thy brother's death, the despair of mind that hath ever since haunted me, the guilty gnawing worm of conscience I feel may be sufficient penance. Thou canst not send me to such a hell, as already there is in my heart. To dispatch me presently is no revenge; it will soon be forgotten: let me die a lingering death; it will be remembered a great deal longer. A lingering death may avail my soul, but it is the illest of ills that can befortune my body. For my soul's health I beg my body's torment: be not thou a devil to torment my soul, and send me to eternal damnation. Thy overhanging sword hides heaven from my sight; I dare not look up, lest I embrace my death's wound unawares. I cannot pray to God, and plead to thee both at once. Ay me, already I see my life buried in the wrinkles of thy brows: say but I shall live, though thou meanest to kill me. Nothing confounds like sudden terror; it thrusts every sense out of office. Poison wrapped up in sugared pills is but half a poison: the fear of death's looks is more terrible than his stroke. The while I view death, my faith is deadened: where a man's fear is, there his heart is. Fear never engenders hope: how can I hope that heaven's father will save me from the hell everlasting, when he gives me over to the hell of thy fury.

"Heraclide now think I on thy tears sown in the dust (thy tears, that my bloody mind made barren). In revenge of thee, God hardens this man's heart against me: yet I did not slaughter thee, though hundreds else my hand hath brought to the shambles. Gentle sir, learn of me what it is to clog your conscience with murder, to have your dreams, your sleep, your solitary walks troubled and disquieted with murder: your shadow by day will affright you; you will not see a weapon unsheathed, but immediately you will imagine it is predestinate for your destruction.

"This murder is a house divided within itself: it suborns a man's own soul to inform against him. His soul (being his accuser) brings forth his two eyes as witnesses against him, and the least eye witness is irrefutable. Pluck out my eyes if thou wilt, and deprive my treacherous soul of her two best witnesses. Dig out my blasphemous tongue with thy dagger; both tongue and eyes will I gladly forgo to have a little more time to think on my journey to heaven.

"Defer but a while thy resolution. I am not at peace with the world, for even but yesterday I fought, and in my fury threatened further vengeance: had I a face to ask forgiveness, I should think half my sins were forgiven. A hundred devils haunt me daily for my horrible murders: the devils when I die will be loth to go to hell with me, for they desired of Christ he would not send them to hell before their time: if they go not to hell, into thee they will go, and hideously vex thee for turning them out of their habitation. Wounds I contemn, life I prize light; it is another world's tranquillity which makes me so timorous: everlasting damnation, everlasting howling and lamentation. It is not from death I request thee to deliver me, but from this terror of torment's eternity. Thy brother's body I only pierced unadvisedly; his soul meant I no harm to at all: my body and soul both shalt thou cast away quite, if thou dost at this moment what thou mayest. Spare me, spare me I beseech thee; by thy own soul's salvation I desire thee, seek not my soul's utter perdition: in destroying me, thou destroyest thyself and me."

Eagerly I replied after this long suppliant oration, "Though I know God will never have mercy on me except I have mercy on thee, yet of thee no mercy would I have. Revenge in our tragedies is continually raised from hell: of hell do I esteem better than heaven, if it afford me revenge. There is no heaven but revenge. I tell thee, I would not have undertook so much toil to gain heaven, as I have done in pursuing thee for revenge. Divine revenge, of which (as of the joys above) there is no fulness or satiety. Look how my feet are blistered with following thee from place to place. I have riven my throat with overstraining it to curse thee. I have ground my teeth to powder with grating and grinding them together for anger when any hath named thee. My tongue with vain threats is blown and waxen too big for

my mouth: my eyes have broken their strings with star-
ing and looking ghastly, as I stood devising how to
frame or set my countenance when I met thee. I have
near spent my strength in imaginary acting on stone
walls, what I determined to execute on thee. Entreat
not, a miracle may not reprieve thee: villain, thus march
I with my blade into thy bowels.

"Stay, stay," exclaimed Esdras, "and hear me but one
word further. Though neither for God nor man thou
carest, but placest thy whole felicity in murder, yet of
thy felicity learn how to make a greater felicity. Respite
me a little from thy sword's point, and set me about
some execrable enterprise, that may subvert the whole
state of Christendom, and make all men's ears tingle
that hear of it. Command me to cut all my kindred's
throats, to burn men, women and children in their beds
in millions, by firing their Cities at midnight. Be it Pope,
Emperor or Turk that displeaseth thee, he shall not
breathe on the earth. For thy sake will I swear and forswear, renounce my baptism, and all interest I have in
any other sacrament; only let me live, how miserable
soever—be it in a dungeon amongst toads, serpents, and
adders, or set up to the neck in dung. No pains I will
refuse however prolonged, to have a little respite to pu-
rify my spirit: oh, hear me, hear me, and thou canst not
be hardened against me."

At this his importunity, I paused a little, not as re-
tiring from my wreakful resolution, but going back to
gather more forces of vengeance, with myself I devised
how to plague him double in his base mind: my thoughts
travelled in quest of some notable new Italianism, whose
murderous platform might not only extend on his body,
but his soul also. The ground work of it was this: that
whereas he had promised for my sake to swear and

forswear and commit Julian-like violence on the highest seals of religion: if he would but this far satisfy me, he should be dismissed from my fury. First and foremost he should renounce God and his laws, and utterly disclaim the whole title or interest he had in any covenant of salvation. Next he should curse him to his face, as Job was willed by his wife, and write an absolute firm obligation of his soul to the devil, without condition or exception. Thirdly and lastly (having done this), he should pray to God fervently never to have mercy upon him, or pardon him.

Scarce had I propounded these articles unto him, but he was beginning his blasphemous abjurations. I wonder the earth opened not and swallowed us both, hearing the bold terms he blasted forth in contempt of Christianity: heaven hath thundered when half less contumelies against it hath been uttered. Able they were to raise Saints and martyrs from their graves, and pluck Christ himself from the right hand of his father. My joints trembled and quaked with attending them; my hair stood upright and my heart was turned wholly to fire. So affectionately and zealously did he give himself over to infidelity, as if Satan had gotten the upper hand of our High Maker. The vein in his left hand that is derived from the heart with no faint blow he pierced, and with the full blood that flowed from it, writ a full obligation of his soul to the devil: yea, he more earnestly prayed unto God never to forgive his soul than many Christians do to save their souls.

These fearful ceremonies brought to an end, I bade him open his mouth and gape wide. He did so (as what will not slaves do for fear?); therewith made I no more ado, but shot him full into the throat with my pistol. No more spake he after; so did I shoot him that he might never speak after or repent him. His body being dead looked as black as a toad: the devil presently branded it for his own.

This is the fault that hath called me hither; no true Italian but will honour me for it. Revenge is the glory of arms, and the highest performance of valour; revenge is whatsoever we call law or justice. The farther we wade in revenge, the nearer come we to the throne of the Almighty. To his scepter it is properly ascribed; his scepter he lends unto man, when he lets one man scourge another. All true Italians imitate me in revenging constantly and dying valiantly. Hangman, to thy task, for I am ready for the utmost of thy rigor.

Here withal the people (outrageously incensed) with one conjoined outcry, yelled mainly, "Away with him, away with him. Executioner, torture him, tear him, or we will tear thee in pieces if thou spare him."

The executioner needed no exhortation hereunto, for of his own nature was he hackster good enough: old excellent he was at a bone-ache. At the first chop with his wood-knife would he fish for a man's heart, and fetch it out as easily as a plum from the bottom of a porridge pot. He would crack necks as fast as a cook cracks eggs: a fiddler cannot turn his pin so soon as he would turn a man off the ladder: bravely did he drum on this Cutwolf's bones, not breaking them outright, but like a saddler knocking in of tacks, jarring on them quaveringly with his hammer a great while together. No joint about him, but with a hatchet he had for the nonce he disjointed half, and then with boiling lead soldered up the wounds from bleeding: his tongue he pulled out, lest he should blaspheme in his torment: venomous stinging worms he thrust into his ears to keep his head ravingly occupied: with cankers scruzed to pieces he rubbed his mouth and his gums: no limb of his but was lingeringly splintered in shivers.

In this horror left they him on the wheel as in hell: where yet living he might behold in the book of our destinies, one murder begetteth another: was never yet bloodshed barren from the beginning of the world to this day.

[FROM *The Unfortunate Traveller*]

III. The Lure of Magic

Christopher Marlowe

THE TRAGICAL HISTORY OF DOCTOR FAUSTUS

DRAMATIS PERSONAE

The Pope.
Cardinal of Lorraine.
The Emperor of Germany.
Duke of Vanholt.
Faustus.
Valdes,
Cornelius, } friends to Faustus.
Wagner, servant to Faustus.
Clown.
Robin.
Ralph.
Vintner.
Horse-Courser.
A Knight.
An Old Man.
Scholars, Friars, and Attendants.
Duchess of Vanholt.

LUCIFER.

BELZEBUB.

MEPHISTOPHILIS.

GOOD ANGEL.

EVIL ANGEL.

THE SEVEN DEADLY SINS.

DEVILS.

Spirits in the shapes of ALEXANDER THE GREAT, of HIS
    PARAMOUR, and of HELEN.

CHORUS.

Enter CHORUS

   CHORUS. Not marching now in fields of Thrasimene,
Where Mars did mate the Carthaginians;
Nor sporting in the dalliance of love;
In courts of kings where state is overturn'd;
Nor in the pomp of proud audacious deeds,
Intends our Muse to vaunt his heavenly verse:
Only this, gentlemen—we must perform
The form of Faustus' fortunes, good or bad:
To patient judgements we appeal our plaud,
And speak for Faustus in his infancy.
Now is he born, his parents base of stock,
In Germany, within a town call'd Rhodes:
Of riper years, to Wittenberg he went,
Whereas his kinsmen chiefly brought him up.
So soon he profits in divinity,
The fruitful plot of scholarism grac'd,
That shortly he was grac'd with doctor's name,
Excelling all whose sweet delight disputes
In heavenly matters of theology;
Till swoln with cunning, of a self-conceit,
His waxen wings did mount above his reach,
And, melting, heavens conspir'd his overthrow;
For, falling to a devilish exercise,
And glutted now with learning's golden gifts,

He surfeits upon cursèd necromancy;
Nothing so sweet as magic is to him,
Which he prefers before his chiefest bliss:
And this the man that in his study sits.   [*Exit.*

SCENE I. FAUSTUS' STUDY

FAUSTUS *discovered.*

FAUSTUS. Settle thy studies, Faustus, and begin
To sound the depth of that thou wilt profess:
Having commenc'd, be a divine in show,
Yet level at the end of every art,
And live and die in Aristotle's works.
Sweet Analytics, 'tis thou hast ravish'd me!
Bene disserere est finis logices.
Is, to dispute well, logic's chiefest end?
Affords this art no greater miracle?
Then read no more; thou hast attain'd that end.
A greater subject fitteth Faustus' wit:
Bid economy farewell, and Galen come,
Seeing, *Ubi desinit philosophus, ibi incipit medicus:*
Be a physician, Faustus; heap up gold,
And be etèrniz'd for some wondrous cure!
Summum bonum medicinae sanitas:
The end of physic is our body's health.
Why, Faustus, hast thou not attain'd that end?
Is not thy common talk found aphorisms?
Are not thy bills hung up as monuments,
Whereby whole cities have escap'd the plague,
And thousand desp'rate maladies been eas'd?
Yet art thou still but Faustus, and a man.
Couldst thou make men to live eternally,
Or, being dead, raise them to life again,
Then this profession were to be esteem'd.
Physic, farewell! Where is Justinian?   [*Reads.*

*Si una eademque res legatur duobus, alter rem, alter
    valorem rei, &c.*

A pretty case of paltry legacies!   [*Reads.*

Exhaereditare filium non potest pater, nisi, &c.

Such is the subject of the institute.

And universal body of the law:

His study fits a mercenary drudge,

Who aims at nothing but external trash;

Too servile and illiberal for me.

When all is done, divinity is best:

Jerome's Bible, Faustus; view it well.   [*Reads.*

Stipendium peccati mors est. Ha! *Stipendium, &c.*

The reward of sin is death: that's hard.   [*Reads.*

*Si peccasse negamus, fallimur, et nulla est in nobis
    veritas:*

If we say that we have no sin, we deceive ourselves,
    and there's no truth in us.

Why, then, belike we must sin, and so consequently die:

Aye, we must die an everlasting death.

What doctrine call you this, *Che, sera, sera:*

What will be, shall be? Divinity, adieu!

These metaphysics of magicians,

And necromantic books are heavenly;

Lines, circles, scenes, letters, and characters;

Aye, these are those that Faustus most desires.

O, what a world of profit and delight,

Of power, of honour, of omnipotence,

Is promis'd to the studious artizan!

All things that move between the quiet poles

Shall be at my command: emperors and kings

Are but obeyèd in their several provinces,

Nor can they raise the wind, or rend the clouds;

But his dominion that exceeds in this,

Stretcheth as far as doth the mind of man;

A sound magician is a mighty god:

Here, Faustus, tire thy brains to gain a deity!

Enter WAGNER.

Wagner, commend me to my dearest friends,
The German Valdes and Cornelius;
Request them earnestly to visit me.

   WAGNER. I will, sir.   [*Exit.*

   FAUSTUS. Their conference will be a greater help to
    me
Than all my labours, plod I ne'er so fast.

   Enter GOOD ANGEL *and* EVIL ANGEL.

   GOOD ANGEL. O, Faustus, lay that damnèd book aside,
And gaze not on it, lest it tempt thy soul,
And heap God's heavy wrath upon thy head!
Read, read the Scriptures—that is blasphemy.

   EVIL ANGEL. Go forward, Faustus, in that famous art
Wherein all Nature's treasure is contain'd:
Be thou on earth as Jove is in the sky,
Lord and commander of these elements. [*Exeunt* Angels.

   FAUSTUS. How am I glutted with conceit of this!
Shall I make spirits fetch me what I please,
Resolve me of all ambiguities,
Perform what desperate enterprise I will?
I'll have them fly to India for gold,
Ransack the ocean for orient pearl,
And search all corners of the new-found world
For pleasant fruits and princely delicates;
I'll have them read me strange philosophy,
And tell the secrets of all foreign kings;
I'll have them wall all Germany with brass,
And make swift Rhine circle fair Wittenberg;
I'll have them fill the public schools with silk,
Wherewith the students shall be bravely clad;
I'll levy soldiers with the coin they bring,
And chase the Prince of Parma from our land,
And reign sole king of all our provinces;

Yea, stranger engines for the brunt of war,
Than was the fiery keel at Antwerp's bridge,
I'll make my servile spirits to invent.

          Enter VALDES *and* CORNELIUS.

Come, German Valdes, and Cornelius,
And make me blest with your sage conference!
Valdes, sweet Valdes, and Cornelius,
Know that your words have won me at the last
To practise magic and concealèd arts:
Yet not your words only, but mine own fantasy,
That will receive no object; for my head
But ruminates on necromantic skill.
Philosophy is odious and obscure;
Both law and physic are for petty wits;
Divinity is basest of the three,
Unpleasant, harsh, contemptible, and vile:
'Tis magic, magic, that hath ravish'd me.
Then, gentle friends, aid me in this attempt;
And I, that have with concise syllogisms
Gravell'd the pastors of the German church,
And made the flowering pride of Wittenberg
Swarm to my problems, as the infernal spirits
On sweet Musaeus when he came to hell,
Will be as cunning as Agrippa was,
Whose shadows made all Europe honour him.

    VALDES. Faustus, these books, thy wit, and our ex-
        perience,
Shall make all nations to canonize us.
As Indian Moors obey their Spanish lords,
So shall the subjects of every element
Be always serviceable to us three;
Like lions shall they guard us when we please;
Like Almain rutters with their horsemen's staves,
Or Lapland giants, trotting by our sides;
Sometimes like women, or unwedded maids,

Shadowing more beauty in their airy brows
Than have the white breasts of the queen of love:
From Venice shall they drag huge argosies,
And from America the golden fleece
That yearly stuffs old Philip's treasury;
If learnèd Faustus will be resolute.

FAUSTUS. Valdes, as resolute am I in this
As thou to live: therefore object it not.

CORNELIUS. The miracles that magic will perform
Will make thee vow to study nothing else.
He that is grounded in astrology,
Enrich'd with tongues, well seen in minerals,
Hath all the principles magic doth require:
Then doubt not, Faustus, but to be renown'd,
And more frequented for this mystery
Than heretofore the Delphian oracle.
The spirits tell me they can dry the sea,
And fetch the treasure of all foreign wrecks,
Aye, all the wealth that our forefathers hid
Within the massy entrails of the earth:
Then tell me, Faustus, what shall we three want?

FAUSTUS. Nothing, Cornelius. O, this cheers my soul!
Come, show me some demonstrations magical,
That I may conjure in some lusty grove,
And have these joys in full possession.

VALDES. Then haste thee to some solitary grove,
And bear wise Bacon's and Albanus' works,
The Hebrew Psalter, and New Testament;
And whatsoever else is requisite
We will inform thee ere our conference cease.

CORNELIUS. Valdes, first let him know the words of
    art;
And then, all other ceremonies learn'd,
Faustus may try his cunning by himself.

VALDES. First I'll instruct thee in the rudiments,

And then wilt thou be perfecter than I.

FAUSTUS. Then come and dine with me, and, after meat,
We'll canvass every quiddity thereof;
For, ere I sleep, I'll try what I can do:
This night I'll conjure, though I die therefore.

[*Exeunt.*

SCENE II. BEFORE FAUSTUS' HOUSE

Enter TWO SCHOLARS.

FIRST SCHOLAR. I wonder what's become of Faustus, that was wont to make our schools ring with *sic probo*.

SECOND SCHOLAR. That shall we know; for see, here comes his boy.

Enter WAGNER.

FIRST SCHOLAR. How now, sirrah! where's thy master?

WAGNER. God in heaven knows.

SECOND SCHOLAR. Why, dost not thou know?

WAGNER. Yes, I know; but that follows not.

FIRST SCHOLAR. Go to, sirrah! leave your jesting, and tell us where he is.

WAGNER. That follows not necessary by force of argument, that you, being licentiate, should stand upon 't: therefore acknowledge your error, and be attentive.

SECOND SCHOLAR. Why, didst thou not say thou knewest?

WAGNER. Have you any witness on 't?

FIRST SCHOLAR. Yes, sirrah, I heard you.

WAGNER. Ask my fellow if I be a thief.

SECOND SCHOLAR. Well, you will not tell us?

WAGNER. Yes, sir, I will tell you: yet, if you were not dunces, you would never ask me such a question; for is not he *corpus naturale?* and is not that *mobile?* then wherefore should you ask me such a question? But that

I am by nature phlegmatic, slow to wrath, it were not
for you to come within forty foot of the place of execution, although I do not doubt to see you both hanged the
next sessions. Thus having triumphed over you, I will
set my countenance like a precisian, and begin to speak
thus: Truly, my dear brethren, my master is within at
dinner, with Valdes and Cornelius, as this wine, if it
could speak, it would inform your worships: and so, the
Lord bless you, preserve you, and keep you, my dear
brethren, my dear brethren!   [*Exit.*

FIRST SCHOLAR. Nay, then, I fear he is fallen into that
damned art for which they two are infamous through the
world.

SECOND SCHOLAR. Were he a stranger, and not allied
to me, yet should I grieve for him. But, come, let us go
and inform the Rector, and see if he by his grave counsel
can reclaim him.

FIRST SCHOLAR. O, but I fear me nothing can reclaim
him!

SECOND SCHOLAR. Yet let us try what we can do.
                                              [*Exeunt.*

SCENE III. A GROVE

Enter FAUSTUS *to conjure.*

FAUSTUS. Now that the gloomy shadow of the earth,
Longing to view Orion's drizzling look,
Leaps from th' antarctic world unto the sky,
And dims the welkin with her pitchy breath,
Faustus, begin thine incantations,
And try if devils will obey thy hest,
Seeing thou hast pray'd and sacrific'd to them.
Within this circle is Jehovah's name,
Forward and backward anagrammatiz'd,
The breviated names of holy saints,

Figures of every adjunct to the heavens,
And characters of signs and erring stars,
By which the spirits are enforc'd to rise:
Then fear not, Faustus, but be resolute,
And try the uttermost magic can perform.

*Sint mihi dei Acherontis propitii! Valeat numen triplex
Jehovae! Ignei, aerii, aquatani spiritus, salvete! Orientis
princeps Belzebub, inferni ardentis monarcha, et Demo-
gorgon, propitiamus vos, ut appareat et surgat Mephistophilis, quod tumeraris: per Jehovam, Gehennam, et
consecratam aquam quam nunc spargo, signumque, signumque crucis quod nunc facio, et per vota nostra, ipse
nunc surgat nobis dicatus Mephistophilis!*

Enter MEPHISTOPHILIS.

I charge thee to return, and change thy shape;
Thou art too ugly to attend on me:
Go, and return an old Franciscan friar;
That holy shape becomes a devil best.

[Exit MEPHISTOPHILIS.

I see there's virtue in my heavenly words:
Who would not be proficient in this art?
How pliant is this Mephistophilis,
Full of obedience and humility!
Such is the force of magic and my spells:
No, Faustus, thou art conjuror laureat,
That canst command great Mephistophilis:
Quin regis Mephistophilis fratris imagine.

Re-enter MEPHISTOPHILIS like a Franciscan friar.

MEPHISTOPHILIS. Now, Faustus, what wouldst thou
  have me do?

FAUSTUS. I charge thee wait upon me whilst I live,
To do whatever Faustus shall command,
Be it to make the moon drop from her sphere,
Or th' ocean to overwhelm the world.

MEPHISTOPHILIS. I am a servant to great Lucifer,

And may not follow thee without his leave:
No more than he commands must we perform.

    FAUSTUS. Did not he charge thee to appear to me?

    MEPHISTOPHILIS. No, I came hither of mine own
      accord.

    FAUSTUS. Did not my conjuring speeches raise thee?
    speak.

    MEPHISTOPHILIS. That was the cause, but yet *per
      accidens;*

For, when we hear one rack the name of God,
Abjure the Scriptures and his Saviour Christ,
We fly, in hope to get his glorious soul;
Nor will we come, unless he use such means
Whereby he is in danger to be damn'd.
Therefore the shortest cut for conjuring
Is stoutly to abjure the Trinity,
And pray devoutly to the prince of hell.

    FAUSTUS. So Faustus hath
Already done; and holds this principle,
There is no chief but only Belzebub;
To whom Faustus doth dedicate himself.
This word 'damnation' terrifies him not,
For he confounds hell in Elysium:
His ghost be with the old philosophers!
But, leaving these vain trifles of men's souls,
Tell me what is that Lucifer thy lord?

    MEPHISTOPHILIS. Arch-regent and commander of all
      spirits.

    FAUSTUS. Was not that Lucifer an angel once?

    MEPHISTOPHILIS. Yes, Faustus, and most dearly lov'd
      of God.

    FAUSTUS. How comes it, then, that he is prince of
      devils?

    MEPHISTOPHILIS. O, by aspiring pride and insolence;
For which God threw him from the face of heaven.

FAUSTUS. And what are you that live with Lucifer?

MEPHISTOPHILIS. Unhappy spirits that fell with Lucifer,

Conspir'd against our God with Lucifer,

And are for ever damn'd with Lucifer.

FAUSTUS. Where are you damn'd?

MEPHISTOPHILIS. In hell.

FAUSTUS. How comes it, then, that thou art out of hell?

MEPHISTOPHILIS. Why, this is hell, nor am I out of it:

Think'st thou that I, who saw the face of God,

And tasted the eternal joys of heaven,

Am not tormented with ten thousand hells,

In being depriv'd of everlasting bliss?

O, Faustus, leave these frivolous demands,

Which strike a terror to my fainting soul!

FAUSTUS. What, is great Mephistophilis so passionate

For being deprivèd of the joys of heaven?

Learn thou of Faustus manly fortitude,

And scorn those joys thou never shalt possess.

Go bear these tidings to great Lucifer:

Seeing Faustus hath incurr'd eternal death

By desp'rate thoughts against Jove's deity,

Say, he surrenders up to him his soul,

So he will spare him four and twenty years,

Letting him live in all voluptuousness;

Having thee ever to attend on me,

To give me whatsoever I shall ask,

To tell me whatsoever I demand,

To slay mine enemies, and aid my friends,

And always be obedient to my will.

Go and return to mighty Lucifer,

And meet me in my study at midnight,

And then resolve me of thy master's mind.

MEPHISTOPHILIS. I will, Faustus.   [*Exit.*

FAUSTUS. Had I as many souls as there be stars,
I'd give them all for Mephistophilis.
By him I'll be great emp'ror of the world,
And make a bridge thorough the moving air,
To pass the ocean with a band of men;
I'll join the hills that bind the Afric shore,
And make that country continent to Spain,
And both contributory to my crown:
The Emp'ror shall not live but by my leave,
Nor any potentate of Germany.
Now that I have obtain'd what I desir'd,
I'll live in speculation of this art,
Till Mephistophilis return again.

SCENE IV. A STREET

Enter WAGNER *and* CLOWN

WAGNER. Sirrah boy, come hither.

CLOWN. How, boy! swowns, boy! I hope you have
seen many boys with such pickadevaunts as I have: boy,
quotha!

WAGNER. Tell me, sirrah, hast thou any comings in?

CLOWN. Aye, and goings out too. You may see else.

WAGNER. Alas, poor slave! see how poverty jesteth
in his nakedness! the villain is bare and out of service,
and so hungry, that I know he would give his soul to the
devil for a shoulder of mutton, though it were blood-
raw.

CLOWN. How! my soul to the devil for a shoulder of
mutton, though 'twere blood-raw! not so, good friend:
by'r lady, I had need have it well roasted, and good
sauce to it, if I pay so dear.

WAGNER. Well, wilt thou serve me, and I'll make thee
go like *Qui mihi discipulus?*

CLOWN. How, in verse?

WAGNER. No, sirrah; in beaten silk and staves-acre.

CLOWN. How, how, knaves-acre! aye, I thought that was all the land his father left him. Do ye hear? I would be sorry to rob you of your living.

WAGNER. Sirrah, I say in staves-acre.

CLOWN. Oho, oho, staves-acre! why, then, belike, if I were your man, I should be full of vermin.

WAGNER. So thou shalt, whether thou beest with me or no. But, sirrah, leave your jesting, and bind yourself presently unto me for seven years, or I'll turn all the lice about thee into familiars, and they shall tear thee in pieces.

CLOWN. Do you hear, sir? You may save that labour; they are too familiar with me already: swowns, they are as bold with my flesh as if they had paid for my meat and drink.

WAGNER. Well, do you hear, sirrah? hold, take these guilders.   [*Gives money.*

CLOWN. Gridirons, what be they?

WAGNER. Why, French crowns.

CLOWN. Mass, but for the name of French crowns, a man were as good have as many English counters. And what should I do with these?

WAGNER. Why, now, sirrah, thou art at an hour's warning, whensoever and wheresoever the devil shall fetch thee.

CLOWN. No, no; here, take your gridirons again.

WAGNER. Truly, I'll none of them.

CLOWN. Truly, but you shall.

WAGNER. Bear witness I gave them him.

CLOWN. Bear witness I give them you again.

WAGNER. Well, I will cause two devils presently to fetch thee away—Baliol and Belcher!

CLOWN. Let your Balio and your Belcher come here, and I'll knock them, they were never so knocked since they were devils: say I should kill one of them, what would folks say? "Do ye see yonder tall fellow in the round slop? he has killed the devil." So I should be called Kill-devil all the parish over.

Enter two DEVILS; *and the* CLOWN *runs up and down crying.*

WAGNER. Baliol and Belcher—spirits, away!

[*Exeunt* DEVILS.

CLOWN. What, are they gone? a vengeance on them! they have vile long nails. There was a he-devil and a she-devil: I'll tell you how you shall know them; all he-devils has horns, and all she-devils has cloven feet.

WAGNER. Well, sirrah, follow me.

CLOWN. But, do you hear? if I should serve you, would you teach me to raise up Banios and Belcheos?

WAGNER. I will teach thee to turn thyself to any thing, to a dog, or a cat, or a mouse, or a rat, or any thing.

CLOWN. How! a Christian fellow to a dog, or a cat, a mouse, or a rat! no, no, sir; if you turn me into any thing, let it be into the likeness of a little pretty frisking flea, that I may be here and there and everywhere.

WAGNER. Well, sirrah, come.

CLOWN. But, do you hear, Wagner?

WAGNER. How—Baliol and Belcher!

CLOWN. O Lord, I pray, sir, let Banio and Belcher go sleep.

WAGNER. Villain, call me Master Wagner, and let thy left eye be diametarily fixed upon my right heel, with *quasi vestigias nostras insistere.* [*Exit.*

CLOWN. God forgive me, he speaks Dutch fustian. Well, I'll follow him; I'll serve him, that's flat. [*Exit.*

SCENE V. FAUSTUS' STUDY

FAUSTUS *discovered.*

FAUSTUS. Now, Faustus, must
Thou needs be damn'd, and canst thou not be sav'd:
What boots it, then, to think of God or heaven?
Away with such vain fancies, and despair;
Despair in God, and trust in Belzebub:
Now go not backward; no, Faustus, be resolute:
Why waver'st thou? O, something soundeth in mine
    ears,
"Abjure this magic, turn to God again!"
Aye, and Faustus will turn to God again.
To God? he loves thee not;
The god thou serv'st is thine own appetite,
Wherein is fix'd the love of Belzebub:
To him I'll build an altar and a church,
And offer lukewarm blood of new-born babes.

Enter GOOD ANGEL *and* EVIL ANGEL.

GOOD ANGEL. Sweet Faustus, leave that execrable art.

FAUSTUS. Contrition, prayer, repentance—what of
    them?

GOOD ANGEL. O, they are means to bring thee unto
    heaven!

EVIL ANGEL. Rather illusions, fruits of lunacy,
That makes men foolish that do trust them most.

GOOD ANGEL. Sweet Faustus, think of heaven and
    heavenly things.

EVIL ANGEL. No, Faustus; think of honour and of
    wealth.   [*Exeunt* ANGELS.

FAUSTUS. Of wealth!
Why, the signiory of Emden shall be mine.
When Mephistophilis shall stand by me,
What god can hurt thee, Faustus? thou art safe:

Cast no more doubts. Come, Mephistophilis,
And bring glad tidings from great Lucifer—
    Is 't not midnight?—come, Mephistophilis,
Veni, veni, Mephistophile!

                    Enter MEPHISTOPHILIS.

Now tell me what says Lucifer, thy lord?
    MEPHISTOPHILIS. That I shall wait on Faustus while
        he lives,
So he will buy my service with his soul.
    FAUSTUS. Already Faustus hath hazarded that for
        thee.
    MEPHISTOPHILIS. But, Faustus, thou must bequeath
        it solemnly,
And write a deed of gift with thine own blood;
For that security craves great Lucifer.
If thou deny it, I will back to hell.
    FAUSTUS. Stay, Mephistophilis, and tell me, what
        good
Will my soul do thy lord?
    MEPHISTOPHILIS. Enlarge his kingdom.
    FAUSTUS. Is that the reason why he tempts us thus?
    MEPHISTOPHILIS. *Solamen miseris socios habuisse*
        doloris.
    FAUSTUS. Why, have you any pain that torture others?
    MEPHISTOPHILIS. As great as have the human souls
        of men.
But tell me, Faustus, shall I have thy soul?
And I will be thy slave, and wait on thee,
And give thee more than thou hast wit to ask.
    FAUSTUS. Aye, Mephistophilis, I give it thee.
    MEPHISTOPHILIS. Then, Faustus, stab thine arm cou-
        rageously,
And bind thy soul, that at some certain day
Great Lucifer may claim it as his own;
And then be thou as great as Lucifer.

FAUSTUS. [*Stabbing his arm*] Lo, Mephistophilis, for
   love of thee,
I cut mine arm, and with my proper blood
Assure my soul to be great Lucifer's,
Chief lord and regent of perpetual night!
View here the blood that trickles from mine arm,
And let it be propitious for my wish.

MEPHISTOPHILIS. But, Faustus, thou must
Write it in manner of a deed of gift.

FAUSTUS. Aye, so I will [*Writes*]. But, Mephistophilis,
My blood congeals, and I can write no more.

MEPHISTOPHILIS. I'll fetch thee fire to dissolve it
   straight.   [*Exit.*

FAUSTUS. What might the staying of my blood por-
   tend?
Is it unwilling I should write this bill?
Why streams it not, that I may write afresh?
Faustus gives to thee his soul: ah, there it stay'd!
Why shouldst thou not? is not thy soul thine own?
Then write again, *Faustus gives to thee his soul.*
   Re-enter MEPHISTOPHILIS *with a chafer of coals.*

MEPHISTOPHILIS. Here's fire; come, Faustus, set it on.

FAUSTUS. So, now the blood begins to clear again;
Now will I make an end immediately.   [*Writes.*

MEPHISTOPHILIS. O, what will not I do to obtain his
   soul?   [*Aside.*

FAUSTUS. *Consummatum est;* this bill is ended,
And Faustus hath bequeath'd his soul to Lucifer.
But what is this inscription on mine arm?
Homo, fuge: whither should I fly?
If unto God, he'll throw me down to hell.
My senses are deceiv'd; here's nothing writ—
I see it plain; here in this place is writ,
Homo, fuge: yet shall not Faustus fly.

MEPHISTOPHILIS. I'll fetch him somewhat to delight
   his mind.   [*Aside, and then exit.*

Re-enter MEPHISTOPHILIS *with* DEVILS, *who give crowns
and rich apparel to* FAUSTUS, *dance, and then depart.*

   FAUSTUS. Speak, Mephistophilis, what means this
   show?

   MEPHISTOPHILIS. Nothing, Faustus, but to delight thy
   mind withal,

And to show thee what magic can perform.

   FAUSTUS. But may I raise up spirits when I please?

   MEPHISTOPHILIS. Aye, Faustus, and do greater things
   than these.

   FAUSTUS. Then there's enough for a thousand souls.

Here, Mephistophilis, receive this scroll,

A deed of gift of body and of soul:

But yet conditionally that thou perform

All articles prescrib'd between us both.

   MEPHISTOPHILIS. Faustus, I swear by hell and Lucifer

To effect all promises between us made!

   FAUSTUS. Then hear me read them.   [*Reads*]

*On these conditions following. First, that Faustus may
be a spirit in form and substance. Secondly, that
Mephistophilis shall be his servant, and at his command.
Thirdly, that Mephistophilis shall do for him, and bring
him whatsoever [he desires]. Fourthly, that he shall be
in his chamb?r or house invisible. Lastly, that he shall
appear to the said John Faustus, at all times, in what
form or shape soever he please. I, John Faustus, of Wittenberg, Doctor, by these presents, do give both body
and soul to Lucifer prince of the east, and his minister
Mephistophilis; and furthermore grant unto them that,
twenty-four years being expired, the articles above written inviolate, full power to fetch or carry the said John
Faustus, body and soul, flesh, blood, or goods, into their
habitation wheresoever. By me,* JOHN FAUSTUS.

MEPHISTOPHILIS. Speak, Faustus, do you deliver this
     as your deed?

FAUSTUS. Aye, take it, and the devil give thee good
     on 't.

MEPHISTOPHILIS. Now, Faustus, ask what thou wilt.

FAUSTUS. First will I question with thee about hell.
Tell me, where is the place that men call hell?

MEPHISTOPHILIS. Under the heavens.

FAUSTUS.   Aye, but whereabout?

MEPHISTOPHILIS. Within the bowels of these ele-
     ments,
Where we are tortur'd and remain for ever:
Hell hath no limits, nor is circumscrib'd
In one self place; for where we are is hell,
And where hell is, there must we ever be:
And, to conclude, when all the world dissolves,
And every creature shall be purified,
All places shall be hell that are not heaven.

FAUSTUS. Come, I think hell's a fable.

MEPHISTOPHILIS. Aye, think so still, till experience
     change thy mind.

FAUSTUS. Why, think'st thou, then, that Faustus shall
     be damn'd?

MEPHISTOPHILIS. Aye, of necessity, for here's the
     scroll
Wherein thou has given thy soul to Lucifer.

FAUSTUS. Aye, and body too: but what of that?
Think'st thou that Faustus is so fond to imagine
That, after this life, there is any pain?
Tush, these are trifles and mere old wives' tales.

MEPHISTOPHILIS. But, Faustus, I am an instance to
     prove the contrary;
For I am damnèd, and am now in hell.

FAUSTUS. How! now in hell!
Nay, an this be hell, I'll willingly be damn'd here:

What! walking, disputing, &c.
But, leaving off this, let me have a wife,
The fairest maid in Germany.

 MEPHISTOPHILIS.   How! a wife!
I pritheee, Faustus, talk not of a wife.

 FAUSTUS. Nay, sweet Mephistophilis, fetch me one;
for I will have one.

 MEPHISTOPHILIS. Well, thou wilt have one? Sit there
  till I come:
I'll fetch thee a wife in the devil's name.   [*Exit.*

 Re-enter MEPHISTOPHILIS *with a* DEVIL *drest like a*
    Woman, *with fireworks.*

 MEPHISTOPHILIS. Tell me, Faustus, how dost thou
like thy wife?

 FAUSTUS. A plague on her!

 MEPHISTOPHILIS. Tut, Faustus,
Marriage is but a ceremonial toy;
If thou lovest me, think no more of it.
She whom thine eye shall like, thy heart shall have,
Be she as chaste as was Penelope,
As wise as Saba, or as beautiful
As was bright Lucifer before his fall.
Hold, take this book, peruse it thoroughly:
          [*Gives book.*

The iterating of these lines brings gold;
The framing of this circle on the ground
Brings whirlwinds, tempests, thunder, and lightning;
Pronounce this thrice devoutly to thyself,
And men in armour shall appear to thee,
Ready to execute what thou desir'st.

 FAUSTUS. Thanks, Mephistophilis; yet fain would I
have a book wherein I might behold all spells and incantations, that I might raise up spirits when I please.

 MEPHISTOPHILIS. Here they are in this book.
          [*Turns to them.*

FAUSTUS. Now would I have a book where I might see all characters and planets of the heavens, that I might know their motions and dispositions.

MEPHISTOPHILIS. Here they are too. [*Turns to them.*

FAUSTUS. Nay, let me have one book more—and then I have done—wherein I might see all plants, herbs, and trees, that grow upon the earth.

MEPHISTOPHILIS. Here they be.

FAUSTUS. O, thou art deceived.

MEPHISTOPHILIS. Tut, I warrant thee.

[*Turns to them.*

SCENE VI. IN THE HOUSE OF FAUSTUS

FAUSTUS. When I behold the heavens, then I repent,
And curse thee, wicked Mephistophilis,
Because thou hast depriv'd me of those joys.

MEPHISTOPHILIS. Why, Faustus,
Thinkest thou heaven is such a glorious thing?
I tell thee, 'tis not half so fair as thou,
Or any man that breathes on earth.

FAUSTUS. How prov'st thou that?

MEPHISTOPHILIS. 'Twas made for man, therefore is man more excellent.

FAUSTUS. If it were made for man, 'twas made for me:
I will renounce this magic and repent.

Enter GOOD ANGEL *and* EVIL ANGEL.

GOOD ANGEL. Faustus, repent; yet God will pity thee.

EVIL ANGEL. Thou art a spirit; God cannot pity thee.

FAUSTUS. Who buzzeth in mine ears I am a spirit?
Be I a devil, yet God may pity me;
Aye, God will pity me, if I repent.

EVIL ANGEL. Aye, but Faustus never shall repent.

[*Exeunt* ANGELS.

FAUSTUS. My heart 's so harden'd, I cannot repent:

Scarce can I name salvation, faith, or heaven,
But fearful echoes thunder in mine ears,
"Faustus, thou art damn'd!" Then swords, and knives,
Poison, guns, halters, and envenom'd steel
Are laid before me to dispatch myself;
And long ere this I should have slain myself,
Had not sweet pleasure conquer'd deep despair.
Have not I made blind Homer sing to me
Of Alexander's love and Oenon's death?
And hath not he, that built the walls of Thebes
With ravishing sound of his melodious harp,
Made music with my Mephistophilis?
Why should I die, then, or basely despair?
I am resolv'd; Faustus shall ne'er repent—
Come, Mephistophilis, let us dispute again,
And argue of divine astrology.
Tell me, are there many heavens above the moon?
Are all celestial bodies but one globe,
As is the substance of this centric earth?

MEPHISTOPHILIS. As are the elements, such are the
    spheres,
Mutually folded in each other's orb,
And, Faustus,
All jointly move upon one axletree,
Whose terminine is term'd the world's wide pole;
Nor are the names of Saturn, Mars, or Jupiter
Feign'd, but are erring stars.

FAUSTUS. But, tell me, have they all one motion, both
situ et tempore?

MEPHISTOPHILIS. All jointly move from east to west
in twenty-four hours upon the poles of the world; but
differ in their motion upon the poles of the zodiac.

FAUSTUS. Tush,
These slender trifles Wagner can decide:
Hath Mephistophilis no greater skill?

Who knows not the double motion of the planets?
The first is finish'd in a natural day;
The second thus: as Saturn in thirty years; Jupiter in
twelve; Mars in four; the Sun, Venus, and Mercury in a
year; the Moon in twenty-eight days. Tush, these are
freshmen's suppositions. But, tell me, hath every sphere
a dominion or *intelligentia?*

MEPHISTOPHILIS. Aye.

FAUSTUS. How many heavens or spheres are there?

MEPHISTOPHILIS. Nine; the seven planets, the firmament, and the empyreal heaven.

FAUSTUS. Well, resolve me in this question: why have
we not conjunctions, oppositions, aspects, eclipses, all
at one time, but in some years we have more, in some
less?

MEPHISTOPHILIS. *Per inaequalem motum respectu
totius.*

FAUSTUS. Well, I am answered. Tell me who made
the world?

MEPHISTOPHILIS. I will not.

FAUSTUS. Sweet Mephistophilis, tell me.

MEPHISTOPHILIS. Move me not, for I will not tell
thee.

FAUSTUS. Villain, have I not bound thee to tell me any
thing?

MEPHISTOPHILIS. Aye, that is not against our kingdom; but this is. Think thou on hell, Faustus, for thou
art damned.

    Re-enter GOOD ANGEL *and* EVIL ANGEL.

GOOD ANGEL. Think, Faustus, upon God that made
   the world.

MEPHISTOPHILIS. Remember this.   [*Exit.*

FAUSTUS. Aye, go, accursèd spirit, to ugly hell! 'Tis
thou has damn'd distressèd Faustus' soul.
Is 't not too late?

EVIL ANGEL. Too late.

GOOD ANGEL. Never too late, if Faustus can repent.

EVIL ANGEL. If thou repent, devils shall tear thee in pieces.

GOOD ANGEL. Repent, and they shall never raze thy skin.   [*Exeunt* ANGELS.

FAUSTUS. Aye, Christ, my Saviour,
Seek to save distressèd Faustus' soul!

Enter LUCIFER, BELZEBUB, *and* MEPHISTOPHILIS.

LUCIFER. Christ cannot save thy soul, for he is just
There 's none but I have int'rest in the same.

FAUSTUS. O, who art thou that look'st so terrible?

LUCIFER. I am Lucifer,
And this is my companion-prince in hell.

FAUSTUS. O, Faustus, they are come to fetch away thy soul!

LUCIFER. We come to tell thee thou dost injure us;
Thou talk'st of Christ, contráry to thy promise:
Thou shouldst not think of God: think of the devil,
And of his dam too.

FAUSTUS. Nor will I henceforth: pardon me in this,
And Faustus vows never to look to heaven,
Never to name God, or to pray to him,
To burn his Scriptures, slay his ministers,
And make my spirits pull his churches down.

LUCIFER. Do so, and we will highly gratify thee.
Faustus, we are come from hell to show thee some pastime: sit down, and thou shalt see all the Seven Deadly Sins appear in their proper shapes.

FAUSTUS. That sight will be as pleasing unto me,
As Paradise was to Adam, the first day
Of his creation.

LUCIFER. Talk not of Paradise nor creation; but mark this show: talk of the devil, and nothing else—Come away!

Enter the SEVEN DEADLY SINS.

Now, Faustus, examine them of their several names and dispositions.

FAUSTUS. What are thou, the first?

PRIDE. I am Pride. I disdain to have any parents. I am like Ovid's flea; I can creep into every corner; sometimes, like a periwig, I sit upon a wench's brow; or, like a fan of feathers, I kiss her lips. But, fie, what a scent is here! I'll not speak another word, except the ground were perfumed, and covered with cloth of arras.

FAUSTUS. What art thou, the second?

COVETOUSNESS. I am Covetousness; and, might I have my wish, I would desire that this house and all the people in it were turned to gold, that I might lock you up in my good chest, O my sweet gold!

FAUSTUS. What art thou, the third?

WRATH. I am Wrath. I had neither father nor mother: I leapt out of a lion's mouth when I was scarce half-an-hour old; and ever since I have run up and down the world with this case of rapiers, wounding myself when I had nobody to fight withal. I was born in hell; and look to it, for some of you shall be my father.

FAUSTUS. What art thou, the fourth?

ENVY. I am Envy, born of a chimney-sweeper and an oyster-wife. I cannot read, and therefore wish all books were burnt. I am lean with seeing others eat. O, that there would come a famine through all the world, that all might die, and I live alone! then thou shouldst see how fat I would be. But must thou sit, and I stand? come down, with a vengeance!

FAUSTUS. Away, envious rascal!—What art thou, the fifth?

GLUTTONY. Who I, sir? I am Gluttony. My parents are all dead, and the devil a penny they have left me, but a bare pension, and that is thirty meals a day and ten bevers—a small trifle to suffice nature. O, I come of a royal parentage! my grandfather was a Gammon of Bacon, my grandmother a Hogshead of Claret-wine; my godfathers were these, Peter Pickle-herring and Martin Martlemas-beef; O, but my godmother, she was a jolly gentlewoman, and well beloved in every good town and city; her name was Mistress Margery March-beer. Now, Faustus, thou hast heard all my progeny; wilt thou bid me to supper?

FAUSTUS. No, I'll see thee hanged; thou wilt eat up all my victuals.

GLUTTONY. Then the devil choke thee!

FAUSTUS. Choke thyself, glutton!—What art thou, the sixth?

SLOTH. I am Sloth. I was born on a sunny bank, where I have lain ever since; and you have done me great injury to bring me from thence: let me be carried thither again by Gluttony and Lechery. I'll not speak another word for a king's ransom.

FAUSTUS. What are you, Mistress Minx, the seventh and last?

LECHERY. Who, I, sir? The first letter of my name begins with Lechery.

LUCIFER. Away, to hell, to hell!   [*Exeunt the* SINS.]
Now, Faustus, how dost thou like this?

FAUSTUS. O, this feeds my soul!

LUCIFER. Tut, Faustus, in hell is all manner of delight.

FAUSTUS. O, might I see hell, and return again,
How happy were I then!

LUCIFER. Thou shalt; I will send for thee at midnight.
In meantime take this book; peruse it throughly,
And thou shalt turn thyself into what shape thou wilt.

FAUSTUS. Great thanks, mighty Lucifer!
This will I keep as chary as my life.

LUCIFER. Farewell, Faustus, and think on the devil.

FAUSTUS. Farewell, great Lucifer. Come, Mephistophilis. [*Exeunt omnes.*

Enter CHORUS.

CHORUS. Learnèd Faustus,

To know the secrets of astronomy
Graven in the book of Jove's high firmament,
Did mount himself to scale Olympus' top,
Being seated in a chariot burning bright,
Drawn by the strength of yoky dragons' necks.
He now is gone to prove cosmography,
And, as I guess, will first arrive at Rome,
To see the Pope and manner of his court,
And take some part of holy Peter's feast,
That to this day is highly solemniz'd. [*Exit.*

SCENE VII. THE POPE'S PRIVY-CHAMBER

Enter FAUSTUS *and* MEPHISTOPHILIS.

FAUSTUS. Having now, my good Mephistophilis,

Pass'd with delight the stately town of Trier,
Environ'd round with airy mountain-tops,
With walls of flint, and deep-entrenchèd lakes,
Not to be won by any conquering prince;
From Paris next, coasting the realm of France,
We saw the river Maine fall into Rhine,
Whose banks are set with groves of fruitful vines;
Then up to Naples, rich Campania,
Whose buildings fair and gorgeous to the eye,
The streets straight forth, and pav'd with finest brick,
Quarter the town in four equivalents;
There saw we learnèd Maro's golden tomb,
The way he cut, an English mile in length,
Thorough a rock of stone, in one night's space;
From thence to Venice, Padua, and the rest,

In one of which a sumptuous temple stands,
That threats the stars with her aspiring top.
Thus hitherto hath Faustus spent his time:
But tell me now what resting-place is this?
Hast thou, as erst I did command,
Conducted me within the walls of Rome?

MEPHISTOPHILIS. Faustus, I have; and, because we
will not be unprovided, I have taken up his Holiness'
privy-chamber for our use.

FAUSTUS. I hope his Holiness will bid us welcome.

MEPHISTOPHILIS. Tut, 'tis no matter, man; we'll be
bold with his good cheer.
And now, my Faustus, that thou may'st perceive
What Rome containeth to delight thee with,
Know that this city stands upon seven hills
That underprop the groundwork of the same:
Just through the midst runs flowing Tiber's stream,
With winding banks that cut it in two parts;
Over the which four stately bridges lean,
That make safe passage to each part of Rome:
Upon the bridge call'd Ponte Angelo
Erected is a castle passing strong,
Within whose walls such store of ordnance are,
And double cannons fram'd of carvèd brass,
As match the days within one cómplete year;
Besides the gates, and high pyramides,
Which Julius Caesar brought from Africa.

FAUSTUS. Now, by the kingdoms of infernal rule,
Of Styx, of Acheron, and the fiery lake
Of ever-burning Phlegethon, I swear
That I do long to see the monuments
And situation of bright-splendent Rome:
Come, therefore, let 's away.

MEPHISTOPHILIS. Nay, Faustus, stay: I know you'd
fain see the Pope,

And take some part of holy Peter's feast,
Where thou shalt see a troop of bald-pate friars,
Whose *summum bonum* is in belly-cheer.

FAUSTUS. Well, I'm content to compass then some
  sport,
And by their folly make us merriment.
Then charm me, that I
May be invisible, to do what I please,
Unseen of any whilst I stay in Rome.

> [MEPHISTOPHILIS *charms him.*

MEPHISTOPHILIS. So, Faustus; now
Do what thou wilt, thou shalt not be discern'd.

Sound a Sonnet. Enter the POPE *and the* CARDINAL OF
  LORRAINE *to the banquet, with* FRIARS *attending.*

POPE. My Lord of Lorraine, will 't please you draw
  near?

FAUSTUS. Fall to, and the devil choke you, an you
  spare!

POPE. How now! who 's that which spake?—Friars,
  look about.

FIRST FRIAR. Here 's nobody, if it like your Holiness.

POPE. My lord, here is a dainty dish was sent me
from the Bishop of Milan.

FAUSTUS. I thank you, sir.   [*Snatches the dish.*

POPE. How now! who 's that which snatched the
meat from me? will no man look?—My lord, this dish
was sent me from the Cardinal of Florence.

FAUSTUS. You say true; I'll ha 't.   [*Snatches the dish.*

POPE. What, again?—My lord, I'll drink to your
grace.

FAUSTUS. I'll pledge your grace. [*Snatches the cup.*

CARDINAL OF LORRAINE. My lord, it may be some
ghost, newly crept out of Purgatory, come to beg a pardon of your Holiness.

POPE. It may be so.—Friars, prepare a dirge to lay

the fury of this ghost.—Once again, my lord, fall to.
> [*The* POPE *crosses himself.*

FAUSTUS. What, are you crossing of yourself?
Well, use that trick no more, I would advise you.
> [*The* POPE *crosses himself again.*

Well, there's the second time. Aware the third;
I give you fair warning.
> [*The* POPE *crosses himself again, and* FAUSTUS *hits*
> *him a box of the ear; and they all run away.*

Come on, Mephistophilis; what shall we do?

MEPHISTOPHILIS. Nay, I know not: we shall be cursed
with bell, book, and candle.

FAUSTUS. How! bell, book, and candle—candle, book,
and bell—
Forward and backward, to curse Faustus to hell!
Anon you shall hear a hog grunt, a calf bleat, and an ass
bray,
Because it is Saint Peter's holiday.

> *Re-enter all the* FRIARS *to sing the Dirge.*

FIRST FRIAR. Come, brethren, let 's about our business with good devotion.

> *They sing.*

*Cursed be he that stole away his Holiness' meat from
the table!* maledicat Dominus!

*Cursed be he that struck his Holiness a blow on the
face!* maledicat Dominus!

*Cursed be he that took Friar Sandelo a blow on the
pate!* maledicat Dominus!

Cursed be he that disturbeth our holy dirge! maledicat Dominus!

Cursed be he that took away his Holiness' wine! maledicat Dominus!

> Et omnes Sancti! Amen!

> [MEPHISTOPHILIS *and* FAUSTUS *beat the* FRIARS
> *and fling fireworks among them; and so exeunt.*

Enter CHORUS

CHORUS. When Faustus had with pleasure ta'en the
    view
Of rarest things, and royal courts of kings,
He stay'd his course, and so returnèd home;
Where such as bear his absence but with grief,
I mean his friends and near'st companions,
Did gratulate his safety with kind words,
And in their conference of what befell,
Touching his journey through the world and air,
They put forth questions of astrology,
Which Faustus answer'd with such learnèd skill
As they admir'd and wonder'd at his wit.
Now is his fame spread forth in every land:
Amongst the rest the Emperor is one,
Carolus the Fifth, at whose palace now
Faustus is feasted 'mongst his noblemen.
What there he did, in trial of his art,
I leave untold; your eyes shall see['t] perform'd.

                          [*Exit.*

SCENE VIII.   NEAR AN INN

Enter ROBIN *the Ostler, with a book in his hand.*

ROBIN. O, this is admirable! here I ha' stolen one of
Doctor Faustus' conjuring-books, and, i'faith, I mean to
search some circles for my own use.

         Enter RALPH, *calling* ROBIN.

RALPH. Robin, prithee, come away; there 's a gentleman tarries to have his horse, and he would have
his things rubbed and made clean: he keeps such a
chafing with my mistress about it; and she has sent me
to look thee out; prithee, come away.

ROBIN. Keep out, keep out, or else you are blown up,

you are dismembered, Ralph: keep out, for I am about a roaring piece of work.

RALPH. Come, what doest thou with that same book? thou canst not read?

ROBIN. Yes, my master and mistress shall find that I can read.

RALPH. Why, Robin, what book is that?

ROBIN. What book! why, the most intolerable book for conjuring that e'er was invented by any brimstone devil.

RALPH. Canst thou conjure with it?

ROBIN. I can do all these things easily with it; first, I can make thee drunk with ippocras at any tavern in Europe for nothing; that 's one of my conjuring works.

RALPH. Our Master Parson says that 's nothing.

ROBIN. True, Ralph: and more, Ralph, if thou hast any mind to Nan Spit, our kitchenmaid—

RALPH. O, brave, Robin! shall I have Nan Spit? On that condition I'll feed thy devil with horse-bread as long as he lives, of free cost.

ROBIN. No more, sweet Ralph; let 's go and make clean our boots, which lie foul upon our hands, and then to our conjuring in the devil's name.   [*Exeunt.*

SCENE IX. THE SAME

Enter ROBIN *and* RALPH *with a silver goblet.*

ROBIN. Come, Ralph: did not I tell thee, we were for ever made by this Doctor Faustus' book? *Ecce, signum!* here 's a simple purchase for horse-keepers: our horses shall eat no hay as long as this lasts.

RALPH. But, Robin, here comes the Vintner.

ROBIN. Hush! I'll gull him supernaturally.

Enter VINTNER.

Drawer, I hope all is paid; God be with you!—Come, Ralph.

VINTNER. Soft, sir; a word with you. I must yet have a goblet paid from you, ere you go.

ROBIN. I a goblet, Ralph, I a goblet!—I scorn you; and you are but a, &c. I a goblet! search me.

VINTNER. I mean so, sir, with your favour.

[*Searches* ROBIN.

ROBIN. How say you now?

VINTNER. I must say somewhat to your fellow.— You, sir!

RALPH. Me, sir! me, sir! search your fill. [VINTNER *searches him.*] Now, sir, you may be ashamed to burden honest men with a matter of truth.

VINTNER. Well, tone of you hath this goblet about you.

RALPH. You lie, drawer, 'tis afore me [*Aside*]. Sirrah you, I'll teach you to impeach honest men—stand by— I'll scour you for a goblet—stand aside you had best, I charge you in the name of Belzebub.—Look to the goblet, Ralph [*Aside to* RALPH].

VINTNER. What mean you, sirrah?

ROBIN. I'll tell you what I mean. [*Reads from a book*] *Sanctobulorum Periphrasticon*—nay, I'll tickle you, Vintner.—Look to the goblet, Ralph [*Aside to* RALPH]. —[*Reads*] *Polypragmos Belseborams framanto pacosti-phos tostu, Mephistophilis, &c.*

Enter MEPHISTOPHILIS, *sets squibs at their backs, and then exit. They run about.*

VINTNER. *O, nomine Domine!* what meanest thou Robin? thou hast no goblet.

RALPH. *Peccatum peccatorum!*—Here 's thy goblet, good Vintner. [*Gives the goblet to* VINTNER, *who exit.*

ROBIN. *Misericordia pro nobis!* what shall I do? Good

devil, forgive me now, and I'll never rob thy library more.

Re-enter MEPHISTOPHILIS.

MEPHISTOPHILIS. Monarch of hell, under whose black survey
Great potentates do kneel with awful fear,
Upon whose altars thousand souls do lie,
How am I vexèd with these villains' charms!
From Constantinople am I hither come,
Only for pleasure of these damnèd slaves.

ROBIN. How, from Constantinople! you have had a great journey: will you take sixpence in your purse to pay for your supper, and be gone?

MEPHISTOPHILIS. Well, villains, for your presumption, I transform thee into an ape, and thee into a dog; and so be gone. [*Exit.*

ROBIN. How, into an ape! that 's brave: I'll have fine sport with the boys; I'll get nuts and apples enow.

RALPH. And I must be a dog.

ROBIN. I' faith, thy head will never be out of the pottage-pot. [*Exeunt.*

SCENE X. THE EMPEROR'S COURT AT INNSBRUCK

Enter EMPEROR, FAUSTUS, *and a* KNIGHT, *with* ATTENDANTS, *among whom* MEPHISTOPHILIS.

EMPEROR. Master Doctor Faustus, I have heard strange report of thy knowledge in the black art, how that none in my empire nor in the whole world can compare with thee for the rare effects of magic: they say thou hast a familiar spirit, by whom thou canst accomplish what thou list. This, therefore, is my request, that thou let me see some proof of thy skill, that mine eyes

may be witnesses to confirm what mine ears have heard
reported: and here I swear to thee, by the honour of
mine imperial crown, that, whatever thou doest, thou
shalt be no ways prejudiced or endamaged.

KNIGHT. I' faith, he looks much like a conjurer.

[Aside.

FAUSTUS. My gracious sovereign, though I must confess myself far inferior to the report men have published,
and nothing answerable to the honour of your imperial
majesty, yet, for that love and duty binds me thereunto,
I am content to do whatsoever your majesty shall command me.

EMPEROR. Then, Doctor Faustus, mark what I shall
say.

As I was sometime solitary set
Within my closet, sundry thoughts arose
About the honour of mine ancestors,
How they had won by prowess such exploits,
Got such riches, subdued so many kingdoms,
As we that do succeed, or they that shall
Hereafter possess our throne, shall
(I fear me) ne'er attain to that degree
Of high renown and great authority:
Amongst which kings is Alexander the Great,
Chief spectacle of the world's pre-eminence,
The bright shining of whose glorious acts
Lightens the world with his reflecting beams,
As when I hear but motion made of him,
It grieves my soul I never saw the man:
If, therefore, thou, by cunning of thine art,
Canst raise this man from hollow vaults below,
Where lies entomb'd this famous conqueror,
And bring with him his beauteous paramour,
Both in their right shapes, gesture, and attire
They us'd to wear during their time of life,

Thou shalt both satisfy my just desire,
And give me cause to praise thee whilst I live.

FAUSTUS. My gracious lord, I am ready to accomplish
your request, so far forth as by art and power of my
spirit I am able to perform.

KNIGHT. I' faith, that 's just nothing at all.   [*Aside.*

FAUSTUS. But, if it like your grace, it is not in my ability to present before your eyes the true substantial bodies
of those deceased princes, which long since are consumed to dust.

KNIGHT. Aye, marry, Master Doctor, now there 's a
sign of grace in you, when you will confess the truth.

[*Aside.*

FAUSTUS. But such spirits as can lively resemble
Alexander and his paramour shall appear before your
grace, in that manner that they both lived in, in their
most flourishing estate; which I doubt not shall sufficiently content your imperial majesty.

EMPEROR. Go to, Master Doctor; let me see them
presently.

KNIGHT. Do you hear, Master Doctor? you bring
Alexander and his paramour before the Emperor!

FAUSTUS. How then, sir?

KNIGHT. I' faith, that 's as true as Diana turned me to
a stag.

FAUSTUS. No, sir; but, when Actaeon died, he left the
horns for you.—Mephistophilis, be gone.

[*Exit* MEPHISTOPHILIS.

KNIGHT. Nay, an you go to conjuring, I'll be gone.

[*Exit.*

FAUSTUS. I'll meet with you anon for interrupting me
so.—Here they are, my gracious lord.

Re-enter MEPHISTOPHILIS *with* SPIRITS *in the shapes of*
ALEXANDER *and his* PARAMOUR.

EMPEROR. Master Doctor, I heard this lady, while

she lived, had a wart or mole in her neck: how shall I know whether it be so or no?

FAUSTUS. Your highness may boldly go and see.

EMPEROR. Sure, these are no spirits, but the true substantial bodies of those two deceased princes.

[*Exeunt* SPIRITS.

FAUSTUS. Will 't please your highness now to send for the knight that was so pleasant with me here of late?

EMPEROR. One of you call him forth.

[*Exit* ATTENDANT.

Re-enter the KNIGHT *with a pair of horns on his head.*

How now, sir knight! Feel on thy head.

KNIGHT. Thou damnèd wretch and execrable dog,
Bred in the concave of some monstrous rock,
How dar'st thou thus abuse a gentleman?
Villain, I say, undo what thou hast done!

FAUSTUS. O, not so fast, sir! there 's no haste: but, good, are you remembered how you crossed me in my conference with the Emperor? I think I have met with you for it.

EMPEROR. Good Master Doctor, at my entreaty release him: he hath done penance sufficient.

FAUSTUS. My gracious lord, not so much for the injury he offered me here in your presence, as to delight you with some mirth, hath Faustus worthily requited this injurious knight; which being all I desire, I am content to release him of his horns—and, sir knight, hereafter speak well of scholars.—Mephistophilis, transform him straight. [MEPHISTOPHILIS *removes the horns.*]— Now, my good lord, having done my duty, I humbly take my leave.

EMPEROR. Farewell, Master Doctor: yet, ere you go, Expect from me a bounteous reward.

[*Exeunt* EMPEROR, KNIGHT, *and* ATTENDANTS.

FAUSTUS. Now, Mephistophilis, the restless course
That time doth run with calm and silent foot,
Short'ning my days and thread of vital life,
Calls for the payment of my latest years:
Therefore, sweet Mephistophilis, let us
Make haste to Wittenberg.

MEPHISTOPHILIS. What, will you go on horse-back or
on foot?

FAUSTUS. Nay, till I'm past this fair and pleasant
green, I'll walk on foot.

Enter a HORSE-COURSER.

HORSE-COURSER. I have been all this day seeking one
Master Fustian: mass, see where he is!—God save you,
Master Doctor!

FAUSTUS. What, horse-courser! you are well met.

HORSE-COURSER. Do you hear, sir? I have brought you
forty dollars for your horse.

FAUSTUS. I cannot sell him so. If thou likest him for
fifty, take him.

HORSE-COURSER. Alas, sir, I have no more!—I pray
you speak for me.

MEPHISTOPHILIS. I pray you, let him have him: he is
an honest fellow, and he has a great charge, neither wife
nor child.

FAUSTUS. Well, come, give me your money [HORSE-
COURSER *gives* FAUSTUS *the money*]: my boy will deliver
him to you. But I must tell you one thing before you
have him; ride him not into the water, at any hand.

HORSE-COURSER. Why, sir, will he not drink of all
waters?

FAUSTUS. O, yes, he will drink of all waters; but ride him not into the water: ride him over hedge or ditch, or where thou wilt, but not into the water.

HORSE-COURSER. Well, sir—Now am I made man for ever: I'll not leave my horse for forty: if he had but the quality of hey-ding-ding, hey-ding-ding, I'd make a brave living on him: he has a buttock as slick as an eel [*Aside*].—Well, God b'wi'ye sir: your boy will deliver him me: but, hark ye, sir; if my horse be sick or ill at ease, you'll tell me what it is?

FAUSTUS. Away, you villain! what, dost think I am a horse-doctor?   [*Exit* HORSE-COURSER.
What art thou, Faustus, but a man condemn'd to die?
Thy fatal time doth draw to final end;
Despair doth drive distrust unto my thoughts:
Confound these passions with a quiet sleep:
Tush, Christ did call the thief upon the Cross;
Then rest thee, Faustus, quiet in conceit.

[*Sleeps in his chair.*
Re-enter HORSE-COURSER, *all wet, crying.*

HORSE-COURSER. Alas, alas! Doctor Fustian, quotha? mass, Doctor Lopus was never such a doctor: has given me a purgation, has purged me of forty dollars; I shall never see them more. But yet, like an ass as I was, I would not be ruled by him, for he bade me I should ride him into no water: now I, thinking my horse had had some rare quality that he would not have had me know of, I, like a venturous youth, rid him into the deep pond at the town's end. I was no sooner in the middle of the pond, but my horse vanished away, and I sat upon a bottle of hay, never so near drowning in my life. But I'll seek out my doctor, and have my forty dollars again, or I'll make it the dearest horse! O, yonder is his snipper-snapper.—Do you hear? you, heypass, where 's your master?

MEPHISTOPHILIS. Why, sir, what would you? you cannot speak with him.

HORSE-COURSER. But I will speak with him.

MEPHISTOPHILIS. Why, he 's fast asleep: come some other time.

HORSE-COURSER. I'll speak with him now, or I'll break his glass-windows about his ears.

MEPHISTOPHILIS. I tell thee, he has not slept this eight nights.

HORSE-COURSER. An he have not slept this eight weeks, I'll speak with him.

MEPHISTOPHILIS. See, where he is, fast asleep.

HORSE-COURSER. Aye, this is he.—God save ye, Master Doctor, Master Doctor, Master Doctor Fustian! forty dollars, forty dollars for a bottle of hay!

MEPHISTOPHILIS. Why, thou seest he hears thee not.

HORSE-COURSER. So-ho, ho! so-ho, ho! [*Holla's in his ear.*] No, will you not wake? I'll make you wake ere I go. [*Pulls* FAUSTUS *by the leg, and pulls it away.*] Alas, I am undone! what shall I do?

FAUSTUS. O, my leg, my leg! Help, Mephistophilis! call the officers! My leg, my leg!

MEPHISTOPHILIS. Come, villain, to the constable.

HORSE-COURSER. O Lord, sir, let me go, and I'll give you forty dollars more!

MEPHISTOPHILIS. Where be they?

HORSE-COURSER. I have none about me: come to my ostry, and I'll give them you.

MEPHISTOPHILIS. Be gone quickly.

[HORSE-COURSER *runs away.*

FAUSTUS. What, is he gone? farewell he! Faustus has his leg again, and the Horse-courser, I take it, a bottle of hay for his labour: well, this trick shall cost him forty dollars more.

Enter WAGNER

How now, Wagner! what 's the news with thee?

WAGNER. Sir, the Duke of Vanholt doth earnestly entreat your company.

FAUSTUS. The Duke of Vanholt! an honourable gentleman, to whom I must be no niggard of my cunning.
—Come, Mephistophilis, let 's away to him.

[*Exeunt.*

SCENE XII. THE COURT OF THE DUKE OF VANHOLT

Enter the DUKE OF VANHOLT, *the* DUCHESS, *and* FAUSTUS.

DUKE OF VANHOLT. Believe me, Master Doctor, this merriment hath much pleased me.

FAUSTUS. My gracious lord, I am glad it contents you so well.—But it may be, madam, you take no delight in this. I have heard that women do long for some dainties or other: what is it, madam? tell me and you shall have it.

DUCHESS OF VANHOLT. Thanks, good Master Doctor: and, for I see your courteous intent to pleasure me, I will not hide from you the thing my heart desires; and, were it now summer, as it is January and the dead time of the winter, I would desire no better meat than a dish of ripe grapes.

FAUSTUS. Alas, madam, that 's nothing—Mephistophilis, be gone. [*Exit* MEPHISTOPHILIS.] Were it a greater thing than this, so it would content you, you should have it.

Re-enter MEPHISTOPHILIS *with grapes.*

Here they be, madam: will 't please you taste on them?

DUKE OF VANHOLT. Believe me, Master Doctor, this makes me wonder above the rest, that being in the dead time of winter and in the month of January, how you should come by these grapes.

FAUSTUS. If it like your grace, the year is divided into two circles over the whole world, that, when it is here winter with us, in the contrary circle it is summer with them, as in India, Saba, and farther countries in the east; and by means of a swift spirit that I have, I had them brought hither, as ye see.—How do you like them, madam? be they good?

DUCHESS OF VANHOLT. Believe me, Master Doctor, they be the best grapes that e'er I tasted in my life before.

FAUSTUS. I am glad they content you so, madam.

DUKE OF VANHOLT. Come, madam, let us in, where you must well reward this learned man for the great kindness he hath showed to you.

DUCHESS OF VANHOLT. And so I will, my lord; and, whilst I live, rest beholding for this courtesy.

FAUSTUS. I humbly thank your grace.

DUKE OF VANHOLT. Come, Master Doctor, follow us, and receive your reward.   [*Exeunt.*

SCENE XIII. A ROOM IN THE HOUSE OF FAUSTUS

Enter WAGNER.

WAGNER. I think my master means to die shortly,
For he hath given to me all his goods:
And yet, methinketh, if that death were near,
He would not banquet, and carouse, and swill
Amongst the students, as even now he doth,
Who are at supper with such belly-cheer
As Wagner ne'er beheld in all his life.
See, where they come! belike the feast is ended.

Enter FAUSTUS *with two or three* SCHOLARS, *and*
MEPHISTOPHILIS.

FIRST SCHOLAR. Master Doctor Faustus, since our
conference about fair ladies, which was the beautiful'st
in all the world, we have determined with ourselves
that Helen of Greece was the admirablest lady that ever
lived: therefore, Master Doctor, if you will do us that
favour, as to let us see that peerless dame of Greece,
whom all the world admires for majesty, we should think
ourselves much beholding unto you.

FAUSTUS. Gentlemen,
For that I know your friendship is unfeign'd,
And Faustus' custom is not to deny
The just requests of those that wish him well,
You shall behold that peerless dame of Greece,
No otherways for pomp and majesty
Then when Sir Paris cross'd the seas with her,
And brought the spoils to rich Dardania.
Be silent, then, for danger is in words.

    [*Music sounds, and* HELEN *passeth over the stage.*

SECOND SCHOLAR. Too simple is my wit to tell her
    praise,
Whom all the world admires for majesty.

THIRD SCHOLAR. No marvel though the angry Greeks
    pursu'd
With ten years' war the rape of such a queen,
Whose heavenly beauty passeth all compare.

FIRST SCHOLAR. Since we have seen the pride of
    Nature's works,
And only paragon of excellence,
Let us depart; and for this glorious deed
Happy and blest be Faustus evermore!

FAUSTUS. Gentlemen, farewell: the same I wish to
    you.   [*Exeunt* SCHOLARS *and* WAGNER.

Enter an OLD MAN.

OLD MAN. Ah, Doctor Faustus, that I might prevail
To guide thy steps unto the way of life,
By which sweet path thou may'st attain the goal
That shall conduct thee to celestial rest!
Break heart, drop blood, and mingle it with tears,
Tears falling from repentant heaviness
Of thy most vile and loathsome filthiness,
The stench whereof corrupts the inward soul
With such flagitious crimes of heinous sins
As no commiseration may expel,
But mercy, Faustus, of thy Saviour sweet,
Whose blood alone must wash away thy guilt.

FAUSTUS. Where art thou, Faustus? wretch, what hast
thou done?
Damn'd art thou, Faustus, damn'd; despair and die!
Hell calls for right, and with a roaring voice
Says, "Faustus, come; thine hour is almost come";
And Faustus now will come to do thee right.

[MEPHISTOPHILIS *gives him a dagger.*

OLD MAN. Ah, stay, good Faustus, stay thy desperate
steps!
I see an angel hovers o'er thy head,
And, with a vial full of precious grace,
Offers to pour the same into thy soul:
Then call for mercy, and avoid despair.

FAUSTUS. Ah, my sweet friend, I feel
Thy words to comfort my distressèd soul!
Leave me a while to ponder on my sins.

OLD MAN. I go, sweet Faustus; but with heavy cheer,
Fearing the ruin of thy hopeless soul.   [*Exit.*

FAUSTUS. Accursèd Faustus, where is mercy now?
I do repent; and yet I do despair:
Hell strives with grace for conquest in my breast:

What shall I do to shun the snares of death?

MEPHISTOPHILIS. Thou traitor, Faustus, I arrest thy
soul
For disobedience to my sovereign lord:
Revolt, or I'll in piece-meal tear thy flesh.

FAUSTUS. Sweet Mephistophilis, entreat thy lord
To pardon my unjust presumption,
And with my blood again I will confirm
My former vow I made to Lucifer.

MEPHISTOPHILIS. Do it, then, quickly, with unfeignèd
heart,
Lest greater danger do attend thy drift.

[FAUSTUS *stabs his arm, and writes on a paper
with his blood.*

FAUSTUS. Torment, sweet friend, that base and
crooked age,
That durst dissuade me from thy Lucifer,
With greatest torments that our hell affords.

MEPHISTOPHILIS. His faith is great; I cannot touch
his soul;
But what I may afflict his body with
I will attempt, which is but little worth.

FAUSTUS. One thing, good servant, let me crave of
thee,
To glut the longing of my heart's desire—
That I might have unto my paramour
That heavenly Helen which I saw of late,
Whose sweet embracings may extinguish clean
These thoughts that do dissuade me from my vow,
And keep mine oath I made to Lucifer.

MEPHISTOPHILIS. Faustus, this, or what else thou
shalt desire,
Shall be perform'd in twinkling of an eye.
                    Re-enter HELEN.

FAUSTUS. Was this the face that launch'd a thousand
    ships,
And burnt the topless towers of Ilium?—
Sweet Helen, make me immortal with a kiss.—

                                    [Kisses her.

Her lips suck forth my soul: see where it flees!—
Come, Helen, come, give me my soul again.
Here will I dwell, for heaven is in these lips,
And all is dross that is not Helena.
I will be Paris, and for love of thee,
Instead of Troy, shall Wittenberg be sack'd
And I will combat with weak Menelaus,
And wear thy colours on my plumèd crest;
Yes, I will wound Achilles in the heel,
And then return to Helen for a kiss.
O, thou art fairer than the evening air
Clad in the beauty of a thousand stars;
Brighter art thou than flaming Jupiter
When he appear'd to hapless Semele;
More lovely than the monarch of the sky
In wanton Arethusa's azur'd arms;
And none but thou shalt be my paramour!   *[Exeunt.*
              Enter the OLD MAN.

OLD MAN. Accursèd Faustus, miserable man,
That from thy soul exclud'st the grace of heaven,
And fly'st the throne of his tribunal-seat!
              Enter DEVILS.
Satan begins to sift me with his pride:
As in this furnace God shall try my faith,
My faith, vile hell, shall triumph over thee.
Ambitious fiends, see how the heavens smile
At your repulse, and laugh your state to scorn!
Hence, hell! for hence I fly unto my God.

      [Exeunt—on one side DEVILS, *on the other* OLD
    MAN.

SCENE XIV. THE SAME

Enter FAUSTUS, *with* SCHOLARS.

FAUSTUS. Ah, gentlemen!

FIRST SCHOLAR. What ails Faustus?

FAUSTUS. Ah, my sweet chamber-fellow, had I lived with thee, then had I lived still! but now I die eternally. Look, comes he not? comes he not?

SECOND SCHOLAR. What means Faustus?

THIRD SCHOLAR. Belike he is grown into some sickness by being over-solitary.

FIRST SCHOLAR. If it be so, we'll have physicians to cure him.—'Tis but a surfeit; never fear, man.

FAUSTUS. A surfeit of deadly sin, that hath damned both body and soul.

SECOND SCHOLAR. Yet, Faustus, look up to heaven; remember God's mercies are infinite.

FAUSTUS. But Faustus' offence can ne'er be pardoned: the serpent that tempted Eve may be saved, but not Faustus. Ah, gentlemen, hear me with patience, and tremble not at my speeches! Though my heart pants and quivers to remember that I have been a student here these thirty years, O, would I had never seen Wittenberg, never read book! and what wonders I have done, all Germany can witness, yea, all the world; for which Faustus hath lost both Germany and the world, yea, heaven itself, heaven, the seat of God, the throne of the blessed, the kingdom of joy; and must remain in hell for ever—hell, ah, hell, for ever! Sweet friends, what shall become of Faustus, being in hell for ever?

THIRD SCHOLAR. Yet, Faustus, call on God.

FAUSTUS. On God, whom Faustus hath abjured! on God, whom Faustus hath blasphemed! Ah, my God, I would weep! but the devil draws in my tears. Gush forth blood, instead of tears! yea, life and soul—O, he stays my tongue! I would lift up my hands; but see, they hold them, they hold them!

ALL. Who, Faustus?

FAUSTUS. Lucifer and Mephistophilis. Ah, gentlemen, I gave them my soul for my cunning!

ALL. God forbid!

FAUSTUS. God forbade it, indeed; but Faustus hath done it: for vain pleasure of twenty-four years hath Faustus lost eternal joy and felicity. I writ them a bill with mine own blood: the date is expired; the time will come, and he will fetch me.

FIRST SCHOLAR. Why did not Faustus tell us of this before, that divines might have prayed for thee?

FAUSTUS. Oft have I thought to have done so; but the devil threatened to tear me in pieces, if I named God, to fetch both body and soul, if I once gave ear to divinity: and now 'tis too late. Gentlemen, away, lest you perish with me.

SECOND SCHOLAR. O, what shall we do to save Faustus?

FAUSTUS. Talk not of me, but save yourselves, and depart.

THIRD SCHOLAR. God will strengthen me; I will stay with Faustus.

FIRST SCHOLAR. Tempt not God, sweet friend; but let us into the next room, and there pray for him.

FAUSTUS. Aye, pray for me, pray for me; and what noise soever ye hear, come not unto me, for nothing can rescue me.

SECOND SCHOLAR. Pray thou, and we will pray that God may have mercy upon thee.

FAUSTUS. Gentlemen, farewell if I live till morning, I'll visit you; if not, Faustus is gone to hell.

ALL. Faustus, farewell.

[*Exeunt* SCHOLARS. *The clock strikes eleven.*

FAUSTUS. Ah, Faustus,
Now hast thou but one bare hour to live,
And then thou must be damn'd perpetually!
Stand still, you ever-moving spheres of heaven,
That time may cease, and midnight never come;
Fair Nature's eye, rise, rise again, and make
Perpetual day; or let this hour be but
A year, a month, a week, a natural day,
That Faustus may repent and save his soul!
O lente, lente currite, noctis equi!
The stars move still, time runs, the clock will strike,
The devil will come, and Faustus must be damn'd.
O, I'll leap up to my God!—Who pulls me down?—
See, see, where Christ's blood streams in the firmament!
One drop would save my soul, half a drop: ah, my
    Christ!—
Ah, rend not my heart for naming of my Christ!
Yet will I call on him: O, spare me, Lucifer!—
Where is it now? 'tis gone; and see, where God
Stretcheth out his arm, and bends his ireful brows!
Mountains and hills, come, come, and fall on me,
And hide me from the heavy wrath of God!
No, no!
Then will I headlong run into the earth:
Earth, gape! O, no, it will not harbour me!
You stars that reign'd at my nativity,
Whose influence hath allotted death and hell,
Now draw up Faustus, like a foggy mist,
Into the entrails of yon lab'ring clouds,
That, when you vomit forth into the air,
My limbs may issue from your smoky mouths,
So that my soul may but ascend to heaven!

                    [*The clock strikes the half-hour.*
Ah, half the hour is past! 'twill all be past anon.

O God,
If thou wilt not have mercy on my soul,
Yet for Christ's sake, whose blood hath ransom'd me,
Impose some end to my incessant pain;
Let Faustus live in hell a thousand years,
A hundred thousand, and at last be sav'd!
O, no end is limited to damnèd souls!
Why wert thou not a creature wanting soul?
Or why is this immortal that thou hast?
Ah, Pythagoras' metempsychosis, were that true,
This soul should fly from me, and I be chang'd
Unto some brutish beast! all beasts are happy,
For, when they die,
Their souls are soon dissolv'd in elements;
But mine must live still to be plagu'd in hell.
Curs'd be the parents that engender'd me!
No, Faustus, curse thyself, curse Lucifer
That hath depriv'd thee of the joys of heaven.
                              [*The clock strikes twelve.*
O, it strikes, it strikes! Now, body, turn to air,
Or Lucifer will bear thee quick to hell!
                              [*Thunder and lightning.*
O soul, be chang'd into little water-drops,
And fall into the ocean, ne'er be found!
                    Enter DEVILS.
My God, my God, look not so fierce on me!
Adders and serpents, let me breathe a while!
Ugly hell, gape not! come not, Lucifer!
I'll burn my books!—Ah, Mephistophilis!
                    [*Exeunt* DEVILS *with* FAUSTUS.
                    Enter CHORUS
  CHORUS. Cut is the branch that might have grown
      full straight,
And burnèd is Apollo's laurel-bough,
That sometime grew within this learnèd man.

Faustus is gone: regard his hellish fall,
Whose fiendful fortune may exhort the wise,
Only to wonder at unlawful things,
Whose deepness doth entice such forward wits
To practise more than heavenly power permits.

[*Exit.*

Terminat hora diem; terminat auctor opus.

John Dee

DR. DEE AND THE SPIRITS

E. K .... Edward Kelley
Δ .... John Dee
NALVAGE ⎫
GABRIEL ⎬ .... Spirits

(*Monday, at Cracow, April 30. At the hour
of six and one-half, in the morning*)

E. K. Now they are here: and Gabriel is all full of
glory, he seemeth to light all places.

Δ. O the mercies of God increased, though his determination be all one.

E. K. Now he is as he was before: and in the time of
this his glorious apparition, Nalvage kneeled down,
somewhat regarding towards Gabriel.

GAB. Give unto him that hath his basket open: But
from him that is not ready, depart.

E. K. There appear here, 7 other like Priests, all in

white, having long hair hanging down behind: their white garments trail after them: having many pleats in them. Me think that I have seen one of them before, and upon that creature appeareth a B upon his clothes, an L in another place, an R upon his other shoulder, another A upon his other shoulder. There is an H upon his breast; there is an I upon his head, and a C upon his side on his garment; and an A under his waist behind: The letters seem to go up and down interchangeably in places. There seemeth an U on him, also an N, a D.

Now cometh a tall man by, all in white, and a great white thing rolled about his neck, and coming down before like a tippet. They all in the Stone (being 9) kneel down unto him.

THE TALL MAN said, "Take this Key, and power: ascend and fill thy vessel, for the River is not pure, and made clean."

E. K. Now he is gone (that said this) in form of a great Millstone of fire.

E. K. Now they go up a Hill, with a great Tankard, as it were, of Bone transparent; now he openeth one door, he, I mean, that had the Letters on his back.

1. There appeareth a Partridge, but it hath one leg like a Kite: This Partridge seemeth to sit on a green place under the gate, one leg is much longer than the other, being like a Kite's leg. This Partridge seemeth to halt.

He biddeth one of his Company take it up. There goeth a bridge to the top of that Hill, all upon arches, and under it goeth a River.

He taketh the Partridge and pulleth all his feathers, and they fall into the River: He cutteth off the longer leg just to the length of the other. They about him cry, "O just judgment."

Now he turneth him off over the Bridge, and he flieth away, for the feathers of his wings were not pulled.

2. He goeth on, and cometh to another Gate; and there the third man unlocketh it, as the second next him unlocked the first Gate; he himself having the Key first delivered him, as above is noted. There appeareth a thing like a Kite, all white, very great. It hath a foul great head. He seemeth to be in a very pleasant Garden, and flieth from place to place of it, and beateth down the Rose trees and other fruit trees. The Garden seemeth very delicate and pleasant. They go all into the Garden: and he saith, Thou art of the Wilderness, thy feathers and carcase are not worthy the spoil of the Garden.

Now the Kite scratcheth and gaspeth at this man; but he taketh the Kite and cutteth her carcase in two equal parts, from the crown of his head, and throweth one half over one side of the Bridge, and the other half over the other side, and said, Fowls must be devoured of Fowls. The rest say, *"O justitia divina,"* clapping their hands over their heads.

3. Now the next in order openeth another Gate (going up upon the same Bridge still). The rest of the building from the Gate inward, seemeth very round and bright: yet there appear no windows in it. It is a frame, made as though the 7 Planets moved in it. The Moon seemeth to be New Moon.

There standeth Armour, and this man putteth on, all white Harness. He seemeth to kick down the Moon, and her frame or Orb; and seemeth to make powder of all. *"For there is no mercy here,"* saith he.

4. Now another of them goeth forward to another Gate, and openeth the Gate, and goeth in; there appear an infinite multitude of men.

There sitteth a man clothed like a Priest, having a great Crown on his head: here are many preaching in this place. He goeth to that Crowned Priest, and he taketh away divers patches of the Vesture which he had, and the patches seemed to be like Owls, and Apes, and such like.

He saith, *"A King is a King, and a Priest is a Priest."*

He taketh from the rest their Keys and Purses, and giveth them *a Staff and a Bottle* in their hands. He goeth from them. He putteth all that he took from them in a house beside the Gate, and writeth on the door, *Cognascat quisque suum.*

5. Now they proceed to another Gate, and another of them opened that Gate. The Bridge continueth still, ascending upward. Now there appeareth (that Gate being opened) a marvelous great Wilderness.

There cometh a great number *of naked wild men to him.* He shaketh that Gate with his hands, and it falleth in pieces, one falleth on one side into the River, and the other falls on the other side into the River,

. . . . *Let both these places be made one. Let the spoil of the first, be the comfort of the last: For from them that have shall be taken, and unto them that have not shall be given.*

6. E. K. Now he goeth, and the last of his Company openeth another Gate; he is longer in opening of that Gate, than any of the rest.

There appeareth a bushy place, and there runneth a great River on the very top of the *Hill,* and a great Gate standeth beyond the Hill, and a very rich Tower all of precious Stones, as it seemeth.

Here he filleth his Tankard in the River, and holdeth his hands up, and maketh shew as he would return.

He said, *"This was my coming, and should be my return."*

E. K. Now they appear suddenly before the first Gate, and there the *Prinicpal man diggeth the earth,* and putteth stones and brambles, and leaves aside. There he taketh out a dead carcase, and bringeth it to a fire, and stroketh it: a very lean carcase it is; it seemeth to be a dead Lion; for it hath a long tail with a bush at the end.

He saith, *"Come let us take him up, and comfort him; for it is in him."*

Now the Lion seemeth to sit up and lick himself, and to drink of the water, and to shake himself, and to roar. The man taketh of the flags by, and stroketh the Lion as he would make his hair smooth.

Now the Lion is become fair, fat, and beautiful.

He saith, *"Tarry you here, till I bring you word again; for I must follow the Lion into the Wilderness."*

E. K. Now all they are gone, except the two our School masters, Gabriel and Nalvage.

GAB. *This is the judgment of God this day. Happy is he that hath judgment to understand it.*

Δ. Thou O Lord knowest the measure of our judgment: Give therefore light, understanding, and the grace to use thy gifts duly.

GAB. *Listen unto my words, for they are a Commandment from above. Behold (Saith he) I have descended to view the Earth, where I will dwell for seven days, and twice seven days: Therefore let them be days of rest to you. But every seventh day, I will visit you, as Now I do.*

E. K. He speaketh as if he spake out of a Trunk.

Δ. I understand that this rest is, that every *Monday*, for three *Mondays* else next after other, we shall await for our lessons, as now we receive, *and that we may all the rest follow our affairs of study or household matters.*

GAB. It is so, for one day shall be as a week: *But those days you must abstain from all things that live upon the Earth.*

Δ. You mean on these three *Mondays*, ensuing next?

GAB. *You shall cover this Table with a new linen cloth.*

(E. K. Pointing to the Table we sat at.)

Δ. Most willingly.

GAB. *Moreover a new Candlestick, with a Taper burning.*

Δ. Obediently (O Lord) it shall be done.

GAB. *And the Candlestick shall be set on the midst of the Table betwixt you two.* (That a day may become a week, and a week as many years.) *For I have put on my upper garment, and have prepared to enter, and it is shortly: and not yet.*

E. K. Now he hath plucked the Curtain, as if he had pulled it round about the Stone; and it seemeth full of little sparks like Stars.

Gloria patri & filio & spiritui sancto; sicut erat in principio, & nunc, & semper, & in secula seculorum.

[FROM *A True Relation of Dr. Dee, His Actions with Spirits, &c.*]

Sir Walter Ralegh

BLACK MAGIC

IT IS true that there are many arts, if we may so call them, which are covered with the name of magic, and esteemed abusively to be as branches of that tree on whose root they never grew. The first of these hath the name of necromancy or *goetia;* and of this again there are divers kinds. The one is an invocation at the graves of the dead, to whom the Devil himself gives answer instead of those that seem to appear. For certain it is, that the immortal souls of men do not inhabit the dust and dead bodies, but they give motion and understanding to the living; death being nothing else but a separation of the body and soul; and therefore the soul is not to be found in the graves.

A second practice of those men who pay tribute, or are in league with Satan, is that of conjuring or of raising up devils, of whom they hope to learn what they list. These men are distract, as they believe that by terrible words they make the Devil to tremble; that being once impaled in a circle (a circle which cannot keep out a mouse) they therein, as they suppose, ensconce themselves against that great monster. Doubtless they forget that the Devil is not terrified from doing ill, and all that is contrary to God and goodness; no, but by the fearful word of the Almighty; and that he feared not to offer to sit in God's seat; that he made no scruple to tempt our Saviour Christ, whom himself called the Son of God. So, forgetting these proud parts of his, an unworthy wretch will yet resolve himself, that he can draw the Devil out of hell, and terrify him with a phrase; whereas in very truth, the obedience which devils seem to use, is but thereby to possess themselves of the bodies and souls of those which raise them up; as his majesty in his book aforenamed hath excellently taught, That the Devils obedience is only *secundum quid, scilicet, ex pacto;* "respective, that is, upon bargain."

I cannot tell what they can do upon those simple and ignorant devils, which inhabit Jamblicus' imagination; but sure I am, the rest are apt enough to come uncalled; and always attending the cogitations of their servants and vassals, do no way need any such enforcement.

Or it may be that these conjurers deal altogether with Cardan's mortal devils, following the opinion of Rabbi Avornathan and of Porphyrius, who taught that these kind of devils lived not above a thousand years; which Plutarch, in his treatise *De Oraculorum Defectu* confirmeth, making example of the great god Pan. For were it true, that the devils were in awe of wicked men, or could be compelled by them, then would they always fear those words and threats, by which at other times they are willingly mastered. But the familiar of Simon Magus, when he had lifted him up in the air, cast him headlong out of his claws, when he was sure he should perish with the fall. If this perhaps were done by St. Peter's prayers (of which St. Peter nowhere vaunteth), yet the same prank at other times upon his own accord the Devil played with Theodotus; who transported (as Simon Magus was supposed to have been), had the same mortal fall that he had. The like success had Budas, a principal pillar of the Manichean heresy, as Socrates in his *Ecclesiastical History* witnesseth; and for a manifest proof hereof, we see it every day, that the Devil leaves all witches and sorcerers at the gallows, for whom at other times he maketh himself a Pegasus, to convey them in haste to places far distant, or at least makes them so think: *For to those that received not the truth,* saith St. Paul, *God shall send them strong illusions.* Of these their supposed transportations (yet agreeing with their confessions) his majesty, in the 2d book and the 4th chapter of the *Dæmonology,* hath confirmed by unanswerable reasons, that they are merely illusive. Another sort there are who take on them to include spirits in glasses and crystals; of whom Cusanus: *Fatui sunt incantatores, qui in ungue et vitro volunt spiritum includere: quia spiritus non clauditur corpore;* "They are foolish enchanters which will shut up their spirits within their nails or in glass; for a spirit cannot be enclosed by a body."

There is also another art besides the aforementioned, which they call *theurgia,* or white magic; a pretended conference with good spirits or angels, whom by sacrifice and invocation they draw out of heaven, and communicate withal. But the administering spirits of God, as they require not any kind of adoration due unto their Creator; so seeing they are most free spirits, there is no man so absurd to think (except the Devil have corrupted his understanding) that they can be constrained or commanded out of heaven by threats. Wherefore let the professors thereof cover themselves how they please by a professed purity of life, by the ministry of infants, by fasting and abstinence in general, yet all those that tamper with immaterial substances and abstract natures, either by sacrifice, vow, or enforcement, are men of evil faith, and in the power of Satan. For good spirits or angels cannot be constrained; and the rest are devils, which willingly obey.

Other sorts there are of wicked divinations; as by fire, called *pyromantia;* by water, called *hydromantia;* by the air, called *matæotechnia,* and the like.

The last, and indeed the worst of all other, is fascination or witchcraft; the practisers whereof are no less envious and cruel, revengeful and bloody, than the Devil himself. And these accursed creatures having sold their souls to the Devil, work two ways; either by the Devil immediately, or by the art of poisoning. The difference between necromancers and witches, his majesty hath excellently taught in a word; that the one (in a sort) command, the other obey the Devil.

There is another kind of petty witchery (if it be not altogether deceit) which they call charming of beasts and birds, of which Pythagoras was accused, because an eagle lighted on his shoulder in the Olympian fields. But if the same exceeded the art of falconry, yet was it no more to be admired than Mahomet's dove, which he had used to feed with wheat out of his ear; which dove, when it was hungry, lighted on Mahomet's shoulder, and thrust his bill therein to find his breakfast; Mahomet persuading the rude and simple Arabians, that it was the Holy Ghost that gave him advice. And certainly if Banks had lived in elder times, he would have shamed all the enchanters in the world; for whosoever was most famous among them, could never master or instruct any beast as he did his horse.

For the drawing of serpents out of their dens, or killing of them in their holes by enchantments (which the Marsians, a people of Italy, practised: *Colubros disrumpit Marsia cantu,* "enchanting Marsia makes the snakes to burst.") That it hath been used, it appears Psalm lviii. 6, though I doubt not but that many impostures may be in this kind, and even by natural causes it may be done. For there are many fumes that will either draw them out or destroy them, as women's hair burnt, and the like. So, many things may be laid in the entrance of their holes that will allure them; and therein I find no other magic or enchantment, than to draw out a mouse with a piece of toasted cheese.

[FROM *History of the World*]

Reginald Scot

WITCHES, INCUBI, AND SKEPTICISM

THE CLOAK OF IGNORANCE

ONE SORT of such as are said to be witches, are women which be commonly old, lame, blear-eyed, pale, foul, and full of wrinkles; poor, sullen, superstitious, and papists; or such as know no religion: in whose drowsy minds the devil hath gotten a fine seat; so as, what mischief, mischance, calamity, or slaughter is brought to pass, they are easily persuaded the same is done by themselves; imprinting in their minds an earnest and constant imagination hereof. They are lean and deformed, shewing melancholy in their faces, to the horror of all that see them. They are doting, scolds, mad, devilish; and not much differing from them that are thought to be possessed with spirits; so firm and steadfast in their opinions, as whosoever shall only have respect to the constancy of their words uttered, would easily believe they were true indeed.

These miserable wretches are so odious unto all their neighbors, and so feared, as few dare offend them, or deny them anything they ask: whereby they take upon them; yea, and sometimes think, that they can do such things as are beyond the ability of human nature. These go from house to house, and from door to door for a pot full of milk, yeast, drink, pottage, or some such relief; without the which they could hardly live: neither obtaining for their service and pains, nor by their art, nor yet at the Devil's hands (with whom they are said to make a perfect and visible bargain) either beauty, money, promotion, wealth, worship, pleasure, honor, knowledge, learning, or any other benefit whatsoever.

It falleth out many times, that neither their necessities, nor their expectation is answered or served, in those places where they beg or borrow; but rather their lewdness is by their neighbors reproved. And further, in tract of time the witch waxeth odious and tedious to her neighbors; and they again are despised and despited of her: so as sometimes she curseth one, and sometimes another; and that from the master of the house, his wife, children, cattle, etc., to the little pig that lieth in the sty. Thus in process of time they have all displeased her, and she hath wished evil luck unto them all; perhaps with curses and imprecations made in form. Doubtless (at length) some of her neighbors die, or fall sick; or some of their children are visited with diseases that vex them strangely: as apoplexies, epilepsies, convulsions, hot fevers, worms, etc. Which by ignorant parents are supposed to be the vengeance of witches. Yea and their opinions and conceits are confirmed and maintained by unskilful physicians, according to the common saying, *Inscitiae pallium maleficium et incantatio:* Witchcraft and enchantment is the cloak of ignorance; whereas indeed evil humors, and not strange words, witches, or spirits are the causes of such diseases. Also some of their cattle perish, either by disease or mischance. Then they, upon whom such adversities fall, weighing the fame that goeth upon this woman (her words, displeasure, and curses meeting so justly with their misfortune) do not only conceive, but also are resolved, that all their mishaps are brought to pass by her only means.

The witch on the other side expecting her neighbors'

mischances, and seeing things sometimes come to pass according to her wishes, curses, and incantations (for Bodin himself confesseth, that not above two in a hundred of their witchings or wishings take effect) being called before a Justice, by due examination of the circumstances is driven to see her imprecations and desires, and her neighbors harms and losses to concur, and as it were to take effect: and so confesseth that she (as a goddess) hath brought such things to pass. Wherein, not only she, but the accuser, and also the Justice are foully deceived and abused; as being through her confession and other circumstances persuaded (to the injury of God's glory) that she hath done, or can do that which is proper only to God himself.

Another sort of witches there are, which be absolutely cozeners. These take upon them, either for glory, fame, or gain, to do anything, which God or the Devil can do: either for foretelling of things to come, betraying of secrets, curing of maladies, or working of miracles. But of these I will talk more at large hereafter.

THE DEVIL HAS BETTER INSTRUMENTS

If witches could do any such miraculous things, as these and other which are imputed to them, they might do them again and again, at any time or place, or at any man's desire: for the Devil is as strong at one time as at another, as busy by day as by night, and ready enough to do all mischief, and careth not whom he abuseth. And in so much as it is confessed, by the most part of witchmongers themselves, that he knoweth not the cogitation of man's heart, he should (methinks) sometimes appear unto honest and credulous persons, in such gross and corporal form, as it is said he doth unto witches: which you shall never hear to be justified by one sufficient witness. For the Devil indeed entereth into the mind, and that way seeketh man's confusion.

The art always presupposeth the power; so as, if they say they can do this or that, they must shew how and by what means they do it; as neither the witches, nor the witchmongers are able to do. For to every action is required the faculty and ability of the agent or doer; the aptness of the patient or subject; and a convenient and possible application. Now the witches are mortal, and their power dependeth upon the analogy and consonancy of their minds and bodies; but with their minds they can but will and understand; and with their bodies they can do no more, but as the bounds and ends of terrain sense will suffer: and therefore their power extendeth not to do such miracles, as surmounteth their own sense, and the understanding of others which are wiser than they; so as here wanteth the virtue and power of the efficient. And in reason, there can be no more virtue in the thing caused, than in the cause, or that which proceedeth of or from the benefit of the cause. And we see, that ignorant and impotent women, or witches, are the causes of incantations and charms; wherein we shall perceive there is none effect, if we will credit our own experience and sense unabused, the rules of philosophy, or the word of God. For alas! What an inept instrument is a toothless, old, impotent, and unwieldly woman to fly in the air? Truly, the Devil little needs such instruments to bring his purposes to pass.

It is strange, that we should suppose, that such persons can work such feats: and it is more strange, that we will imagine that to be possible to be done by a witch, which to nature and sense is impossible; especially when our neighbor's life dependeth upon our credulity therein; and when we may see the defect of ability, which always is an impediment both to the act, and also to the presumption thereof. And because there is nothing possible in law, that in nature is impossible; therefore the judge doth not attend or regard what the accused man saith; or yet would do: but what is proved to have been committed, and naturally falleth in man's power and will to do. For the law saith, that to will a thing impossible, is a sign of a mad man, or of a fool, upon whom no sentence or judgement taketh hold. Furthermore, what Jury will condemn, or what Judge will give sentence or judgement against one for killing a man at Berwicke; when they themselves, and many other saw that man at London, that very day, wherein the murder was committed; yea though the party confess himself guilty therein, and twenty witnesses depose the same? But in this case also I say the Judge is not to weigh their testimony, which is weakened by law; and the Judge's authority is to supply the imperfection of the case, and to maintain the right and equity of the same.

Seeing therefore that some other things might naturally be the occasion and cause of such calamities as witches are supposed to bring; let not us that profess the Gospel and knowledge of Christ, be bewitched to believe that they do such things, as are in nature impossible, and in sense and reason incredible. If they say it is done through the Devil's help, who can work miracles; why do not thieves bring their business to pass miraculously, with whom the Devil is as conversant as with the other? Such mischiefs as are imputed to witches, happen where no witches are; yea and continue when witches are hanged and burnt: why then should we attribute such effect to that cause, which being taken away, happeneth nevertheless?

BAWDY INCUBUS

Of witchmongers' opinions concerning evil spirits, how they frame themselves in more excellent sort than God made us.

James Sprenger and Henrie Institor, in M. Mal. agreeing with Bodin, Barth, Spineus, Danaeus, Erastus, Hemingius, and the rest, do make a bawdy discourse; labouring to prove by a foolish kind of philosophy, that evil spirits cannot only take earthly forms and shapes of men; but also counterfeit hearing, seeing, etc. and likewise, that they can eat and devour meats, and also retain, digest, and avoid the same: and finally, use diverse kinds of activities, but specially excel in the use and art of venery. For M. Mal. saith, that the eyes and ears of the mind are far more subtle than bodily eyes or carnal ears. Yea it is there affirmed, that as they take bodies and the likeness of members; so they take minds and similitudes of their operations. But by the way, I would have them answer this question. Our minds and souls are spiritual things. If our corporeal ears be stopped, what can they hear or conceive of any external wisdom? And truly, a man of such a constitution of body, as they imagine of these spirits, which make themselves, etc. were of far more excellent substance, etc. than the bodies of them that God made in paradise; and so the Devil's workmanship should exceed the handiwork of God the Father and Creator of all things.

Of bawdy Incubus and Succubus, and whether the action of venery may be performed between witches and devils, and when witches first yielded to Incubus.

Heretofore (they say) Incubus was fain to ravish women against their will, until Anno 1400: but now since that time witches consent willingly to their desires: in so much as some one witch exerciseth that trade of lechery with Incubus twenty or thirty years together; as was confessed by forty and eight witches burned at Ravenspurge. But what goodly fellows Incubus begetteth upon these witches, is proved by Thomas of Aquine, Bodin, M. Mal. Hyperius, etc.

This is proved first by the Devil's cunning, in discerning the difference of the seed which falleth from men. Secondly, by his understanding of the aptness of the women for the receipt of such seed. Thirdly, by his knowledge of the constellations, which are friendly to such corporeal effects. And lastly, by the excellent complexion of such as the Devil maketh choice of, to beget such notable personages upon, as are the causes of the greatness and excellence of the child thus begotten.

And to prove that such bawdy doings betwixt the Devil and witches is not feigned, S. Augustine is alleged, who saith, that all superstitious arts had their beginning of the pestiferous society betwixt the Devil and man. Wherein he saith truly; for that in paradise, betwixt the Devil and man, all wickedness was so contrived, that man ever since hath studied wicked arts: yea and the Devil will be sure to be at the middle and at both ends of every mischief. But that the Devil engendereth with a woman, in manner and form as is supposed, and naturally begetteth the wicked, neither is it true, nor Augustine's meaning in this place.

Howbeit M. Mal. proceedeth, affirming that all witches take their beginning from such filthy actions, wherein the Devil in likeness of a pretty wench, lieth prostitute as Succubus to the man, and retaining his nature and seed, conveyeth it unto the witch, to whom he delivereth it as Incubus. Wherein also is refuted the opinion of them that hold a spirit to be unpalpable. M. Mal. saith, There can be rendered no infallible rule, though a probable distinction may be set down, whether Incubus in the act of venery do always pour seed out of his assumed body. And this is the distinction; either she is old and barren or young and pregnant. If she be barren, then doth Incubus use her without decision of seed; because such seed should serve for no purpose. And the Devil avoideth superfluity as much as he may; and yet for her pleasure and condemnation together, he goeth to work with her. But by the way, if the Devil were so compendious, what should he need to use such circumstances, even in these very actions, as to make these assemblies, conventicles, ceremonies, etc. when he hath already bought their bodies, and bargained for their souls? Or what reason had he, to make them kill so many infants, by whom he rather loseth than gaineth anything; because they are, so far as either he or we know, in better case than we of riper years by reason of their innocence? Well, if she be not past children, then stealeth he seed away (as hath been said) from some wicked man being about that lecherous business and therewith getteth young witches upon the old.

And note, that they affirm that this business is better accomplished with seed thus gathered, than that which is shed in dreams, through superfluity of humours: because that is gathered from the virtue of the seed generative. And if it be said that the seed will wax cold by the way, and so lose his natural heat, and consequently the virtue: M. Mal., Danaeus, and the rest do answer, that the devil can so carry it, as no heat shall go from it, etc.

Furthermore, old witches are sworn to procure as many young virgins for Incubus as they can, whereby in time they grow to be excellent bawds: but in this case the priest playeth Incubus. For you shall find, that confession to a priest, and namely this word Benedicite, driveth Incubus away, when Ave Maries, crosses, and all other charms fail.

Of the devil's visible and invisible dealing with witches in the way of lechery.

But as touching the Devil's visible or invisible execution of lechery, it is written, that to such witches, as before have made a visible league with the priest (the devil I should say), there is no necessity that Incubus should appear invisible: marry to the standers by he is for the most part invisible. For proof hereof James Sprenger and Institor affirm, that many times witches are seen in the fields, and woods, prostituting themselves uncovered and naked up to the navel, wagging and moving their members in every part, according to the disposition of one being about that act of concupiscence, and yet nothing seen of the beholders upon her; saving that after such a convenient time as is required about such a piece of work, a black vapor of the length and bigness of a man, hath been seen as it were to depart from her, and to ascend from that place. Nevertheless, many times the husband seeth Incubus making him cuckold, in the likeness of a man, and sometimes striketh off his head with his sword: but because the body is nothing but air, it closeth together again: so as, although the goodwife be sometimes hurt thereby; yet she maketh him believe he is mad or possessed, and that he doth he knoweth not what. For she hath more pleasure and delight (they say) with Incubus that way, than with any mortal man: whereby you may perceive that spirits are palpable.

That the power of generation is both outwardly and inwardly impeached by witches, and of divers that had their genitals taken from them by witches, and by the same means again restored.

They also affirm, that the virtue of generation is impeached by witches, both inwardly, and outwardly: for intrinsically they repress the courage, and they stop the passage of the man's seed, so as it may not descend to the vessels of generation: also they hurt extrinsically, with images, herbs, etc. And to prove this true, you shall hear certain stories out of M. Mal. worthy to be noted.

A young priest at Mespurge in the diocese of Constance was bewitched so as he had no power to occupy any other or more women than one; and to be delivered out of that thraldom, sought to fly into another country, where he might use that priestly occupation more freely. But all in vain; for evermore he was brought as far backward by night, as he went forward in the day before; sometimes by land, sometimes in the air, as though he flew. And if this be not true, I am sure that James Sprenger doth lie.

For the further confirmation of our belief in Incubus, M. Mal. citeth a story of a notable matter executed at Ravenspurge, as true and as cleanly as the rest. A young man lying with a wench in that town (saith he) was faine to leave his instruments of venery behind him, by means of that prestigious art of witchcraft: so as in that place nothing could be seen or felt but his plain body. This young man was willed by another witch, to go to her whom he suspected, and by fair or foul means to require her help: who soon after meeting with her, entreated her fair, but that was in vain; and therefore he caught her by the throat, and with a towel strangled her, saying: "Restore me my tool, or thou shalt die for it." So as she being swollen and black in the face, and through his boisterous handling ready to die, said, "Let me go, and I will help thee." And whilst he was loosing the towel, she put her hand into his codpiece, and touched the place; saying, "Now hast thou thy desire," and even at that instant he felt himself restored.

Item, a reverend father, for his life holiness, and knowledge notorious, being a friar of the order and company of Spire, reported, that a young man at shrift made lamentable moan unto him for the like loss: but his gravity suffered him not to believe lightly any such reports, and therefore made the young man untruss his codpiece point, and saw the complaint to be true and just. Whereupon he advised or rather enjoined the youth to go to the witch whom he suspected, and with flattering words to entreat her, to be so good unto him, as to restore him his instrument: which by that means he obtained, and soon after returned to shew himself thankful; and told the holy father of his good success in that behalf: but he so believed him, as he would needs be *Oculatus testis*, and made him pull down his breeches, and so was satisfied of the truth and certainty thereof.

Another young man being in that very taking, went to a witch for the restitution thereof, who brought him to a tree, where she shewed him a nest, and bade him climb up and take it. And being in the top of the tree, he took out a mighty great one, and shewed the same to her, asking her if he might not have the same. "Nay," quoth she, "that is our parish priest's tool, but take any other which thou wilt." And it is there affirmed, that some have found 20 and some 30 of them in one nest, being there preserved with provender, as it were at the rack and manger, with this note, wherein there is no contradiction (for all must be true that is written against witches) that if a witch deprive one of his privities, it is done only by prestigious means, so as the senses are but illuded. Marry by the Devil it is really taken away, and in like sort restored. These are no jests, for they be written by them that were and are judges upon the lives and deaths of those persons.

Of Bishop Sylvanus his lechery opened and covered again; how maids having yellow hair are most encumbered with Incubus; how married men are bewitched to use other men's wives, and to refuse their own.

You shall read in the legend, how in the nighttime Incubus came to a lady's bedside, and made hot love unto her: whereat she being offended, cried out so loud, that company came and found him under her bed in the likeness of the holy bishop Sylvanus, which holy man was much defamed thereby, until at the length this infamy was purged by the confession of a Devil made at S. Jerome's tomb. Oh excellent piece of witchcraft or cozening wrought by Sylvanus! Item, S. Christine would needs take unto her another maid's Incubus, and lie in her room: and the story saith, that she was shrewdly accloyed. But she was a shrew indeed, that would needs change beds with her fellow, that was troubled every night with Incubus, and deal with him herself. But here the inquisitor's note may not be forgotten, to wit: that Maids having yellow hair are most molested with this spirit. Also it is written in the Legend, of S. Barnard, that a pretty wench that had had the use of Incubus his body by the space of six or seven years in Aquitania (being belike weary of him for that he waxed old) would needs go to S. Barnard another while. But Incubus told her, that if she would so forsake him, being so long her true lover, he would be revenged upon her, etc. But befall what would, she went to S. Barnard, who took her his staff, and bade her lay it in the bed beside her. And indeed the devil fearing the bedstaff, or that S. Barnard lay there himself, durst not approach into her chamber that night: what he did afterwards, I am uncertain. Marry you may find other circumstances hereof, and many other like bawdy lies in the golden Legend. But here again we may not forget the inquisitor's note, to wit; that many are so bewitched that they cannot use their own wives: but any other bodies they may well enough away withal. Which witchcraft is practiced among many bad husbands, for whom it were a good excuse to say they were bewitched.

[FROM *The Discovery of Witchcraft*]

PART THREE
The Rise of Protestantism

John Foxe

THE DEATH OF
RIDLEY AND LATIMER

THEN THE wicked sermon being ended, Dr. Ridley and Master Latimer kneeled down upon their knees to my lord Williams of Tame, the vice-chancellor of Oxford, and divers other commissioners appointed for that purpose, who sate upon a form thereby; unto whom Master Ridley said, "I beseech you, my Lord, even for Christ's sake, that I may speak but two or three words." And whilst my lord bent his head to the mayor and vice-chancellor, to know (as it appeared) whether he might have leave to speak, the bailiffs and Dr. Marshal, the vice-chancellor, ran hastily unto him, and with their hands stopped his mouth, and said, "Master Ridley, if you will revoke your erroneous opinions, and recant the same, you shall not only have liberty so to do, but also the benefit of a subject, that is, have your life." "Not otherwise?" said Master Ridley. "No," quoth Dr. Marshal: "therefore if you will not do so, then there is no remedy but you must suffer for your deserts." "Well," quoth Master Ridley, "so long as the breath is in my body I will never deny my Lord Christ, and his known truth: God's will be done in me." And with that he rose up, and said with a loud voice, "Well, then I commit our cause to Almighty God, who will indifferently judge all." To whose saying, Mr. Latimer added his old posy, "Well, there is nothing hid but it shall be opened." And he said, he could answer Smith well enough, if he might be suffered.

Incontinently they were commanded to make themselves ready, which they all meekness obeyed. Master Ridley took his gown and his tippet, and gave it to his brother-in-law Master Shipside, who all his time of imprisonment, although he might not be suffered to come to him, lay there at his own charges to provide him necessaries, which from time to time he sent him by the sergeant that kept him. Some other of his apparel that was little worth, he gave away, the others the bailiffs took.

He gave away besides, divers other small things to gentlemen standing by, and divers of them pitifully weeping, as to Sir Henry Lea he gave a new groat; and to divers of my lord William's gentlemen, some napkins, some nutmegs, and races of ginger, his dial, and such other things as he had about him, to every one that stood next him. Some plucked the points off his hose. Happy was he that might get any rag of him.

Master Latimer gave nothing, but very quietly suffered his keeper to pull off his hose, and his other array, which to look unto was very simple: and being stripped into his shroud, he seemed as comely a person to them that were there present, as one should lightly see; and whereas in his clothes he appeared a withered and crooked silly old man, he now stood bolt upright, as comely a father as one might behold.

Then Master Ridley, standing as yet in his truss, said to his brother, "It were best for me to go in my truss still." "No," quoth his brother, "it will put you to more pain: and the truss will do a poor man good." Whereunto Dr. Ridley said, "Be it, in the name of God," and so unlaced himself. Then being in his shirt, he stood upon the foresaid stone, and held up his hand and said, "O heavenly Father, I give unto thee most hearty thanks, for that thou hast called me to be a professor of thee, even unto death; I beseech thee, Lord God, take mercy on this realm of England, and deliver the same from all her enemies."

Then the smith took a chain of iron, and brought the same about both Dr. Ridley's and Master Latimer's middle: and, as he was knocking in a staple, Dr. Ridley took the chain in his hand and shaked the same, for it did gird in his belly; and looking aside to the smith, said, "Good fellow, knock it in hard, for the flesh will have his course." Then his brother did bring him a bag of gunpowder, and would have tied it about his neck. Master Ridley asked him what it was; his brother said, "Gunpowder." "Then," said he, "I will take it to be sent of God, therefore I will receive it as sent from him. And have you any," said he, "for my brother?" (meaning Master Latimer). "Yea, sir, that I have," quoth his brother. "Then give it unto him," said he, "betime; lest ye come too late." So his brother went and carried off the same gunpowder to Mr. Latimer.

In the mean time Dr. Ridley spake unto my lord Williams, and said, "My lord, I must be a suitor unto your lordship in the behalf of divers poor men, and especially in the cause of my poor sister: I have made a supplication to the queen's majesty in their behalfs. I beseech your lordship for Christ's sake, to be a mean to her grace for them. My brother here hath the supplication, and will resort to your lordship to certify you hereof. There is nothing in all the world that troubleth my conscience, I praise God, this only excepted. Whilst I was in the see of London, divers poor men took leases of me, and agreed with me for the same. Now I hear say the bishop that now occupieth the same room, will not allow my grants unto them made, but contrary to all law and conscience, hath taken from them their livings, and will not suffer them to enjoy the same. I beseech you, my lord, be a mean for them: you shall do a good deed, and God will reward you."

Then they brought a faggot kindled with fire, and laid the same down at Dr. Ridley's feet. Thereupon Master Latimer said, "Be of good comfort, Master Ridley, and play the man, we shall this day light such a candle, by God's grace, in England, as I trust shall never be put out." And so the fire being given unto them, when Dr. Ridley saw the fire flaming up towards him, he cried with a wonderful loud voice, *In manus tuas, Domine, commendo spiritum meum: Domine recipe spiritum meum.* And after, repeated this latter part often in English, "Lord, Lord, receive my spirit." Master Latimer crying as vehemently on the other side, "O Father of heaven, receive my soul!" who received the flame as it were embracing of it. After that he had stroked his face with his hands, and as it were bathed them a little in the fire, he soon died (as it appeareth) with very little pain or none. And thus much concerning the end of this old and faithful servant of God, Master Latimer, for whose laborious travails, fruitful life, and constant death the whole realm hath cause to give thanks to Almighty God.

But Master Ridley, by reason of the evil making of the fire unto him, because the wooden faggots were laid about the gorse, and over-high built, the fire burnt first beneath, being kept down by the wood; which when he felt, he desired them for Christ's sake to let the fire come unto him. Which his brother-in-law heard, but not well understood, intending to rid him out of his pain (for which cause he gave attendance) as one in such sorrow, not well advised what he did, heaped faggots upon him, so that he clean covered him, which made the fire more vehement beneath, that it burned clean all his nether parts, before it touched the upper; and that made him leap up and down under the faggots, and often desire them to let the fire come unto him, saying, "I cannot burn." Which indeed appeared well; for, after his legs were consumed by reason of his struggling through the pain (whereof he had no release, but only his contentation God) he showed that side toward us clean, shirt and all untouched with flame. Yet in all this torment he forgot not to call unto God still, having in his mouth, "Lord, have mercy upon me," intermingling his cry, "Let the fire come unto me, I cannot burn." In which pangs he laboured till one of the standers-by with his bill pulled off the faggots above, and where he saw the fire flame up, he wrested himself unto that side. And when the flame touched the gunpowder, he was seen to stir no more, but burned on the other side, falling down at Master Latimer's feet: which some said, happened by reason that the chain loosed; others said, that he fell over the chain by reason of the poise of his body, and the weakness of the nether limbs.

Some said, that before he was like to fall from the stake, he desired them to hold him to it with their bills. However it was, surely it moved hundreds to tears, in beholding the horrible sight; for I think there were none that had not clean exiled all humanity and mercy which would not have lamented to behold the fury of the fire so to rage upon their bodies. Signs there were of sorrow on every side. Some took it grievously to see their deaths, whose lives they held full dear; some pitied their persons, that thought their souls had no need thereof. His brother moved many men, seeing his miserable case, seeing (I say) him compelled to such infelicity, that he thought then to do him best service when he hastened his end. Some cried out of the fortune, to see his endeavour (who most dearly loved him, and sought his release), turn to his greater vexation, and increase of pain. But whoso considered their preferments in time past, the places of honour that they sometime occupied in this commonwealth, the favour they were in with their princes, and the opinion of learning they had in the university where they studied, could not choose but sorrow with tears to see so great dignity, honour and estimation, so necessary members sometime accounted, so many godly virtues, the study of so many years, such excellent learning, to be put into the fire, and consumed in one moment. Well! dead they are, and the reward of this world they have already. What reward remaineth for them in heaven, the day of the Lord's glory, when he cometh with his saints, shall shortly, I trust, declare.

[FROM *Acts and Monuments*]

Book of Common Prayer

DAILY DEVOTIONALS

A PRAYER AT THE PUTTING ON OF OUR CLOTHES.

MOST GRACIOUS and merciful Saviour, Jesus Christ, thou knowest how we be born, clothed and clogged with the grievous and heavy burthen of the first man, who fell away unto fleshliness thorough disobedience. Vouchsafe, therefore, I beseech thee, to strip me out of the old corrupt Adam, which, being soaked in sin, transformeth himself into all incumbrances and diseases of the mind, that may lead away from thee.

Rid me also quite and clean of that his tempter, the deceitful Eve, which turneth us away from the obedience of thy Father. Clothe me with thyself, O my redeemer and sanctifier, clothe me with thyself, which art the second man, and hast yielded thyself obedient in all things to God thy Father, to rid away all lusts of the flesh, and to destroy the kingdom thereof through righteousness.

Be thou our clothing and apparel, to keep us warm from the cold of this world. For, if thou be away, by and by all things become numb, weak, and stark dead: whereas, if thou be present, they be lively, sound, strong, and lusty. And, therefore, like as I wrap my body in these clothes, so clothe thou me all over, but specially my soul, with thine own self. Amen.

A PRAYER TO BE SAID AT THE SETTING OF THE SUN.

Wretched are they, O Lord, to whom thy day-sun goeth down,—I mean that sun of thine, which never setteth to thy saints, but is always at the noon-point with them, ever bright, and ever shining. A droopy night ever deepeth the minds of them, even at high noontide, which depart from thee. But unto them, that are conversant with thee, it is continually clear day-light. This day-sun, that shineth in the sky, goeth and cometh by turns: but thou (if we love thee in deed) dost never go away from us. O that thou wouldest remove away this impediment of sin from us, that it might always be day-light in our hearts! Amen.

ANOTHER PRAYER FOR THE CHURCH, AND ALL THE STATES THEREFORE, BY JOHN FOXE.

Lord Jesus Christ, Son of the living God, who wast crucified for our sins, and didst rise again for our justification, and, ascending up to heaven, reignest now at the right hand of the Father, with full power and authority, ruling and disposing all things according to thine own gracious and glorious purpose: we, sinful creatures, and yet servants and members of Thy church, do prostrate ourselves and our prayers before thy imperial majesty, having no other patron nor advocate to speed our suits, or to resort unto, but thee alone, beseeching thee to be good to thy poor church militant here in this wretched earth; sometime a rich church, a large church, an universal church, spread far and wide, through the whole compass of the earth; now driven into a narrow corner of the world, and hath much need of thy gracious help.

First, the Turk with his sword, what lands, what nations, and countries, what empires, kingdoms, and provinces, with cities innumerable, hath he won, not from us, but from thee. Where thy name was wont to be invocated, thy word preached, thy sacraments administered, there now remaineth barbarous Mahumet, with his filthy Alcoran. The flourishing churches in Asia, the learned churches of Grecia, the manifold churches in Africa, which were wont to serve thee, now are gone from thee. The seven churches of Asia with their candlesticks (whom thou didst so well forewarn) are now removed. All the churches, where thy diligent apostle St Paul, thy apostles Peter and John, and other apostles, so laboriously travailed, preaching and writing to plant thy gospel, are now gone from thy gospel. In all the kingdom of Syria, Palestina, Arabia, Persia, in all Armenia, and the empire of Cappadocia, through the whole compass of Asia, with Egypt, and with Africa also (unless among the far Ethiopians some old steps of Christianity peradventure do yet remain), either else in all Asia and Africa thy church hath not one foot of free land, but is all turned either to infidelity or to captivity, whatsoever pertaineth to thee. And if Asia and Africa only were decayed, the decay were great, but yet the defection were not so universal.

Now of Europa a great part also is shrunk from thy church. All Thracia, with the empire of Constantinople, all Grecia, Epirus, Illyricum, and now of late all the kingdom almost of Hungaria, with much of Austria, with lamentable slaughter of Christian blood, is wasted, and all become Turks. Only a little angle of the West parts yet remaineth in some profession of thy name.

But here (alack) cometh another mischief, as great, or greater than the other. For the Turk with his sword is not so cruel, but the bishop of Rome on the other side is more fierce and bitter against us; stirring up his bishops to burn us, his confederates to conspire our destruction, setting kings against their subjects, and subjects disloyally to rebel against their princes, and all for thy name.

Such dissention and hostility Satan hath sent among us, that Turks be not more enemies to Christians, than Christians to Christians, papists to protestants: yea, protestants with protestants do not agree, but fall out for trifles. So that the poor little flock of thy church, distressed on every side, hath neither rest without, nor peace within, nor place almost in the world, where to abide, but may cry now from the earth, even as thine own reverence cried once from the cross: My God, my God, why hast thou forsaken me?

Amongst us Englishmen here in England, after so great storms of persecution and cruel murther of so many martyrs, it hath pleased thy grace to give us these Alcyon days, which yet we enjoy, and beseech thy merciful goodness still they may continue.

But here also (alack) what should we say? so many enemies we have, that envy us this rest and tranquillity, and do what they can to disturb it. They which be friends and lovers of the bishop of Rome, although they eat the fat of the land, and have the best preferments and offices, and live most at ease, and ail nothing, yet are they not therewith content. They grudge, they mutter and murmur, they conspire and take on against us. It fretteth them, that we live by them, or with them, and cannot abide, that we should draw the bare breathing of the air, when they have all the most liberty of the land.

And albeit thy singular goodness hath given them a Queen so calm, so patient, so merciful, more like a natural mother than a princess, to govern over them, such as neither they nor their ancestors ever read of in the stories of this land before: yet all this will not calm them, their unquiet spirit is not yet content; they repine and rebel, and needs would have, with the frogs of Aesop, a stork, an Italian stranger, the bishop of Rome, to play Rex over them, and care not, if all the world were set a fire, so that they, with their Italian lord, might reign alone. So fond are we Englishmen of strange and foreign things: so unnatural to ourselves, so greedy of newfangle novelties, never contented with any state long to continue, be it never so good; and, furthermore, so cruel one to another, that we think our life not quiet, unless it be seasoned with the blood of other. For that is their

hope, that is all their gaping and looking, that is their
golden day, their day of Jubilee, which they thirst for so
much: not to have the Lord to come in the clouds, but
to have our blood, and to spill our lives. That, that is it,
which they would have, and long since would have had
their wills upon us, had not thy gracious pity and mercy
raised up to us this our merciful Queen, thy servant
Elizabeth, somewhat to stay their fury: for whom as we
most condignly give thee thanks, so likewise we beseech
thy heavenly majesty, that, as thou hast given her unto
us, and hast from so manifold dangers preserved her,
before she was queen, so now, in her royal estate, she
may continually be preserved not only from the hands,
but from all malignant devices wrought, attempted, or
conceived, of enemies, both ghostly and bodily, against
her.

In this her government be her governor, we beseech
thee, so shall her majesty well govern us, if first she be
governed by thee. Multiply her reign with many days,
and her years with much felicity, with abundance of
peace and life ghostly: that, as she hath now doubled
the years of her sister and brother, so (if it be thy pleasure) she may overgrow in reigning the reign of her
father.

And because no government can long stand without
good counsel, neither can any counsel be good, except it
be prospered by thee: bless, therefore, we beseech thee,
both her majesty, and her honourable council, that both
they rightly understand what is to be done, and she accordingly may accomplish that they do counsel, to thy
glory, and furtherance of the gospel, and public wealth
of this realm.

Furthermore, we beseech thee, Lord Jesu, who with
the majesty of thy generation dost drown all nobility,
being the only Son of God, heir and Lord of all things,

bless the nobility of this realm, and of other Christian realms, so as they (Christianly agreeing among themselves) may submit their nobility to serve thee; or else let them feel, O Lord, what a frivolous thing is the nobility, which is without thee.

Likewise, to all magistrates, such as be advanced to authority, or placed in office, by what name or title soever, give, we beseech thee, a careful conscience uprightly to discharge their duty; that, as they be public persons to serve the common wealth, so they abuse not their office to their private gain, nor private revenge of their own affections, but that, justice being administered without bribery, and equity balanced without cruelty or partiality, things that be amiss may be reformed, vice abandoned, truth supported, innocency relieved, God's glory maintained, and the commonwealth truly served.

But especially, to thy spiritual ministers, bishops, and pastors of thy church, grant, we beseech thee, O Lord, Prince of all pastors, that they, following the steps of thee, of thy apostles, and holy martyrs, may seek those things which be not their own, but only which be thine, not caring how many benefices nor what great bishopricks they have, but how well they can guide those they have. Give them such zeal of thy church, as may devour them, and grant them such salt, wherewith the whole people may be seasoned, and which may never be unsavoury, but quickened daily by thy Holy Spirit, whereby Thy flock by them may be preserved.

In general, give to all the people, and the whole state of this realm, such brotherly unity in knowledge of thy truth, and such obedience to their superiors, as they neither provoke the scourge of God against them, nor their prince's sword to be drawn against her will out of the scabbard of long sufferance, where it hath been long hid. Especially, give thy gospel long continuance amongst us. And, if our sins have deserved the contrary, grant us, we beseech thee, with an earnest repentance of that which is past, to join a hearty purpose of amendment to come.

And forasmuch as the bishop of Rome is wont on every Good Friday to accurse us, [as] damned heretics, we curse not him, but pray for him, that he with all his partakers either may be turned to a better truth; or else, we pray thee, gracious Lord, that we never agree with him in doctrine, and that he may so curse us still, and never bless us more, as he blessed us in queen Mary's time. God, of thy mercy keep away that blessing from us.

Finally, instead of the pope's blessing give us thy blessing, Lord, we beseech thee, and conserve the peace of thy church, and course of thy blessed gospel. Help them that be needy and afflicted. Comfort them that labour and be heavy laden. And, above all things, continue and increase our faith.

And forasmuch as thy poor little flock can scarce have any place or rest in this world, come, Lord, we beseech thee, with thy *factum est,* and make an end, that this world may have no more time nor place here, and that thy church may have rest for ever.

For these, and all other necessities requisite to be begged and prayed for, asking in thy Christ's name, and as he hath taught us, we say: Our Father, which art in heaven &c.

A PRAYER FOR THE QUEEN'S MAJESTY.

Wonderful, O most excellent and almighty God, is the depth of thy judgments. Thou King of kings, Lord of lords; thou, which at thy pleasure dost take away and transpose, root out and plant, confound and establish, kingdoms; thou, of thy singular goodness, hast delivered our Queen, thy handmaid, when she was almost at death's door: yea, thou hast delivered her out of prison, and settled her in her father's throne. To thee, therefore, do we render thanks: to thee do we sing laud and praise: thy name do we honour day and night.

Thou hast restored again the liberty of our country, and the sincerity of thy doctrine, with peace and tranquillity of thy church. Thine, thine was the benefit: the means, the labour, and service, was hers. A burthen too heavy (alas) for a woman's shoulders, yet easy and tolerable by thy helping hand.

Assist her, therefore, O most merciful Father: neither respect her offences, or the deserts of her parents, or the manifold sins of us, her people; but think upon thy wonted compassion, always at hand to thy poor afflicted.

Preserve her kingdom, maintain religion, defend thy cause, our Queen, us, thy sheep and her people. Scatter thine enemies, which thirst after war. Let them be ashamed and confounded, that worship idols. Let us not be a prey to the nations, that know not thee, neither call upon thy name.

Strengthen and confirm, O Lord, that good work, which thou hast begun. Inspire our gracious Queen, thy servant, and us, thy poor flock with thy Holy Spirit; that with uncorrupt life we may so join purity of religion, as we may not yield and bring forth wild and bastard fruits, but mild and sweet grapes, and fruits beseeming repentance, and meet and convenient for thy gospel, to the intent we may enjoy this immortal treasure immortally, and that, living and dying in thee, we may finally possess the inheritance of thy heavenly kingdom. Through Jesus Christ our Lord. For thine is the kingdom, the power, and the glory, for ever. Amen.

[FROM *Book of Common Prayers,* 1578]

The Authorized Version
of the Bible

THE WOOING OF REBEKAH

AND ABRAHAM was old, and well stricken in age: and the Lord had blessed Abraham in all things. And Abraham said unto his eldest servant of his house, that ruled over all that he had, "Put, I pray thee, thy hand under my thigh: and I will make thee swear by the Lord, the God of heaven, and the God of the earth, that thou shalt not take a wife unto my son of the daughters of the Canaanites, among whom I dwell: but thou shalt go unto my country, and to my kindred, and take a wife unto my son Isaac."

And the servant said unto him, "Peradventure the woman will not be willing to follow me unto this land: must I needs bring thy son again unto the land from whence thou camest?" And Abraham said unto him, "Beware thou that thou bring not my son thither again. The Lord God of heaven, which took me from my father's house, and from the land of my kindred, and which spake unto me, and that sware unto me, saying, Unto thy seed will I give this land; he shall send his angel before thee, and thou shalt take a wife unto my son from thence. And if the woman will not be willing to follow thee, then thou shalt be clear from this my oath: only bring not my son thither again."

And the servant put his hand under the thigh of Abraham his master, and sware to him concerning that matter. And the servant took ten camels of the camels of his master, and departed; for all the goods of his master were in his hand: and he arose, and went to Mesopotamia, unto the city of Nahor. And he made his camels to kneel down without the city by a well of water at the time of the evening, even the time that women go out to draw water, and he said, "O Lord God of my master Abraham, I pray thee, send me good speed this day, and show kindness unto my master Abraham. Behold, I stand here by the well of water; and the daughters of the men of the city come out to draw water: and let it come to pass, that the damsel to whom I shall say, Let down thy pitcher, I pray thee, that I may drink; and she shall say, Drink, and I will give thy camels drink also: let the same be she that thou hast appointed for thy servant Isaac; and thereby shall I know that thou hast showed kindness unto my master."

And it came to pass, before he had done speaking, that, behold, Rebekah came out, who was born to Bethuel, son of Milcah, the wife of Nahor, Abraham's brother, with her pitcher upon her shoulder: and the damsel was very fair to look upon, a virgin, neither had any man known her: and she went down to the well, and filled her pitcher, and came up. And the servant ran to meet her, and said, "Let me, I pray thee, drink a little water of thy pitcher." And she said, "Drink, my lord": and she hasted, and let down her pitcher upon her hand, and gave him drink. And when she had done giving him drink, she said, "I will draw water for thy camels also, until they have done drinking." And she hasted, and emptied her pitcher into the trough, and ran again unto the well to draw water, and drew for all his camels; and the man wondering at her held his peace, to wit whether the Lord had made his journey prosperous or not.

And it came to pass, as the camels had done drinking,

that the man took a golden earring of half a shekel weight, and two bracelets for her hands of ten shekels weight of gold; and said, "Whose daughter art thou? tell me, I pray thee: is there room in thy father's house for us to lodge in?" And she said unto him, "I am the daughter of Bethuel the son of Milcah, which she bare unto Nahor." She said moreover unto him, "We have both straw and provender enough, and room to lodge in." And the man bowed down his head, and worshipped the Lord. And he said, "Blessed be the Lord God of my master Abraham, who hath not left destitute my master of his mercy and his truth: I being in the way, the Lord led me to the house of my master's brethren."

And the damsel ran, and told them of her mother's house these things. And Rebekah had a brother, and his name was Laban: and Laban ran out unto the man, unto the well. And it came to pass, when he saw the earring and bracelets upon his sister's hands, and when he heard the words of Rebekah his sister, saying, "Thus spake the man unto me," that he came unto the man; and, behold, he stood by the camels at the well. And he said, "Come in, thou blessed of the Lord; wherefore standest thou without? for I have prepared the house, and room for the camels." And the man came into the house: and he ungirded his camels, and gave straw and provender for the camels, and water to wash his feet, and the men's feet that were with him. And there was set meat before him to eat: but he said, "I will not eat, until I have told mine errand." And he said, "Speak on." And he said,

"I am Abraham's servant. And the Lord hath blessed my master greatly; and he is become great: and he hath given him flocks, and herds, and silver, and gold, and menservants, and maidservants, and camels, and asses. And Sarah my master's wife bare a son to my master when she was old: and unto him hath he given all that he hath. And my master made me swear, saying, Thou shalt not take a wife to my son of the daughters of the Canaanites, in whose land I dwell: but thou shalt go unto my father's house, and to my kindred, and take a wife unto my son. And I said unto my master, Peradventure the woman will not follow me. And he said unto me, The Lord, before whom I walk, will send his angel with thee, and prosper thy way; and thou shalt take a wife for my son of my kindred, and of my father's house: then shalt thou be clear from this my oath, when thou comest to my kindred; and if they give not thee one, thou shalt be clear from my oath. And I came this day unto the well, and said, O Lord God of my master Abraham, if now thou do prosper my way which I go: behold, I stand by the well of water; and it shall come to pass, that when the virgin cometh forth to draw water, and I say to her, Give me, I pray thee, a little water of thy pitcher to drink; and she say to me, Both drink thou, and I will also draw for thy camels: let the same be the woman whom the Lord hath appointed out for my master's son. And before I had done speaking in mine heart, behold, Rebekah came forth with her pitcher on her shoulder; and she went down unto the well, and drew water: and I said unto her, Let me drink, I pray thee. And she made haste, and let down her pitcher from her shoulder, and said, Drink, and I will give thy camels drink also: so I drank, and she made the camels drink also. And I asked her, and said, Whose daughter art thou? and she said, The daughter of Bethuel, Nahor's son, whom Milcah bare unto him. And I put the earring upon her face, and the bracelets upon her hands. And I bowed down my head, and worshipped the Lord, and blessed the Lord God of my master Abraham, which had led me in the right way to take my master's brother's daughter unto his son. And now if ye will deal kindly and truly with my master, tell me: and if not, tell me; that I may turn to the right hand, or to the left."

Then Laban and Bethuel answered and said, "The thing proceedeth from the Lord: we cannot speak unto thee bad or good. Behold, Rebekah is before thee, take her, and go, and let her be thy master's son's wife, as the Lord hath spoken."

And it came to pass, that, when Abraham's servant heard their words, he worshipped the Lord, bowing himself to the earth. And the servant brought forth jewels of silver, and jewels of gold, and raiment, and gave them to Rebekah: he gave also to her brother and to her mother precious things. And they did eat and drink, he and the men that were with him, and tarried all night; and they rose up in the morning, and he said, "Send me away unto my master." And her brother and her mother said, "Let the damsel abide with us a few days, at the least ten; after that she shall go." And he said unto them, "Hinder me not, seeing the Lord hath prospered my way; send me away that I may go to my master."

And they said, "We will call the damsel, and inquire at her mouth." And they called Rebekah, and said unto her, "Wilt thou go with this man?" And she said, "I will go." And they sent away Rebekah their sister, and her nurse, and Abraham's servant, and his men. And they blessed Rebekah, and said unto her, "Thou art our sister, be thou the mother of thousands of millions, and let thy seed possess the gate of those which hate them." And Rebekah arose, and her damsels, and they rode upon the camels, and followed the man: and the servant took Rebekah, and went his way.

And Isaac came from the way of the well Lahai-roi; for he dwelt in the south country. And Isaac went out to meditate in the field at the eventide: and he lifted up his eyes, and saw, and, behold, the camels were coming.

And Rebekah lifted up her eyes, and when she saw Isaac, she lighted off the camel. For she had said unto the servant, "What man is this that walketh in the field to meet us?" and the servant had said, "It is my master": therefore she took a veil, and covered herself. And the servant told Isaac all things that he had done. And Isaac brought her into his mother Sarah's tent, and took Rebekah, and she became his wife; and he loved her: and Isaac was comforted after his mother's death.

[*Genesis* xxiv]

JEW OR GENTILE

Now there are diversities of gifts, but the same Spirit. And there are differences of administrations, but the same Lord. And there are diversities of operations, but it is the same God which worketh all in all. But the manifestation of the Spirit is given to every man to profit withal. For to one is given by the Spirit the word of wisdom; to another the word of knowledge by the same Spirit; to another faith by the same Spirit; to another the gifts of healing by the same Spirit; to another the working of miracles; to another prophecy; to another discerning of spirits; to another divers kinds of tongues; to another the interpretation of tongues: but all these worketh that one and the selfsame Spirit, dividing to every man severally as he will.

For as the body is one, and hath many members, and all the members of that one body, being many, are one body: so also is Christ. For by one Spirit are we all baptized into one body, whether we be Jews or Gentiles, whether we be bond or free; and have been all made to drink into one Spirit. For the body is not one member, but many. If the foot shall say, Because I am not the hand, I am not of the body; is it therefore not of the

body? And if the ear shall say, Because I am not the eye,
I am not of the body; is it therefore not of the body? If
the whole body were an eye, where were the hearing? If
the whole were hearing, where were the smelling? But
now hath God set the members every one of them in the
body, as it hath pleased him. And if they were all one
member, where were the body? But now are they many
members, yet but one body. And the eye cannot say unto
the hand, I have no need of thee: nor again the head to
the feet, I have no need of you. Nay, much more those
members of the body, which seem to be more feeble, are
necessary: and those members of the body, which we
think to be less honourable, upon these we bestow more
abundant honour; and our uncomely parts have more
abundant comeliness. For our comely parts have no
need: but God hath tempered the body together, having
given more abundant honour to that part which lacked:
that there should be no schism in the body, but that the
members should have the same care one for another.
And whether one member suffer, all the members suffer
with it; or one member be honoured, all the members
rejoice with it. Now ye are the body of Christ, and members in particular. And God hath set some in the church,
first apostles, secondarily prophets, thirdly teachers,
after that miracles, then gifts of healings, helps, govern-
ments, diversities of tongues. Are all apostles? are all
prophets? are all teachers? are all workers of miracles?
Have all the gifts of healing? do all speak with tongues?
do all interpret? But covet earnestly the best gifts.

And yet show I unto you a more excellent way.
Though I speak with the tongues of men and of angels,
and have not love, I am become as sounding brass, or a
tinkling cymbal. And though I have the gift of prophecy,
and understand all mysteries, and all knowledge; and
though I have all faith, so that I could remove moun-

tains, and have not love, I am nothing. And though I bestow all my goods to feed the poor, and though I give my body to be burned, and have not love, it profiteth me nothing. Love suffereth long, and is kind; love envieth not; vaunteth not itself, is not puffed up, doth not behave itself unseemly, seeketh not her own, is not easily provoked, thinketh no evil; rejoiceth not in iniquity, but rejoiceth in the truth; beareth all things, believeth all things, hopeth all things, endureth all things. Love never faileth: but whether there be prophecies, they shall fail; whether there be tongues, they shall cease; whether there be knowledge, it shall vanish away. For we know in part, and we prophesy in part. But when that which is perfect is come, then that which is in part shall be done away. When I was a child I spake as a child, I understood as a child, I thought as a child: but when I became a man, I put away childish things. For now we see through a glass, darkly; but then face to face; now I know in part; but then shall I know even as also I am known. And now abideth faith, hope, love, these three; but the greatest of these is love.

[*I Corinthians*, xii, 4-31; xiii]

THE PARABLE OF THE PRODIGAL SON

And [1] hee said, A certaine man had two sonnes: and the yonger of them said to his father, Father, giue me the portion of goods that falleth to me. And he diuided vnto them his liuing. And not many dayes after, the yonger sonne gathered al together, and tooke his iourney into a farre countrey, and there wasted his substance with riotous liuing. And when he had spent all, there arose a mighty famine in that land, and he beganne to be in want. And he went and ioyned himselfe to a citizen

---

[1] Spelling of this and next extract not modernized.

of that countrey, and he sent him into his fields to feed
swine. And he would faine haue filled his belly with the
huskes that the swine did eate: & no man gaue vnto him.
And when he came to himselfe, he said, How many
hired seruants of my fathers haue bread inough and to
spare, and I perish with hunger? I will arise and goe to
my father, and will say vnto him, Father, I haue sinned
against heauen and before thee. And am no more worthy
to be called thy sonne: make me as one of thy hired
seruants. And he arose and came to his father. But when
he was yet a great way off, his father saw him, and had
compassion, and ranne, and fell on his necke, and kissed
him. And the sonne said vnto him, Father, I haue sinned
against heauen, and in thy sight, and am no more
worthy to be called thy sonne. But the father saide to
his seruants, Bring foorth the best robe, and put it on
him, and put a ring on his hand, and shooes on his feete.
And bring hither the fatted calfe, and kill it, and let vs
eate and be merrie. For this my sonne was dead, and is
aliue againe; hee was lost, & is found. And they began to
be merie.

Now his elder sonne was in the field, and as he came
and drew nigh to the house, he heard musicke & daunc-
ing, And he called one of the seruants, and asked what
these things meant. And he said vnto him, Thy brother
is come, and thy father hath killed the fatted calfe, because he hath receiued him safe and sound. And he was
angry, and would not goe in: therefore came his father
out, and intreated him. And he answering said to his
father, Loe, these many yeeres doe I serue thee, neither
transgressed I at any time thy commandement, and yet
thou neuer gauest mee a kid, that I might make merry
with my friends: But as soone as this thy sonne was come,
which hath deuoured thy liuing with harlots, thou hast
killed for him the fatted calfe. And he said vnto him,

Sonne, thou art euer with me, and all that I haue is thine. It was meete that we should make merry, and be glad: for this thy brother was dead, and is aliue againe: and was lost, and is found.

[*St. Luke* xv. 11-32]

MARY MAGDALENE AT THE SEPULCHRE

But Mary stood without at the sepulchre, weeping: & as shee wept, she stouped downe, and looked into the Sepulchre, And seeth two Angels in white, sitting, the one at the head, and the other at the feete, where the body of Jesus had layen: And they say vnto her, Woman, why weepest thou? Shee saith vnto them, Because they haue taken away my Lord, and I know not were they haue laied him. And when she had thus said, she turned herselfe backe, and saw Jesus standing, and knew not that it was Jesus. Jesus saith vnto her, Woman, why weepest thou? whom seekest thou? She supposing him to be the gardiner, saith vnto him, Sir, if thou haue borne him hence, tell me where thou hast laied him, and I will take him away. Jesus saith vnto her, Mary. She turned herselfe, and saith vnto him, Rabboni, which is to say, Master.

[*St. John* xx. 11-16]

Richard Hooker

OF THE LAWS OF THE UNIVERSE

ALL THINGS that are, have some operation not violent or casual. Neither doth any thing ever begin to exercise the same, without some fore-conceived end for which it worketh. And the end which it worketh for is not obtained, unless the work be also fit to obtain it by. For unto every end every operation will not serve. That which doth assign unto each thing the kind, that which doth moderate the force and power, that which doth appoint the form and measure, of working, the same we term a law. So that no certain end could ever be attained, unless the actions whereby it is attained were regular; that is to say, made suitable, fit and correspondent unto their end, by some canon, rule or law. Which thing doth first take place in the works even of God himself.

All things therefore do work after a sort according to law: all other things according to a law, whereof some superior, unto whom they are subject, is author; only the works and operations of God have him both for their worker, and for the law whereby they are wrought. The being of God is a kind of law to his working; for that perfection which God is, giveth perfection to that he doth. Those natural, necessary, and internal operations of God, the Generation of the Son, the Proceeding of the

Spirit, are without the compass of my present intent: which is to touch only such operations as have their beginning and being by a voluntary purpose, wherewith God hath eternally decreed when and how they should be. Which eternal decree is that we term an eternal law.

Dangerous it were for the feeble brain of man to wade far into the doings of the Most High; whom although to know be life, and joy to make mention of his name; yet our soundest knowledge is to know that we know him not as indeed he is, neither can know him: and our safest eloquence concerning him is our silence, when we confess without confession that his glory is inexplicable, his greatness above our capacity and reach. He is above, and we upon earth; therefore it behoveth our words to be wary and few.

Our God is one, or rather very Oneness, and mere unity, having nothing but itself in itself, and not consisting (as all things do besides God) of many things. In which essential Unity of God a Trinity personal nevertheless subsisteth, after a manner far exceeding the possibility of man's conceit. The works which outwardly are of God, they are in such sort of him being one, that each Person hath in them somewhat peculiar and proper. For being Three, and they all subsisting in the essence of one Deity; from the Father, by the Son, though the Spirit, all things are. That which the Son doth hear of the Father, and which the Spirit doth receive of the Father and the Son, the same we have at the hands of the Spirit as being the last, and therefore the nearest unto us in order, although in power the same with the second and the first.

The wise and learned among the very heathens themselves have all acknowledged some First Cause, whereupon originally the being of all things dependeth.

Neither have they otherwise spoken of that cause than as an Agent, which knowing what and why it worketh, observeth in working a most exact order or law. Thus much is signified by that which Homer mentioneth, Διὸς δ᾽ ἐτελείετο βουλή. Thus much acknowledged by Mercurius Trismegistus, Τὸν πάντα κόσμον ἐποίησεν ὁ δημιουργὸς οὐ χερσὶν ἀλλὰ λόγῳ. Thus much confest by Anaxagoras and Plato, terming the Maker of the world an *intellectual* Worker. Finally the Stoics, although imagining the first cause of all things to be fire, held nevertheless, that the same fire having art, did ὁδῷ βαδίζειν ἐπὶ γενέσει κόσμου. They all confess therefore in the working of that first cause, that counsel is used, reason followed, a way observed; that is to say, constant order and law is kept; whereof itself must needs be author unto itself. Otherwise it should have some worthier and higher to direct it, and so could not itself be the first. Being the first, it can have no other than itself to be the author of that law which it willingly worketh by.

God therefore is a law both to himself, and to all other things besides. To himself he is a law in all those things, whereof our Saviour speaketh, saying, "My Father worketh as yet, so I." God worketh nothing without cause. All those things which are done by him have some end for which they are done; and the end for which they are done is a reason of his will to do them. His will had not inclined to create woman, but that he saw it could not be well if she were not created. *Non est bonum*, "It is not good man should be alone; therefore let us make a helper for him." That and nothing else is done by God, which to leave undone were not so good.

If therefore it be demanded, why God having power and ability infinite, the effects notwithstanding of that power are all so limited as we see they are: the reason hereof is the end which he hath proposed, and the law whereby his wisdom hath stinted the effects of his power in such sort, that it doth not work infinitely, but correspondently unto that end for which it worketh, even "all things χρηστῶς, in most decent and comely sort," all things in measure, number, and weight.

The general end of God's external working is the exercise of his most glorious and most abundant virtue. Which abundance doth shew itself in variety, and for that cause this variety is oftentimes in Scripture exprest by the name of *riches*. "The Lord hath made all things for his own sake." Not that any thing is made to be beneficial unto him, but all things for him to shew beneficence and grace in them.

The particular drift of every act proceeding externally from God we are not able to discern, and therefore cannot always give the proper and certain reason of his works. Howbeit undoubtedly a proper and certain reason there is of every finite work of God, inasmuch as there is a law imposed upon it; which if there were not, it should be infinite, even as the worker himself is.

They err therefore who think that of the will of God to do this or that there is no reason besides his will. Many times no reason known to us; but that there is no reason thereof I judge it most unreasonable to imagine, inasmuch as he worketh all things κατὰ τὴν βουλὴν τοῦ θελήματος αὐτοῦ, not only according to his own will, but "the Counsel of his own will." And whatsoever is done with counsel or wise resolution hath of necessity some reason why it should be done, albeit that reason be to us in some things so secret, that it forceth the wit of man to stand, as the blessed Apostle himself doth, amazed thereat: "O the depth of the riches both of the wisdom and knowledge of God! how unsearchable are his judgements," &c. That law eternal which God himself hath made to himself, and thereby worketh all things whereof he is the cause and author; that law in the admirable frame whereof shineth with most perfect beauty the countenance of that wisdom which hath testified concerning herself," "The Lord possessed me in the beginning of his way, even before his works of old I was set up;" that law, which hath been the pattern to make, and is the card to guide the world by; that law which hath been of God and with God everlastingly; that law, the author and observer whereof is one only God to be blessed for ever: how should either men or angels be able perfectly to behold? The book of this law we are neither able nor worthy to open and look into. That little thereof which we darkly apprehend we admire, the rest with religious ignorance we humbly and meekly adore.

Seeing therefore that according to this law he worketh, "of whom, through whom, and for whom, are all things;" although there seem unto us confusion and disorder in the affairs of this present world: *Tamen quoniam bonus mundum rector temperat, recte fieri cuncta ne dubites:*" "let no man doubt but that every thing is well done, because the world is ruled by so good a guide," as transgresseth not his own law: than which nothing can be more absolute, perfect, and just.

The law whereby he worketh is eternal, and therefore can have no show or colour of mutability: for which cause, a part of that law being opened in the promises which God hath made (because his promises are nothing else but declarations what God will do for the good of men) touching those promises the Apostle hath witnessed, that God may as possibly "deny himself" and not be God, as fail to perform them. And concerning the counsel of God, he termeth it likewise a thing "unchangeable;" the counsel of God, and that law of God whereof now we speak, being one.

Nor is the freedom of the will of God any whit abated, let, or hindered, by means of this; because the imposition of this law upon himself is his own free and voluntary act.

This law therefore we may name eternal, being "that order which God before all ages hath set down with himself, for himself to do all things by."

I am not ignorant that by "law eternal" the learned for the most part do understand the order, not which God hath eternally purposed himself in all his works to observe, but rather that which with himself he hath set down as expedient to be kept by all his creatures, according to the several conditions wherewith he hath endued them. They who thus are accustomed to speak apply the name of law unto that only rule of working which superior authority imposeth; whereas we somewhat more enlarging the sense thereof term any kind of rule or canon, whereby actions are framed, a law. Now that law which, as it is laid up in the bosom of God, they call eternal, receiveth according unto the different kinds of things which are subject unto it different and sundry kinds of names. That part of it which ordereth natural agents we call usually Nature's law; that which Angels do clearly behold and without any swerving observe is a law celestial and heavenly; the law of reason, that which bindeth creatures reasonable in this world, and with which by reason they may most plainly perceive themselves bound; that which bindeth them, and is not known but by special revelation from God, divine law; human law, that which out of the law either of reason or of God men probably gathering to be expedient, they make it a law. All things therefore, which are as they ought to be, are conformed unto *this second law eternal;* and even those things which to this eternal law are not conformable are notwithstanding in some sort ordered by *the first eternal law*. For what good or evil is here under the sun, what action correspondent or repugnant unto the law which God hath imposed upon his creatures, but in or upon it God doth work according to the law which himself hath eternally purposed to keep; that is to say, the *first law eternal?* So that a twofold law eternal being thus made, it is not hard to conceive how they both take place in all things. . . .

Of law there can be no less acknowledged, than that her seat is the bosom of God, her voice the harmony of the world; all things in heaven and earth do her homage, the very least as feeling her care, and the greatest as not exempted from her power; both Angels and men and creatures of what condition soever, though each in different sort and manner, yet all with uniform consent, admiring her as the mother of their peace and joy.

[FROM *Of the Laws of Ecclesiastical Polity*, Book I]

John Donne

CORRUPTION AND REDEMPTION

CORRUPTION in the skin, says Job; in the outward beauty, these be the records of vellum, these be the parchments and indictments, and the evidences that shall condemn many of us, at the last day, our own skins; we have the Book of God, the Law, written in our hearts; we have the image of God imprinted in our own souls; we have the character, and seal of God stamped in us, in our baptism; and, all this is bound up in this vellum, in this parchment in this skin of ours, and we neglect Book, and image, and character, and seal, and all for the covering. It is not a clear case, if we consider the original words properly, that Jezebel did paint; and yet all translators, and expositors have taken a just occasion, out of the ambiguity of those words, to cry down that abomination of painting. It is not a clear case, if we consider the propriety of the words, that Absalom was hanged by the hair of the head; and yet the Fathers and others have made use of that indifferency, and verisimilitude, to explode that abomination, of cherishing and curling hair, to the inveigling, and ensnaring, and entangling of others. *Judicium patietur aeternum*, says St. Jerome, Thou art guilty of a murder, though nobody die; *Quia vinum attulisti, si fuisset qui bibisset;* Thou hast poisoned a cup, if any would drink, thou hast prepared a temptation, if any would swallow it. Tertullian thought he had done enough, when he had writ his book *De Habitu muliebri*, against the excess of women in clothes, but he was fain to add another with more vehemence, *De cultu faeminarum*, that went beyond their clothes to their skin. And he concludes, *Illud ambitionis crimen*, there's vainglory in their excess of clothes, but *Hoc prostitutionis*, there's prostitution in drawing the eye to the skin. Pliny says, that when their thin silk stuffs were first invented at Rome, *Excogitatum ad faeminas denudandas;* it was but an invention that women might go naked in clothes, for their skins might be seen through those clothes, those thin stuffs. Our women are not so careful, but they expose their nakedness professedly, and paint it, to cast bird lime for the passenger's eye.

Beloved, good diet makes the best complexion, and a good conscience is a continual feast; a cheerful heart makes the best blood, and peace with God is the true cheerfulness of heart. Thy Saviour neglected his skin so much, as that at last, he scarce had any; all was torn with the whips, and scourges; and thy skin shall come to that absolute corruption, as that, though a hundred years after thou art buried, one may find thy bones, and say, this was a *tall* man, this was a *strong* man, yet we shall soon be past saying, upon any relic of thy skin, This was a *fair* man. Corruption seizes the skin, all outward beauty, quickly, and so it does the body, the whole frame and constitution, which is another consideration: After my skin, my Body.

If the whole body were an eye, or an ear, where were the body, says St. Paul; but, when of the whole body there is neither eye nor ear, nor any member left, where is the body? And what should an eye do there, where there is nothing to be seen but loathsomeness; or a nose there, where there is nothing to be smelt, but putrefaction; or an ear, where in the grave they do not praise God? Doth not that body that boasted but yesterday of that privilege above all creatures, that it only could go upright, lie today as flat upon the earth as the body of a horse, or of a dog? And doth it not tomorrow lose his other privilege, of looking up to heaven? Is it not farther removed from the eye of heaven, the Sun, than any dog, or horse, by being covered with the earth, which they are not? Painters have presented to us with some horror, the skeleton, the frame of the bones of a man's body; but the state of a body, in the dissolution of the grave, no pencil can present to us. Between that excremental jelly that thy body is made of at first, and that jelly which thy body dissolves to at last; there is not so noisome, so putrid a thing in nature. This skin (this outward beauty) this body (this whole constitution) must be destroyed, says Job, in the next place.

The word is well chosen, by which all this is expressed, in this text, *Nakaph,* which is a word of as heavy a signification, to express an utter abolition, and annihilation, as perchance can be found in all the Scriptures. Tremellius hath mollified it in his translation; there is but one *confodere,* to pierce. And yet it is such a piercing, such a sapping, such an undermining, such a demolishing of a fort or castle, as may justly remove us from any high valuation, or any great confidence, in that skin, and in that body, upon which this *confoderint* must fall. But in the great Bible it is *contriverint,* thy skin, and thy body shall be ground away, trod away upon the ground. Ask where that iron is that is ground off a knife, or axe; ask that marble that is worn off of a threshold in the church porch by continual treading, and with that iron, and with that marble, thou mayst find thy Father's skin, and body; *contrita sunt,* the knife, the marble, the skin, the body are ground away, trod away, they are destroyed. Who knows the revolutions of dust? Dust upon the King's highway, and dust upon the King's grave, are both, or neither, Dust Royal, and may change places. Who knows the revolutions of dust?

Even in the dead body of Christ Jesus himself, one dram of the decree of his Father, one sheet, one sentence of the prediction of the Prophets preserved his body from corruption, and incineration, more than all Joseph's new tombs, and fine linen, and great proportion of spices could have done. O, who can express this inexpressible mystery? The soul of Christ Jesus, which took no harm by him, contracted no original sin, in coming to him, was guilty of no more sin, when it went out, than when it came from the breath and bosom of God; yet this soul left this body in death. And the Divinity, the Godhead, incomparably better than that soul, which soul was incomparably better than all the Saints, and Angels in heaven, that Divinity, that Godhead did not forsake the body, though it were dead. If we might compare things infinite in themselves; it was nothing so much, that God did assume man's nature, as that God did still cleave to that man, then when he was no man, in the separation of body and soul, in the grave. But fall we from incomprehensible mysteries; for, there is mortification enough (and mortification is vivification, and edification) in this obvious consideration: skin and body, beauty and substance must be destroyed; and, destroyed by worms, which is another descent in this humiliation, and exinanition of man, in death; after my skin, worms shall destroy this body.

I will not insist long upon this, because it is not in the Original. In the Original there is no mention of worms. But because in other places of Job there is (They shall lie down alike in the dust, and the worms shall cover them) (The womb shall forget them, and the worm shall feed sweetly on them; and because the word Destroying is presented in that form and number, *contriverint*, when they shall destroy, they and no other persons, no other creatures named) both our later translations (for indeed, our first translation hath no mention of worms) and so very many others, even Tremellius that adheres most to the letter of the Hebrew, have filled up this place, with that addition, Destroyed by worms. It makes the destruction the more contemptible; thou that wouldest not admit the beams of the Sun upon thy skin, and yet hast admitted the spirit of lust, and unchaste solicitations to breathe upon thee, in execrable oaths, and blasphemies, to vicious purposes; thou, whose body hath (as far as it can) putrefied and corrupted even the body of thy Saviour, in an unworthy receiving thereof, in this skin, in this body, must be the food of worms, the prey of destroying worms. After a low birth thou mayst pass an honorable life, after a sentence of an ignominious death, thou mayst have an honorable end. But, in the grave canst thou make these worms silk worms? They were bold and early worms that eat up Herod before he died; they are bold and everlasting worms, which after thy skin and body is destroyed, shall remain as long as God remains, in an eternal gnawing of thy conscience; long, long after the destroying of skin and body, by bodily worms. . . .

[FROM *Sermon XIV*]

II

God made the first Marriage, and man made the first Divorce; God married the Body and Soul in the Creation, and man divorced the Body and Soul by death through sin, in his fall. God doth not admit, not justify, not authorize such super-inductions upon such Divorces, as some have imagined: that the soul departing from one body, should become the soul of another body, in a perpetual revolution and transmigration of souls through bodies, which hath been the giddiness of some Philosophers to think; Or that the body of the dead should become the body of an evil spirit, that that spirit might at his will, and to his purposes inform, and inanimate that dead body; God allows no such super-inductions, no such second Marriages upon such Divorces by death, no such disposition of soul or body, after their dissolution by death.

But because God hath made the band of Marriage indissoluble but by death, farther than man can die, this Divorce cannot fall upon man. As far as man is immortal, man is a married man still, still in possession of a soul, and a body too. And man is forever immortal in both: immortal in his soul by preservation, and immortal in his body by reparation in the Resurrection. For, though they be separated *a Thoro et Mensa*, from Bed and Board, they are not divorced; though the soul be at the Table of the Lamb, in Glory, and the body but at the table of the Serpent, in dust; though the soul be *in lecto florido*, in that bed which is always green, in an everlasting spring, in Abraham's Bosom; and the body but in that green-bed, whose covering is but a yard and a half of Turf, and a Rug of Grass, and the sheet but a winding sheet, yet they are not divorced; they shall return to one another again, in an inseparable reunion in the Resurrection. . . .

How imperfect is all our knowledge! What one thing do we know perfectly? Whether we consider Arts, or Sciences, the servant knows but according to the proportion of his Master's knowledge in that Art, and the Scholar knows but according to the proportion of his Master's knowledge in that Science; young men mend not their sight by using old men's Spectacles; and yet we look upon Nature, but with Aristotle's Spectacles, and upon the body of man, but with Galen's, and upon the frame of the world, but with Ptolemy's Spectacles. Almost all knowledge is rather like a child that is embalmed to make Mummy, than that is nursed to make a Man; rather conserved in the stature of the first age, than grown to be greater; And if there be any addition to knowledge, it is rather a new knowledge, than a greater knowledge; rather a singularity in a desire of proposing something that was not known at all before, than an improving, an advancing, a multiplying of former inceptions; and by that means, no knowledge comes to be perfect. . . .

But we must not insist upon his Consideration of knowledge; for, though knowledge be of a spiritual nature, yet it is but as a terrestrial Spirit, conversant upon Earth; Spiritual things, of a more rarified nature than knowledge, even faith itself, and all that grows from that in us, falls within this Rule, which we have in hand; That even in spiritual things, nothing is perfect. . . .

When we consider with a religious seriousness the manifold weaknesses of the strongest devotions in time of Prayer, it is a sad consideration. I throw myself down in my Chamber, and I call in, and invite God, and his Angels thither, and when they are there, I neglect God and his Angels, for the noise of a Fly, for the rattling of a Coach, for the whining of a door; I talk on, in the same posture of praying; eyes lifted up; knees bowed down; as though I prayed to God; and, if God, or his Angels should ask me, when I thought last of God in that prayer, I cannot tell: sometimes I find that I had forgot what I was about, but when I began to forget it, I cannot tell. A memory of yesterday's pleasures, a fear of tomorrow's dangers, a straw under my knee, a noise in mine ear, a light in mine eye, an anything, a nothing, a fancy, a Chimera in my brain, troubles me in my prayer. So certainly is there nothing, nothing in spiritual things, perfect in this world. . . .

I need not call in new Philosophy, that denies a settledness, an acquiescence in the very body of the Earth, but makes the Earth to move in that place, where we thought the Sun had moved; I need not that help, that the Earth itself is in Motion, to prove this, that nothing upon Earth is permanent; the Assertion will stand of itself, till some man assign me some instance, something that a man may rely upon, and find permanent. Consider the greatest Bodies upon Earth, the Monarchies; Objects, which one would think, Destiny might stand and stare at, but not shake; consider the smallest bodies upon Earth, the hairs of our head, Objects, which one would think, Destiny would not observe, or could not discern. And yet, Destiny (to speak to a natural man) and God (to speak to a Christian) is no more troubled to make a

Monarchy ruinous, than to make a hair gray. Nay, nothing needs be done to either, by God, or Destiny; a Monarchy will ruin, as a hair will grow gray, of itself. In the Elements themselves, of which all sub-elementary things are composed, there is no acquiescence, but a vicissitudinary transmutation into one another; air condensed becomes water, a more solid body, and air rarified becomes fire, a body more disputable, and inapparent.

It is so in the conditions of men too; a Merchant condensed, kneaded and packed up in a great estate, becomes a Lord; and a Merchant rarified, blown up by a perfidious Factor, or by a riotous Son, evaporates into air, into nothing, and is not seen. And if there were anything permanent and durable in this world, yet we got nothing by it, because howsoever that might last in itself, yet we could not last to enjoy it; if our goods were not amongst Movables, yet we ourselves are; if they could stay with us, yet we cannot stay with them; which is another consideration in this part.

The world is a great Volume, and man the Index of that Book: Even in the body of man, you may turn to the whole world; this body is an illustration of all Nature; God's recapitulation of all that he had said before in his *Fiat lux,* and *Fiat firmamentum,* and in all the rest, said or done, in all the six days. Propose this body to thy consideration in the highest exaltation thereof; as it is the Temple of the Holy Ghost: Nay, not in a metaphor, or comparison of a Temple, or any other similitudinary thing, but as it was really and truly the very Body of God, in the person of Christ, and yet this body must wither, must decay, must languish, must perish. When Goliath had armed and fortified this body, and Jezebel had painted and perfumed this body, and Dives had pampered and larded this body, as God said to Ezekiel, when he brought him to the dry bones, *Fili hominis,* Son of Man, dost thou think these bones can live? They said in their hearts to all the world, Can these bodies die? And they are dead. Jezebel's dust is not Amber, nor Goliath's dust *Terra sigillata,* Medicinal; nor does the Serpent, whose meat they are both, find any better relish in Dives' dust than in Lazarus'. But as in our former part, where our foundation was, that in nothing, no spiritual thing, there was any perfectness, which we illustrated in the weaknesses of Knowledge, and Faith, and Hope, and Charity, yet we concluded, that for all those defects, God accepted those their religious services; so in this part, where our foundation is, that nothing in temporal things is permanent, as we have illustrated that, by the decay of that which is God's noblest piece in Nature, the body of man; so we shall also conclude that, with this goodness of God, that for all this dissolution, and putrefaction he affords this Body a Resurrection.

The Gentiles, and their Poets, describe the sad state of Death so, *Nox una obeunda,* that it is one everlasting night; to them, a Night; but to a Christian, it is *Dies Mortis,* and *Dies Resurrectionis,* the day of Death, and the day of Resurrection. We die in the light in the sight of God's presence, and we rise in the light in the sight of his very Essence. Nay, God's corrections, and judgements upon us in this life, are still expressed so, *Dies visitationis,* still it is a Day, though a Day of visitation; and still we may discern God to be in the action. The Lord of Life was the first that named Death; *Morte morieris,* says God, Thou shalt die the Death. I do the less fear, or abhor Death, because I find it in his mouth.

Even a malediction hath a sweetness in his mouth; for there is a blessing wrapped up in it; a mercy in every correction a Resurrection upon every Death. When

Jezebel's beauty, exalted to that height which it had by
art, or higher than that, to that height which it had in
her own opinion, shall be infinitely multiplied upon
everybody; and as God shall know no man from his own
Son, so as not to see the very righteousness of his own
Son upon that man; so the Angels shall know no man
from Christ, so as not to desire to look upon that man's
face, because the most deformed wretch that is there,
shall have the very beauty of Christ himself. So shall
Goliath's armor, and Dives' fulness, be doubled, and re-
doubled upon us, and every thing that we can call good,
shall first be infinitely exalted in the goodness, and then
infinitely multiplied in the proportion, and again infinitely extended in the duration. And since we are in an
action of preparing this dead Brother of ours to that
state (for the Funeral is the Easter-eve, the Burial is the
depositing of that man for the Resurrection) as we have
held you, with the Doctrine of Mortification, by extending the Text, from Martha to this occasion; so shall we
dismiss you with Consolation, by a like occasional in-
verting the Text, from passion in Martha's mouth, Lord,
if thou hadst been here, my Brother had not died, to joy
in ours, Lord, because thou wast here, our Brother is not
dead.

The Lord was with him in all these steps; with him in
his life; with him in his death; he is with him in his
funerals, and he shall be with him in his Resurrection;
and therefore, because the Lord was with him, our
Brother is not dead. He was with him in the beginning of
his life, in this manifestation, that though he were of
Parents of a good, of a great Estate, yet his possibility
and his expectation from them, did not slacken his own
industry; which is a Canker that eats into, nay that hath
eat up many a family in this City, that relying wholly
upon what the Father hath done, the Son does nothing

for himself. And truly, it falls out too often, that he that labors not for more, does not keep his own. God imprinted in him an industrious disposition, though such hopes from such parents might have excused some slackness, and God prospered his industry so, as that when his Father's estate came to a distribution by death, he needed it not. God was with him, as with David in a Dilatation, and then in a Repletion; God enlarged him, and then he filled him; he gave him a large and comprehensive understanding, and with it, a public heart; and such as perchance in his way of education, and in our narrow and contracted times, in which every man determines himself in himself, and scarce looks farther, it would be hard to find many Examples of such largeness.

You have, I think a phrase of driving a Trade; and you have, I know a practise of driving away Trade, by other use of money; and you have lost a man, that drove a great Trade, the right way in making the best use of our home-commodity. To fetch in Wine, and Spice, and Silk, is but a drawing of Trade; the right driving of trade, is, to vent our own outward; and yet, for the drawing in of that, which might justly seem most behooveful, that is, of Arts, and Manufactures, to be employed upon our own Commodity within the Kingdom, he did his part, diligently, at least, if not vehemently, if not passionately. This City is a great Theater, and he acted great and various parts in it; and all well.

And when he went higher (as he was often heard in Parliaments, at Council tables, and in more private accesses to the late King of ever blessed memory) as, for that comprehension of those businesses, which he pretended to understand, no man doubts, for no man lacks arguments and evidences of his ability therein, so for his manner of expressing his intentions, and digesting and uttering his purposes, I have sometimes heard the greatest Master of Language and Judgement, which these times, or any other did, or do, or shall give (that good and great King of ours) say of him, that he never heard any man of his breeding, handle businesses more rationally, more pertinently, more elegantly, more persuasively. And when his purpose was, to do a grace to a Preacher, of very good abilities, and good note in his own Chapel, I have heard him say, that his language, and accent, and manner of delivering himself, was like this man.

This man hath God accompanied all his life; and by performance thereof seems to have made that Covenant with him, which he made to Abraham, *Multiplicabote vehementer,* I will multiply thee exceedingly. He multiplied his estate so, as was fit to endow many and great Children; and he multiplied his Children so, both in their number, and in their quality, as they were fit to receive a great Estate. God was with him all the way, in a Pillar of Fire, in the brightness of prosperity, and in the Pillar of Clouds, too, in many dark, and sad, and heavy crosses. So great a Ship, required a great Ballast, so many blessings, many crosses; and he had them, and sailed on his course the steadier for them; the Cloud as well as the Fire, was a Pillar to him; his crosses, as well as his blessings established his assurance in God. And so, in all the course of his life, the Lord was here, and therefore our Brother is not dead; not dead in the evidences and testimonies of life; for he, whom the world hath just cause to celebrate, for things done, when he was alive, is alive still in their celebration.

The Lord was here, that is, with him at his death too. He was served with the Process here in the City, but his cause was heard in the Country; here he sickened, There he languished, and died there. In his sickness there, those that assisted him, are witnesses, of his many expressings, of a religious and a constant heart towards God, and of his pious joining with them, even in the holy declaration of kneeling, then, when they, in favor of his weakness, would dissuade him from kneeling. I must not defraud him of this testimony for myself, that into this place where we are now met, I have observed him to enter with much reverence, and compose himself in this place with much declaration of devotion. And truly it is that reverence, which those persons who are of the same rank that he was in the City, that reverence that they use in this place, when they come hither, is that that makes us, who have now the administration of this Choir, glad, that our Predecessors, but a very few years before our time (and not before all our times neither) admitted these Honorable and worshipful Persons of this City, to sit in this Choir, so, as they do upon Sundays. The Church receives an honor in it; but the honor is more in their reverence, than in their presence; though in that too: and they receive an honor, and an ease in it; and therefore they do piously towards God, and prudently for themselves, and gratefully towards us, in giving us, by their reverent comportment here, so just occasion of continuing that honor, and that ease to them here, which to less reverent, and unrespective persons, we should be less willing to do.

To return to him in his sickness; he had but one day's labor, and all the rest were Sabbaths, one day in his sickness he converted to business thus; he called his family, and friends together; thankfully he acknowledged God's manifold blessings, and his own sins as penitently. And then, to those who were to have the disposing of his estate, jointly with his Children, he recommended his servants, and the poor, and the Hospitals, and the Prisons, which, according to his purpose, have been all taken into consideration. And after this (which

mandment to Wife and Children was Christ's last commandment to his Spouse the Church, in the Apostles, to
love one another. He blest them, and the Estate de-
volved upon them, unto them. And by God's grace shall
prove as true a Prophet to them in that blessing, as he
was to himself, when in entering his last bed, two days
before his Death, he said, "Help me off with my earthly
habit, and let me go to my last bed." Where, in the
second night after, he said, "Little know ye what pain
I feel this night, yet I know I shall have joy in the
morning." And in that morning he died.

The form in which he implored his Saviour, was evermore, towards his end, this, "Christ Jesus, which died on
the Cross, forgive me my sins; have mercy upon me."
And his last and dying words were the repetition of the
name of Jesus; and when he had not strength to utter
that name distinctly and perfectly, they might hear it
from within him, as from a man afar off; even then,
when his hollow and remote naming of Jesus, was rather
a certifying of them, that he was with his Jesus, than a
prayer that he might come to him. And so the Lord was
here, here with him in his Death; and because the Lord
was here, our Brother is not dead; not dead in the eyes
and ears of God; for as the blood of Abel speaks yet, so
doth the zeal of God's Saints; and their last prayers
(though we hear them not) God continues still; and
they pray in Heaven, as the Martyrs under the Altar,
even till the Resurrection.

He is with him now too; here in his Funerals. Burial,
and Christian Burial, and Solemn Burial are all evidences, and testimonies of God's presence. God forbid
we should conclude, or argue an absence of God, from
the want of Solemn Burial, or Christian Burial, or any
Burial; but neither must we deny it, to be an evidence of
his favor and presence, where he is pleased to afford

Burial; but neither must we deny it, to be an evidence of his favor and presence, where he is pleased to afford these. So God makes that the seal of all his blessings to Abraham, that he should be buried in a good age; God established Jacob with that promise, That his Son Joseph should have care of his Funerals. And Joseph does cause his servants, the Physicians, to embalm him, when he was dead. Of Christ it was Prophesied, that he should have a glorious Burial; and therefore Christ interprets well that profuse, and prodigal piety of the Woman that poured out the Ointment upon him, that she did it to bury him. And so shall Joseph of Arimathea be ever celebrated, for his care in celebrating Christ's Funerals. If we were to send a Son, or a friend, to take possession of any place in Court, or foreign parts, we would send him out in the best equipage. Let us not grudge to set down our friends, in the Ante-chamber of Heaven, the Grave, in as good manner, as without vain-gloriousness, and wastefulness we may. And, in inclining them, to whom that care belongs, to express that care as they do this day, the Lord is with him, even in this Funeral; and because the Lord is here, our brother is not dead; Not dead in the memories and estimation of men.

And lastly, that we may have God present in all his Manifestations, he that was, and is, and is to come, was with him, in his life and death, and is with him in this holy Solemnity, and shall be with him again in the Resurrection. God says to Jacob, "I will go down with thee into Egypt, and I will also surely bring thee up again." God goes down with a good man into the Grave, and will surely bring him up again. When? The Angel promised to return to Abraham and Sarah, for the assurance of the birth of Isaac, according to the time of life; that is, in such time, as by nature a woman may have a child. God will return to us in the Grave, according to the time of life; that is, in such time, as he, by his gracious Decree, hath fixed for the Resurrection. And in the meantime, no more than the Godhead departed from the dead body of our Saviour, in the grave, doth his power, and his presence depart from our dead bodies in that darkness; But that which Moses said to the whole Congregation, I say to you all, both to you that hear me, and to him that does not, "All ye that did cleave unto the Lord your God, are alive, every one of you this day." Even he whom we call dead, is alive this day. In the presence of God, we lay him down; in the power of God, he shall rise; in the person of Christ, he is risen already. And so into the same hands that have received his soul, we commend his body; beseeching his blessed Spirit, that as our charity inclines us to hope confidently of his good estate, our faith may assure us of the same happiness, in our own behalf; And that for all our sakes, but especially for his own glory, he will be pleased to hasten the consummation of all, in that kingdom which that Son of God hath purchased for us, with the inestimable price of his incorruptible blood. *Amen.*

[Sermon LXXX, *preached at the funeral of Sir William Cokayne*]

PART FOUR

The Creed of the Court

I. The Perfect Courtier

Fulke Greville

THE PRESIDENT OF CHIVALRY:
SIR PHILIP SIDNEY

I MUST lift him above the censure of subjects, and give you an account of what respect and honor his worth won him amongst the most eminent monarchs of that time: as first with that chief and best of princes, his most excellent Majesty, then King of Scotland, to whom his service was affectionately devoted, and from whom he received many pledges of love and favor.

In like manner, with the late renowned Henry of France, then of Navarre, who having measured and mastered all the spirits in his own Nation, found out this master-spirit among us, and used him like an equal in nature, and so fit for friendship with a king.

Again, that gallant prince Don John of Austria, Viceroy in the Low Countries for Spain, when this gentleman in his embassage to the Emperor came to kiss his hand, though at the first, in his Spanish hauteur, he gave him access as by descent, to a youth of grace as to a stranger, and in particular competition—as he conceived—to an enemy; yet after a while, when he had taken his just altitude, he found himself so stricken with this extraordinary planet, that the beholders wondered to see what ingenuous tribute that brave and high-minded prince paid to his worth; giving more honor and respect to this hopeful young gentleman, than to the ambassadors of mighty princes.

But to climb yet a degree higher: in what due estimation his extraordinary worth was, even amongst enemies, will appear by his death. When Mendoza, a secretary of many treasons amongst us, acknowledged openly that howsoever he was glad King Philip, his master, had lost, in a private gentleman, a dangerous enemy to his estate; yet he could not but lament to see Christendom deprived of so rare a light in those cloudy times; and bewail poor widow England—so he termed her—that having been many years in breeding one eminent spirit, was in a moment bereaved of him, by the hands of a villain.

Indeed he was a true model of worth; a man fit for Conquest, Plantation, Reformation, or what action soever is greatest and hardest amongst men: withal, such a lover of mankind and goodness, that whoever had any real parts, in him found comfort, participation, and protection to the uttermost of his power: like Zephyrus he giving life where he blew. The Universities abroad and at home, accounted him a general Maecenas of learning; dedicated their books to him; and communicated every invention, or improvement of knowledge, with him. Soldiers honored him, and were so honored by him as no man thought he marched under the true banner of Mars, that had not obtained Sir Philip Sidney's approbation. Men of affairs in most parts of Christendom, entertained correspondence with him. But what speak I of these, with whom his own ways and ends did concur? Since—to descend—his heart and capacity were so

large that there was not a cunning Painter, a skilful
Engineer, an excellent Musician, or any other artificer of
extraordinary fame, that made not himself known to this
famous spirit, and found him his true friend without
hire; and the common Rendezvous of Worth in his time.

Now let princes vouchsafe to consider, of what importance it is to the honor of themselves and their estates, to have one man of such eminence; not only as a
nourisher of virtue in their Courts or service, but besides
for a reformed standard, by which even the most hu-
morous persons could not but have a reverent kind of
ambition to be tried, and approved current. This I do
the more confidently affirm, because it will be confessed
by all men, that this one man's example and personal
respect, did not only encourage Learning and Honour in
the Schools, but brought the affection and true use
thereof both into the Court and Camp. Nay more, even
many gentlemen excellently learned amongst us, will
not deny, but that they affected to row and steer their
course in his wake. Besides which honour of unequal
nature and education his very ways in the world, did
generally add reputation to his Prince and Country, by
restoring amongst us the ancient majesty of noble and
true dealing: as a manly wisdom, that can no more be
weighed down by any effeminate craft, than Hercules
could be overcome by that contemptible army of dwarfs.
And this was it which, I profess, I loved dearly in him,
and still shall be glad to honour in the great men of this
time: I mean, that his heart and tongue went both one
way, and so with every one that went with the Truth;
as knowing no other kindred, party, or end.

Above all, he made the Religion he professed, the
firm basis of his life: for this was his judgement—as he
often told me—that our true-heartedness to the Reformed Religion in the beginning, brought peace and

safety and freedom to us; concluding that the wisest and best way was that of the famous William, Prince of Orange, who never divided the consideration of Estate from the consideration of Religion, nor gave that sound party occasion to be jealous, or distracted, upon any appearance of safety whatsoever; prudently resolving, that to temporize with the enemies of our Faith, was but— as among sea gulls—a strife, not to keep upright, but aloft upon the top of every billow: which falseheartedness to God and man, would in the end find itself forsaken of both; as Sir Philip conceived. For to this active spirit of his, all depths of the devil proved but shallow fords; he piercing into men's counsels and ends, not by their words, oaths, or compliments, all barren in that age, but by fathoming their hearts and powers, by their deeds, and found no wisdom where he found no courage, nor courage without wisdom, nor either without honesty and truth. With which solid and active reaches of his, I am persuaded, he would have found or made a way through all the traverses, even of the most weak and irregular times. But it pleased God in this decrepit age of the world, not to restore the image of her ancient vigor in him, otherwise than as in a lightning before death.

Neither am I—for my part—so much in love with this life, nor believe so little in a better to come, as to complain of God for taking him, and such like exorbitant worthiness from us: fit—as it were by an ostracism—to be divided, and not incorporated with our corruptions: yet for the sincere affection I bear to my Prince and Country, my prayer to God is, that his worth and way may not fatally be buried with him; in respect, that before his time and since, experience hath published the usual discipline of greatness to have been tender of itself only; making honour a triumph, or rather trophy of

desire, set up in the eyes of mankind, either to be worshipped as idols, or else as rebels to perish under her
glorious oppressions.

Notwithstanding, when the pride of flesh, and power
of favour shall cease in these by death or disgrace; what
then hath Time to register, or fame to publish, in these
great men's names, that will not be offensive and infec-
tious to others? What pen without blotting can write the
story of their deeds? Or what herald blaze their arms
without a blemish? And as for their counsels and projects, when they come once to light, shall not they live
as noisome and loathsomely above ground, as their authors' carcasses lie in the grave? So that the return of
such greatness to the world and themselves, can be but
private reproach, public ill example, and a fatal scorn to
the Government they live in. Sir Philip Sidney is none
of this number; for the greatness which he affected was
built upon true worth; esteeming fame more than riches,
and noble actions far above nobility itself.

THE QUARREL ON THE TENNIS COURT

Thus stood the Court at that time; and thus stood this
ingenuous spirit in it. If dangerously in men's opinions
who are curious of the present, and in it rather to do
craftly, than well: yet, I say, that princely heart of hers
was a sanctuary unto him; and as for the people, in
whom many times the lasting images of Worth are preferred before the temporary visions of art of favour, he
could not fear to suffer anything there, which would not
prove a kind of trophy to him. So that howsoever he
seemed to stand alone, yet he stood upright; kept his
access to her Majesty as before; a liberal conversation
with the French, reverenced amongst the worthiest of
them for himself, and bound in too strong a fortification

of nature for the less worthy to accost, either with question, familiarity, or scorn.

In this freedom, even whilst the greatest spirits and estates seemed hoodwinked or blind; and the inferior sort of men made captive by hope, fear, ignorance; did he enjoy the freedom of his thoughts, with all recreations worthy of them.

And in this freedom of heart being one day at tennis, a peer of this realm, born great, greater by alliance, and superlative in the Prince's favor, abruptly came into the Tennis Court; and speaking out of these three paramount authorities, he forgot to entreat that which he could not legally command. When by the encounter of a steady object, finding unrespectiveness in himself— though a great lord—not respected by this princely spirit, he grew to expostulate more roughly. The returns of which style coming still from an understanding heart, that knew what was due to itself, and what it owed to others, seemed—through the mists of my lord's passion, swollen with the winds of this faction then reigning—to provoke in yielding. Whereby, the less amazement or confusion of thoughts he stirred up in Sir Philip, the more shadows this great lord's own mind was possessed with: till at last with rage—which is ever ill-disciplined —he commands them to depart the Court.

To this Sir Philip temperately answers; that if his lordship had been pleased to express desire in milder characters, perchance he might have led out those, that he should now find would not be driven out with any scourge of fury. This answer—like a bellows—blowing up the sparks of excess already kindled, made my lord scornfully call Sir Philip by the name of "puppy."

In which progress of heat, as the tempest grew more and more vehement within, so did their hearts breathe out their perturbations in a more loud and shrill accent.

The French Commissioners unfortunately had that day audience, in those private galleries, whose windows looked into the Tennis Court. They instantly drew all to this tumult: every sort of quarrels sorting well with their humors, especially this. Which Sir Philip perceiving, and rising with an inward strength by the prospect of a mighty faction against him; asked my lord, with a loud voice, that which he heard clearly enough before. Who —like an echo, that still multiplies by reflections—repeated this epithet of "puppy" the second time. Sir Philip resolving in one answer to conclude both the attentive hearers and passionate actor, gave my lord a lie, impossible—as he averred—to be retorted; in respect all the world knows, puppies are gotten by dogs, and children by men.

Hereupon those glorious inequalities of fortune in his Lordship were put to a kind of pause, by a precious inequality of nature in this gentleman. So that they both stood silent a while, like a dumb show in a Tragedy; till Sir Philip sensible of his own wrong, the foreign and factious spirits that attended; and yet, even in this question between him, and his superior, tender of his Country's honour; with some words of sharp accent, led the way abruptly out of the Tennis Court, as if so unexpected an accident were not fit to be decided any farther in that place. Whereof the great lord making another sense, continues his play, without any advantage of reputation; as by the standard of humors in those times it was conceived.

A day Sir Philip remains in suspense. Then, hearing nothing of or from the Lord, he sends a gentleman of worth to awake him out of his trance; wherein the French would assuredly think any pause, if not death, yet a lethargy of true honour in both. This stirred up a resolution in his lordship to send Sir Philip a challenge.

Notwithstanding, these thoughts in the great lord wandered so long between glory and anger and inequality of state, as the lords of her Majesty's Council took notice of these differences, commanded peace, and labored a reconciliation between them—but needlessly in one respect, and bootlessly in another. The great lord being—as it should seem—either not hasty to adventure many inequalities against one, or inwardly satisfied with the progress of his own acts: Sir Philip, on the other side confident, he neither had nor would lose, or let fall anything of his right. Which her Majesty's Council quickly perceiving, recommended this work to herself.

The Queen, who saw that by the loss or disgrace of either, she could gain nothing, presently undertakes Sir Philip; and—like an excellent Monarch—lays before him the difference in degree between earls and gentlemen; the respect inferiors owed to their superiors; and the necessity in princes to maintain their own creations, as degrees descending between the people's licentiousness and the anointed sovereignty of crowns: how the gentleman's neglect of the nobility taught the peasant to insult upon both.

Whereunto Sir Philip, with such reverence as became him, replied: First, that place was never intended for privilege to wrong: witness herself, who how sovereign soever she were by throne, birth, education, and nature; yet was she content to cast her own affections into the same molds her subjects did, and govern all her rights by their laws. Again he besought her Majesty to consider, that although he were a great lord by birth, alliance, and grace; yet he was no lord over him: and therefore the difference of degrees between free men, could not challenge any other homage than precedence. And by her father's act—to make a princely wisdom become the more familiar—he did instance the govern-

ment of King Henry VIII, who gave the gentry free and
safe appeal unto his feet, against the oppressions of the
grandees; and found it wisdom, by the stronger corporation in number, to keep down the greater in power: in-
ferring else, that if they should unite, the overgrown
might be tempted by still coveting more, to fall—as the
angels did—by affecting equality with their Maker.

This constant tenor of truth he took upon him; which
as a chief duty in all creatures, both to themselves and
the sovereignty above them, protected this gentleman—
though he obeyed not—from the displeasure of his sovereign. Wherein he left an authentical precedent to after
ages, that howsoever tyrants allow of no scope, stamp, or
standard, but their own will; yet with princes there is
a latitude for subjects to reserve native and legal freedom, by paying humble tribute in manner, though not in
matter, to them.

"THY NEED IS GREATER THAN MINE"

When that unfortunate stand was to be made before
Zutphen, to stop the issuing out of the Spanish Army
from a strait; with what alacrity soever he went to actions of honor, yet remembering that upon just grounds
the ancient sages describe the worthiest persons to be
ever best armed, he had completely put on his; but meeting the marshall of the Camp lightly armed—whose
honour in that art would not suffer this unenvious Themistocles to sleep—the unspotted emulation of his heart,
to venture without any inequality, made him cast off his
cuisses, and so, by the secret influence of destiny, to
disarm that part, where God—it seems—had resolved
to strike him. Thus they go on, every man in the head of
his own troop; and the weather being misty, fell unawares upon the enemy, who had made a strong stand to

receive them, near to the very walls of Zutphen; by reason of which accident their troops fell, not only unexpectedly to be engaged within the level of the great shot that played from the *rampiers,* but more fatally within shot of their muskets, which were laid in ambush within their own trenches.

Now whether this were a desperate cure in our leaders, for a desperate disease; or whether misprision, neglect, audacity, or what else induced it, it is no part of my office to determine, but only to make the narration clear, and deliver rumour, as it passed then, without any stain or enamel.

Howsoever, by this stand, an unfortunate hand out of those forespoken trenches, brake the bone of Sir Philip's thigh with a musket-shot. The horse he rode upon, was rather furiously choleric, than bravely proud, and so forced him to forsake the field, but not his back, as the noblest and fittest bier to carry a martial commander to his grave. In which sad progress, passing along by the rest of the army, where his uncle the general was, and being thirsty with excess of bleeding, he called for drink, which was presently brought him.

But as he was putting the bottle to his mouth he saw a poor soldier carried along, who had eaten his last at the same feast, ghastly casting up his eyes at the bottle. Which Sir Philip perceiving, took it from his head, before he drank, and delivered it to the poor man, with these words, "Thy necessity is yet greater than mine." And when he had pledged this poor soldier, he was presently carried to Arnheim.

DEATH

First, he called the Ministers unto him; who were all excellent men, of divers Nations, and before them made such a confession of Christian faith, as no book but the heart can truly and feelingly deliver. Then he desired them to accompany him in prayer, wherein he besought leave to lead the assembly, in respect—as he said—that the secret sins of his own heart were best known to himself, and out of that true sense, he more properly instructed to apply the eternal Sacrifice of our Saviour's Passion and Merits to him. His religious zeal prevailed with this humbly devout and afflicted company; in which well-chosen progress of his, howsoever they were all moved, and those sweet motions witnessed by sighs and tears, even interrupting their common devotion; yet could no man judge in himself, much less in others, whether this rack of heavenly agony, whereupon they all stood, was forced by reason of sorrow for him, or admiration of him; the fire of this phoenix being hardly able out of any ashes to produce his equal, as they conceived.

Here this first mover stayed the motions in every man, by staying himself. Whether to give rest to that frail wounded flesh of his, unable to bear the bent of eternity so much affected any longer; or whether to abstract that spirit more inwardly, and by chewing as it were the cud of meditation, to imprint these excellent images in his soul; who can judge but God? Notwithstanding, in this change—it would seem—there was little or no change in the object. For instantly after prayer, he entreated his choir of divine philosophers about him, to deliver the opinion of the ancient heathen, touching the immortality of the soul: First to see what true knowledge she retains of her own essence, out of the light of herself; then to parallel with it the most pregnant authorities of the Old and New Testament, as supernatural revelations, sealed up from our flesh, for the divine light of faith to reveal and work by. Not that he wanted instruction or assurance; but because this fixing of a lover's thoughts upon those eternal beauties, was not only a cheering up of his decaying spirits, but as it were a taking possession of that immortal inheritance, which was given unto him by his brotherhood in Christ.

The next change used, was the calling for his Will; which though at first sight it may seem a descent from heaven to earth again; yet he that observes the distinction of those offices, which he practised in bestowing his own, shall discern, that as the soul of man is all in all and all in every part; so was the goodness of his nature equally dispersed, into the greatest and least actions of his too short life. Which Will of his, will ever remain for a witness to the world, that those sweet and large, even dying affections in him, could no more be contracted with the narrowness of pain, grief, and sickness, than any sparkle of our immortality can be privately buried in the shadow of death.

Here again this restless soul of his—changing only the air, and not the cords of her harmony—calls for music; especially that song which himself had entitled, *La cuisse rompue:* partly—as I conceive by the name— to shew that the glory of mortal flesh was shaken in him: and by the music itself, to fashion and enfranchise his heavenly soul into that everlasting harmony of angels, whereof these concords were a kind of terrestrial echo: and in this supreme, or middle orb of contemplation, he blessedly went on, within a circular motion, to the end of all flesh.

The last scene of this tragedy, was the parting of the two brothers: the weaker showing infinite strength in suppressing sorrow, and the stronger infinite weakness in expressing it. So far did invaluable worthiness, in the dying brother, enforce the living to descend beneath his own worth, and by abundance of childish tears, bewail the public, in his particular loss. Yea, so far was his true remission of mind transformed into lamentation, that Sir Philip—in whom all earthly passion did even as it were flash, like lights ready to burn out—recalls those spirits together with a strong virtue, but weak voice; mildly blaming him for relaxing the frail strengths left to support him, in this final combat of separation at hand. And to stop this natural torrent of affection in both, took his leave, in these admonishing words:

"Love my memory, cherish my friends; their faith to me may assure you they are honest. But above all, govern your will and affections, by the will and Word of your Creator; in me, beholding the end of this world, with all her vanities."

And with this farewell, he desired the company to lead him away. Here the noble gentleman ended the too short line of his life; in which path, whosoever is not confident that he walked the next way to eternal rest, will be found to judge uncharitably.

[FROM *The Life of the Renowned Sir Philip Sidney*]

Sir Robert Naunton

ELIZABETH'S ESSEX

MY LORD of ESSEX (as Sir Henry Wotton, a gentleman of great parts, and partly of his time and retinue, observes) had his introduction by my Lord of Leicester, who had married his Mother, a tie of affinity, which, besides a more urgent obligation, might have invited his care to advance him, his Fortune being then (and through his Father's infelicity) grown low. But that the son of a Lord Ferrers of Chartley, Viscount Hartford, and Earl of Essex, who was of the ancient Nobility, and formerly in the Queen's good grace, could not have room in her favour, without the assistance of Leicester, was beyond the rule of her nature, which as I have elsewhere taken into observation, was ever inclinable to favour the Nobility. Sure it is, that he no sooner appeared in Court, but he took with the Queen and Courtiers; and I believe, they all could not choose but look through the Sacrifice of the Father, on his living Son, whose image, by the remembrance of former passages, was afresh (like the bleeding of men murdered) represented to the Court, and offered up as a subject of compassion to all the Kingdom. There was in this young Lord, together with a most goodly Person, a kind of urbanity or innate courtesy, which both won the Queen, and too much took upon the people, to gaze upon the new adopted son of her favour.

And as I go along, it were not amiss to take into observation two notable quotations. The first was, a violent indulgence of the Queen (which is incident to old age, where it encounters with a pleasing and suitable object) towards this Lord; all which argued a non-perpetuity. The second was, a fault in the Object of her grace, my Lord himself, who drew in too fast, like a child sucking on an over-uberous Nurse; and had there been a more decent decorum observed in both, or either of those, without doubt the unity of their affections had been more permanent, and not so in and out as they were, like an Instrument ill tuned, and lapsing to discord.

The great error of the two (though unwillingly) I am constrained to impose on my Lord of Essex, or rather on his youth; and none of the least of his blame on those that stood Sentinels about him, who might have advised him better, but that like men intoxicated with hopes, they likewise had sucked in with the most, and of their Lord's receipt, and so like Caesars would have all or none: a rule quite contrary to nature, and the most indulgent Parents, who though they may express more affection to one in the abundance of bequests, yet cannot forget some Legacies, just distributives, and dividends to others of their begetting. And how hateful partiality proves, every day's experience tells us, out of which common consideration might have framed to their hands a maxim of more discretion for the conduct and management of their now graced Lord and Master.

But to omit that of infusion, and to do right to truth: My Lord of Essex (even of those that truly loved and honoured him) was noted for too bold an engrosser both of fame and favour; and of this (without offense to the living, or treading on the sacred urn of the dead) I shall present a truth, and a passage yet in memory.

My Lord Mountjoy (who was another child of her favour), being newly come to Court, and then but Sir Charles Blunt (for my Lord William, his elder brother, was then living), had the good fortune one day to run very well a Tilt; and the Queen therewith was so well pleased, that she sent him in token of her favour, a Queen at Chess of gold richly enameled, which his servants had the next day fastened on his Arm with a Crimson ribbon; which my Lord of Essex, as he passed through the Privy Chamber espying, with his cloak cast under his Arm, the better to commend it to the view, enquired what it was, and for what cause there fixed? Sir Fulke Greville told him, that it was the Queen's favour, which the day before, and after the Tilting she had sent him, whereat my Lord of Essex, in a kind of emulation, and as though he would have limited her favour, said, "Now I perceive every fool must have a favour."

This bitter and public affront came to Sir Charles Blunt's ear, who sent him a challenge, which was accepted by my Lord, and they met near Marybone, where my Lord was hurt in the thigh and disarmed. The Queen missing the men, was very curious to learn the truth; and when at last it was whispered out, she swore by God's death, it was fit that someone or other should take him down, and teach him better manners, otherwise there would be no rule with him. And here I note the inition of my Lord's friendship with Mountjoy, which the Queen herself did then conjure.

Now for the same, we need not go far; for my Lord of Essex having borne a grudge to General Norris, who had (unwittingly) offered to undertake the action of Britain with fewer men, than my Lord had before demanded: on his return with victory, and a glorious report of his valour, he was then thought the only man for the Irish War; wherein my Lord of Essex so wrought, by despising the number and quality of Rebels, that Norris was sent over with a scanted force, joined with the relics of the veteran troops of Britain, of set purpose (as it fell out) to ruin Norris; and the Lord Burrowes, by my Lord's procurement, sent at his heels, and to command in chief; and to confine Norris only to his government at Munster, which broke the great heart of the General, to see himself undervalued and undermined by my Lord and Burrowes, which was as the Proverb speaks it, *Imberbes docere senes.*

My Lord Burrowes, in the beginning of his prosecution died; whereupon the Queen was fully bent to have sent over Mountjoy, which my Lord of Essex utterly disliked, and opposed with many reasons, and by arguments of contempt against Mountjoy, his then professed friend and familiar; so predominant were his words, to reap the honour of closing up that War, and all other.

Now the way being opened and planned by his own workmanship, and so handled that none durst appear to stand for the place, at last with much ado he obtained his own ends, and withal his fatal destruction, leaving the Queen and the Court (where he stood firm and impregnable in her grace) to men that long had sought and watched their times to give him the trip, and could never find any opportunity but this of his absence, and of his own creation. And these are the true observations of his appetite and inclinations, which were not of any true proportion, but carried and transported with an over-desire and thirstiness after fame, and that deceitful fame of popularity.

And to help on his Catastrophe, I observe likewise two sorts of people that had a hand in his fall; the first was the Soldiery, which all flocked unto him, as foretelling a mortality; and are commonly of blunt and too rough counsels, and many times dissonant from the time of the Court and the State. The other sort were of his family, his servants, and his own creatures, such as were bound by the rules of safety, and obligations of fidelity, to have looked better to the steering of that Boat, wherein they themselves were carried, and not have suffered it to float and run aground, with those empty Sails of Fame and Rumour of popular applause.

Methinks one honest man or other, that had but the office of brushing his clothes, might have whispered in his ear, "My Lord, look to it, this multitude that follows you, will either devour you, or undo you; strive not to rule, and over-rule all, for it will cost hot water, and it will procure envy; and if needs your Genius must have it so, let the Court, and the Queen's presence be your station."

But as I have said, they had sucked too much of their Lord's milk, and instead of withdrawing, they blew the coals of his ambition, and infused into him too much of the spirit of glory; yea, and mixed the goodness of his nature with a touch of revenge, which is ever accompanied with a destiny of the same fate. And of this number there were some insufferable Natures about him, that towards his last gave desperate advice, such as his integrity abhorred, and his fidelity forbade; Amongst whom, Sir Henry Wotton notes (without injury) his Secretary Cuffe, a vile man, and of a perverse nature.

I could also name others, that when he was in the right course of recovery, and settling to moderation, would not suffer a recess in him, but stirred up the dregs of those rude humours, which by time, and his affliction, out of his own judgement he sought to repose; or to give them all a vomit. And thus I conclude this noble Lord, as a mixture between prosperity and adversity; once the Child of his great Mistress' favour, but the son of Bellona.

[FROM *Fragmenta Regalia, or, Observations on the Late Queen Elizabeth, Her Times and Favourites*]

Thomas Dekker

HOW A GALLANT SHOULD BEHAVE HIMSELF IN A PLAYHOUSE

THE THEATER is your Poets' Royal Exchange, upon which their Muses (that are now turned to Merchants), meeting, barter away that light commodity of words for a lighter ware than words, Plaudits, and the breath of the great Beast; which (like the threatenings

of two Cowards) vanish all into air. Players and their
Factors, who put away the stuff, and make the best of
it they possibly can (as indeed it is their parts so to do),
your Gallant, your Courtier, and your Captain had wont
to be the soundest paymasters; and I think are still the
surest chapmen: and these, by means that their heads
are well stocked, deal upon this comical freight by the
gross: when your Groundling and Gallery-commoner
buys his sport by the penny, and, like a Haggler, is glad
to utter it again by retailing.

Since then the place is so free in entertainment, allowing a stool as well to the Farmer's son as to your Tem-
pler: that your Stinkard has the self-same liberty to be
there in his Tobacco Fumes, which your sweet Courtier
hath: and that your Carman and Tinker claim as strong
a voice in their suffrage, and sit to give judgement on the
play's life and death, as well as the proudest Momus
among the tribe of Critic, it is fit that he, whom the
most tailors' bills do make room for, when he comes,
should not be basely (like a viol) cased up in a corner.

Whether therefore the gatherers of the public or
private Playhouse stand to receive the afternoon's rent,
let our Gallant (having paid it) presently advance himself up to the Throne of the Stage. I mean not into the
Lords' room (which is now but the stage's Suburbs):
No, those boxes by the iniquity of custom, conspiracy of
waiting-women and Gentlemen-Ushers, that there sweat
together, and the covetousness of Sharers, are contempt-
ibly thrust into the rear, and much new Satin is there
damned, by being smothered to death in darkness. But
on the very Rushes where the Comedy is to dance, yea,
and under the state of Cambises himself must our feath-
ered Ostrich, like a piece of Ordnance, be planted valiantly (because impudently) beating down the mews
and hisses of the opposed rascality.

For do but cast up a reckoning, what large comings-in are pursed up by sitting on the Stage. First a conspicuous Eminence is gotten; by which means, the best and most essential parts of a Gallant (good clothes, a proportionable leg, white hand, the Persian lock, and a tolerable beard) are perfectly revealed.

By sitting on the Stage, you have a signed patent to engross the whole commodity of Censure; may lawfully presume to be a Girder; and stand at the helm to steer the passage of scenes; yet no man shall once offer to hinder you from obtaining the title of an insolent, overweening Coxcomb.

By sitting on the Stage, you may (without travelling for it) at the very next door ask whose play it is: and, by that Quest of Inquiry the law warrants you to avoid much mistaking: if you know not the author, you may rail against him: and peradventure so behave yourself, that you may enforce the Author to know you.

By sitting on the Stage, if you be a Knight, you may happily get you a Mistress: if a mere Fleet-Street Gentleman, a wife: but assure yourself, by continual residence, you are the first and principal man in election to begin the number of We Three.

By spreading your body on the Stage, and by being a Justice in examining of plays, you shall put yourself into such true scenical authority, that some Poet shall not dare to present his Muse rudely upon your eyes, without first having unmasked her at a tavern, when you most knightly shall, for his pains, pay for both their suppers.

By sitting on the Stage, you may (with small cost) purchase the dear acquaintance of the boys: have a good stool for sixpence: at any time know what particular part any of the infants present: get your match lighted, examine the playsuits' lace, and perhaps win wagers upon

laying 'tis copper, etc. And to conclude, whether you be
a fool or a Justice of peace, or a Captain, a Lord Mayor's
son, or a dawcock, a knave, or an under-Sheriff; of what
stamp soever you be, current, or counterfeit, the Stage,
like time, will bring you to most perfect light and lay you
open: neither are you to be hunted from thence, though
the Scarecrows in the yard hoot at you, hiss at you, spit
at you, yea, throw dirt even in your teeth: it is most
Gentlemanlike patience to endure all this, and to laugh
at the silly Animals: but if the Rabble, with a full throat,
cry, away with the fool, you were worse than a madman
to tarry by it: for the Gentleman, and the fool should
never sit on the Stage together.

Marry, let this observation go hand in hand with the
rest: or rather, like a country serving-man, some five
yards before them. Present not yourself on the Stage
(especially at a new play) until the quaking prologue
hath (by rubbing) got colour into his cheeks, and is ready
to give the trumpets their Cue, that he is upon point to
enter: for then it is time, as though you were one of the
Properties, or that you dropped out of the Hangings, to
creep from behind the Arras, with your Tripos or three-
footed stool in one hand, and a teston mounted between
a forefinger and a thumb in the other: for if you should
bestow your person upon the vulgar, when the belly of
the house is but half full, your apparel is quite eaten up,
the fashion lost, and the proportion of your body in more
danger to be devoured than if it were served up in the
Counter amongst the Poultry: avoid that as you would
the Bastome.

It shall crown you with rich commendation to laugh
aloud in the middle of the most serious and saddest
scene of the terriblest Tragedy: and to let that clapper
(your tongue) be tossed so high, that all the house may
ring of it: your Lords use it; your Knights are Apes to

the Lords, and do so too: your Inns-of-Court man is Zany to the Knights, and (marry very scurvily) comes likewise limping after it. Be thou a beagle to them all, and never leave snuffing, till you have scented them: for by talking and laughing (like a Ploughman in a Morris) you heap Pelion upon Ossa, glory upon glory: As first, all the eyes in the galleries will leave walking after the Players, and only follow you: the simplest dolt in the house snatches up your name, and when he meets you in the streets, or that you fall into his hands in the middle of a Watch, his word shall be taken for you. He'll cry, "He's such a gallant," and you pass. Secondly, you publish your temperance to the world, in that you seem not to resort thither to taste vain pleasures with a hungry appetite: but only as a gentleman to spend a foolish hour or two, because you can do nothing else. Thirdly, you mightily relish the Audience and disgrace the Author: marry, you take up (though it be at the worst hand) a strong opinion of your own judgement, and enforce the Poet to take pity on your weakness, and, by some dedicated sonnet, to bring you into a better paradise, only to stop your mouth.

If you can (either for love or money) provide yourself a lodging by the waterside: for, above the convenience it brings to shun Shoulder-clapping, and to ship away your Cockatrice betimes in the morning, it adds a kind of state unto you, to be carried from thence to the stairs of your Playhouse: hate a Sculler (remember that) worse than to be acquainted with one of the Scullery. No, your Oars are your only sea-crabs, board them, and take heed you never go twice together with one pair: often shifting is a great credit to Gentlemen; and that dividing of your fare will make the poor water-snakes be ready to pull you in pieces to enjoy your custom. No matter whether upon landing, you have money or no: you may swim in twenty of their boats over the river upon Ticket: marry, when silver comes in, remember to pay treble their fare, and it will make your Flounder-catchers to send more thanks after you, when you do not draw, than when you do, for they know, it will be their own another day.

Before the Play begins, fall to cards: you may win or lose (as Fencers do in a prize) and beat one another by confederacy, yet share the money when you meet at supper: notwithstanding, to gull the Raggamuffins that stand aloof gaping at you, throw the cards (having first torn four or five of them) round about the Stage, just upon the thirds sound, as though you had lost: it skills not if the four knaves lie on their backs, and outface the Audience; there's none such fools as dare take exception to them, because, ere the Play go off, better knaves than they will fall into the company.

Now sir, if the writer be a fellow that hath either epi- grammed you, or hath had a flirt at your mistress, or hath brought either your feather, or your red beard, or your little legs etc. on the stage, you shall disgrace him worse than by tossing him in a blanket, or giving him the bastinado in a Tavern, if, in the middle of his Play (be it Pastoral or Comedy, Moral or Tragedy), you rise with a screwed and discontented face from your stool to be gone: no matter whether the Scenes be good or no; the better they are the worse do you distaste them: and, being on your feet, sneak not away like a coward, but salute all your gentle acquaintances, that are spread either on the rushes, or on stools about you, and draw what troop you can from the stage after you: the Mimics are beholden to you, for allowing them elbow-room: their Poet cries, perhaps, "A pox go with you," but care not for that—there's no music without frets.

Marry, if either the company, or indisposition of the

weather bind you to sit it out, my counsel is then that you turn plain Ape, take up a rush, and tickle the earnest ears of your fellow Gallants, to make other fools fall a-laughing: mew at passionate speeches, blare at merry, find fault with the music, whew at the children's Action, whistle at the songs: and above all, curse the sharers, that whereas the same day you had bestowed forty shillings on an embroidered Felt and Feather (Scotch-fashion), for your mistress in the Court, within two hours after, you encounter with the very same block on the Stage, when the haberdasher swore to you the impression was extant but that morning.

To conclude, hoard up the finest play-scraps you can get, upon which your lean wit may most favorably feed, for want of other stuff, when the Arcadian and Euphuized gentlewomen have their tongues sharpened to set upon you: that quality (next to your shuttlecock) is the only furniture to a Courtier that is but a new beginner, and is but in his A B C of compliment. The next places that are filled, after the Playhouses be emptied, are (or ought to be) Taverns: into a Tavern then let us next march, where the brains of one Hogshead must be beaten out to make up another.

II. The Religion of Beauty in Women

Edmund Spenser

THE FAERIE QUEENE

THE AUTHOR'S INTRODUCTION

A LETTER of the Author's expounding his whole intention in the course of this work: which for that it giveth great light to the reader, for the better understanding is hereunto annexed.

SIR, knowing how doubtfully all allegories may be construed, and this book of mine, which I have entitled *The Faerie Queene*, being a continued allegory, or dark conceit, I have thought good as well for avoiding of jealous opinions and misconstructions, as also for your better light in reading thereof (being so by you commanded), to discover unto you the general intention and meaning, which in the whole course thereof I have fashioned, without expressing of any particular purposes or by-accidents therein occasioned. The general end therefore of all the book is to fashion a gentleman or noble person in virtuous and gentle discipline: which for that I conceived should be most plausible and pleasing, being coloured with an historical fiction, the which the most part of men delight to read rather for variety of matter than for profit of the ensample: I chose the history of King Arthur, as most fit for the excellency of his person, being made famous by many men's former works, and also furthest from the danger of envy, and suspicion of present time. In which I have followed all the antique poets historical, first Homer, who in the persons of Agamemnon and Ulysses hath ensampled a good governor and a virtuous man, the one in his *Ilias,* the other in his *Odysseis:* then Virgil, whose like intention was to do in the person of Aeneas: after him Ariosto comprised them both in his *Orlando:* and lately Tasso dissevered them again, and formed both parts in two persons, namely that part which they in Philosophy call Ethic, or virtues of a private man, coloured in his *Rinaldo:* the other named Politic in his *Godfredo.* By ensample of which excellent poets, I labour to portray in Arthur, before he was king, the image of a brave knight, perfected in the twelve private moral virtues, as Aristotle hath devised, the which is the purpose of these first twelve books: which if I find to be well accepted, I may be perhaps encouraged to frame the other part of politic virtues in his person, after that he came to be king. To some I know this method will seem displeasant, which had rather have good discipline delivered plainly in way of precepts, or sermoned at large, as they use, than thus cloudily enwrapped in allegorical devices. But such, meseem, should be satisfied with the use of these days, seeing all things accounted by their shows, and nothing esteemed of that is not delightful and pleasing to common sense. For this cause is Xenophon preferred before Plato, for that the one in the exquisite depth of his judgement, formed a Commonwealth such as it should be, but the other in the person of Cyrus and the Persians fashioned a government such as might best be:

so much more profitable and gracious is doctrine by ensample than by rule. So have I laboured to do in the person of Arthur: whom I conceive after his long education by Timon, to whom he was by Merlin delivered to be brought up, so soon as he was born of the Lady Igrayne, to have seen in a dream or vision the Faerie Queene, with whose excellent beauty ravished, he awaking resolved to seek her out, and so being by Merlin armed, and by Timon thoroughly instructed, he went to seek her forth in Faeryland. In that Faerie Queene I mean glory in my general intention, but in my particular I conceive the most excellent and glorious person of our sovereign the Queene, and her kingdom in Faeryland. And yet in some places else, I do otherwise shadow her. For considering she beareth two persons, the one of a most royal Queene or Empress, the other of a most virtuous and beautiful Lady, this latter part in some places I do express in Belphoebe, fashioning her name according to your own excellent concept of Cynthia (Phoebe and Cynthia being both names of Diana). So in the person of Prince Arthur I set forth magnificence in particular, which virtue for that (according to Aristotle and the rest) it is the perfection of all the rest, and containeth in it them all, therefore in the whole course I mention the deeds of Arthur applyable to that virtue, which I write of in that book. But of the twelve other virtues, I make twelve other knights the patrons, for the more variety of the history: of which these three books contain three, the first of the knight of the Redcross, in whom I express Holiness: the second of Sir Guyon, in whom I set forth Temperance: the third of Britomartis a Lady knight, in whom I picture Chastity. But because the beginning of the whole work seemeth abrupt and as depending upon other antecedents, it needs that ye know the occasion of these three knights' several adventures. For the method of a Poet historical is not such as of an Historiographer. For an Historiographer discourseth of affairs orderly as they were done, accounting as well the times as the actions, but a Poet thrusteth into the midst, even where it most concerneth him, and there recoursing to the things forepast, and divining of things to come, maketh a pleasing analysis of all. The beginning therefore of my history, if it were to be told by an Historiographer, should be the twelfth book, which is the last, where I devise that the Faerie Queene kept her annual feast twelve days, upon which twelve several days, the occasions of the twelve several adventures happened, which being undertaken by twelve several knights, are in these twelve books severally handled and discoursed. The first was this. In the beginning of the feast, there presented himself a tall clownish young man, who falling before the Queene of Faeries desired a boon (as the manner then was) which during that feast she might not refuse: which was that he might have the achievement of any adventure which during that feast should happen; that being granted, he rested him on the floor, unfit through his rusticity for a better place. Soon after entered a fair lady in mourning weeds, riding on a white ass, with a dwarf behind her leading a warlike steed, that bore the arms of a knight, and his spear in the dwarf's hand. She falling before the Queene of Faeries, complained that her father and mother, an ancient King and Queene, had been by a huge dragon many years shut up in a brazen castle, who thence suffered them not to issue: and therefore besought the Faerie Queene to assign her some one of her knights to take on him that exploit. Presently that clownish person upstarting, desired that adventure: whereat the Queene much wondering, and the lady much gainsaying, yet he earnestly importuned his desire. In the end the lady told him that unless that armour which she brought would serve him (that is the armour of a Christian man specified by St. Paul, v. *Ephes.*) that he could not succeed in that enterprise, which being forthwith put upon him with due furnitures thereunto, he seemed the goodliest man in all that company, and was well liked of the lady. And eftsoon taking on him knighthood, and mounting on that strange courser, he went forth with her on that adventure: where beginneth the first book, viz.

A gentle knight was pricking on the plain, &c.

The second day there came in a palmer bearing an infant with bloody hands, whose parents he complained to have been slain by an enchantress called Acrasia: and therefore craved of the Faerie Queene to appoint him some knight to perform that adventure, which being assigned to Sir Guyon, he presently went forth with that same palmer: which is the beginning of the second book and the whole subject thereof. The third day there came in a groom who complained before the Faerie Queene that a vile enchanter called Busirane had in hand a most fair lady called Amoretta, whom he kept in most grievous torment, because she would not yield him the pleasure of her body. Whereupon Sir Scudamour the lover of that lady presently took on him that adventure. But being unable to perform it by reason of the hard enchantments, after long sorrow, in the end met with Britomartis, who succoured him, and rescued his love.

But by occasion hereof, many other adventures are intermeddled, but rather as accidents than intendments. As the love of Britomart, the overthrow of Marinell, the misery of Florimell, the virtuousness of Belphoebe, the lasciviousnesss of Hellenora, and many the like.

Thus much, Sir, I have briefly overrun to direct your

understanding to the well-head of the history, that from thence gathering the whole intention of the conceit, ye may as in a handful grip all the discourse, which otherwise may haply seem tedious and confused. So humbly craving the continuance of your honourable favour towards me, and the eternal establishment of your happiness, I humbly take leave.

Yours most humbly affectionate,
ED. SPENSER.

23 January, 1589.

Sir Philip Sidney

ASTROPHEL AND STELLA

I

Loving in truth, and fain in verse my love to show,
    That she, dear she, might take some pleasure of my
        pain,
    Pleasure might cause her read, reading might make
        her know,
    Knowledge might pity win, and pity grace obtain—
I sought fit words to paint the blackest face of woe;
    Studying inventions fine, her wits to entertain,
    Oft turning others' leaves to see if thence would flow
    Some fresh and fruitful showers upon my sun-burned
        brain.
But words came halting forth, wanting invention's stay;
    Invention, Nature's child, fled step-dame Study's
        blows,
    And others' feet still seemed but strangers in my way.

Thus, great with child to speak, and helpless in my
    throes,
  Biting my truant pen, beating myself for spite,
  Fool, said my muse to me, look in thy heart and
    write. . . .

II

It is most true that eyes are formed to serve
  The inward light, and that the heavenly part
  Ought to be king, from whose rules who do swerve,
  Rebels to nature, strive for their own smart.
It is most true what we call Cupid's dart
  An image is which for ourselves we carve,
  And, fools, adore in temple of our heart
  Till that good god make church and churchman
    starve.
True, that true beauty virtue is indeed,
  Whereof this beauty can be but a shade,
  Which elements with mortal mixture breed.
True, that on earth we are but pilgrims made,
  And should in soul up to our country move;
  True, and yet true that I must Stella love. . . .

III

Alas, have I not pain enough, my friend,
  Upon whose breast a fiercer gripe doth tire
  Than did on him who first stole down the fire,
  While Love on me doth all his quiver spend—
But with your rhubarb words ye must contend,
  To grieve me worse, in saying that desire
  Doth plunge my well-formed soul even in the mire
  Of sinful thoughts which do in ruin end?
If that be sin which doth the manners frame,
  Well stayed with truth in word and faith of deed,

Ready of wit and fearing nought but shame;
If that be sin which in fixed hearts doth breed
    A loathing of all loose unchastity,
    Then love is sin, and let me sinful be. . . .

IV

Fly, fly, my friends, I have my death wound, fly;
    See there that boy, that murth'ring boy, I say,
    Who, like a thief, hid in dark bush doth lie
    Till bloody bullet get him wrongful prey.
So tyrant he no fitter place could spy,
    Nor so fair level in so secret stay,
    As that sweet black which veils the heav'nly eye:
    There himself with his shot he close doth lay.
Poor passenger, pass now thereby I did,
    And stayed, pleased with the prospect of the place,
    While that black hue from me the bad guest hid;
But straight I saw motions of lightning grace,
    And then descried the glist'ring of his dart;
    But ere I could fly thence, it pierced my heart. . . .

V

Whether the Turkish new-moon minded be
    To fill his horns this year on Christian coast;
    How Poles' right king means without leave of host
    To warm with ill-made fire cold Muscovy;
If French can yet three parts in one agree;
    What now the Dutch in their full diets boast;
    How Holland hearts, now so good towns be lost,
    Trust in the shade of pleasing Orange-tree;
How Ulster likes of that same golden bit
    Wherewith my father once made it half tame;
    If in the Scotch Court be no welt'ring yet:
These questions busy wits to me do frame.

I, cumbered with good manners, answer do,
But know not how, for still I think of you.

VI

With how sad steps, O moon, thou climb'st the skies!
   How silently, and with how wan a face!
   What! may it be that even in heav'nly place
   That busy archer his sharp arrows tries?
Sure, if that long-with-love-acquainted eyes
   Can judge of love, thou feel'st a lover's case;
   I read it in thy looks—thy languished grace
   To me, that feel the like, thy state descries.
Then, ev'n of fellowship, O moon, tell me,
   Is constant love deemed there but want of wit?
   Are beauties there as proud as here they be?
Do they above love to be loved, and yet
   Those lovers scorn whom that love doth possess?
   Do they call virtue there ungratefulness? . . .

VII

Come, let me write. And to what end? To ease
   A burthened heart. How can words ease, which are
   The glasses of thy daily vexing care?
   Oft cruel fights well pictured forth do please.
Art not ashamed to publish thy disease?
   Nay, that may breed my fame, it is so rare.
   But will not wise men think thy words fond ware?
   Then be they close, and so none shall displease.
What idler thing than speak and not be heard?
   What harder thing than smart and not to speak?
   Peace, foolish wit! with wit my wit is marred.
Thus write I, while I doubt to write, and wreak
   My harms on ink's poor loss. Perhaps some find
   Stella's great powers, that so confuse my mind. . . .

VIII

Come sleep! O sleep, the certain knot of peace,
  The baiting place of wit, the balm of woe,
  The poor man's wealth, the prisoner's release,
  Th' indifferent judge between the high and low;
With shield of proof shield me from out the prease
  Of those fierce darts despair at me doth throw;
  O make in me those civil wars to cease;
  I will good tribute pay, if thou do so.
Take thou of me smooth pillows, sweetest bed,
  A chamber deaf to noise and blind to light,
  A rosy garland and a weary head;
And if these things, as being thine by right,
  Move not thy heavy grace, thou shalt in me,
  Livelier than elsewhere, Stella's image see. . . .

IX

Having this day my horse, my hand, my lance
  Guided so well that I obtained the prize,
  Both by the judgment of the English eyes
  And of some sent from that sweet enemy, France;
Horsemen my skill in horsemanship advance,
  Town-folks my strength; a daintier judge applies
  His praise to sleight which from good use doth rise;
  Some lucky wits impute it but to chance;
Others, because of both sides I do take
  My blood from them who did excel in this,
  Think nature me a man of arms did make.
How far they shot awry! The true cause is,
  Stella looked on, and from her heav'nly face
  Sent forth the beams which made so fair my race.

X

Because I breathe not love to every one,
 Nor do not use set colors for to wear,
 Nor nourish special locks of vowëd hair,
 Nor give each speech a full point of a groan,
The courtly nymphs, acquainted with the moan
 Of them who in their lips Love's standard bear,
 What, he! say they of me, Now I dare swear
 He cannot love; no, no, let him alone.
And think so still, so Stella know my mind;
 Profess indeed I do not Cupid's art;
 But you, fair maids, at length this true shall find,
That his right badge is but worn in the heart;
 Dumb swans, not chatt'ring pies, do lovers prove;
 They love indeed who quake to say they love. . . .

XI

O grammar-rules, O now your virtues show;
 So children still read you with awful eyes,
 As my young dove may, in your precepts wise,
 Her grant to me by her own virtue know;
For late, with heart most high, with eyes most low,
 I craved the thing which ever she denies;
 She, lightning Love displaying Venus' skies,
 Lest once should not be heard, twice said, No, No!
Sing then, my muse, now Io Pæan sing;
 Heav'ns envy not at my high triumphing,
 But grammar's force with sweet success confirm;
For grammar says—O this, dear Stella, weigh—
 For grammar says—to grammar who says nay?
 That in one speech two negatives affirm! . . .

XII

No more, my dear, no more these counsels try;
   O give my passions leave to run their race;
   Let fortune lay on me her worst disgrace;
   Let folk o'ercharged with brain against me cry;
Let clouds bedim my face, break in mine eye;
   Let me no steps but of lost labor trace;
   Let all the earth with scorn recount my case,
   But do not will me from my love to fly.
I do not envy Aristotle's wit,
   Nor do aspire to Caesar's bleeding fame;
   Nor aught do care though some above me sit;
Nor hope nor wish another course to frame,
   But that which once may win thy cruel heart;
   Thou art my wit, and thou my virtue art. . . .

XIII

Stella, think not that I by verse seek fame,
   Who seek, who hope, who love, who live but thee;
   Thine eyes my pride, thy lips mine history;
   If thou praise not, all other praise is shame.
Nor so ambitious am I as to frame
   A nest for my young praise in laurel tree;
   In truth, I swear I wish not there should be
   Graved in mine epitaph a poet's name.
Nay, if I would, I could just title make,
   That any laud to me thereof should grow,
   Without my plumes from others' wings I take;
For nothing from my wit or will doth flow,
   Since all my words thy beauty doth endite,
   And love doth hold my hand and makes me write. . . .

XIV. ASTROPHEL'S LOVE IS DEAD

Ring out your bells, let mourning shows be spread;
For Love is dead—
   All Love is dead, infected
With plague of deep disdain;
   Worth, as nought worth, rejected,
And Faith fair scorn doth gain.
    From so ungrateful fancy,
    From such a female franzy,
    From them that use men thus,
    Good Lord, deliver us!

Weep, neighbors, weep; do you not hear it said
That Love is dead?
   His death-bed, peacock's folly;
His winding-sheet is shame;
   His will, false-seeming holy;
His sole exec'tor, blame.
    From so ungrateful, &c.

Let dirge be sung and trentals rightly read,
For Love is dead;
   Sir Wrong his tomb ordaineth
My mistress Marble-heart,
   Which epitaph containeth,
Her eyes were once his dart.
    From so ungrateful, &c.

Alas, I lie, rage hath this error bred;
Love is not dead;
   Love is not dead, but sleepeth
In her unmatchëd mind,
   Where she his counsel keepeth,

Till due desert she find.
  Therefore from so vile fancy,
  To call such wit a franzy,
  Who Love can temper thus,
  Good Lord, deliver us!

XV

Thou blind man's mark, thou fool's self-chosen snare,
Fond fancy's scum, and dregs of scattered thought;
Band of all evils, cradle of causeless care;
Thou web of will, whose end is never wrought;
Desire, desire! I have too dearly bought,
With price of mangled mind, thy worthless ware;
Too long, too long, asleep thou hast me brought,
Who should my mind to higher things prepare.
But yet in vain thou hast my ruin sought;
In vain thou madest me to vain things aspire;
In vain thou kindlest all thy smoky fire;
For virtue hath this better lesson taught—
Within myself to seek my only hire,
Desiring nought but how to kill desire.

XVI

Leave me, O love which reachest but to dust;
And thou, my mind, aspire to higher things;
Grow rich in that which never taketh rust,
Whatever fades but fading pleasure brings.
Draw in thy beams, and humble all thy might
To that sweet yoke where lasting freedoms be;
Which breaks the clouds and opens forth the light,
That doth both shine and give us sight to see.
O take fast hold; let that light be thy guide
In this small course which birth draws out to death,
And think how evil becometh him to slide,

Who seeketh heav'n, and comes of heav'nly breath.
Then farewell, world; thy uttermost I see;
Eternal Love, maintain thy life in me.

Splendidis longum valedico nugis.

PART FIVE

The Common Man

Gabriel Harvey

IN PRAISE OF THE ARTISAN

CHAUCER'S CONCLUSIONS of the Astrolabe, still in *esse*. Pregnant rules to many worthy purposes.

His familiar Staff, newly published this 1590. The Instrument itself, made and sold by M. Kynvin, of London, near Paul's. A fine workman, and my kind friend: first commended unto me by M. Digges, and M. Blagrave himself. Meaner artificers much praised by Cardan, Gauricus, and others, than he, and old Humphrey Cole, my mathematical mechanicians. As M. Lucar newly commends John Reynolds, John Read, Christopher Paine, Londoners, for making Geometrical Tables, with their feet, frames, rulers, compasses, and squares, M. Blagrave also in his Familiar Staff, commends John Read, for a very artificial workman.

Mr. Kynvin selleth the Instrument in brass.

[On the verses: "The Author in his own Defense."
"A child but yesterday, and now to scale the sky?
Where gathered he his skill? What tutor told him in?
The Universities deny That ere he dwelt therein."]

An Youth: & no University man. The more shame for some Doctors of Universities, that may learn of him. . . . Scholars have the books: and practitioners the Learning.

[FROM Marginalia]

427

He that remembereth Humfrey Cole, a Mathematical Mechanician, Mathew Baker a shipwright, John Shute, an Architect, Robert Norman a Navigator, William Bourne a Gunner, John Hester, a Chemist, *or any like cunning, and subtle Empiric* (Cole, Baker, Shute, Norman, Bourne, Hester, will be remembered, when greater Clerks shall be forgotten) is a proud man, if he contemn *expert artisans, or any sensible industrious Practitioner, howsoever Unlectured in Schools, or Unlettered in Books.*

[FROM *Pierce's Supererogation*]

Thomas Dekker

THE SHOEMAKER'S HOLIDAY

OR A PLEASANT COMEDY OF THE GENTLE CRAFT.

DRAMATIS PERSONÆ

THE KING.
THE EARL OF CORNWALL.
SIR HUGH LACY, Earl of Lincoln.
ROWLAND LACY, otherwise HANS, } His Nephews.
ASKEW
SIR ROGER OATELEY, Lord Mayor of London.
Master HAMMON ⎫
Master WARNER ⎬ Citizens of London.
Master SCOTT ⎭
SIMON EYRE, the Shoemaker.
ROGER, commonly called ⎫
    HODGE   ⎬ EYRE'S Journeymen.
FIRK   ⎭
RALPH
LOVELL, a Courtier.
DODGER, Servant to the EARL OF LINCOLN.
A DUTCH SKIPPER.
A BOY.
   Courtiers, Attendants, Officers, Soldiers, Hunters,
      Shoemakers, Apprentices, Servants.

ROSE, Daughter of SIR ROGER.
SYBIL, her Maid.
MARGERY, Wife of SIMON EYRE.
JANE, Wife of RALPH.

SCENE—LONDON and OLD FORD.

ACT THE FIRST

SCENE I.—*A Street in London.*

Enter the LORD MAYOR *and the* EARL OF LINCOLN.

LINCOLN. My lord mayor, you have sundry times
Feasted myself and many courtiers more:
Seldom or never can we be so kind
To make requital of your courtesy.
But leaving this, I hear my cousin Lacy
Is much affected to your daughter Rose.

L. MAYOR. True, my good lord, and she loves him so
well
That I mislike her boldness in the chase.

LINCOLN. Why, my lord mayor, think you it then a
shame,
To join a Lacy with an Oateley's name?

L. MAYOR. Too mean is my poor girl for his high
birth;
Poor citizens must not with courtiers wed,
Who will in silks and gay apparel spend
More in one year than I am worth, by far:
Therefore your honour need not doubt my girl.

LINCOLN. Take heed, my lord, advise you what you
do!
A verier unthrift lives not in the world,
Than is my cousin; for I'll tell you what:

'Tis now almost a year since he requested
To travel countries for experience;
I furnished him with coin, bills of exchange,
Letters of credit, men to wait on him,
Solicited my friends in Italy
Well to respect him. But to see the end:
Scant had he journeyed through half Germany,
But all his coin was spent, his men cast off,
His bills embezzled, and my jolly coz,
Ashamed to show his bankrupt presence here,
Became a shoemaker in Wittenberg,
A goodly science for a gentleman
Of such descent! Now judge the rest by this:
Suppose your daughter have a thousand pound,
He did consume me more in one half year;
And make him heir to all the wealth you have,
One twelvemonth's rioting will waste it all.
Then seek, my lord, some honest citizen
To wed your daughter to.

    L. MAYOR.   I thank your lordship.
(*Aside*) Well, fox, I understand your subtilty.
As for your nephew, let your lordship's eye
But watch his actions, and you need not fear,
For I have sent my daughter far enough.
And yet your cousin Rowland might do well,
Now he hath learned an occupation;
And yet I scorn to call him son-in-law.

    LINCOLN. Ay, but I have a better trade for him;
I thank his grace, he hath appointed him
Chief colonel of all those companies
Mustered in London and the shires about,
To serve his highness in those wars of France.
See where he comes!—

        Enter LOVELL, LACY, *and* ASKEW.

               Lovell, what news with you?

LOVELL. My Lord of Lincoln, 'tis his highness' will,
That presently your cousin ship for France
With all his powers; he would not for a million,
But they should land at Dieppe within four days.

LINCOLN. Go certify his grace, it shall be done.

[*Exit* LOVELL.

Now, cousin Lacy, in what forwardness
Are all you companies?

LACY.   All well prepared.
The men of Hertfordshire lie at Mile-end,
Suffolk and Essex train in Tothill-fields,
The Londoners and those of Middlesex,
All gallantly prepared in Finsbury,
With frolic spirits long for their parting hour.

L. MAYOR. They have their imprest, coats, and furni-
    ture;
And, if it please your cousin Lacy come
To the Guildhall, he shall receive his pay;
And twenty pounds besides my brethren
Will freely give him, to approve our loves
We bear unto my lord, your uncle here.

LACY. I thank your honour.

LINCOLN.   Thanks, my good lord mayor.

L. MAYOR. At the Guildhall we will expect your
    coming.   [*Exit.*

LINCOLN. To approve your loves to me? No subtilty!
Nephew, that twenty pound he doth bestow
For joy to rid you from his daughter Rose.
But, cousins both, now here are none but friends,
I would not have you cast an amorous eye
Upon so mean a project as the love
Of a gay, wanton, painted citizen.
I know, this churl even in the height of scorn
Doth hate the mixture of his blood with thine.
I pray thee, do thou so! Remember, coz,

What honourable fortunes wait on thee:
Increase the king's love, which so brightly shines,
And gilds thy hopes. I have no heir but thee—
And yet not thee, if with a wayward spirit
Thou start from the true bias of my love.

    LACY. My lord, I will for honour, not desire
Of land or livings, or to be your heir,
So guide my actions in pursuit of France,
As shall add glory to the Lacys' name.

    LINCOLN. Coz, for those words here's thirty Portu-
        guese
And, nephew Askew, there's a few for you.
Fair Honour, in her loftiest eminence,
Stays in France for you, till you fetch her thence.
Then, nephews, clap swift wings on your designs:
Begone, begone, make haste to the Guildhall;
There presently I'll meet you. Do not stay:
Where honour beckons, shame attends delay.   [*Exit.*

    ASKEW. How gladly would your uncle have you gone!

    LACY. True, coz, but I'll o'erreach his policies.
I have some serious business for three days,
Which nothing but my presence can dispatch.
You, therefore, cousin, with the companies,
Shall haste to Dover; there I'll meet with you:
Or, if I stay past my prefixèd time,
Away for France; we'll meet in Normandy.
The twenty pounds my lord mayor gives to me
You shall receive, and these ten Portuguese,
Part of mine uncle's thirty. Gentle coz,
Have care to our great charge; I know, your wisdom
Hath tried itself in higher consequence.

    ASKEW. Coz, all myself am yours: yet have this care,
To lodge in London with all secrecy;
Our uncle Lincoln hath, besides his own,
Many a jealous eye, that in your face

Stares only to watch means for your disgrace.

LACY. Stay, cousin, who be these?

Enter SIMON EYRE, MARGERY *his wife*, HODGE, FIRK, JANE, *and* RALPH *with a pair of shoes*.

EYRE. Leave whining, leave whining! Away with this whimpering, this puling, these blubbering tears, and these wet eyes! I'll get thy husband discharged, I warrant thee, sweet Jane; go to!

HODGE. Master, here be the captains.

EYRE. Peace, Hodge; hush, ye knave, hush!

FIRK. Here be the cavaliers and the colonels, master.

EYRE. Peace, Firk; peace, my fine Firk! Stand by with your pishery-pashery, away! I am a man of the best presence; I'll speak to them, an they were Popes.—Gentlemen, captains, colonels, commanders! Brave men, brave leaders, may it please you to give me audience. I am Simon Eyre, the mad shoemaker of Tower Street; this wench with the mealy mouth that will never tire, is my wife, I can tell you; here's Hodge, my man and my foreman; here's Firk, my fine firking journeyman, and this is blubbered Jane. All we come to be suitors for this honest Ralph. Keep him at home, and as I am a true shoemaker and a gentleman of the gentle craft, buy spurs yourselves, and I'll find ye boots these seven years.

MARG. Seven years, husband?

EYRE. Peace, midriff, peace! I know what I do. Peace!

FIRK. Truly, master cormorant, you shall do God good service to let Ralph and his wife stay together. She's a young new-married woman; if you take her husband away from her a night, you undo her; she may beg in the daytime; for he's as good a workman at a prick and an awl, as any is in our trade.

JANE. O let him stay, else I shall be undone.

FIRK. Ay, truly, she shall be laid at one side like a pair of old shoes else, and be occupied for no use.

LACY. Truly, my friends, it lies not in my power:
The Londoners are pressed, paid, and set forth
By the lord mayor; I cannot change a man.

HODGE. Why, then you were as good be a corporal as
a colonel, if you cannot discharge one good fellow; and
I tell you true, I think you do more than you can answer,
to press a man within a year and a day of his marriage.

EYRE. Well said, melancholy Hodge; gramercy, my
fine foreman.

MARG. Truly, gentlemen, it were ill done for such as
you, to stand so stiffly against a poor young wife, considering her case, she is new-married, but let that pass:
I pray, deal not roughly with her; her husband is a
young man, and but newly entered, but let that pass.

EYRE. Away with your pishery-pashery, your pols and
your edipols! Peace, midriff; silence, Cicely Bumtrinket!
Let your head speak.

FIRK. Yea, and the horns too, master.

EYRE. Too soon, my fine Firk, too soon! Peace, scoundrels! See you this man? Captains, you will not release
him? Well, let him go; he's a proper shot; let him vanish!
Peace, Jane, dry up thy tears, they'll make his powder
dankish. Take him, brave men; Hector of Troy was an
hackney to him, Hercules and Termagant scoundrels,
Prince Arthur's Round-table—by the Lord of Ludgate—
ne'er fed such a tall, such a dapper swordsman; by the
life of Pharaoh, a brave, resolute swordsman! Peace,
Jane! I say no more, mad knaves.

FIRK. See, see, Hodge, how my master raves in commendation of Ralph!

HODGE. Ralph, th'art a gull, by this hand, an thou
goest not.

ASKEW. I am glad, good Master Eyre, it is my hap
To meet so resolute a soldier.
Trust me, for your report and love to him,

A common slight regard shall not respect him.

LACY. Is thy name Ralph?

RALPH. Yes, sir.

LACY. Give me thy hand;
Thou shalt not want, as I am a gentleman.
Woman, be patient; God, no doubt, will send
Thy husband safe again; but he must go,
His country's quarrel says it shall be so.

HODGE. Th'art a gull, by my stirrup, if thou dost not
go. I will not have thee strike thy gimlet into these weak
vessels; prick thine enemies, Ralph.

Enter DODGER.

DODGER. My lord, your uncle on the Tower-hill
Stays with the lord mayor and the aldermen,
And doth request you with all speed you may,
To hasten thither.

ASKEW. Cousin, let's go.

LACY. Dodger, run you before, tell them we come.—
This Dodger is mine uncle's parasite, [*Exit* DODGER.
The arrant'st varlet that e'er breathed on earth;
He sets more discord in a noble house
By one day's broaching of his pickthank tales,
Than can be salved again in twenty years,
And he, I fear, shall go with us to France,
To pry into our actions.

ASKEW. Therefore, coz,
It shall behove you to be circumspect.

LACY. Fear not, good cousin.—Ralph, hie to your
colours.

RALPH. I must, because there's no remedy;
But, gentle master and my loving dame,
As you have always been a friend to me,
So in mine absence think upon my wife.

JANE. Alas, my Ralph.

MARG. She cannot speak for weeping.

EYRE. Peace, you cracked groats, you mustard tokens, disquiet not the brave soldier. Go thy ways, Ralph!

JANE. Ay, ay, you bid him go; what shall I do
When he is gone?

FIRK. Why, be doing with me or my fellow Hodge; be not idle.

EYRE. Let me see thy hand, Jane. This fine hand, this white hand, these pretty fingers must spin, must card, must work; work, you bombast-cotton-candle-queen; work for your living, with a pox to you.—Hold thee, Ralph, here's five sixpences for thee; fight for the honour of the gentle craft, for the gentlemen shoemakers, the courageous cordwainers, the flower of St. Martin's, the mad knaves of Bedlam, Fleet Street, Tower Street, and Whitechapel; crack me the crowns of the French knaves; a pox on them, crack them; fight, by the Lord of Ludgate; fight, my fine boy!

FIRK. Here, Ralph, here's three twopences: two carry into France, the third shall wash our souls at parting, for sorrow is dry. For my sake, firk the *Basa mon cues*.

HODGE. Ralph, I am heavy at parting; but here's a shilling for thee. God send thee to cram thy slops with French crowns, and thy enemies' bellies with bullets.

RALPH. I thank you, master, and I thank you all.
Now, gentle wife, my loving lovely Jane,
Rich men, at parting, give their wives rich gifts,
Jewels and rings, to grace their lily hands.
Thou know'st our trade makes rings for women's heels:
Here take this pair of shoes, cut out by Hodge,
Stitched by my fellow Firk, seamed by myself,
Made up and pinked with letters for thy name.
Wear them, my dear Jane, for thy husband's sake;
And every morning, when thou pull'st them on,

Remember me, and pray for my return.
Make much of them; for I have made them so,
That I can know them from a thousand mo'.

Drum sounds. Enter the LORD MAYOR, *the* EARL *of*
LINCOLN, LACY, ASKEW, DODGER, *and* Soldiers.
They pass over the stage; RALPH *falls in amongst
them;* FIRK *and the rest cry* "Farewell," *etc., and
so exeunt.*

ACT THE SECOND.

SCENE I.—*A Garden at Old Ford.*

Enter ROSE, *alone, making a garland.*

ROSE. Here sit thou down upon this flow'ry bank,
And make a garland for thy Lacy's head.
These pinks, these roses, and these violets,
These blushing gilliflowers, these marigolds,
The fair embroidery of his coronet,
Carry not half such beauty in their cheeks,
As the sweet countenance of my Lacy doth.
O my most unkind father! O my stars,
Why lowered you so at my nativity,
To make me love, yet live robbed of my love?
Here as a thief am I imprisonëd
For my dear Lacy's sake within those walls,
Which by my father's cost were builded up
For better purposes; here must I languish
For him that doth as much lament, I know,
Mine absence, as for him I pine in woe.

Enter SYBIL.

SYBIL. Good morrow, young mistress. I am sure you
make that garland for me; against I shall be Lady of the
Harvest.

ROSE. Sybil, what news at London?

SYBIL. None but good; my lord mayor, your father, and master Philpot, your uncle, and Master Scot, your cousin, and Mistress Frigbottom by Doctors' Commons, do all, by my troth, send you most hearty commendations.

ROSE. Did Lacy send kind greetings to his love?

SYBIL. O yes, out of cry, by my troth. I scant knew him; here 'a wore a scarf; and here a scarf, here a bunch of feathers, and here precious stones and jewels, and a pair of garters—O, monstrous! like one of our yellow silk curtains at home here in Old Ford house, here in Master Belly-mount's chamber. I stood at our door in Cornhill, looked at him, he at me indeed, spake to him, but he not to me, not a word; marry go-up, thought I, with a wanion! He passed by me as proud—Marry foh! are you grown humourous, thought I; and so shut the door, and in I came.

ROSE. O Sybil, how dost thou my Lacy wrong!
My Rowland is as gentle as a lamb,
No dove was ever half so mild as he.

SYBIL. Mild? yea, as a bushel of stamped crabs. He looked upon me as sour as verjuice. Go thy ways, thought I; thou may'st be much in my gaskins, but nothing in my nether-stocks. This is your fault, mistress, to love him that loves not you; he thinks scorn to do as he's done to; but if I were as you, I'd cry: Go by, Jeronimo, go by!

> I'd set mine old debts against my new driblets,
> And the hare's foot against the goose giblets,
> For if ever I sigh, when sleep I should take,
> Pray God I may lose my maidenhead when I wake.

ROSE. Will my love leave me then, and go to France?

SYBIL. I know not that, but I am sure I see him stalk

before the soldiers. By my troth, he is a proper man;
but he is proper that proper doth. Let him go snick-up,
young mistress.

ROSE. Get thee to London, and learn perfectly,
Whether my Lacy go to France, or no.
Do this, and I will give thee for thy pains
My cambric apron and my Romish gloves,
My purple stockings and a stomacher.
Say, wilt thou do this, Sybil, for my sake?

SYBIL. Will I, quoth a? At whose suit? By my troth,
yes I'll go. A cambric apron, gloves, a pair of purple
stockings, and a stomacher! I'll sweat in purple, mistress,
for you; I'll take anything that comes a God's name. O
rich! a cambric apron! Faith, then have at "up tails all."
I'll go jiggy-joggy to London, and be here in a trice,
young mistress.   [*Exit.*

ROSE. Do so, good Sybil. Meantime wretched I
Will sit and sigh for his lost company.   [*Exit.*

SCENE II.—*A Street in London.*

Enter LACY, *disguised as a Dutch Shoemaker.*

LACY. How many shapes have gods and kings de-
                                              vised,
Thereby to compass their desired loves!
It is no shame for Rowland Lacy, then,
To clothe his cunning with the gentle craft,
That, thus disguised, I may unknown possess
The only happy presence of my Rose.
For her have I forsook my charge in France,
Incurred the king's displeasure, and stirred up
Rough hatred in mine uncle Lincoln's breast.
O love, how powerful art thou, that canst change
High birth to baseness, and a noble mind

To the mean semblance of a shoemaker!
But thus it must be. For her cruel father,
Hating the single union of our souls,
Has secretly conveyed my Rose from London,
To bar me of her presence; but I trust,
Fortune and this disguise will further me
Once more to view her beauty, gain her sight.
Here in Tower Street with Eyre the shoemaker
Mean I a while to work; I know the trade,
I learnt it when I was in Wittenberg.
Then cheer thy hoping spirits, be not dismayed,
Thou canst not want: do Fortune what she can,
The gentle craft is living for a man.   [*Exit.*

SCENE III.—*An open Yard before* EYRE'S *House.*

Enter EYRE, *making himself ready.*

EYRE. Where be these boys, these girls, these drabs, these scoundrels? They wallow in the fat brewiss of my bounty, and lick up the crumbs of my table, yet will not rise to see my walks cleansed. Come out, you powder-beef queens! What, Nan! what, Madge Mumble-crust Come out, you fat midriff-swag-belly-whores, and sweep me these kennels that the noisome stench offend not the noses of my neighbours. What, Firk, I say; what, Hodge! Open my shop-windows! What, Firk, I say!

Enter FIRK.

FIRK. O master, is't you that speak bandog and Bedlam this morning? I was in a dream, and mused what madman was got into the street so early; have you drunk this morning that your throat is so clear?

EYRE. Ah, well said, Firk; well said, Firk. To work, my fine knave, to work! Wash thy face, and thou'lt be more blest.

FIRK. Let them wash my face that will eat it. Good master, send for a souse-wife, if you'll have my face cleaner.

Enter HODGE.

EYRE. Away, sloven! avaunt, scoundrel!—Good-morrow, Hodge; good-morrow, my fine foreman.

HODGE. O master, good-morrow; y'are an early stirrer. Here's a fair morning.—Good-morrow, Firk, I could have slept this hour. Here's a brave day towards.

EYRE. Oh, haste to work, my fine foreman, haste to work.

FIRK. Master, I am dry as dust to hear my fellow Roger talk of fair weather; let us pray for good leather, and let clowns and ploughboys and those that work in the fields pray for brave days. We work in a dry shop; what care I if it rain?

Enter MARGERY.

EYRE. How now, Dame Margery, can you see to rise? Trip and go, call up the drabs, your maids.

MARG. See to rise? I hope 'tis time enough, 'tis early enough for any woman to be seen abroad. I marvel how many wives in Tower Street are up so soon. Gods me, 'tis not noon—here's a yawling!

EYRE. Peace, Margery, peace! Where's Cicely Bumtrinket, your maid? She has a privy fault, she farts in her sleep. Call the queen up; if my men want shoe-thread, I'll swinge her in a stirrup.

FIRK. Yet, that's but a dry beating; here's still a sign of drought.

Enter LACY *disguised, singing.*

LACY. *Der was een bore van Gelderland*
  Frolick sie byen;
   He was als dronck he cold nyet stand,
   Upsolce sie byen.

Tap eens de canneken,
Drincke, schone mannekin.

FIRK. Master, for my life, yonder's a brother of the
gentle craft; if he bear not St. Hugh's bones, I'll forfeit
my bones; he's some uplandish workman: hire him, good
master, that I may learn some gibble-gabble; 'twill make
us work the faster.

EYRE. Peace, Firk! A hard world! Let him pass, let
him vanish; we have journeymen enow. Peace, my fine
Firk!

MARG. Nay, nay, y'are best follow your man's counsel; you shall see what will come on't: we have not men
enow, but we must entertain every butter-box; but let
that pass.

HODGE. Dame, 'fore God, if my master follow your
counsel, he'll consume little beef. He shall be glad of
men, and he can catch them.

FIRK. Ay, that he shall.

HODGE. 'Fore God, a proper man, and I warrant, a
fine workman. Master, farewell; dame, adieu; if such a
man as he cannot find work, Hodge is not for you.

                                        [*Offers to go.*

EYRE. Stay, my fine Hodge.

FIRK. Faith, an your foreman go, dame, you must take
a journey to seek a new journeyman; if Roger remove,
Firk follows. If St. Hugh's bones shall not be set a-work,
I may prick mine awl in the walls, and go play. Fare ye
well, master; good-bye, dame.

EYRE. Tarry, my fine Hodge, my brisk foreman! Stay,
Firk! Peace, pudding-broth! By the Lord of Ludgate, I
love my men as my life. Peace, you gallimafry! Hodge,
if he want work, I'll hire him. One of you to him; stay—
he comes to us.

LACY. *Goeden dach, meester, ende u vro oak.*[1]

FIRK. Nails, if I should speak after him without drinking, I should choke. And you, friend Oake, are you of the gentle craft?

LACY. *Yaw, yaw, ik bin den skomawker.*[2]

FIRK. *Den skomaker,* quoth a! And hark you, *skomaker,* have you all your tools, a good rubbing-pin, a good stopper, a good dresser, your four sorts of awls, and your two balls of wax, your paring-knife, your hand- and thumb-leathers, and good St. Hugh's bones to smooth up your work?

LACY. *Yaw, yaw; be niet vorveard. Ik hab all de dingen voour mack skooes groot and cleane.*[3]

FIRK. Ha, ha! Good master, hire him; he'll make me laugh so that I shall work more in mirth than I can in earnest.

EYRE. Hear ye, friend, have ye any skill in the mystery of cordwainers?

LACY. *Ik weet niet wat yow seg; ich verstaw you niet.*[4]

FIRK. Why, thus, man: (*Imitating by gesture a shoemaker at work*) *Ich verste u niet,* quoth a.

LACY. *Yaw, yaw, yaw; ick can dat wel doen.*[5]

FIRK. *Yaw, yaw!* He speaks yawing like a jackdaw that gapes to be fed with cheese-curds. Oh, he'll give a villanous pull at a can of double-beer; but Hodge and I have the vantage, we must drink first, because we are the eldest journeymen.

EYRE. What is thy name?

LACY. Hans—Hans Meulter.

EYRE. Give me thy hand; th'art welcome.—Hodge,

---

[1] Good day, master, and your wife too.

[2] Yes, yes, I am a shoemaker.

[3] Yes, yes; be not afraid. I have everything, to make boots big and little.

[4] I don't know what you say; I don't understand you.

[5] Yes, yes, yes; I can do that very well.

entertain him; Firk, bid him welcome; come, Hans. Run, wife, bid your maids, your trullibubs, make ready my fine men's breakfasts. To him, Hodge!

HODGE. Hans, th'art welcome; use thyself friendly, for we are good fellows; if not, thou shalt be fought with, wert thou bigger than a giant.

FIRK. Yea, and drunk with, wert thou Gargantua. My master keeps no cowards, I tell thee.—Ho, boy, bring him an heel-block, here's a new journeyman.

Enter Boy.

LACY. *O, ich wersto you; ich moet een halve dossen cans betaelen; here, boy, nempt dis skilling, tap eens freelicke.*[6]

[*Exit* Boy.

EYRE. Quick, snipper-snapper, away! Firk, scour thy throat, thou shalt wash it with Castilian liquor.

Enter Boy.

Come, my last of the fives, give me a can. Have to thee, Hans; here, Hodge; here, Firk; drink, you mad Greeks, and work like true Trojans, and pray for Simon Eyre, the shoemaker. Here, Hans, and th'art welcome.

FIRK. Lo, dame, you would have lost a good fellow that will teach us to laugh. This beer came hopping in well.

MARG. Simon, it is almost seven.

EYRE. Is't so, Dame Clapper-dudgeon? Is't seven a clock, and my men's breakfast not ready? Trip and go, you soused conger, away! Come, you mad hyperboreans; follow me, Hodge; follow me, Hans; come after, my fine Firk; to work, to work a while, and then to breakfast!

FIRK. Soft! *Yaw, yaw,* good Hans, though my master have no more wit but to call you afore me, I am not so

---

[6] O, I understand you; I must pay for half-a-dozen cans; here, boy, take this shilling, tap this once freely.

foolish to go behind you, I being the elder journeyman.

[*Exeunt*

SCENE IV.—*A Field near Old Ford.*

Holloaing within. Enter Master WARNER *and*
Master HAMMON, *attired as* Hunters.

HAM. Cousin, beat every brake, the game's not far,
This way with wingèd feet he fled from death,
Whilst the pursuing hounds, scenting his steps,
Find out his highway to destruction.
Besides, the miller's boy told me even now,
He saw him take soil, and he holloaed him,
Affirming him to have been so embost
That long he could not hold.

WARN.   If it be so,
'Tis best we trace these meadows by Old Ford.

A noise of Hunters *within. Enter a* Boy.

HAM. How now, boy? Where's the deer? speak, saw'st
thou him?

BOY. O yea; I saw him leap through a hedge, and
then over a ditch, then at my lord mayor's pale, over he
skipped me, and in he went me, and "holla" the hunters
cried, and "there, boy; there, boy!" But there he is, 'a
mine honesty.

HAM. Boy, God amercy. Cousin, let's away;
I hope we shall find better sport today.   [*Exeunt.*

SCENE V.—*Another part of the Field.*

Hunting within. Enter ROSE *and* SYBIL.

ROSE. Why, Sybil, wilt thou prove a forester?

SYBIL. Upon some, no; forester, go by; no, faith, mistress. The deer came running into the barn through the
orchard and over the pale; I wot well, I looked as pale as
a new cheese to see him. But whip, says Goodman Pin-

close, up with his flail, and our Nick with a prong, and
down he fell, and they upon him, and I upon them. By
my troth, we had such sport; and in the end we ended
him; his throat we cut, flayed him, unhorned him, and
my lord mayor shall eat of him anon, when he comes.

[*Horns sound within.*

ROSE. Hark, hark, the hunters come; y'are best take
    heed,
    They'll have a saying to you for this deed.

Enter Master HAMMON, Master WARNER, Huntsmen,
    and Boy.

HAM. God save you, fair ladies.

SYBIL.   Ladies! O gross!

WARN. Came not a buck this way?

ROSE.   No, but two does.

HAM. And which way went they? Faith, we'll hunt at
    those.

SYBIL. At those? upon some, no: when, can you tell?

WARN. Upon some, ay?

SYBIL.   Good Lord!

WARN.   Wounds! Then farewell!

HAM. Boy, which way went he?

BOY.   This way, sir, he ran.

HAM. This way he ran indeed, fair Mistress Rose;
Our game was lately in your orchard seen.

WARN. Can you advise, which way he took his flight?

SYBIL. Follow your nose; his horns will guide you
    right.

WARN. Th'art a mad wench.

SYBIL.   O, rich!

ROSE.   Trust me, not I.
It is not like that the wild forest-deer
Would come so near to places of resort;
You are deceived, he fled some other way.

WARN. Which way, my sugar-candy, can you shew?

SYBIL. Come up, good honeysops, upon some, no.

ROSE. Why do you stay, and not pursue your game?

SYBIL. I'll hold my life, their hunting-nags be lame.

HAM. A deer more dear is found within this place.

ROSE. But not the deer, sir, which you had in chase.

HAM. I chased the deer, but this dear chaseth me.

ROSE. The strangest hunting that ever I see.

But where's your park?   [*She offers to go away.*

HAM.   'Tis here: O stay!

ROSE. Impale me, and then I will not stray.

WARN. They wrangle, wench; we are more kind than
     they.

SYBIL. What kind of hart is that dear heart, you seek?

WARN. A hart, dear heart.

SYBIL.   Who ever saw the like?

ROSE. To lose your heart, is't possible you can?

HAM. My heart is lost.

ROSE.   Alack, good gentleman!

HAM. This poor lost hart would I wish you might find.

ROSE. You, by such luck, might prove your hart a
     hind.

HAM. Why, Luck had horns, so have I heard some
     say.

ROSE. Now, God, an't be his will, send Luck into your
     way.

     Enter the LORD MAYOR *and* Servants.

L. MAYOR. What, Master Hammon? Welcome to Old
     Ford!

SYBIL. Gods pittikins, hands off, sir! Here's my lord.

L. MAYOR. I hear you had ill luck, and lost your game.

HAM. Tis true, my lord.

L. MAYOR.   I am sorry for the same.

What gentleman is this?

HAM.   My brother-in-law.

L. MAYOR. Y'are welcome both; sith Fortune offers
    you
Into my hands, you shall not part from hence,
Until you have refreshed your wearied limbs.
Go, Sybil, cover the board! You shall be guest
To no good cheer, but even a hunter's feast.

HAM. I thank your lordship.—Cousin, on my life,
For our lost venison I shall find a wife.   [Exeunt.

L. MAYOR. In, gentlemen; I'll not be absent long.—
This Hammon is a proper gentleman,
A citizen by birth, fairly allied;
How fit an husband were he for my girl!
Well, I will in, and do the best I can,
To match my daughter to this gentleman.   [Exit.

ACT THE THIRD

SCENE I.—A Room in EYRE'S House.

Enter LACY otherwise HANS, SKIPPER, HODGE,
and FIRK.

SKIP. Ick sal yow wat seggen, Hans; dis skip, dat
comen from Candy, is al vol, by Got's sacrament, van
sugar, civet, almonds, cambrick, end alle dingen, towsand towsand ding. Nempt it, Hans, nempt it vor v
meester. Daer be de bils van laden. Your meester Simon
Eyre sal hae good copen. Wat seggen yow, Hans?[7]

FIRK. Wat seggen de reggen de copen, slopen—laugh,
Hodge, laugh!

HANS. Mine liever broder Firk, bringt Meester Eyre

---

[7] I'll tell you what, Hans; this ship that is come from Candia,
is quite full, by God's sacrament, of sugar, civet, almonds, cambric,
and all things; a thousand, thousand things. Take it, Hans, take
it for your master. There are the bills of lading. Your master, Simon
Eyre, shall have a good bargain. What say you, Hans?

tot det signe vn Swannekin; daer sal yow finde dis skip-
per end me. Wat seggen yow, broder Firk? Doot it,
Hodge.[8]

Come, skipper. [*Exeunt.*

FIRK. Bring him, quoth you? Here's no knavery, to
bring my master to buy a ship worth the lading of two
or three hundred thousand pounds. Alas, that's nothing;
a trifle, a bauble, Hodge.

HODGE. The truth is, Firk, that the merchant owner
of the ship dares not shew his head, and therefore this
skipper that deals for him, for the love he bears to Hans,
offers my master Eyre a bargain in the commodities.
He shall have a reasonable day of payment; he may sell
the wares by that time, and be an huge gainer himself.

FIRK. Yea, but can my fellow Hans lend my master
twenty porpentines as an earnest penny?

HODGE. Portuguese, thou wouldst say; here they be,
Firk; hark, they jingle in my pocket like St. Mary Overy's
bells.

Enter EYRE *and* MARGERY.

FIRK. Mum, here comes my dame and my master.
She'll scold, on my life, for loitering this Monday; but
all's one, let them all say what they can, Monday's our
holiday.

MARG. You sing, Sir Sauce, but I beshrew your heart,
   I fear, for this your singing we shall smart.

FIRK. Smart for me, dame; why, dame, why?

HODGE. Master, I hope you'll not suffer my dame to
take down your journeymen.

FIRK. If she take me down, I'll take her up; yea, and
take her down too, a button-hole lower.

---

[8] My dear brother Firk, bring Master Eyre to the sign of the
Swan; there shall you find this skipper and me. What say you,
brother Firk? Do it, Hodge.—[There were at this time two inns
with the sign of the Swan in London, one at Dowgate, the other
in Old Fish Street.]

EYRE. Peace, Firk; not I, Hodge; by the life of Pharaoh, by the Lord of Ludgate, by this beard, every hair
whereof I value at a king's ransom, she shall not meddle
with you.—Peace, you bombast-cotton-candle-queen;
away, queen of clubs; quarrel not with me and my men,
with me and my fine Firk; I'll firk you, if you do.

MARG. Yea, yea, man, you may use me as you please;
but let that pass.

EYRE. Let it pass, let it vanish away; peace! Am I
not Simon Eyre? Are not these my brave men, brave
shoemakers, all gentlemen of the gentle craft? Prince am
I none, yet am I nobly born, as being the sole son
of a shoemaker. Away, rubbish! vanish, melt; melt like
kitchen-stuff.

MARG. Yea, yea, 'tis well; I must be called rubbish,
kitchen-stuff, for a sort of knaves.

FIRK. Nay, dame, you shall not weep and wail in woe
for me. Master, I'll stay no longer; here's an inventory
of my shop-tools. Adieu, master; Hodge, farewell.

HODGE. Nay, stay, Firk; thou shalt not go alone.

MARG. I pray, let them go; there be more maids than
Mawkin, more men than Hodge, and more fools than
Firk.

FIRK. Fools? Nails! if I tarry now, I would my guts
might be turned to shoe-thread.

HODGE. And if I stay, I pray God I may be turned to
a Turk, and set in Finsbury for boys to shoot at.—Come,
Firk.

EYRE. Stay, my fine knaves, you arms of my trade,
you pillars of my profession. What, shall a tittle-tattle's
words make you forsake Simon Eyre?—Avaunt, kitchen-
stuff! Rip, you brown-bread Tannikin, out of my sight!
Move me not! Have not I ta'en you from selling tripes in
Eastcheap, and set you in my shop, and made you hail-
fellow with Simon Eyre, the shoemaker? And now do

you deal thus with my journeymen? Look, you powder-beef-queen, on the face of Hodge, here's a face for a lord.

FIRK. And here's a face for any lady in Christendom.

EYRE. Rip, you chitterling, avaunt! Boy, bid the tap-ster of the Boar's Head fill me a dozen cans of beer for my journeymen.

FIRK. A dozen cans? O, brave! Hodge, now I'll stay.

EYRE. (*In a low voice to the* Boy). An the knave fills any more than two, he pays for them. (*Exit* Boy. *Aloud.*) A dozen cans of beer for my journeymen. (*Re-enter* Boy.) Here, you mad Mesopotamians, wash your livers with this liquor. Where be the odd ten? No more, Madge, no more.—Well said. Drink and to work!—What work dost thou, Hodge? what work?

HODGE. I am a making a pair of shoes for my lord mayor's daughter, Mistress Rose.

FIRK. And I a pair of shoes for Sybil, my lord's maid. I deal with her.

EYRE. Sybil? Fie, defile not thy fine workmanly fingers with the feet of kitchenstuff and basting-ladles. Ladies of the court, fine ladies, my lads, commit their feet to our apparelling; put gross work to Hans. Yark and seam, yark and seam!

FIRK. For yarking and seaming let me alone, an I come to't.

HODGE. Well, master, all this is from the bias. Do you remember the ship my fellow Hans told you of? The skipper and he are both drinking at the Swan. Here be the Portuguese to give earnest. If you go through with it, you cannot choose but be a lord at least.

FIRK. Nay, dame, if my master prove not a lord, and you a lady, hang me.

MARG. Yea, like enough, if you may loiter and tipple thus.

FIRK. Tipple, dame? No, we have been bargaining with Skellum Skanderbag. Can you Dutch spreaken for a ship of silk Cyprus, laden with sugar-candy?

Enter Boy *with a velvet coat and an Alderman's gown.*
EYRE *puts them on.*

EYRE. Peace, Firk; silence, Tittle-tattle! Hodge, I'll go through with it. Here's a seal-ring, and I have sent for a guarded gown and a damask cassock. See where it comes; look here, Maggy; help me, Firk; apparel me, Hodge; silk and satin, you mad Philistines, silk and satin.

FIRK. Ha, ha, my master will be as proud as a dog in a doublet, all in beaten damask and velvet.

EYRE. Softly, Firk, for rearing of the nap, and wearing threadbare my garments. How dost thou like me, Firk? How do I look, my fine Hodge?

HODGE. Why, now you look like yourself, master. I warrant you, there's few in the city, but will give you the wall, and come upon you with the right worshipful.

FIRK. Nails, my master looks like a threadbare cloak new turned and dressed. Lord, lord, to see what good raiment doth! Dame, dame, are you not enamoured?

EYRE. How say'st thou, Maggy, am I not brisk? Am I not fine?

MARG. Fine? By my troth, sweetheart, very fine! By my troth, I never liked thee so well in my life, sweetheart; but let that pass. I warrant, there be many women in the city have not such handsome husbands, but only for their apparel; but let that pass too.

Re-enter HANS *and* Skipper.

HANS. *Godden day, mester. Dis be de skipper dat heb de skip van marchandice; de commodity ben good; nempt it, master, nempt it.*[9]

---

[9] Good day master. This is the skipper that has the ship of merchandise; the commodity is good; take it, master, take it.

EYRE. Godamercy, Hans; welcome, skipper. Where lies this ship of merchandise?

SKIP. *De skip ben in revere; dor be van Sugar, cyvet, almonds, cambrick, and a towsand towsand tings, gotz sacrament; nempt it, mester: ye sal heb good copen.*[10]

FIRK. To him, master! O sweet master! O sweet wares! Prunes, almonds, sugar-candy, carrot-roots, turnips, O brave fatting meat! Let not a man buy a nutmeg but yourself.

EYRE. Peace, Firk! Come, skipper, I'll go aboard with you.—Hans, have you made him drink?

SKIP. *Yaw, yaw, ic heb veale gedrunck.*[11]

EYRE. Come, Hans, follow me.—Skipper, thou shalt have my countenance in the city.   [*Exeunt.*

FIRK. *Yaw, heb veale gedrunck,* quoth a. They may well be called butter-boxes, when they drink fat veal and thick beer too. But come, dame, I hope you'll chide us no more.

MARG. No, faith, Firk; no, perdy, Hodge. I do feel honor creep upon me, and which is more, a certain rising in my flesh; but let that pass.

FIRK. Rising in your flesh do you feel, say you? Ay, you may be with child, but why should not my master feel a rising in his flesh, having a gown and a gold ring on? But you are such a shrew, you'll soon pull him down.

MARG. Ha, ha! prithee, peace! Thou mak'st my worship laugh; but let that pass. Come, I'll go in; Hodge, prithee, go before me; Firk, follow me.

FIRK. Firk doth follow: Hodge, pass out in state.
                                    [*Exeunt.*

---

[10] The ship lies in the river; there are sugar, civet, almonds, cambric, and a thousand thousand things, by God's sacrament, take it, master; you shall have a good bargain.

[11] Yes, yes, I have drunk well.

SCENE II.—*London: a Room in* LINCOLN'S *House.*

Enter the EARL OF LINCOLN *and* DODGER.

LINCOLN. How now, good Dodger, what's the news in
    France?

DODGER. My lord, upon the eighteenth day of May
The French and English were prepared to fight;
Each side with eager fury gave the sign
Of a most hot encounter. Five long hours
Both armies fought together; at the length
The lot of victory fell on our side.
Twelve thousand of the Frenchmen that day died,
Four thousand English, and no man of name
But Captain Hyam and young Ardington,
Two gallant gentlemen, I knew them well.

LINCOLN. But Dodger, prithee, tell me, in this fight
How did my cousin Lacy bear himself?

DODGER. My lord, your cousin Lacy was not there.

LINCOLN. Not there?

DODGER.   No, my good lord.

LINCOLN.   Sure, thou mistakest.
I saw him shipped, and a thousand eyes beside
Were witnesses of the farewells which he gave,
When I, with weeping eyes, bid him adieu.
Dodger, take heed.

DODGER.   My lord, I am advised,
That what I spake is true: to prove it so,
His cousin Askew, that supplied his place,
Sent me for him from France, that secretly
He might convey himself thither.

LINCOLN.   Is't even so?
Dares he so carelessly venture his life
Upon the indignation of a king?
Has he despised my love, and spurned those favours

Which I with prodigal hand poured on his head?
He shall repent his rashness with his soul;
Since of my love he makes no estimate,
I'll make him wish he had not known my hate.
Thou hast no other news?

DODGER.   None else, my lord.

LINCOLN. None worse I know thou hast.—Procure
    the king
To crown his giddy brows with ample honours,
Send him chief colonel, and all my hope
Thus to be dashed! But 'tis in vain to grieve,
One evil cannot a worse relieve.
Upon my life, I have found out his plot;
That old dog, Love, that fawned upon him so,
Love to that puling girl, his fair-cheeked Rose,
The lord mayor's daughter, hath distracted him,
And in the fire of that love's lunacy
Hath he burnt up himself, consumed his credit,
Lost the king's love, yea, and I fear, his life,
Only to get a wanton to his wife,
Dodger, it is so.

DODGER.   l fear so, my good lord.

LINCOLN. It is so—nay, sure it cannot be!
I am at my wits' end. Dodger!

DODGER.   Yea, my lord.

LINCOLN. Thou art acquainted with my nephew's
    haunts;
Spend this gold for thy pains; go seek him out;
Watch at my lord mayor's—there if he live,
Dodger, thou shalt be sure to meet with him.
Prithee, be diligent.—Lacy, thy name
Lived once in honour, now 'tis dead in shame.—
Be circumspect.   [*Exit.*

DODGER.   I warrant you, my lord.   [*Exit.*

SCENE III.—*London: a Room in the* LORD MAYOR'S
House.

Enter the LORD MAYOR *and* Master SCOTT.

L. MAYOR. Good Master Scott, I have been bold with
    you,
To be a witness to a wedding-knot
Betwixt young Master Hammon and my daughter.
O, stand aside; see where the lovers come.

    Enter Master HAMMON *and* ROSE.

ROSE. Can it be possible you love me so?
No, no, within those eyeballs I espy
Apparent likelihoods of flattery.
Pray now, let go my hand.

HAM.   Sweet Mistress Rose,
Misconstrue not my words, nor misconceive
Of my affection, whose devoted soul
Swears that I love thee dearer than my heart.

ROSE. As dear as your own heart? I judge it right,
Men love their hearts best when th'are out of sight.

HAM. I love you, by this hand.

ROSE.   Yet hands off now!
If flesh be frail, how weak and frail's your vow!

HAM. Then by my life I swear.

ROSE.   Then do not brawl;
One quarrel loseth wife and life and all.
Is not your meaning thus?

HAM.   In faith, you jest.

ROSE. Love loves to sport; therefore leave love, y'are
    best.

L. MAYOR. What? square they, Master Scott?

SCOTT.   Sir, never doubt,
Lovers are quickly in, and quickly out.

HAM. Sweet Rose, be not so strange in fancying me.
Nay, never turn aside, shun not my sight:
I am not grown so fond, to fond my love
On any that shall quit it with disdain;
If you will love me, so—if not, farewell.

L. MAYOR. Why, how now, lovers, are you both
    agreed?

HAM. Yes, faith, my lord.

L. MAYOR.   'Tis well, give me your hand.
Give me yours, daughter—How now, both pull back!
What means this, girl?

ROSE.   I mean to live a maid.

HAM. But not to die one; pause, ere that be said.

                            [Aside.

L. MAYOR. Will you still cross me, still be obstinate?

HAM. Nay, chide her not, my lord, for doing well;
If she can live an happy virgin's life,
'Tis far more blessed than to be a wife.

ROSE. Say, sir, I cannot: I have made a vow,
Whoever be my husband, 'tis not you.

L. MAYOR. Your tongue is quick; but Master Ham-
    mon, know,
I bade you welcome to another end.

HAM. What, would you have me pule and pine and
        pray,
    With "lovely lady," "mistress of my heart,"
  "Pardon your servant," and the rhymer play,
    Railing on Cupid and his tyrant's-dart;
Or shall I undertake some martial spoil,
Wearing your glove at tourney and at tilt,
And tell how many gallants I unhorsed—
Sweet, will this pleasure you?

ROSE.   Yea, when wilt begin?
What, love rhymes, man? Fie on that deadly sin!

L. MAYOR. If you will have her, I'll make her agree.

HAM. Enforced love is worse than hate to me.

(*Aside*.) There is a wench keeps shop in the Old
     Change,

To her will I; it is not wealth I seek,

I have enough, and will prefer her love

Before the world. (*Aloud*.) My good lord mayor, adieu.

Old love for me, I have no luck with new.   [*Exit*.

L. MAYOR. Now, mammet, you have well behaved
     yourself,

But you shall curse your coyness if I live.—

Who's within there? See you convey your mistress

Straight to th'Old Ford! I'll keep you straight enough.

Fore God. I would have sworn the puling girl

Would willingly accepted Hammon's love;

But banish him, my thoughts!—Go, minion, in!

                                   [*Exit* ROSE.

Now tell me, Master Scott, would you have thought

That Master Simon Eyre, the shoemaker,

Had been of wealth to buy such merchandise?

SCOTT. 'Twas well, my lord, your honour and myself

Grew partners with him; for your bills of lading

Shew that Eyre's gains in one commodity

Rise at the least to full three thousand pound

Besides like gain in other merchandise.

L. MAYOR. Well, he shall spend some of his thou-
     sands now,

For I have sent for him to the Guildhall.

                   Enter EYRE.

See, where he comes.—Good morrow, Master Eyre.

EYRE. Poor Simon Eyre, my lord, your shoemaker.

L. MAYOR. Well, well, it likes yourself to term you so.

                  Enter DODGER.

Now, Master Dodger, what's the news with you?

DODGER. I'd gladly speak in private to your honour.

L. MAYOR. You shall, you shall.—Master Eyre and
    Master Scott,
I have some business with this gentleman;
I pray, let me entreat you to walk before
To the Guildhall; I'll follow presently.
Master Eyre, I hope ere noon to call you sheriff.

EYRE. I would not care, my lord, if you might call me
King of Spain.—Come, Master Scott.

                         [*Exeunt* EYRE *and* SCOTT.

L. MAYOR. Now, Master Dodger, what's the news
you bring?

DODGER. The Earl of Lincoln by me greets your lord-
    ship,
And earnestly requests you, if you can,
Inform him, where his nephew Lacy keeps.

L. MAYOR. Is not his nephew Lacy now in France?

DODGER. No, I assure your lordship, but disguised
Lurks here in London.

L. MAYOR.   London? is't even so?
It may be; but upon my faith and soul,
I know not where he lives, or whether he lives:
So tell my Lord of Lincoln.—Lurks in London?
Well, Master Dodger, you perhaps may start him;
Be but the means to rid him into France,
I'll give you a dozen angels for your pains:
So much I love his honour, hate his nephew.
And, prithee, so inform thy lord from me.

DODGER. I take my leave.   [*Exit* DODGER.

L. MAYOR.   Farewell, good Master Dodger.
Lacy in London? I dare pawn my life,
My daughter knows thereof, and for that cause
Denied young Master Hammon in his love.
Well, I am glad I sent her to Old Ford.

Gods Lord, 'tis late; to Guildhall I must hie;
I know my brethren stay my company.   [*Exit.*

SCENE IV.—*London: a Room in* EYRE'S *House.*

Enter FIRK, MARGERY, HANS, *and* ROGER.

MARG. Thou goest too fast for me, Roger. O, Firk!

FIRK. Ay, forsooth.

MARG. I pray thee, run—do you hear?—run to Guildhall, and learn if my husband, Master Eyre, will take
that worshipful vocation of Master Sheriff upon him.
Hie thee, good Firk.

FIRK. Take it? Well, I go; an' he should not take it,
Firk swears to forswear him. Yes, forsooth, I go to Guildhall.

MARG. Nay, when? thou art too compendious and
tedious.

FIRK. O rare, your excellence is full of eloquence;
how like a new cartwheel my dame speaks, and she
looks like an old musty ale-bottle going to scalding.

MARG. Nay, when? thou wilt make me melancholy.

FIRK. God forbid your worship should fall into that
humour—I run.   [*Exit.*

MARG. Let me see now, Roger and Hans.

HODGE. Ay, forsooth, dame—mistress I should say,
but the old term so sticks to the roof of my mouth, I can
hardly lick it off.

MARG. Even what thou wilt, good Roger; dame is a
fair name for any honest Christian; but let that pass.
How dost thou, Hans?

HANS. *Mee tanck you, vro.*[12]

MARG. Well, Hans and Roger, you see, God hath
blest your master, and, perdy, if ever he comes to be

---

[12] I thank you, mistress!

Master Sheriff of London—as we are all mortal—you shall see, I will have some odd thing or other in a corner for you: I will not be your back-friend; but let that pass. Hans, pray thee, tie my shoe.

HANS. *Yaw, ic sal, vro.*[13]

MARG. Roger, thou know'st the size of my foot; as it is none of the biggest, so I thank God, it is handsome enough; prithee, let me have a pair of shoes made, cork, good Roger, wooden heel too.

HODGE. You shall.

MARG. Art thou acquainted with never a farthingale-maker, nor a French hood-maker? I must enlarge my bum, ha, ha! How shall I look in a hood, I wonder! Perdy, oddly, I think.

HODGE. As a cat out of a pillory: very well, I warrant you, mistress.

MARG. Indeed, all flesh is grass; and, Roger, canst thou tell where I may buy a good hair?

HODGE. Yes, forsooth, at the poulterer's in Gracious Street.

MARG. Thou art an ungracious wag; perdy, I mean a false hair for my periwig.

HODGE. Why, mistress, the next time I cut my beard, you shall have the shavings of it; but they are all true hairs.

MARG. It is very hot, I must get me a fan or else a mask.

HODGE. So you had need to hide your wicked face.

MARG. Fie, upon it, how costly this world's calling is; perdy, but that it is one of the wonderful works of God, I would not deal with it. Is not Firk come yet? Hans, be not so sad, let it pass and vanish, as my husband's worship says.

---

[13] Yes, I shall, mistress!

HANS. *Ick bin vrolicke, lot see yow soo.*[14]

HODGE. Mistress, will you drink a pipe of tobacco?

MARG. Oh, fie upon it, Roger, perdy! These filthy tobacco-pipes are the most idle slavering baubles that ever I felt. Out upon it! God bless us, men look not like men that use them.

Enter RALPH, *lame.*

ROGER. What, fellow Ralph? Mistress, look here, Jane's husband! Why, how now, lame? Hans, make much of him, he's a brother of our trade, a good workman, and a tall soldier.

HANS. You be welcome, broder.

MARG. Perdy, I knew him not. How dost thou, good Ralph? I am glad to see thee well.

RALPH. I would to God you saw me, dame, as well As when I went from London into France.

MARG. Trust me, I am sorry, Ralph, to see thee impotent. Lord, how the wars have made him sunburnt! The left leg is not well; 'twas a fair gift of God the infirmity took not hold a little higher, considering thou camest from France; but let that pass.

RALPH. I am glad to see you well, and I rejoice To hear that God hath blest my master so Since my departure.

MARG. Yea, truly, Ralph, I thank my Maker; but let that pass.

HODGE. And, sirrah Ralph, what news, what news in France?

RALPH. Tell me, good Roger, first, what news in England? How does my Jane? When didst thou see my wife? Where lives my poor heart? She'll be poor indeed, Now I want limbs to get whereon to feed.

HODGE. Limbs? Hast thou not hands, man? Thou

---

[14] I am merry; let's see you so too!

shalt never see a shoemaker want bread, though he have but three fingers on a hand.

RALPH. Yet all this while I hear not of my Jane.

MARG. O Ralph, your wife—perdy, we know not what's become of her. She was here a while, and because she was married, grew more stately than became her; I checked her, and so forth; away she flung, never returned, nor said bye nor bah; and, Ralph, you know, "ka me, ka thee." And so, as I tell ye—Roger, is not Firk come yet?

HODGE. No, forsooth.

MARG. And so, indeed, we heard not of her, but I hear she lives in London; but let that pass. If she had wanted, she might have opened her case to me or my husband, or to any of my men; I am sure, there's not any of them, perdy, but would have done her good to his power. Hans, look if Firk be come.

HANS. *Yaw, ik sal, vro.*[15]   [*Exit* HANS.

MARG. And so, as I said—but, Ralph, why dost thou weep? Thou knowest that naked we came out of our mother's womb, and naked we must return; and, therefore, thank God for all things.

HODGE. No, faith, Jane is a stranger here; but, Ralph, pull up a good heart, I know thou hast one. Thy wife, man, is in London; one told me, he saw her a while ago very brave and neat; we'll ferret her out, an' London hold her.

MARG. Alas, poor soul, he's overcome with sorrow; he does but as I do, weep for the loss of any good thing. But, Ralph, get thee in, call for some meat and drink, thou shalt find me worshipful towards thee.

RALPH. I thank you, dame; since I want limbs and
            lands,
I'll trust to God, my good friends, and my hands. [*Exit.*

---

[15] Yes, I shall, dame!

Enter HANS *and* FIRK *running.*

FIRK. Run, good Hans! O Hodge, O mistress! Hodge, heave up thine ears; mistress, smug up your looks; on with your best apparel; my master is chosen, my master is called, nay, condemned by the cry of the country to be sheriff of the city for this famous year now to come. And time now being, a great many men in black gowns were asked for their voices and their hands and my master had all their fists about his ears presently, and they cried, "Ay, ay, ay, ay"—and so I came away—

> Wherefore without all other grieve
> I do salute you, Mistress Shrieve.

HANS. *Yaw, my mester is de groot man, de shrieve.*

HODGE. Did not I tell you, mistress? Now I may boldly say: Good-morrow to your worship.

MARG. Good-morrow, good Roger. I thank you, my good people all.—Firk, hold up thy hand: here's a three-penny piece for thy tidings.

FIRK. 'Tis but three-half-pence, I think. Yes, 'tis three-pence, I smell the rose.

HODGE. But, mistress, be ruled by me, and do not speak so pulingly.

FIRK. 'Tis her worship speaks so, and not she. No, faith, mistress, speak me in the old key: "To it, Firk," "there, good Firk," "ply your business, Hodge," "Hodge, with a full mouth," "I'll fill your bellies with good cheer, till they cry twang."

Enter EYRE *wearing a gold chain.*

HANS. *See, myn liever broder, heer compt my meester.*

MARG. Welcome home, Master Shrieve; I pray God continue you in health and wealth.

EYRE. See here, my Maggy, a chain, a gold chain for Simon Eyre. I shall make thee a lady; here's a French hood for thee; on with it, on with it! dress thy brows with this flap of a shoulder of mutton, to make thee look lovely. Where be my fine men? Roger, I'll make over my shop and tools to thee; Firk, thou shalt be the foreman; Hans, thou shalt have an hundred for twenty. Be as mad knaves as your master Sim Eyre hath been, and you shall live to be Sheriffs of London. How dost thou like me, Margery? Prince am I none, yet am I princely born. Firk, Hodge, and Hans!

ALL THREE. Ay forsooth, what says your worship, Master Sheriff?

EYRE. Worship and honour, you Babylonian knaves, for the gentle craft. But I forgot myself, I am bidden by my lord mayor to dinner to Old Ford; he's gone before, I must after. Come, Madge, on with your trinkets! Now, my true Trojans, my fine Firk, my dapper Hodge, my honest Hans, some device, some odd crotchets, some morris, or such like, for the honour of the gentlemen shoemakers. Meet me at Old Ford, you know my mind. Come, Madge, away. Shut up the shop, knaves, and make holiday. [*Exeunt.*

FIRK. O rare! O brave! Come, Hodge; follow me, Hans;

We'll be with them for a morris-dance. [*Exeunt.*

SCENE V.—*A Room at Old Ford.*

Enter the LORD MAYOR, ROSE, EYRE, MARGERY *in a French hood*, SYBIL, *and other* Servants.

L. MAYOR. Trust me, you are as welcome to Old Ford As I myself.

MARG. Truly, I thank your lordship.

L. MAYOR. Would our bad cheer were worth the thanks you give.

EYRE. Good cheer, my lord mayor, fine cheer! A fine house, fine walls, all fine and neat.

L. MAYOR. Now, by my troth, I'll tell thee, Master
    Eyre,
It does me good, and all my brethren
That such a madcap fellow as thyself
Is entered into our society.

MARG. Ay, but, my lord, he must learn now to put on
    gravity.

EYRE. Peace, Maggy, a fig for gravity! When I go to
Guildhall in my scarlet gown, I'll look as demurely as a
saint, and speak as gravely as a justice of peace; but
now I am here at Old Ford, at my good lord mayor's
house, let it go by, vanish, Maggy, I'll be merry; away
with flip-flap, these fooleries, these gulleries. What,
honey? Prince am I none, yet am I princely born. What
says my lord mayor?

L. MAYOR. Ha, ha, ha! I had rather than a thousand
pound, I had an heart but half so light as yours.

EYRE. Why, what should I do, my lord? A pound of
care pays not a dram of debt. Hum, let's be merry,
whiles we are young; old age, sack and sugar will steal
upon us, ere we be aware.

THE FIRST THREE-MEN'S SONG.

O the month of May, the merry month of May,
    So frolick, so gay, and so green, so green, so green!
O, and then did I unto my true love say:
    "Sweet Peg, thou shalt be my summer's queen!

"Now the nightingale, the pretty nightingale,
    The sweetest singer in all the forest's choir,
Entreats thee, sweet Peggy, to hear thy true love's tale;
    Lo, yonder she sitteth, her breast against a brier.

"But O, I spy the cuckoo, the cuckoo, the cuckoo;
    See where she sitteth: come away, my joy;

Come away, I prithee: I do not like the cuckoo
   Should sing where my Peggy and I kiss and toy."

O the month of May, the merry month of May,
   So frolick, so gay, and so green, so green, so green!
And then did I unto my true love say:
   "Sweet Peg, thou shalt be my summer's queen!"

L. MAYOR. It's well done; Mistress Eyre, pray, give
      good counsel
To my daughter.

MARG. I hope, Mistress Rose will have the grace to
take nothing that's bad.

L. MAYOR. Pray God she do; for i' faith, Mistress
      Eyre,
I would bestow upon that peevish girl
A thousand marks more than I mean to give her,
Upon condition she'd be ruled by me;
The ape still crosseth me. There came of late
A proper gentleman of fair revenues,
Whom gladly I would call son-in-law:
But my fine cockney would have none of him.
You'll prove a coxcomb for it, ere you die:
A courtier, or no man must please your eye.

EYRE. Be ruled, sweet Rose: th'art ripe for a man.
Marry not with a boy that has no more hair on his face
than thou hast on thy cheeks. A courtier, wash, go by,
stand not upon pishery-pashery: those silken fellows are
but painted images, outsides, outsides, Rose; their inner
linings are torn. No, my fine mouse, marry me with a
gentleman grocer like my lord mayor, your father; a
grocer is a sweet trade: plums, plums. Had I a son or
daughter should marry out of the generation and blood
of the shoemakers, he should pack; what, the gentle
trade is a living for a man through Europe, through the
world.   [A *noise within of a tabor and a pipe.*

L. MAYOR. What noise is this?

EYRE. O my lord mayor, a crew of good fellows that for love to your honour are come hither with a morris-dance. Come in, my Mesopotamians, cheerily.

Enter HODGE, HANS, RALPH, FIRK, *and other* SHOE-MAKERS, *in a morris; after a little dancing the* LORD MAYOR *speaks.*

L. MAYOR. Master Eyre, are all these shoemakers?

EYRE. All cordwainers, my good lord mayor.

ROSE. [*Aside*]. How like my Lacy looks yond' shoe-maker!

HANS. [*Aside*.] O that I durst but speak unto my love!

L. MAYOR. Sybil, go fetch some wine to make these drink. You are all welcome.

ALL. We thank your lordship.

[ROSE *takes a cup of wine and goes to* HANS.

ROSE. For his sake whose fair shape thou represent'st, Good friend, I drink to thee.

HANS. *Ic bedancke, good frister.*[16]

MARG. I see, Mistress Rose, you do not want judge-ment; you have drunk to the properest man I keep.

FIRK. Here be some have done their parts to be as proper as he.

L. MAYOR. Well, urgent business calls me back to London:

Good fellows, first go in and taste our cheer;

And to make merry as you homeward go,

Spend these two angels in beer at Stratford-Bow.

EYRE. To these two, my mad lads, Sim Eyre adds an-other; then cheerily, Firk; tickle it, Hans, and all for the honour of shoemakers.   [*All go dancing out.*

L. MAYOR. Come, Master Eyre, let's have your com-pany.   [*Exeunt.*

---

[16] I thank you, good maid!

ROSE. Sybil, what shall I do?

SYBIL. Why, what's the matter?

ROSE. That Hans the shoemaker is my love Lacy,
Disguised in that attire to find me out.
How should I find the means to speak with him?

SYBIL. What, mistress, never fear; I dare venture my
maidenhead to nothing, and that's great odds, that Hans
the Dutchman, when we come to London, shall not only
see and speak with you, but in spite of all your father's
policies steal you away and marry you. Will not this
please you?

ROSE. Do this, and ever be assured of my love.

SYBIL. Away, then, and follow your father to London,
lest your absence cause him to suspect something:

    Tomorrow, if my counsel be obeyed,

    I'll bind you prentice to the gentle trade. [*Exeunt.*

ACT THE FOURTH.

SCENE I.—*A Street in London.*

JANE *in a Seamster's shop, working; enter* Master
    HAMMON, *muffled; he stands aloof.*

HAM. Yonder's the shop, and there my fair love sits.
She's fair and lovely, but she is not mine.
O, would she were! Thrice have I courted her,
Thrice hath my hand been moistened with her hand,
Whilst my poor famished eyes do feed on that
Which made them famish. I am unfortunate:
I still love one, yet nobody loves me.
I muse, in other men what women see,
That I so want! Fine Mistress Rose was coy,
And this too curious! Oh, no, she is chaste,
And for she thinks me wanton, she denies
To cheer my cold heart with her sunny eyes.

How prettily she works, oh pretty hand!
Oh happy work! It doth me good to stand
Unseen to see her. Thus I oft have stood
In frosty evenings, a light burning by her,
Enduring biting cold, only to eye her.
One only look hath seemed as rich to me
As a king's crown; such is love's lunacy.
Muffled I'll pass along, and by that try
Whether she know me.

JANE.   Sir, what is't you buy?
What is't you lack, sir, calico, or lawn,
Fine cambric shirts, or bands, what will you buy?

HAM. [*Aside.*] That which thou wilt not sell. Faith,
      yet I'll try:
How do you sell this handkerchief?

JANE.   Good cheap.

HAM. And how these ruffs?

JANE.   Cheap too.

HAM.   And how this band?

JANE. Cheap too.

HAM.   All cheap; how sell you then this hand?

JANE. My hands are not to be sold.

HAM.   To be given then!
Nay, faith, I come to buy.

JANE.   But none knows when.

HAM. Good sweet, leave work a little while; let's play.

JANE. I cannot live by keeping holiday.

HAM. I'll pay you for the time which shall be lost.

JANE. With me you shall not be at so much cost.

HAM. Look, how you wound this cloth, so you wound
me.

JANE. It may be so.

HAM.   'Tis so.

JANE.   What remedy?

HAM. Nay, faith, you are too coy.

JANE.   Let go my hand.

HAM. I will do any task at your command,
I would let go this beauty, were I not
In mind to disobey you by a power
That controls kings: I love you!

JANE.   So, now part.

HAM. With hands I may, but never with my heart.
In faith, I love you.

JANE.   I believe you do.

HAM. Shall a true love in me breed hate in you?

JANE. I hate you not.

HAM.   Then you must love?

JANE.   I do.
What are you better now? I love not you.

HAM. All this, I hope, is but a woman's fray,
That means: come to me, when she cries: away!
In earnest, mistress, I do not jest,
A true chaste love hath entered in my breast.
I love you dearly, as I love my life,
I love you as a husband loves a wife;
That, and no other love, my love requires,
Thy wealth, I know, is little; my desires
Thirst not for gold. Sweet, beauteous Jane, what's mine
Shall, if thou make myself thine, all be thine.
Say, judge, what is thy sentence, life or death?
Mercy or cruelty lies in thy breath.

JANE. Good sir, I do believe you love me well;
For 'tis a silly conquest, silly pride
For one like you—I mean a gentleman—
To boast that by his love-tricks he hath brought
Such and such women to his amorous lure;
I think you do not so, yet many do,
And make it even a very trade to woo.
I could be coy, as many women be,
Feed you with sunshine smiles and wanton looks,

But I detest witchcraft; say that I
Do constantly believe, you constant have—

    HAM. Why dost thou not believe me?

    JANE.   I believe you;
But yet, good sir, because I will not grieve you
With hopes to taste fruit which will never fall,
In simple truth this is the sum of all:
My husband lives, at least, I hope he lives.
Pressed was he to these bitter wars in France;
Bitter they are to me by wanting him.
I have but one heart, and that heart's his due.
How can I then bestow the same on you?
Whilst he lives, his I live, be it ne'er so poor,
And rather be his wife than a king's whore.

    HAM. Chaste and dear woman, I will not abuse thee,
Although it cost my life, if thou refuse me.
Thy husband, pressed for France, what was his name?

    JANE. Ralph Damport.

    HAM.   Damport? Here's a letter sent
From France to me, from a dear friend of mine,
A gentleman of place; here he doth write
Their names that have been slain in every fight.

    JANE. I hope death's scroll contains not my love's
        name.

    HAM. Cannot you read?

    JANE.   I can.

    HAM.   Peruse the same.
To my remembrance such a name I read
Amongst the rest. See here.

    JANE.   Ay me, he's dead!
He's dead! if this be true, my dear heart's slain!

    HAM. Have patience, dear love.

    JANE.   Hence, hence!

    HAM.   Nay, sweet Jane,
Make not poor sorrow proud with these rich tears.

I mourn thy husband's death, because thou mourn'st.

JANE. That bill is forged; 'tis signed by forgery.

HAM. I'll bring thee letters sent besides to many,
Carrying the like report: Jane, 'tis too true.
Come, weep not: mourning, though it rise from love,
Helps not the mourned, yet hurts them that mourn.

JANE. For God's sake, leave me.

HAM. Whither dost thou turn?
Forget the dead, love them that are alive;
His love is faded, try how mine will thrive.

JANE. 'Tis now no time for me to think on love.

HAM. 'Tis now best time for you to think on love,
Because your love lives not.

JANE. Though he be dead,
My love to him shall not be buried;
For God's sake, leave me to myself alone.

HAM. 'Twould kill my soul, to leave thee drowned in
moan.
Answer me to my suit, and I am gone;
Say to me yea or no.

JANE. No.

HAM. Then farewell!
One farewell will not serve, I come again;
Come, dry these wet cheeks; tell me, faith, sweet Jane,
Yea or no, once more.

JANE. Once more I say: no;
Once more be gone, I pray; else will I go.

HAM. Nay, then I will grow rude, by this white hand,
Until you change that cold "no"; here I'll stand
Till by your hard heart—

JANE. Nay, for God's love, peace!
My sorrows by your presence more increase.
Not that you thus are present, but all grief
Desires to be alone; therefore in brief
Thus much I say, and saying bid adieu:

If ever I wed man, it shall be you.

HAM. O blessed voice! Dear Jane, I'll urge no more,
Thy breath hath made me rich.

JANE. Death makes me poor.

[*Exeunt.*

SCENE II.—*London: a Street before* HODGE'S *Shop.*

HODGE, *at his shop-board,* RALPH, FIRK, HANS, *and a*
Boy *at work.*

ALL. Hey, down a down, down derry.

HODGE. Well said, my hearts; ply your work today,
we loitered yesterday; to it pell-mell, that we may live
to be lord mayors, or aldermen at least.

FIRK. Hey, down a down, derry.

HODGE. Well said, i' faith! How say'st thou, Hans,
doth not Firk tickle it?

HANS. *Yaw, mester.*

FIRK. Not so neither, my organ-pipe squeaks this
morning for want of liquoring. Hey, down a down,
derry!

HANS. *Forward, Firk, tow best un jolly youngster.
Hort, I, mester, ic bid yo, cut me un pair vampres vor
Mester Jeffre's boots.*[17]

HODGE. Thou shalt, Hans.

FIRK. Master!

HODGE. How now, boy?

FIRK. Pray, now you are in the cutting vein, cut me
out a pair of counterfeits, or else my work will not pass
current; hey, down a down!

HODGE. Tell me, sirs, are my cousin Mrs. Priscilla's
shoes done?

---

[17] Forward, Firk, thou art a jolly youngster. Hark, ay, master,
I bid you cut me a pair of vamps for Master Jeffrey's boots.

FIRK. Your cousin? No, master; one of your aunts, hang her; let them alone.

RALPH. I am in hand with them; she gave charge that none but I should do them for her.

FIRK. Thou do for her? then 'twill be a lame doing, and that she loves not. Ralph, thou might'st have sent her to me, in faith, I would have yearked and firked your Priscilla. Hey, down a down, derry. This gear will not hold.

HODGE. How say'st thou, Firk, were we not merry at Old Ford?

FIRK. How, merry? why, our buttocks went jiggy-joggy like a quagmire. Well, Sir Roger Oatmeal, if I thought all meal of that nature, I would eat nothing but bagpuddings.

RALPH. Of all good fortunes my fellow Hans had the best.

FIRK. 'Tis true, because Mistress Rose drank to him.

HODGE. Well, well, work apace. They say, seven of the aldermen be dead, or very sick.

FIRK. I care not, I'll be none.

RALPH. No, nor I; but then my Master Eyre will come quickly to be lord mayor.

Enter SYBIL.

FIRK. Whoop, yonder comes Sybil.

HODGE. Sybil, welcome, i'faith; and how dost thou, mad wench?

FIRK. Syb-whore, welcome to London.

SYBIL. Godamercy, sweet Firk; good lord, Hodge, what a delicious shop you have got! You tickle it, i'faith.

RALPH. Godamercy, Sybil, for our good cheer at Old Ford.

SYBIL. That you shall have, Ralph.

FIRK. Nay, by the mass, we had tickling cheer, Sybil;

and how the plague dost thou and Mistress Rose and my lord mayor? I put the women in first.

SYBIL. Well, Godamecry; but God's me, I forget myself, where's Hans the Fleming?

FIRK. Hark, butter-box, now you must yelp out some *spreken.*

HANS. *Wat begaie you? Vat vod you, Frister?*[18]

SYBIL. Marry, you must come to my young mistress, to pull on her shoes you made last.

HANS. *Vare ben your egle fro, vare ben your mistris?*[19]

SYBIL. Marry, here at our London house in Cornhill.

FIRK. Will nobody serve her turn but Hans?

SYBIL. No, sir. Come, Hans, I stand upon needles.

HODGE. Why then, Sybil, take heed of pricking.

SYBIL. For that let me alone. I have a trick in my budget. Come, Hans.

HANS. *Yaw, yaw, ic sall meete yo gane.*[20]

[*Exit* HANS *and* SYBIL.

HODGE. Go, Hans, make haste again. Come, who lacks work?

FIRK. I, master, for I lack my breakfast; 'tis munching-time, and past.

HODGE. Is't so? why, then leave work, Ralph. To breakfast! Boy, look to the tools. Come, Ralph; come, Firk.   [*Exeunt.*

SCENE III.—*The Same.*

Enter a Serving-man.

SERV. Let me see now, the sign of the Last in Tower Street. Mass, yonder's the house. What, haw! Who's within?

---

[18] What do you want (was begehrt ihr), what would you, girl?
[19] Where is your noble lady, where is your mistress?
[20] Yes, yes, I shall go with you.

Enter RALPH.

RALPH. Who calls there? What want you, sir?

SERV. Marry, I would have a pair of shoes made for a gentlewoman against to-morrow morning. What, can you do them?

RALPH. Yes, sir, you shall have them. But what length's her foot?

SERV. Why, you must make them in all parts like this shoe; but, at any hand, fail not to do them, for the gentlewoman is to be married very early in the morning.

RALPH. How? by this shoe must it be made? by this? Are you sure, sir, by this?

SERV. How, by this? Am I sure, by this? Art thou in thy wits? I tell thee, I must have a pair of shoes dost thou mark me? a pair of shoes, two shoes, made by this very shoe, this same shoe, against to-morrow morning by four a clock. Dost understand me? Canst thou do't?

RALPH. Yes, sir, yes—I—I—I can do't. By this shoe, you say? I should know this shoe. Yes, sir, yes, by this shoe, I can do't. Four a clock, well. Whither shall I bring them?

SERV. To the sign of the Golden Ball in Watling Street; enquire for one Master Hammon, a gentleman, my master.

RALPH. Yea, sir; by this shoe, you say?

SERV. I say, Master Hammon at the Golden Ball; he's the bridegroom, and those shoes are for his bride.

RALPH. They shall be done by this shoe; well, well, Master Hammon at the Golden Shoe—I would say, the Golden Ball; very well, very well. But I pray you, sir, where must Master Hammon be married?

SERV. At St. Faith's Church, under Paul's. But what's that to thee? Prithee, dispatch those shoes, and so farewell.   [*Exit.*

RALPH. By this shoe, said he. How am I amazed

At this strange accident! Upon my life,
This was the very shoe I gave my wife,
When I was pressed for France; since when, alas!
I never could hear of her: it is the same,
And Hammon's bride no other but my Jane.

Enter FIRK.

FIRK. 'Snails, Ralph, thou hast lost thy part of three
pots, a countryman of mine gave me to breakfast.

RALPH. I care not; I have found a better thing.

FIRK. A thing? away! Is it a man's thing, or a woman's
thing?

RALPH. Firk, dost thou know this shoe?

FIRK. No, by my troth; neither doth that know me!
I have no acquaintance with it, 'tis a mere stranger to
me.

RALPH. Why, then I do; this shoe, I durst be sworn,
Once covered the instep of my Jane.
This is her size, her breadth, thus trod my love;
These true-love knots I pricked; I hold my life,
By this old shoe I shall find out my wife.

FIRK. Ha, ha! Old shoe, that wert new! How a mur-
rain came this ague-fit of foolishness upon thee?

RALPH. Thus, Firk: even now here came a serving-
     man;
By this shoe would he have a new pair made
Against to-morrow morning for his mistress,
That's to be married to a gentleman.
And why may not this be my sweet Jane?

FIRK. And why may'st not thou be my sweet ass? Ha,
ha!

RALPH. Well, laugh and spare not! But the truth is
     this:
Against tomorrow morning I'll provide
A lusty crew of honest shoemakers,
To watch the going of the bride to church.

If she prove Jane, I'll take her in despite
From Hammon and the devil, were he by.
If it be not my Jane, what remedy?
Hereof I am sure, I shall live till I die,
Although I never with a woman lie.   [*Exit.*

FIRK. Thou lie with a woman to build nothing but
Cripple-gates! Well, God sends fools fortune, and it may
be, he may light upon his matrimony by such a device;
for wedding and hanging goes by destiny.   [*Exit.*

SCENE IV.—*London: a Room in the* LORD MAYOR'S
House.

Enter HANS *and* ROSE, *arm in arm.*

HANS. How happy am I by embracing thee!
Oh, I did fear such cross mishaps did reign,
That I should never see my Rose again.

ROSE. Sweet Lacy, since fair opportunity
Offers herself to further our escape,
Let not too over-fond esteem of me
Hinder that happy hour. Invent the means,
And Rose will follow thee through all the world.

HANS. Oh, how I surfeit with excess of joy,
Made happy by thy rich perfection!
But since thou pay'st sweet interest to my hopes,
Redoubling love on love, let me once more
Like to a bold-faced debtor crave of thee,
This night to steal abroad, and at Eyre's house,
Who now by death of certain aldermen
Is mayor of London, and my master once,
Meet thou thy Lacy, where in spite of change,
Your father's anger, and mine uncle's hate,
Our happy nuptials will we consummate.

Enter SYBIL.

SYBIL. Oh God, what will you do, mistress? Shift for yourself, your father is at hand! He's coming, he's coming! Master Lacy, hide yourself in my mistress! For God's sake, shift for yourselves!

HANS. Your father come, sweet Rose—what shall I do? Where shall I hide me? How shall I escape?

ROSE. A man, and want wit in extremity?
Come, come, be Hans still, play the shoemaker,
Pull on my shoe.

Enter the LORD MAYOR.

HANS. Mass, and that's well remembered.

SYBIL. Here comes your father.

HANS. *Forware, metresse, 'tis un good skow, it sal vel dute, or ye sal neit betallen.*[21]

ROSE. Oh God, it pincheth me; what will you do?

HANS. [*Aside.*] Your father's presence pincheth, not the shoe.

L. MAYOR. Well done; fit my daughter well, and she shall please thee well.

HANS. *Yaw, yaw, ick weit dat well; forware, 'tis un good skoo, 'tis gimait van neits leither; se euer, mine here.*[22]

Enter a Prentice.

L. MAYOR. I do believe it—What's the news with you?

PRENTICE. Please you, the Earl of Lincoln at the gate Is newly 'lighted, and would speak with you.

L. MAYOR. I do believe it.—What's the news with me?
Well, well, I know his errand. Daughter Rose,

---

[21] Indeed, mistress, 'tis a good shoe, it shall fit well, or you shall not pay.
[22] Yes, yes, I know that well; indeed, 'tis a good shoe, 'tis made of neat's leather, see here, good sir!

Send hence your shoemaker, dispatch, have done!
Syb, make things handsome! Sir boy, follow me.

[*Exit.*

HANS. Mine uncle come! Oh, what may this portend?
Sweet Rose, this of our love threatens an end.

ROSE. Be not dismayed at this; whate'er befall,
Rose is thine own. To witness I speak truth,
Where thou appoint'st the place, I'll meet with thee.
I will not fix a day to follow thee,
But presently steal hence. Do not reply:
Love which gave strength to bear my father's hate,
Shall now add wings to further our escape.   [*Exeunt.*

SCENE V.—*Another Room in the same House.*

Enter the LORD MAYOR *and the* EARL OF LINCOLN.

L. MAYOR. Believe me, on my credit, I speak truth:
Since first your nephew Lacy went to France,
I have not seen him. It seemed strange to me,
When Dodger told me that he stayed behind,
Neglecting the high charge the king imposed.

LINCOLN. Trust me, Sir Roger Oateley, I did think
Your counsel had given head to this attempt,
Drawn to it by the love he bears your child.
Here I did hope to find him in your house;
But now I see mine error, and confess,
My judgment wronged you by conceiving so.

L. MAYOR. Lodge in my house, say you? Trust me,
my lord,
I love your nephew Lacy too too dearly,
So much to wrong his honour; and he hath done so,
That first gave him advice to stay from France.
To witness I speak truth, I let you know,
How careful I have been to keep my daughter
Free from all conference or speech of him;

Not that I scorn your nephew, but in love
I bear your honour, lest your noble blood
Should by my mean worth be dishonoured.

    LINCOLN. [*Aside.*] How far the churl's tongue wanders
        from his heart!
Well, well, Sir Roger Oateley, I believe you,
With more than many thanks for the kind love,
So much you seem to bear me. But, my lord,
Let me request your help to seek my nephew,
Whom if I find, I'll straight embark for France.
So shall your Rose be free, my thoughts at rest,
And much care die which now lies in my breast.

                Enter SYBIL.

    SYBIL. Oh Lord! Help, for God's sake! my mistress;
oh, my young mistress!

    L. MAYOR. Where is thy mistress? What's become of
her?

    SYBIL. She's gone, she's fled!

    L. MAYOR. Gone! Whither is she fled?

    SYBIL. I know not, forsooth; she's fled out of doors
with Hans the shoemaker; I saw them scud, scud, scud,
apace, apace!

    L. MAYOR. Which way? What, John! Where be my
men? Which way?

    SYBIL. I know not, an it please your worship.

    L. MAYOR. Fled with a shoemaker? Can this be true?

    SYBIL. Oh Lord, sir, as true as God's in Heaven.

    LINCOLN. Her love turned shoemaker? I am glad of
        this.

    L. MAYOR. A Fleming butter-box, a shoemaker!
Will she forget her birth, requite my care
With such ingratitude? Scorned she young Hammon
To love a honniken, a needy knave?
Well, let her fly, I'll not fly after her,
Let her starve, if she will; she's none of mine.

LINCOLN. Be not so cruel, sir.

Enter FIRK *with shoes.*

SYBIL.   I am glad, she's 'scaped.

L. MAYOR. I'll not account of her as of my child.
Was there no better object for her eyes
But a foul drunken lubber, swill-belly,
A shoemaker? That's brave!

FIRK. Yea, forsooth; 'tis a very brave shoe, and as fit
as a pudding.

L. MAYOR. How now, what knave is this? From
whence comest thou?

FIRK. No knave, sir. I am Firk the shoemaker, lusty
Roger's chief lusty journeyman, and I have come hither
to take up the pretty leg of sweet Mistress Rose, and
thus hoping your worship is in as good health, as I was
at the making hereof, I bid you farewell, yours, Firk.

L. MAYOR. Stay, stay, Sir Knave!

LINCOLN. Come hither, shoemaker!

FIRK. 'Tis happy the knave is put before the shoemaker, or else I would not have vouchsafed to come
back to you. I am moved, for I stir.

L. MAYOR. My lord, this villain calls us knaves by
craft.

FIRK. Then 'tis by the gentle craft, and to call one
knave gently, is no harm. Sit your worship merry! Syb,
your young mistress—I'll so bob them, now my Master
Eyre is lord mayor of London.

L. MAYOR. Tell me, sirrah, who's man are you?

FIRK. I am glad to see your worship so merry. I have
no maw to this gear, no stomach as yet to a red petticoat.

[*Pointing to* SYBIL.

LINCOLN. He means not, sir, to woo you to his maid,
But only doth demand who's man you are.

FIRK. I sing now to the tune of Rogero. Roger, my
fellow, is now my master.

LINCOLN. Sirrah, know'st thou one Hans, a shoe-maker?

FIRK. Hans, shoemaker? Oh yes, stay, yes, I have him. I tell you what, I speak it in secret: Mistress Rose and he are by this time—no, not so, but shortly are to come over one another with "Can you dance the shaking of the sheets?" It is that Hans—[*Aside.*] I'll so gull these diggers!

L. MAYOR. Know'st thou, then, where he is?

FIRK. Yes, forsooth; yea, marry!

LINCOLN. Canst thou, in sadness—

FIRK. No, forsooth; no, marry!

L. MAYOR. Tell me, good honest fellow, where he is, And thou shalt see what I'll bestow on thee.

FIRK. Honest fellow? No, sir; not so, sir; my profes-sion is the gentle craft; I care not for seeing, I love feel-ing; let me feel it here; *aurium tenus,* ten pieces of gold; *genuum tenus,* ten pieces of silver; and then Firk is your man in a new pair of stretchers.

L. MAYOR. Here is an angel, part of thy reward, Which I will give thee; tell me where he is.

FIRK. No point! Shall I betray my brother? no! Shall I prove Judas to Hans? no! Shall I cry treason to my corporation? no, I shall be firked and yerked then. But give me your angel; your angel shall tell you.

LINCOLN. Do so, good fellow; 'tis no hurt to thee.

FIRK. Send simpering Syb away.

L. MAYOR. Huswife, get you in. [*Exit* SYBIL.

FIRK. Pitchers have ears, and maids have wide mouths; but for Hans Prauns, upon my word, to-morrow morning he and young Mistress Rose go to this gear, they shall be married together, by this rush, or else turn Firk to a firkin of butter, to tan leather withal.

L. MAYOR. But art thou sure of this?

FIRK. Am I sure that Paul's steeple is a handful higher

than London Stone, or that the Pissing-Conduit leaks nothing but pure Mother Bunch? Am I sure I am lusty Firk? God's nails, do you think I am so base to gull you?

LINCOLN. Where are they married? Dost thou know the church?

FIRK. I never go to church, but I know the name of it; it is a swearing church—stay a while, 'tis—ay, by the mass, no, no,—'tis—ay, by my troth, no, nor that; 'tis —ay, by my faith, that, that, 'tis, ay, by my Faith's Church under Paul's Cross. There they shall be knit like a pair of stockings in matrimony; there they'll be inconie.

LINCOLN. Upon my life, my nephew Lacy walks
In the disguise of this Dutch shoemaker.

FIRK. Yes, forsooth.

LINCOLN. Doth he not, honest fellow?

FIRK. No, forsooth; I think Hans is nobody but Hans, no spirit.

L. MAYOR. My mind misgives me now, 'tis so, indeed.

LINCOLN. My cousin speaks the language, knows the trade.

L. MAYOR. Let me request your company, my lord;
Your honourable presence may, no doubt,
Refrain their headstrong rashness, when myself
Going alone perchance may be o'erborne.
Shall I request this favour?

LINCOLN.   This, or what else.

FIRK. Then you must rise betimes, for they mean to fall to their hey-pass and repass, pindy-pandy, which hand will you have, very early.

L. MAYOR. My care shall every way equal their haste.
This night accept your lodging in my house,
The earlier shall we stir, and at St. Faith's
Prevent this giddy hare-brained nuptial.
This traffic of hot love shall yield cold gains:

They ban our loves, and we'll forbid their banns.   [*Exit.*

LINCOLN. At St. Faith's Church thou say'st?

FIRK. Yes, by their troth.

LINCOLN. Be secret, on thy life.   [*Exit.*

FIRK. Yes, when I kiss your wife! Ha, ha, here's no
craft in the gentle craft. I came hither of purpose with
shoes to Sir Roger's worship, whilst Rose, his daughter,
be cony-catched by Hans. Soft now; these two gulls
will be at St. Faith's Church to-morrow morning, to take
Master Bridegroom and Mistress Bride napping, and
they, in the mean time, shall chop up the matter at the
Savoy. But the best sport is, Sir Roger Oateley will find
my fellow lame Ralph's wife going to marry a gentleman,
and then he'll stop her instead of his daughter. Oh brave!
there will be fine tickling sport. Soft now, what have I
to do? Oh, I know; now a mess of shoemakers meet at
the Woolsack in Ivy Lane, to cozen my gentleman of
lame Ralph's wife, that's true.

> Alack, alack!
> Girls, hold out tack!
> For now smocks for this jumbling
> Shall go to wrack.   [*Exit.*

ACT THE FIFTH.

SCENE I.—*A Room in* EYRE'S *House.*

Enter EYRE, MARGERY, HANS, *and* ROSE.

EYRE. This is the morning, then; stay, my bully, my
honest Hans, is it not?

HANS. This is the morning that must make us two
happy or miserable; therefore, if you—

EYRE. Away with these ifs and ands, Hans, and these
et caeteras! By mine honour, Rowland Lacy, none but

the king shall wrong thee. Come, fear nothing, am not I Sim Eyre? Is not Sim Eyre lord mayor of London? Fear nothing, Rose: let them all say what they can; dainty, come thou to me—laughest thou?

MARG. Good my lord, stand her friend in what thing you may.

EYRE. Why, my sweet Lady Madgy, think you Simon Eyre can forget his fine Dutch journeyman? No, vah! Fie, I scorn it, it shall never be cast in my teeth, that I was unthankful. Lady Madgy, thou had'st never covered thy Saracen's head with this French flap, nor loaden thy bum with this farthingale ('tis trash, trumpery, vanity); Simon Eyre had never walked in a red petticoat, nor wore a chain of gold, but for my fine journeyman's Portuguese. And shall I leave him? No! Prince am I none, yet bear a princely mind.

HANS. My lord, 'tis time for us to part from hence.

EYRE. Lady Madgy, Lady Madgy, take two or three of my pie crust-eaters, my buff-jerkin varlets, that do walk in black gowns at Simon Eyre's heels; take them, good Lady Madgy; trip and go, my brown queen of periwigs, with my delicate Rose and my jolly Rowland to the Savoy; see them linked, countenance the marriage; and when it is done, cling, cling together, you Hamborow turtle-doves. I'll bear you out, come to Simon Eyre; come, dwell with me, Hans, thou shalt eat minced-pies and marchpane. Rose, away, cricket; trip and go, my Lady Madgy, to the Savoy; Hans, wed, and to bed; kiss, and away! Go, vanish!

MARG. Farewell, my lord.

ROSE. Make haste, sweet love.

MARG.   She'd fain the deed were done.

HANS. Come, my sweet Rose; faster than deer we'll run.   [*Exeunt* HANS, ROSE, *and* MARGERY.

EYRE. Go, vanish, vanish! Avaunt, I say! By the Lord

of Ludgate, it's a mad life to be a lord mayor; it's a stirring life, a fine life, a velvet life, a careful life. Well, Simon Eyre, yet set a good face on it, in the honour of St. Hugh. Soft, the king this day comes to dine with me, to see my new buildings; his majesty is welcome, he shall have good cheer, delicate cheer, princely cheer. This day, my fellow prentices of London come to dine with me too, they shall have fine cheer, gentlemanlike cheer. I promised the mad Cappadocians, when we all served at the Conduit together, that if ever I came to be mayor of London, I would feast them all, and I'll do't, I'll do't, by the life of Pharaoh; by this beard, Sim Eyre will be no flincher. Besides, I have procured that upon every Shrove Tuesday, at the sound of the pancake bell, my fine dapper Assyrian lads shall clap up their shop windows, and away. This is the day, and this day they shall do't, they shall do't.

Boys, that day are you free, let masters care,
And prentices shall pray for Simon Eyre.   [*Exit.*

SCENE II.—*A Street near St. Faith's Church.*

Enter HODGE, FIRK, RALPH, *and five or six* Shoemakers,
all with cudgels or such weapons.

HODGE. Come, Ralph; stand to it, Firk. My masters, as we are the brave bloods of the shoemakers, heirs apparent to St. Hugh, and perpetual benefactors to all good fellows, thou shalt have no wrong; were Hammon a king of spades, he should not delve in thy close without thy sufferance. But tell me, Ralph, art thou sure 'tis thy wife?

RALPH. Am I sure this is Firk? This morning, when I stroked on her shoes, I looked upon her, and she upon me, and sighed, asked me if ever I knew one Ralph. Yes, said I. For his sake, said she—tears standing in her eyes—and for thou art somewhat like him, spend this piece of gold. I took it; my lame leg and my travel beyond sea made me unknown. All is one for that: I know she's mine.

FIRK. Did she give thee this gold? O glorious glittering gold! She's thine own, 'tis thy wife, and she loves thee; for I'll stand to't, there's no woman will give gold to any man, but she thinks better of him, than she thinks of them she gives silver to. And for Hammon, neither Hammon nor hangman shall wrong thee in London. Is not our old master Eyre, lord mayor? Speak, my hearts.

ALL. Yes, and Hammon shall know it to his cost.

Enter HAMMON, *his* Serving-man, JANE *and* Others.

HODGE. Peace, my bullies; yonder they come.

RALPH. Stand to't, my hearts. Firk, let me speak first.

HODGE. No, Ralph, let me.—Hammon, whither away so early?

HAM. Unmannerly, rude slave, what's that to thee?

FIRK. To him, sir? Yes, sir, and to me, and others. Good-morrow, Jane, how dost thou? Good Lord, how the world is changed with you! God be thanked!

HAM. Villains, hands off! How dare you touch my love?

ALL. Villains? Down with them! Cry clubs for prentices!

HODGE. Hold, my hearts! Touch her, Hammon? Yea, and more than that: we'll carry her away with us. My masters and gentlemen, never draw your bird-spits; shoemakers are steel to the back, men every inch of them, all spirit.

THOSE OF HAMMON'S SIDE. Well, and what of all this?

HODGE. I'll show you.—Jane, dost thou know this man? 'Tis Ralph, I can tell thee; nay, 'tis he in faith, though he be lamed by the wars. Yet look not strange, but run to him, fold him about the neck and kiss him.

JANE. Lives then my husband? Oh God, let me go,
Let me embrace my Ralph.

HAM.   What means my Jane?

JANE. Nay, what meant you, to tell me, he was slain?

HAM. Pardon me, dear love, for being misled.
(TO RALPH.) 'Twas rumoured here in London, thou
        wert dead.

FIRK. Thou seest he lives. Lass, go, pack home with
him. Now, Master Hammon, where's your mistress, your
wife?

SERV. 'Swounds, master, fight for her! Will you thus
lose her?

ALL. Down with that creature! Clubs! Down with
him!

HODGE. Hold, hold!

HAM. Hold, fool! Sirs, he shall do no wrong.
Will my Jane leave me thus, and break her faith?

FIRK. Yea, sir! She must, sir! She shall, sir! What
then? Mend it!

HODGE. Hark, fellow Ralph, follow my counsel: set
the wench in the midst, and let her choose her man, and
let her be his woman.

JANE. Whom should I choose? Whom should my
        thoughts affect
But him whom Heaven hath made to be my love?
Thou art my husband, and these humble weeds
Makes thee more beautiful than all his wealth.
Therefore, I will but put off his attire,
Returning it into the owner's hand,
And after ever be thy constant wife.

HODGE. Not a rag, Jane! The law's on our side; he
that sows in another man's ground, forfeits his harvest.
Get thee home, Ralph; follow him, Jane; he shall not
have so much as a busk-point from thee.

FIRK. Stand to that, Ralph; the appurtenances are thine own. Hammon, look not at her!

SERV. O, swounds, no!

FIRK. Blue coat, be quiet, we'll give you a new livery else; we'll make Shrove Tuesday Saint George's Day for you. Look not, Hammon, leer not! I'll firk you! For thy head now, one glance, one sheep's eye, anything, at her! Touch not a rag, lest I and my brethren beat you to clouts.

SERV. Come, Master Hammon, there's no striving here.

HAM. Good fellows, hear me speak; and, honest Ralph,

Whom I have injured most by loving Jane,

Mark what I offer thee: herein fair gold

Is twenty pound, I'll give it for thy Jane;

If this content thee not, thou shalt have more.

HODGE. Sell not thy wife, Ralph; make her not a whore.

HAM. Say, wilt thou freely cease thy claim in her,

And let her be my wife?

ALL. No, do not, Ralph.

RALPH. Sirrah Hammon, Hammon, dost thou think a shoemaker is so base to be a bawd to his own wife for commodity? Take thy gold, choke with it! Were I not lame, I would make thee eat thy words.

FIRK. A shoemaker sell his flesh and blood? Oh indignity!

HODGE. Sirrah, take up your pelf, and be packing.

HAM. I will not touch one penny, but in lieu

Of that great wrong I offered thy Jane,

To Jane and thee I give that twenty pound.

Since I have failed of her, during my life,

I vow, no woman else shall be my wife.

Farewell, good fellows of the gentle trade:

Your morning mirth my mourning day hath made. [*Exit.*

FIRK. (*To the* Serving-man.) Touch the gold, creature, if you dare! Y'are best be trudging. Here, Jane, take thou it. Now let's home, my hearts.

HODGE. Stay! Who comes here? Jane, on again with thy mask!

Enter the EARL *of* LINCOLN, *the* LORD MAYOR *and*
Servants.

LINCOLN. Yonder's the lying varlet mocked us so.

L. MAYOR. Come hither, Sirrah!

FIRK. I, sir? I am sirrah? You mean me, do you not?

LINCOLN. Where is my nephew married?

FIRK. Is he married? God give him joy, I am glad of it. They have a fair day, and the sign is in a good planet, Mars in Venus.

L. MAYOR. Villain, thou toldst me that my daughter
           Rose
This morning should be married at St. Faith's;
We have watched there these three hours at the least,
Yet see we no such thing.

FIRK. Truly, I am sorry for't; a bride's a pretty thing.

HODGE. Come to the purpose. Yonder's the bride and bridegroom you look for, I hope. Though you be lords, you are not to bar by your authority men from women, are you?

L. MAYOR. See, see, my daughter's masked.

LINCOLN.   True, and my nephew,
To hide his guilt, counterfeits him lame.

FIRK. Yea, truly; God help the poor couple, they are lame and blind.

L. MAYOR. I'll ease her blindness.

LINCOLN.   I'll his lameness cure.

FIRK. Lie down, sirs, and laugh! My fellow Ralph is taken for Rowland Lacy, and Jane for Mistress Damask Rose. This is all my knavery.

L. MAYOR. What, have I found you, minion?

LINCOLN.   O base wretch

Nay, hide thy face, the horror of thy guilt

Can hardly be washed off. Where are thy powers?

What battles have you made? O yes, I see,

Thou fought'st with Shame, and Shame hath conquered
    thee.

This lameness will not serve.

L. MAYOR.   Unmask yourself.

LINCOLN. Lead home your daughter.

L. MAYOR.   Take your nephew hence.

RALPH. Hence! Swounds, what mean you? Are you
mad? I hope you cannot enforce my wife from me.
Where's Hammon?

L. MAYOR. Your wife?

LINCOLN. What, Hammon?

RALPH. Yea, my wife; and, therefore, the proudest of
you that lays hands on her first, I'll lay my crutch 'cross
his pate.

FIRK. To him, lame Ralph! Here's brave sport!

RALPH. Rose call you her? Why, her name is Jane.
Look here else; do you know her now?

                              [*Unmasking* JANE.

LINCOLN. Is this your daughter?

L. MAYOR.   No, nor this your nephew.
My Lord of Lincoln, we are both abused
By this base, crafty varlet.

FIRK. Yea, forsooth, no varlet; forsooth, no base; forsooth, I am but mean; no crafty neither, but of the gentle craft.

L. MAYOR. Where is my daughter Rose? Where is my
    child?

LINCOLN. Where is my nephew Lacy married?

FIRK. Why, here is good laced mutton, as I promised
you.

LINCOLN. Villain, I'll have thee punished for this wrong.

FIRK. Punish the journeyman villain, but not the journeyman shoemaker.

Enter DODGER.

DODGER. My lord, I come to bring unwelcome news.
Your nephew Lacy and your daughter Rose
Early this morning wedded at the Savoy,
None being present but the lady mayoress.
Besides, I learnt among the officers,
The lord mayor vows to stand in their defence
'Gainst any that shall seek to cross the match.

LINCOLN. Dares Eyre the shoemaker uphold the deed?

FIRK. Yes, sir, shoemakers dare stand in a woman's quarrel, I warrant you, as deep as another, and deeper too.

DODGER. Besides, his grace today dines with the mayor;
Who on his knees humbly intends to fall
And beg a pardon for your nephew's fault.

LINCOLN. But I'll prevent him! Come, Sir Roger Oateley;
The king will do us justice in this cause.
Howe'er their hands have made them man and wife,
I will disjoin the match, or lose my life.   [*Exeunt.*

FIRK. Adieu, Monsieur Dodger! Farewell, fools! Ha, ha! Oh, if they had stayed, I would have so lammed them with flouts! O heart, my codpiece-point is ready to fly in pieces every time I think upon Mistress Rose; but let that pass, as my lady mayoress says.

HODGE. This matter is answered. Come, Ralph; home with thy wife. Come, my fine shoemakers, let's to our master's, the new lord mayor, and there swagger this Shrove Tuesday. I'll promise you wine enough, for Madge keeps the cellar.

ALL. O rare! Madge is a good wench.

FIRK. And I'll promise you meat enough, for simp'r-ing Susan keeps the larder. I'll lead you to victuals, my brave soldiers; follow your captain. O brave! Hark, hark!

[*Bell rings.*

ALL. The pancake-bell rings, the pancake-bell! Tri-lill, my hearts!

FIRK. Oh brave! Oh sweet bell! O delicate pancakes! Open the doors, my hearts, and shut up the windows! keep in the house, let out the pancakes! Oh rare, my hearts! Let's march together for the honour of St. Hugh to the great new hall in Gracious Street-corner, which our master, the new lord mayor, hath built.

RALPH. O the crew of good fellows that will dine at my lord mayor's cost to-day!

HODGE. By the Lord, my lord mayor is a most brave man. How shall prentices be bound to pray for him and the honour of the gentlemen shoemakers! Let's feed and be fat with my lord's bounty.

FIRK. O musical bell, still! O Hodge, O my brethren! There's cheer for the heavens: venison-pasties walk up and down piping hot, like sergeants; beef and brewess comes marching in dry-vats, fritters and pancakes comes trowling in in wheel-barrows; hens and oranges hopping in porters'-baskets, collops and eggs in scuttles, and tarts and custards comes quavering in in malt-shovels.

Enter more PRENTICES.

ALL. Whoop, look here, look here!

HODGE. How now, mad lads, whither away so fast?

1ST PRENTICE. Whither? Why, to the great new hall, know you not why? The lord mayor hath bidden all the prentices in London to breakfast this morning.

ALL. Oh brave shoemaker, oh brave lord of incompre-hensible good-fellowship! Whoo! Hark you! The pan-cake-bell rings.

[*Cast up caps.*

FIRK. Nay, more, my hearts! Every Shrove Tuesday is our year of jubilee; and when the pancake-bell rings, we are as free as my lord mayor; we may shut up our shops, and make holiday. I'll have it called St. Hugh's Holiday.

ALL. Agreed, agreed! St. Hugh's Holiday.

HODGE. And this shall continue for ever.

ALL. Oh brave! Come, come, my hearts! Away, away!

FIRK. O eternal credit to us of the gentle craft! March fair, my hearts! Oh rare!   [*Exeunt.*

SCENE III.—*A Street in London.*

Enter the KING *and his* Train *across the stage.*

KING. Is our lord mayor of London such a gallant?

NOBLEMAN. One of the merriest madcaps in your land.
Your grace will think, when you behold the man,
He's rather a wild ruffian than a mayor.
Yet thus much I'll ensure your majesty.
In all his actions that concern his state,
He is as serious, provident, and wise,
As full of gravity amongst the grave,
As any mayor hath been these many years.

KING. I am with child, till I behold this huff-cap.
But all my doubt is, when we come in presence,
His madness will be dashed clean out of countenance.

NOBLEMAN. It may be so, my liege.

KING.   Which to prevent,
Let some one give him notice, 'tis our pleasure
That he put on his wonted merriment.
Set forward!

ALL. On afore!   [*Exeunt.*

SCENE IV.—*A Great Hall.*

Enter EYRE, HODGE, FIRK, RALPH, *and other* Shoe-
    makers, *all with napkins on their shoulders.*

EYRE. Come, my fine Hodge, my jolly gentlemen
shoemakers; soft, where be these cannibals, these varlets, my officers? Let them all walk and wait upon my
brethren; for my meaning is, that none but shoemakers,
none but the livery of my company shall in their satin
hoods wait upon the trencher of my sovereign.

FIRK. O my lord, it will be rare!

EYRE. No more, Firk; come, lively! Let your fellow-
prentices want no cheer; let wine be plentiful as beer,
and beer as water. Hang these penny-pinching fathers,
that cram wealth in innocent lamb-skins. Rip, knaves,
avaunt! Look to my guests!

HODGE. My lord, we are at our wits' end for room;
those hundred tables will not feast the fourth part of
them.

EYRE. Then cover me those hundred tables again,
and again, till all my jolly prentices be feasted. Avoid,
Hodge! Run, Ralph! Frisk about, my nimble Firk! Carouse me fathom-healths to the honour of the shoemakers. Do they drink lively, Hodge? Do they tickle
it, Firk?

FIRK. Tickle it? Some of them have taken their liquor
standing so long that they can stand no longer; but for
meat, they would eat it, an they had it.

EYRE. Want they meat? Where's this swag-belly, this
greasy kitchenstuff cook? Call the varlet to me! Want
meat? Firk, Hodge, lame Ralph, run, my tall men, be-
leaguer the shambles, beggar all Eastcheap, serve me
whole oxen in chargers, and let sheep whine upon the

tables like pigs for want of good fellows to eat them. Want meat? Vanish, Firk! Avaunt, Hodge!

HODGE. Your lordship mistakes my man Firk; he means, their bellies want meat, not the boards; for they have drunk so much, they can eat nothing.

THE SECOND THREE-MEN'S SONG.

Cold's the wind, and wet's the rain,
   St. Hugh be our good speed:
Ill is the weather that bringeth no gain,
   Nor helps good hearts in need.

Trowl the bowl, the jolly nut-brown bowl,
   And here, kind mate, to thee:
Let's sing a dirge for St. Hugh's soul,
   And down it merrily.

Down a down heydown a down,
   Hey derry derry, down a down!
    (*Close with the tenor boy*)
Ho, well done; to me let come!
   Ring, compass, gentle joy.

Trowl the bowl, the nut-brown bowl,
   And here, kind mate, to thee: etc.
   [*Repeat as often as there be men to drink;
   and at last when all have drunk, this verse:*

Cold's the wind, and wet's the rain,
   St. Hugh be our good speed:
Ill is the weather that bringeth no gain,
   Nor helps good hearts in need.

   Enter HANS, ROSE, *and* MARGERY.

MARG. Where is my lord?

EYRE. How now, Lady Madgy?

MARG. The king's most excellent majesty is new come; he sends me for thy honour; one of his most worshipful peers bade me tell thou must be merry, and so forth; but let that pass.

EYRE. Is my sovereign come? Vanish, my tall shoe-makers, my nimble brethren; look to my guests, the prentices. Yet stay a little! How now, Hans? How looks my little Rose?

HANS. Let me request you to remember me.
I know, your honour easily may obtain
Free pardon of the king for me and Rose,
And reconcile me to my uncle's grace.

EYRE. Have done, my good Hans, my honest journey-man; look cheerily! I'll fall upon both my knees, till they be as hard as horn, but I'll get thy pardon.

MARG. Good my lord, have a care what you speak to his grace.

EYRE. Away, you Islington whitepot! hence, you hop-perarse! you barley-pudding, full of maggots! you broiled carbonado! avaunt, avaunt, avoid, Mephistophi-les! Shall Sim Eyre learn to speak of you, Lady Madgy? Vanish, Mother Miniver-cap; vanish, go, trip and go; meddle with your partlets and your pishery-pashery, your flewes and your whirligigs; go, rub, out of mine alley! Sim Eyre knows how to speak to a Pope, to Sultan Soliman, to Tamburlaine, an he were here; and shall I melt, shall I droop before my sovereign? No, come, my Lady Madgy! Follow me, Hans! About your business, my frolic free-booters! Firk, frisk about, and about, and about, for the honour of mad Simon Eyre, lord mayor of London.

FIRK. Hey, for the honour of the shoemakers.

[*Exeunt.*

SCENE V.—*An Open Yard before the Hall.*

A long flourish, or two. Enter the KING, NOBLES, EYRE,
MARGERY, LACY, ROSE. LACY *and* ROSE *kneel.*

KING. Well, Lacy, though the fact was very foul
Of your revolting from our kingly love
And your own duty, yet we pardon you.
Rise both, and, Mistress Lacy, thank my lord mayor
For your young bridegroom here.

EYRE. So, my dear liege, Sim Eyre and my brethren,
the gentlemen shoemakers, shall set your sweet majesty's
image cheek by jowl by St. Hugh for this honour you
have done poor Simon Eyre. I beseech your grace, pardon my rude behaviour; I am a handicraftsman, yet my
heart is without craft; I would be sorry at my soul, that
my boldness should offend my king.

KING. Nay, I pray thee, good lord mayor, be even as
    merry
As if thou wert among thy shoemakers;
It does me good to see thee in this humour.

EYRE. Say'st thou me so, my sweet Diocletian? Then,
humph! Prince am I none, yet am I princely born. By
the Lord of Ludgate, my liege, I'll be as merry as a pie.

KING. Tell me, in faith, mad Eyre, how old thou art.

EYRE. My liege, a very boy, a stripling, a younker;
you see not a white hair on my head, not a gray in this
beard. Every hair, I assure thy majesty, that sticks in
this beard, Sim Eyre values at the King of Babylon's
ransom, Tamar Cham's beard was a rubbing brush to't:
yet I'll shave it off, and stuff tennis-balls with it, to
please my bully king.

KING. But all this while I do not know your age.

EYRE. My liege, I am six and fifty years old, yet I can
cry humph! with a sound heart for the honour of St.

Hugh. Mark this old wench, my king: I danced the shaking of the sheets with her six and thirty years ago, and yet I hope to get two or three young lord mayors, ere I die. I am lusty still, Sim Eyre still. Care and cold lodging brings white hairs. My sweet Majesty, let care vanish, cast it upon thy nobles, it will make thee look always young like Apollo, and cry humph! Prince am I none, yet am I princely born.

KING. Ha, ha!
Say, Cornwall, didst thou ever see his like?

CORNWALL. Not I, my lord.

Enter the EARL OF LINCOLN *and the* LORD MAYOR.

KING.   Lincoln, what news with you?

LINCOLN. My gracious lord, have care unto yourself,
For there are traitors here.

ALL. Traitors? Where? Who?

EYRE. Traitors in my house? God forbid! Where be my officers? I'll spend my soul, ere my king feel harm.

KING. Where is the traitor, Lincoln?

LINCOLN.   Here he stands.

KING. Cornwall, lay hold on Lacy!—Lincoln, speak,
What canst thou lay unto thy nephew's charge?

LINCOLN. This, my dear liege: your Grace, to do me
    honour,
Heaped on the head of this degenerate boy
Desertless favours; you made choice of him,
To be commander over powers in France.
But he—

KING. Good Lincoln, prithee, pause a while!
Even in thine eyes I read what thou wouldst speak.
I know how Lacy did neglect our love,
Ran himself deeply, in the highest degree,
Into vile treason—

LINCOLN.   Is he not a traitor?

KING. Lincoln, he was; now have we pardoned him.

'Twas not a base want of true valour's fire,
That held him out of France, but love's desire.

LINCOLN. I will not bear his shame upon my back.

KING. Nor shalt thou, Lincoln; I forgive you both.

LINCOLN. Then, good my liege, forbid the boy to wed
One whose mean birth will much disgrace his bed.

KING. Are they not married?

LINCOLN.   No, my liege.

BOTH.   We are.

KING. Shall I divorce them then? O be it far,
That any hand on earth should dare untie
The sacred knot, knit by God's majesty;
I would not for my crown disjoin their hands,
That are conjoined in holy nuptial bands.
How say'st thou, Lacy, wouldst thou lose thy Rose?

LACY. Not for all India's wealth, my sovereign.

KING. But Rose, I am sure, her Lacy would forego?

ROSE. If Rose were asked that question, she'd say no.

KING. You hear them, Lincoln?

LINCOLN.   Yea, my liege, I do.

KING. Yet canst thou find i'th' heart to part these two?
Who seeks, besides you, to divorce these lovers?

L. MAYOR. I do, my gracious lord, I am her father.

KING. Sir Roger Oateley, our last mayor, I think?

NOBLEMAN. The same, my liege.

KING.   Would you offend Love's laws?
Well, you shall have you wills, you sue to me,
To prohibit the match. Soft, let me see—
You both are married, Lacy, art thou not?

LACY. I am, dread sovereign.

KING.   Then, upon thy life,
I charge thee, not to call this woman wife.

L. MAYOR. I thank your grace.

ROSE.   O my most gracious lord!
                                            [Kneels.

KING. Nay, Rose, never woo me; I tell you true,
Although as yet I am a bachelor,
Yet I believe, I shall not marry you.

ROSE. Can you divide the body from the soul,
Yet make the body live?

KING. Yea, so profound?
I cannot, Rose, but you I must divide.
This fair maid, bridegroom, cannot be your bride.
Are you pleased, Lincoln? Oateley, are you pleased?

BOTH. Yes, my lord.

KING. Then must my heart be eased;
For, credit me, my conscience lives in pain,
Till these whom I divorced, be joined again.
Lacy, give me thy hand; Rose, lend me thine!
Be what you would be! Kiss now! So, that's fine.
At night, lovers, to bed!—Now, let me see,
Which of you all mislikes this harmony.

L. MAYOR. Will you then take from me my child perforce?

KING. Why, tell me, Oateley: shines not Lacy's name
As bright in the world's eye as the gay beams
Of any citizen?

LINCOLN. Yea, but, my gracious lord,
I do dislike the match far more than he;
Her blood is too, too base.

KING. Lincoln, no more.
Dost thou not know that love respects no blood,
Cares not for difference of birth or state?
The maid is young, well born, fair, virtuous,
A worthy bride for any gentleman.
Besides, your nephew for her sake did stoop
To bare necessity, and, as I hear,
Forgetting honours and all courtly pleasures,
To gain her love, became a shoemaker.
As for the honour which he lost in France,

Thus I redeem it: Lacy, kneel thee down!—
Arise, Sir Rowland Lacy! Tell me now,
Tell me in earnest, Oateley, canst thou chide,
Seeing thy Rose a lady and a bride?

 L. MAYOR. I am content with what your grace hath
  done.

 LINCOLN. And I, my liege, since there's no remedy.

 KING. Come on, then, all shake hands: I'll have you
  friends;

Where there is much love, all discord ends.
What says my mad lord mayor to all this love?

 EYRE. O my liege, this honour you have done to my
fine journeyman here, Rowland Lacy, and all these
favours which you have shown to me this day in my
poor house, will make Simon Eyre live longer by one
dozen of warm summers more than he should.

 KING. Nay, my mad lord mayor, that shall be thy
  name,

If any grace of mine can length thy life,
One honour more I'll do thee: that new building,
Which at thy cost in Cornhill is erected,
Shall take a name from us; we'll have it called
The Leadenhall, because in digging it
You found the lead that covereth the same.

 EYRE. I thank your majesty.

 MARG. God bless your grace!

 KING. Lincoln, a word with you!

 Enter HODGE, FIRK, RALPH, *and more* Shoemakers.

 EYRE. How now, my mad knaves? Peace, speak softly,
yonder is the king.

 KING. With the old troop which there we keep in pay,
We will incorporate a new supply.
Before one summer more pass o'er my head,
France shall repent, England was injured.
What are all those?

LACY.　　　　　　　All shoemakers, my liege,
Sometime my fellows; in their companies
I lived as merry as an emperor.

KING. My mad lord mayor, are all these shoemakers?

EYRE. All shoemakers, my liege; all gentlemen of the gentle craft, true Trojans, courageous cordwainers; they all kneel to the shrine of holy St. Hugh.

ALL THE SHOEMAKERS. God save your Majesty!

KING. Mad Simon, would they anything with us?

EYRE. Mum, mad knaves! Not a word! I'll do't; I warrant you. They are all beggars, my liege; all for themselves, and I for them all on both my knees do entreat, that for the honour of poor Simon Eyre and the good of his brethren, these mad knaves, your grace would vouchsafe some privilege to my new Leadenhall, that it may be lawful for us to buy and sell leather there two days a week.

KING. Mad Sim, I grant your suit, you shall have
　　　patent
To hold two market-days in Leadenhall,
Mondays and Fridays, those shall be the times.
Will this content you?

ALL. Jesus bless your grace!

EYRE. In the name of these my poor brethren shoemakers, I most humbly thank your grace. But before I rise, seeing you are in the giving vein and we in the begging, grant Sim Eyre one boon more.

KING. What is it, my lord mayor?

EYRE. Vouchsafe to taste of a poor banquet that stands sweetly waiting for your sweet presence.

KING. I shall undo thee, Eyre, only with feasts;
Already have I been too troublesome;
Say, have I not?

EYRE. O my dear king, Sim Eyre was taken unawares

upon a day of shroving, which I promised long ago to
the prentices of London.

    For, an't please your highness, in time past,
    I bare the water-tankard, and my coat
    Sits not a whit the worse upon my back;
    And then, upon a morning, some mad boys,
    It was Shrove Tuesday, even as 'tis now,
Gave me my breakfast, and I swore then by the stopple
of my tankard, if ever I came to be lord mayor of London, I would feast all the prentices. This day, my liege,
I did it, and the slaves had an hundred tables five times
covered; they are gone home and vanished;

    Yet add more honour to the gentle trade,
    Taste of Eyre's banquet, Simon's happy made.

    KING. Eyre, I will taste of thy banquet, and will say,
I have not met more pleasure on a day.
Friends of the gentle craft, thanks to you all,
Thanks, my kind lady mayoress, for our cheer.—
Come, lords, a while let's revel it at home!
When all our sports and banquetings are done,
Wars must right wrongs which Frenchmen have begun.

                            [*Exeunt.*

Broadside Ballads

A SONG BETWEEN THE QUEEN'S MAJESTY AND ENGLAND

E[ngland]. Come over the bourn, Bessy,
    Come over the bourn, Bessy,
Sweet Bessy, come over to me;
    And I shall thee take
    And my dear lady make,
Before all other that ever I see.

B[essy]. Methink I hear a voice
    At whom I do rejoice,
And answer thee now I shall:
    Tell me, I say,
    What art thou that bids me come away,
And so earnestly dost me call?

E.   I am thy lover fair,
    Hath chose thee to mine heir,
And my name is merry England;
    Therefore come away,
    And make no more delay,
Sweet Bessy, give me thy hand!

B.   Here is my hand,
    My dear lover, England;

I am thine both with mind and heart,
    Forever to endure,
    Thou mayest be sure,
Until death us two depart.

E. Lady, this long space
    Have I loved thy grace,
More than I durst well say;
    Hoping at the last,
    When all storms were past,
For to see this joyful day.

B. Yet, my lover England,
    Ye shall understand
How fortune on me did lour;
    I was tumbled and tossed
    From pillar to post,
And prisoner in the Tower.

E. Dear Lady, we do know
    How tyrants, not a few,
Went about for to seek thy blood;
    And contrary to right
    They did what they might,
That now bear two faces in one hood.

B. Then was I carried to Woodstock,
    And kept close under lock,
That no man might with me speak;
    And against all reason
    They accused me of treason,
And terribly they did me threat.

E. Oh, my lover fair!
    My darling and mine heir!

Full sore for thee I did lament;
　　But no man durst speak,
　　But they would him threat
And quickly make him repent.

B.　Then was I delivered their hands,
　　But was fain to put in bands
And good sureties for my forthcoming;
　　Not from my house to depart,
　　Nor nowhere else to start,
As though I had been away running.

E.　Why, dear Lady, I trow,
　　Those madmen did not know
That ye were daughter unto King Harry,
　　And a princess of birth,
　　One of the noblest on earth,
And sister unto Queen Mary.

B.　Yes, yet I must forgive
　　All such as do live,
If they will hereafter amend;
　　And for those that are gone,
　　God forgive them every one,
And his mercy on them extend.

E.　Yet, my lover dear,
　　Tell me now here,
For what cause had ye this punishment?
　　For the commons did not know,
　　Nor no man would them show,
The chief cause of your imprisonment.

B.　No, nor they themself,
　　That would have decayed my wealth,

But only by power and abusion,
> They could not detect me,
> But that they did suspect me,
That I was not of their religion.

E. Oh, cruel tyrants,
> And also monstrous giants,
That would such a sweet blossom devour!
> But the Lord, of his might,
> Defended thee in right,
And shortened their arm and power.

B. Yet, my lover dear,
> Mark me well here,
Though they were men of the devil,
> The Scripture plainly saith,
> All they that be of faith
Must needs do good against evil.

E. O sweet virgin pure!
> Long may ye endure
To reign over us in this land;
> For your works do accord,
> Ye are the handmaid of the Lord,
For he hath blessed you with his hand.

B. My sweet realm, be obedient
> To God's holy commandment,
And my proceedings embrace;
> And for that that is abused,
> Shall be better used,
And that within short space.

E. Dear Lady and Queen,
> I trust it shall be seen

Ye shall reign quietly without strife;
    And if any traitors there be,
    Of any kind or degree,
I pray God send them short life.

B.   I trust all faithful hearts
    Will play true subjects' parts,
Knowing me their Queen and true heir by right;
    And that much the rather
    For the love of my father,
That worthy prince, King Henry th' Eight.

E.   Therefore let us pray
    To God both night and day,
Continually and never to cease,
    That he will preserve your grace
    To reign over us long space
In tranquility, wealth, and peace.

Both. All honor, laud, and praise
    Be to the Lord God always,
Who hath all princes' hearts in his hands;
    That by his power and might,
    He may guide them right,
For the wealth of all Christian lands.

                  WILLIAM BIRCHE

A NEW COURTLY SONNET,
OF THE LADY GREENSLEEVES

(To the new tune of "Greensleeves")

Greensleeves was all my joy,
    Greensleeves was my delight;

Greensleeves was my heart of gold,
    And who but Lady Greensleeves?

Alas, my love, ye do me wrong
    To cast me off discourteously;
And I have lovëd you so long,
    Delighting in your company.

Greensleeves was all my joy,
    Greensleeves was my delight;
Greensleeves was my heart of gold,
    And who but Lady Greensleeves?

I have been ready at your hand
    To grant whatever you would crave;
I have both wagëd life and land,
    Your love and good will for to have.

Greensleeves was all my joy, &c.

I bought thee kerchiefs to thy head,
    That were wrought fine and gallantly;
I kept thee both at board and bed,
    Which cost my purse well favouredly.

Greensleeves was all my joy, &c.

I bought thee petticoats of the best,
    The cloth so fine as fine might be;
I gave thee jewels for thy chest,
    And all this cost I spent on thee.

Greensleeves was all my joy, &c.

Thy smock of silk both fair and white,
    With gold embroidered gorgeously;
Thy petticoat of sendal right,
    And thus I bought thee gladly.

Greensleeves was all my joy, &c.

Thy girdle of gold so red,
    With pearls bedeckèd sumptuously,
The like no other lasses had,
    And yet thou wouldst not love me.

Greensleeves was all my joy, &c.

Thy purse and eke thy gay gilt knives,
    Thy pin-case, gallant to the eye,
No better wore the burgess' wives,
    And yet thou wouldst not love me.

Greensleeves was all my joy, &c.

Thy crimson stockings all of silk,
    With gold all wrought above the knee,
Thy pumps as white as was the milk,
    And yet thou wouldst not love me.

Greensleeves was all my joy, &c.

Thy gown was of the grossy green,
    Thy sleeves of satin hanging by,
Which made thee be our harvest queen,
    And yet thou wouldst not love me.

Greensleeves was all my joy, &c.

Thy garters fringëd with the gold,
    And silver aglets hanging by,
Which made thee blithe for to behold,
    And yet thou wouldst not love me.

Greensleeves was all my joy, &c.

My gayest gelding I thee gave,
    To ride wherever liked thee;
No lady ever was so brave,
    And yet thou wouldst not love me.

Greensleeves was all my joy, &c.

My men were clothëd all in green,
    And they did ever wait on thee;
All this was gallant to be seen,
    And yet thou wouldst not love me.

Greensleeves was all my joy, &c.

They set thee up, they took thee down,
    They served thee with humility;
Thy foot might not once touch the ground,
    And yet thou wouldst not love me.

Greensleeves was all my joy, &c.

For every morning when thou rose
    I sent thee dainties orderly,
To cheer thy stomach from all woes,
    And yet thou wouldst not love me.

Greensleeves was all my joy, &c.

Thou couldst desire no earthly thing,
 But still thou hadst it readily;
Thy music still to play and sing,
 And yet thou wouldst not love me.

Greensleeves was all my joy, &c.

And who did pay for all this gear
 That thou didst spend when pleased thee?
Even I that am rejected here,
 And thou disdain'st to love me.

Greensleeves was all my joy, &c.

Well, I will pray to God on high
 That thou my constancy mayest see;
And that yet once before I die
 Thou wilt vouchsafe to love me.

Greensleeves was all my joy, &c.

Greensleeves, now farewell, adieu,
 God I pray to prosper thee;
For I am still thy lover true,
 Come once again and love me.

Greensleeves was all my joy, &c.

A PROPER NEW SONG MADE BY A
STUDENT IN CAMBRIDGE

(*To the tune of* "I wish to see those happy days")

I which was once a happy wight
  and high in fortune's grace,
And which did spend my golden prime
  in running pleasure's race,
    Am now enforced of late
      contrariwise to mourn,
    Since fortune joys into annoys
      my former state to turn.

The toiling ox, the horse, the ass
  have time to take their rest;
Yea, all things else which nature wrought
  sometimes have joys in breast,
    Save only I, and such
      which vexèd are with pain;
    For still in tears my life it wears,
      and so I must remain.

How oft have I in folded arms
  enjoyèd my delight!
How oft have I excuses made,
  of her to have a sight!
    But now to fortune's will
      I causèd am to bow,
    And for to reap a hugy heap
      which youthful years did sow.

Wherefore all ye which do as yet
  remain and bide behind,

Whose eyes Dame Beauty's blazing beams
    as yet did never blind,
        Example let me be
            to you and other more
        Whose heavy heart hath felt the smart,
            subdued by Cupid's lore.

Take heed of gazing over-much
    on damsels fair unknown,
For oftentimes the snake doth lie
    with roses overgrown;
        And under fairest flowers
            do noisome adders lurk,
        Of whom take heed, I thee areed,
            lest that thy cares they work.

What though that she doth smile on thee?
    perchance she doth not love;
And though she smack thee once or twice,
    she thinks thee so to prove;
        And when that thou dost think
            she loveth none but thee,
        She hath in store perhaps some more
            which so deceivëd be.

Trust not therefore the outward show,
    beware in any case:
For good conditions do not lie
    where is a pleasant face.
        But if it be thy chance
            a lover true to have,
        Be sure of this, thou shalt not miss
            each thing that thou wilt crave.

And whenas thou, good reader, shalt
    peruse this scroll of mine,

Let this a warning be to thee,
  and say a friend of thine
    Did write thee this of love
      and of a Zealous mind,
    Because that he sufficiently
      hath tried the female kind.

Here, Cambridge, now I bid farewell!
  adieu to students all!
Adieu unto the Colleges
  and unto Gonville Hall!
    And you, my fellows once,
      pray unto Jove that I
    May have relief for this my grief,
      and speedy remedy.

And that he shield you everyone
  from beauty's luring looks,
Whose bait hath brought me to my bane
  and caught me from my books.
    Wherefore, for you my prayer shall be
      to send you better grace,
    That modesty with honesty
      may guide your youthful race.
               THOMAS RICHARDSON

AS YOU CAME FROM THE HOLY
LAND OF WALSINGHAM

As you came from the holy land
  Of Walsingham
Met you not with my true love,
  By the way as you came?
How should I know your true love,

That have met many a one,
As I came from the holy land,
    That have come, that have gone?

She is neither white nor brown,
    But as the heavens fair;
There is none hath her form so divine,
    On the earth, in the air.
Such a one did I meet, good sir,
    With angel-like face,
Who like a nymph, like a queen did appear
    In her gait, in her grace.

She hath left me here alone,
    All alone unknown,
Who sometime loved me as her life,
    And callëd me her own.
What is the cause she hath left thee alone,
    And a new way doth take,
That sometime did thee love as herself,
    And her joy did thee make?

I have loved her all my youth,
    But now am old as you see;
Love liketh not the falling fruit,
    Nor the withered tree.
For love is a careless child,
    And forgets promise past;
He is blind, he is deaf, when he list,
    And in faith never fast.

His desire is fickle found,
    And a trustless joy;
He is won with a world of despair,
    And is lost with a toy.

Such is the love of women-kind,
   Or the word, love, abused,
Under which many childish desires
   And conceits are excused.

But love, it is a durable fire
   In the mind ever burning,
Never sick, never dead, never cold,
   From itself never turning.

THOMAS DELONEY (?)

MARY AMBREE

(*The tune is* "The blind beggar")

When Captain Courageous, whom death could not
   daunt,
Had roundly besiegëd the city of Gaunt,
And manly they marched by two and by three,
And foremost in battle was Mary Ambree.

Thus being enforced to fight with her foes,
On each side most fiercely they seemed to close;
Each one sought for honor in every degree,
But none so much won it as Mary Ambree.

When brave Sergeant Major was slain in the fight,
Who was her own true love, her joy and delight,
She swore unrevenged his blood should not be;
Was not this a brave bonny lass, Mary Ambree?

She clothed herself from the top to the toe
With buff of the bravest and seemly to show;
A fair shirt of mail over that striped she;
Was not this a brave bonny lass, Mary Ambree?

A helmet of proof she put on her head,
A strong armed sword she girt on her side,
A fairly goodly gauntlet on her hand wore she;
Was not this a brave bonny lass, Mary Ambree?

Then took she her sword and her target in hand,
And called all those that would be of her band—
To wait on her person there came thousands three;
Was not this a brave bonny lass, Mary Ambree?

Before you shall perish, the worst of you all,
Or come to any danger of enemy's thrall,
This hand and this life of mine shall set you free;
Was not this a brave bonny lass, Mary Ambree?

The drums and the trumpets did sound out alarm,
And many a hundred did lose leg and arm,
And many a thousand she brought on their knee;
Was not this a brave bonny lass, Mary Ambree?

The sky then she filled with smoke of her shot,
And her enemies' bodies with bullets so hot,
For one of her own men, a score killed she;
Was not this a brave bonny lass, Mary Ambree?

And then her false gunner did spoil her intent,
Her powder and bullets away he had spent,
And then with her weapon she slashed them in three;
Was not this a brave bonny lass, Mary Ambree?

Then took she her castle where she did abide,
Her enemies besieged her on every side;
To beat down her castle walls they did agree,
And all for to overcome Mary Ambree.

Then took she her sword and her target in hand,
And on her castle walls stoutly did stand,
So daring the captains to match any three;
Oh, what a brave captain was Mary Ambree!

At her then they smiled, not thinking in heart
That she could have performed so valorous a part;
The one said to the other, we shortly shall see
This gallant brave captain before us to flee.

Why, what do you think or take me to be?
Unto these brave soldiers so valiant spoke she.
A knight, sir, of England, and captain, quoth they,
Whom shortly we mean to take prisoner away.

No captain of England behold in your sight,
Two breasts in my bosom, and therefore no knight;
No knight, sir, of England, nor captain, quoth she,
But even a poor bonny lass, Mary Ambree.

But art thou a woman as thou dost declare,
That hath made us thus spend our armor in war?
The like in our lives we never did see,
And therefore we'll honor brave Mary Ambree.

The Prince of great Parma heard of her renown,
Who long had advanced for England's fair crown;
In token he sent a glove and a ring,
And said she should be his bride at his wedding.

Why, what do you think or take me to be?
Though he be a prince of great dignity,
It shall never be said in England so free
That a stranger did marry with Mary Ambree.

Then unto fair England she back did return,
Still holding the foes of brave England in scorn;
In valor no man was ever like she;
Was not this a brave bonny lass, Mary Ambree?

In this woman's praises I'll here end my song,
Whose heart was approved in valor most strong;
Let all sorts of people, whatever they be,
Sing forth the brave valors of Mary Ambree.

WILLIAM ELDERTON (?)

Thomas Nashe

I CAUGHT THE BIRD

TO CUT off blind ambages by the highway side, we made a long stride and got to Venice in short time, where having scarce looked about us, a precious supernatural pander apparelled in all points like a gentleman, and having half a dozen several languages in his purse, entertained us in our own tongue very paraphrastically and eloquently, and maugre all other pretended acquaintance, would have us in a violent kind of courtesy to be guests of his appointment. His name was Petro de Campo Frego, a notable practitioner in the policy of bawdry. The place whither he brought us was a pernicious courtesan's house named Tabitha the Temptress's, a wench that could set as civil a face on it as chastity's first martyr Lucretia.

What will you conceit to be in any saint's house that was there to seek? Books, pictures, beads, crucifixes—why there was a haberdasher's shop of them in every chamber. I warrant you should not see one set of her neckerchief perverted or turned awry, not a piece of a hair displaced. On her beds there was not a wrinkle of any wallowing to be found, her pillows bare out as smooth as a groaning wife's belly, and yet she was a Turk and an infidel, and had more doings than all her neighbours besides. Us for our money they used like Emperors. I was master as you heard before, and my master the Earl was but as my chief man whom I made my companion. So it happened (as iniquity will out at one time or other) that she perceiving my expense had no more vents, than it should have, fell in with my supposed servant, my man, and gave him half a promise of marriage if he would help to make me away, that she and he might enjoy the jewels and wealth that I had.

The indifficulty of the condition thus she explained unto him, her house stood upon vaults, which in two hundred years together were never searched; who came into her house none took notice of. His fellow servants that knew of his master's abode there, should be all dispatched by him as from his master, into sundry parts of the city about business, and when they returned, answer should be made that he lay not there anymore, but had moved to Padua since their departure, and thither they must follow him.

"Now," quoth she, "if you be disposed to make him away in their absence, you shall have my house at command. Stab, poison or shoot him through with a pistol. All is one; into the vault he shall be thrown when the deed is done."

On my bare honesty, it was a crafty queen, for she had enacted with herself if he had been my legitimate servant, as he was one that served and supplied my necessities, when he had murdered me, to have accused him of the murder, and made all that I had hers (as I carried all my master's wealth—money, jewels, rings, or bills of exchange, continually about me). He very subtly consented to her stratagem at the first motion, kill me he would, that heavens could not withstand, and a pistol was the predestinate engine which must deliver the parting blow. God wot I was a raw young squire, and my master dealt Judasly with me, for he told me but everything that she and he agreed of. Wherefore I could not possibly prevent it, but as a man would say, avoid it. The execution day aspired to his utmost devolution; into my chamber came my honorable attendant with his pistol charged by his side, very suspiciously and sullenly. Lady Tabitha and Petro de Campo Frego, her pander, followed him at the hard heels.

At their entrance I saluted them very familiarly and merrily, and began to impart unto them what disquiet dreams had disturbed me the last night.

"I dreamed," quoth I, "that my man Brunquell here (for no better name got he of me) came into my chamber with a pistol charged under his arm to kill me, and that he was suborned by you, Mistress Tabitha, and my very good friend Petro de Campo Frego. God send it turn to good, for it hath affrighted me above measure."

As they were ready to enter into a colourable commonplace of the deceitful frivolousness of dreams, my trusty servant Brunquell stood quivering and quaking every joint of him, and as it was before compacted between us, let his pistol drop from him on the sudden, wherewith I started out of my bed, and drew my rapier, and cried, "Murder, murder!"—which made good wife Tabitha ready to bepiss her.

My servant or my master, which you will, I took roughly by the collar, and threatened to run him through incontinent if he confessed not the truth. He, as it were stricken with remorse of conscience (God be with him, for he could counterfeit most daintily), down on his knees, asked me forgiveness, and impeached Tabitha and Petro de Campo Frego as guilty of subornation. I very mildly and gravely, gave him audience. Rail on them I did not after his tale was ended, but said I would try what the law could do. Conspiracy by the custom of their country was a capital offense, and what custom or justice might afford, they should be all sure to feel. I could, quoth I, acquit myself otherwise, but it is not for a stranger to be his own carver in revenge.

Not a word more with Tabitha, but die she would before God or the Devil would have her. She swooned and revived, and then swooned again, and after she revived again, sighed heavily, spoke faintly and pitifully, yea, and so pitifully, as if a man had not known the pranks of harlots before, he would have melted into commiseration.

Tears, sighs, and doleful tuned words could not make any forcible claim to my stony ears. It was the glittering crowns that I hungered and thirsted after, and with them for all her mock holy day gestures she was fain to come off, before I condescended to any bargain of silence. So it fortuned (fie upon that unfortunate word of Fortune) that this whore, this queen, this courtesan, this common of ten thousand, so bribing me not to betray her, had given me a great deal of counterfeit gold, which she had received of a coiner to make away a little before. Amongst the gross sum of my bribery, I, silly milksop, mistrusting no deceit, under an angel of light took what she gave me, never turned it over, for which (O falsehood in fair shew) my master and I had like to have been turned over.

He that is a knight errant, exercised in the affairs of Ladies and Gentlewomen, hath more places to send money to than the Devil hath to send his spirits to. There was a delicate wench named Flavia Aemilia lodging in St. Mark's Street at a goldsmith's, which I would fain have had to the grand test, to try whether she were cunning in alchemy or no. Aye me, she was but a counterfeit slip, for she not only gave me the slip, but had well nigh made me a slip string.

To her I sent my gold to beg an hour of grace, ah graceless fornicatress, my hostess and she were confederate, who having gotten but one piece of my ill gold in their hands, devised the means to make me immortal. I could drink for anger till my head ached, to think how I was abused.

Shall I shame the Devil and speak the truth? To prison was I sent as principal, and my master as accessary, nor was it to a prison neither, but to the master of the mint's house, who though partly our judge, and a most severe upright justice in his own nature, extremely seemed to condole our ignorant estate, and without all peradventure a present redress he had ministered, if certain of our countrymen, hearing an English Earl was apprehended for coining, had not come to visit us.

An ill planet brought them thither, for at the first glance they knew the servant of my secrecies to be the Earl of Surrey, and I (not worthy to be named I) an outcast of his cup or pantouffles. Thence, thence sprung the full period of our infelicity.

The master of the mint, our whilom refresher and consolation, now took part against us. He thought we had a mint in our heads of mischievous conspiracies against their state. Heavens bear witness with us it was not so (heavens will not always come to witness when they are called). To a straiter ward were we committed: that which we have imputatively transgressed must be answered. O heathen high pass, and the intrinsical legerdemain of our special approved good pander Petro de Campo Frego. He, although he dipped in the same dish with us every day, seeming to labour our cause very importunately, and had interpreted for us to the State from the beginning, yet was one of those treacherous Brother Trulies, and abused us most clerkly. He interpreted to us with a pestilence, for whereas we stood obstinately upon it, we were wrongfully detained, and that it was naught but a malicious practise of sinful Tabitha our late hostess, he by a fine coney-catching corrupt translation, made us plainly to confess and cry Miserere, ere we had need of our neck-verse.

Detestable, detestable, that the flesh and the Devil should deal by their factors. I'll stand to it there is not a pander but hath bowed paganism. The Devil himself is not such a devil as he, so be he perform his function aright. He must have the back of an ass, the snout of an elephant, the wit of a fox, and the teeth of a wolf. He must faun like a spaniel, crouch like a Jew, lie like a sheepbiter. If he be half a Puritan, and have scripture continually in his mouth, he speeds the better. I can tell you it is a trade of great promotion, and let none ever think to mount by service in foreign courts, or creep near to some magnificent Lords, if they be not seen in this science. O it is the art of arts, and ten thousand times goes beyond the intelligencer. None but a staid grave civil man is capable of it. He must have exquisite courtship in him or else he is not old: he wants the best point in his tables.

God be merciful to our pander (and that were for God to work a miracle); he was seen in all the seven liberal deadly sciences, not a sin but he was as absolute in as Satan himself. Satan could never have supplanted us so as he did. I may say to you, he planted in us the first Italianate wit that we had.

During the time we lay close and took physic in this

castle of contemplation, there was a Magnifico's wife of good calling sent to bear us company. Her husband's name was Castaldo; she hight Diamante. The cause of her committing, was an ungrounded jealous suspicion which her doting husband had conceived of her chastity. One Isaac Medicus, a burgomaster was the man he chose to make him a monster—who, being a courtier, and repairing to his house very often, neither for love of him nor his wife, but only with a drift to borrow money of a pawn of wax and parchment, when he saw his expectation deluded, and that Castaldo was too chary for him to close with, he privily with purpose of revenge gave out amongst his copesmates, that he resorted to Castaldo's house for no other end but to cuckold him, and doubtfully he talked that he had and he had not obtained his suit. Rings which he borrowed of a light courtesan that he used, he would feign to be taken from her fingers, and in sum, so handled the matter, that Castaldo exclaimed, "Out, whore, strumpet, sixpenny hackster. Away with her to prison!"

As glad were we almost as if they had given us liberty, that fortune lent us such a sweet pew-fellow. A pretty round faced wench was it, with black eyebrows, a high forehead, a little mouth, and a sharp nose, as fat and plump every part of her as a plover, a skin as slick and soft as the back of a swan; it doth me good when I remember her. Like a bird she tripped on the ground, and bore out her belly as majestical as an Ostrich. With a lecherous rolling eye fixed piercing on the earth, and sometimes scornfully darted on the tone side, she figured forth a high discontented disdain, much like a prince puffing and storming at the treason of some mighty subject fled lately out of his power. Her very countenance repiningly wrathful, and yet clear and unwrinkled, would have confirmed the clearness of her conscience to the austerest judge in the world. If in anything she were culpable, it was in being too melancholy chaste, and shewing herself as covetous of her beauty as her husband was of his bags.

Many are honest, because they know not how to be dishonest: she thought there was no pleasure in stolen bread, because there was no pleasure in an old man's bed. It is almost impossible that any woman should be excellently witty and not make the utmost penny of her beauty. This age and this country of ours admits of some miraculous exceptions, but former times are my constant informers. Those that have quick motions of wit have quick motions in everything; iron only needs many strokes; only iron wits are not won without a long siege of entreaty. Gold easily bends; the most ingenious minds are easiest moved: *ingenium nobis molle thalia dedit*, saith Sappho to Phao. Who hath no merciful mild mistress, I will maintain, hath no witty, but a clownish, dull, phlegmatic puppy to his mistress.

This Magnifico's wife was a good loving soul, that had metal enough in her to make a good wit of, but being never removed from under her mother and her husband's wing, it was not molded and fashioned as it ought. Causeless distrust is able to drive deceit into a simple woman's head. I durst pawn the credit of a page, which is worth an ace at all times, that she was immaculate honest till she met with us in prison.

Marry, what temptations she had then, when fire and flax were put together, conceit with yourselves, but hold my master excusable. Alack, he was too virtuous to make her vicious; he stood upon religion and conscience: what a heinous thing it was to subvert God's ordinance! This was all the injury he would offer her: sometimes, in a melancholy humour, he would imagine her to be his Geraldine, and court her in terms correspondent. Nay, he would swear she was his Geraldine, and take her white hand and wipe his eyes with it, as though the very touch of her might staunch his anguish. Now would he kneel and kiss the ground as holy ground which she vouch-safed to bless from barrenness by her steps.

Who would have learned to write an excellent passion, might have been a perfect tragic poet, had he but attended half the extremity of his lament. Passion upon passion would throng one on another's neck; he would praise her beyond the moon and the stars, and that so sweetly and ravishingly, as I persuade myself he was more in love with his own curious forming fancy than her face. And truth it is, many become passionate lovers, only to win praise to their wits.

He praised, he prayed, he desired and besought her to pity him that perished for her. From this, his entranced mistaking ecstasy, could no man remove him. Who loveth resolutely, will include every thing under the name of his love. From prose he would leap into verse, and with these or such like times assault her:

If I must die, O let me choose my death,
Suck out my soul with kisses, cruel maid,
In thy breasts' crystal balls embalm my breath,
Dole it all out in sighs when I am laid.
Thy lips on mine like cupping glasses clasp,
Let our tongues meet and strive as they would sting,
Crush out my wind with one strait girting grasp;
Stabs on my heart keep time while thou dost sing.
Thy eyes like searing irons burn out mine.
In thy fair tresses stifle me outright,
Like Circe change me to a loathsome swine,
So I may live forever in thy sight.
   Into heaven's joys none can profoundly see,
    Except that first they meditate on thee.

Sadly and verily, if my master said true, I should, if I were a wench, make many men quickly immortal. What is it, what is it for a maid fair and fresh to spend a little lip-salve on a hungry lover? My master beat the bush and kept a coil and a prattling, but I caught the bird—simplicity and plainness shall carry it away in another world.

God wot he was Petro Desperato, when I, stepping to her with a dunstable tale, made up my market. A holy requiem to their souls that think to woo a woman with riddles. I had some cunning plot you must suppose, to bring this about. Her husband had abused her, and it was very necessary she should be revenged: seldom do they prove patient martyrs who are punished unjustly. One way or other they will cry quittance whatsoever it cost them. No other apt means had this poor captive, to work her hoddie peak husband a proportionable plague for his jealousy, but to give his head his full loading of infamy. She thought she would make him complain for *something*, that now was so hard bound with an heretical opinion. How I dealt with her, guess gentle reader, Subaudi that I was in prison, and she my silly Jailer.

[FROM *The Unfortunate Traveller*]

PART SIX
The Well of the Past

Sir Walter Ralegh

MEDITATIONS ON HISTORY

To me it belongs in the first part of this preface, following the common and approved custom of those who have left the memories of time past to after-ages, to give, as near as I can, the same right to history which they have done. Yet seeing therein I should but borrow other men's words, I will not trouble the reader with the repetition. True it is, that among many other benefits, for which it hath been honoured, in this one it triumpheth over all human knowledge, that it hath given us life in our understanding, since the world itself had life and beginning, even to this day: yea it hath triumphed over time, which, besides it, nothing but eternity hath triumphed over: for it hath carried our knowledge over the vast and devouring space of so many thousands of years, and given so fair and piercing eyes to our mind, that we plainly behold living now, as if we had lived then, that great world, *magni Dei sapiens opus*, "the wise work," saith Hermes, "of a great God," as it was then, when but new to itself.

By it, I say, it is, that we live in the very time when it was created; we behold how it was governed; how it was covered with waters, and again repeopled; how kings and kingdoms have flourished and fallen; and for what virtue and piety God made prosperous, and for what vice and deformity he made wretched, both the one and the other. And it is not the least debt which we owe unto history, that it hath made us acquainted with our dead ancestors; and, out of the depth and darkness of the earth, delivered us their memory and fame. In a word, we may gather out of history a policy no less wise than eternal; by the comparison and application of other men's fore-passed miseries with our own like errors and ill deservings.

But it is neither of examples the most lively instructions, nor the words of the wisest men, nor the terror of future torments, that hath yet so wrought in our blind and stupified minds, as to make us remember that the infinite eye and wisdom of God doth pierce through all our pretences; as to make us remember, that the justice of God doth require none other accuser than our own consciences: which neither the false beauty of our apparent actions, nor all the formality which (to pacify the opinions of men) we put on, can in any or the least kind cover from his knowledge. And so much did that heathen wisdom confess, no way as yet qualified by the knowledge of a true God. If any (saith Euripides) having in his life committed wickedness, think he can hide it from the everlasting gods, he thinks not well.

To repeat God's judgements in particular upon those of all degrees which have played with his mercies, would require a volume apart: for the sea of examples hath no bottom. The marks set on private men are with their bodies cast into the earth; and their fortunes written only in the memories of those that lived with them: so as they who succeed, and have not seen the fall of others, do not fear their own faults. God's judgements upon the greater and greatest have been left to posterity; first, by those happy hands which the Holy Ghost hath guided; and secondly, by their virtue who have gathered the acts and ends of men, mighty and remarkable in the world.

Now to point far off, and to speak of the conversion of angels into devils for ambition; or of the greatest and most glorious kings, who have gnawn the grass of the earth with beasts, for pride and ingratitude towards God; or of that wise working of Pharaoh, when he slew the infants of Israel, ere they had recovered their cradles; or of the policy of Jezebel, in covering the murder of Naboth by a trial of the elders, according to the law; with many thousands of the like: what were it other than to make an hopeless proof, that far-off examples would not be left to the same far-off respects as heretofore? For who hath not observed what labour, practice, peril, bloodshed, and cruelty, the kings and princes of the world have undergone, exercised, taken on them, and committed, to make themselves and their issues masters of the world? And yet hath Babylon, Persia, Egypt, Syria, Macedon, Carthage, Rome, and the rest, no fruit, flower, grass, nor leaf, springing upon the face of the earth, of those seeds. No; their very roots and ruins do hardly remain.

Omnia quæ manu hominum facta sunt, vel manu hominum evertuntur, vel stando et durando deficiunt: "All that the hand of man can make is either overturned by the hand of man, or at length by standing and continuing consumed." The reasons of whose ruins are diversely given by those that ground their opinions on second causes. All kingdoms and states have fallen (say the politicians) by outward and foreign force, or by inward negligence and dissension, or by a third cause arising from both. Others observe, that the greatest have sunk down under their own weight; of which Livy hath a touch: *Eo crevit, ut magnitudine laboret sua.* Others,

that the divine providence (which Cratippus objected
to Pompey) hath set down the date and period of every
estate, before their first foundation and erection. But
hereof I will give myself a day over to resolve. . . .

Generally concerning the order of the work, I have
only taken counsel from the argument. For of the Assyrians, which, after the downfall of Babel, take up the first
part, and were the first great kings of the world, there
came little to the view of posterity: some few enterprises,
greater in fame than faith, of Ninus and Semiramis excepted.

It was the story of the Hebrews, of all before the
Olympiads, that overcame the consuming disease of
time, and preserved itself from the very cradle and beginning to this day: and yet not so entire, but that the
large discourses thereof (to which in many scriptures we
are referred) are nowhere found. The fragments of other
stories, with the actions of those kings and princes which
shot up here and there in the same time, I am driven to
relate by way of digression; of which we may say with
Virgil,

Apparent rari nantes in gurgite vasto.
They appear here and there floating in the great gulf of
　　time.

To the same first ages do belong the report of many
inventions therein found, and from them derived to us;
though most of the authors' names have perished in so
long a navigation. For those ages had their laws; they
had diversity of government; they had kingly rule; nobility, policy in war; navigation; and all or the most of
needful trades. To speak therefore of these (seeing in a
general history we should have left a great deal of nakedness by their omission) it cannot properly be called a

digression. True it is that I have also made many others, which, if they shall be laid to my charge, I must cast the fault into the great heap of human error. For, seeing we digress in all the ways of our lives, yea, seeing the life of man is nothing else but digression, I may the better be excused in writing their lives and actions. I am not altogether ignorant in the laws of history, and of the kinds.

The same hath been taught by many, but by no man better, and with greater brevity, than by that excellent learned gentleman, Sir Francis Bacon. Christian laws are also taught us by the prophets and apostles, and every day preached unto us. But we still make large digressions; yea, the teachers themselves do not (in all) keep the path which they point out to others.

For the rest; after such time as the Persians had wrested the empire from the Chaldeans, and had raised a great monarchy, producing actions of more importance than were elsewhere to be found; it was agreeable to the order of story to attend this empire, whilst it so flourished, that the affairs of the nations adjoining had reference thereunto. The like observance was to be used towards the fortunes of Greece, when they again began to get ground upon the Persians, as also towards the affairs of Rome, when the Romans grew more mighty than the Greeks.

As for the Medes, the Macedonians, the Sicilians, the Carthaginians, and other nations, who resisted the beginnings of the former empires, and afterwards became but parts of their composition and enlargement; it seemed best to remember what was known of them from their several beginnings, in such times and places as they in their flourishing estates opposed those monarchies, which, in the end, swallowed them up. And herein I have followed the best geographers, who seldom give names to those small brooks, whereof many, joined together, make great rivers; till such time as they become united, and run in a main stream to the ocean sea. If the phrase be weak, and the style not everywhere like itself; the first shews their legitimation and true parent; the second will excuse itself upon the variety of matter. For Virgil, who wrote his Eclogues *gracili avena,* used stronger pipes when he sounded the wars of Aeneas.

It may also be laid to my charge, that I use divers Hebrew words in my first book, and elsewhere; in which language others may think, and I myself acknowledge it, that I am altogether ignorant; but it is true, that some of them I find in Montanus, others in Latin character in S. Senensis, and of the rest I have borrowed the interpretation of some of my learned friends. But say I had been beholden to neither, yet were it not to be wondered at, having had eleven years' leisure to attain the knowledge of that or of any other tongue.

I know that it will be said by many, that I might have been more pleasing to the reader, if I had written the story of mine own times, having been permitted to draw water as near the well-head as another. To this I answer, that whosoever, in writing a modern history, shall follow truth too near the heels, it may happily strike out his teeth. There is no mistress or guide that hath led her followers and servants into greater miseries. He that goes after her too far off, loseth her sight, and loseth himself; and he that walks after her at a middle distance, I know not whether I should call that kind of course temper or baseness. It is true, that I never travelled after men's opinions, when I might have made the best use of them; and I have now too few days remaining to imitate those, that, either out of extreme ambition or extreme cowardice, or both, do yet (when death hath them on his shoulders) flatter the world between the bed and the grave.

It is enough for me (being in that state I am) to write of the eldest times; wherein also, why may it not be said, that, in speaking of the past, I point at the present, and tax the vices of those that are yet living, in their persons that are long since dead; and have it laid to my charge. But this I cannot help, though innocent. And certainly, if there be any, that, finding themselves spotted like the tigers of old time, shall find fault with me for painting them over anew, they shall therein accuse themselves justly, and me falsely.

For I protest before the majesty of God, that I malice no man under the sun. Impossible I know it is to please all, seeing few or none are so pleased with themselves, or so assured of themselves, by reason of their subjection to their private passions, but that they seem diverse persons in one and the same day. Seneca hath said it, and so do I: *Unus mihi pro populo erat:* and to the same effect Epicurus, *Hoc ego non multis, sed tibi;* or (as it hath since lamentably fallen out) I may borrow the resolution of an ancient philosopher, *Satis est unus, satis est nullus.* For it was for the service of that inestimable prince Henry, the successive hope, and one of the greatest of the Christian world, that I undertook this work. It pleased him to peruse some part thereof, and to pardon what was amiss. It is now left to the world without a master; from which all that is presented hath received both blows and thanks. *Eadem probamus, eadem reprehendimus: his exitus est omnis judicii, in quo lis secundum plures datur.*

But these discourses are idle. I know that as the charitable will judge charitably, so against those *qui gloriantur in malitia* my present adversity hath disarmed me. I am on the ground already, and therefore have not far to fall; and for rising again, as in the natural privation there is no recession to habit; so it is seldom seen in the privation politic. I do therefore forbear to style my readers *gentle, courteous,* and *friendly,* thereby to beg their good opinions, or to promise a second and third volume (which I also intend) if the first receive grace and good acceptance. For that which is already done may be thought enough, and too much; and it is certain, let us claw the reader with never so many courteous phrases, yet shall we evermore be thought fools that write foolishly. For conclusion; all the hope I have lies in this, that I have already found more ungentle and uncourteous readers of my love towards them, and well-deserving of them, than ever I shall do again. For had it been otherwise, I should hardly have had this leisure to have made myself a fool in print.

[FROM Preface, *History of the World*]

George Chapman

From HOMER'S *ILIAD*

ACHILLES PREPARES FOR BATTLE

The host set forth, and poured his steel waves far out
    of the fleet.
And as from air the frosty north wind blows a cold thick
    sleet
That dazzles eyes, flakes after flakes incessantly de-
    scending;
So thick, helms, curets, ashen darts, and round shields,
    never ending,
Flowed from the navy's hollow womb. Their splendours
    gave heaven's eye

His beams again. Earth laughed to see her face so like
    the sky;
Arms shined so hot, and she such clouds made with the
    dust she cast,
She thundered, feet of men and horse importuned her
    so fast.
In midst of all, divine Achilles his fair person armed,
His teeth gnashed as he stood, his eyes so full of fire
    they warmed,
Unsuffered grief and anger at the Trojans so combined.
His greaves first used, his goodly curets on his bosom
    shined,
His sword, his shield that cast a brightness from it like
    the moon.
And as from sea sailors discern a harmful fire let run
By herdsmen's faults, till all their stall flies up in wras-
    tling flame,
Which being on hills is seen far off, but being alone,
    none came
To give it quench, at shore no neighbours, and at sea
    their friends
Driven off with tempests; such a fire from his bright
    shield extends
His ominous radiance, and in heaven impressed his fer-
    vent blaze.
His crested helmet, grave and high, had next triumphant
    place
On his curled head, and like a star it cast a spurry ray,
About which a bright thick'ned bush of golden hair did
    play,
Which Vulcan forged him for his plume. Thus com-
    plete armed, he tried
How fit they were, and if his motion could with ease
    abide

Their brave instruction; and so far they were from hin-
    d'ring it,
That to it they were nimble wings, and made so light
    his spirit,
That from the earth the princely captain they took up to
    air.
    Then from his armoury he drew his lance, his father's
      spear,
Huge, weighty, firm, that not a Greek but he himself
    alone
Knew how to shake; it grew upon the mountain Pelion,
From whose height Chiron hewed it for his sire, and
    fatal 'twas
To great-souled men, of Peleus and Pelion surnamed
    Pelias.
    Then from the stable their bright horse Automedon
      withdraws
And Alcymus; put poitrils on, and cast upon their jaws
Their bridles, hurling back the reins, and hung them on
    the seat.
The fair scourge then Automedon takes up, and up doth
    get
To guide the horse. The fight's seat last Achilles took
    behind,
Who looked so armed as if the sun, there fall'n from
    heaven, had shined,
And terribly thus charged his steeds: "Xanthus and
    Balius,
Seed of the Harpy, in the charge ye undertake of us,
Discharge it not as when Patroclus ye left dead in field,
But, when with blood, for this day's fast observed, re-
    venge shall yield
Our heart satiety, bring us off." Thus, since Achilles
    spake

As if his awed steeds understood, 'twas Juno's will to
    make
Vocal the palate of the one, who shaking his fair head
(Which in his mane, let fall to earth, he almost buried)
Thus Xanthus spake: "Ablest Achilles, now, at least, our
    care
Shall bring thee off; but not far hence the fatal minutes
    are
Of thy grave ruin. Nor shall we be then to be reproved,
But mightiest Fate, and the great God. Nor was thy best
    beloved
Spoiled so of arms by our slow pace, or courage's impair,
The best of Gods, Latona's son, that wears the golden
    hair,
Gave him his death's wound, though the grace he gave
    to Hector's hand.
We, like the spirit of the west that all spirits can com-
    mand
For pow'r of wing, could run him off; but thou thyself
    must go,
So fate ordains, God and a man must give thee over-
    throw."
    This said, the Furies stopped his voice. Achilles, far
    in rage,
Thus answered him: "It fits not thee thus proudly to
    presage
My overthrow. I know myself it is my fate to fall
Thus far from Phthia; yet that fate shall fail to vent her
    gall
Till mine vent thousands." These words used, he fell to
    horrid deeds,
Gave dreadful signal, and forthright made fly his one-
    hoofed steeds.

                        [FROM *Book XIX*]

PRIAM BEGS FOR THE BODY OF HECTOR

　　　　　　　　　　Forthwith they reached the tent
Of great Achilles, large and high, and in his most ascent
A shaggy roof of seedy reeds mown from the meads; a
　　hall
Of state they made their king in it, and strength'ned it
　　withal
Thick with fir rafters, whose approach was let in by a
　　door
That had but one bar, but so big that three men ever-
　　more
Raised it to shut, three fresh take down, which yet
　　Aeacides
Would shut and ope himself. And this with far more
　　ease
Hermes set ope, ent'ring the king, then leaped from
　　horse, and said:
　　"Now know, old king, that Mercury, a God, hath
　　given this aid
To thy endeavour, sent by Jove; and now away must I,
For men would envy thy estate to see a Deity
Affect a man thus. Enter thou, embrace Achilles' knee,
And by his sire, son, mother, pray his ruth and grace to
　　thee."
　　This said, he high Olympus reached. The king then
　　left his coach
To grave Idaeus, and went on, made his resolved ap-
　　proach,
And entered in a goodly room, where with his princes
　　sate
Jove-loved Achilles, at their feast; two only kept the
　　state

Of his attendance, Alcimus, and lord Automedon,
At Priam's entry. A great time Achilles gazed upon
His wondered-at approach, nor ate; the rest did nothing
    see,
While close he came up, with his hands fast holding the
    bent knee
Of Hector's conqueror, and kissed that large man-
    slaught'ring hand
That much blood from his sons had drawn. And as in
    some strange land,
And great man's house, a man is driv'n (with that ab-
    horred dismay
That follows wilful bloodshed still, his fortune being to
    slay
One whose blood cries aloud for his) to plead protec-
    tion,
In such a miserable plight as frights the lookers on;
In such a stupefied estate Achilles sat to see
So unexpected, so in night, and so incredibly,
Old Priam's entry. All his friends one on another stared
To see his strange looks, seeing no cause. Thus Priam
    then prepared
His son's redemption: "See in me, O godlike Thetis' son,
Thy aged father, and perhaps even now being outrun
With some of my woes, neighbour foes, thou absent,
    taking time
To do him mischief, no mean left to terrify the crime
Of his oppression; yet he hears thy graces still survive,
And joys to hear it, hoping still to see thee safe arrive
From ruined Troy; but I, cursed man, of all my race
    shall live
To see none living. Fifty sons the Deities did give
My hopes to live in, all alive when near our trembling
    shore

The Greek ships harboured, and one womb nineteen of
    those sons bore.

Now Mars a number of their knees hath strengthless
    left, and he

That was, of all, my only joy, and Troy's sole guard, by
    thee,

Late fighting for his country, slain; whose tendered per-
    son now

I come to ransom. Infinite is that I offer you,

Myself conferring it, exposed alone to all your odds,

Only imploring right of arms. Achilles! Fear the Gods,

Pity an old man like thy sire, different in only this,

That I am wretcheder, and bear that weight of miseries

That never man did, my cursed lips enforced to kiss that
    hand

That slew my children." This moved tears, his father's
    name did stand,

Mentioned by Priam, in much help to his compassion,

And moved Aeacides so much he could not look upon

The weeping father. With his hand he gently put away

His grave face. Calm remission now did mutually dis-
    play

Her power in either's heaviness. Old Priam, to record

His son's death and his deathsman see, his tears and
    bosom poured

Before Achilles; at his feet he laid his reverend head.

Achilles' thoughts, now with his sire, now with his
    friend, were fed.

Betwixt both sorrow filled the tent. But now Aeacides

⟨Satiate at all parts with the ruth of their calamities⟩

Start up, and up he raised the king. His milk-white head
    and beard

With pity he beheld, and said: "Poor man, thy mind is
    scared

With much affliction. How durst thy person thus alone

Venture on his sight that hath slain so many a worthy
    son,
And so dear to thee? Thy old heart is made of iron. Sit,
And settle we our woes, though huge, for nothing profits
    it.
Cold mourning wastes but our lives' heats. The Gods
    have destinate
That wretched mortals must live sad: 'tis the Immortal
    State
Of Deity that lives secure. Two tuns of gifts there lie
In Jove's gate, one of good, one ill, that our mortality
Maintain, spoil, order; which when Jove doth mix to any
    man,
One while he frolics, one while mourns. If of his mourn-
    ful can
A man drinks only, only wrongs he doth expose him to,
Sad hunger in th' abundant earth doth toss him to and
    fro,
Respected nor of Gods nor men. The mixed cup Peleus
    drank
Even from his birth; Heaven blest his life; he lived not
    that could thank
The Gods for such rare benefits as set forth his estate.
He reigned among his Myrmidons most rich, most fortu-
    nate,
And, though a mortal, had his bed decked with a death-
    less dame.
And yet, with all this good, one ill God mixed, that takes
    all name
From all that goodness; his name now, whose preserva-
    tion here
Men count the crown of their most good, not blessed
    with power to bear
One blossom but myself, and I shaken as soon as blown;
Nor shall I live to cheer his age, and give nutrition

To him that nourished me. Far off my rest is set in Troy
To leave thee restless and thy seed; thyself that did enjoy,
As we have heard, a happy life, what Lesbos doth contain,
In times past being a blessed man's seat, what th' unmeasured main
Of Hellespontus, Phrygia, holds, are all said to adorn
Thy empire, wealth and sons enow, but, when the Gods did turn
Thy blest state to partake with bane, war and the bloods of men
Circled thy city, never clear. Sit down and suffer then,
Mourn not inevitable things; thy tears can spring no deeds
To help thee, nor recall thy son; impatience ever breeds
Ill upon ill, makes worst things worse, and therefore sit."
    He said:
"Give me no seat, great seed of Jove, when yet unransomed
Hector lies riteless in thy tents, but deign with utmost speed
His resignation, that these eyes may see his person freed,
And thy grace satisfied with gifts. Accept what I have brought,
And turn to Phthia; 'tis enough thy conquering hand hath fought
Till Hector faltered under it, and Hector's father stood
With free humanity safe." He frowned and said: "Give not my blood
Fresh cause of fury. I know well I must resign thy son,
Jove by my mother utter'd it, and what besides is done
I know as amply; and thyself, old Priam, I know too.
Some God hath brought thee, for no man durst use a thought to go

On such a service. I have guards, and I have gates to
    stay
Easy accesses; do not then presume thy will can sway,
Like Jove's will, and incense again my quenched blood,
    lest nor thou
Nor Jove get the command of me." This made the old
    king bow,
And down he sat in fear. The prince leaped like a lion
    forth,
Automedon and Alcimus attending; all the worth
Brought for the body they took down and brought in,
    and with it
Idæus, herald to the king; a coat embroidered yet,
And two rich cloaks, they left to hide the person. Thetis'
    son
Called out his women to anoint and quickly overrun
The corse with water, lifting it in private to the coach,
Lest Priam saw, and his cold blood embraced a fiery
    touch
Of anger at the turpitude profaning it, and blew
Again his wrath's fire to his death. This done, his women
    threw
The coat and cloak on, but the corse Achilles' own hand
    laid
Upon a bed, and with his friends to chariot it conveyed.
For which forced grace, abhorring so from his free mind,
    he wept,
Cried out for anger, and thus prayed: "O friend, do not
    except
Against this favour to our foe, if in the deep thou hear,
And that I give him to his sire; he gave fair ransom;
    dear
In my observance is Jove's will; and whatsoever part
Of all these gifts by any mean I fitly may convert

To thy renown here, and will there, it shall be poured
upon

Thy honoured sepulchre." This said, he went, and what
was done

Told Priam, saying: "Father, now thy will's fit rites are
paid,

Thy son is given up; in the morn thine eyes shall see
him laid

Decked in thy chariot on his bed; in mean space let us
eat.

The rich-haired Niobe found thoughts that made her
take her meat,

Though twelve dear children she saw slain, six daughters, six young sons.

The sons incensed Apollo slew; the maids' confusions

Diana wrought, since Niobe her merits durst compare

With great Latona's, arguing that she did only bear

Two children and herself had twelve, for which those
only two

Slew all her twelve. Nine days they lay steeped in their
blood, her woe

Found no friend to afford them fire, Saturnius had turned

Humans to stones. The tenth day yet the good Celestials
burned

The trunks themselves, and Niobe, when she was tired
with tears,

Fell to her food, and now with rocks and wild hills
mixed she bears

In Sipylus the Gods' wraths still, in that place where 'tis
said,

The Goddess Fairies use to dance about the funeral bed

Of Achelous, where, though turned with cold grief to a
stone,

Heaven gives her heat enough to feel what plague comparison

With his pow'rs made by earth deserves. Affect not then
    too far
Without grief, like a God, being a man, but for a man's
    life care,
And take fit food: thou shalt have time beside to mourn
    thy son;
He shall be tearful, thou being full, not here, but Ilion
Shall find the weeping-rooms enow." He said, and so
    arose,
And caused a silver-fleeced sheep killed: his friends'
    skills did dispose
The flaying, cutting of it up, and cookly spitted it,
Roasted, and drew it artfully. Automedon, as fit,
Was for the reverend sewer's place, and all the brown
    joints served
On wicker vessels to the board; Achilles' own hands
    kerved,
And close they fell to. Hunger stanched, talk, and ob-
    serving time,
Was used of all hands. Priam sat amazed to see the
    prime
Of Thetis' son, accomplished so with stature, looks, and
    grace,
In which the fashion of a God he thought had changed
    his place.
Achilles fell to him as fast, admired as much his years
Told in his grave and good aspect, his speech even
    charmed his ears,
So ordered, so material. With this food feasted too,
Old Priam spake thus: "Now, Jove's seed, command that
    I may go,
And add to this feast grace of rest. These lids ne'er
    closed mine eyes
Since under thy hands fled the soul of my dear son;
    sighs, cries,

And woes, all use from food and sleep have taken; the
    base courts
Of my sad palace made my beds, where all the abject
    sorts
Of sorrow I have varied, tumbled in dust, and hid;
No bit, no drop, of sustenance touched." Then did
    Achilles bid
His men and women see his bed laid down, and covered
With purple blankets, and on them an arras coverlid,
Waistcoats of silk plush laying by. The women straight
    took lights,
And two beds made with utmost speed, and all the other
    rites
Their lord named used, who pleasantly the king in hand
    thus bore:
    "Good father, you must sleep without, lest any coun-
    sellor
Make his access in depth of night, as oft their industry
Brings them t' impart our war-affairs, of whom should
    any eye
Discern your presence, his next steps to Agamemnon fly,
And then shall I lose all these gifts. But go to, signify,
And that with truth, how many days you mean to keep
    the state
Of Hector's funerals; because so long would I rebate
Mine own edge set to sack your town, and all our host
    contain
From interruption of your rites." He answered: "If you
    mean
To suffer such rites to my son, you shall perform a part
Of most grace to me. But you know with how dismayed
    a heart
Our host took Troy, and how much fear will therefore
    apprehend
Their spirits to make out again, so far as we must send

For wood to raise our heap of death; unless I may assure
That this your high grace will stand good, and make
    their pass secure;
Which if you seriously confirm, nine days I mean to
    mourn,
The tenth keep funeral and feast, th' eleventh raise and
    adorn
My son's fit sepulcher, the twelfth, if we must needs,
    we'll fight."
    "Be it," replied Aeacides, "do Hector all this right;
I'll hold war back those whole twelve days; of which, to
    free all fear,
Take this my right hand." This confirmed, the old king
    rested there;
His herald lodged by him; and both in forepart of the
    tent;
Achilles in an inmost room of wondrous ornament,
Whose side bright-cheeked Briseis warmed.

                             [Book XXIV]

Sir Thomas North

ANTONY'S FLIGHT

So, when Antonius had determined to fight by sea,
he set all the other ships on fire but threescore ships
of Egypt, and reserved only but the best and greatest
galleys, from three banks unto ten banks of oars. Into
them he put two-and-twenty thousand fighting men,
with two thousand darters and slingers. Now, as he was
setting his men in order of battle, there was a captain,

and a valiant man, that had served Antonius in many battles and conflicts, and had all his body hacked and cut: who, as Antonius passed by him, cried out unto him and said: "O noble emperor, how cometh it to pass that you trust to these vile brittle ships? What, do you mistrust these wounds of mine and this sword? Let the Egyptians and Phoenicians fight by sea, and set us on the mainland, where we use to conquer, or to be slain on our feet." Antonius passed by him and said never a word, but only beckoned to him with his hand and head, as though he willed him to be of good courage, although indeed he had no great courage himself. For, when the masters of the galleys and pilots would have let their sails alone, he made them clap them on, saying to colour the matter withal, that not one of his enemies should scape. All that day and the three days following, the sea rose so high and was so boisterous, that the battle was put off. The fifth day the storm ceased and the sea calmed again, and then they rowed with force of oars in battle one against the other, Antonius leading the right wing with Publicola, and Caelius the left, and Marcus Octavius and Marcus Justeius the midst. Octavius Caesar, on the other side, had placed Agrippa in the left wing of his army, and had kept the right wing for himself. For the armies by land, Canidius was general of Antonius' side, and Taurus of Caesar's side: who kept their men in battle array the one before the other, upon the seaside, without stirring one against the other. Further, touching both the chieftains: Antonius, being in a swift pinnace, was carried up and down by force of oars through his army, and spake to his people to encourage them to fight valiantly, as if they were on mainland, because of the steadiness and heaviness of their ships: and commanded the pilots and masters of the galleys that they should not stir, none otherwise than if they were at anchor, and so to receive the first charge of their enemies, and that they should not go out of the strait of the gulf. Caesar betimes in the morning, going out of his tent to see his ships throughout, met a man by chance that drove an ass before him. Caesar asked the man what his name was. The poor man told him that his name was Eutychus, to say, Fortunate: and his ass's name Nicon, to say, Conqueror. Therefore Caesar after he had won the battle setting out the marketplace with the spurs of the galleys he had taken, for a sign of his victory, he caused also the man and his ass to be set up in brass. When he had visited the order of his army throughout, he took a little pinnace, and went to the right wing, and wondered when he saw his enemies lie still in the strait, and stirred not. For, discerning them afar off, men would have thought they had been ships riding at anchor, and a good while he was so persuaded. So he kept his galleys eight furlong from his enemies. About noon there rose a little gale of wind from the sea, and then Antonius' men waxing angry with tarrying so long, and trusting to the greatness and height of their ships, as if they had been invincible, they began to march forward with their left wing. Caesar seeing that was a glad man, and began a little to give back from the right wing, to allure them to come farther out of the strait and gulf, to the end that he might with his light ships well manned with watermen turn and environ the galleys of the enemies, the which were heavy of yarage, both for their bigness as also for lack of watermen to row them. When the skirmish began, and that they came to join, there was no great hurt at the first meeting, neither did the ships vehemently hit one against the other, as they do commonly in fight by sea. For, on the one side, Antonius' ships for their heaviness could not have the strength and swiftness to make their blows of any force:

and Caesar's ships, on the other side, took great heed
not to rush and shock with the forecastles of Antonius'
ships, whose prows were armed with great brazen spurs.
Furthermore they durst not flank them, because their
points were easily broken, which way so ever they came
to set upon his ships, that were made of great main
square pieces of timber, bound together with great
iron pins: so that the battle was much like to a battle by
land, or, to speak more properly, to the assault of a city.
For there were always three or four of Caesar's ships
about one of Antonius' ships, and the soldiers fought
with their pikes, halberds, and darts, and threw pots
and darts with fire. Antonius' ships on the other side
bestowed among them, with their cross-bows and engines of battery, great store of shot from their high
towers of wood that were upon their ships. Now Publicola seeing Agrippa put forth his left wing of Caesar's
army, to compass in Antonius' ships that fought, he
was driven also to loose off to have more room, and,
going a little at one side, to put those farther off that
were afraid, and in the midst of the battle. For they
were sore distressed by Arruntius. Howbeit the battle
was yet of even hand, and the victory doubtful, being
indifferent to both: when suddenly they saw the threescore ships of Cleopatra busy about their yard-masts,
and hoisting sail to fly. So they fled through the midst
of them that were in fight, for they had been placed
behind the great ships, and did marvellously disorder
the other ships. For the enemies themselves wondered
much to see them sail in that sort with full sail towards
Peloponnesus. There Antonius showed plainly, that he
had not only lost the courage and heart of an emperor,
but also of a valiant man, and that he was not his own
man (proving that true which an old man spake in
mirth, that the soul of a lover lived in another body, and

not in his own): he was so carried away with the vain love of this woman, as if he had been glued unto her, and that she could not have removed without moving of him also. For, when he saw Cleopatra's ship under sail, he forgot, forsook, and betrayed them that fought for him, and embarked upon a galley with five banks of oars, to follow her that was already begun to overthrow him, and would in the end be his utter destruction. When she knew his galley afar off, she lift up a sign in the poop of her ship, and so Antonius coming to it was plucked up where Cleopatra was: howbeit he saw her not at his first coming, nor she him, but went and sat down alone in the prow of his ship, and said never a word, clapping his head between both his hands.

[FROM Plutarch's *Life of Antony*, translated from the French of Amyot]

CLEOPATRA'S DEATH

WHEN THIS was told Cleopatra, she requested Caesar that it would please him to suffer her to offer the last oblations of the dead unto the soul of Antonius. This being granted her, she was carried to the place where his tomb was, and there falling down on her knees, embracing the tomb with her women, the tears running down her cheeks, she began to speak in this sort: "O my dear lord Antonius, not long since I buried thee here, being a free woman: and now I offer unto thee the funeral springlings and oblations, being a captive and prisoner, and yet I am forbidden and kept from tearing and murdering this captive body of mine with blows, which they carefully guard and keep, only to triumph of thee: look therefore henceforth for no other honours, offerings nor sacrifices from me, for these are the last which Cleopatra can give thee, since now they carry her away. Whilst we lived together, nothing could sever our companies: but now at our death I fear me they will make us change our countries. For as thou being a Roman hast been buried in Egypt, even so, wretched creature, I, an Egyptian, shall be buried in Italy, which shall be all the good that I have received by thy country. If therefore the gods where thou art now have any power and authority, since our gods here have forsaken us, suffer not thy true friend and lover to be carried away alive, that in me they triumph of thee: but receive me with thee, and let me be buried in one self tomb with thee. For though my griefs and miseries be infinite, yet none hath grieved me more, nor that I could less bear withal, than this small time which I have been driven to live alone without thee." Then, having ended these doleful plaints, and crowned the tomb with garlands and sundry nosegays, and marvellous lovingly embraced the same, she commanded they should prepare her bath, and when she had bathed and washed herself she fell to her meat, and was sumptuously served. Now whilst she was at dinner there came a countryman, and brought her a basket. The soldiers that warded at the gates asked him straight what he had in his basket. He opened the basket, and took out the leaves that covered the figs, and showed them that they were figs he brought. They all of them marvelled to see so goodly figs. The countryman laughed to hear them, and bade them take some if they would. They believed he told them truly, and so bade him carry them in. After Cleopatra had dined, she sent a certain table written and sealed unto Caesar, and commanded them all to go out of the tombs where she was, but the two women: then she shut the doors to her. Caesar, when he received this table, and began to read her lamentation and petition, requesting him that he would let her be buried with

Antonius, found straight what she meant, and thought to have gone thither himself: howbeit he sent one before in all haste that might be, to see what it was. Her death was very sudden. For those whom Caesar sent unto her ran thither in all haste possible, and found the soldiers standing at the gate, mistrusting nothing, nor understanding of her death. But when they had opened the doors they found Cleopatra stark dead, laid upon a bed of gold, attired and arrayed in her royal robes, and one of her two women, which was called Iras, dead at her feet: and her other woman called Charmion half-dead, and trembling, trimming the diadem which Cleopatra wore upon her head. One of the soldiers, seeing her, angrily said unto her: "Is that well done, Charmion?" "Very well," said she again, "and meet for a princess descended from the race of so many noble kings." She said no more, but fell down dead hard by the bed. Some report that this aspic was brought unto her in the basket with figs, and that she had commanded them to hide it under the fig-leaves, that, when she should think to take out the figs, the aspic should bite her before she should see her: howbeit that, when she would have taken away the leaves for the figs, she perceived it, and said, "Art thou here then?" And so, her arm being naked, she put it to the aspic to be bitten. Others say again, she kept it in a box, and that she did prick and thrust it with a spindle of gold, so that the aspic, being angered withal, leapt out with great fury, and bit her in the arm. Howbeit few can tell the truth. For they report also, that she had hidden poison in a hollow razor which she carried in the hair of her head: and yet was there no mark seen of her body, or any sign discerned that she was poisoned, neither also did they find this serpent in her tomb. But it was reported only, that there were seen certain fresh steps or tracks where it had gone, on the tomb side toward the sea, and specially by the door side. Some say also, that they found two little pretty bitings in her arm, scant to be discerned: the which it seemeth Caesar himself gave credit unto, because in his triumph he carried Cleopatra's image, with an aspic biting of her arm. And thus goeth the report of her death. Now Caesar, though he was marvellous sorry for the death of Cleopatra, yet he wondered at her noble mind and courage, and therefore commanded she should be nobly buried, and laid by Antonius: and willed also that her two women should have honourable burial. Cleopatra died being eight-and-thirty years old, after she had reigned two-and-twenty years, and governed above fourteen of them with Antonius. And for Antonius, some say that he lived three-and-fifty years: and others say, six-and-fifty.

[FROM Plutarch's *Life of Antony*]

Raphael Holinshed

THE BATTLE OF AGINCOURT

THE FRENCH king being at Rouen, and hearing that King Henry was passed the river of Somme, was much displeased therewith, and assembling his council to the number of five-and-thirty, asked their advice what was to be done. There was amongst these five-and-thirty, his son the Dauphin, calling himself King of Sicily; the Dukes of Berri and Brittany, the Earl of Ponthieu the king's youngest son, and other high estates. At length thirty of them agreed that the Englishmen should not depart unfought withal, and five were of a contrary opinion, but the greater number ruled the matter: and so Montjoy King-at-Arms was sent to the King of England to defy him as the enemy of France, and to tell him that he should shortly have battle. King Henry advisedly answered: "Mine intent is to do as it pleaseth God, I will not seek your master at this time; but if he or his seek me, I will meet with them God willing. If any of your nation attempt once to stop me in my journey now towards Calais, at their jeopardy be it; and yet I wish not any of you so unadvised, as to be the occasion that I dye your tawny ground with your red blood."

When he had thus answered the herald, he gave him a princely reward, and licence to depart. Upon whose return, with this answer, it was incontinently on the French side proclaimed, that all men of war should resort to the Constable to fight with the King of England. Whereupon, all men apt for armour and desirous of honour, drew them toward the field. The Dauphin sore desired to have been at the battle, but he was prohibited by his father: likewise Philip Earl of Charleroi would gladly have been there, if his father the Duke of Bourgogne would have suffered him: many of his men stole away, and went to the Frenchmen. The King of England hearing that the Frenchmen approached, and that there was another river for him to pass with his army by a bridge, and doubting lest if the same bridge should be broken, it would be greatly to his hindrance, appointed certain captains with their bands to go thither with all speed before him, and to take possession thereof, and so to keep it till his coming thither.

Those that were sent, finding the Frenchmen busy to break down their bridge, assailed them so vigorously that they discomfited them, and took and slew them; and so the bridge was preserved till the King came, and passed the river by the same with his whole army. This was on the two-and-twentieth day of October. The Duke of York that led the vanguard (after the army was passed the river) mounted up to the height of an hill with his people, and sent out scouts to discover the country, the which upon their return advertised him that a great army of Frenchmen was at hand, approaching towards them. The Duke declared to the King what he had heard, and the King thereupon, without all fear or trouble of mind, caused the battle which he led himself to stay, and incontinently rode forth to view his adversaries, and that done, returned to his people, and with cheerful countenance caused them to be put in order of battle, assigning to every captain such room and place as he thought convenient, and so kept them still in that order till night was come, and then determined to seek a place to encamp and lodge his army in for that night.

There was not one amongst them that knew any certain place whither to go, in that unknown country: but by chance they happened upon a beaten way, white in sight; by the which they were brought unto a little village, where they were refreshed with meat and drink somewhat more plenteously than they had been divers days before. Order was taken by commandment from the King after the army was first set in battle array, that no noise or clamour should be made in the host; so that in marching forth to this village, every man kept himself quiet: but at their coming into the village, fires were made to give light on every side, as there likewise were in the French host, which was encamped not past two hundred and fifty paces distant from the English. The chief leaders of the French host were these: the Constable of France, the Marshal, the Admiral, the Lord Rambures master of the crossbows, and other of the

French nobility, which came and pitched down their standards and banners in the county of Saint Paul, within the territory of Agincourt, having in their army (as some write) to the number of threescore thousand horsemen, besides footmen, wagoners and other.

They were lodged even in the way by the which the Englishmen must needs pass towards Calais, and all that night after their coming thither, made great cheer and were very merry, pleasant, and full of game. The Englishmen also for their parts were of good comfort, and nothing abashed of the matter, and yet they were both hungry, weary, sore travelled, and vexed with many cold diseases. Howbeit reconciling themselves with God by housel and shrift, requiring assistance at his hands that is the only giver of victory, they determined rather to die than to yield, or flee. The day following was the five-and-twentieth of October in the year 1415, being then Friday, and the feast of Crispin and Crispinian, a day fair and fortunate to the English, but most sorrowful and unlucky to the French.

In the morning the French captains made three battles, in the vanward were eight thousand helms of knights and esquires, four thousand archers, and fifteen hundred crossbows which were guided by the Lord de la Brette, Constable of France, having with him the Dukes of Orleans and Bourbon, the Earls of Ewe and Richmond, the Marshal Bouciquault, and the master of the crossbows, the Lord Dampier Admiral of France, and other captains. The Earl of Vendôme with sixteen hundred men of arms were ordered for a wing to that battle. And the other wing was guided by Sir Guichard Dolphine, Sir Clugnet of Brabant, and Sir Lewis Bourdon, with eight hundred men of arms, of elect chosen persons. And to break the shot of the Englishmen were appointed Sir Guilliam de Saueuses, with Hector and

Philip his brethren, Ferrie de Maillie, and Alen de Gaspanes, with other eight hundred of arms.

In the middle ward were assigned as many persons, or more, as were in the foremost battle, and the charge thereof was committed to the Dukes of Bar and Alençon, the Earls of Nevers, Vaudemont, Blamont, Salinges, Grand Pré, and of Russie. And in the rearward were all the other men of arms guided by the Earls of Marle, Dampmartin, Fauconberg, and the Lord of Lourreie, Captain of Arde, who had with him the men of the frontiers of Bolonois. Thus the Frenchmen being ordered under their standards and banners, made a great show: for surely they were esteemed in number six times as many or more than was the whole company of the Englishmen, with wagoners, pages and all. They rested themselves, waiting for the bloody blast of the terrible trumpet, till the hour between nine and ten of the clock of the same day, during which season the Constable made unto the captains and other men of war a pithy oration, exhorting and encouraging them to do valiantly, with many comfortable words and sensible reasons. King Henry also, like a leader, and not as one led, like a sovereign and not an inferior, perceiving a plot of ground very strong and meet for his purpose, which on the back-half was fenced with the village, wherein he had lodged the night before, and on both sides defended with hedges and bushes, thought good there to embattle his host, and so ordered his men in the same place, as he saw occasion, and as stood for his most advantage.

First he sent privily two hundred archers into a low meadow, which was near to the vanguard of his enemies, but separated with a great ditch; commanding them there to keep themselves close till they had a token to them given, to let drive at their adversaries: beside this he appointed a vanward, of the which he made captain Edward, Duke of York, who of an haughty courage had desired that office, and with him were the Lords Beaumont, Willoughby, and Fanhope, and this battle was all of archers. The middle ward was governed by the king himself, with his brother the Duke of Gloucester, and the Earls of Marshall, Oxford, and Suffolk, in the which were all the strong billmen. The Duke of Exeter, uncle to the King, led the rearward, which was mixed both with billmen and archers. The horsemen like wings went on every side of the battle.

Thus the King having ordered his battles, feared not the puissance of his enemies, but yet to provide that they should not with the multitude of horsemen break the order of his archers, in whom the force of his army consisted (for in those days the yeomen had their limbs at liberty, since their hosen were then fastened with one point, and their jacks long and easy to shoot in; so that they might draw bows of great strength, and shoot arrows of a yard long, beside the head), he caused stakes bound with iron, sharp at both ends, of the length of five or six foot to be pitched before the archers, and of each side the footmen like an hedge, to the intent that if the barded horses ran rashly upon them, they might shortly be gored and destroyed. Certain persons also were appointed to remove the stakes, as by the moving of the archers occasion and time should require, so that the footmen were hedged about with stakes, and the horsemen stood like a bulwark between them and their enemies, without the stakes. This device of fortifying an army was at this time first invented; but since that time they have devised caltrops, harrows, and other new engines against the force of horsemen; so that if the enemies run hastily upon the same, either are their horses wounded with the stakes, or their feet hurt with the other engines, so as thereby the beasts are gored, or else made unable to maintain their course.

King Henry, by reason of his small number of people to fill up his battles, placed his vanguard so on the right hand of the main battle, which himself led, that the distance betwixt them might scarce be perceived, and so in like case was the rearward joined on the left hand, that the one might the more readily succour another in time of need. When he had thus ordered his battles, he left a small company to keep his camp and carriage, which remained still in the village, and then calling his captains and soldiers about him, he made to them a right grave oration, moving them to play the men, whereby to obtain a glorious victory, as there was hope certain they should, the rather if they would but remember the just cause for which they fought, and whom they should encounter, such faint-hearted people as their ancestors had so often overcome. To conclude, many words of courage he uttered, to stir them to do manfully, assuring them that England should never be charged with his ransom, nor any Frenchman triumph over him as a captive; for either by famous death or glorious victory would he (by God's grace) win honour and fame.

It is said, that as he heard one of the host utter his wish to another thus: "I would to God there were with us now so many good soldiers as are at this hour within England!" the King answered: "I would not wish a man more here than I have; we are indeed in comparison to the enemies but a few, but if God of his clemency do favour us, and our just cause (as I trust he will) we shall speed well enough. But let no man ascribe victory to our own strength and might, but only to God's assistance, to whom I have no doubt we shall worthily have cause to give thanks therefor. And if so be that for our offences' sakes we shall be delivered into the hands of our enemies, the less number we be, the less damage shall the realm of England sustain: but if we should fight in trust of multitude of men, and so get the victory (our minds being prone to pride) we should thereupon peradventure ascribe the victory not so much to the gift of God as to our own puissance, and thereby provoke his high indignation and displeasure against us: and if the enemy get the upper hand, then should our realm and country suffer more damage and stand in further danger. But be you of good comfort, and show yourselves valiant, God and our just quarrel shall defend us, and deliver these our proud adversaries with all the multitude of them which you see (or at the least the most of them) into our hands." Whilst the King was yet thus in speech, either army so maligned the other, being as then in open sight, that every man cried: "Forward, forward." The Dukes of Clarence, Gloucester, and York were of the same opinion, yet the king stayed a while, lest any jeopardy were not foreseen, or any hazard not prevented. The Frenchmen in the meanwhile, as though they had been sure of victory, made great triumph, for the captains had determined before how to divide the spoil, and the soldiers the night before had played the Englishmen at dice. The noblemen had devised a chariot, wherein they might triumphantly convey the King captive to the city of Paris, crying to their soldiers: "Haste you to the spoil, glory and honour"; little weening (God wot) how soon their brags should be blown away.

Here we may not forget how the French thus in their jollity sent an herald to King Henry, to inquire what ransom he would offer. Whereunto he answered, that within two or three hours he hoped it would so happen, that the Frenchmen should be glad to common rather

with the Englishmen for their ransoms, than the English
to take thought for their deliverance, promising for his
own part that his dead carcass should rather be a prize
to the Frenchmen, than that his living body should pay
any ransom. When the messenger was come back to the
French host, the men of war put on their helmets, and
caused their trumpets to blow to the battle. They
thought themselves so sure of victory, that divers of
the noblemen made such haste towards the battle, that
they left many of their servants and men of war behind
them, and some of them would not once stay for their
standards: as amongst other the Duke of Brabant, when
his standard was not come, caused a banner to be taken
from a trumpet and fastened to a spear, the which he
commanded to be borne before him instead of his standard. But when both these armies coming within danger
either of other, set in full order of battle on both sides,
they stood still at the first, beholding either other's
demeanour, being not distant in sunder past three bow-
shots. And when they had on both parts thus stayed a
good while without doing anything (except that certain
of the French horsemen advancing forwards, betwixt
both the hosts, were by the English archers constrained
to return back) advice was taken amongst the Englishmen what was best for them to do. Thereupon all things
considered, it was determined that since the Frenchmen
would not come forward, the King with his army em-
battled (as ye have heard) should march towards them,
and so leaving their truss and baggage in the village
where they lodged the night before, only with their
weapons, armour, and stakes prepared for the purpose,
as ye have heard.

These made somewhat forward, before whom there
went an old knight, Sir Thomas Erpingham (a man of
great experience in the war) with a warder in his hand;

and when he cast up his warder, all the army shouted, but that was a sign to the archers in the meadow, which therewith shot wholly altogether at the vanward of the Frenchmen, who when they perceived the archers in the meadow, and saw they could not come at them for a ditch that was betwixt them, with all haste set upon the foreward of King Henry; but ere they could join, the archers in the forefront and the archers on that side which stood in the meadow so wounded the footmen, galled the horses, and cumbered the men of arms, that the footmen durst not go forward, the horsemen ran together upon plumps without order, some overthrew such as were next them, and the horses overthrew their masters, and so at the first joining, the Frenchmen were foully discomforted and the Englishmen highly encouraged.

When the French vanward were thus brought to confusion, the English archers cast away their bows, and took into their hands axes, malls, swords, bills, and other hand-weapons, and with the same slew the Frenchmen, until they came to the middle ward. Then approached the King, and so encouraged his people, that shortly the second battle of the Frenchmen was overthrown and dispersed, not without great slaughter of men; howbeit, divers were relieved by their varlets, and conveyed out of the field. The English were so busied in fighting, and taking of the prisoners at hand, that they followed not in chase of their enemies, nor would once break out of their array of battle. Yet sundry of the French strongly withstood the fierceness of the English, when they came to handy strokes, so that the fight sometimes was doubtful and perilous. Yet as part of the French horsemen set their courses to have entered upon the King's battle, with the stakes overthrown, they were either taken or slain. Thus this battle continued three long hours.

The King that day showed himself a valiant knight, albeit almost felled by the Duke of Alençon; yet with plain strength he slew two of the duke's company, and felled the duke himself; whom when he would have yielded, the King's guard (contrary to his mind) slew out of hand. In conclusion, the King minding to make an end of that day's journey, caused his horsemen to fetch a compass about, and to join with him against the rearward of the Frenchmen, in the which was the greatest number of people. When the Frenchmen perceived his intent, they were suddenly amazed and ran away like sheep, without order or array. Which when the King perceived, he encouraged his men, and followed so quickly upon the enemies, that they ran hither and thither, casting away their armour; many on their knees desired to have their lives saved.

In the mean season, while the battle thus continued, and that the Englishmen had taken a great number of prisoners, certain Frenchmen on horseback, whereof were Captains Robinet of Borneville, Rifflart of Clamas, Isambert of Agincourt, and other men of arms, to the number of six hundred horsemen, which were the first that fled, hearing that the English tents and pavilions were a good way distant from the army, without any sufficient guard to defend the same, either upon a covetous meaning to gain by the spoil, or upon a desire to be revenged, entered upon the King's camp, and there spoiled the hails, robbed the tents, brake up chests, and carried away caskets, and slew such servants as they found to make any resistance. For which treason and haskardie in thus leaving their camp at the very point of fight, for winning of spoil where none to defend it, very many were after committed to prison, and had lost their lives, if the Dauphin had longer lived.

But when the outcry of the lackeys and boys, which

ran away for fear of the Frenchmen thus spoiling the camp, came to the King's ears, he doubting lest his enemies shall gather together again, and begin a new field; and mistrusting further that the prisoners would be an aid to his enemies, or the very enemies to their takers indeed if they were suffered to live, contrary to his accustomed gentleness, commanded by sound of trumpet that every man (upon pain of death) should incontinently slay his prisoner. When this dolorous decree, and pitiful proclamation was pronounced, pity it was to see how some Frenchmen were suddenly sticked with daggers, some were brained with pole-axes, some slain with malls, others had their throats cut, and some their bellies paunched, so that in effect, having respect to the great number, few prisoners were saved.

When this lamentable slaughter was ended, the Englishmen disposed themselves in order of battle, ready to abide a new field, and also to invade, and newly set on their enemies, with great force they assailed the Earls of Marle and Fauconberg, and the Lords of Lourreie and of Thine, with six hundred men of arms, who had all that day kept together, but now slain and beaten down out of hand. Some write, that the King perceiving his enemies in one part to assemble together, as though they meant to give a new battle for preservation of the prisoners, sent to them an herald, commanding them either to depart out of his sight, or else to come forward at once, and give battle: promising herewith, that if they did offer to fight again, not only those prisoners which his people already had taken; but also so many of them as in this new conflict which they thus attempted should fall into his hands, should die the death without redemption.

The Frenchmen fearing the sentence of so terrible a decree, without further delay parted out of the field.

And so about four of the clock in the afternoon, the King when he saw no appearance of enemies caused the retreat to be blown; and gathering his army together, gave thanks to almighty God for so happy a victory, causing his prelates and chaplains to sing this psalm: *In exitu Israel de Aegypto,* and commanded every man to kneel down on the ground at this verse: *Non nobis Domine, non nobis, sed nomini tuo da gloriam.* Which done, he caused *Te Deum* with certain anthems to be sung, giving laud and praise to God, without boasting of his own force or any human power. That night he and his people took rest, and refreshed themselves with such victuals as they found in the French camp, but lodged in the same village where he lay the night before.

In the morning, Montjoy King-at-Arms and four other French heralds came to the king to know the number of prisoners, and to desire burial for the dead. Before he made them answer (to understand what they would say) he demanded of them why they made to him that request, considering that he knew not whether the victory was his or theirs? When Montjoy by true and just confession had cleared that doubt to the high praise of the King, he desired of Montjoy to understand the name of the castle near adjoining; when they had told him that it was called Agincourt, he said, "Then shall this conflict be called the battle of Agincourt." He feasted the French officers of arms that day, and granted them their request, which busily sought through the field for such as were slain. But the Englishmen suffered them not to go alone, for they searched with them, and found many hurt, but not in jeopardy of their lives, whom they took prisoners, and brought them to their tents. When the King of England had well refreshed himself, and his soldiers, that had taken the spoil of such as were slain, he with his prisoners in good order returned to his town of Calais.

[FROM *Chronicles of England, Scotland, and Ireland*]

Edward Hall

THE WARS OF THE ROSES

DURING this time the King called a parliament, in the city of Coventry, in the which the Duke of York and all his confederates were attainted of high treason, and their goods and lands confiscated and forfeited: and to prohibit their landing in all parts, haven towns were watched, and the sea coasts were garnished with beacons. And Sir Simon Montfort with a great crew, was appointed to keep the Downs, and the Five Ports, and all men passing into Flanders, were, upon pain of death, prohibited to pass by Calais, lest the lords there, should borrow of them any money, as they did, pressed of the merchants of the staple late before, which was a great displeasure to the King and a more corasey to the Queen. The lords lying at Calais were not ignorant of all these doings and provisions, but daily were ascertained what was done in the King's privy chamber: wherefore first they sent a company to Sandwich which conquered the town, and apprehended Sir Simon Montford, and brought him with all his mates to the Haven of Calais, where incontinent, he with twelve of his chief fellows, lost their heads on the sands, before Risebank. After the King's navy gained, and his captains on the arrival of the sea taken and destroyed, the lords living at Calais, hoping in their friends within the realm determined to pass the sea and to land in England. And after they had put the castle and town of Calais in sure and safe custody to their only use, they passed the sea and landed at Sandwich. And so passing through Kent, there came to them the Lord Cobham, John Guildford, William Peche, Robert Horne, and many other gentlemen, which conveyed them to the city of London. But the fame of their landing once known, gentlemen repaired and yeomen resorted out of all the southern parts of the realm: upon which rumour Thomas Lord Scales, a man in great favour with the King and Queen, accompanied with the Earl of Kendale, a Gascoyn, and the Lord Lovel, resorted to London with a great company of armed men; declaring to the Mayor of the city, that their repair only was to defend, and to keep the city from the spoil and robbery of such traitors, as the King was credibly informed would thither make access. To whom the Mayor answered, that he well knew both his own oath, and bounden duty toward his sovereign lord and prince, and needed neither of prompter nor yet of co-adjutor; either to defend or govern the city to him committed in charge. With which answer, the Lord Scales and his associates not a little displeased, entered into the Tower of London, daily with new inventions, doing displeasures and damages to the citizens of the city whom they sore suspected rather to favour than to hate, the Earls of March and Warwick and others of their band and affinity. Which earls with a great army came shortly to London, and were of the Mayor and citizens joyously received, to whom resorted the Archbishop of Canterbury, the Bishops of London, Ely and Exeter, with many prelates and religious persons. These lords nothing slacking the purpose that they came for, daily consulted and assembled together in the house of the

Friars Franciscan within the city. After long debating, and secret consultation had, it was agreed, that they with their whole puissance should march forward towards the King: determining either by force or fair means to bring their purpose to a conclusion.

When this council was dissolved, the Earls of March and Warwick, Thomas Lord Faulconbridge, Henry Lord Bouchier, called Earl of Eue, with a great number of men which came out of Kent, Essex, Surrey and Sussex to the number as some persons affirm of 25,000 persons departed from London, towards the King lying at Coventry, then called the Queen's secret arbour, leaving behind them to keep the Londoners in their fidelity from reverting from their part, the Earl of Salisbury, the Lord Cobham, and Sir John Wenlock: which Lord Cobham with certain aldermen of the City, so kept the west side against the Tower, and Sir John Wenlock with others so vigilantly watched the east part towards St. Katharine's, that no person either could issue out or enter in, to the great displeasure of the Lord Scales and his company, which daily shot their ordnance out and had likewise great ordnance shot at them, to the hurt and no pleasure of both parties.

The King not ignorant of all these doings, assembled a great army and accompanied by the Duke of Somerset, which was lately come from Guisnes, and the Duke of Buckingham, and divers other great lords of his party and faction came to the town of Northampton, where the Queen encouraged her friends, and promised great rewards to her helpers: for the King studied nothing but of peace, quiet and solitary life. When the King's host was assembled, and that the Queen perceived that her power was able to match with the forces of her adversaries, she caused her army to issue out of the towne and to pass the river Nene, and there in the new field, between Harsington and Sandiford, the captains strongly emparked themselves with high banks and deep trenches.

The Earl of March being lusty, and in the flower of his courageous youth—lying betweene Towcester and Northampton, determined to set on the King's army without longer protracting of time. In the night-season he removed his camp towards Northampton, and in marching forward set his men in good order of battle, whereof the vanguard was conducted by the Earl of Warwick, which either by stealth or strength, malgré the Lord Beauman, which kept a straight going towards the King's camp, entered freshly, and began the battle about seven of the clock, the ninth day of July. After whom followed the Earl of March with the banner of his father.

This fight continued in doubtful judgment till the hour of nine, at which time the King's army was profligate and discomfitted, and of the same, slain, and drowned in the river few less than 10,000 tall Englishmen, and the King himself left alone disconsolate, was taken and apprehended, as a man born and predestinate to trouble, misery and calamity. . . .

ARTICLES OF AGREEMENT BETWEEN KING HENRY VI. AND RICHARD DUKE OF YORK

AFTER long arguments made and deliberate consultation had among the peers, prelates and commons of the realm: upon the Vigil of All Saints, it was condescended and agreed by the three Estates, for so much as King Henry had been taken as king by the space of thirty-eight years and more, that he should enjoy the name and title of King and have possession of the realm during his life natural: and if he either died or resigned or forfeited the same, for infringing any point of this concord, then the said crown and authority royal, should immediately be divoluted to the Duke of York, if he then lived or else to the next heir of his line or lineage, and that the duke from thenceforth should be protector and regent of the land. Provided always that if the King did closely or aptly study or go about to break or alter this agreement to compass or imagine the death or destruction of the said Duke or his blood, then he to forfeit the crown, and the Duke of York to take it. The articles, with many other, were not only written, sealed and sworn by the two parties, but also enacted, in the High Court of Parliament. For joy whereof, the King having in his company the said Duke, rode to the Cathedral Church of Saint Paul, within the city of London and there on the Day of All Saints, went solemnly with the diadem on his head, in procession, and was lodged a good space after in the bishop's palace near to the said Church. And upon the Saturday next issuing, Richard Duke of York was by the sound of a trumpet solemnly proclaimed heir apparent to the crown of England and protector of the realm.

After this the parliament kept at Coventry the last year was declared to be a devilish council and only celebrate for the destruction of the nobility; and no lawful parliament because they which were returned were never elected according to the due order of the law, but secretly named by them which desired more the destruction than the enhancement of the public wealth and common profit. When these agreements were done and enacted, the King dissolved his Parliament, which was the last parliament that ever he ended. . . .

The Duke of York well knowing, that the Queen

would spurn and impugn the conclusions agreed and
taken in this parliament, caused her and her son to be
sent for by the King; but she being a manly woman,
using to rule and not be ruled, and thereto counselled
by the Dukes of Exeter and Somerset, not only denied
not to come but also assembled together a great army,
intending to take the King by fine force, out of the lords'
hands, and to set them to a new school. The protector
living in London, having perfect knowledge of all these
doings; assigned the Duke of Norfolk and the Earl of
Warwick, his trusty friends to be about the King, and
he with the Earls of Salisbury and Rutland: with a convenient company departed out of London, the second
day of December—northward, and sent to the Earl of
March his eldest son to follow him with all his power.

The Duke by small journeys came to his castle of
Sandall, beside Wakefield on Christmas Eve, and there
began to assemble his tenants and friends. The Queen
being thereof ascertained, determined to couple with
him while his power was small and his aid not come.
And so having in her company, the prince her son, the
Dukes of Exeter and Somerset, the Earl of Devonshire,
the Lord Clifford, the Lord Rosse and in effect all the
lords of the north part, with eighteen thousand men, or
as some write twenty two thousand, marched from York
to Wakefield, and bade base to the Duke even before his
castle, he having with him not fully five thousand persons, determined incontinent to issue out and to fight
with his enemies, and although Sir Davy Halle, his old
servant and chief counsellor advised him to keep his
castle and to defend the same with his small number, till
his son the Earl of March were come with his power of
Marchmen and Welsh soldiers.

Yet he would not be counselled, but in a great fury
said, "O Davy, Davy, hast thou loved me so long and

now wouldest have me dishonoured? Thou never sawest
me keep fortress when I was Regent in Normandy, when
the Dauphin himself with his puissance came to besiege
me, but like a man and not like a bird enclosed in a cage,
I issued and fought with mine enemies to their loss, ever
(I thank God) and to my honour. If I have not kept myself within walls for fear of a great and strong prince,
nor hid my face from any man living, wouldst thou that
I for dread of a scolding woman, whose weapon is only
her tongue, and her nails should incarcerate myself and
shut my gates, then all men might of me wonder and
all creatures may of me report dishonour, that a woman
hath made me a dastard, who no man ever to this day
could yet prove a coward: And surely my mind is,
rather to die with honour than to live with shame. For
of honour cometh fame, and of dishonour riseth infamy.
Their great number shall not appal my spirits, but encourage them, for surely, I think that I have there as
many friends as enemies, which at joining will either fly
or take my part. Therefore, advance my banner. In the
name of God and Saint George, for surely I will fight
with them though I should fight alone."

[FROM Hall's *Chronicle*]

PART SEVEN

An Age of Song

Sir Philip Sidney

AN APOLOGY FOR POETRY

B<small>UT SINCE</small> the authors of most of our sciences were the Romans, and before them the Greeks, let us a little stand upon their authorities, but even so far as to see what names they have given unto this now scorned skill. Among the Romans a poet was called *vates*, which is as much as a diviner, forseer, or prophet, as by his conjoined words, *vaticinium* and *vaticinari*, is manifest; so heavenly a title did that excellent people bestow upon this heart-ravishing knowledge. And so far were they carried into the admiration thereof, that they thought in the chanceable hitting upon any such verses great foretokens of their following fortunes were placed; whereupon grew the word of *Sortes Virgilianæ*, when by sudden opening Virgil's book they lighted upon some verse of his making. Whereof the histories of the emperors' lives are full: as of Albinus, the governor of our island, who in his childhood met with this verse,

Arma amens capio, nec sat rationis in armis,

and in his age performed it. Although it were a very vain and godless superstition, as also it was to think that spirits were commanded by such verses—whereupon this word charms, derived of *carmina*, cometh—so yet serveth it to show the great reverence those wits were held in, and altogether not without ground, since both

587

the oracles of Delphos and Sibylla's prophecies were wholly delivered in verses; for that same exquisite observing of number and measure in words, and that high-flying liberty of conceit proper to the poet, did seem to have some divine force in it.

And may not I presume a little further to show the reasonableness of this word *vates,* and say that the holy David's Psalms are a divine poem? If I do, I shall not do it without the testimony of great learned men, both ancient and modern. But even the name of psalms will speak for me, which, being interpreted, is nothing but songs; then, that it is fully written in meter, as all learned Hebricians agree, although the rules be not yet fully found; lastly and principally, his handling his prophecy, which is merely poetical. For what else is the awaking his musical instruments, the often and free changing of persons, his notable *prosopopœias,* when he maketh you, as it were, see God coming in his majesty, his telling of the beasts' joyfulness and hills' leaping, but a heavenly poesy, wherein almost he showeth himself a passionate lover of that unspeakable and everlasting beauty to be seen by the eyes of the mind only cleared by faith? But truly now having named him, I fear I seem to profane that holy name, applying it to poetry, which is among us thrown down to so ridiculous an estimation. But they that with quiet judgments will look a little deeper into it, shall find the end and working of it such as, being rightly applied, deserveth not to be scourged out of the church of God.

But now let us see how the Greeks named it and how they deemed of it. The Greeks called him ποιητήν, which name hath, as the most excellent, gone through other languages. It cometh of this word ποιεῖν, which is "to make"; wherein I know not whether by luck or wisdom we Englishmen have met with the Greeks in calling him a maker. Which name how high and incomparable a title it is, I had rather were known by marking the scope of other sciences than by any partial allegation. There is no art delivered unto mankind that hath not the works of nature for his principal object, without which they could not consist, and on which they so depend as they become actors and players, as it were, of what nature will have set forth. So doth the astronomer look upon the stars, and, by that he seeth, set down what order nature hath taken therein. So do the geometrician and arithmetician in their divers sorts of quantities. So doth the musician in times tell you which by nature agree, which not. The natural philosopher thereon hath his name, and the moral philosopher standeth upon the natural virtues, vices, and passions of man; and "follow nature," saith he, "therein, and thou shalt not err." The lawyer saith what men have determined, the historian what men have done. The grammarian speaketh only of the rules of speech, and the rhetorician and logician, considering what in nature will soonest prove and persuade, thereon give artificial rules, which still are compassed within the circle of a question, according to the proposed matter. The physician weigheth the nature of man's body, and the nature of things helpful or hurtful unto it. And the metaphysic, though it be in the second and abstract notions, and therefore be counted supernatural, yet doth he, indeed, build upon the depth of nature.

Only the poet, disdaining to be tied to any such subjection, lifted up with the vigor of his own invention, doth grow, in effect, into another nature, in making things either better than nature bringeth forth, or, quite anew, forms such as never were in nature, as the heroes, demi-gods, cyclops, chimeras, furies, and such like; so as he goeth hand in hand with nature, not enclosed within the narrow warrant of her gifts, but freely rang-

ing within the zodiac of his own wit. Nature never set
forth the earth in so rich tapestry as divers poets have
done; neither with pleasant rivers, fruitful trees, sweet-
smelling flowers, nor whatsoever else may make the too-
much-loved earth more lovely; her world is brazen, the
poets only deliver a golden.

But let those things alone, and go to man—for whom
as the other things are, so it seemeth in him her uttermost cunning is employed—and know whether she have
brought forth so true a lover as Theagenes; so constant
a friend as Pylades; so valiant a man as Orlando; so
right a prince as Xenophon's Cyrus; so excellent a man
every way as Virgil's Aeneas? Neither let this be jest-
ingly conceived, because the works of the one be essential, the other in imitation or fiction; for any understanding knoweth the skill of each artificer standeth in that
idea, or fore-conceit of the work, and not in the work
itself. And that the poet hath that idea is manifest, by
delivering them forth in such excellency as he hath
imagined them. Which delivering forth, also, is not
wholly imaginative, as we are wont to say by them that
build castles in the air; but so far substantially it
worketh, not only to make a Cyrus, which had been but
a particular excellency, as nature might have done, but
to bestow a Cyrus upon the world to make many
Cyruses, if they will learn aright why and how that
maker made him. Neither let it be deemed too saucy a
comparison to balance the highest point of man's wit
with the efficacy of nature; but rather give right honor to
the heavenly Maker of that maker, who, having made
man to his own likeness, set him beyond and over all the
works of that second nature. Which in nothing he showeth so much as in poetry, when with the force of a divine
breath he bringeth things forth far surpassing her
doings, with no small argument to the incredulous of

that first accursed fall of Adam—since our erected wit maketh us know what perfection is, and yet our infected will keepeth us from reaching unto it. But these arguments will by few be understood, and by fewer granted; thus much I hope will be given me, that the Greeks with some probability of reason gave him the name above all names of learning.

Now let us go to a more ordinary opening of him, that the truth may be the more palpable; and so, I hope, though we get not so unmatched a praise as the etymology of his names will grant, yet his very description, which no man will deny, shall not justly be barred from a principal commendation.

Poesy, therefore, is an art of imitation, for so Aristotle termeth it in his word μίμησις, that is to say, a representing, counterfeiting, or figuring forth; to speak metaphorically, a speaking picture, with this end—to teach and delight.

Of this have been three general kinds. The chief, both in antiquity and excellency, were they that did imitate the inconceivable excellencies of God. Such were David in his Psalms; Solomon in his Song of Songs, in his Ecclesiastes and Proverbs; Moses and Deborah in their hymns; and the writer of Job; which, beside other, the learned Emanuel Tremellius and Franciscus Junius do entitle the poetical part of the Scripture. Against these none will speak that hath the Holy Ghost in due holy reverence. In this kind, though in a full wrong divinity, were Orpheus, Amphion, Homer in his hymns, and many other, both Greeks and Romans. And this poesy must be used by whosoever will follow St. James' counsel in singing psalms when they are merry; and I know is used with the fruit of comfort by some, when, in sorrowful pangs of their death-bringing sins, they find the consolation of the never-leaving goodness.

The second kind is of them that deal with matters philosophical: either moral, as Tyrtæus, Phocylides, and Cato; or natural, as Lucretius and Virgil's *Georgics;* or astronomical, as Manilius and Pontanus; or historical, as Lucan; which who mislike, the fault is in their judgment quite out of taste, and not in the sweet food of sweetly uttered knowledge.

But because this second sort is wrapped within the fold of the proposed subject, and takes not the free course of his own invention, whether they properly be poets or no let grammarians dispute; and go to the third, indeed right poets, of whom chiefly this question ariseth. Betwixt whom and these second is such a kind of difference as betwixt the meaner sort of painters, who counterfeit only such faces as are set before them, and the more excellent, who having no law but wit, bestow that in colors upon you which is fittest for the eye to see —as the constant though lamenting look of Lucretia, when she punished in herself another's fault; wherein he painteth not Lucretia, whom he never saw, but painteth the outward beauty of such a virtue. For these third be they which most properly do imitate to teach and delight; and to imitate borrow nothing of what is, hath been, or shall be; but range, only reined with learned discretion, into the divine consideration of what may be and should be. These be they that, as the first and most noble sort may justly be termed *vates,* so these are waited on in the excellentest languages and best understandings with the foredescribed name of poets. For these, indeed, do merely make to imitate, and imitate both to delight and teach, and delight to move men to take that goodness in hand, which without delight they would fly as from a stranger; and teach to make them know that goodness whereunto they are moved; which being the noblest scope to which ever any learning was directed, yet want there not idle tongues to bark at them. . . .

Now therein of all sciences—I speak still of human, and according to the human conceit—is our poet the monarch. For he doth not only show the way, but giveth so sweet a prospect into the way as will entice any man to enter into it. Nay, he doth, as if your journey should lie through a fair vineyard, at the very first give you a cluster of grapes, that full of that taste you may long to pass further. He beginneth not with obscure definitions, which must blur the margent with interpretations, and load the memory with doubtfulness. But he cometh to you with words set in delightful proportion, either accompanied with, or prepared for, the well-enchanting skill of music; and with a tale, forsooth, he cometh unto you with a tale which holdeth children from play, and old men from the chimney-corner, and, pretending no more, doth intend the winning of the mind from wickedness to virtue; even as the child is often brought to take most wholesome things, by hiding them in such other as have a pleasant taste—which, if one should begin to tell them the nature of the aloes or rhubarb they should receive, would sooner take their physic at their ears than at their mouth. So is it in men, most of which are childish in the best things, till they be cradled in their graves—glad they will be to hear the tales of Hercules, Achilles, Cyrus, Aeneas; and, hearing them, must needs hear the right description of wisdom, valor, and justice; which, if they had been barely, that is to say philosophically, set out, they would swear they be brought to school again.

That imitation whereof poetry is, hath the most conveniency to nature of all other; insomuch that, as Aristotle saith, those things which in themselves are horrible, as cruel battles, unnatural monsters, are made in poetical imitation delightful. Truly, I have known men, that even with reading *Amadis de Gaule*, which, God knoweth, wanteth much of a perfect poesy, have found their hearts moved to the exercise of courtesy, liberality, and especially courage. Who readeth Aeneas carrying old Anchises on his back, that wisheth not it were his fortune to perform so excellent an act? Whom do not those words of Turnus move, the tale of Turnus having planted his image in the imagination?

Fugientem hæc terra videbit?
Usque adeone mori miserum est?

Where the philosophers, as they scorn to delight, so must they be content little to move—saving wrangling whether virtue be the chief or the only good, whether the contemplative or the active life do excel—which Plato and Boethius well knew, and therefore made Mistress Philosophy very often borrow the masking raiment of Poesy. For even those hard-hearted evil men who think virtue a school-name, and know no other good but *indulgere genio,* and therefore despise the austere admonitions of the philosopher, and feel not the inward reason they stand upon, yet will be content to be delighted, which is all the good-fellow poet seemeth to promise; and so steal to see the form of goodness—which seen, they cannot but love—ere themselves be aware, as if they took a medicine of cherries. . . .

Is it the lyric that most displeaseth, who with his tuned lyre and well-accorded voice giveth praise, the reward of virtue, to virtuous acts; who giveth moral precepts and natural problems; who sometimes raiseth up his voice to the height of the heavens, in singing the lauds of the immortal God? Certainly I must confess mine own barbarousness; I never heard the old song of Percy and Douglas that I found not my heart moved more than with a trumpet; and yet it is sung but by some blind crowder, with no rougher voice than rude style; which being so evil apparelled in the dust and cobwebs of that uncivil age, what would it work, trimmed in the gorgeous eloquence of Pindar? In Hungary I have seen it the manner at all feasts, and other such meetings, to have songs of their ancestors' valour, which that right soldier-like nation think the chiefest kindlers of brave courage. The incomparable Lacedæmonians did not only carry that kind of music ever with them to the field, but even at home, as such songs were made, so were they all content to be singers of them; when the lusty men were to tell what they did, the old men what they had done, and the young men what they would do. And where a man may say that Pindar many times praiseth highly victories of small moment, matters rather of sport than virtue; as it may be answered, it was the fault of the poet, and not of the poetry, so indeed the chief fault was in the time and custom of the Greeks, who set those toys at so high a price that Philip of Macedon reckoned a horserace won at Olympus among his three fearful felicities. But as the unimitable Pindar often did, so is that kind most capable and most fit to awake the thoughts from the sleep of idleness, to embrace honorable enterprises. . . .

But I, that before ever I durst aspire unto the dignity am admitted into the company of the paper-blurrers, do find the very true cause of our wanting estimation is want of desert, taking upon us to be poets in despite of Pallas. Now wherein we want desert were a thankworthy labor to express; but if I knew, I should have mended myself. But as I never desired the title, so have I neglected the means to come by it; only, overmastered by some thoughts, I yielded an inky tribute unto them. Marry, they that delight in poesy itself should seek to know what they do and how they do; and especially look themselves in an unflattering glass of reason, if they be inclinable unto it. For poesy must not be drawn by the ears, it must be gently led, or rather it must lead; which was partly the cause that made the ancient learned affirm it was a divine gift, and no human skill, since all other knowledges lie ready for any that hath strength of wit, a poet no industry can make if his own genius be not carried into it. And therefore is it an old proverb: *orator fit, poeta nascitur.* . . .

Chaucer, undoubtedly, did excellently in his *Troilus and Cressida;* of whom, truly, I know not whether to marvel more, either that he in that misty time could see so clearly, or that we in this clear age walk so stumblingly after him. Yet had he great wants, fit to be forgiven in so reverend antiquity. I account the *Mirror of Magistrates* meetly furnished of beautiful parts; and in the Earl of Surrey's lyrics many things tasting of a noble birth, and worthy of a noble mind. *The Shepherd's Calendar* hath much poetry in his eclogues, indeed worthy the reading, if I be not deceived. That same framing of his style to an old rustic language I dare not allow, since neither Theocritus in Greek, Virgil in Latin, nor Sannazzaro in Italian did affect it. Besides these, I do not remember to have seen but few (to speak boldly) printed, that have poetical sinews in them. For proof whereof, let but most of the verses be put in prose, and then ask the meaning, and it will be found that one verse did but beget another, without ordering at the first what should be at the last; which becomes a confused mass of words, with a tinkling sound of rhyme, barely accompanied with reason.

Our tragedies and comedies not without cause cried out against, observing rules neither of honest civility nor of skillful poetry, excepting *Gorboduc* (again I say of those that I have seen), which notwithstanding as it is full of stately speeches and well-sounding phrases, climbing to the height of Seneca's style, and as full of notable morality, which it doth most delightfully teach, and so obtain the very end of poesy; yet in truth it is very defectious in the cricumstances, which grieveth me, because it might not remain as an exact model of all tragedies. For it is faulty both in place and time, the two necessary companions of all corporal actions; for where the stage should always represent but one place, and the uttermost time presupposed in it should be, both by Aristotle's precept and common reason, but one day, there is both many days and many places inartificially imagined.

But if it be so in *Gorboduc,* how much more in all the rest? where you shall have Asia of the one side, and Afric of the other, and so many other under-kingdoms, that the player, when he cometh in, must ever begin with telling where he is, or else the tale will not be conceived. Now ye shall have three ladies walk to gather flowers, and then we must believe the stage to be a garden. By and by we hear news of shipwreck in the same place, and then we are to blame if we accept it not for a rock. Upon the back of that comes out a hideous monster with fire and smoke, and then the miserable beholders are bound to take it for a cave. While in the meantime two armies fly in, represented with four swords and bucklers, and then what hard heart will not receive it for a pitched field?

Now of time they are much more liberal. For ordinary it is that two young princes fall in love; after many traverses she is got with child, delivered of a fair boy, he is lost, groweth a man, falleth in love, and is ready to get another child—and all this in two hours' space; which how absurd it is in sense even sense may imagine, and art hath taught, and all ancient examples justified, and at this day the ordinary players in Italy will not err in. Yet will some bring in an example of *Eunuchus* in Terence, that containeth matter of two days, yet far short of twenty years. True it is, and so was it to be played in two days, and so fitted to the time it set forth. And though Plautus have in one place done amiss, let us hit with him, and not miss with him. But they will say, How then shall we set forth a story which containeth both many places and many times? And do they not know that a tragedy is tied to the laws of poesy, and not of history; not bound to follow the story, but having liberty either to feign a quite new matter, or to frame the history to the most tragical conveniency? Again, many things may be told which cannot be showed—if they know the difference betwixt reporting and representing. As for example I may speak, though I am here, of Peru, and in speech digress from that to the description of Calicut; but in action I cannot represent it without Pacolet's horse. And so was the manner the ancients took, by some *nuntius* to recount things done in former time or other place.

Lastly, if they will represent a history, they must not, as Horace saith, begin *ab ovo*, but they must come to the principal point of that one action which they will represent. By example this will be best expressed. I have a story of young Polydorus, delivered for safety's sake, with great riches, by his Father Priamus to Polymnestor, King of Thrace, in the Trojan war time. He, after some years, hearing the overthrow of Priamus, for to make the treasure his own murdereth the child; the body of the child is taken up by Hecuba; she, the same day, findeth a sleight to be revenged most cruelly of the tyrant. Where now would one of our tragedy-writers begin, but with the delivery of the child? Then should

he sail over into Thrace, and so spend I know not how
many years, and travel numbers of places. But where
doth Euripides? Even with the finding of the body, leaving the rest to be told by the spirit of Polydorus. This
needs no further to be enlarged; the dullest wit may conceive it.

But, besides these gross absurdities, how all their
plays be neither right tragedies nor right comedies, min-
gling kings and clowns, not because the matter so carrieth it, but thrust in the clown by head and shoulders
to play a part in majestical matters, with neither decency
nor discretion; so as neither the admiration and commiseration, nor the right sportfulness, is by their mongrel
tragi-comedy obtained. I know Apuleius did somewhat
so, but that is a thing recounted with space of time, not
represented in one moment; and I know the ancients
have one or two examples of tragi-comedies, as Plautus
hath *Amphytrio*. But, if we mark them well, we shall
find that they never, or very daintily, match hornpipes
and funerals. So falleth it out that, having indeed no
right comedy in that comical part of our tragedy, we
have nothing but scurrility, unworthy of any chaste ears,
or some extreme show of doltishness, indeed fit to lift up
a loud laughter, and nothing else; where the whole tract
of a comedy should be full of delight, as the tragedy
should be still maintained in a well-raised admiration.

But our comedians think there is no delight without
laughter, which is very wrong; for though laughter may
come with delight, yet cometh it not of delight, as
though delight should be the cause of laughter; but well
may one thing breed both together. Nay, rather in themselves they have, as it were, a kind of contrariety. For
delight we scarcely do but in things that have a conveniency to ourselves, or to the general nature; laughter
almost ever cometh of things most disproportioned to

ourselves and nature. Delight hath a joy in it either permanent or present; laughter hath only a scornful tickling. For example, we are ravished with delight to see a fair woman, and yet are far from being moved to laughter. We laugh at deformed creatures, wherein certainly we cannot delight. We delight in good chances, we laugh at mischances. We delight to hear the happiness of our friends and country, at which he were worthy to be laughed at that would laugh. We shall, contrarily, laugh sometimes to find a matter quite mistaken and go down the hill against the bias, in the mouth of some such men, as for the respect of them one shall be heartily sorry he cannot choose but laugh, and so is rather pained than delighted with laughter. Yet deny I not but that they may go well together. For as in Alexander's picture well set out we delight without laughter, and in twenty mad antics we laugh without delight; so in Hercules, painted, with his great beard and furious countenance, in woman's attire, spinning at Omphale's commandment, it breedeth both delight and laughter; for the representing of so strange a power in love procureth delight, and the scornfulness of the action stirreth laughter.

But I speak to this purpose, that all the end of the comical part be not upon such scornful matters as stir laughter only, but mixed with it that delightful teaching which is the end of poesy. And the great fault, even in that point of laughter, and forbidden plainly by Aristotle, is that they stir laughter in sinful things, which are rather execrable than ridiculous; or in miserable, which are rather to be pitied than scorned. For what is it to make folks gape at a wretched beggar or a beggarly clown, or, against law of hospitality, to jest at strangers because they speak not English so well as we do? What do we learn? since it is certain,

Nil habet infelix paupertas durius in se,
Quam quod ridiculos homines facit.

But rather a busy loving courtier; a heartless threatening Thraso; a self-wise-seeming schoolmaster; a wry-transformed traveler: these if we saw walk in stage-names, which we play naturally, therein were delightful laughter and teaching delightfulness—as in the other, the tragedies of Buchanan do justly bring forth a divine admiration.

But I have lavished out too many words of this play-matter. I do it, because as they are excelling parts of poesy, so is there none so much used in England, and none can be more pitifully abused; which, like an unmannerly daughter, showing a bad education, causeth her mother Poesy's honesty to be called in question.

Other sorts of poetry almost have we none, but that lyrical kind of songs and sonnets, which, Lord if he gave us so good minds, how well it might be employed, and with how heavenly fruits both private and public, in singing the praises of the immortal beauty, the immortal goodness of that God who giveth us hands to write, and wits to conceive—of which we might well want words, but never matter; of which we could turn our eyes to nothing, but we should ever have new-budding occasions.

But truly, many of such writings as come under the banner of unresistible love, if I were a mistress would never persuade me they were in love; so coldly they apply fiery speeches, as men that had rather read lovers' writings, and so caught up certain swelling phrases—which hang together like a man which once told me the wind was at north-west and by south, because he would be sure to name winds enough—than that in truth they feel those passions, which easily, as I think, may be bewrayed by that same forcibleness, or *energia* (as the Greeks call it) of the writer. But let this be a sufficient, though short note, that we miss the right use of the material point of poesy.

Now for the outside of it, which is words, or (as I may term it) diction, it is even well worse, so is that honey-flowing matron eloquence apparelled, or rather disguised, in a courtesan-like painted affectation: one time with so far-fet words, that many seem monsters—but must seem strangers—to any poor Englishman; another time with coursing of a letter, as if they were bound to follow the method of a dictionary; another time with figures and flowers extremely winter-starved.

But I would this fault were only peculiar to versifiers, and had not as large possession among prose-printers, and, which is to be marvelled, among many scholars, and, which is to be pitied, among some preachers. Truly I could wish—if at least I might be so bold to wish in a thing beyond the reach of my capacity—the diligent imitators of Tully and Demosthenes (most worthy to be imitated) did not so much keep Nizolian paper-books of their figures and phrases, as by attentive translation, as it were, devour them whole, and make them wholly theirs. For now they cast sugar and spice upon every dish that is served to the table; like those Indians, not content to wear earrings at the fit and natural place of the ears, but they will thrust jewels through their nose and lips, because they will be sure to be fine. . . .

Now of versifying there are two sorts, the one ancient, the other modern. The ancient marked the quantity of each syllable, and according to that framed his verse; the modern observing only number, with some regard of the accent, the chief life of it standeth in that like sounding of the words, which we call rhyme. Whether of these be the more excellent would bear many speeches; the ancient no doubt more fit for music, both words and tune observing quantity; and more fit lively to express divers passions, by the low or lofty sound of the well-weighed syllable. The latter likewise with his rhyme striketh a certain music to the ear; and, in fine, since it doth delight, though by another way, it obtaineth the same purpose; there being in either, sweetness, and wanting in neither, majesty. Truly the English, before any other vulgar language I know, is fit for both sorts. For, for the ancient, the Italian is so full of vowels that it must ever be cumbered with elisions; the Dutch so, of the other side, with consonants, that they cannot yield the sweet sliding fit for a verse. The French in his whole language hath not one word that hath his accent in the last syllable saving two, called antepenultima, and little more hath the Spanish; and therefore very gracelessly may they use dactyls. The English is subject to none of these defects. Now for rhyme, though we do not observe quantity, yet we observe the accent very precisely, which other languages either cannot do, or will not do so absolutely. That cæsura, or breathing-place in the midst of the verse, neither Italian nor Spanish have, the French and we never almost fail of.

Lastly, even the very rhyme itself the Italian cannot put in the last syllable, by the French named the masculine rhyme, but still in the next to the last, which the French call the female, or the next before that, which the Italians term *sdrucciola*. The example of the former is *buono: suono;* of the *sdrucciola* is *femina: semina.* The French, of the other side, hath both the male, as *bon: son,* and the female, as *plaise: taise;* but the *sdrucciola* he hath not. Where the English hath all three, as *due: true; father: rather; motion: potion;* with much more which might be said, but that already I find the triflingness of this discourse is much too much enlarged.

So that since the ever praiseworthy poesy is full of virtue-breeding delightfulness, and void of no gift that ought to be in the noble name of learning; since the blames laid against it are either false or feeble; since the cause why it is not esteemed in England is the fault of poet-apes, not poets; since, lastly, our tongue is most fit to honor poesy, and to be honored by poesy; I conjure you all that have had the evil luck to read this ink-wasting toy of mine, even in the name of the Nine Muses, no more to scorn the sacred mysteries of poesy; no more to laugh at the name of poets, as though they were next inheritors to fools; no more to jest at the reverend title of a "rhymer"; but to believe, with Aristotle, that they were the ancient treasurers of the Grecians' divinity; to believe, with Bembus, that they were the first bringers-in of all civility; to believe, with Scaliger, that no philosopher's precepts can sooner make you an honest man than the reading of Virgil; to believe, with Clauserus, the translator of Cornutus, that it pleased the heavenly deity by Hesiod and Homer, under the veil of fables, to give us all knowledge, logic, rhetoric, philosophy natural and moral, and *quid non;* to believe, with me, that there are many mysteries contained in poetry which of purpose were written darkly, lest by profane wits it should be abused; to believe, with Landino, that they are so beloved of the gods, that whatsoever they write proceeds of a divine fury; lastly, to believe themselves, when they tell you they will make you immortal by their verses. . . .

But if—fie of such a but!—you be born so near the dull-making cataract of Nilus, that you cannot hear the planet-like music of poetry; if you have so earth-creeping a mind that it cannot lift itself up to look to the sky of poetry, or rather, by a certain rustical disdain, will become such a mome as to be a Momus of poetry; then, though I will not wish unto you the ass's ears of Midas, nor to be driven by a poet's verses, as Bubonax was, to hang himself; nor to be rhymed to death, as is said to be done in Ireland; yet thus much curse I must send you in the behalf of all poets: that while you live you live in love, and never get favor for lacking skill of a sonnet; and when you die, your memory die from the earth for want of an epitaph.

Sir Thomas Wyatt

SONNETS AND LYRICS

WHOSO LIST TO HUNT

Whoso list to hunt, I know where is a hind,
    But as for me—alas, I may no more.
    The vain travail has wearied me so sore,
    I am of them that farthest come behind.
Yet may I, by no means, my wearied mind
    Draw from the deer; but as she fleeth afore
    Fainting I follow. I leave off therefore,
    Since in a net I seek to hold the wind.
Who list her hunt, I put him out of doubt,
    As well as I, may spend his time in vain.
    And graven with diàmonds in letters plain
There is written, her fair neck round about:
    Noli me tangere, for Caesar's I am,
    And wilde for to hold, though I seem tame.

TO A LADY, TO ANSWER DIRECTLY
WITH YEA OR NAY

Madam, withouten many words,
Once I am sure, you will or no;
And if you will, then leave your bordes,
And use your wit, and show it so;
For with a beck you shall me call.
And if of one that burns alway
Ye have pity or ruth at all,
Answer him fair, with yea or nay:
If it be yea, I shall be fain;
If it be nay, friends as before;
You shall another man obtain,
And I mine own, and yours no more.

THE LOVER SHOWETH HOW HE IS FORSAKEN
OF SUCH AS HE SOMETIME ENJOYED

They flee from me, that sometime did me seek,
With naked foot stalking within my chamber.
Once have I seen them gentle, tame, and meek,
That now are wild, and do not once remember
That sometime they have put themselves in danger
To take bread at my hand; and now they range,
Busily seeking in continual change.
　　Thanked be fortune it hath been otherwise,
Twenty times better; but once especïal,
In thin array, after a pleasant guise,
When her loose gown did from her shoulders fall,
And she me caught in her arms long and small,
And therewithal so sweetly did me kiss
And softly said, Dear heart, how like you this?

It was no dream, for I lay broad awaking.
But all is turned now, through my gentleness,
Into a bitter fashion of forsaking;
And I have leave to go, of her goodness,
And she also to use newfangleness.
But since that I unkindly so am served,
How like you this? what hath she now deserved?

FORGET NOT YET

Forget not yet the tried intent
Of such a truth as I have meant,
My great travail, so gladly spent,
        Forget not yet.

Forget not yet when first began
The weary life ye know, since when
The suit, the service none tell can,
        Forget not yet.

Forget not yet the great assays,
The cruel wrong, the scornful ways;
The painful patience in denays,
        Forget not yet.

Forget not yet, forget not this,
How long ago hath been, and is,
The mind that never meant amiss—
        Forget not yet.

Forget not, then, thine own approved,
The which so long hath thee so loved,
Whose steadfast faith yet never moved,
        Forget not yet.

BLAME NOT MY LUTE

Blame not my lute, for he must sound
Of this and that as liketh me;
For lack of wit the lute is bound
To give such tunes as pleaseth me;
Though my songs be somewhat strange,
And speaks such words as touch thy change,
       Blame not my lute.

My lute, alas, doth not offend,
Though that perforce he must agree
To sound such tunes as I intend
To sing to them that heareth me;
Then though my songs be somewhat plain
And toucheth some that use to feign,
       Blame not my lute.

My lute and strings may not deny,
But as I strike they must obey;
Break not them then so wrongfully,
But wreak thyself some wiser way;
And though the songs which I indite
To quit thy change with rightful spite,
       Blame not my lute.

Spite asketh spite, and changing change,
And falsèd faith must needs be known;
The fault so great, the case so strange,
Of right it must abroad be blown.
Then since that by thine own desart
My songs do tell how true thou art,
       Blame not my lute.

Blame but thy self that hast misdone
And well deservèd to have blame;
Charge thou thy way, so evil begun,
And then my lute shall sound that same;
But if till then my fingers play,
By thy desert, their wonted way,
          Blame not my lute.

Farewell, unknown, for though thou break
My strings in spite, with great disdain,
Yet have I found out for thy sake
Strings for to string my lute again:
And if perchance this seely rhyme
Do make thee blush at any time,
          Blame not my lute.

THE LOVER COMPLAINETH THE
UNKINDNESS OF HIS LOVE

My lute, awake, perform the last
Labor that thou and I shall waste,
And end that I have now begun;
And when this song is sung and past,
My lute, be still, for I have done.

  As to be heard where ear is none,
As lead to grave in marble stone,
My song may pierce her heart as soon.
Should we then sigh, or sing, or moan?
No, no, my lute, for I have done.

  The rocks do not so cruelly
Repulse the waves continually,
As she my suit and affection;
So that I am past remedy,
Whereby my lute and I have done.

Proud of the spoil that thou hast got
Of simple hearts, through lovë's shot;
By whom unkind thou hast them won,
Think not he hath his bow forgot,
Although my lute and I have done.

Vengeance shall fall on thy disdain,
That makest but game on earnest pain;
Think not alone under the sun
Unquit to cause thy lovers plain,
Although my lute and I have done.

May chance thee lie withered and old,
In winter nights that are so cold,
Plaining in vain unto the moon;
Thy wishes then dare not be told.
Care then who list, for I have done.

And then may chance thee to repent
The time that thou hast lost and spent
To cause thy lovers sigh and swoon;
Then shalt thou know beauty but lent,
And wish and want as I have done.

Now cease, my lute, this is the last
Labor that thou and I shall waste,
And ended is that we begun.
Now is this song both sung and past,
My lute, be still, for I have done.

Elizabeth

WHEN I WAS FAIR AND YOUNG

When I was fair and young, and favor gracèd me,
Of many was I sought, their mistress for to be;

But I did scorn them all, and answered them therefore,
    "Go, go, go, seek some otherwhere,
      Impòrtune me no more!"

How many weeping eyes I made to pine with woe,
    How many sighing hearts, I have no skill to show;
Yet I the prouder grew, and answered them therefore,
    "Go, go, go, seek some otherwhere,
      Impòrtune me no more!"

Then spake fair Venus' son, that proud victorious boy,
    And said, "Fine dame, since that you be so coy,
I will so pluck your plumes that you shall say no more,
    'Go, go, go, seek some otherwhere,
      Impòrtune me no more!'"

When he had spake these words, such change grew in
    my breast
    That neither night nor day since that, I could take
    any rest.
Then lo! I did repent that I had said before,
    "Go, go, go, seek some otherwhere,
      Impòrtune me no more!"

Robert Devereux, Earl of Essex

TO ELIZABETH

CHANGE THY MIND

Change thy mind, since she doth change!
Let not fancy still abuse thee.
Thy untruth can not seem strange

When her falsehood doth excuse thee.
  Love is dead and thou art free,
  She doth live, but dead to thee.

Whilst she loved thee best a while,
See how she hath still delayed thee,
Using shows for to beguile
Those vain hopes that have deceived thee.
  Now thou seest, although too late,
  Love loves truth, which women hate.

Love no more, since she is gone—
She is gone, and loves another.
Being once deceived by one,
Leave her love, but love none other.
  She was false—bid her adieu;
  She was best, but yet untrue.

Love, farewell, more dear to me
Than my life, which thou preservest.
Life, all joys are gone from thee,
Others have what thou deservest.
  Oh, my death doth spring from hence,
  I must die for her offence.

Die, but yet before thou die,
Make her know what she hath gotten;
She, in whom my hopes did lie,
Now is changed—I, quite forgotten.
  She is changed, but changèd base,
  Baser in so vild a place.

[TO PLEAD MY FAITH]

To plead my faith where faith had no reward,
To move remorse where favor is not borne,
To heap complaints where she doth not regard—
Were fruitless, bootless, vain, and yield but scorn.

I lovëd her whom all the world admired,
I was refused of her that can love none;
And my vain hopes, which far too high aspired,
Is dead, and buried, and for ever gone.

Forget my name, since you have scorned my love,
And woman-like do not too late lament;
Since for your sake I do all mischief prove,
I none accuse nor nothing do repent.

I was as fond as ever she was fair,
Yet loved I not more than I now despair.

A PASSION

Happy were he could finish forth his fate
In some unhaunted desert, more obscure
From all society, from love and hate
Of worldly folk, there might he sleep secure;
There wake again, and give God ever praise,
Content with hips and haws and brambleberry,
In contemplation passing still his days,
And change of holy thoughts to make him merry.
    That when he dies, his tomb might be a bush,
    Where harmless Robin dwells with gentle thrush.

Sir Walter Ralegh

POEMS

A DESCRIPTION OF LOVE

Now what is Love, I pray thee, tell?
It is that fountain and that well
Where pleasure and repentance dwell;
It is perhaps the saucing bell
That tolls all into heaven or hell:
And this is Love, as I hear tell.

Yet what is Love, I pray thee, say?
It is a work on holy-day,
It is December matched with May,
When lusty bloods in fresh array
Hear ten months after of the play:
And this is Love, as I hear say.

Yet what is Love, I pray thee sain?
It is a sunshine mixed with rain;
It is a toothache, or like pain,
It is a game where none hath gain;
The lass saith no, yet would full fain:
And this is Love, as I hear sain.

Yet what is Love, I pray thee say?
It is a yea, it is a nay,
A pretty kind of sporting fray,
It is a thing will soon away.

614

Then take the vantage while you may:
And this is Love, as I hear say.

Yet what is Love, I pray thee show?
A thing that creeps, it cannot go,
A prize that passeth to and fro,
A thing for one, a thing for mo,
And he that proves shall find it so;
And this is Love, sweet friend, I trow.

A VISION UPON THIS CONCEIT OF THE FAERIE QUEENE

Methought I saw the grave where Laura lay,
Within that temple where the vestal flame
Was wont to burn; and passing by that way
To see that buried dust of living fame,
Whose tomb fair Love and fairer Virtue kept,
All suddenly I saw the Faerie Queene
At whose approach the soul of Petrarch wept,
And from thenceforth those graces were not seen,
For they this Queen attended; in whose stead
Oblivion laid him down on Laura's hearse.
Hereat the hardest stones were seen to bleed,
And groans of buried ghosts the heavens did pierce;
　　Where Homer's sprite did tremble all for grief,
　　And cursed th' access of that celestial thief.

THE NYMPH'S REPLY TO THE SHEPHERD

If all the world and love were young,
And truth in every shepherd's tongue,
These pretty pleasures might me move
To live with thee and be thy love.

Time drives the flocks from field to fold
When rivers rage and rocks grow cold,
And Philomel becometh dumb;
The rest complains of cares to come.

The flowers do fade, and wanton fields
To wayward winter reckoning yields;
A honey tongue, a heart of gall,
Is fancy's spring, but sorrow's fall.

Thy gowns, thy shoes, thy beds of roses,
Thy cap, thy kirtle, and thy posies
Soon break, soon wither, soon forgotten—
In folly ripe, in reason rotten.

Thy belt of straw and ivy buds,
Thy coral clasps and amber studs,
All these in me no means can move
To come to thee and be thy love.

But could youth last and love still breed,
Had joys no date nor age no need,
Then these delights my mind might move
To live with thee and be thy love.

TO HIS SON

Three things there be that prosper all apace
And flourish, while they grow asunder far;
But on a day they meet all in one place,
And when they meet, they one another mar.
And they be these: the wood, the weed, the wag.
The wood is that which makes the gallows tree;
The weed is that which strings the hangman's bag;
The wag, my pretty knave, betokens thee.

Now mark, dear boy: while these assemble not,
Green springs the tree, hemp grows, the wag is wild;
But when they meet, it makes the timber rot,
It frets the halter, and it chokes the child.
    Then bless thee, and beware, and let us pray
    We part not with thee at this meeting day.

[NATURE, THAT WASHED HER HANDS]

Nature, that washed her hands in milk,
    And had forgot to dry them,
Instead of earth took snow and silk,
    At Love's request to try them,
If she a mistress could compose
To please Love's fancy out of those.

Her eyes he would should be of light,
    A violet breath, and lips of jelly;
Her hair not black, nor overbright,
    And of the softest down her belly;
As for her inside he'ld have it
Only of wantonness and wit.

At Love's entreaty such a one
    Nature made, but with her beauty
She hath framed a heart of stone;
    So as Love, by ill destiny,
Must die for her whom nature gave him,
Because her darling would not save him.

But Time, which Nature doth despise
    And rudely gives her love the lie,
Makes hope a fool, and sorrow wise,
    His hands doth neither wash nor dry;

But being made of steel and rust,
Turns snow, and silk, and milk to dust.

The light, the belly, lips and breath,
　　He dims, discolors, and destroys;
With those he feeds but fills not death,
　　Which sometimes were the food of joys.
Yea, Time doth dull each lively wit,
And dries all wantonness with it.

Oh, cruel Time, which takes in trust
　　Our youth, our joys, and all we have,
And pays us but with age and dust;
　　Who in the dark and silent grave
When we have wandered all our ways
Shuts up the story of our days.

THE LIE

Go, soul, the body's guest,
Upon a thankless arrant.
Fear not to touch the best;
The truth shall be thy warrant.
　　Go, since I needs must die,
　　And give the world the lie.

Say to the court, it glows
And shines like rotten wood;
Say to the church, it shows
What's good, and doth no good:
　　If church and court reply,
　　Then give them both the lie.

Tell potentates, they live
Acting by others' action,

Not loved unless they give,
Not strong but by affection:
    If potentates reply,
    Give potentates the lie.

Tell men of high condition
That manage the estate,
Their purpose is ambition,
Their practice only hate:
    And if they once reply,
    Then give them all the lie.

Tell them that brave it most,
They beg for more by spending,
Who, in their greatest cost,
Like nothing but commending:
    And if they make reply,
    Then give them all the lie.

Tell zeal it wants devotion;
Tell love it is but lust;
Tell time it meets but motion;
Tell flesh it is but dust:
    And wish them not reply,
    For thou must give the lie.

Tell age it daily wasteth;
Tell honor how it alters;
Tell beauty how she blasteth;
Tell favor how it falters:
    And as they shall reply,
    Give every one the lie.

Tell wit how much it wrangles
In tickle points of niceness;

Tell wisdom she entangles
Herself in over-wiseness:
   And when they do reply,
   Straight give them both the lie.

Tell physic of her boldness;
Tell skill it is prevention;
Tell charity of coldness;
Tell law it is contention:
   And as they do reply,
   So give them still the lie.

Tell fortune of her blindness;
Tell nature of decay;
Tell friendship of unkindness;
Tell justice of delay:
   And if they will reply,
   Then give them all the lie.

Tell arts they have no soundness,
But vary by esteeming;
Tell schools they want profoundness,
And stand too much on seeming:
   If arts and schools reply,
   Give arts and schools the lie.

Tell faith it's fled the city;
Tell how the country erreth;
Tell, manhood shakes off pity,
Tell, virtue least preferrëd:
   And if they do reply,
   Spare not to give the lie.

So when thou hast, as I
Commanded thee, done blabbing,

Because to give the lie
Deserves no less than stabbing,
　　Stab at thee he that will—
　　No stab thy soul can kill.

THE PASSIONATE MAN'S PILGRIMAGE, SUPPOSED TO BE WRITTEN BY ONE AT THE POINT OF DEATH

Give me my scallop-shell of quiet,
My staff of faith to walk upon,
My scrip of joy, immortal diet,
My bottle of salvation,
My gown of glory, hope's true gage,
And thus I'll take my pilgrimage.

Blood must be my body's balmer,
No other balm will there be given,
Whilst my soul like a white palmer
Travels to the land of heaven,
Over the silver mountains,
Where spring the nectar fountains;
And there I'll kiss
The bowl of bliss,
And drink my eternal fill
On every milken hill.
My soul will be a-dry before,
But after it will ne'er thirst more;
And by the happy blissful way
More peaceful pilgrims I shall see,
That have shook off their gowns of clay
And go appareled fresh like me.
I'll bring them first
To slake their thirst,

And then to taste those nectar suckets,
At the clear wells
Where sweetness dwells,
Drawn up by saints in crystal buckets.

And when our bottles and all we
Are filled with immortality,
Then the holy paths we'll travel,
Strewed with rubies thick as gravel,
Ceilings of diamonds, sapphire floors,
High walls of coral, and pearl bowers.

From thence to heaven's bribeless hall
Where no corrupted voices brawl,
No conscience molten into gold,
Nor forged accusers bought and sold,
No cause deferred, nor vain-spent journey,
For there Christ is the king's attorney,
Who pleads for all without degrees,
And he hath angels, but no fees.
When the grand twelve million jury
Of our sins and sinful fury,
'Gainst our souls black verdicts give,
Christ pleads his death, and then we live.
Be thou my speaker, taintless pleader,
Unblotted lawyer, true proceeder,
Thou movest salvation even for alms,
Not with a bribèd lawyer's palms.

And this is my eternal plea
To him that made heaven, earth, and sea,
Seeing my flesh must die so soon,
And want a head to dine next noon,
Just at the stroke when my veins start and spread,

Set on my soul an everlasting head.
Then am I ready, like a palmer fit,
To tread those blest paths which before I writ.

Edmund Spenser

THE BOWER OF BLISS

I

There, whence that music seemed heard to be,
 Was the fair witch herself now solacing,
 With a new lover, whom through sorcery
 And witchcraft, she from far did thither bring;
 There she had him now laid a slumbering,
 In secret shade, after long wanton joys,
 Whilst round about them pleasantly did sing
 Many fair ladies and lascivious boys,
That ever mixt their song with light licentious toys.

II

And all that while, right over him she hung
 With her false eyes fast fixed in his sight,
 As seeking medicine, whence she was stung,
 Or greedily depasturing delight;
 And oft inclining down with kisses light,
 For fear of waking him, his lips bedewd,
 And through his humid eyes did suck his spright,
 Quite molten into lust and pleasure lewd;
Wherewith she sighed soft, as if his case she rued.

III

The whiles some one did chant this lovely lay:
  Ah see, who so fair thing doest fain to see,
  In springing flower the image of thy day;
  Ah see the virgin rose, how sweetly she
  Doth first peep forth with bashful modesty,
  That fairer seems, the less ye see her may;
  Lo see soon after, how more bold and free
  Her bared bosom she doth broad display;
Lo see soon after, how she fades, and falls away.

IV

So passeth, in the passing of a day,
  Of mortal life the leaf, the bud, the flower;
  Ne more doth flourish after first decay,
  That erst was sought to deck both bed and bower,
  Of many a ladie, and many a paramour:
  Gather therefore the rose, whilst yet is prime,
  For soon comes age that will her pride deflower:
  Gather the rose of love, whilst yet is time,
Whilst loving thou mayst loved be with equal crime.

EPITHALAMION

Ye learned sisters, which have oftentimes
Been to me aiding, others to adorn,
Whom ye thought worthy of your graceful rhymes,
That even the greatest did not greatly scorn
To hear their names sung in your simple lays,
But joyéd in their praise;
And when ye list your own mishaps to mourn,

Which death, or love, or fortune's wreck did raise,
Your string could soon to sadder tenor turn,
And teach the woods and waters to lament
Your doleful dreariment.
Now lay those sorrowful complaints aside;
And having all your heads with girlands crowned,
Help me mine own love's praises to resound;
Ne let the same of any be envide:
So Orpheus did for his own bride!
So I unto myself alone will sing;
The woods shall to me answer, and my echo ring.

Early, before the world's light-giving lamp
His golden beam upon the hills doth spread,
Having dispersed the night's uncheerful damp,
Do ye awake; and with fresh lustihead
Go to the bower of my belovéd love,
My truest turtle-dove,
Bid her awake; for Hymen is awake,
And long since ready forth his mask to move,
With his bright tead that flames with many a flake,
And many a bachelor to wait on him,
In their fresh garments trim.
Bid her awake therefore, and soon her dight,
For lo! the wishéd day is come at last,
That shall, for all the pains and sorrows past,
Pay to her usury of long delight:
And whilst she doth her dight,
Do ye to her of joy and solace sing,
That all the woods may answer, and your echo ring.

Bring with you all the nymphs that you can hear
Both of the rivers and the forests green,
And of the sea that neighbours to her near:

All with gay girlands goodly well beseen.
And let them also with them bring in hand
Another gay girland,
For my fair love, of lilies and of roses,
Bound true-love wise, with a blue silk riband.
And let them make great store of bridal posies,
And let them eke bring store of other flowers,
To deck the bridal bowers.
And let the ground whereas her foot shall tread,
For fear the stones her tender foot should wrong,
Be strewed with fragrant flowers all along,
And diap'red like the discoloured mead.
Which done, do at her chamber door await,
For she will waken straight;
The whiles do ye this song unto her sing,
The woods shall to you answer, and your echo ring.

Ye nymphs of Mulla, which with careful heed
The silver scaly trouts do tend full well,
And greedy pikes which use therein to feed
(Those trouts and pikes all others do excel);
And ye likewise, which keep the rushy lake,
Where none do fishes take:
Bind up the locks the which hang scattered light,
And in his waters, which your mirror make,
Behold your faces as the crystal bright,
That when you come whereas my love doth lie,
No blemish she may spy.
And eke, ye lightfoot maids, which keep the deer,
That on the hoary mountain used to tower;
And the wild wolves, which seek them to devour,
With your steel darts do chase from coming near;
Be also present here,
To help to deck her, and to help to sing,
That all the woods may answer, and your echo ring.

Wake now, my love, awake! for it is time;
The rosy Morn long since left Tithone's bed,
All ready to her silver coach to climb;
And Phoebus gins to shew his glorious head.
Hark! how the cheerful birds do chant their lays
And carol of Love's praise.
The merry lark her matins sings aloft;
The thrush replies; the mavis descant plays:
The ouzel shrills; the ruddock warbles soft;
So goodly all agree, with sweet consent,
To this day's merriment.
Ah! my dear love, why do ye sleep thus long,
When meeter were that ye should now awake,
T' await the coming of your joyous make,
And harken to the birds' love-learnéd song,
The dewy leaves among!
For they of joy and pleasance to you sing,
That all the woods them answer, and their echo ring.

My love is now awake out of her dreams,
And her fair eyes, like stars that dimméd were
With darksome cloud, now shew their goodly beams
More bright than Hesperus his head doth rear.
Come now, ye damsels, daughters of delight,
Help quickly her to dight:
But first come, ye fair hours, which were begot
In Jove's sweet paradise of Day and Night;
Which do the seasons of the year allot,
And all, that ever in this world is fair,
Do make and still repair:
And ye three handmaids of the Cyprian Queen,
The which do still adorn her beauty's pride,
Help to adorn my beautifullest bride:
And, as ye her array, still throw between
Some graces to be seen;

And, as ye use to Venus, to her sing,
The whiles the woods shall answer, and your echo ring.

Now is my love all ready forth to come:
Let all the virgins therefore well await:
And ye fresh boys, that tend upon her groom,
Prepare yourselves, for he is coming straight.
Set all your things in seemly good array,
Fit for so joyful day:
The joyfull'st day that ever sun did see.
Fair sun! shew forth thy favourable ray,
And let thy lifeful heat not fervent be,
For fear of burning her sunshiny face,
Her beauty to disgrace.
O fairest Phoebus! father of the Muse!
If ever I did honour thee aright,
Or sing the thing that mote thy mind delight,
Do not thy servant's simple boon refuse;
But let this day, let this one day, be mine;
Let all the rest be thine.
Then I thy sovereign praises loud will sing,
That all the woods shall answer, and their echo ring.

Hark: how the minstrels gin to shrill aloud
Their merry music that resounds from far,
The pipe, the tabor, and the trembling croud,
That well agree withouten breach or jar.
But, most of all, the damsels do delight
When they their timbrels smite,
And thereunto do dance and carol sweet,
That all the senses they do ravish quite;
The whiles the boys run up and down the street,
Crying aloud with strong confuséd noise,
As if it were one voice,
Hymen, iö Hymen, Hymen, they do shout;

That even to the heavens their shouting shrill
Doth reach, and all the firmament doth fill;
To which the people standing all about,
As in approvance, do thereto applaud,
And loud advance her laud;
And evermore they Hymen, Hymen sing,
That all the woods them answer, and their echo ring.

Lo! where she comes along with portly pace,
Like Phoebe, from her chamber of the east,
Arising forth to run her mighty race,
Clad all in white, that 'seems a virgin best.
So well it her beseems, that ye would ween
Some angel she had been.
Her long loose yellow locks like golden wire,
Sprinkled with pearl, and purling flowers atween,
Do like a golden mantle her attire;
And, being crownéd with a girland green,
Seem like some maiden queen.
Her modest eyes, abashéd to behold
So many gazers as on her do stare,
Upon the lowly ground affixéd are;
Ne dare lift up her countenance too bold,
But blush to hear her praises sung so loud,
So far from being proud.
Nathless do ye still loud her praises sing,
That all the woods my answer, and your echo ring.

Tell me, ye merchants' daughters, did ye see
So fair a creature in your town before;
So sweet, so lovely, and so mild as she,
Adorned with beauty's grace and virtue's store?
Her goodly eyes like sapphires shining bright,
Her forehead ivory white,
Her cheeks like apples which the sun hath rudded,

Her lips like cherries charming men to bite,
Her breast like to a bowl of cream uncrudded,
Her paps like lilies budded,
Her snowy neck like to a marble tower;
And all her body like a palace fair,
Ascending up, with many a stately stair,
To honour's seat and chastity's sweet bower.
Why stand ye still, ye virgins, in amaze,
Upon her so to gaze,
Whiles ye forget your former lay to sing,
To which the woods did answer, and your echo ring?

But if ye saw that which no eyes can see,
The inward beauty of her lively sprite,
Garnisht with heavenly gifts of high degree,
Much more then would ye wonder at that sight,
And stand astonisht like to those which read
Medusa's mazeful head.
There dwells sweet love, and constant chastity,
Unspotted faith, and comely womanhood,
Regard of honour, and mild modesty;
There virtue reigns as queen in royal throne,
And giveth laws alone,
The which the base affections do obey,
And yield their services unto her will;
Ne thought of thing uncomely ever may
Thereto approach to tempt her mind to ill.
Had ye once seen these her celestial treasures,
And unrevealéd pleasures,
Then would ye wonder, and her praises sing,
That all the woods should answer, and your echo ring.

Open the temple gates unto my love,
Open them wide that she may enter in,
And all the posts adorn as doth behove,

And all the pillars deck with girlands trim,
For to receive this saint with honour due,
That cometh in to you.
With trembling steps, and humble reverence,
She cometh in, before th' Almighty's view;
Of her ye virgins learn obedience,
Whenso ye come into those holy places,
To humble your proud faces:
Bring her up to th' high altar, that she may
The sacred ceremonies there partake,
The which do endless matrimony make;
And let the roaring organs loudly play
The praises of the Lord in lively notes;
The whiles, with hollow throats,
The choristers the joyous anthem sing,
That all the woods may answer, and their echo ring.

Behold, whiles she before the altar stands,
Hearing the holy priest that to her speaks,
And blesseth her with his two happy hands,
How the red roses flush up in her cheeks,
And the pure snow, with goodly vermeil stain
Like crimson dyed in grain:
That even th' angels, which continually
About the sacred altar do remain,
Forget their service and about her fly,
Oft peeping in her face, that seems more fair
The more they on it stare.
But her sad eyes, still fastened on the ground,
Are governéd with goodly modesty,
That suffers not one look to glance awry,
Which may let in a little thought unsound.
Why blush ye, love, to give to me your hand,
The pledge of all our band!
Sing, ye sweet angels, Alleluia sing,

That all the woods may answer, and your echo ring.
Now all is done: bring home the bride again;
Bring home the triumph of our victory:
Bring home with you the glory of her gain,
With joyance bring her and with jollity.
Never had man more joyful day than this,
Whom heaven would heap with bliss.
Make feast therefore now all this livelong day;
This day for ever to me holy is.
Pour out the wine without restraint or stay,
Pour not by cups, but by the bellyful,
Pour out to all that wull,
And sprinkle all the posts and walls with wine,
That they may sweat, and drunken be withal.
Crown ye God Bacchus with a coronal,
And Hymen also crown with wreaths of vine;
And let the Graces dance unto the rest,
For they can do it best:
The whiles the maidens do their carol sing,
To which the woods shall answer, and their echo ring.

Ring ye the bells, ye young men of the town,
And leave your wonted labours for this day:
This day is holy; do ye write it down,
That ye for ever it remember may.
This day the sun is in his chiefest height,
With Barnaby the bright,
From whence declining daily by degrees,
He somewhat loseth of his heat and light,
When once the Crab behind his back he sees.
But for this time it ill ordainéd was,
To choose the longest day in all the year,
And shortest night, when longest fitter were:
Yet never day so long, but late would pass.
Ring ye the bells, to make it wear away,

And bonfires make all day;
And dance about them, and about them sing,
That all the woods may answer, and your echo ring.

Ah! when will this long weary day have end,
And lend me leave to come unto my love?
How slowly do the hours their numbers spend!
How slowly does sad Time his feathers move!
Haste thee, O fairest planet, to thy home,
Within the western foam:
Thy tired steeds long since have need of rest.
Long though it be, at last I see it gloom,
And the bright evening-star with golden crest
Appear out of the east.
Fair child of beauty! glorious lamp of love!
That all the host of heaven in ranks dost lead,
And guidest lovers through the night's sad dread,
How cheerfully thou lookest from above,
And seem'st to laugh atween thy twinkling light,
As joying in the sight
Of these glad many, which for joy do sing,
That all the woods them answer, and their echo ring!

Now cease, ye damsels, your delights forepast;
Enough it is that all the day was yours:
Now day is done, and night is nighing fast,
Now bring the bride into the bridal bowers.
The night is come, now soon her disarray,
And in her bed her lay;
Lay her in lilies and in violets,
And silken curtains over her display,
And odoured sheets, and arras coverlets.
Behold how goodly my fair love does lie,
In proud humility!
Like unto Maia, whenas Jove her took

In Tempe, lying on the flow'ry grass,
'Twixt sleep and wake, after she weary was,
With bathing in the Acidalian brook.
Now it is night, ye damsels may be gone,
And leave my love alone,
And leave likewise your former lay to sing:
The woods no more shall answer, nor your echo ring.

Now welcome, night! thou night so long expected,
That long day's labour dost at last defray,
And all my cares, which cruel Love collected,
Hast summed in one, and cancelléd for aye:
Spread thy broad wing over my love and me,
That no man may us see;
And in thy sable mantle us enwrap,
From fear of peril and foul horror free.
Let no false treason seek us to entrap,
Nor any dread disquiet once annoy
The safety of our joy;
But let the night be calm, and quietsome,
Without tempestuous storms or sad affray:
Like as when Jove with fair Alcmena lay,
When he begot the great Tirynthian groom:
Or like as when he with thyself did lie
And begot Majesty.
And let the maids and young men cease to sing,
Ne let the woods them answer, nor their echo ring.

Let no lamenting cries, nor doleful tears,
Be heard all night within, nor yet without:
Ne let false whispers, breeding hidden fears,
Break gentle sleep with misconceivéd doubt.
Let no deluding dreams, nor dreadful sights,
Make sudden sad affrights;
Ne let house-fires, nor lightning's helpless harms,

Ne let the Pouke, nor other evil sprites,
Ne let mischievous witches with their charms,
Ne let hobgoblins, names whose sense we see not,
Fray us with things that be not:
Let not the shriek-owl nor the stork be heard,
Nor the night-raven, that still deadly yells;
Nor damnéd ghosts, called up with mighty spells,
Nor grisly vultures, make us once afeard:
Ne let th' unpleasant quire of frogs still croaking
Make us to wish their choking.
Let none of these their dreary accents sing;
Ne let the woods them answer, nor their echo ring.

But let still silence true night-watches keep,
That sacred peace may in assurance reign,
And timely sleep, when it is time to sleep,
May pour his limbs forth on your pleasant plain;
The whiles an hundred little wingéd loves,
Like divers-feathered doves,
Shall fly and flutter round about your bed,
And in the secret dark, that none reproves,
Their pretty stealths shall work, and snares shall spread
To filch away sweet snatches of delight,
Concealed through covert night.
Ye sons of Venus, play your sports at will!
For greedy pleasure, careless of your toys,
Thinks more upon her paradise of joys,
Than what ye do, albeit good or ill.
All night therefore attend your merry play,
For it will soon be day:
Now none doth hinder you, that say or sing;
Ne will the woods now answer, nor your echo ring.

Who is the same, which at my window peeps?
Or whose is that fair face that shines so bright?

Is it not Cynthia, she that never sleeps,
But walks about high heaven all the night?
O! fairest goddess, do thou not envý
My love with me to spy:
For thou likewise didst love, though now unthought,
And for a fleece of wool, which privily
The Latmian shepherd once unto thee brought,
His pleasures with thee wrought.
Therefore to us be favourable now;
And sith of women's labours thou hast charge,
And generation goodly dost enlarge,
Incline thy will t' effect our wishful vow,
And the chaste womb inform with timely seed,
That may our comfort breed:
Till which we cease our hopeful hap to sing;
Ne let the woods us answer, nor our echo ring.

And thou, great Juno! which with awful might
The laws of wedlock still dost patronize;
And the religion of the faith first plight
With sacred rites hast taught to solemnize;
And eke for comfort often callèd art
Of women in their smart;
Eternally bind thou this lovely band,
And all thy blessings unto us impart.
And thou, glad Genius! in whose gentle hand
The bridal bower and genial bed remain,
Without blemish or stain:
And the sweet pleasures of their love's delight
With secret aid dost succour and supply,
Till they bring forth the fruitful progeny;
Send us the timely fruit of this same night.
And thou, fair Hebe! and thou, Hymen free!
Grant that it may so be.

Till which we cease your further praise to sing;
Ne any woods shall answer, nor your echo ring.

And ye high heavens, the temple of the gods,
In which a thousand torches flaming bright
Do burn, that to us wretched earthly clods
In dreadful darkness lend desiréd light;
And all ye powers which in the same remain,
More than we men can feign,
Pour out your blessing on us plenteously,
And happy influence upon us rain,
That we may raise a large posterity,
Which from the earth, which they may long possess
With lasting happiness,
Up to your haughty palaces may mount;
And, for the guerdon of their glorious merit,
May heavenly tabernacles there inherit,
Of blessed saints for to increase the count.
So let us rest, sweet love, in hope of this,
And cease till then our timely joys to sing;
The woods no more us answer, nor our echo ring!

Song! made in lieu of many ornaments,
With which my love should duly have been deckt,
Which cutting off through hasty accidents,
Ye would not stay your due time to expect,
But promised both to recompense;
Be unto her a goodly ornament,
And for short time an endless monument.

Nicholas Breton

SONGS

A SWEET LULLABY

Come, little babe; come, silly soul,
Thy father's shame, thy mother's grief,
Born, as I doubt, to all our dole
And to thyself unhappy chief:
   Sing lullaby, and lap it warm,
   Poor soul that thinks no creature harm.

Thou little think'st and less dost know
The cause of this thy mother's moan,
Thou want'st the wit to wail her woe,
And I myself am all alone.
   Why dost thou weep? why dost thou wail?
   And knowest not yet what thou dost ail.

Come, little wretch—ah, silly heart,
Mine only joy, what can I more?
If there be any wrong thy smart,
That may the destinies implore,
   'Twas I, I say, against my will;
   I wail the time, but be thou still.

And dost thou smile? Oh, thy sweet face,
Would God himself he might thee see;
No doubt thou wouldst soon purchase grace,
I know right well, for thee and me.

But come to mother, babe, and play,
For father false is fled away.

Sweet boy, if it by fortune chance
Thy father home again to send,
If death do strike me with his lance,
Yet mayst thou me to him commend;
　If any ask thy mother's name,
　Tell how by love she purchased blame.

Then will his gentle heart soon yield;
I know him of a noble mind.
Although a lion in the field,
A lamb in town thou shalt him find.
　Ask blessing, babe, be not afraid;
　His sugared words hath me betrayed.

Then mayst thou joy and be right glad,
Although in woe I seem to moan.
Thy father is no rascal lad,
A noble youth of blood and bone;
　His glancing looks, if he once smile,
　Right honest women may beguile.

Come, little boy, and rock asleep,
Sing lullaby, and be thou still;
I that can do nought else but weep
Will sit by thee and wail my fill.
　God bless my babe, and lullaby,
　From this thy father's quality.

SAY THAT I SHOULD SAY

Say that I should say I love ye,
    Would you say 'tis but a saying?
But if love in prayers move ye,
    Will you not be moved with praying?

Think I think that love should know ye,
    Will you think 'tis but a thinking?
But if love the thought do show ye,
    Will ye lose your eyes with winking?

Write that I do write you blessed,
    Will you write 'tis but a writing?
But if truth and love confess it,
    Will ye doubt the true inditing?

No: I say, and think, and write it—
    Write, and think, and say your pleasure.
Love and truth and I indite it,
    You are blessed out of measure.

PHILLIDA AND CORIDON

In the merry month of May,
In a morn by break of day
Forth I walked by the wood-side,
Whenas May was in his pride.
There I spiéd, all alone,
Phillida and Coridon.
Much ado there was, God wot,
He would love and she would not.
She said, Never man was true;

He said, None was false to you.
He said he had loved her long.
She said, Love should have no wrong.
Coridon would kiss her then;
She said maids must kiss no men
Till they did for good and all.
Then she made the shepherd call
All the heavens to witness truth,
Never loved a truer youth.
Thus, with many a pretty oath,
Yea and nay, and faith and troth,
Such as silly shepherds use
When they will not love abuse,
Love which had been long deluded
Was with kisses sweet concluded.
And Phillida with garlands gay
Was made the lady of the May.

AN ODD CONCEIT

Lovely kind, and kindly loving,
Such a mind were worth the moving;
Truly fair, and fairly true,
Where are all these but in you?

Wisely kind, and kindly wise—
Blessed life, where such love lies!
Wise, and kind, and fair, and true,
Lovely live all these in you.

Sweetly dear, and dearly sweet—
Blessed, where these blessings meet!
Sweet, fair, wise, kind, blessed, true,
Blessed be all these in you!

Robert Greene

SONGS

SEPHESTIA'S SONG TO HER CHILD

Weep not, my wanton, smile upon my knee,
When thou art old there's grief enough for thee.
    Mother's wag, pretty boy,
    Father's sorrow, father's joy,
    When thy father first did see
    Such a boy by him and me,
    He was glad, I was woe;
    Fortune changed made him so,
    When he left his pretty boy,
    Last his sorrow, first his joy.

Weep not, my wanton, smile upon my knee,
When thou art old there's grief enough for thee.
    Streaming tears that never stint,
    Like pearl-drops from a flint,
    Fell by course from his eyes,
    That one another's place supplies.
    Thus he grieved in every part;
    Tears of blood fell from his heart,
    When he left his pretty boy,
    Father's sorrow, father's joy.

Weep not, my wanton, smile upon my knee,
When thou art old there's grief enough for thee.
    The wanton smiled, father wept,
    Mother cried, baby leapt;

More he crowed, more we cried,
Nature could not sorrow hide.
He must go, he must kiss
Child and mother, baby bliss,
For he left his pretty boy,
Father's sorrow, father's joy.
Weep not, my wanton, smile upon my knee,
When thou art old there's grief enough for thee.

THE SHEPHERD'S WIFE'S SONG

Ah, what is love? It is a pretty thing,
As sweet unto a shepherd as a king—
    And sweeter too,
For kings have cares that wait upon a crown,
And cares can make the sweetest love to frown.
    Ah then, ah then,
If country loves such sweet desires do gain,
What lady would not love a shepherd swain?

His flocks once folded, he comes home at night
As merry as a king in his delight—
    And merrier too,
For kings bethink them what the state require,
Where shepherds careless carol by the fire.
    Ah then, ah then,
If country loves such sweet desires gain,
What lady would not love a shepherd swain?

He kisseth first, then sits as blithe to eat
His cream and curds as doth the king his meat—
    And blither too,
For kings have often fears when they do sup,
Where shepherds dread no poison in their cup.
    Ah then, ah then,

If country loves such sweet desires gain,
What lady would not love a shepherd swain?

To bed he goes, as wanton then, I ween,
As is a king in dalliance with a queen—
            More wanton too,
For kings have many griefs, affects to move,
Where shepherds have no greater grief than love.
            Ah then, ah then,
If country loves such sweet desires gain,
What lady would not love a shepherd swain?

Upon his couch of straw he sleeps as sound
As doth the king upon his beds of down—
            More sounder too,
For cares cause kings full oft their sleep to spill,
Where weary shepherds lie and snort their fill.
            Ah then, ah then,
If country loves such sweet desires gain,
What lady would not love a shepherd swain?

Thus with his wife he spends the year, as blithe
As doth the king, at every tide or sithe—
            And blither too,
For kings have wars and broils to take in hand,
Where shepherds laugh and love upon the land.
            Ah then, ah then,
If country loves such sweet desires gain,
What lady would not love a shepherd swain?

SWEET ARE THE THOUGHTS

Sweet are the thoughts that savor of content,
    The quiet mind is richer than a crown;
Sweet are the nights in careless slumber spent,

The poor estate scorns fortune's angry frown:
Such sweet content, such minds, such sleep, such bliss,
Beggars enjoy, when princes oft do miss.

The homely house that harbors quiet rest,
    The cottage that affords no pride nor care,
The mean that grees with country music best,
    The sweet consort of mirth and music's fare,
Obscurëd life sets down a type of bliss;
A mind content both crown and kingdom is.

PHILOMELA'S ODE THAT SHE SUNG
IN HER ARBOR

Sitting by a river side
Where a silent stream did glide,
Muse I did of many things
That the mind in quiet brings.
I gan think how some men deem
Gold their god; and some esteem
Honour is the chief content
That to man in life is lent;
And some others do contend
Quiet none like to a friend;
Others hold there is no wealth
Compared to a perfect health;
Some man's mind in quiet stands
When he is lord of many lands:
But I did sigh, and said all this
Was but a shade of perfect bliss;
And in my thoughts I did approve
Nought so sweet as is true love.
Love 'twixt lovers passeth these,
When mouth kisseth and heart grees,

With folded arms and lippës meeting,
Each soul another sweetly greeting;
For by the breath the soul fleeteth
And soul with soul in kissing meeteth.
If love be so sweet a thing,
That such happy bliss doth bring,
Happy is love's sugared thrall;
But unhappy maidens all,
Who esteem your virgin's blisses
Sweeter than a wife's sweet kisses.
No such quiet to the mind
As true love with kisses kind;
But if a kiss prove unchaste,
Then is true love quite disgraced.
Though love be sweet, learn this of me:
No love sweet but honesty.

Thomas Lodge

SONGS

ROSALIND'S MADRIGAL

Love in my bosom like a bee
　　Doth suck his sweet;
Now with his wings he plays with me,
　　Now with his feet.
Within mine eyes he makes his nest,
His bed amidst my tender breast,
My kisses are his daily feast,
And yet he robs me of my rest—
　　Ah, wanton, will ye?

And if I sleep, then percheth he
    With pretty flight,
And makes his pillow of my knee
    The livelong night.
Strike I my lute, he tunes the string,
He music plays if so I sing,
He lends me every lovely thing,
Yet cruel he my heart doth sting—
    Whist, wanton, still ye!

Else I with roses every day
    Will whip you hence,
And bind you, when you long to play,
    For your offence.
I'll shut mine eyes to keep you in,
I'll make you fast it for your sin,
I'll count your power not worth a pin;
Alas! what hereby shall I win
    If he gainsay me?

What if I beat the wanton boy
    With many a rod?
He will repay me with annoy,
    Because a god.
Then sit thou safely on my knee,
And let thy bower my bosom be,
Lurk in mine eyes, I like of thee.
O Cupid, so thou pity me,
    Spare not, but play thee!

MY MISTRESS WHEN SHE GOES

My mistress when she goes
To pull the pink and rose

Along the river bounds,
And trippeth on the grounds,
And runs from rocks to rocks
With lovely scattered locks,
Whilst amorous wind doth play
With hairs so golden gay;
The water waxeth clear,
The fishes draw her near,
The sirens sing her praise,
Sweet flowers perfume her ways,
And Neptune, glad and fain,
Yields up to her his reign.

PHILLIS

I

My Phillis hath the morning sun
  At first to look upon her,
And Phillis hath morn-waking birds
  Her risings for to honour.
My Phillis hath prime-feathered flowers
  That smile when she treads on them,
And Phillis hath a gallant flock
  That leaps since she doth own them.
But Phillis hath so hard a heart
  (Alas, that she should have it!)
As yields no mercy to desert
  Nor grace to those that crave it.
  Sweet sun, when thou lookest on,
  Pray her regard my moan;
  Sweet birds, when you sing to her,
  To yield some pity woo her;
  Sweet flowers, whenas she treads on,

Tell her, her beauty deads one;
And if in life her love she nill agree me,
Pray her, before I die she will come see me.

II

I'll teach thee, lovely Phillis, what love is:
It is a vision, seeming such as thou,
That flies as fast as it assaults mine eyes;
It is affection that doth reason miss;
    It is a shape of pleasure like to you,
Which meets the eye, and seen on sudden dies;
It is a doubled grief, a spark of pleasure
Begot by vain desire. And this is love,
    Whom in our youth we count our chiefest treasure,
In age, for want of power, we do reprove.
    Yea, such a power is love, whose loss is pain,
    And having got him, we repent our gain.

Michael Drayton

DOWSABELL

Far in the country of Arden
There wonned a knight hight Cassemen,
    As bold as Isenbras;
Fell was he and eager bent
In battle and in tournament,
    As was the good Sir Thopas.
He had, as antique stories tell,
A daughter clepëd Dowsabell,
    A maiden fair and free;

And for she was her father's heir,
Full well she was yconned the lere
   Of mickle courtesy.
The silk well couth she twist and twine,
And make the fine marchpine,
   And with the needle work;
And she couth help the priest to say
His matins on a holy-day,
   And sing a psalm in kirk.
She ware a frock of frolic green
Might well beseem a maiden queen,
   Which seemly was to see;
A hood to that so neat and fine,
In color like the columbine,
   Ywrought full featously.
Her feature all as fresh above
As is the grass that grows by Dove,
   As lithe as lass of Kent;
Her skin as soft as Lemster wool,
As white as snow on Peakish hull,
   Or swan that swims in Trent.
This maiden in a morn betime
Went forth when May was in her prime
   To get sweet cetywall,
The honeysuckle, the harlock,
The lily, and the lady-smock,
   To deck her summer hall.
Thus as she wandered here and there,
Ypicking of the bloomëd breer,
   She chancëd to espy
A shepherd sitting on a bank;
Like chanticleer he crowëd crank,
   And piped with merry glee.
He leared his sheep as he him list,
When he would whistle in his fist,

To feed about him round,
Whilst he full many a carol sung,
Until the fields and meadows rung,
    And that the woods did sound.
In favor this same shepherd's swain
Was like the bedlam Tamburlaine,
    Which held proud kings in awe.
But meek he was as lamb mought be,
Ylike that gentle Abel he,
    Whom his lewd brother slaw.
This shepherd ware a sheep-grey cloak,
Which was of the finest loke
    That could be cut with shear;
His mittens were of bauzens' skin,
His cockers were of cordiwin,
    His hood of meniveere;
His awl and lingel in a thong,
His tar-box on his broad belt hung,
    His breech of cointrie blue.
Full crisp and curlèd were his locks,
His brows as white as Albion rocks,
    So like a lover true.
And piping still he spent the day,
So merry as the popinjay;
    Which likèd Dowsabell,
That would she aught or would she nought
This lad would never from her thought,
    She in love-longing fell.
At length she tuckèd up her frock,
White as the lily was her smock,
    She drew the shepherd nigh.
But then the shepherd piped a good
That all his sheep forsook their food
    To hear his melody.
Thy sheep, quoth she, cannot be lean,

That have a jolly shepherd's swain
　　The which can pipe so well.
Yea but, saith he, their shepherd may,
If piping thus he pine away
　　In love of Dowsabell.
Of love, fond boy, take thou no keep,
Quoth she, look well unto thy sheep
　　Lest they should hap to stray.
Quoth he, So had I done full well,
Had I not seen fair Dowsabell
　　Come forth to gather may.
With that she gan to vail her head;
Her cheeks were like the roses red,
　　But not a word she said.
With that the shepherd gan to frown;
He threw his pretty pipes adown,
　　And on the ground him laid.
Saith she, I may not stay till night
And leave my summer hall undight,
　　And all for long of thee.
My cote, saith he, nor yet my fold,
Shall neither sheep nor shepherd hold,
　　Except thou favor me.
Saith she, Yet liefer I were dead,
Than I should lose my maidenhead,
　　And all for love of men.
Saith he, Yet are you too unkind,
If in your heart you cannot find
　　To love us now and then;
And I to thee will be as kind
As Colin was to Rosalind,
　　Of courtesy the flower.
Then will I be as true, quoth she,
As ever maiden yet might be
　　Unto her paramour.

With that she bent her snow-white knee;
Down by the shepherd kneelëd she,
   And him she sweetly kissed.
With that the shepherd whooped for joy;
Quoth he, There's never shepherd's boy
   That ever was so blist.

SONNETS

Into these loves who but for passion looks,
At this first sight here let him lay them by,
And seek elsewhere, in turning other books
Which better may his labor satisfy.
No far-fetched sigh shall ever wound my breast,
Love from mine eye a tear shall never wring,
Nor in *Ah me's* my whining sonnets dressed.
A libertine, fantastically I sing;
My verse is the true image of my mind,
Ever in motion, still desiring change.
And as thus to variety inclined,
So in all humors sportively I range;
   My muse is rightly of the English strain,
   That cannot long one fashion entertain.

Like an adventurous seafarer am I,
Who hath some long and dang'rous voyage been,
And called to tell of his discovery,
How far he sailed, what countries he had seen;
Proceeding from the port whence he put forth,
Shows by his compass how his course he steered,
When east, when west, when south, and when by north,
As how the pole to ev'ry place was reared,
What capes he doubled, of what continent,

The gulfs and straits that strangely he had passed,
Where most becalmed, where with foul weather spent,
And on what rocks in peril to be cast:
    Thus in my love, time calls me to relate
    My tedious travels and oft-varying fate.

How many paltry, foolish, painted things,
That now in coaches trouble ev'ry street,
Shall be forgotten, whom no poet sings,
Ere they be well wrapped in their winding sheet!
Where I to thee eternity shall give,
When nothing else remaineth of these days,
And queens hereafter shall be glad to live
Upon the alms of thy superfluous praise;
Virgins and matrons reading these my rhymes
Shall be so much delighted with thy story
That they shall grieve they lived not in these times,
To have seen thee, their sex's only glory.
    So shalt thou fly above the vulgar throng,
    Still to survive in my immortal song.

To nothing fitter can I thee compare
Than to the son of some rich penny-father,
Who having now brought on his end with care,
Leaves to his son all he had heaped together;
This new-rich novice, lavish of his chest,
To one man gives, doth on another spend,
Then here he riots; yet amongst the rest
Haps to lend some to one true honest friend.
Thy gifts thou in obscurity dost waste,
False friends thy kindness, born but to deceive thee;
Thy love, that is on the unworthy placed;
Time hath thy beauty, which with age will leave thee;

Only that little which to me was lent,
I give thee back, when all the rest is spent.

An evil spirit, your beauty, haunts me still,
Wherewith, alas, I have been long possessed,
Which ceaseth not to tempt me to each ill,
Nor gives me once but one poor minute's rest;
In me it speaks, whether I sleep or wake,
And when by means to drive it out I try,
With greater torments then it me doth take,
And tortures me in most extremity;
Before my face it lays down my despairs,
And hastes me on unto a sudden death,
Now tempting me to drown myself in tears,
And then in sighing to give up my breath.
　　Thus am I still provoked to every evil
　　By this good wicked spirit, sweet angel devil.

In pride of wit, when high desire of fame
Gave life and courage to my lab'ring pen,
And first the sound and virtue of my name
Won grace and credit in the ears of men;
With those the throngèd theaters that press
I in the circuit for the laurel strove,
Where the full praise, I freely must confess,
In heat of blood, a modest mind might move.
With shouts and claps at ev'ry little pause,
When the proud round on ev'ry side hath rung,
Sadly I sit, unmoved with the applause,
As though to me it nothing did belong.
　　No public glory vainly I pursue,
　　All that I seek is to eternize you.

Since there's no help, come let us kiss and part;
Nay, I have done, you get no more of me,
And I am glad, yea glad with all my heart
That thus so cleanly I myself can free;
Shake hands forever, cancel all our vows,
And when we meet at any time again,
Be it not seen in either of our brows
That we one jot of former love retain.
Now at the last gasp of love's latest breath,
When, his pulse failing, passion speechless lies,
When faith is kneeling by his bed of death,
And innocence is closing up his eyes,
   Now if thou wouldst, when all have given him over,
   From death to life thou mightst him yet recover.

Thomas Campion

FIFTEEN SONGS

MY LOVE BOUND ME

My love bound me with a kiss
   That I should no longer stay;
When I felt so sweet a bliss
   I had less power to pass away.
Alas! that women do not know
Kisses make men loath to go.

Yet she knows it but too well,
   For I heard when Venus' dove
In her ear did softly tell
   That kisses were the seals of love.

Oh, muse not then though it be so,
Kisses make men loath to go.

Wherefore did she thus inflame
    My desires, heat my blood,
Instantly to quench the same
    And starve whom she had given food?
I the common sense can show:
Kisses make men loath to go.

Had she bid me go at first
    It would ne'er have grieved my heart;
Hope delayed had been the worst.
    But ah! to kiss and then to part!
How deep it struck; speak, gods, you know
Kisses make men loath to go.

WHAT IF A DAY

What if a day, or a month, or a year
Crown thy delights with a thousand sweet contentings?
Cannot a chance of a night or an hour
Cross thy desires with as many sad tormentings?
            Fortune, honour, beauty, youth
            Are but blossoms dying;
            Wanton pleasure, doting love
            Are but shadows flying.
            All our joys are but toys,
            Idle thoughts deceiving,
            None have power of an hour
            In their lives' bereaving.

Earth's but a point to the world, and a man
Is but a point to the world's compared centure;

Shall then the point of a point be so vain
As to triumph in a seely point's adventure?
       All is hazard that we have,
       There is nothing biding;
       Days of pleasure are like streams
       Through fair meadows gliding.
       Weal and woe, time doth go,
       Time is never turning;
       Secret fates guide our states,
       Both in mirth and mourning.

MY SWEETEST LESBIA

My sweetest Lesbia, let us live and love,
And though the sager sort our deeds reprove,
Let us not weigh them. Heav'n's great lamps do dive
Into their west, and straight again revive,
But soon as once set is our little light,
Then must we sleep one ever-during night.

If all would lead their lives in love like me,
Then bloody swords and armour should not be;
No drum nor trumpet peaceful sleeps should move,
Unless alarm came from the camp of love.
But fools do live, and waste their little light,
And seek with pain their ever-during night.

When timely death my life and fortune ends,
Let not my hearse be vexed with mourning friends,
But let all lovers, rich in triumph, come
And with sweet pastimes grace my happy tomb;
And Lesbia, close up thou my little light,
And crown with love my ever-during night.

WHEN TO HER LUTE CORINNA SINGS

When to her lute Corinna sings,
Her voice revives the leaden strings,
And doth in highest notes appear
As any challenged echo clear;
But when she doth of mourning speak,
Ev'n with her sighs the strings do break.

And as her lute doth live or die,
Led by her passion, so must I:
For when of pleasure she doth sing,
My thoughts enjoy a sudden spring,
But if she doth of sorrow speak,
Ev'n from my heart the strings do break.

FOLLOW YOUR SAINT

Follow your saint, follow with accents sweet;
Haste you, sad notes, fall at her flying feet.
There, wrapped in cloud of sorrow, pity move,
And tell the ravisher of my soul I perish for her love.
But if she scorns my never-ceasing pain,
Then burst with sighing in her sight and ne'er return
    again.

All that I sung still to her praise did tend,
Still she was first, still she my songs did end.
Yet she my love and music both doth fly,
The music that her echo is and beauty's sympathy.
Then let my notes pursue her scornful flight:
It shall suffice that they were breathed and died for her
    delight.

THOU ART NOT FAIR

Thou art not fair for all thy red and white,
   For all those rosy ornaments in thee;
Thou art not sweet, though made of mere delight,
   Nor fair nor sweet, unless you pity me.
I will not soothe thy fancies; thou shalt prove
That beauty is no beauty without love.

Yet love not me, nor seek thou to allure
   My thoughts with beauty, were it more divine;
Thy smiles and kisses I cannot endure,
   I'll not be wrapped up in those arms of thine.
Now show it, if thou be a woman right—
Embrace, and kiss, and love me in despite.

THE MAN OF LIFE UPRIGHT

The man of life upright,
   Whose guiltless heart is free
From all dishonest deeds,
   Or thought of vanity;

The man whose silent days
   In harmless joys are spent,
Whom hopes cannot delude,
   Nor sorrow discontent;

That man needs neither towers
   Nor armor for defence,
Nor secret vaults to fly
   From thunder's violence.

He only can behold
  With unaffrighted eyes
The horrors of the deep
  And terrors of the skies.

Thus, scorning all the cares
  That fate or fortune brings,
He makes the heav'n his book,
  His wisdom heav'nly things,

Good thoughts his only friends,
  His wealth a well-spent age,
The earth his sober inn
  And quiet pilgrimage.

HARK, ALL YOU LADIES

Hark, all you ladies that do sleep!
  The fairy queen Proserpina
Bids you awake and pity them that weep.
  You may do in the dark
    What the day doth forbid;
  Fear not the dogs that bark,
    Night will have all hid.

But if you let your lovers moan,
  The fairy queen Proserpina
Will send abroad her fairies ev'ry one,
  That shall pinch black and blue
    Your white hands and fair arms
  That did not kindly rue
    Your paramours' harms.

In myrtle arbors on the downs
　　The fairy queen Proserpina,
This night by moonshine leading merry rounds,
　　Holds a watch with sweet love,
　　　　Down the dale, up the hill;
　　No plaints or groans may move
　　　　Their holy vigil.

All you that will hold watch with love,
　　The fairy queen Proserpina
Will make you fairer than Dione's dove;
　　Roses red, lilies white,
　　　　And the clear damask hue,
　　Shall on your cheeks alight;
　　　　Love will adorn you.

All you that love, or loved before,
　　The fairy queen Proserpina
Bids you increase that loving humor more;
　　They that yet have not fed
　　　　On delight amorous,
　　She vows that they shall lead
　　　　Apes in Avernus.

ROSE-CHEEKED LAURA

Rose-cheeked Laura, come,
Sing thou smoothly with thy beauty's
Silent music, either other
　　　　Sweetly gracing.

Lovely forms do flow
From concent divinely framèd;
Heav'n is music, and thy beauty's
　　　　Birth is heavenly.

These dull notes we sing
Discords need for helps to grace them;
Only beauty purely loving
          Knows no discord,

But still moves delight,
Like clear springs renewed by flowing,
Ever perfect, ever in them-
          Selves eternal.

I CARE NOT FOR THESE LADIES

I care not for these ladies,
That must be wooed and prayed:
Give me kind Amarillis,
The wanton country maid.
Nature art disdaineth,
Her beauty is her own,
    Her when we court and kiss,
    She cries, Forsooth, let go!
    But when we come where comfort is,
    She never will say No!

If I love Amarillis,
She gives me fruit and flowers:
But if we love these ladies,
We must give golden showers,
Give them gold, that sell love,
Give me the nut-brown lass,
    Who, when we court and kiss,
    She cries, Forsooth, let go!
    But when we come where comfort is,
    She never will say No!

These ladies must have pillows,
And beds by strangers wrought;
Give me a bower of willows,
Of moss and leaves unbought,
And fresh Amarillis,
With milk and honey fed;
  Who, when we court and kiss,
  She cries, Forsooth, let go!
  But when we come where comfort is,
  She never will say No!

NOW WINTER NIGHTS ENLARGE

Now winter nights enlarge
  The number of their hours,
And clouds their storms discharge
  Upon the airy towers.

Let now the chimneys blaze
  And cups o'erflow with wine;
Let well-tuned words amaze
  With harmony divine.

Now yellow waxen lights
  Shall wait on honey love,
While youthful revels, masks, and courtly sights
  Sleep's leaden spells remove.

This time doth well dispense
  With lovers' long discourse;
Much speech hath some defence,
  Though beauty no remorse.

All do not all things well:
  Some measures comely tread;

Some knotted riddles tell;
  Some poems smoothly read.

The summer hath his joys,
  And winter his delights;
Though love and all his pleasures are but toys,
  They shorten tedious nights.

NEVER LOVE UNLESS YOU CAN

Never love unless you can
Bear with all the faults of man;
Men sometimes will jealous be,
Though but little cause they see,
  And hang the head, as discontent,
  And speak what straight they will repent.

Men that but one saint adore
Make a show of love to more;
Beauty must be scorned in none,
Though but truly served in one;
  For what is courtship but disguise?
  True hearts may have dissembling eyes.

Men when their affairs require
Must a while themselves retire,
Sometimes hunt, and sometimes hawk,
And not ever sit and talk.
  If these and such like you can bear,
  Then like, and love, and never fear.

THERE IS A GARDEN

There is a garden in her face,
Where roses and white lilies grow;
  A heav'nly paradise is that place,
Wherein all pleasant fruits do flow.
    There cherries grow which none may buy
    Till cherry-ripe themselves do cry.

Those cherries fairly do enclose
Of orient pearl a double row,
  Which when her lovely laughter shows,
They look like rosebuds filled with snow.
    Yet them nor peer nor prince can buy,
    Till cherry-ripe themselves do cry.

Her eyes like angels watch them still;
Her brows like bended bows do stand,
  Threat'ning with piercing frowns to kill
All that attempt with eye or hand
    Those sacred cherries to come nigh,
    Till cherry-ripe themselves do cry.

YOUNG AND SIMPLE THOUGH I AM

Young and simple though I am,
I have heard of Cupid's name;
Guess I can what thing it is
Men desire when they do kiss.
    Smoke can never burn, they say,
    But the flames that follow may.

I am not so foul or fair
To be proud, nor to despair;
Yet my lips have oft observed,
Men that kiss them press them hard,
    As glad lovers use to do
    When their new-met loves they woo.

Faith, 'tis but a foolish mind,
Yet methinks a heat I find,
Like thirst-longing, that doth bide
Ever on my weaker side,
    Where they say my heart doth move.
    Venus, grant it be not love.

If it be, alas, what then?
Were not women made for men?
As good 'twere a thing were past,
That must needs be done at last.
    Roses that are over-blown
    Grow less sweet, then fall alone.

Yet nor churl nor silken gull
Shall my maiden blossom pull;
Who shall not I soon can tell,
Who shall, would I could as well;
    This I know, whoe'er he be,
    Love he must, or flatter me.

FAIN WOULD I WED

Fain would I wed a fair young man that night and day
    could please me,
When my mind or body grieved that had the power to
    ease me.

Maids are full of longing thoughts that breed a bloodless
  sickness,
And that, oft I hear men say, is only cured by quickness.
Oft I have been wooed and praised, but never could be
  movëd;
Many for a day or so I have most dearly lovëd,
But this foolish mind of mine straight loathes the thing
  resolvëd;
If to love be sin in me, that sin is soon absolvëd.
Sure I think I shall at last fly to some holy order;
When I once am settled there, then can I fly no farther.
Yet I would not die a maid, because I had a mother,
As I was by one brought forth, I would bring forth
  another.

Ben Jonson

LYRICS

EPITAPH ON ELIZABETH, L. H.

Wouldst thou hear what man can say
  In a little? Reader, stay.
Underneath this stone doth lie
  As much beauty as could die;
Which in life did harbor give
  To more virtue than doth live.
If at all she had a fault,
  Leave it buried in this vault.
One name was Elizabeth,
  Th' other let it sleep with death;
Fitter, where it died to tell,
  Than that it lived at all. Farewell.

WHY I WRITE NOT OF LOVE

Some act of Love's bound to rehearse,
I thought to bind him in my verse;
Which when he felt, Away, quoth he,
Can poets hope to fetter me?
It is enough they once did get
Mars and my mother in their net;
I wear not these my wings in vain.
With which he fled me, and again
Into my rhymes could ne'er be got
By any art. Then wonder not
That since my numbers are so cold,
When Love is fled, and I grow old.

SONG, TO CELIA [1]

Come, my Celia, let us prove
While we may the sports of love;
Time will not be ours forever,
He at length our good will sever.
Spend not then his gifts in vain;
Suns that set may rise again,
But if once we lose this light,
'Tis with us perpetual night.
Why should we defer our joys?
Fame and rumor are but toys.
Cannot we delude the eyes
Of a few poor household spies?
Or his easier ears beguile,
So removèd by our wile?
'Tis no sin love's fruit to steal;
But the sweet theft to reveal,

To be taken, to be seen,
These have crimes accounted been.

SONG, TO CELIA [2]

Drink to me only with thine eyes,
    And I will pledge with mine;
Or leave a kiss but in the cup,
    And I'll not look for wine.
The thirst that from the soul doth rise
    Doth ask a drink divine;
But might I of Jove's nectar sup,
    I would not change for thine.

I sent thee late a rosy wreath,
    Not so much honoring thee,
As giving it a hope that there
    It could not withered be.
But thou thereon didst only breathe,
    And sent'st it back to me,
Since when it grows and smells, I swear,
    Not of itself, but thee.

HIS EXCUSE FOR LOVING

Let it not your wonder move,
Less your laughter, that I love.
Though I now write fifty years,
I have had, and have, my peers;
Poets though divine are men,
Some have loved as old again.
And it is not always face,
Clothes, or fortune, gives the grace,
Or the feature, or the youth;

But the language and the truth,
With the ardor and the passion,
Gives the lover weight and fashion.

If you then will read the story,
First prepare you to be sorry
That you never knew till now
Either whom to love, or how;
But be glad, as soon with me,
When you know that this is she
Of whose beauty it was sung:
She shall make the old man young,
Keep the middle age at stay,
And let nothing high decay;
Till she be the reason why
All the world for love may die.

HER TRIUMPH

See the chariot at hand here of love,
  Wherein my lady rideth!
Each that draws is a swan or a dove,
  And well the car love guideth.
As she goes all hearts do duty
    Unto her beauty,
And enamoured do wish so they might
    But enjoy such a sight,
That they still were to run by her side,
Through swords, through seas, whither she would ride.

Do but look on her eyes; they do light
  All that love's world compriseth!
Do but look on her hair; it is bright
  As love's star when it riseth!

Do but mark, her forehead's smoother
  Than words that soothe her;
And from her arched brows, such a grace
  Sheds itself through the face,
As alone there truimphs to the life
All the gain, all the good of the elements' strife.

Have you seen but a bright lily grow
  Before rude hands have touched it?
Ha' you marked but the fall o' the snow
  Before the soil hath smutched it?
Ha' you felt the wool of beaver,
    Or swan's down ever?
Or have smelt o' the bud o' the briar?
    Or the nard in the fire?
Or have tasted the bag of the bee?
O so white! O so soft! O so sweet is she!

BEGGING ANOTHER [KISS], ON COLOR OF MENDING THE FORMER

For love's sake, kiss me once again;
I long, and should not beg in vain,
  Here's none to spy or see;
    Why do you doubt or stay?
  I'll taste as lightly as the bee
That doth but touch his flower and flies away.

Once more, and faith I will be gone;
Can he that loves ask less than one?
  Nay, you may err in this
    And all your bounty wrong;
  This could be called but half a kiss,
What we're but once to do, we should do long.

I will but mend the last, and tell
Where, how it would have relished well;
   Join lip to lip, and try,
     Each suck other's breath.
  And whilst our tongues perplexëd lie,
Let who will, think us dead or wish our death.

THE PLANT AND FLOWER OF LIGHT

It is not growing like a tree
In bulk, doth make man better be;
Or standing long an oak, three hundred year,
To fall a log at last, dry, bald, and sere;
A lily of a day
Is fairer far in May,
Although it fall and die that night,
It was the plant and flower of light.
In small proportions we just beauties see;
And in short measures, life may perfect be.

TO CYNTHIA

Queen and huntress, chaste and fair,
Now the sun is laid to sleep,
Seated in thy silver chair
State in wonted manner keep;
   Hesperus entreats thy light,
   Goddess excellently bright.

Earth, let not thy envious shade
Dare itself to interpose;
Cynthia's shining orb was made
Heaven to clear, when day did close;
   Bless us then with wishëd sight,
   Goddess excellently bright.

Lay thy bow of pearl apart,
And thy crystal shining quiver;
Give unto the flying hart
Space to breathe, how short soever,
    Thou that mak'st a day of night,
    Goddess excellently bright.

IF I FREELY MAY DISCOVER

If I freely may discover
What would please me in my lover:
    I would have her fair and witty,
    Savoring more of court than city;
    A little proud, but full of pity;
    Light and humorous in her toying,
    Oft building hopes and soon destroying;
    Long, but sweet, in the enjoying;
Neither too easy, nor too hard,
All extremes I would have barred.

She should be allowed her passions,
So they were but used as fashions;
    Sometimes froward, and then frowning,
    Sometimes sickish, and then swowning,
    Every fit with change still crowning.
    Purely jealous I would have her;
    Then only constant when I crave her,
    'Tis a virtue should not save her.
Thus, nor her delicates would cloy me,
Neither her peevishness annoy me.

STILL TO BE NEAT

Still to be neat, still to be dressed
As you were going to a feast;
Still to be powdered, still perfumed:
Lady, it is to be presumed,
Though art's hid causes are not found,
All is not sweet, all is not sound.

Give me a look, give me a face
That makes simplicity a grace;
Robes loosely flowing, hair as free:
Such sweet neglect more taketh me
Than all th' adulteries of art;
They strike mine eyes, but not my heart.

John Donne

POEMS

SONG

Go, and catch a falling star,
    Get with child a mandrake root,
Tell me, where all past years are,
    Or who cleft the Devil's foot,
Teach me to hear Mermaids singing,
    Or to keep off envy's stinging,
        And find
        What wind
Serves to advance an honest mind.

If thou be'st born to strange sights,
   Things invisible to see,
Ride ten thousand days and nights,
   Till age snow white hairs on thee,
Thou, when thou return'st, wilt tell me
All strange wonders that befell thee,
      And swear
      No where
Lives a woman true, and fair.

If thou find'st one, let me know,
   Such a Pilgrimage were sweet;
Yet do not, I would not go,
   Though at next door we might meet,
Though she were true, when you met her,
And last, till you write your letter,
      Yet she
      Will be
False, ere I come, to two, or three.

THE SUN RISING

Busy old fool, unruly sun,
   Why dost thou thus
Through windows and through curtains call on us?
Must to thy motions lovers' seasons run?
   Saucy pedantic wretch, go chide
   Late schoolboys and sour prentices,
Go tell court-huntsmen that the King will ride,
   Call country ants to harvest offices;
Love, all alike, no season knows, nor clime,
Nor hours, days, months, which are the rags of time.

Thy beams, so reverend and strong
    Why shouldst thou think?
I could eclipse and cloud them with a wink,
But that I would not lose her sight so long;
    If her eyes have not blinded thine,
    Look, and tomorrow late tell me
    Whether both the' Indias of spice and mine
    Be where thou left'st them, or lie here with me.
Ask for those kings whom thou saw'st yesterday,
And thou shalt hear, all here in one bed lay.

    She is all states, and all princes I;
        Nothing else is.
Princes do but play us; compared to this,
All honour's mimic, all wealth alchemy.
        Thou, sun, art half as happy'as we,
        In that the world's contracted thus;
    Thine age asks ease, and since thy duties be
    To warm the world, that's done in warming us.
Shine here to us, and thou art everywhere;
This bed thy center is, these walls thy sphere.

A LECTURE UPON THE SHADOW

Stand still, and I will read to thee
A lecture, love, in love's philosophy.
    These three hours that we have spent
    Walking here, two shadows went
Along with us, which we ourselves produced;
    But, now the sun is just above our head,
    We do those shadows tread,
And to brave clearness all things are reduced.
    So whilst our infant loves did grow,

Disguises did, and shadows, flow
From us and our cares, but now 'tis not so.

That love hath not attained the high'st degree,
Which is still diligent lest others see.
Except our loves at this noon stay,
We shall new shadows make the other way.
    As the first were made to blind
    Others, these which come behind
Will work upon ourselves, and blind our eyes.
    If our loves faint, and westwardly decline,
    To me thou falsely thine,
And I to thee, mine actions shall disguise.
    The morning shadows wear away,
    But these grow longer all the day;
    But oh, love's day is short, if love decay.

Love is a growing, or full constant light,
And his short minute after noon, is night.

THE ECSTASY

Where, like a pillow on a bed,
    A pregnant bank swelled up to rest
The violet's reclining head,
    Sat we two, one another's best.
Our hands were firmly cémented
    With a fast balm, which thence did spring;
Our eye-beams twisted, and did thread
    Our eyes upon one double string;
So to entergraft our hands, as yet
    Was all the means to make us one,
And pictures in our eyes to get
    Was all our propagation.

As 'twixt two equal armies fate
   Suspends uncertain victory,
Our souls, which to advance their state
   Were gone out, hung 'twixt her and me.
And whilst our souls negotiate there,
   We like sepulchral statues lay;
All day, the same our postures were,
   And we said nothing, all the day.
If any, so by love refined
   That he soul's language understood,
And by good love were grown all mind,
   Within convenient distance stood,
He, though he knew not which soul spake,
   Because both meant, both spake the same,
Might thence a new concoction take
   And part far purer than he came.
This ecstasy doth unperplex,
   We said, and tell us what we love:
We see by this it was not sex,
   We see we saw not what did move;
But as all several souls contain
   Mixture of things, they know not what,
Love these mixed souls doth mix again
   And makes both one, each this and that.
A single violet transplant,
   The strength, the color, and the size,
All which before was poor and scant,
   Redoubles still, and multiplies.
When love with one another so
   Interinanimates two souls,
That abler soul, which thence doth flow,
   Defects of loneliness controls.
We then, who are this new soul, know
   Of what we are composed and made,
For th' atomies of which we grow

Are souls, whom no change can invade.
But oh, alas, so long, so far,
    Our bodies why do we forbear?
They are ours, though not we; we are
    The intelligences, they the sphere.
We owe them thanks, because they thus
    Did us to us at first convey,
Yielded their forces, sense, to us,
    Nor are dross to us, but allay.
On man heaven's influence works not so,
    But that it first imprints the air;
For soul into the soul may flow,
    Though it to body first repair.
As our blood labors to beget
    Spirits, as like souls as it can,
Because such fingers need to knit
    That subtle knot which makes us man,
So must pure lovers' souls descend
    T' affections, and to faculties,
Which sense may reach and apprehend,
    Else a great prince in prison lies.
To our bodies turn we then, that so
    Weak men on love revealed may look;
Love's mysteries in souls do grow,
    But yet the body is his book.
And if some lover, such as we,
    Have heard this dialogue of one,
Let him still mark us, he shall see
    Small change when we're to bodies gone.

TO HIS MISTRESS GOING TO BED

Come, madam, come, all rest my powers defy;
Until I labour, I in labour lie.

The foe oft-times, having the foe in sight,
Is tired with standing, though he never fight.
Off with that girdle, like Heaven's zone glittering,
But a far fairer world encompassing.
Unpin that spangled breast-plate, which you wear,
That th' eyes of busy fools may be stopp'd there.
Unlace yourself, for that harmonious chime
Tells me from you that now it is bed-time.
Off with that happy busk, which I envy,
That still can be, and still can stand so nigh.
Your gown going off such beauteous state reveals,
As when from flowery meads th' hill's shadow steals.
Off with your wiry coronet, and show
The hairy diadems which on you do grow.
Off with your hose and shoes; then softly tread
In this love's hallow'd temple, this soft bed.
In such white robes heaven's angels used to be
Revealed to men; thou, angel, bring'st with thee
A heaven-like Mahomet's paradise; and though
Ill spirits walk in white, we easily know
By this these angels from an evil sprite;
Those set our hairs, but these our flesh upright.
    License my roving hands, and let them go
Before, behind, between, above, below.
Oh, my America, my Newfoundland,
My kingdom, safest when with one man mann'd,
My mine of precious stones, my empery;
How am I blest in thus discovering thee!
To enter in these bonds, is to be free;
Then, where my hand is set, my soul shall be.
    Full nakedness! All joys are due to thee;
As souls embodied, bodies unclothed must be
To taste whole joys. Gems which you women use
Are like Atlanta's ball cast in men's views;
That, when a fool's eye lighteth on a gem,

His earthly soul might court that, not them.
Like pictures, or like books' gay coverings made
For laymen, are all women thus array'd.
Themselves are only mystic books, which we
—Whom their imputed grace will dignify—
Must see reveal'd. Then, since that I may know,
As liberally as to thy midwife show
Thyself; cast all, yea, this white linen hence;
There is no penance due to innocence:
To teach thee, I am naked first; why then,
What needst thou have more covering than a man?

THE UNDERTAKING

I have done one braver thing
    Than all the worthies did,
And yet a braver thence doth spring,
    Which is, to keep that hid.

It were but madness now t' impart
    The skill of specular stone,
When he which can have learned the art
    To cut it, can find none.

So if I now should utter this,
    Others, because no more
Such stuff to work upon there is,
    Would love but as before.

But he who loveliness within
    Hath found, all outward loathes,
For he who colour loves, and skin,
    Loves but their oldest clothes.

If, as I have, you also do
   Virtue attired in woman see,
And dare love that, and say so too,
   And forget the he and she;

And if this love, though placëd so,
   From profane men you hide,
Which will no faith on this bestow,
   Or, if they do, deride,

Then you have done a braver thing
   Than all the worthies did;
And a braver thence will spring,
   Which is, to keep that hid.

THE RELIC

When my grave is broke up again
Some second guest to entertain—
For graves have learned that woman-head,
   To be to more than one a bed—
     And he that digs it, spies
A bracelet of bright hair about the bone,
     Will he not let's alone,
And think that there a loving couple lies,
Who thought that this device might be some way
To make their souls, at the last busy day,
Meet at this grave, and make a little stay?

If this fall in a time or land
   Where mis-devotion doth command,
Then he that digs us up will bring
   Us to the bishop and the king,
     To make us relics; then

Thou shalt be a Mary Magdalen, and I
    A something else thereby;
All women shall adore us, and some men;
And since at such time miracles are sought,
I would have that age by this paper taught
What miracles we harmless lovers wrought.

    First, we loved well and faithfully,
    Yet knew not what we loved, nor why,
    Difference of sex no more we knew
    Than our guardian angels do;
      Coming and going, we
Perchance might kiss, but not between those meals;
      Our hands ne'er touched the seals,
Which nature, injured by late law, sets free;
These miracles we did, but now alas,
All measure and all language I should pass,
Should I tell what a miracle she was.

THE ANNIVERSARY

    All kings, and all their favorites,
    All glory of honours, beauties, wits,
The sun itself, which makes times as they pass,
Is elder by a year now, than it was
When thou and I first one another saw;
All other things to their destruction draw,
    Only our love hath no decay;
This no tomorrow hath, nor yesterday,
Running, it never runs from us away,
But truly keeps his first, last, everlasting day.

    Two graves must hide thine and my corse;
    If one might, death were no divorce.

Alas, as well as other princes, we,
Who prince enough in one another be,
Must leave at last in death these eyes and ears,
Oft fed with true oaths, and with sweet salt tears;
    But souls where nothing dwells but love,
All other thoughts being inmates, then shall prove
This, or a love increasèd there above,
When bodies to their graves, souls from their graves,
    remove.

    And then we shall be throughly blest,
    But we no more than all the rest;
Here upon earth we're kings, and none but we
Can be such kings, nor of such subjects be.
Who is so safe as we, where none can do
Treason to us, except one of us two?
    True and false fears let us refrain;
Let us love nobly, and live, and add again
Years and years unto years, till we attain
To write threescore; this is the second of our reign.

SONNETS

At the round earth's imagined corners, blow
Your trumpets, angels; and arise, arise
From death, you numberless infinities
Of souls, and to your scattered bodies go;
All whom the flood did, and fire shall o'erthrow,
All whom war, dearth, age, agues, tyrannies,
Despair, law, chance hath slain, and you whose eyes
Shall behold God and never taste death's woe.
But let them sleep, Lord, and me mourn a space,
For if above all these my sins abound,
'Tis late to ask abundance of thy grace

When we are there; here on this lowly ground
Teach me how to repent; for that's as good
As if thou'dst sealed my pardon with thy blood.

Death, be not proud, though some have callëd thee
Mighty and dreadful, for thou art not so;
For those whom thou think'st thou dost overthrow
Die not, poor Death, nor yet canst thou kill me.
From rest and sleep, which but thy pictures be,
Much pleasure; then from thee much more must flow,
And soonest our best men with thee do go,
Rest of their bones, and soul's delivery.
Thou art slave to fate, chance, kings, and desperate men,
And dost with poison, war, and sickness dwell,
And poppy or charms can make us sleep as well
And better than thy stroke; why swell'st thou then?
One short sleep past, we wake eternally,
And death shall be no more; Death, thou shalt die.

GOOD FRIDAY, 1613. RIDING WESTWARD

Let man's soul be a sphere, and then in this
The intelligence that moves, devotion is;
And as the other spheres, by being grown
Subject to foreign motion, lose their own,
And being by others hurried every day
Scarce in a year their natural form obey,
Pleasure or business, so, our souls admit
For their first mover, and are whirled by it.
Hence is 't that I am carried towards the west
This day, when my soul's form bends towards the east.
There I should see a sun, by rising set,
And by that setting, endless day beget;

But that Christ on this cross did rise and fall,
Sin had eternally benighted all.
Yet dare I'almost be glad I do not see
That spectacle of too much weight for me.
Who sees God's face, that is self life, must die;
What a death were it then to see God die!
It made his own lieutenant, nature, shrink;
It made his footstool crack, and the sun wink.
Could I behold those hands which span the poles
And tune all spheres at once, pierced with those holes?
Could I behold that endless height, which is
Zenith to us and our antipodes,
Humbled below us? or that blood which is
The seat of all our souls, if not of his,
Made dirt of dust, or that flesh which was worn
By God for his apparel, ragg'd and torn?
If on these things I durst not look, durst I
Upon his miserable mother cast mine eye,
Who was God's partner here, and furnished thus
Half of that sacrifice which ransomed us?
Though these things, as I ride, be from mine eye,
They're present yet unto my memory,
For that looks towards them; and thou look'st towards
    me,
O Saviour, as thou hang'st upon the tree;
I turn my back to thee but to receive
Corrections, till thy mercies bid thee leave.
Oh, think me worth thine anger, punish me,
Burn off my rusts, and my deformity;
Restore thine image, so much, by thy grace,
That thou mayst know me, and I'll turn my face.

A HYMN TO GOD THE FATHER

Wilt thou forgive that sin where I begun,
　Which was my sin, though it were done before?
Wilt thou forgive that sin through which I run,
　And do run still, though still I do deplore?
　　When thou hast done, thou hast not done,
　　　For I have more.

Wilt thou forgive that sin which I have won
　Others to sin, and made my sin their door?
Wilt thou forgive that sin which I did shun
　A year or two, but wallowed in a score?
　　When thou hast done, thou hast not done,
　　　For I have more.

I have a sin of fear, that when I have spun
　My last thread, I shall perish on the shore;
But swear by thyself, that at my death thy Son
　Shall shine as he shines now, and heretofore;
　　And having done that, thou hast done;
　　　I fear no more.